I0699658

CASCADING LIGHT

THE VAST COLLECTIVE FINALE

Nicole Hayes

Library of Congress Control Number: 2023909055

ISBN (Hardcover Edition) 979-8-9877243-4-7
ISBN (Softcover Edition) 979-8-9877243-5-4
ISBN (Ebook Edition) 979-8-9877243-7-8

Printed in the USA

Iona Print
nicolehayesauthor@gmail.com
nicolehayeswriter.com/

THE VAST COLLECTIVE SERIES

Last of Daylight
By the Pale Moonlight
Asylum in Firelight
Nox's Verse
Glass Chains
Pyrite Prison
Restraining Silver
Korac's Verse
Thirst
Levee
Flood
Xelan's Verse
Cascading Light

Winter's Verse
Copper & Snow
Polar Axis

*For those seeking peace of mind—
seeking forgiveness—
seeking belonging—
This one is for us.*

CONTENTS

ACKNOWLEDGMENTS

It's such a full circle. These books started as me writing down my nightmares to get them out of my head, and now I'm afraid to write these last moments because I'll never see them again.

Batman, thirteen books later, and I think we've never been more in love. Thank you for inspiring me to start writing: sitting me down in front of the computer, tirelessly remodeling my space; and providing emotional support through the ups and downs. I appreciate you more everyday. Thank you for rescuing me.

Firefly, oh boy, where do I begin? Your insights have helped me write myself out of a corner many a time, and I dub you an expert in all things Vast Collective. With every character moment you cherished, I pocketed motivation to keep going. Thank you for your tireless readings and encouragement to try harder. Hopefully, you'll forgive me for shelving Korac's POV after this, but I think it's time. Much love and kudos.

To everyone who reads, thank you for making it this far.

Welcome to the end.

PART I
IGNITE

I SPARK

RAYNE WAS DEAD. As the explosion reached critical mass, her body disintegrated and scattered like phosphorous butterflies. The light blinded her for only a second, embracing its destiny—

The end of Enki.

Rayne was neither alone nor afraid. She was warm in Nox's arms. There were no tears. No pain. He shouldered that burden. In the last second of Rayne's life, she cupped Nox's jaw, clenched in agony. The pain he asked to take from her.

Then nothing.

For a little while.

Rayne first became aware of her regenerating body when a freshly grown tendon tugged on a reflex and alerted her to the presence of an arm. Two, in fact. Eyes were forthcoming. She laid on a surface, one she understood was a resurrection casket, but with no idea of how she was in it. She only knew it was taking a while.

Time was hard to measure without a watch. Or a body. Especially without knowing how it had taken to constitute the two arms and half a leg—maybe an entire brain—Growing a new body was exhausting.

And boring.

Rayne had lain there for a long time before she could twitch a finger. Then the voice came.

"Daughter."

Kindness in a familiar baritone. Nox had inherited his voice from Elden. This wasn't Rayne's first time speaking to the deity. He always came to Rayne at her darkest hour. The first time, Elden had come to Rayne heartbeats after she'd slayed Nox. The second time happened while she was dying in the heart of Enki, an hour before the Weapon fully detonated. But how...

"Elden?" No voice yet. Rayne asked the question with her consciousness, hoping to reach him. She wanted so badly to open her eyes, but maybe they still needed to form. Ew.

Light permeated Rayne's mindscape and under Elden's construct, her consciousness became an empty white expanse like on TV. Stood inside it, wearing her last outfit, Rayne checked the metal links holding the blue full-body suit together. Her hair was the same, too. Into the white, Rayne called again, "Elden?"

"Daughter."

Rayne turned to find an enormous figure behind her. Charcoal gray skin with molten gold tattoos, dancing along the striations of his corded arms. They framed his face—Elden was extremely handsome and a little bashful about Rayne's inner monologue, if the blue flush to his cheeks was any indication. His eyes... They were hers in Atramentous. Li blazed in them.

Although it was an honor to see Elden's face for the first time, Rayne was spellbound by his hair: black on the underside of each strand and white on the topside. He was an Icarus. How did he have Aegis-esque features?

A sadness competed with the kindness in his voice as Elden said, "A mystery for another time. We have much work to do, daughter."

After a reverent pause, Rayne spoke with her mind again. "How am I alive… grandfather? Dad? Throw me an endearment here."

Elden's chuckle was rich and filled Rayne like a plate of her mom's cooking: comforting and gone. He said, "'Forefather,' if you would. And *I* would be so honored." The deity of the Icarean race—of the entire galaxy—bowed to Rayne.

She was proud to say, "Forefather."

With strides as graceful as a jaguar—the cat for which the Shadow was named—Elden crossed the white space and held out his closed fist. Rayne stared down at it until he opened his slender fingers, revealing a nacre. A white one. His. Incomplete with one empty chink and one amber sliver from her nacre.

Elden said, "There is nothing which will stabilize the Weapon in you. Even now, it wishes to begin again. To fulfill your promise, you require instruments more advanced." He held up the nacre, pinched in his fingers so that Rayne viewed him through it. "This will see my children and Cinder safe. Will you accept it, Rayne Echo Callahan of Earth and Cinder?"

Rayne's heart said to reach for it without hesitation, but her wisdom told her to consider with caution. She wet her lips before saying, "Tell me of its composition. Its upgrade history? What about you? Will you—"

"I will be within, but apart from you." This rang with truth as Elden's eyes burned with sincerity. As much as an exploding star could look sincere. He said, "This is Quet's nacre, the Tritan Primary who created and wronged my Silence. He was the strongest and most intelligent of his kind. I am uninformed of its history before the Aegis granted it to him. Seek which Aegis created it, if this is significant to you. The upgrades are made from constructs based on my understanding of the now. Are there more questions?"

Elden gave the avian head tilt of an Icarean warrior. Thin gold rings, piercing Elden's ears and nose, moved with the gesture. His shadow, too, but it wasn't only his. Silhouettes of Elden's descendants formed the shade he cast. Massive man, massive family.

Considering Elden's proposal, Rayne tucked a strand of hair behind her ear. After a few heartbeats—and she had a heart to beat—Rayne asked, "Will I be able to communicate with you? Or will you have any influence over me?"

"Yes."

Rayne's eyes widened a little. She asked, "To what end?"

Elden straightened and his fist closed over the nacre once more. He gave Rayne the full weight of his burning stare as he said, "I want to take the life of the perversion. The woman who spurns the gift of life. Celindria."

Of course. "She's what you mean by 'seeing your children and Cinder safe.'"

In a familiar gesture which broke Rayne's heart, Elden bit his thumbnail, paced, and explained, "Yes. Celindria poses the only indomitable threat to my children's empire. To Cinder. And to Pax."

The smallest peak of a figure in Elden's shadow gave a little wave.

Rayne blinked at it and shook the odd sensation from her head before asking, "How much time will you give me? Until you decide to take my body into your own hands—Turn me into a weapon like everyone else?"

Elden's back was to her while she watched him stiffly lower his hand. His voice wasn't only in three pitches. More like a million. It was hard to even understand the words cascaded into her head.

"One year."

With her hands covering her ears, this was enough to choke Rayne. Even here in her consciousness, tears—hot and scalding—rolled down her cheeks. Pouring her heart aloud, Rayne begged... to anyone who was listening. "Will someone give me a choice? Ever? Why am I only *this*?!" Lost, she fell to her knees and let her head hang with the weight of her constant responsibility and sorrow.

Thunder rumbled all around.

Elden's voice was back to one pitch, and he let some gentleness into it as he assured, "None of my arrangement is permanent. If we kill the perversion within the year, you can return me to the nacre chamber and take a neutral nacre."

A thought occurred to Rayne, and she enthusiastically wiped the tears from her face. "Why can't you resurrect yourself like me? You can have your own body and—"

"Part of my nacre must always remain with Cinder to keep the Sphere functional. Forgive me. I want better for you, which is why I offer this. Take my nacre. Leave yours here with a sliver from mine. And you and I can defeat Celindria—A mission you already wish to undertake. Only with this arrangement can I assist you."

Alive with Elden...

"What about Nox?" Will there be two Icari in Rayne's head? She glanced around, searching for him, and frowned. "Where is he?"

Elden's eyes narrowed a touch, but enough for Rayne to notice. The Icarean deity said, "I love all my descendants, but perhaps one among them disappoints me. Nox died in an act of true selflessness, so I honor him as fitting to the son of the Icarus who ruined my daughter. Nox's nacre occupies Umbra's pedestal in the nacre chamber, shining alongside all the Coalition who'd sacrificed themselves so Cinder could survive. Appropriate, is it not?"

Nox's words came to Rayne. The words he'd said when they'd lived his greatest sin against her together. *"I'll regret it until I'm gone, until I'm dust, and long after."*

Lightning branched in an arc of kinetic energy behind Elden, striking the white space in a shower of sparks.

"Elden, I'll agree, but only if you let me resurrect Nox, as well."

So, yes. Elden's eyes reflected his view of Li, a red giant, from the nacre chamber. And, yes. Like all Icari, he was differently emotive in his facial expressions and body language. But there was no mistaking it.

Elden grinned bright enough to light his eyes. It was such a perfect echo of Xelan's signature smile that it squeezed Rayne's heart to see it. The behemoth of a god said, "Granted."

Rayne took Elden's white nacre from his hand and swallowed it.

Cheers to another year as someone's weapon, but at least this time, Rayne was given a choice.

"You are worth more to me."

Rayne's words were the first thing to trickle into Nox's consciousness—

A living consciousness.

Nox opened his eyes—his own eyes—and immediately panicked. "Rayne?!" Her name was hard to form, as if his tongue was unfinished.

Still, it proved effective as Rayne called to Nox from... Where were they? He couldn't see through a blurry haze.

"I'm here," she said with more gentleness than he deserved. "Try not to panic, okay? You're not... exactly done yet."

A form appeared at Nox's side, a Rayne-shaped blob haloed by the glow of her skin. Relief washed over him. They were momentarily fine. Even more so. Whatever situation they currently faced, together they could endure anything. Rayne had taught Nox that. With this in mind, he asked with his half-formed tongue, "What. Of. Enki?"

Rayne's smile was in her voice, sad and melancholy. "Gone." Something had transpired while Nox was resurrecting to cause the tremor in the word.

Nox's next attempt at speaking came easier. "Tell. Me." Even with all the adrenaline from waking half-made, unaware of his surroundings, he rallied enough consideration to add, "Please."

"We died." Rayne made a little noise at how preposterous her sentence sounded. "Elden resurrected me, and we're in the nacre chamber. I started your resurrection about ten hours ago."

Started his...

Nox couldn't keep the astonishment out of his voice. "Voluntarily?"

Rayne laughed, and there was irony in it. The gradually focusing blur of her moved a mass of hair over her shoulder as she said, "Yes. You still have work to do, soldier, unless... Well, I never thought to ask your consent. Nox, would you want to be resurrected—"

"Yes. Yes." Nox swallowed to say, "Absolutely." A sudden thought made him frown. "The. Weapon?"

Now Nox wished he could see, because Rayne's voice never sounded so beautiful. Elation suited her. "Gone. We're free." There was a slight tinge to the words, which he found curious, but excitement took precedence.

Free.

Seven million years as a killing machine—A nightmare sicked on the galaxy and aimed at the girl beside Nox. For the first time in his life, he could act without the trained impulse to harm and avoid contact of any other nature.

"You're crying. I know you can't see yet, but your tear ducts are working."

Rayne had bestowed a gift onto Nox. Her small hand slipped into his heavy palm and squeezed. Chronic anxiety washed over him as he waited for the words, 'Calibrating. Optimizing. Stabilizing … Unable to stabilize—'

But they never came.

The anxiety couldn't recede. Not fully, not yet. Instead, Nox heard Rayne's sniffles and smelled the salt of their tears. She *understood*. Aside from Korac, Rayne was the only person in the Vast Collective who could understand.

Rayne said, "No more warning. Rest now. It'll speed up the process if you don't interfere. I'll be right here." She took back her hand, but the warmth lingered. More so, Rayne hummed Queen's *Somebody to Love.*

Nox fell asleep to her gentle voice and the smell of ocean spray, seashells, and strawberry ice cream.

A heartbeat.

Strong, but …

Nox's resting heart rate beat once every two hours. This … this was a flurry of activity. Not since his childhood had Nox's pulse rushed this fast. With his eyes closed, he calmed himself, counting.

Fifty.

Per Minute.

Impossible.

Nox opened his eyes. Amber glass comprised the dome above him and, through it, Li blazed on. The same view in Rayne's Atramentous eyes.

"Rayne?"

A shuffling sound drew his attention to the right. As Rayne stood and approached, Nox's pulse increased by one beat per minute. He could see in his periphery. Long dark hair braided back from her face had left the angles of her cheeks and jaw in stark relief. Bright blue eyes searched Nox over with her brows drawn lightly in concern. Her lips were rosier than normal, like she'd bitten them with worry. Rayne had changed out of her Enki explosion gear into denim shorts and a cropped tank covered by a long sweater. She folded her arms into it, hugging herself, as she reached out and brushed a strand of hair from Nox's face. She looked small and tired.

"How are you feeling?" Rayne asked with a little bounce, like she'd been waiting a while.

Nox took account of his digits, extremities, mouth— He made a fist and clenched his jaw. *His* jaw. He could turn his head and look up at Rayne, fortunate as he was—

Was Nox clothed?!

The momentary anxiety sent his pulse racing, but Nox was indeed dressed in the same black t-shirt and jeans Rayne had made him wear in her consciousness.

Nox said, "I believe I'm finished. Except…" He wet his lips before adding, "My pulse is awfully quick for an Icarus nearing eight million."

Without a word, Rayne took Nox's hand and placed his fingers on her wrist.

The same.

Not only the number of beats per minute, but the rhythms were identical.

Nox frowned with the question Rayne was already answering. "Remember when Silence gave me the virus to permanently entrap me with my nacre? How mine almost absorbed yours? I kept ours separate as best I could, but this is a byproduct. Even with Elden's nacre, we still share the fusion from the one shard inside me."

"Elden's nacre?" Nox sat up inside the resurrection casket, frowning at her. "You took it?"

Rayne bit her thumbnail, nodding.

Nox's eyes widened, bewildered. "Why?"

Around her thumbnail, she said, "He asked me to. It's complicated, but it will help me with my mission.

I couldn't use mine. The shield virus kept the Weapon active, unlike yours, which dissipated when you detonated on Volcano Day. So, here I am, infused with your deity." She switched her eyes to Atramentous. It was still the view from the nacre chamber of Li's explosion, but there was a mirror of the image on the bottom. A vista of flames stretching on for eons—

"Nox." Rayne steadied him and switched her eyes back to a brilliant blue. "Sorry. I wish I had a mirror to see what it looks like."

With a shake of his head, Nox assured, "It looks impossible, but beautiful. In a terrifying way." Restored, he climbed out of the resurrection casket, nodding to Rayne as she stepped out of his way. Only when they stood face-to-face did Nox notice the touch of pink to her cheeks at his compliment. He looked away and cleared his throat into his fist to say, "You mentioned a mission."

Rayne's sweater brushed the tops of her combat boots as she swirled to walk away, presumably to hide her reaction to him calling her beautiful. With her back to him, she said, "The same mission as always: keep our people safe. But you saw her, Nox." Rayne turned and faced him, braids moving with the action. With appropriate gravity, she said, "Celindria's alive."

So grave. So tired.

While Rayne explained the deal with Elden, Nox boxed with his shadow, cast by the sun along the dome of Aegis bones. Nacre ore. Unbreakable—His fist went into it. Broke right into it, splintering broken glass in a spiderweb. With shards of nacre glass slithered under his skin, Nox announced, "This is new." He couldn't break nacre glass before ...

Rayne ran over and timidly checked Nox's fist as the ore regenerated around his bleeding hand. With a wince and a hiss of air through her teeth, she tried to pry it free, asking, "Are you okay?"

Absolutely not. Elden, Nox's ancestral father and leader of Cinder's Icari, was taking advantage of

Rayne like all the other planetary leaders in her life—Nox, included. Slamming his fist into the wall was therapeutic, all things considered. Only…

The genuine concern in Rayne's eyes told Nox he'd need to find a better outlet for his frustration around her. He couldn't have her worried about him every time he punched something in his lifetime of pain-induced catharsis.

"There. Can you remove your fist from the glass—Right, like that." Rayne sucked air through her teeth again, and, with more of her gentle demeanor, she said, "Let me see."

Nox tried not to look at her this close until Rayne asked knowingly, "Did it help?"

"Yes." Always honest with her.

Rayne kept her eyes on the healing wound, nodding. "I understand." When she met Nox's eyes, there was something close to appreciation in hers. "I get it, but we can't do this anymore, Nox. Let's take some of the healthier outlets we learned in my consciousness and use them in the real world. We're better than this."

Nox's pulse fluttered while he stared down at her, and they both looked away. Still, he assured, "I can't guarantee my success, but I will try." He stared at his fists, flexing it and wondering at the efficiency of this nacre upgrade. While she paced away, he asked, "About the mission? How do you want me?"

In seven million years, Nox could count maybe twenty times he'd wanted to retract a sentence the moment he said it. *That* was number twenty-one.

Another thrill raced through Nox's pulse before Rayne turned and crossed the entire nacre chamber from him, weaving between the pedestals. She said, "I want to give you the option to be on your own. Out in the world without a weaponized nacre. You could do anything you wanted and leave the rest to me and Elden—"

"Martyr."

Rayne stopped and stiffened with her back to him.

Nox examined the nacre on Elden's pedestal, saying, "I told you once, I wouldn't entertain your self-sacrificing notions, as your friends have done. Yet I understand… It's simply your nature. No, I don't believe I'll let you be rid of me so easily, your majesty." The nacre was Rayne's, all intermixed with Nox's forefather's nacre. A massive explosion waited inside this tiny pearl. What waited inside of Elden's?

Rayne was quiet for too long, so Nox turned to find her… smiling at him. With a sigh of relief, she said, "All right. I've sorted through Razor's dossier. There are some mutual contacts between him and Celindria on all the planets, even Earth and Cinder, which warrant some investigation. Obviously, it would go faster if you and I split up and rendezvous once we finished our assigned planets."

Split up.

Rayne trusted Nox on his own. Did he trust himself? He tapped his fist in his palm, considering. "Which planets will I take?"

Now Rayne beamed as she said, "Pil, Lukemore, and Reipon."

All the planets least likely to recognize Nox. Smart. He said, "Which leaves Lacceirus Capra, Cinder, Earth, Yu, and Mon3 for you. What about Thailea? And Ishkur?"

"There were no contacts on Yu. Legir's against all things Enki and Imminent, and I'm even more impressed those agencies didn't infiltrate his people. Thailea's murky in the dossier. Razor kept it off limits. Once we interrogate our marks, we'll rendezvous on Ishkur."

A thought occurred to Nox. He asked, "Do you have access to Elden's memories?"

Rayne shook her head, expression intensely grave.

Ah. So the arrangement was more of a benefit to the Icarean forefather than to her.

Rayne bit her lip before changing the subject, while the worry from earlier returned to her eyes. "I've been trying to reach Xelan, but he's not sleeping. I want him to know I'm alive because I'm worried about how he'll grieve for me otherwise."

After Savis died, Xelan had spent months in his labs before Colita convinced him to leave. And only then so he could see Korac at Nox's coronation while apparently stealing books from the castle. Nox confessed, "I believe your concern is merited, but you'll find your way to him. Of that I'm sure—"

A lurching groan resounded, disrupting their conversation. Nox was surprised it corresponded with the empty ache in his stomach.

An appetite. For Elden's sake, when was the last time Nox had wanted food?

Rayne snickered into her hand.

Nox crooked a brow at her.

"Oh no. Don't give me that look," Rayne said, giggling in her words. "I'm starving."

Affixed to the very northernmost point of Elden's sphere like a blister, the nacre chamber was only accessible via Seamswalking. Nox asked, "How do we leave?"

To answer his question, a conduit opened.

Elden?

Nox stepped up to the conduit, peering out. Red soil stretched on as far as the eye could see, ensconced in black mountains. Cinder. He stepped aside and bowed to the lady in the room, like the son his mother had raised. "After you."

Rayne had many smiles. Sad ones, happy ones. They were all beautiful, but this one... This one was special. Her eyes sparkled with it as she stepped through the conduit.

Nox followed her and instantly regretted his second chance.

Rayne's blood momentarily left her body, leaving her faint and nauseous. The conduit had led them into Nox's castle, standing on the observation platform right beside Elden's throne. Would this nightmare ever end? Why did Elden open the conduit to here?

Lightning flashed on the horizon.

Rayne couldn't face Nox. Couldn't think about him. Or think at all. The only thing Rayne could hear or see was her whimpers and the faces in the crowd who'd watched Nox decimate the existing trust and feelings between them.

It felt so long ago now. Living seven million years with Nox had extended Rayne's understanding of a lifetime. She wasn't the girl from that night, and he wasn't that Icarus. Not anymore.

Rehabilitation required trust, and this Icarus with a broken past had earned his second chance.

With her heart racing, Rayne turned to face Nox and found him—

Mirrors. Nox's Atramentous always transformed his eyes into mirrors, reflecting his victims' last moments back at them. Elden's throne was framed in Nox's eyes. He'd clenched his teeth and fists so tight the striations and veins popped. Their shared heart rate pounded beneath the skin.

"I'll regret it until I'm gone, until I'm dust, and long after."

Rayne tried to keep her voice calm, despite the emotional storm inside. "Nox." Thunder rumbled, echoing in the valley.

It drew Nox's attention to her. She looked so small—scared—in the mercury of his eyes.

"We move forward. I haven't forgiven you, but I won't hold it over your head. I know your remorse…" Nox winced at the word and Rayne softened her voice in apology as she continued. "…is genuine—I've *felt* it." She gestured at the throne, saying, "We leave this behind us and return to our mission."

Strangled, Nox strove to say, "I…" He didn't finish his thought. The former King of Cinder crossed the platform, lifted the massive symbol of so much wrong, and, with a great heave, hurled it into the valley below. Seconds later, a cacophony of exploding rock resounded.

Unable to stop herself, Rayne went to the edge and peered down. Stronger now, Nox had reduced Elden's throne to rubble. The site of Silence's introduction to Elden, where Umbra had raped Savis to conceive Nox, and—

Behind them.

Rayne put it behind them, and so did Nox, as he peered over the edge with her. Already more relaxed than earlier, his eyes had even returned to normal.

Impressed, Rayne said, "I don't even need to ask if *that* helped."

Nox gave a single nod.

The lightning and thunder ceased, and Rayne knew it was time. She asked, "Nox, are you prepared to move forward and take to your task?"

Nox admitted, "I could use the exercise."

Icari and their jokes.

"I'll miss you," Rayne blurted without thinking, and instantly regretted it. Her face went red before Nox glanced at her with brows raised. To save face, she stammered, "I mean. You've been good company, and I'll miss having you around to talk to." Was that really saving face if it was the absolute truth?

Nox conceded the point with a nod, but he also took in Rayne's features before turning away. With another clearing of his throat, Nox promised, "We'll see each other again. Soon." He punctuated the last with a crooked smile in Rayne's direction.

She marveled at the unpracticed expression, considering Korac's words, *"Nox actually smiled. That's right. Take a moment to let that sink in. I think I can count on one hand how often that happened in those years. In public. Xelan would remember better."*

In Rayne's brief life, she'd experienced more love and affection than Nox had received in his seven million years of existence. This lent to more smiles for her, but in the last two years with Nox, she was sure he'd smiled more worth her than in his entire lifetime.

"Rayne."

Too long in her head, Rayne blinked at him. "I'm sorry, what?"

Was that the ghost of a smirk? Nox asked, apparently again, "Who am I investigating?"

A little ego looked good on the enormous Icarus, but Rayne rallied her dignity. "An apprentice of Pil's head mechanized engineer, 2Lip. His former student had once helped package Progeny weapon designs for Celindria."

"The Seamswalking capsules?" Nox had hit the nail on the head.

Rayne nodded. "Exactly." She carried on listing off suspicious individuals and their alleged offenses per Razor's handy notes. Now and again wondering what were the enigmatic Pain Curator's true motivations? By the time she'd finished, Nox's stomach had growled four more times. Rayne giggled after each one, ignoring her own hunger pangs. "Okay. Do you think you can handle it?"

Nox looked on the verge of asking her something, but instead, he said, "Most certainly, your majesty."

Two conduits opened: one to Pil and one to L. Capra.

Alone.

They would go out alone, and only now did Rayne's heart trip with anxiety. She'd never really traveled alone before and had spent the last three years with the constant presence of another.

Lonely.

Rayne would feel lonely without Nox.

Maybe it was a good thing to be on her own for a bit? Certainly, it would benefit Nox to live away from his obsession with her. This was the right thing to do.

Rayne smiled as she took up beside her exit, promising, "We'll meet again in Ishkur. I'll let you decide when. Who knows? It might do you some good being out in the world without an explosive nacre."

There was... an anxiety in Nox. It tightened his shoulders and stiffened his speech as he stared into the conduit to Pil. "Quite," he offered out of hand.

Rayne stepped up to him, making Nox look down at her. She put all her best optimism into her face, eyes, and voice. "You deserve this second chance, and I think you'll find people will warm up to you as they did when you were younger."

Love.

Their pulse pounded with it.

Nox couldn't help how he responded to Rayne, and the devotion was in his eyes before he could look away. "I will find you when it's time."

There was no doubt about it. Nox would always find Rayne.

They stepped through and went to work. For the Shadow, for Elden, and for Iona Pax.

This would be the end.

⸻

"This one. This Icarus follows Surra and finds her beautiful."

A voice.

It had come to the Icarus in his sleep. How did he come to be asleep? Why couldn't he remember?

A second male said, "We must be wary. Are we certain this Probability will produce optimal results?"

The first one replied, "Your caution may be well-founded but a might tardy, One. The specimen is already in our midst and forever altered. Look at his hair."

Eyes closed, listening, breathing. Don't wake and don't alarm them. Let them carry on while the Icarus listened, laid out on a cold slab in a space which smelled of blood. No blood the Icarus had ever smelled before, but still the metallic tang couldn't be mistaken.

The second male, called 'One,' said, "His reaction to the Seam was unpredictable. Do you suppose the Feast of Roses could kill him?"

The deeper voice moved further from the slab. His footsteps sounded heavy compared to One. The larger man boomed, "No time to run tests. You freed Surra as Zero had instructed, and now we have set these events in motion. The Icarus listens. Order him to submerge in our blood. I cannot stay while the other Primaries are on high alert. Be careful, One."

"Be careful, Tumu."

Rayne, startled awake, sat upright on her cot. Into the silence, she breathed, "Tumu." Did she just dream of herself as Elden with Tumu in the room? The Feast of Roses was a space in the Seam, wasn't it? Where Sagan had dipped into a pool of Aegis blood and surfaced with enough power to bisect a planet?

Razor's dossier had mentioned Aegis agents of his father, Zero, once spied on him before the Tritans confined the Aegis within Gait's core, but something kept recurring in the Pain Curator's notes.

ONE IS STILL MISSING.

Rayne had taken it to mean 'one of them,' but what if Razor had meant someone *named* 'One' was missing?

With a fist scrunched in her hair, Rayne tried to calm her rapid pulse. No need to alert Nox. Five months had passed since she'd last seen him, and Rayne was starting to worry he couldn't find her because of all the lookalikes. Thousands of girls surrounded her at any location with her eye color, nearly identical bone structure, and black hair. It was… comforting after so many nasty-meaning people like Abresson had went on about how beautiful she was.

Anonymity was nice, and it let Rayne secure this bed in a random hostel on Monarch 3. When she had checked in, the drone at the door commented, "You're close, honey, but your eyes are a little too big and not far enough apart. But the hair?" He gave Rayne two thumbs up.

She couldn't wait to tell Nox about it. And her dream. And all the people she'd interrogated. And...

A sliver of light shone in through the window. Rayne craved the moonlight, but being inside a giant tree, she settled for the milky street lamp outside. She lifted her palms into it and closed them, trying to capture it.

Rayne missed Nox.

Somehow, the dream had left her even lonelier than before. The apprehension left her unsettled, especially with the lingering suspicion of Tumu. And who was One?

Rayne missed Xelan, too. Several times a day, every day, she tried to reach him in his dreams—Communicating across the galaxy with nacre fibers she'd woven into a bridge based on Elden's constructs.

Someone snored, and another person rolled over and scratched their side. The noises were amplified in the dark, so Rayne went still to listen beyond the room. People wandered along the avenues outside, some returning to their hives, while visitors sought a bed like the ones in this hostel. Their heartbeats betrayed their race to Rayne. Lamias beat closer to human heart rate where the drones fluttered in the realm of two hundred beats per minute.

All of them were waiting...

Waiting for the next battle.

The Concerted Empire of Iona Pax was a peace-loving effort among all the planets and Ishkur. Rayne was so proud of the Shadow, but here, in the outer worlds, an undercurrent of violence stirred.

Celindria.

The former Cult of Night Justice Rayne had interrogated on Earth confirmed it. He'd said, "Celindria came here two weeks ago and collected her pawns."

Rayne had narrowed her eyes, asking, "Pawns?"

The man took a heavy drink of his scotch, humphing in the affirmative before saying, "Those who she'd granted nacres for their diligent service. They left with her, unable to turn her down."

What a strange way to put it.

It was the same story on Lacceirus Capra and Cinder. The Caprent contact and the mad Icarus both raved about choice. Mostly about not having one when Celindria came to call.

Rayne looked forward to meeting this last contact here on Mon3 and regrouping with Nox. She most looked forward to making him smile at her jokes. For an Icarus with black eyes, they sure sparkled—

Why was Rayne's brain doing this to her in the middle of the night? Giving up on sleep, she gathered her things and joined the heartbeats outside. A stroll and some fresh tree air sounded nice.

Out here, Rayne focused more on the Shadow. Tameka and Sagan. Pax and Echo. The precious moments she was missing out here on her own. She couldn't wait for Xelan to sleep so she could get some news out of him—

"Our wedding will be a public event. We invite the entire Iona Pax to attend."

As if summoned by Rayne's wishful thinking, Sagan's voice carried out of a bar on a side street. Hurrying to the entrance, Rayne listened for the rest of the announcement.

Over the projection, Korac said, "Join us for the reception on the Palatial Grounds in Ishkur. Celebrate the union of Earth and Cinder—the formation of Iona Pax with us." He gave the date and exact location.

One month from now.

Rayne beamed. There was no way she was missing this. A little pain twinged her heart. While she would attend, she couldn't let the Shadow know she was there, but at least this way she could see how everyone was doing.

One more contact, and Rayne was free to rendezvous with Nox on Ishkur. She couldn't help but wonder if he'd attend the wedding, too.

━━━━━━━━━━━━━━━━━━━━━━━━━━━━━━━━━

In the two plus years in which Nox had lived within Rayne's consciousness, never once did he let himself imagine inhabiting his own body again. And never once did he imagine leaving her side. When Rayne proposed separate, dual missions, he'd swallowed the aversion to letting her go. Now...

Reipon boasted green oceans and four moons in the night sky. Nox easily lifted twice more than the other dock hands and carried the cargo over to a Prince's ship. Or yacht, luxury cruiser—Whatever. The royal Lamia's harem of women from all around Iona Pax giggled and waved at Nox while he worked undercover for his last contact. Millions of years of practice ignoring advances made it easy for Nox to lower his eyes and stay focused on the task. One deck below and two right turns brought him aft with the engines. There, a Lamia in coveralls with a utility belt waited.

"It *is* you," Celindria's contact said, drawing out the 'S' sound.

Nox ignored the recognition, not willing to argue. The last two contacts had made him before the bruising started as well, but Nox was generous enough to leave them breathing. Imminent filth. He couldn't keep the disdain from his voice as he said, "Tell me everything. Or don't. I came here for information, and if you give me what I want, I'll leave your jaw intact."

The Lamia jeered, "The angel will be so pleased to know you're alive—"

Thrown up against the wall, face smashed into the Lukemore plaster—Celindria's contact would need to bill her for his two front fangs.

Nox growled against the back of the Lamian engineer's head, "Why is Celindria recruiting? And why are these people so indebted to her that they can't refuse her?"

"Debt?" The Lamia choked the word out through purple blood and drywall dust. He drawled more on his 'S's as he said, "It's why they exist. Celindria won't care if you kill me, but you already know how casually she murders."

Frustrated, Nox let Celindria's contact go and stepped back.

Cartilage popped and adjusted as the minion hissed, "Join Celindria. No one will survive her procession through the empire. You could be Emperor to her Empress. Why fight it?"

Nox scoffed. "You fool. Have you not read the Verses? She's wronged me and the ones under my ward unforgivably."

"One need not forgive to accept their fate. Unless…" The sneer which spread across the engineer's face sickened Nox as the contact insisted, "I could understand preferring Rayne to Celindria, but she's dead. Is she not?"

Nox remained silent.

As if his quiet confirmed the truth, a grin split the Lamia's face in a poisoned crescent. He said, "What a magical lay the War King must've been. You bedded her once for the entire Vast Collective to see, and now you're some redeeming saint. I wonder if fucking her righteousness would absolve me of my sins?"

Nox spent the next hour detaching the Lamia's scales, one by one, until he tore out the bastard's nacre. Intelligence derived under duress wasn't trustworthy, but none of this was forthright.

Volition.

Nox had wrenched that much from the contact. Celindria was dallying once more in volition—

"We invite the entire Iona Pax to attend."

Sagan.

The Lamia's severed hand opened a seal to his engineering quarters. Nox entered, listening to the wedding announcement and public invitation.

"Join us for the reception on the Palatial Grounds in Ishkur. Celebrate the union of Earth and Cinder— the formation of Iona Pax with us."

Perfect.

After a well-concealed body disposal, Nox grabbed more cargo and hauled it off the ship under the guise of his 'job.' Once on the dock, he stopped to admire the ocean, dripping in moonlight. Often when things went quiet, mostly in the easiness of the night, his thoughts turned to Rayne. How was she doing alone in her head with all those memories and emotions he'd experienced with her? In their extreme intensity. Was the quiet strength she'd developed to endure them enough to get her through each night?

Rayne should afford herself more breaks. Enjoy what warmed her, what she found beautiful. What made her laugh. Nox wanted this for her. More than anyone he had ever known, Rayne deserved peace.

Once more on the docks, Nox stared out at the ocean, where waves yawned and stretched beneath their sleeping silver lovers.

It was time to return to Rayne. This spell apart was good for them, an exercise in independence, but in his bones he knew. Nox was sure of the perfect occasion for the rendezvous.

"All of Iona Pax knows why we gather today."

That was Iuo's voice coming over the speakers throughout the Palatial Grounds as Nox wended through the crowd. Yes. He was wearing a cloak with the hood pulled dramatically over his head. Some part of him knew Korac would find this hilarious. Even Rayne would snicker, but it was out of necessity. Nox's features were too recognizable.

The King Elect of Reipon continued, "Welcome to the union of General Sagan Sterling and General Korac of Cinder. In a beautiful blending of two races with a tempestuous history, this couple honors their unioned traditions to celebrate the establishment of our unified galaxy. The strife may not completely end with this ceremony, but hope will convey beyond it. A beacon we'll trust to follow on our journey to Eternity. So, no pressure, you two."

Over the speakers, Nox made out giggling. Definitely Sagan. Korac's laughter followed, and Nox smiled at the familiar sound.

Those among the Shadow made bets on how long this union would last. Some voices were familiar, while others were new.

Nox smirked at how each of them grossly underestimated Korac's obsession with his Progeny partner as Nox picked his way through the crowd. Most female attendees were Rayne tributes, but Nox had spent his life with her. They couldn't confuse his senses. He sought the beach and summer vacation. The gentle glow to her skin, and the fullness of her hair. Their heart beat was slowed for her, at peace, as was Nox even in his search for Rayne.

At the absurd gambling amounts, Sagan laughed until Korac said, "One million credits."

The audio went silent in the wake of his proclamation to the persistence of their relationship.

Nox couldn't stop himself from grinning with a chuckle.

Iuo started again. "Ahem. Yes. In front of those who stand witness, exchange your vows of union. From these words forth, you are wedded and belonging to each other."

Korac's smirk was in his voice. "Sagan Sterling, state your terms."

Elation in her words, Sagan said, "All of it to you."

After a pause blazing with joy, Korac offered, "Take from me what you need."

Sagan's voice trembled. "Give to me what you want."

Together, they finished, "Until Eternity takes me, I'm yours."

Korac was unioned, and Nox had been alive to see it. His chest swelled, and he hoped to one day congratulate his former General in person—

There.

Nox recognized Rayne, in hooded coat with her back to him. Even so, he knew without a doubt it was her. The cut of her shoulders fit the smell of Earth ice cream. Rayne watched on as the Shadow filed into the wedding reception and took up the dance floor.

She looked lonely, and that was an affront Nox wouldn't abide. "Why don't you go to them?"

A rush flooded through their shared pulse, flushing Nox with a thrill. This was unexpected. What did this reaction mean?

Under her hood, Rayne faked composure with a sideways glance in his direction. She said, "It might be hard to explain you."

Nox smirked, asking, "Can you imagine the gift it would be?"

Rayne shifted uncomfortably before saying, "It's better this way. Look at them—Thriving. They don't even know their enemy is alive, let alone at this event."

Nox's hood shifted as he looked down at her. "You believe Celindria is here?"

"I know." Rayne sounded beyond certain. "But it's far too public to attack and not really her style."

The very notion of their enemy so close to his nephew and best friend left Nox nauseated and enraged all at once.

Rayne changed the subject, gazing out at the reception. "I've never known a couple so perfect for each other."

"Quite."

Straightening her shoulders and raising her chin, Rayne asked, "Are you ready to get back to work?"

With sarcasm thick in his voice, Nox declared, "To defend the Concerted Empire anonymously against its greatest threat? Why, yes. I'm always ready."

"Let's go."

{CINDER | NEAR 6,000BCE}

The first ten nights in Nox's bed were a blur of erotic stimulation and steady infusions of oxytocin, serotonin, and dopamine. Celindria laid under an Icarean cotton sheet, eyes closed, surveying her body. Deliciously sore, she stretched and surveyed her internal functions. Mild dehydration and the beginnings of hunger—

Three days.

Sex with Nox had left Celindria unconscious for three days.

Wow.

Why had she even awakened—

Flowers.

Celindria's eyes snapped open. Blossoms of all colors and shapes filled the room in massive bouquets. There were other scents. She sought them out. Jasmine and oils...

Behind one impressive display of lilies at the foot of Nox's bed, Celindria spied a tub filled with steaming blue water and petals. The water on Cinder was black, so Nox needed to have this bath imported from Earth.

Celindria could become accustomed to such indulgences.

But we know we should not.

Why not? Are we not entitled to pleasure and comfort?

We ruin Nox—Always.

Perhaps this time will be different. It must be.

But we already know Nox deviates from Imminent's initial predictions. Remorse told us so, and we already bore the Tritan's young.

A woman can have multiple histories without them condemning her—

Not a woman like us.

Celindria dunked her head under the water, bathing her locs and braids. Oils lined the brim of the tub to cleanse and moisturize her skin and hair.

Nox was always so considerate.

Until Celindria condemns her lover to the Wrong Side of Eternity.

{PALATIAL GROUNDS | SAGAN AND KORAC'S WEDDING}

To witness the world through a billion lenses required a disciplined mind and a wealth of patience. Celindria watched the Shadow and each of their alternate realities file into Sagan's conduit for the stronghold in a kaleidoscope of colors, fabrics, and smiles.

Father stole the proverbial spotlight from his former lover. It was so richly petty. Celindria approved.

Xelan's Verse would soon surface, as had all the others, and Celindria wouldn't miss it for the Probability Matrix. Her golden gown spun with her turn as Celindria faced her armament. Her soldiers' eyes stared blankly beneath their hoods as she danced inside their minds.

Twelve hundred.

It was such a clean number for an escort force. A dozen hundred. Each of them had surrendered their volition in exchange for favors, while none of them understood what they had signed away. This mixed assortment of Icari, drones, Lamias, humans, and dwarves was only a taste.

Bored of the scene, Celindria stepped into the nearest shadow and walked into an alternate grounds some seven thousand Probabilities removed. From this Ishkur's barren wasteland, Celindria traveled anonymously through a series of conduits to this universe's Cinder. Once there, she flew hundreds of kilometers to a cave dwelling in Cinder's conglomeration of apartments, careful she wasn't followed. The small abode smelled of ash, as with all of Cinder. But under the pervading stench of Li's scorching punishment, Celindria made out the aroma of fresh baked bread and love.

As not to alarm the girl, Celindria called out, "Hope, I came to visit."

"Mother!" With a toddler on her hip, Hope peered around the kitchen corner. "Did you come to see Raisin?" She gave her two-year-old grandchild an extra bounce to indicate her.

Hope wasn't allowed outside. She was born with black hair, deep skin, and blue eyes—A perfect replica of Celindria. As Hope grew older, her skin had transitioned into Tritan blue, so she spent her life in hiding. Minus one irritating spurt of rebellion around 4000BCE. It was during this stunt which Celindria came out of seclusion to tame her daughter's dangerous adventure for the safety of their line.

Remorse and Abresson wouldn't have hesitated to snatch Hope and restrain her in stirrups like Silence.

Celindria let the shudder roll down her spine, but refused to give into it. It was only a concern in this one Probability. In all the others, Hope died a young mother. This was the only Probability in which Celindria met her daughter.

She brought herself back to the now, blinking at Raisin—Celindria's fifteenth great granddaughter—toddling toward her.

We could bring our family to Father, and he would ensure their safety as he did with us.

No. Father wouldn't let them cross the Probabilities. He wouldn't understand our ability, and he'd insist on learning more. Experiments, tests—No. There isn't time.

"How was the wedding?" Hope asked from the kitchen, where she pulled fresh bread from the clay oven.

Celindria lifted the toddler and kissed Raisin's coiled black hair. Her skin was richly purple, like Celindria's. Her genetics were strong.

What would Nox's daughter look like—
We never speak of this.

"It was beautiful, as expected." Celindria twirled Raisin around while the toddler squealed in delight. She said to Hope, "Any changes here?"

A utensil dropped in the kitchen, alarming Celindria. She turned the corner to find Hope's back to her.

The Tritan/Progeny girl sounded distraught as she asked, "You didn't talk to Grandfather, did you?"

Celindria sighed and set Raisin down, restraining from a power surge. She did *not* want this argument with her child. "Hope—"

"Mother! You promised you would at least discuss the options with him. You don't know. He may not try to perform tests on us. He might say, 'Yes.' Isn't it worth trying? One way or the other Remorse will find us here—"

"No."

In this Probability, Razor and Remorse both survived Rayne's destruction of Enki, as planned, and amassed their army of Rayne lookalike weapons to establish *their* empire. One of vice and breeding control.

Celindria held up her hand to stave any further arguments. She said, "Remorse won't find you as long as you stay within the conglomeration. I've already devised a transfer of leadership to me within the Shadow's Iona Pax. I won't leave you drifting in this half-life forever."

Hope's position was reasonable. "You've been saying that for eight thousand years."

"It's never been closer to the truth." Celindria gestured at herself. "Only I can shadow walk across the Probability Matrix, but I have soldiers who will meet the source on Thailea as I did. Then I'll fulfill my promise."

Hope chafed her arm, looking uncertain. Her voice was thin as she asked, "Will you need to hurt anyone? I've grown fond of the people you describe in the Shadow. Especially Korac. He sounds worth meeting."

Kill her.

Celindria contained herself. For only a fraction of a second did her eyes threaten to transition into Atramentous. No one who witnessed it could live. Celindria would endeavor to not kill her child over one innocent remark.

To the mundane and simple-minded, the Shadow's wholesome family aura emanated belonging and love.

To Celindria, the Shadow represented a fundamental imbalance in sense and logical decision-making. They drew too much from their emotions and put themselves in the position of relying on each other—

Vulnerability was lethal.

What about us? We want love.

We've only felt it from two people, and we ruined them both.

For power.

For Imminence.

"No, dear Hope. No one will feel a thing."

II   FLiCKER

{ISHKUR | CINDER II | FIVE DAYS AFTER THE WEDDING}
"I'M NOT ALONE, XELAN, AND NEITHER ARE YOU. Hang tight for me. It's almost over."

In their dream, Rayne let Xelan see Elden for reassurance, but the Icarean deity wasn't who was keeping her from being alone.

Nox stood guard for five days while Rayne convened with Xelan. After the wedding reception, the pair had opted to spend the night in the Palatial Grounds: a massive park of flora from all across Iona Pax. Water and fire features greeted every turn and delighted all those welcome to experience this majesty.

One such feature had captivated Rayne, and with little effort, she encouraged Nox to follow her on the path inside a ring of waterfalls. She'd expected a fountain inside. Instead they found a round alcove lined with blooming wisteria. Lounge chairs and chess tables were scattered within.

Like every night since Elden had resurrected her, Rayne had hoped to find Xelan dreaming. Finally, he let her in. Five days later, Rayne awakened on a lounger.

With no way of knowing this encounter had taken place, Nox had let Rayne sleep undisturbed. Now he stood with his back to her, defending the secret entrance.

Unbidden, Rayne thought of her confession to Xelan, *"I can't love Nox because you won't let me."* She hadn't lied, but it wasn't the complete truth. Rayne harbored feelings for Nox, but she wouldn't have guessed they were close to love until Xelan had asked her how she felt about Nox. Until she'd gone six months without Nox's presence. Until she opened her eyes and found him protecting her right now.

"Did you meet with Xelan?" the former Icarean King asked without turning around.

How did Nox know Rayne was awake?

Disheveled, she slipped her black boots over her cranberry leather-net leggings and readjusted her black tunic to drape off her shoulders. Still half-lost in her thoughts, Rayne peered down at her coat. It matched her leggings—The native color of Cinder's vegetation. Rayne awakened to find it covering her, but she didn't recall using it as a blanket.

To answer Nox's questions, she said, "Yes."

As if he knew Rayne was composing herself, Nox continued to face the entrance. There was a trace of regard in his voice as he asked, "Did you find him well?"

Rayne followed the lit trail across the violet-veined marble slab. When she stepped around Nox's front to meet his eyes, Rayne forced herself not to frown.

Nox's black shirt wrapped diagonally across his shoulders and chest, like the two halves weren't connected. When the two of them had first reunited at the wedding reception, the supplies belt he'd worn crossed on his chest and fastened his shirt. Now with it off, the soft material gaped, revealing the gray expanse of his chest. It reminded Rayne of Xelan's revelation about why his older brother had stopped wearing shirts altogether.

Umbra—rat bastard and the first King of Cinder—used to snatch Nox by his robes when in a foul mood. One day, Nox had endured enough and strangled his father with the robes. Their mother intervened. Xelan revealed it all in his Verse.

{"I grow tired of his hands on me."

"Then stop wearing your robes," Savis offered this as if it made utter sense. Not as if she were excusing Umbra's part in the conflict. "Your father will have no purchase on you."

The next thing Nox said only made sense in the hindsight of him discovering her rebellion, her willingness to have me murdered, and Nox usurping Umbra's throne. "Sensible, as always, Lady Savis. Yes. Let me disgrace this family with my lack of decorum to better reflect the savagery contained within these walls." He let Umbra go and never wore a shirt again.}

Rayne stared up at this Icarus, who'd compromised for her sake, and she tried to measure what it meant to her. She held out her hand, palm up. "You can see how Xelan is for yourself. He told me his Verse, and while I won't share our personal conversations with you, the rest he'll publicize. Letting you see it early won't be a breach of privacy."

An emotion—anxiety maybe?—tightened Nox's eyes before he took what Rayne offered. The entire transaction took place in seconds, while she watched his reactions closely. When he resurfaced, Nox stared over Rayne's head at the water spilling around them. She peered down at where he still held her hand.

Maybe it was a mistake letting Nox see the arguments between Korac and Xelan. Maybe Rayne's guardian wouldn't want those candid moments shared with his older brother. But dammit. The whole reason these Verses existed in the first place was because these three grown Icari never communicated like rational adults—

"The Ten Million Icari who'd sacrificed themselves for Earth's Sphere deserve tribute. Tameka was wise to suggest them for the next Iona." After learning about all of Xelan's history, that granular detail was Nox's takeaway from the Verse.

It left Rayne uneasy and a little hurt.

Especially so when Nox let go of her hand to reach for his bag. He said, "It's time to move from this place, unless you have further need of it?"

Rayne couldn't control her frown. Hell, she wanted to pout as she looked away. This wasn't the reaction she'd expected—

"I'm grateful to you." Nox's baritone was unexpectedly soft. It made her meet his eyes once more as he continued. "We can discuss his Verse once we reach a less exposed location."

Rayne wet her lips to say, "Xelan confirmed his hideouts for me toward the end. There's only one place safe enough for us, but it may not be safe to reach."

Nox quirked a brow at her, and Rayne tried not to appreciate the humor in his eyes. But it certainly cheered her up.

"Thailea."

As Rayne said the planet's name, Elden opened a conduit.

Nox wanted a word with his forefather. His abilities exceeded all those legends hidden throughout the annals and Verses across the galaxy. Who knew what bearing Elden's nacre was inflicting on Rayne?

Later.

Nox trusted in her capabilities and let Rayne proceed first. She stepped into the blizzard on the other side, and he thought to grab her coat before following. Before taking in his surroundings, Nox draped Rayne's coat over her shoulders, sheltering the exposed tattooed script of Elden's Verse on her back.

"Thank you," Rayne shouted over the howling wind.

Snow pelted them heavy enough to blanket them into their surroundings. The eastbound wind cut like an obsidian knife, but it couldn't distract from the view. Some of the snow wasn't snow at all. Among the white fluffy flakes, particles of iridescent shavings fell in a shimmering rainbow. Drifts of the stuff mounded all around them until they stood inside a prism with just enough light to illuminate the repeated diamond carets of ground and sky. The light came from within the planet as no star could pierce the volume of storm clouds above.

Rayne asked, "This is Thailea?"

Nox recognized the scent. In his Verse, Xelan had referred to it as 'harnessed potential:' the strike of steel against steel. Metallic and potent, there was no mistaking it. "This is Thailea."

And it would bury them in the phenomenal snow.

Rayne was up to her knees in it. She put her hood up, muttering, "Why isn't it cold?"

"It doesn't need to be if it can smother us to death. We need to keep moving. What direction, your majesty?" Nox reseated his cloak and followed her example, raising his hood, while he considered the spectacle accumulating around his ankles. His boots climbed to mid-thigh, performing admirably, but Rayne…

Through the netted leather material, the "snow" touched her skin. This bothered Nox.

With an attempt forward, Rayne nodded at the west, saying, "Elden brought us close to the coordinates. If we move west for about half an hour, we should find the location in Razor's dossier. He said it was inside a tree."

A tree?

Nox looked to the west and barely discerned a faint silhouette of tall structures through the blizzard. Those might be trees. With a glance at Rayne, he opened his wings. "You'll need to fly."

A single laugh escaped her as Rayne gestured at her knee-deep situation. "No shit. I'm almost buried over here." She detracted her wings, so sheer Nox could only see them for the gold flecks twinkling within. "Beat you to the treeline."

If those were even trees—

Rayne rocketed to the west.

Nox wasn't entirely competitive, but he knew it was good for Kings to lose occasionally. With that in mind, he went after Rayne. It wasn't easy. The wind kept throwing them around like toys, and conduits appeared randomly along their journey. He almost flew into Lukemore, but eventually caught up to Rayne.

Eyes front, she stayed the course, but there was a smirk tugging at the corner of her lips. It was enough to make Nox fold his wings down for better aerodynamics. He passed Rayne and beat her to the treeline.

It was, indeed, a forest filled with strange trees. Rather than roots, their bases were colossal pedestals of gray wood. The trunks emerged from these castle-sized foundations and stretched almost high enough to touch the clouds. There, they spread into branches with twinkling silver leaves. Thick and immense, the chrome canopy sheltered the forest from the snow.

Rayne alighted on the glowing forest floor and marveled at the first blossom she met, as blue as her eyes. "I've never heard of any place like this."

Nox agreed with a nod. Xelan had explored so many wonders during his Verse. The second half of his life was so completely removed from the childhood they'd shared that it surprised Nox the Traitor Prince could still care for the Icari at all. Or that he could care for his older brother at all.

The conversations Rayne had left out between her and Xelan involved Nox. He was certain of this. Their back and forth likely centered on Xelan's disdain for his older brother and any involvement between Nox and Rayne.

Would Rayne admit to bringing Nox to victory with her? Confess to sharing in a rehabilitation unlike any in the galaxy? Reveal she'd resurrected Nox—

"The tree we're looking for is this way." Rayne interrupted his thoughts with cheerful optimism in her sweet voice. She'd taken off her coat and stuffed it in her pack. When Rayne turned away and headed further west, her dense braids didn't conceal the tattoos on her back, despite the considerable volume and length of her hair. Over her shoulder, she called, "I thought we could walk and explore a bit on the way. It should only take us ten minutes to find it, considering how easy the cleared floor is to walk through. I kinda love it. Are there fairies on Thailea?"

Nox was looking at one. He followed Rayne as he always would and tried to keep his focus on the walk rather than Xelan's Verse or Rayne's graceful stride.

This went on for an hour.

"I swear—It should be right here." Rayne clicked her tongue while surveying a tree with one hand on her hip and the other thumbnail to her teeth. "I wonder how we keep missing it."

Nox offered unhelpfully, "That makes four circles now." He made sure to sound bemused, sitting on a tree root big enough to fashion an Icarean clipper.

Rayne sighed, and there was so much frustration in it that Nox chuckled. He said, "Patience, your majesty. You'll find it."

The next sound she made wasn't very feminine and reminded him of a growl. "I must be standing right on it." She thudded her palm against one of the tree's bases—

"Ow!"

Nox straightened and hopped off the root to her side. "What is it?"

Rayne pouted, beguiling Nox, but the sight of her blood in her palm, bright red and dripping, affected him. He dropped his hands and looked anywhere else. The fallen silver leaves, the glistening gray bark on the trees, the door opening beside them—

Nox pointed.

Excitement glittered in Rayne's eyes as she wiped the blood on her coat. "Hey! No way! That was almost movie-convenient."

He shook his head incredulous, smirking. "Complain about misgivings, not gifts, King Rayne."

The frown returned to her face.

"What is it?" Nox asked.

Rayne shouldered her supplies, ready to enter, before admitting, "I think I'm sad I'm not a King anymore. They're elected now, and Tempest won. She totally deserves it, but I kinda liked being the first female King."

Nox bundled his gear, hauled it over his shoulder, and went first this time.

"You're the only King to whom I'd kneel, your majesty."

Rayne let Nox go inside first while her cheeks flamed. The old Icarean King would've incited the sudden thrill in her pulse, but in this moment, she wondered if he knew the effect of his words. Biting her lip, she took a steadying breath and shored herself.

Living with Nox.

Nox and Rayne. Alone together in a hideout.

Sleeping, and dressing, and showering where Nox also did those things.

Right. She had this.

Rayne stepped inside the tree's foundation and gaped. This was a marvel of nanite engineering and oozed with Wingmaster decor syndrome. The "treeloft," as Razor referred to it, was a hollowed-out basin and smelled of fresh growth. Rayne stood in a living area with an L-shaped couch to the side, partnered with a little coffee table. All of it was laser cut by nanites from the natural wood with cushions piled on top. To her left was a wall with stairs mounted into it, also carved out of the tree.

In the corner ahead, Xelan had carved out a library and filled it with tabs and books. Rayne couldn't wait to nestle in some of the cushioned chairs and geek out at whatever her guardian found interesting enough to store here. She rounded the corner to the left. This area was for dining. Tables and chairs, a bar—All in gray wood. Again, the wall was on her left. It climbed to the loft upstairs, and Rayne wondered what was up there.

Directly across from her was another corner and the kitchen. More tech was in here than anywhere else in the house, and yup—Stove and sink still worked. What a relief. There was even a small refrigeration unit and some root storage. Plenty of counter space, down the length of which Rayne spotted Nox.

He was standing in an open space with holes drilled into the floor and into the ceiling high above. It was the last area of the downstairs. Rayne asked, "What is it?" before wandering over to the far wall.

Nox frowned. "I'm uncertain, but I think—"

His face went completely flat when Rayne brushed her fingers on the far wall and activated the high-tech shower taps.

Incredulous, Nox glared, dripping wet.

"Sorry!" She rushed to turn them off, but found the dryer instead.

Nox looked like he was in a music video with his arms folded and his hair billowing everywhere.

Rayne died with laughter, held her ribs and everything. "I promise I'm more sorry than I seem." She finally found the off switch and blinked.

How did Nox look better than a few minutes ago? If Rayne had stood under the water and the dryer, her makeup would've run down her face, and her hair would've fallen flat, frizzed out.

But not Nox. He looked like the cover of a 90s romance novel.

This notion gave Rayne a case of the giggles, which stayed with her all the way around the corners.

Nox called after her, "What do you find so amusing?"

"Nothing. Nothing at all," Rayne said, climbing the stairs.

He followed, his footfalls heavier than hers, and the enormous Icarus was almost too broad for the staircase. When they arrived on the landing, they both stopped and peered into the loft.

This hideout was U-shaped, and the upstairs area took up the inside of the U.

With a bed.

That's it. A bed and one wardrobe for storing clothes. Spanning the entire upstairs loft, the mattress was enormous. And singular. As in one.

"Dibs on the bed." Rayne called it.

Nox humphed as she ran and jumped into it.

Sweet, heavenly softness, but the mattress was still firm enough to treat Rayne's back right. She sighed, saying, "Finally, a real bed." From up here, she peered around at the loft. All the furniture and finishes were black, gray, and white, with pops of color here and there. It made Rayne smile. "Good ol' Wingmaster."

Nox's heavy boots on the steps drew her attention back to him. Rayne asked, "Will you be all right with the couch?"

He'd descended far enough to fold his arms on the loft floor and lean forward. Nox assured, "I'm accustomed to hunting for weeks with nothing. Not even a tent. If the ashen ground of Cinder was good enough, I'm sure the couch will suit me. I'm more concerned about the openness of the shower."

Rayne's eyes widened a little as she considered showering without cover of any kind. She'd gone communal with the rest of the Shadow in the Ionas, but… Nox was different.

He seemed to understand it, too. "I'll fasten a sheet. One from this bed should span the kitchen and keep the spaces separate." Without waiting for her to respond, he went through the drawers until he pulled out a sheet.

A fresh one.

Rayne climbed out of the bed, saying, "We should probably clean, anyway. I'm surprised there's no dust."

As he descended the stairs, Nox said, "Xelan automated a nanite cleaning schedule. Leave this one chore to me and settle in, your majesty."

Rayne admitted, "This is my first time living with someone other than family. If you don't count the couple of months with the Shadow after Invasion Day." Climbing back into the bed, she moved to the upstairs banister to peer down at him.

After a second of consideration, Nox shrugged and confessed, "In a way, neither have I. I was alone or near my brothers." He glanced up at her, and Rayne recognized the gravity which weighted his eyes when Nox sought something more meaningful from her. He asked, "Should we set some ground rules?"

Nox set about his task of hanging the sheet across a line from the loft to the kitchen with this absurdly sized sheet. Light emanated from all the tree's surfaces and from a window high enough above them to come from within the tree's trunk. Meanwhile, he took in the tale-tale silence of Rayne over thinking his question.

After a few more heartbeats, she said, "I know you dress more for my comfort."

Ah.

Nox stopped stretching to hang this thing and glanced over his shoulder at Rayne, waiting for her to continue.

Kindness filled her voice as she offered, "You can go around without a shirt in the treeloft. I mean…" Pink kissed Rayne's cheeks, and Nox returned to his task, eyes off of her. She continued to explain, "I want you to be comfortable here."

Quite.

Did Rayne realize how much she martyred herself? Nox made her uncomfortable, with only a gap in his shirt. Yes, the material on his skin grated. However, he understand something vital to this arrangement.

Rayne would never clutch at Nox out of malice or control, and frankly, she was welcome to clutch at him anyway she wanted.

"I'm fine as I am."

Did she mutter something? "What was that?"

Rayne asked, "How was your last six months?" Movement from above indicated she was unpacking.

Nox was fairly certain that's not what she'd said. He crossed from the kitchen to the stairs in fifteen steps. He thought better of knocking when Rayne came to the railing and greeted him with a curious smile.

Nox said, "I met my contacts, as I'm sure you met yours. It was an experience different from any other to work among regular people, almost completely anonymous." He felt silly as he climbed into the compensation-sized bed to drape the sheet down the line on the other side.

Rayne sat on the bed with a sigh. "Yeah. I know what you mean. There's so many Rayne tributes,

I mostly blended in. I still think some people can sense that… whatever thing the Tritans said about me—"

"Your biorhythms are synchronized within yourself and the Probability Matrix, but it's not the only reason you stand out." When Nox righted, he accidentally bumped into Rayne. Catching her from falling off the bed meant searing his hand on her back tattoos…

Rayne blinked into his face, inches away. She breathed, "You can touch gold."

Nox considered this lack of another weakness he attributed to the resurrection—

He took entirely too much notice of the softness of Rayne's skin and the firmness of the well-toned muscle beneath.

Rayne breathed against his hand, staring into his eyes, and their pulse raced. Nox tried to resist, but his gaze went to her lips, the color of rose petals and fuller still.

Rayne bolted up from the bed and cleared her throat, resuming her task of settling in. She spared not one glance in his direction.

There was a time when Nox would find Rayne's reaction arousing, stimulating the chase. He'd once relished such a streak of confusion and self-doubt cultivated over endless nights of reminding Rayne how small and fragile her body was. It had become more satisfying after Rayne grew stronger and more sure of herself that she'd still felt threatened by Nox's physical prowess.

Now Rayne's internal turmoil only hurt Nox. Deeply wounded him in ways he needed to unpack before he could reassure her in the only language he understood between them. Nox vowed, "I won't take anymore pieces from you, Rayne."

She stopped midway through folding a shirt and hugged it to her chest. Was Rayne on the verge of tears? Nox didn't want this. Not anymore. He stood slowly and kept his distance from her as he went to the stairs. Perhaps, after some privacy, she could withstand his presence—

"Nox."

Halfway down, he turned and faced the woman he loved and had wronged irrevocably.

Rayne lifted her chin a little higher as she said, "I know you won't hurt me. That's not why I got off the bed. It's less about you than you think because Eternity knows you love me."

Nox considered the softness of her voice—the sadness in it. A thought occurred to him. "Is it because of Xelan?"

The answer was in Rayne's eyes before she could hide it. So that's what she and Xelan had discussed in their private conversation.

After running a hand through his hair, frustrated, Nox said, "Whatever he told you, he's right. We can forget this moment ever happened and get back to work. The curtain's up for the shower." He glanced around, taking in the loft's openness. "There's not much privacy, but I promise to respect your space. I'll go out and check our surroundings, and perhaps find something to eat."

"Nox, wait." Rayne followed him down the stairs and stood on eye-level with him three steps up. "I agree focusing on work is best for us, but I want us to be friends here. Like we were before."

"I'll miss you."

Nox would never forget Rayne's confession before they'd parted. Looking into her eyes now, he knew she had, in fact, missed him. As he had missed her. He nodded to assure her before asking, "How will we go about killing Celindria?"

Rayne held up a finger as she climbed the stairs and returned with a tablet. "This is how."

Nox glanced through the files—histories, eyewitness accounts, locations. Impressed, he asked, "Where did you get all of this?"

"Mostly Xelan. As you saw in his Verse, he'd planned to take on Imminent all along. But matters grew more complicated and out of his hands. Now, we'll pick up his work."

Nox frowned a little. "And he approves?"

Rayne insisted with a nod. "Xelan wants to come in on it at some point, but I want to keep the Shadow at bay for as long as possible. He has a kid. Then Korac and Sagan have Echo. I—we—have nothing holding us back."

Free agents. It seemed wrong Rayne lived her life this way, broken and unattached because she was never granted purchase. But Nox understood. He held up his index finger. "I insist on one caveat."

"Anything."

Recovering, he said, "We bring Korac in first. Sagan, too."

Rayne beamed, and it melted Nox. "You got it, Night King."

Oh, yes. Their time here would prove quite interesting, indeed.

═══════════════════

Rayne grew tired of waiting for Nox to return, so she went on an expedition of her own. The ethereal glow of the trees made the forest magical, as she wandered through the maze of tree bases. Flowers blossomed phosphorescent petals, yielding to persistent and luminescent bees. All around, leaves rained from the canopy, twinkling in their descent. Rayne picked them from her braids, smiling.

"No conduits," she muttered to herself.

Bird song sounded from all around, and occasionally, one walloped. There wasn't another word for the bizarre call, likely a mating one. Rayne giggled at the notion and silently wished the fella good luck on his mission.

Since they'd spent six months apart, this time alone wasn't so hard on Rayne as were those first weeks. Before she'd spent lifetimes with Nox in her head, friends and family had fully enveloped her life. School stuff, hangouts, and training with…

Xelan.

Rayne was worried about her guardian. Heart heavy with concern, she strolled back to the treeloft, all the while thanking Xelan for letting her do this without him. For now.

One prick of her blood let Rayne through the door. It reminded her of so long ago when Xelan had asked Rayne to give her blood to a disc for the stronghold. Maybe it was an all-access pass?

Rayne froze in the doorway.

The shower was on.

Nox was in the shower.

Visuals filled her head, ones Rayne made herself shake away. Tucking her hair behind her ear, Rayne turned the first corner, calling, "I'm back!"

Through the splashing, Nox said, "Food is in the kitchen."

Oh?

Curious and starving, Rayne rounded the next corner into the kitchen/bathroom space. She couldn't help but reflect on a time when she'd suppressed her appetite—

Nox was in the shower.

Okay.

Rayne already knew that, but the sheet…

The light from the window above and the surrounding glowing wood cast a perfect silhouette of Nox against the white sheet, like a screen in a movie. A dirty movie.

Although Rayne's cheeks blazed, she couldn't tear her eyes away. Not from *that*.

Nox was running soap across his shoulders, chest, stomach—He paused before he went any lower and stared at the sheet. In the Icarean way, he gave an avian head tilt, peering. After another heartbeat, he started walking toward—

Toward Rayne.

In a panic, she went to the vegetables and—was that a plucked bird?—on the counter and tried to look busy preparing dinner.

The sheet pulled back, and Nox called, "Did you need anything?"

Need.

Rayne bit her lip and hoped he couldn't see her burning blush from over there. To control the breathy, shakiness of her voice, she kept her answer short. "No. Thanks."

The sheet reseated, and the shower turned off after a few more minutes.

In those minutes, Rayne cut *one* parsnip-looking root. But it's not like she could concentrate. Not while she kept seeing—

"The door works for my blood as well. It must be DNA based, but it seems rather clumsy of Xelan. Why not bio-lock it to keep me out?" Nox found a towel and squeezed his hair dry while he padded into the room wearing far more clothes than five minutes ago. A long-sleeved shirt held together with buckles, and soft pants Rayne would steal if they'd fit her. He set the towel aside and peered at her, eyes narrowed. "What do you make of it, your majesty?"

Oh, right. The door.

Rayne turned and tried to focus on the potato-thing while saying, "Uhm, I agree. It does seem curious, but convenient, so I don't think we should worry about it much. Did you check out the files?"

Nox came up beside her and hauled the bird over to the kitchen island. There, he butchered it with the precision of one long accustomed to hunting. He said, "Yes. When do we begin?"

At least Rayne could speak to this with a clear head. "Tomorrow."

"Then you should appraise the shower before bed. A spring supplies the water, but for the life of me, I can't find the source. Another of my brother's mysteries to solve."

Ah, but that could wait. Rayne asked, "Can we talk about Xelan's Verse now?"

Nox chopped harder, which didn't bode well for the conversation. It hurt Rayne that so much had come between the three—Korac, Xelan, and Nox—but she mourned the brothers' relationship especially.

Please. Say something.

"When Xelan left us for the Vacating, I never imagined he thought anything good of our childhood—our time as brothers. The story of the festival was unexpected, and it troubles me that he recalled any instance of mother's abuse. No matter how heroic Xelan's recollection made me seem, I never wanted the toddler he was at the time to remember those brawls with Umbra to protect Savis."

There was a finality to the thunk of the knife in the butcher block, and the reverberation throbbed in Rayne's heart. The emptiness which followed made her want to turn around and console Nox. Until he said, "I would've killed her sooner if I'd known she'd threatened my brother. Ever, let alone at such a young age. How cold she was. Telling him she would force him to kill Many Feet. Why did we deserve constant punishment—"

Nox stopped speaking abruptly, and Rayne whirled to reach out to him. "I'm sorry for bringing it up—"

"No, Rayne." He kept his back to her, shoulders slumped, but his voice softened as he said, "You're right for asking us to face it." Nox gave a bitter laugh before admitting, "It doesn't make it without complications though, does it?"

Rayne worried her lips with her teeth until an idea struck her. She put herself in Nox's line of sight, and she saw her reflection in his Atramentous gaze. "Tell me one thing you liked about his Verse. Something which made you happy to read."

A tiny frown wrinkled Nox's dark brows as he considered her request. After a few seconds, the Atramentous dissipated and he listed on his fingers, "Everything involving Pax, Xelan's confrontation with Abresson over the children of Gait, and..." His lips—full and soft—crooked into a smirk as he said, "Mercury Turbo."

Could one groan and laugh at the same time? Because that's the noise Rayne made. "What was Xelan thinking?!"

Nox turned, hands back-gripping the counter as he leaned his ass on it. "Indeed."

Rayne's grin softened into a smile the longer she stared at him until she said, "Tell me whatever you want about it when you're ready. I won't push anymore. Let's cook this poor creature you slaughtered and eat it in thanks."

They cooked a while in companionable silence before Nox interrupted another round of Rayne imagining him in the shower.

"There was one other aspect I liked. I only caught glimpses of it, of course."

Rayne checked the vegetables roasting in the oven, calling over her shoulder, "Hmm?"

Nox confessed, "The way Xelan treats you."

Nox knew Rayne stiffened only because she missed her guardian something terribly. They never reunited properly after his resurrection, and it was long past due. When she turned and faced Nox, tears glittered in her brilliant blue eyes. Her brief nod said more than words.

Rayne loved Xelan like a father, and she would need to see him again soon.

The savory smell of the spit rotisserie within the kitchen island triggered Nox's appetite for food rather than the woman in the room with him. He said, "I'll see if we have plates."

Two minutes later, they sat together at the small dining area. It seemed so bizarre, Nox eating dinner with Rayne, but there was an easiness between them which lent to more talk of Xelan's Verse.

Well-meaning in her curiosity, Rayne asked, "Did the conversations between Korac and Xelan make you angry with your brother all over again?"

"I'm not angry with him. I'm angry that he's right." Nox looked away to shake his head, shamed. Being honest with himself, he said, "Xelan has every right to hate me."

"I don't think he hates you or he wouldn't distribute your Verse to the entire empire."

A good point.

Nox conceded with a nod of his head, but knew without a doubt there was little love left between the brothers. He glanced up at Rayne.

Except hers. Her kindness was holding this triumvirate of relationships together: Nox, Korac, and Xelan. And Rayne was winning.

Also, hungry. Her plate was empty before Nox's.

Rayne patted her stomach. "I was living off scraps for the last six months. You're an excellent chef, by the way. I'll clear the dishes."

With his mouth full, Nox stopped Rayne by touching her hand. Electricity traveled from his fingers to other places in response. Swallowing more than his food, Nox said, "You shower. We should wake early tomorrow for sparring."

The grin which blossomed on Rayne's face melted Nox. "Thanks. I've been dying to try the water out. You said it was… what had you said?"

"Effervescent. There's no other way to describe it, and I'm determined to find its source before our work here is done."

"Thanks," Rayne repeated before heading around the corner to the kitchen/shower.

Nox collected their plates and the roast platter and rounded the corner to the kitchen sink—

Frozen in place, Nox watched as Rayne receded all of her clothes in an unusual display, projected against the white sheet. He damned near dropped the plates as the shower started, and Rayne loosed her hair under the spray. He imagined his hands on her breasts while she turned her face up to the water and smoothed her hair back—

Stop.

Look away.

Nox took the dishes to the sink, finding a nanite scrubbing device. He would leave this room, and he would *not* look back—

Rayne made a sound.

An involuntary moan.

It drew his eyes back to her. Suds sluiced from everywhere on Rayne, and her hands traveled lower with it—

This…

Was familiar.

Earlier, Rayne came into the kitchen while Nox was showering. About this point in his cleansing, Nox swore honeysuckle bloomed and perfumed the air—

"Oh, wow. You were right." The taps turned off while Rayne said, "It was… frothy. So much fun. I've never felt anything like it."

Nox stared straight down at the dishes he'd yet to wash and tried to blink those undeserved images of Rayne away.

They persisted.

"We definitely have to find where it comes from and see if we can swim it." Rayne was already drying herself and growing more clothing.

The sound of her bare feet padding on the floor did something to Nox. Never had he imagined this level of trust between them. This comfortable companionship. Earlier, they'd almost… Well, Nox wasn't certain what exactly had transpired, but he'd been a breath away from kissing her, and Rayne didn't exactly protest to it so much as say things were too complicated—

"I owe you some strawberry ice cream."

Rayne stood behind him when Nox turned around, looking small in a baseball shirt barely covering her thighs. Near-sheer cotton contained all the capable muscle and the swells of her curves beneath it. During their dinner, whatever passed for night in this area of Thailea fell, and the treeloft grew considerably cooler. But never did Nox notice it so much as looking at Rayne in that shirt right now.

"Ow."

Her complaint brought Nox back to reality. He asked, "What is it?"

Rayne was combing her fingers through her hair— Well, not exactly. It was tangling. She pouted and whined cutely. "I don't think the water likes my hair." To further her pout, she glanced at Nox's hair. "How is yours so healthy?"

With a chuckle at her pitiful face, Nox rummaged through his things until he found the bottle he wanted. Shaking it, he gestured for her to turn around. Once she did, he explained, "Mother told her sons to always keep sleh oil with us at all times." He smoothed the liquid, warmed in his palms, through the considerable length of her thick hair.

Rayne giggled.

Nox took a comb and ran it through the ends, asking, "What's so amusing?"

"It's funny taking hair advice from you, is all."

For some Elden forsaken reason, Rayne's words twinged. Nox defended himself. "I try to look nice. We can't all be as naturally gorgeous as Korac." The comb glided through the silky ends in a soothing rhythm.

Rayne's voice was soft as she said, "It's not that. I always liked your hair. It's so soft and shiny. My fingers wouldn't tangle in it—"

She clapped a hand over her mouth.

Too late.

Every compliment Rayne paid Nox reminded him of their situation. He loved her, and she couldn't forgive him. And she was right. But...

"I'm sorry for making things awkward," Rayne gently offered. She turned back around and gazed up at Nox, vulnerable and undressed beneath her night clothes.

There was trust.

There was respect.

But there was also a daily reminder Nox lived with his desire for her. He stemmed it and tried to respect her personal space. But the idea she could admire even a small part of him tested Nox.

No, he would do nothing she didn't want. But Rayne danced passionately, fought passionately, sang, trained—even slept passionately. She held nothing back. He could grip her by the arms now and kiss her, which would inevitably lead to deeper intimacy. Nox had taken advantage of that once, and he refused to do it again.

"You did nothing wrong," he assured. After swallowing his restraint, Nox said, "I'm ready to sleep." Which was true. Before his resurrection, he'd only sleep once per year—Such was his age. Now, Nox slept once a week, and he'd spent the last one watching over Rayne while she spoke to Xelan. He could use the rest.

A sweet smile spread across her lips. "You're right. Big day tomorrow."

Nox followed Rayne back around the corner, through the dining space, and to the stairs. She climbed until he looked away, as the shirt revealed more than her legs.

Almost nervously, Rayne waved to him as she ascended. "Good night, Nox."

"Good night, your majesty," he said while spreading a blanket across the long end of the L-shaped couch.

The sight must've been amusing, because she giggled on her way up.

Nox loved the sound.

The memory of her silhouetted against the sheet nearly chased him into sleep before Rayne asked from the upper loft, "What's the 'Eternal Bind'?"

Ah.

Celindria talk before bed would surely give Nox nightmares. Still, he said, "I believe it's a myth regarding the Probability Matrix. Xelan or Tumu would be better to ask—Silence—or anyone more familiar with the Matrix."

The sound of Rayne shifting in the sheets as she rolled over left Nox imagining her in bed. She asked, "But why would Celindria think you two are it when you don't even know what 'it' is?"

That was a good question. One Nox had contemplated over these last six months. He said, "My more immediate concern is with how she plans to 'revive' me, as promised. The Tritans took regular samples of my nacre at different intervals in my upgrades. There are a multitude of versions to choose from."

Some of them were not as humane as Nox's current incarnation.

Rayne sighed and said, "Sorry for bringing it up. It's the reason I could never sleep growing up. All my thoughts wait for me at the end of the day."

Nox could relate. "Sleep well knowing our people are safe and capable of defending themselves against anything. We will see it so."

There was a smile in Rayne's voice as she said, "Thanks. Icari always know the exact right thing to say."

"Seven million years of practice. Get some rest." Gorgeous warrior of Nox's dreams.

Too much. Too much had happened in the last twenty-four hours. Ready for bed, he stretched out on the couch and—

His feet dangled off the end, and Nox nearly barked out a laugh.

But of course they did.

{CINDER | NEAR 6,000BCE}

It was nearing time. Every day on Cinder, Celindria worked toward securing her Imminence and the power to mend her heart and mind—soul—whatever word described a conscience and the ability to experience love. For the last one hundred years in Nox's Castle, she'd captured glimpses of joy, charity, and love in all its forms. Breaths half-taken and gone in a heartbeat.

Here and now Celindria felt loss. Naked, she had draped herself in a sheet when she took to the balcony. Li spanned above while ashen Cinder stretched below. The view perhaps contributed to her melancholy. Celindria mourned love, potent in its brevity and only captured with—

"Celindria."

She closed her eyes and soaked in the sound of her name from Nox's lips. He awoke from where she'd left him sleeping, deeper in the room. Able to touch only Celindria, Nox stood behind her and gripped her biceps. His front was warm against her back, and Celindria leaned against him. Staring at the wrong in the galaxy had stolen the life from her, and so much of it was her doing.

A sob broke from Celindria's lips, and she choked on another.

Nox kissed the top of her locs. "Tell me what troubles you."

Tears squeezed from Celindria's eyes, but she shook her head, unwilling to tell the truth and unwilling to lie. Instead, Celindria turned and climbed to her tiptoes, taking her lover's face in her hands and bringing Nox down to sear her with his kiss. To slip the sheet from Celindria's shoulders and put his hands on her.

Nox backed them onto a chaise on the balcony and sat with Celindria straddling him.

Loss.

Love.

Through her tears, Celindria took love from Nox— The only time she ever felt it completely was in his arms.

And she would destroy him for it.

Celindria would keep this pregnancy only to end it. For Imminence, for Nox's resurrection, and for consecrating the Eternal Bind—No image of a blue-eyed girl in Cascading Light could stop it.

{Now}

Celindria awakened, frightened for the first time in eight thousand years.

The Probabilities were shrinking.

This shouldn't occur until later, after Celindria's Nox was ready. What could this mean for the Eternal Bind? Her calculations were clear: once the pair who comprised the Eternal Bind united, the Probabilities would vanish until only one remained.

The only true existence.

The initial fear abated, and now Celindria felt nothing as she wandered across her chambers. A backward glance at the vacant bed, in all its grandeur, reminded the First Progeny of her most important task. Nox would wake today.

Naked as before, Celindria walked onto her balcony. A nacre shield prevented the wind from slashing at her, one thousand stories into the air. From up here, the Empress could look down upon her empire.

Ishkur never looked so beautiful.

Under Celindria's rule, the galaxy was an Eden. All the people were her, and they were closer to happiness than she could ever be. Not since she'd stepped into Cascading Light's source on Thailea.

In this reality, Razor's last act against Celindria's invasion was to split the Aegis planet in half with the Chorus.

It was a pity, as Celindria couldn't migrate her forces to other universes. This Probability's Remorse had enjoyed taunting her about it in his last moments. "The one man you never fucked, fucked you in the end, you bitch." His mad laughter bayed like a hyena, knowing his end was near.

Primary Rem had died on his knees, screaming.

This was Celindria's favorite reality. She only needed Nox to complete it. In all the Probabilities passed, when he'd resurrected on Gait, he'd first confront Celindria about the loss of their child.

Nox called it murder.

Celindria called it costly.

The price she paid for this empire. The one she'd named Paradise.

Once Celindria explained to him how she fought for everything while feeling nothing—For him, for them, for everyone—Nox always came around because that's who they were.

The Eternal Bind.

All the other Probabilities in the Matrix eventually fell in line, proving Celindria's hypothesis about their relationship. And yet...

They were shrinking.

This felt above her, beyond her—Ancient.

But how?

During Imminent's calls, Razor had warned Remorse that his father—the Exalted, Zero, leader of the Aegis—maintained one or two pure bred agents disguised within the Twelve Worlds. Was it possible these carefully orchestrated manipulations of the Probability Matrix legitimized the Pain Curator's guilt-induced paranoia as valid concerns?

Aegis.

Beings of incredible intellect and patience. Even a single one free in the galaxy posed a threat to Celindria's machinations, but explained so much of the trouble Imminent had encountered within the dominant Probability.

Nox danced with Rayne.

Korac fell in love with the Seamswalker.

Nox took Rayne for all of Cinder to see.

Rayne disintegrated Nox's nacre.

Silence awakened and sided with the Shadow.

Andrew was exposed to Cascading Light.

Xelan resurrected.

Sagan destroyed their source of Aegis blood and ore.

Pax stayed with his family.

Razor killed Remorse and Bol.

Never mind the countless deaths, survivals, and alliances—broken and formed.

Celindria leaned on the balcony's balustrade and stared out at the glittering lights miles below. Across the galaxy, she worked the populace. Every single being contributed to the operation of Paradise, and they all loved it. Inside their mindscapes, they cried with grateful tears and thanked Celindria for releasing them from the constant threat of decision. Saving them from heartache and loss.

Two experiences Celindria both never wanted to endure again and begged to feel with every heartbeat.

Once she finished creating Nox and exposed him to Cascading Light's source, they could bring Hope here. Afterward, they'd establish this as the dominant reality and reduce the others until none but Paradise remained.

Only then would Celindria feel love again.

III   HEAT

SAGAN WAS LAYING OUT ON A SECLUDED BEACH ON AN UNKNOWN PLANET AND TAKING IN SOME RAYS. Yeah, she was naked. Tan lines weren't her thing. Besides, the only two people here were her and—

Korac emerged from the surf with the sun setting at his back. Purple water sluiced down his chest, abs, hips—

"God damn," Sagan muttered to herself.

The sexy smirk spreading on Korac's lips told Sagan she was doing the thing again. Drooling. Knowingly, he smoothed his soaking wet hair back from his face and turned to give her his side profile against the sunset.

Was Korac walking in slow motion, or was Sagan imagining it? Why did this beach smell like watermelon and frost-tipped pine?

Realizing her mouth was open, Sagan snapped it shut, but not before he said, "I love the way you look at me." He raked his eyes over her bare skin, blond hair to cute toes, which she wiggled for effect.

When Korac laughed, it was like a gift to Sagan, especially considering his history. He rewarded her with a peck on her forehead, dripping water on her tan.

Sagan promised, "I'm getting in that water with you as soon as I'm done cooking."

Korac took a drink from a water bottle, perhaps intentionally letting it stream from his lips down his chin, throat, chest...

Drooling.

With all the love in her, Sagan swatted him. "Quit it. I know this is our honeymoon, but we can't *only* have sex and ogle each other the entire time."

"Why not?"

Sagan's laugh was only half-incredulous because it all sounded so appealing.

Korac sobered abruptly and swallowed hard enough for Sagan to see it before he asked, "Actually, amos, could you take me somewhere?"

A little concerned, she propped herself up. "Of course. Where?"

"Well..." Korac dried himself off and squeezed the water from his hair, taking his time to consider his next words. Eventually, he said, "I want to go to the nacre chamber as a pilgrimage of sorts. Ask for Elden's blessing in person."

Sagan wasn't sure why that was so hard for him to ask, but she was happy to say, "Yeah, let me get dressed. I don't think the Coalition needs to see us naked."

"That's a damned shame."

Ten minutes later, they were dressed in beachwear, and Sagan opened a conduit to the nacre chamber. Together, they stepped into the amber-colored dome. The sight of it against the exploding star always took her breath away.

Curiously, Sagan noticed the resurrection caskets Celindria had once used were still on the highest dais. Putting the notion aside, she offered, "I'll let you have some privacy and stay down here on the bottom tier."

Korac had tied his hair back in a long ponytail, which moved with him as he nodded to Sagan. Without a word, he climbed the broad steps to Elden's pedestal, and she watched his hair sway. His shoulders seemed tighter than usual, indicating this was hard for him.

Privacy, as promised, Sagan examined the lower nacres. They were different colors, and the first one she sought was purple like her eyes. Strange—

"Thank you for bringing me," Korac said, as he headed back down. He was a master at schooling his face into a mask of composure, but his eyes were drawn tight. A stress he wasn't willing to share. Yet.

Sagan beamed at him. "Are you ready to go back to the beach?"

Korac smirked, saying, "Night swimming with you? What're we waiting for?"

They made love in the ocean—several times—until Sagan suggested a snack break. Under a blanket of stars unmarred by light pollution, they fed each other in a cutesy display sure to make Pehton sick. Speaking of, "How are Bones and Pehton doing on their mission?"

Korac, lying on his side with his head propped in his hand, stared out at the two moons reflected on the water's surface. He said, "They're investigating a case on Pil. Since Matt and Lucy took Bethany there, I wanted to make sure there was backup available to them. Not to mention, they only look into human trafficking, and we can't have that shit in Iona Pax."

Xelan certainly set the bar high with the vice industry. It wasn't completely outlawed, but heavily regulated. At least this world was safer for Echo. Wingmaster wanted the brightest future for their children.

Xelan.

"You're frowning, babe." The endearment always sounded so silly coming from Korac, but damn it sure cheered Sagan up.

She asked, "Do you think Xelan and Tameka will be okay? I mean... You can't hold everything together all the time, right?"

Korac rolled over and rifled through their things, but still answered, "They'll be fine. Not only are they more resilient than they'll ever give each other credit for, but they also called in professional help. I don't necessarily want to speak to a shrink, but I will do it to be a better man for you."

Warmth filled Sagan's chest until a tear fell from her lashes. "Thank you." She'd already had her own sessions to cope with the Razor trauma. More than anything, Sagan wanted to regain some of the girl Korac had met in the beginning.

"Aha. Our time in the stronghold wasn't completely wasted." Korac found whatever he was looking for and rolled back over with—

"Is that a riding crop?" Sagan's eyes widened as Korac switched it on. Electricity buzzed from it, sending a thrill through her. "Did you steal this from Xelan's secret bunker in the study?"

The grin on Korac's face was sexy, anticipatory, and a little wild. "Oh, I certainly did."

Sagan laughed, incredulous, but she couldn't keep the goofy smile off her face as she asked, "What're your terms?"

"All of it to me."

Somehow, Sagan knew Korac would say that.

Tameka loved Xelan. So, so much. No quirks or unhealthy coping mechanisms could change that. He was strong for her when she needed it. Helped her—helped all the Progeny—discover their own inner strengths. Now, Tameka could be strong for Xelan.

"But why did you name it Mercury Turbo, daddy?! You're so silly."

Pax giggled as Xelan tucked him, telling his son more stories. "Because I'm cool, kiddo. That's why."

Xelan had slept every night for the last two days. Ten hours the first night, and eight the second. After they had found him hiding in the Divine Booth, mumbling about Rayne, Tameka stayed with him on watch. Tonight, she leaned in Pax's doorway, watching her little family play and laugh.

This was therapy.

Speaking of, Tameka liked the Lamian psychologist the most of the fifteen professionals called in to help the Shadow manage. The people of Reipon, known for maintaining the old regime's histories, were such good listeners. And good at keeping secrets.

"You want a reprieve, Peaches?"

Tameka closed the door, as she greeted Tumu with a smile. He and Lamassau opted to stay a few extra days once the others had left, following the spectacular finale to Xelan's Verse. While chafing her arms, she said, "He's been doing better since the first night of sleep, and Legir has some herbal remedies to help with the chronic insomnia."

Tumu shook his head, a little smile on his lipless mouth. "You tough Progeny—I wasn't asking about him."

Tameka blew the air from her cheeks and let her head hang for a heartbeat. She was fine. Really. So why couldn't she say it to Tumu? She lifted her chin and met his voids, realizing she couldn't lie to him.

After ensuring the door was indeed closed, Tameka blurted in a whisper, "How long before an Icarean male can smell pregnancy in his mate?"

Tumu took Tameka's hand in both of his and gently squeezed. "I'm glad you finally told someone. It won't be a secret for much longer. I'd say another week, and Xelan will know."

Pregnancy was determined by the health and mentality of the nacre-bearing female. Tameka wanted another baby with Xelan, and this time, he'd help with the delivery. Maybe a little girl this go-around? With Xelan's hair and Tameka's eyes.

But the conception had taken place in a world without Celindria and without doubt.

Unfortunately, the last two days were filled with both—

A hand, much bigger than hers, moved to Tameka's shoulder. Tumu asked, "Would you care for my advice?"

Tameka very much would. Unable to voice as much, she nodded.

"We've learned from our history that the world is never certain and never safe. I supported you while you brought Pax into this galaxy during the worst of it I'd seen since the Aegis-Tritan wars. You were so magnificent, Peaches. Why should now be any different? It's safer than ever before, and your children are sure to live more securely than any in the empire. Especially with you and Xelan as parents."

Okay. A tear totally squeezed out. Tameka brushed it away, feeling better. She asked, "Do you think it's a good time with Xelan and all?"

Tumu leaned back so he could take in her face, thumbing away tears, and fixing her coiled red hair. All the while saying, "I've never been more certain of anything. Xelan will adore your daughter, and all the potential she represents."

Daughter.

She.

Tameka beamed.

"There's Peaches." Tumu pinched her chin briefly before looking at the door. "He's coming. I think it's best to tell him before he finds out on his own, and

I want to take over for you tonight. I'll ensure he sleeps."

Feeling worlds better, Tameka nodded. "Thank you, Tumu."

The door opened, and Xelan offered a weak smile. "My paranoia's telling me you two were talking about me."

Tameka exchanged a glance with Tumu before admitting, "We were. I think I'm gonna check in on our elected Kings and get some work done tonight. Are you okay with a shift change?"

Xelan smiled graciously, with only a faint hint of shame. Better than yesterday. He asked, "So Tumu's my guard tonight?"

"If you think all this," Tumu gestured at himself, "Is too distracting for you to sleep, then I can always ask Lam to play watchman."

Tameka snickered. It was a good laugh, and her first one in days.

With a ghost of his signature grin, Xelan said to Tumu, "I think I'll still manage just fine." To Tameka, he said, "Let me know if you need my help with any of it."

"Ah, ah, ah." Tumu wagged his finger. "One week of no work. We all know the doctor's orders."

"Right." The smile vanished from Xelan's face, and he looked ready to escape the three-way conversation. After clearing his throat, he asked, "Shall we?"

Tameka couldn't leave it like this. She jumped and adhered to her mate, searing to Xelan's bones with the beat of her heart.

A kiss.

Xelan returned in kind, though with more gratitude and the apology he'd kept repeating since he confessed to letting Celindria go.

During the moment, Tameka forgot they had an audience until a camera snapped. An old-fashioned shutter noise.

Mid-kiss, they both stopped and turned stiffly to find Iuo at the end of the hall, waving awkwardly.

"Hi."

As if she weighed nothing, Xelan easily held onto Tameka while he asked, "King Elect, what do you have to say for yourself?"

Tumu chuckled, as if he already knew the answer.

"Well," Iuo started with an awkward reach for the back of his neck. "I have this series in mind, starring the imperial family. You know? Really humanize everyone along with the Verses and Rayne's biopic. 'Your Warrior Majesties.' Eh?"

Tameka exchanged an incredulous look with Tumu, but Xelan beamed. "I love it. Let's discuss it more tomorrow. And Iuo? Have you been here this whole time?"

Reipon's King Elect gave a sheepish smile. "Yes. Yes, I have."

Lamassau came around the corner. "We can't seem to make him go home." The green Tritan punctuated his statement by pouring a bag of Chili Cheese Frito into his mouth.

This was a bit much, and Tameka still needed to do a lot of work. Not to mention, she felt the same hunger pangs she'd experienced with Pax's pregnancy. "We can all chat tomorrow. Iuo, you're welcome to stay for however long you want. In fact, I may borrow you for some work. Xelan, you and Tumu—"

"And me," Lam chimed.

"—I'll see you when I come to bed."

"OoooOooo." All the men in this hallway but Xelan were twelve-year-olds.

Tameka wouldn't trade this for the worlds, and as Co-Emperor, she didn't have to.

An hour later, Tameka was looking over the tablets on Xelan's desk. Iuo sat on the sofa, governing his own planet remotely. Aria and Torch meditated at the door. Lam and Tumu were downstairs with Xelan.

The stronghold was quiet. The perfect time to make an unpleasant call.

A voice filled with gravel answered the palm device. "Co-Emperor."

"Caedes, please call me Tameka. You earned it long ago."

The little display of him blushed blue before he offered a "humph" in response.

Tameka sighed, asking, "Have you uncovered any reports about Celindria?"

"Chris and I took Andrius out with us on our rounds. He was right. *Suggestion* is beyond convenient for security work. The guard who was stationed on the load of Pil platinum paid six million credits each to keep his coworkers quiet while he left with the supplies."

Damn. "I thought we screened them all with Kyle and Andrew?"

Caedes nodded. "We did, and until this occurred, the other guards considered the thief an upstanding citizen of the empire. His background check and track record are clean. It's almost as if one day he simply decided to commit the crime and disappear."

"Disappear?" Iuo asked from across the room.

Tameka frowned, considering the abrupt change in personality. "This reeks of volition."

Again, Caedes nodded. "Andrius thinks so. Chris has some follow-up questions. With his firsthand experience, I'm letting him lead the investigation on the other planets. Especially those who benefited from the stolen supplies. I notified Bones since he's out with Pehton to check on the orphanage Xelan suspects Celindria established. The hospital on Reipon, too."

Tameka didn't like this. She muttered, "We're following in her footsteps rather than predicting her next move."

"I'll get my people on Reipon to see about the hospital. You focus your people on anticipating patterns." Iuo's idea was a great one.

Caedes agreed. "I think that works, and I think I have a solid lead on Cinder. We want to see Twenty-One and Miy off on a safe journey to Tumu's homeworld. Not a journey contaminated by this woman's infection."

It was a good word for the malignancy the First Progeny spread across the galaxy.

Keeping a promise, Tameka offered, "I'll send T.A.O. with you to speed things along. She's eager to find Celindria, too."

"Understandably," Caedes said before changing the subject. "How is Pax?"

Heartwarming and wholesome—Caedes was such a surprise, considering how he'd started with the Shadow. It made Tameka smile as she said, "He's asleep and can't wait to see you and Auntie Pehton again soon."

"Please get some rest, Tameka. Good night."

Caedes disappeared from her palm without waiting for a reply. Gruff as always, and such a good friend—

"An investor once offered me half a billion credits to produce a film of your forbidden relationship."

"Forbidden—What?!"

Iuo held up his hands. "Hear me out. A throuple with you, Xelan, and Caedes."

Tameka scoffed and threw a paperweight at the back of the Lamia's head.

Iuo laughed as he caught it, stood, and backed away with his hands out in surrender. "I turned it down. Relax."

"Go. Home."

Kyle's bedroom in Merit's Iona smelled of lilies, cannabis, and cucumbers. The latter meant Smith was getting off outside the door again, fucking voyeur. Silence didn't care. She liked to put on a show. As a woman who was accustomed to public sex with a deity lover, who could blame her?

Not Kyle who presently enjoyed her long nails gripping the sheets beneath them while he repaid in kind against Silence's hips. He loved how her curves fit in his hands and relished how her hair moved when she threw her head back.

Yeah, Smith might as well listen 'cause he was missing one helluva show.

After a few hours, they finished—many, many times—and cuddled up with each other for sleep. Every night was like this, and Kyle enjoyed every second. Especially since...

Well.

Kyle couldn't shake this feeling that something would take Silence away from him soon. Call it paranoia after losing her once before, but it lingered in his chest and burned like acid. Even while he idly brushed the blue streak of Silence's black hair out of her steel eyes, he couldn't ignore the inkling.

Silence purred so beautifully in satisfaction as she shifted even closer still, until she laid half across Kyle's chest. She kissed over his nacre—The woman who'd invented the custom, and thereby understood more than anyone its significance. A promise to live and die together as one.

Kyle kissed the top of her head and let her snuggle while he stared up at the ceiling.

Silence never slept. Her nacres were ancient, taken from two Gargantuan Tritans. Pablo and Lynn cured those nacres of the shield virus which blocked incoming upgrades and nanite transmissions. She was also fully vaccinated from volition—It was required as of two days ago.

Fucking Xelan.

Kyle must've sighed, because Silence asked, "Will you give your troubles to me, so I may share in them? Or keep me in the dark?"

She would be fine with either because she understood bearing certain burdens alone.

But that wasn't Kyle's style. "With Celindria out there, I'm worried about Bethany on Pil with Matt and Lucy."

Silence lifted her head to meet Kyle's eyes and said, "Your concern is natural. Celindria hungers for those with extraordinary talents such as Bethany, but your sister… Her eagerness to live as Matt and Lucy—two predators—would eventually lead to unhappiness here if you'd kept her from going on a hunt."

Unhappiness in Bethany manifested in awful fits and self harm, and Kyle hated to see it in his baby sister.

Silence lowered her cheek back to his chest and asked against his skin, "Do you blame Ross?"

This was a hard question to answer, but if put simply, Kyle would say, "No."

"But you hold her accountable?"

This line of question was the sort of depth which made Kyle avoid the therapists Tameka and Xelan brought in to treat the Shadow's PTSD. His voice was soft as he confessed, "Maybe." Splaying his fingers against Silence's bare back soothed him as he considered her question more. "And no. I was the oldest, and it was my job to protect them. I did the best I could, and I don't blame myself at all for what happened because Bethany's recovery should be in Ross' hands. I protected her, so she could protect the baby." Mind him, Bethany had only been twelve, and Ross only fifteen when Invasion Day had torn their family apart.

Silence lived up to her name, and the kind of quiet she could create told Kyle he was wrong.

He sighed. "I know. I know it's not fair, and I promise, I'll see the first psychologist I run into tomorrow."

With all the wisdom of her long life, Silence said, "That is best, and in solidarity, so will I."

"Do you think Bethany will be all right out there?"

Her lips spread into a smile against his chest. "The little huntress will feed and be home before you know it."

Why was the thought of Kyle's little sister out there kicking ass so fucking comforting?

<hr>

Andrew awakened in an empty bed.

Again.

It was the second night in a row since they'd returned to the zeppelin outside Nikki's Iona after Xelan's Verse. Both nights, Andrew dreamt of Celindria decimating Iona Pax with her mad ambitions. And both nights, he awakened to cold sheets and the ginger scent of Lucas lingering on his pillow.

Andrew had ignored it the first time, but not tonight. With a quick hop into some shorts, he left their room in search of his lover with a clandestine past.

Bathroom.

Kitchen.

Closet.

Living Space—

Where the hell was Lucas?!

Andrew didn't understand the source of the panic. Maybe it was residual from his nightmare? Maybe it resulted from Xelan's confession? Whatever the reason, Andrew's heart threatened to choke him until he ran out the door and opened his wings.

"Lucas?!" Where the fuck—

"Up here."

Andrew gazed up to the very top of the zeppelin where Lucas sat, waving at him. Within seconds, the Progeny flew up to meet his Icarean partner. The neatness of whom intimidated Andrew, flustered in his shorts. Lucas had already donned a three-piece suit, gelled his sandy-blond hair, and pulled it back to let his molten gold eyes have center stage. Only they were red-rimmed, and the scent of salt permeated the surrounding air.

Concerned, Andrew sat beside Lucas and plopped his chin on the other man's shoulder. Andrew asked, "Do you want to talk about it?" He could check his lover's intentions, but doubted he'd find an honest answer there.

Lucas sat with his elbows resting on his knees, hands hanging down. They stared out at the ocean where a non-mutated whaleshark spouted red water into the pre-dawn air. Gull-like birds with horns circled above. It would make for a beautiful sunrise, and Xelan did his best to program realistic ones to the shields, turning around Ishkur's unnamed star.

So Andrew would sit here, cuddling Lucas, until the Icarus volunteered his woes or the sun greeted them on the horizon.

Several minutes later, when the rays first streaked the sky, Lucas confessed, "I miss my people."

"The Brethren?"

Lucas shook his head, staring at the beach and not meeting Andrew's eyes. The ancient spy said, "My father and my brothers."

They'd never discussed his family before. Andrew assumed it was information Lucas would volunteer if or when he was ready. Wrapping his arms around his lover's middle, Andrew squeezed and asked, "Can you visit them?"

Lucas shook his head. That was all. He stared out at the rising sun and envisioned a family Andrew couldn't see, lamenting a loss untold—

Light bulb. Eureka. Epiphany—Whatever. Andrew declared, "You can."

Now Lucas finally looked at Andrew. With something shifting in his golden eyes, he asked, "How's that, amos?"

Okay. So. Andrew totally indulged too much in Lucas calling him the pet name Icari often gave their partners. That aside, he said, "Kyle can return you to the memories, and you can relive them. We did the interactive memory walk with the girls and the gorge. Do you remember? We were in Tumu's sanctum, waiting for the battle—"

"Yes. Yes. I recall, but…" Lucas looked back out to the horizon and swallowed before he said, "I'm afraid that isn't so in my case." With a big inhale, moving Andrew a bit with him, Lucas said, "Andrew, thank you for this."

Still stuck on the whole 'isn't so in my case' bit, Andrew frowned at his lover's gratitude. "For what?"

Lucas hugged him, saying, "This." He patted one of Andrew's hands. "Now come on. We have a long day of work ahead of us, trying to narrow down why the Probability Matrix is shrinking. I won't fail the Kings and our Emperors."

They shifted and opened their wings. In flight, Andrew asked, "Do you think Celindria is behind it?"

Back on the ground already, Lucas straightened his bow tie while saying, "We can't rule her out."

"You don't sound certain," Andrew said while they returned to the zeppelin. He didn't mind running around the Shadow without a shirt on, but he liked to dress for work to get a semblance of compartmentalization of his life.

From the doorway, Lucas said, "There can always be multiple factors contributing to the dilemma. No need to assume Celindria is entirely responsible."

Dressed and outside once again, Andrew asked, "You've been around Celindria for a while. What was it like?"

They passed through the conduit to their place and entered the Shadow… Foyer? Landing? The place where all their conduits met. As they traveled, Lucas said, "It was like witnessing a powerful toddler throw a tantrum while holding the multi-verse in her hands."

Andrew gave a bewildered, conceding nod as they entered Ishkur's bridge. There, they stared down into the swirling maelstrom of Cascading Light while walking along nanite-railed gangplanks. Dizzying and dangerous.

Silence and Smith waited on the level below, ready to begin. One grinned and glowed in her bikini and labcoat. The other smirked because Smith communicated mostly in smiles.

Andrew asked, "Where's T.A.O.? I thought she wanted to join us—"

The eldest Seamswalker appeared beside him with her violet Atramentous eyes set on the vortex. "There are fewer."

Silence shot Andrew and Lucas a curious glance.

Smith hopped his ass on the glass gangplank and dangled his legs over the whirlpool. His smirk shifted into something more challenging, as if he dared anyone to tell him to move.

Andrew ignored the look and answered Silence's wordless question. "It's true. The Probabilities have been shrinking, especially within the last five days."

Lucas handed out diagnostic reports on the Matrix, and they all glimpsed over the irrefutable data. Their job today was to meet and discern any patterns. Brainstorm. It might take hours or days, even—

"It's natural," Lucas said after swiping one-page of the five-volume analysis.

Silence nodded, agreeing.

Smith, who never once looked at it, stared across the nightmare below and simply did not contribute.

Andrew exchanged a glance with T.A.O., who was the only person that looked confused or even concerned. He said, "I'm sorry. Can you three please share your findings with the rest of the class?"

Lucas did the thing where he gave Andrew a sexy smirk, which Lucas did when he found Andrew adorable for something young or obvious. The Icarus pointed to the readings on the tab. "See this dissolution marker here? And here? It means those Probabilities died of natural causes to put it frankly."

At Andrew's frown, Silence explained, "Their Verse ended from some resolution."

"The end of their story?" T.A.O. seemed faster on the uptake than Andrew.

Musing to himself, Smith asked, "I wonder if it was happy?"

Lucas spared his comrade a bemused look before meeting Andrew's eyes again. He said, "You're right, though. We should be concerned. Probabilities rarely end this way—Especially so young. Yet, here we are with evidence of it in our hands. It may even mean our world is at risk of dissolution. We should investigate their endings to learn what brought them on."

End.

End of the Verse—A universal apocalypse.

And the three most knowledgeable people in the room didn't look alarmed at all. There was something to this pattern. Something familiar.

Andrew would work with his team to solve this, but he'd also consult some outside help. Sources with less suspicious ties to the Probability Matrix.

Tumu was the first person who came to mind. Andrew only hoped the Tritan Primary wasn't too busy helping with Xelan to spare a few minutes to brainstorm about the world ending.

So this was simply a normal day at the office.

{6,000BCE}

In every Probability, Celindria returned from meeting with Remorse in the Ignis Desert to find Nox in bed with Colita.

And in every Probability, it masticated Celindria's heart. The sound of Nox finding pleasure with someone else, but especially with a lower being. The smell of cinnamon, clove, and sex—It was nauseating and left Celindria dizzy with disgust. The hurt in Nox's eyes when he spied Celindria watching.

It's our fault.

We brought this on ourselves.

Every. Single. Time.

We didn't have to let the Tritan inside us. Nor did we have to let Nox overhear our plans for it to happen again. We could always choose Nox, and we always choose to hurt him.

Bitch.

Korac's disapproval culminated in his cold white eyes was almost refreshing compared to the pain in Nox's or the satisfaction in Colita's. Celindria knew from Korac's grip on her arm that he would relish enforcing her punishment—He always did. She'd been a threat to their triumvirate from the beginning, and Korac couldn't understand how little consequence it was to Celindria's calculations.

Nox was hers. Even now, her lover couldn't stand to watch the lashings. Not out of cowardice, but because he knew as well as she, this felt wrong. Neither of them should force the other one to suffer. And yet—

The whip struck the moment Celindria deactivated her nacre. Pain lanced as the lashing split her back wide open. For the gathered audience, she cried out.

Skin came off the bone with the second strike, and the night air cooled Celindria's blood as it spilled down her exposed back. Copper filled her mouth where she'd bit her tongue from the exquisite blow. There was a scent on the air other than iron and salt. Peppermint and winter. Korac lived up to his reputation.

During this pause, Celindria gauged the crowd—Shock and concern. They knew her for good deeds. Now here the Icari treated her so badly—

Nox.

In every Probability, after the second blow, he regretted assigning the punishment, and came around the corner to stop it. He always gaped at the horror he'd put Celindria through.

We always forgive Nox, because we know it wasn't his fault.

It's ours.

And Korac's.

The insurrection which forged the Vacating must always happen. Celindria shouted to the crowd, "I am like you! I am not like your Icarean masters. They beat me to frighten you. But know that I am not afraid." For effect, she glared at Nox with madness in her eyes. "Keep beating me. I will free them in the end."

With little convincing, Korac posed to continue, but Nox—

His eyes.

They'd shifted into Atramentous, and Celindria saw her battered body in his reflection. The picture of betrayal and all things Nox would come to hate.

More lashes; more bleeding and screaming for the masses. Until…

"Stop!"

Celindria could always count on her maker.

{Now}

Celindria's lab occupied three hundred and fifty floors of the imperial space-scraper. Each one was furnished in glass and steel surfaces, projected monitors, and instruments from the best minds across Paradise—Razor and 2Lip included. Her inspiration preferred the first floor.

Nacre glass, body slice displays greeted Celindria in the foyer. Remarkable bodies—Those of the Progeny. Like all else in this Probability, they'd fallen to her volition, but unlike the rest of the populace, the Progeny were perfect specimens for research once kept apart, alive and unable to regenerate.

They forgave us, and we reduced them to this.

Father approved of it.

Lies. Father is dead in all but the dominant Probability. Ask if he'd approve now!
Why do we lie to ourselves so much?
STOP!

The lights dimmed and lit again.

Celindria opened her eyes, straightened her white pantsuit, and resumed course.

The body sliced Progeny and their young lined the walk down the lab's main aisle. Pax waved from his station as she went by, and she nodded on her way deeper into the lab. The prize of Celindria's creativity waited at the end.

Nox stood sentinel over Paradise.

Or at least her replica of him. This one possessed a nacre templated after Nox had invaded Earth, but before he'd captured Rayne. When Remorse and Abresson harassed Nox for breaking their precious beauty's arm, they'd sampled his DNA then.

Celindria's favorite Nox: flushed with victory and high on malice.

The fight sex would only be bested by the makeup sex.

Unfortunately, one ingredient remained. When Razor bisected Thailea, Celindria had lost her source of Aegis blood and Cascading Light. She could return with both from the dominant Probability to perfect her creation. Except Korac was the last remaining Aegis to Celindria's knowledge after Razor had departed the worlds in a publicity stunt.

Before Rayne destroyed Enki, the Silver General only ascended into the Atheneum in two realities: the dominant one and one where Korac and Razor ruled together as Aegis brothers. Korac died in all the others.

We kill him.
Always. We dismiss Korac's execution as a mercy.
No need to let him suffer alone without Xelan and Nox.

Celindria smiled at the recollection of every instance. Korac died the same—left mad and alone inside the nacre chamber. A fitting tomb.

Now, Celindria gazed into Nox's empty eyes and knew she'd move Eternity to steal the Silver General's DNA. She need only activate the proper leverage.

The slave boy betrayed his brother-in-arms once for Cinder.

Let us see if Korac would do it again.

IV   FLAME

SURRA'S EYES REMINDED ELDEN OF STORM CLOUDS THE SECOND BEFORE LIGHTNING SPLIT THE SKY. He gazed into them, tilting his head left and right to memorize every facet of cold gray. This was the first time he'd seen them with the blessing—The white pearl Surra had asked him to swallow. Elden trembled from its awesome might as he reached to touch the magnificent angles of her face. So soft. So beautiful.

But when Surra's eyes widened, Elden let his hand fall, not wishing to offend—

"No!" His goddess brought his palm back to her cheek and leaned into it.

Sweet tears spilled from Surra's lashes. Unable to bear it, Elden brushed them away with his thumb, saying, "I am honored by your grace, Surra."

With this pearl, Elden could admire the subtleties of her expressions. Sparkling eyes framed by gently arching brows. The pull on Surra's lips in a soft smile. How her skin pulsed with a blue light, emphasizing the streak in her hair.

Surra said, "You reveled in my presence, and the moment you can speak, you speak only of me. What does Elden desire?"

A question Elden could answer with pure certainty and a smirk on his lips. "You." Forever he'd waited for this moment, to voice his desire—To show Surra what she meant to him. Elden cupped her cheek, leaned down, and claimed Surra's lips in a searing kiss.

The Icari swarmed and consumed the foreigner's corpse while Elden carried his goddess back to her throne, where they spent many nights in each other's arms.

All the while, Elden lamented that Surra never got to see his eyes before One and Tumu poured Li into them.

In her sleep, Rayne's legs scissored together for sweet friction, gripping the sheets to hold on to—

Rayne's eyes snapped open. Her heart pounded, and the bed was hot from… Well, Elden's memory was vivid, and every sensation was burned onto her skin. Hands, lips, tongues—

Honeysuckle.

Oh, shit.

Nox.

Flustered and frustrated, Rayne tiptoed to the edge of the loft and peered out. Her roommate was laid out on the couch—mostly on the couch—with an arm flung over his face so she couldn't see his eyes. While she stared at Nox, who looked so at ease in this place, Rayne couldn't help but notice he had taken his shirt off during the night. Who could blame him? The temperature was always perfect with a nacre, but dressing down was best for sleeping—

Who was Rayne kidding?!

Nox had spent millions of years honing his physique into peak fighting shape, and oh, Eternity, did it show. The only ounce of fat on the man perfectly filled out the back of his pants. Everything about

Nox exhibited the power contained in him and made Rayne think of how he'd used it to help her. To seek redemption in saving their people. Which meant more to Rayne, since she was sure a good percentage of those people wouldn't approve of this partnership.

Xelan.

Rayne turned away from Nox and went to develop some kind of morning self care routine when she glimpsed herself in the mirror. Her hair—It was wavy. And so much fun to play with. Yay, sleh oil!

With that, Rayne tiptoed down the stairs to keep from waking her distractingly attractive roomie and padded around the corner to the kitchen. From her own provisions, she ate a Vittle crop supplement and boiled some tea for breakfast, all while trying to keep quiet. It was nice living with someone else, so far anyway. While her tea steeped, Rayne mused to herself about building a bigger couch for Nox. Then she grabbed a tablet, curled up in the nook Xelan had built into the library wall, and sipped from her obscenely large tea mug.

Somehow the tech in this treeloft updated itself with current events, including Xelan's Verse which had gone live two hours ago. Rayne sifted through public reactions. Still fresh in its establishment, Iona Pax's King Elects voiced nothing but support for their Co-Emperors. People lauded all three Icari—Nox, Korac, and Xelan—as the bravest souls in the galaxy.

This reception could only mean Xelan didn't publicize that Celindria was still breathing. It was probably for the best. A public uproar would only hinder Rayne and Nox's work.

With a sip of her never-ending tea, she filtered through more news for reports of unusual activity, like the orphanage on Pil and the hospital on Reipon. The missing civic workers, and so on.

Wait.

There was something new from Pil. Five months ago, three hundred people were saved in a mudslide—No casualties. All the survivors claimed a man pulled them from the rushing mud at significant risk to himself. A fly-er with Icarean wings.

Rayne shuffled through more reports, this time from Lukemore. Three months ago, a mysterious stranger had stopped an underground slave ring—An attempt to maintain the old regime.

LUKEMORE'S ANGEL FREED ONE THOUSAND CHILDREN DESTINED FOR UNDERGROUND VICE TRADE AND SILK MILLS BEFORE DEPARTING WITHOUT A WORD.

Then one more from last month in Reipon.

SERIAL PEDOPHILE FOUND DEAD, RIPPED APART, ON PRINCE'S YACHT.

From her corner in the loft, Rayne peered over at Nox, still asleep.

What would Xelan make of his brother now? Would Nox's good deeds ever compensate for the wrong he'd brought into these worlds? And how could Rayne show Xelan that his brother was a man worth knowing, a man worth forgiving? Could Rayne ever convince him to see Nox for what he was?

A man worth loving.

Nox had heard Rayne tiptoe down the stairs, and he'd cracked an eye open to watch her round the corner. After some quiet shuffling in the kitchen, she'd returned to the corner lined with books, holding a mug the size of her face. Like a languid cat, she'd climbed into a nook and curled up to read on her device.

It was tranquil, and Nox didn't want to interrupt Rayne's morning's peace. Soon they would start training for the mission ahead, and nothing would stop the momentum from there.

Besides, the smell of a beautiful woman making tea in the morning was nice to wake up to. No matter how much the three abrupt seconds of honeysuckle had puzzled Nox.

Somehow, Rayne finished the fishbowl full of tea and looked in his direction again. He wondered what she was thinking and found the unknown enticing. Nox's skin couldn't stand clothing while he'd tried to sleep, and at first, he'd mistaken Rayne's glances as discomfort. Until the curious look on her face bloomed into a sweet smile. At Nox.

Partly out of his own curiosity and partly for his amusement, Nox stirred on the couch—

Rayne bolted up the stairs like a skittish kitten caught in the creamery, and Nox fought not to chuckle. Upstairs, he heard her busying herself while he went through his provisions for Vittle bars. Foul things, but they abated his hunger. To say his appetite had accelerated since his resurrection was an understatement. In his body before, Nox could survive on one feeding every year. Now, he craved sustenance several times a day. The supplements kept it at bay for twenty-four hours at a time, and at this rate, he'd need to buy more.

Rayne asked from above, "Do you want me to knock before I come downstairs, or...?"

Her consideration brought a smile to Nox's lips as he assured, "No need. We will become quite acquainted the longer we stay here, and it's not as if you don't already know my darkest secrets."

Nox knew Rayne meant more for the sake of decency and modesty, but he enjoyed the way she squirmed to say, "I meant for dressing and getting ready in the morning."

"Come whenever you like."

That was not an occasion when Nox wanted to retract his words. He enjoyed the blush on Rayne's cheeks too much to recant it. Perhaps he was still a bastard after all, but some light teasing and flirting between two people as close as they shouldn't harm their comfortable relationship—

"Well, then you can come upstairs whenever you like."

Interesting.

Not only was their heart racing, but there was a challenge to the set of Rayne's shoulders as she made her declaration—Drew her line in the sand, so to speak. And not for the first time, Nox wasn't sure what to do about it.

So, he got up and stretched, half-naked. When he glanced back upstairs, Rayne was gone from the banister. She called from further upstairs, "Did you see what the sleh oil did to my hair? I love it, of course. Thanks again…"

Nox heard Rayne's words, but he focused on the tremor in her voice. It was all he could do not to comment on their quickening pulse. It was unkind to tease her, and that's not the man Nox wanted to be. Not anymore.

As a peace offering, he said, "I've never seen anything like it. It's beautiful." He could still pay Rayne compliments while he dressed.

A flutter thrilled through Nox's head—his heart.

Rayne.

Something had occurred between their conversation last night and when Nox had awakened this morning. A paradigm had shifted in her. Whatever had taken place, Nox wanted to reclaim their comfortable rapport. Flustered-Rayne was cute—more like incredibly sexy and tempting—but it wouldn't help their dynamic for them to frustrate each other.

Staring at the loft, Nox said, "I apologize."

Rayne reappeared at the banister, looking intrigued. "Hm?"

Frustrated, Nox ran a hand through his hair as he said, "I should be more careful with my feelings for you, and I shouldn't antagonize you. This living situation may take some adjustment for both of us. I'll keep my peace."

Without realizing what she was doing, Rayne glided down the stairs, displaying every inch of her toned, bare legs exposed by those little shorts. All the while, she said, "I appreciate how considerate you're being, but I'm a big girl. A little elevated heart rate won't kill me. Hell, it might do me some good to feel... to *feel*. I think you're good for me, former King of Cinder." Rayne stopped at the bottom of the stairs and folded her arms across her sports bra, ready for a workout.

Despite himself, Nox smirked. "Is this a gauntlet you truly wish to throw down?"

Rayne strode across the room until she stared up at him, inches from touching. With a defiant gleam in her eyes, she said, "I think I've already proven more than a match for you."

Never had Nox felt his heart pounding this hard— Blood raced through his veins all in a southernly direction as he looked into Rayne's eyes and fought not to kiss her. To take her.

The honeysuckle alone drove Nox insane with desire—

But this was a game. With all the composure he could muster, Nox accepted her challenge. "Meet you outside, your majesty."

Nox ignored the stabbing pain in his heart— because that was it. That was an opportunity spurned. Oh, he would meet Rayne on this battlefield.

Nox only hoped he didn't lose her in the process.

May the best warrior win.

Rayne watched from her perch on a silver bough as Nox emerged from their loft. He'd dressed for training, and that black tank looked so, so good stretched across his shoulders and chest.

Rayne had lied.

She was in way over her head. The smell of cloves—warm and spicy—had chased her out the door and all the way up this tree, like a frightened kitten. More like an excited kitten.

How long ago had she last felt this way?

Sagan.

Rayne winced. How would her lover—forever her lover and best friend—feel about Rayne flirting with Nox? Would Sagan think less of her?

No time to ponder it because Nox disappeared from the forest floor. Rayne focused on her senses, searching for a warning before he—

With a flip off the branch, she avoided his kick from above. Opening her wings, Rayne faced Nox in the canopy of metallic leaves. He never looked arrogant about his physical capabilities. Prowess had defined him ever since he'd asked for the strength to defend his mother and brother, and it was hard not to think about it, standing across from him in combat.

Rayne said, "We like to meet this way, I think."

There was a slight pull to his lips before Nox said, "We find ourselves here often, facing one another as equals."

Curious, she asked, "Do you have a favorite move I've pulled on you?"

It was unexpected enough to make him laugh, and Rayne cherished the sound. He considered her question for a moment while gripping his chin. After a few anticipatory heartbeats, Nox said, "A tie, I think. Between the take down at your school and..."

The take down was all Xelan, but Rayne would claim some credit for executing it. For the second one, she pressed, "And...?"

Nox's eyes were pitch black and still they grew darker as he said, "When you broke my ribs by squeezing them between your thighs."

Their heart rate spiked as Rayne stared at Nox. She was so gonna lose this game. Before she could form a comprehensive thought and respond, he came for her with a punch to the jaw.

Reflexively, Rayne blocked and kneed him in the gut—But Nox was already flying backward to evade.

The pure joy in his grin affected her. The ocean inside amassed a tidal wave, drawn to the volcano—Eager for the steam.

Rayne rocketed at him at her fastest, but Nox was more like her now and easily saw her coming.

They collided only for him to use her momentum and fling her into a nearby tree trunk.

Her back slammed into it. And wasn't that a familiar sensation? Trees with smooth surfaces didn't lose bark. Instead, she left a Rayne-shaped tree crater as she slid to the branch below.

Their heart rate was definitely up, and Rayne needed to catch her breath after the tree had knocked it out of her. Nox wasn't giving her time. He landed on the branch with a run-up.

Rayne had seconds to stand and prepare herself for—

In a defiance of physics, Nox ran down the side and disappeared under the branch.

For a quick heartbeat, she commended him for these bizarre maneuvers. They were exactly the sort of stunts Celindria would pull—

Nox's arms encircled Rayne from behind, locking her in his grip. He was hot against her back as he leaned closer to whisper in her ear, "What was *your* favorite of my techniques?"

Their kiss during the dance was all that came to mind, given the proximity.

Think.

Think of an answer and think of the next move.

Rayne regretted leaving so much skin exposed. Not because of any potential damage to it, but because Nox was against all of her—

It was so unfair that her tattoo no longer affected him.

Elden.

He could open a conduit, and then they could—

Fall.

They were falling.

Rayne needed a way to communicate with Elden on exactly where she wanted conduits to open for her. The deity's sense of humor sent them falling through the tree branch down to the forest floor.

However, the maneuver had worked, because Nox released her out of sheer awkwardness when the bottom fell out.

Rayne let her wings catch her, but so had Nox, and he disappeared again. She muttered, "Clever motherfucker." She closed her eyes and paid attention to her other senses.

Nox always smelled warm, like a bakery, but there wasn't any wind in the forest. So scent wasn't entirely helpful.

Fuck it.

Rayne shifted into Atramentous and opened the magnesium field. From her eyes, white light burned and surrounded her, spreading out and out—

"That's cheating!"

Nox's admonishment made Rayne grin.

Under this cover, she retrieved an old friend. Wrenching Night Killer—Rayne's bladed staff—from her nacre always hurt like a son of a bitch. Yet the weight of it, the spin of it, and the reminder of its forger...

Night Killer was home.

Rayne lowered the magnesium field and let Nox come for her. To answer his earlier questions, she shouted into the forest, "In one of our dreams, we fought with batons." She unlocked the connecting mechanism in Night Killer's center and separated the staff into two weapons. "Your blows came at me so fast, I could barely keep you from pummeling me. Swift and twirling, flipping and spinning. Then you lit them on fire. Honestly, what could be cooler?" She flipped her own weapons, honoring the memory.

Nox's laughter carried through the trees, making it difficult to tell where it was coming from—

Warm bread.

Rayne spun and blocked Nox's attack with her weapons crossed. Daggers. He'd attacked her with matte black daggers.

Their eyes meet between the blades. He was grinning, a mirror of herself. Nox said, "Why, your majesty, I believe you are flushed with the thrill of combat."

Rayne added a little cockiness to her smile as she assured, guaranteed, and vowed, "Because I know I'll win."

Elden, the Icarus' chuckle was dangerously sexy—

Nox flipped backward, and Rayne pursued. He couldn't block as well with those weapons as she could, but he evaded like a dancer. The twin components of Night Killer were longer than his daggers, but his arms reached farther than hers. It was quite the match.

While spinning one half of Night Killer and lunging with the other, Rayne tried to lock and sweep one of Nox's ankles.

Light on his feet for a man his size, he twirled to the side, spun the other way, and jabbed a dagger at Rayne's throat.

She ducked and used the blunt ends of Night Killer to punch him in the stomach—

Nox shouted as he tumbled backward, losing his footing on a . . .

Rayne cried, "What the hell?!"

He grabbed one end of Night Killer, and they both fell through a conduit.

Would Tumu and One return? To modify more Icari as they had Elden?

Surra seemed concerned about the like. Every day, she trained their people to fend against the foreigners—Millions of Icari capable of so much death.

And yet, she must know how to make them like Elden. Able to speak and think. But nothing he said convinced her. Why? Was there a cost?

As on every turn of Li, Elden asked, "Surra, how can I make my people like me? To protect themselves?"

A sorrow greater than the sun's loneliness filled those steel-gray eyes. This time was different. This time, Surra said, "Let me show you, amos. Pick ten most loyal to you, and we will make them like you."

Elden knew exactly which ten, and he assembled them all at Surra's throne. When she came to him, her limbs looked heavy with a weight she wouldn't share. It broke his heart, for her burdens were his, but the Icari... They needed him.

"Please, Surra."

Her voice trembled as she said, "I will grant you the only wish you have ever asked of me. Now close your eyes and know that I love your weeping heart."

Elden did as she asked. As he stood before her with his eyes shut, he thought of their future. Thought of how Umbra, Vinco, Mirx—all of them—could serve the Icarean race. How badly he wanted the Icari to advance enough to meet the foreigners on even ground and ask them to stop hurting each other—

Elden screamed as something broke through his sternum, opening a sucking wound, filling and spilling precious blood. His eyes opened of their own accord to find a most fearsome sight. Surra plowed into his chest, wrist deep, as Elden fell to his knees. "Why..."

"Because you asked." Tears spilled down her face even while she pilfered into his nacre and...

Chink.

A break. A tear. Or a hole—Partial. Not whole or complete—

Failure.

Elden felt it.

Surra shattered his nacre.

"Shh... Shh... You will survive this, amos. Go to sleep."

The certainty in her voice—the love and kindness in it—assured Elden Surra would keep her promise.

"Rayne. Can you hear me?"

Nox came to on the forest floor with Rayne laying on top of him, her hair spilled all around them. Her skin felt hot, and she was muttering—

"Nox?"

Rayne shifted and lifted her head. The fine tremor across her entire body made Nox chafe her arms. Her pupils were dilated as their gazes met. "What... What happened?"

Nox brushed her hair from her face, cradling her head to see if there were signs of trauma or concussion. Meanwhile, he said, "Elden opened a conduit, and we fell through it. I don't recall why we fell unconscious or how we came to be here. You awakened seconds after I did."

He wasn't aware of it, but his thumb was grazing her cheek reassuringly. It was Rayne's reaction to it which drew his awareness—She smiled, half out of it. Little dull gray leaves peppered the wavy curtain of her hair, adding to her charms.

Drunk on some cosmic coincidence, Nox answered her smile with one of his own. He said, "Hi."

Wow.

Rayne's eyes became sparkling sapphires as her smile turned into a goofy grin. "Hi."

Well, this was it. This was the sexiest moment of Nox's long life. This preposterous, silly, warm, clumsy—

A bird walloped somewhere directly above them.

They both scanned the canopy before meeting eyes again. A heartbeat passed in the exchange, followed by a shared burst of laughter.

Nox asked, "Do you think he'll ever find her?" Referring to the bird's quest for a mate.

Laying atop him while staring up at the branches, Rayne mused, "I hope so." With a cute grunt and groan, she climbed off of Nox. He couldn't help but notice the faint pinkness to her cheeks as Rayne extended a hand. "Come on. Let's shower and get into town somewhere. I need to find a Vittle vendor, and I'm curious what people are thinking of Xelan's Verse."

Nox took her hand and let Rayne pull him to his feet. Only then did he realize they were standing right outside the loft.

As she went inside, Rayne muttered, "I don't know what Elden's thinking, but we should get to the mission soon. I made a promise."

In an insane misfire between his brain and his mouth, Nox said, "We could get to it sooner if we showered together."

That made her freeze with her back to him, but Rayne sounded certain as she said, "You're absolutely right." She turned, a little flushed but resolute. "We're both adults, and the shower is more than big enough for ten people—Which I plan to ask Xelan about one day." Her silly grin offset the stiffness of her posture. "Get your stuff ready, and I'll meet you in there."

Rayne marched around the corner like a woman facing execution and was too proud to let the crowd see her fear.

Was Nox a bastard for suggesting it? He didn't know anymore. Half the time, Rayne was initiating whatever this was between them. Her attraction was clear, and it was an honor she bestowed upon him. Truly.

Anytime Rayne gave Nox an opening, he refused—the number of those opportunities staggered him—he worried it could lead to hurt feelings of shame and rejection. But Nox would never reject Rayne. If she ever came to him of her own person, he'd give her the stars along with his heart. Until such a time came, she was safe from him.

Or so Nox kept repeating as he made his way to the shower. He got as far as the kitchen before the water came on, and, through the sheet, he glimpsed Rayne's clothes receding into her. A million, million years could pass, and he would never tire of this view—Her hair pulled up in a bun and her curves unveiled to the water. Lucky, lucky water—

"You hit like a girl," Rayne called from the other side.

It was so outside of Nox's thoughts that he barked out a laugh. Considering the statement, he said, "I'll take it as a compliment. The strongest warrior I know is a woman." A mesmerizing woman, currently naked in this room.

Fuck him. Nox was in way over his head.

He stripped out of his clothes the old-fashioned way before slipping by the sheet's barrier. Nox tried to keep his eyes on the floor spouts and not on Rayne's creamy skin. Her back was to him, and he did the same. It worked until…

Was Rayne aware of the sounds she was making? Soft moans and little sighs.

Aside from that, she was right. They were mature adults, and the shower was uneventful. Well, except… When Nox lathered his backside…

Impossible.

He did *not* catch Rayne looking.

Surely.

She left the shower first and stood outside the sheet, assembling her clothes. While Nox dressed where she couldn't see, Rayne asked, "Did you have any trouble buying a fake persona from Razor's contacts?"

"I am a veteran of the Icarean army named Schu with a free labor visa. You?"

Rayne was smiling when Nox emerged. She said, "I'm Becca, a hairdresser from Earth, eager to explore fashion and style across the galaxy—And you look *amazing* in red."

Nox felt his cheeks warm, which always seemed silly given his age, but she brought it out in him. He was thinking of her when he'd picked out the asymmetrical shirt. He cleared his throat to say, "Thank you. You look…" Tempting. "Honestly, your majesty, I've never seen you look anything but gorgeous in everything you've worn."

Warm cheeks all around.

Nox maintained eye contact, but he kept glimpsing the lacy burgundy bra exposed by the low scoop of Rayne's gray sleeveless shirt. The black leather pants were patchwork—aerated, suede, shiny, and matte—and they were practically poured onto her skin. As Rayne turned to grab her hair supplies, he admired the tattoos, but when she bent over to check her boots, he had to look away.

The lacy panties Nox glimpsed matched the bra, sitting below the alluring dimples on her back.

Rayne faced him again and held out the comb. He took it and brushed her hair when she turned for him. He asked, "Do we have signals in case this mission gets messy?"

Nox helped Rayne weave braids along her scalp and pull the massive curtain of her wavy hair into a ponytail. All the while, she said, "We could always use 'banana.'" She snickered.

With an incredulous shake of his head, Nox said, "I think it's an imperial favorite now thanks to the Verses."

"Oh, good point." Rayne bit her thumbnail before offering, "How about 'pomegranate?'"

Nox quirked a brow. "'Pomegranate.'" The word tasted right. "Fitting. Are you ready?" He finished with her hair.

Rayne faced him, smirked, and patted her nacre where Night Killer lived. Her voice was… Well, Nox assumed she didn't know the sultry effect of it as she said, "I'm looking forward to working with you, Nox. This way, I can show you how it's done."

Down their eleven-inch height difference, Nox stared into Rayne's eyes and grinned. "Yes, your majesty. I'm sure there's plenty you can teach me."

Until then—if it ever happened—Nox would savor the raw anticipation.

{6,000BCE}

Celindria sat on the floor of the shower in Xelan's stronghold, the blood long washed away. She hugged her knees to her chest, buried her face in them, and cried.

This was always the worst moment of Celindria's lives.

Our baby. We killed our baby.

It had to be done. It must always be done.

We will never know if she'd have Nox's eyes and our skin. His smile and our nose. Strength and grace—

Please. Please stop.

When the multitude of her voices ceased, Nox's voice invaded the vacuum. *"Celindria, rule Earth and Cinder with me. We can raise our daughter together. We could lead together."*

Next came her awful retort. *"Conceived in rape. Cultivated by a monster. A history of violence so erratic that you almost killed your own brother. What kind of father would you make?"*

Nauseated by her own words, Celindria rolled to her side and vomited into the drain, tears and blood along with it—A wash of blue, red, and yellow.

The way Nox's throat tightened when he begged Celindria to stop and the venom in her hateful, digging spur. *"You soft creature."*

Celindria screamed. She shrieked and clawed the horror out of her forearms. Thrashed and pulled her hair out.

Yet she would never ask 'why.' The answer was always the same.

Power.

Nox deserves better.

Everyone deserves better. That's why we bring them to Paradise.

What would father make of our Paradise?

Xelan's kind kiss lingered on Celindria's forehead from when he'd stopped and confronted her. *"Was it Nox's child?"*

She'd confirmed the truth and ignored the ugly impulse to let Xelan believe Nox had caused the termination.

Never.

Celindria wouldn't let anyone believe that of Nox. Not for sport, nor for spite. Nox always made for a wonderful father, and she would *not* let anyone think otherwise.

Father would never understand, so Celindria would make the worlds understand.

Bring them to Paradise and make Nox strong enough to withstand the trials ahead.

Yes.

*But what about the **one**?*

Celindria's eyes fluttered closed as she let herself breathe for a second—a mere second—in the Probability where she'd refused power and gave into love.

One Probability where Celindria and Nox raise their beautiful daughter together.

A cool spring breeze touched her face, smelling of her favorite orange blossoms. There were clouds, not Li, in the sky. Tiny laughter tinkered nearby, followed by the heavy chuckle of a proud father. If Celindria could only stay here a little while longer…

A single breath. Then Celindria returned to all the realities without little Surra. The air here was hotter, heavier. It stank of ash and impossibility. Hatred.

This was where Celindria thrived.

{NOW}

Monarch 3 in Paradise was a gaseous farm—Kilometers of gigantic trees occupied with busy worker drones. The Queens lived in luxury, all at Celindria's hand, of course. She granted most every request presented by the lady insects—Earnest in reminding them that this was a mutually beneficial arrangement.

Control the queen, control the hive. Much less work for Celindria in the long run to claim volition of their rulers from the start. How she'd gained control varied across each Probability. For Paradise, Celindria had recently cured a hive from blight death. In the Queen's delirious gratitude, she'd repeated Elden's Tenements of Volition.

Easy enough.

The dominant Probability had proven more resilient, as in all things. Unlike here in Paradise, in the dominant Probability, there was enmity between Celindria and F8, something Celindria detested.

When one was a goddess of their realm, they need but travel to the enemy's fortress and walk inside. Everything in Paradise was in the same position as in the dominant Probability, including the shadows.

Within Paradise, Celindria stood inside F8's hive. After a step into the shadows, Celindria stood inside F8's hive of the dominant Probability. Billions surrounded it, all under Celindria's command, ready to tear the wings off this aggressive butterfly.

When Celindria and Remorse had established the gas factory beneath the Queen's Fare, she'd implanted those queens with volition protocols. It had proven a worthwhile investment. Out and out, the trees and their hives stretched. Billions and billions. All the drones had awakened this morning under Celindria's command.

We are brilliant.

Yes, the others will fall quickly.

But first, a proud woman must relinquish it all.

The brave King Elect of Monarch 3 kept her voice steady as she assured Celindria, "The emperors will stop you, abomination."

"They will never see me coming."

F8 stood from her throne and put her fist to her chest, facing destruction and she was fierce still. No wonder they were friends in Paradise. With her chin held high, the proud insect queen said, "Xelan will never see these worlds diminished to you."

Stood in the middle of an impregnable hive, Celindria let the colors and fog obscure the shift of Atramentous in her gaze. Pleased with her own success, she said in one deep pitch, "Father will, or he will see them diminished to nothing." She crossed the room, billowing wafts of pheromone smoke in her wake until she stood within inches of F8's tiny frame. Celindria said, "Tell me the words I want to hear, and I'll let your people live."

F8 sought something in Celindria's Atramentous eyes before frowning. There was pity in F8's facets as she said, "You have crossed the line, child. There will be no coming back."

"Old friend, I crossed it long ago."

We must kill her soon. No one can see us like this.

Are we in a mood to care?

No. There are no emotions here.

As if F8 saw the apathy in Celindria's eyes, F8 recited, "'Under my own will, I forfeit my volition. Perfectly and consensually until she returns me unto myself.'"

Inside the King Elect's head, Celindria smiled, saying, "You've made the right decision, F8."

"Remind me after the Shadow have wiped us both out. Kill me, and you lose control of the hive, child." The butterfly was pinned to the floor of her mindscape, unable to lift her head higher than a few inches.

Celindria crossed the space and looked down at her, asking, "Why do the Queens never enforce control over their subjects? I've always wondered."

F8 let her head fall and took a few deep breaths to rally enough incredulity to say, "Because it's wrong, child—"

"I have lived infinite lives, and I am no child."

With labored breaths, F8 forced out, "You are a daughter throwing a tantrum for her father's affections if I ever saw one."

F8 fell silent as Celindria forced her into sleep. Her earlier warning fell on deaf ears. Father would never kill F8, even to fell one of Celindria's advantages. To kill the queens would condemn their species to extinction, and Father was no Aegis nor Razor.

The plan continued. Celindria would secure Hope and Nox in Paradise with Korac's blood, and the Shadow were the only thing standing in her way.

We'll need more soldiers.

Indeed.

Off to Earth and Cinder.

V SEAR

NOX SCRUBBING HIS BACK WOULD NOT STOP FLASHING IN FRONT OF RAYNE'S EYES, LIKE A SEXY NEON SIGN. She giggled at the visual, and the Icarus in question quirked a brow at her. With a warding wave, she assured, "You don't even want to know."

With a shrug, Nox looked back at the conduit leading to a location on Ishkur. Lights, people, music— So much movement. It was dizzying to Rayne, who'd spent the last few years in a box.

Nox nodded toward it, asking, "Is this our destination?"

Elden had opened the conduit to the right club. The logo, W^3, flashed on the cathedral ceiling. "This is it. Remember, we're looking for a way upstairs. There, we should find our targets. They're responsible for off-sphere human trafficking, so there's no need to play nice."

Nox smirked down at Rayne, eyes glinting with hunger. She wondered if hers looked the same as Rayne contemplated her appetite.

Violence.

"Let's go." She walked in first, grateful Elden had placed their entrance in a secluded corner—

"Harder, Jay, please!"

Unnerved by the moans and sighs, Rayne's eyes involuntarily searched for the source. To her right, a couple went at it pretty hot and heavy, ignoring Nox walking into the club from thin air. Once he realized the nature of their company, he glanced down at Rayne.

So not going there.

She glanced up at the mezzanine bordering the perimeter upstairs. Trying to ignore the climax of the show, Rayne nodded at the second floor, saying, "I'll head up. You take the downstairs."

Nox always trusted Rayne to handle herself. In answer, he tapped the thick belt strapped across his chest, indicating his daggers. Before Nox lifted his hood to leave, his gaze raked down Rayne and up again, expression inscrutable. Then he turned and left without a word. Those soft leather pants on that ass looked spectacular walking away.

Rayne shook herself.

Focus.

When the couple found the finish line, she rolled her eyes. It was as if Eternity itself wanted her to jump Nox's bones with all these hints.

Never mind that, because Rayne was in the thick of it—Her first vice den. Dagger's *Warehouse of Wild Wonders* was a knockoff Pain Curator establishment built in the first six weeks of Ishkur's freshly developed underground. Like its namesake implied, it was a warehouse with a space-scraper mounted on its roof.

Rayne never saw Razor's Emporium of Exotic Experiences in person, but this pitiful imitation made her wish for whiskey-lit, antiqued mirrors. Instead, she got multi-colored track lighting, fog machines, and a place so packed with bodies, every movement counted as first base.

Near some booths, Rayne overheard patrons discussing the Verses.

A short Lamia muttered, "I can't imagine they'll let Xelan keep his title."

"What're you talking about? Remorse, Razor, and Celindria were all crazy and didn't give a shit about us. At least the Mad Emperor looks after us," a dwarf argued.

The Lamia scoffed, "Who started calling him that? Traitor Prince, deadliest warrior in the galaxy, Mad Emperor—Is he giving himself these names?!"

A female Icarus said, "Perhaps they're pet names from Korac? Now there's a pair I'd like to join."

Both men humphed.

With a bemused shake of her head, Rayne headed up. As she climbed the stairs, she glanced about and easily spotted Nox. The hood from his shirt could hide his eyes, but nothing could hide his build. He towered above everyone, even the drones. As if he sensed her watching, Nox glanced right at Rayne across the crowd.

Their pulse gave one of them away. Who knew eye contact could be so thrilling?

Rayne looked away first and focused on the mission. Elevator or stairs? She cut through the center of a chatty group to investigate the next level of wraparound catwalks—

"Hey, gorgeous!" Someone snaked an arm around her waist, slurring as he said, "How about I get you a drink, and you hang out with us for a while?"

Rayne faced the Lamia, who dropped his arm the moment they made eye contact. He blinked, big and kinda stupid. "You... I..."

He couldn't seem to find his words, but his date could. "Sorry, love." The second male Lamia smiled apologetically, saying, "He's simply never seen a woman as beautiful as you. Would you care to join us?"

"Oh, say you will," the drone in their group said. With his needle nose and multi-faceted eyes, he looked Rayne over, but not sexually. It was more measuring. "You are the most convincing Rayne tribute I've ever seen." There was something wrong with how he said it.

Rayne was already overwhelmed, but she wouldn't allow herself to forget she was a tough, badass world savior. She beamed, and the first Lamia stepped back with a gasp as Rayne said, "Thanks so much, but I'm just trying to find a friend. Have a nice night."

She left them without incident except for a clawing itch on the back of her neck. Rayne spared a glance behind her to see the drone...

Why was he glaring at her?

Okay. Next time, Rayne would wear a hood or a mask or something. Maybe she should invest in colored contact lenses. She made her way to the VIP rope, working on a cover story to let her inside, when something caught her eye at the bar downstairs.

The extremely busy mixologist behind the diorite counter was making time to flirt with her latest customer. Nox leaned against it, with his eyes on the crowd, and sipped a neon pink drink with an umbrella. Meanwhile, the Lyrik tending the bar ignored all her other customers to lean her breasts on the counter in his face.

They were nice breasts—God, Rayne missed boobs. But this poor woman wasn't getting anywhere. Nox was either oblivious or politely disinterested. Rayne could tell by his heart rate and the fact that he kept scanning his surroundings for a threat. She would talk to him about socializing. They might be on a mission, but some interaction with outsiders could do them both some good.

She said as she neared a tight crowd, trying to enter the door at mezzanine's end.

With a brief prayer to Elden, Rayne approached the rope and opened her mouth to spill the story about having a brother inside and needing to drag his ass back to his wife—

"G'head."

The bouncer took one look at Rayne and opened the door.

Although grateful, it made her glance at her own breasts. What magic was this?

There was no time to signal Nox, and she doubted this Tritan—an older one by the lighter cast to his complexion—would let Nox in without reservation. Confident in her own capabilities, Rayne went in and immediately regretted it.

Well, at least now she knew why the bouncer had let her in.

People were having sex everywhere, in every way, with everyone. Mud pools, oil pools, food pools, hot tubs, on the counter, on the beds, on the ceiling—

Would Rayne ever forget Tameka sharing her first time with Xelan?

Rope lights were strung everywhere, glowing an ethereal cyan color, but not bright enough to illuminate a single participant's features. Bass throbbed in Rayne's chest from the music—Something between techno and New Age spa music. The smell—Oh, Eternity, the smell.

Florals and spices culminated in a cloud of heady sensory overload. Between the fog of pheromones and the low lighting, it was almost impossible to make anything out—

Wait.

On the far side of this vice arena was an elevator. Rayne only needed to cross the gauntlet of grabbing hands and voyeurs without drawing suspicion. Tucking loose strands behind both ears, she took a step around the first pool. The partners seemed consensual and quite happy with their decision to participate, so need to pay any further attention.

Another step, another obstacle. This time, it was a sunken hot tub from which a hand reached out and clutched Rayne's boot while the Caprent hit their crescendo. Fortunately, she was strong enough to let them cling on and then release her once finished.

Was this night one blazing sign?

RAYNE, GET LAID.

The next few steps were uneventful. Everyone seemed too involved in their kink to notice her. In fact, Rayne almost made it through this football field of orgasms to the door when someone whispered, "Yo."

She silently cursed before facing whoever caught her with a wave. "Hello." Boy, could Rayne be any less cool? It's like she was trained by the best or something.

It was a bartender from Lukemore, which explained why he whispered rather than shouted. The young—judging by the brightness of his kelp dreads—man beamed at Rayne with genuine friendliness asking in a whisper, "Where you going, missy?"

Rayne swallowed before pointing at the ceiling. "Upstairs."

The Luk shook his head, saying, "Not without having some fun first. You new or something?" He waved for her to follow.

Again, Rayne reminded herself she could level the space-scraper with a few well-placed punches. She followed him to his bar and sat down. Oozing inexperience, she gave a shy smile. "You caught me. I wasn't expecting this."

As if on cue, someone finished. Loudly.

This Luk's jellyfish cap/kilt was blue, and it glowed to match the atmosphere. He caught her looking and winked, saying, "I'm Dagger."

The fact that Rayne's jaw didn't immediately hit the bar top was a miracle. How was she so unlucky to run into the owner while trying to work her way to the top?

Please, let Nox be having better luck—

The door on the far end opened, and the devil—very handsome devil—stepped into the arena. Rayne was amused to see Nox's reaction was at least similar to hers.

Dagger chuckled, muttering, "Newbies."

Rayne tried to ignore Nox, pretending not to know him, and feigned a bit of shy curiosity. "So, what's the upstairs like if *this* is so wild?"

The Luk quirked a kelp brow at her before saying, "Darling, if you're too green to handle this, there's no way you're heading up the shaft. Get my drift?"

Okay. Innuendos, for all. Damn, Rayne wished she'd taken lessons from Lucy. After a heartbeat to collect herself, she pouted, faking eagerness and having something to prove. "I can take it."

This time, Dagger threw his head back and laughed outright. It was a friendly sound in a whisper, but Rayne could tell he obviously modeled it after Razor. Having met the genuine article in a three-piece, she could say there was no contest. Undiluted sociopathic charm won every time.

Still, Dagger oozed sincerity like a pro. "Sweet thing, if you can climb that mountain over there without breaking into a blush, then we can talk. Until then, can I get you something to drink?"

No way in hell was Rayne drinking something from here. She didn't even bother answering his question.

Nox.

'Climb' Nox and get upstairs.

On second thought, pummeling her way up sounded good, too.

***

The smell was intoxicating, dizzying, and crushing. It reminded Nox of the public consummation ceremonies. Reminded him of home.

Perhaps not the best of Cinder, but an aspect of her nonetheless.

Across the sea of potent stimulation, Rayne met Nox's eyes with a primal craving in her gaze. And it wasn't carnal. No, Nox found this element of Rayne far more intriguing.

Violence in her stride, she crossed the arena. The Luk behind the bar watched Rayne go with a smirk, mistaking her intentions. Nox recognized the storm in her eyes, and as Rayne waded nearer through the sea of sex and onlookers, Nox felt their heart racing.

Her or him? Which one's chest had started the pounding anticipation? And why was Nox more aroused by the potential between them than the entire vice arena?

Rayne stopped within inches of Nox and let him see it.

He glanced around, taking in the space and all the strange coincidences lately. It made him smirk as he mused, "Do you ever feel the universe is trying to send you a message?"

Rayne smiled like a predator with sharp teeth. "That's exactly what I've been thinking."

"That's Dagger." She turned and waved to the Luk, who returned the gesture while she said, "He won't let me up the elevator without paying a price."

With a shrug, Nox reached for his stash of credits. "It's not a king's ransom, but I can pay…"

Without turning back to face Nox, Rayne shook her head. Her voice was nearing Atramentous. "He wants something he has no right to ask."

Thunder cracked overhead, drawing the attention of a few onlookers.

"Did he accost you, your majesty?" Nox was careful to keep his lethal response in its cage and out of his voice.

Now Rayne faced him, searching his eyes before saying, "For you. He asked me to be with you here, or he won't let me up."

Nox chuckled. "Is the price so high, your majesty?"

Frustrated, she swatted his arm. "You know that's not—Ugh." Rayne rubbed her shoulders with a groan, not happy about her next confession. "If it were ever to happen between us again, I'd want us to be alone and not in this place."

Nox's stare was hard and confounded. Did Rayne... did she just admit to wanting him? Or occasionally considering it? Enough to determine the circumstances under which their pairing would take place?

That was enough for Nox.

He gave Rayne's bicep a gentle squeeze as he headed for the bar. The Luk—Dagger—looked less intrigued with the turn of events and more ready to press his panic button. Sometimes Nox's intimidating build proved beneficial.

"I didn't realize you and the Rayne Tribute knew each other." Dagger shrank behind the bar the more he talked. "My bad. But didn't it make my offer more inviting?"

Rayne leaned against the counter, keeping her eye on the sexed-out customers.

Nox slapped a stack of credits on the bar, saying, "You take this, apologize to her, and let us up the elevator."

Dagger was prey.

His panicked glances between the two combined with the sharp smell of fear. Higher-pitched, Dagger's voice lost its counterfeit elegance as he said, "I did nothing to her worth apologizing for, but fine. I'm sorry, darling." He gave Nox all the wide-eyed contact as Dagger trembled with his next words. "But I won't—*cannot*—let you in that elevator."

"Nox."

At the hardness of her tone, he turned and—

Ah.

Rayne and Nox stared out at the arena as naked customers emerged from the pit, armed and ready for combat.

Her voice shook with nervous laughter as she said, "Well, I never imagined this kind of fight in store tonight." She met Nox's eyes and grinned radiantly. "You up for this?"

Was the euphemism intended? Nox returned the grin and faced their attackers, so he didn't see Rayne's face when he said, "I'm always up for this with you."

Rayne's laughter was full of affection for his absurd remark. After which, she said, "Try non-lethal force—"

The first throwing knife hit Nox's nanite shield, upgraded to stop any projectile faster than 20MPH. With his construct abilities learned from Rayne, he reconstructed the blade in his hand and threw it back into the crowd. "So much for non-lethal, your majesty."

But Rayne was already charging into battle with an endearing cartwheel kick, uppercutting into some naked opponent's chin. She'd held back, too, because the human's head didn't explode.

Nox's next comer grappled his Caprent-bent arms with Nox's. Slippery. This one had been in the oil pit. In a lock, the Caprent loaded up for an acid spit. The former King of Cinder snarled as he tried repeatedly to get a grip on his slick, naked opponent and lost. Thinking with his head, he bashed it into the Caprent's face, cracking his skull, before they both slid to the floor.

Two—No, three more fighters jumped on Nox's back. Mud rained down on him as he flipped and crushed them. Fortunately, the vice fighters came here to copulate and weren't well armed—

Nox growled from the familiar lance of a blade in his side. He grabbed the muddy bastard by the arm and pulled until Nox heard the wet socket suction of a dislocated shoulder. When the limb fell loose, Nox's appetite was satisfied. Only then did he recognize the black hair and brown eyes of his own kind.

The Icarus stared up at Nox and something close to recognition clarified the agonizing daze. "Your… your majesty?"

"This is a bad dream. Go to sleep." Nox pressed his thumb against the young male's carotid until the Icarus fell unconscious. Possessed with guilt, Nox popped his former subject's joint back in place, to speed along the recovery.

Covered in caked mud, Nox flipped back onto his feet—

Not for long.

A female Lamia plowed into Nox with a high-pitched battle squeal. He let them fall over, using her momentum to flip her off him into a hot tub. Nox grabbed her by the hair and punched her once in the face, knocking her out without breaking her nose. He even laid her on the side of the tub to keep her from drowning.

Non-lethal.

It was taking more time than simply executing them. Rayne could blind them all with one sweep of her magnesium field, but it was too signature and easily recognizable by their enemies.

At a time like this—a naked battle in a vice den—Nox could do with some of Korac's humor. And perhaps some of Xelan's awkward zeal.

Present company suited just fine.

Rayne in combat was a waltz of grace and vigor. Twirling kicks, swirling throws, and all the while, bone crunched and shattered. Blood, in all colors, was sprayed across her face, neck, and breasts. Her eyes flashed brighter, almost to Atramentous, and her skin glowed with her ethereal vitality.

Not even remotely breathless, Rayne asked mid-punch, "Did you swap contact frequencies with her?"

A human and a dwarf in each hand, Nox knocked their heads together and answered, perplexed. "What are you on about?"

Rayne swept a Lamia's feet out from under him and stomped him unconscious, saying, "The gorgeous Lyriki bartender downstairs."

With a flip over his opponent's head and a blow to their kidneys, Nox considered her question.

Oh.

He didn't even notice at the time but... "She was interested in me?" He felled the next Icarean naked fighter, covered in cake icing, with a toss into the nearest wall.

Rayne's laughter was incredulous as she let two of her combatants run into each other. Knocked out cold, but her laughter was for Nox. "Are you serious? She was captivated, mesmerized, ready to take you to the nearest dark corner and—"

"I comprehend your point perfectly clear."

The number of naked fighters was dissipating, thankfully, and Nox was happy to continue the battle. Unfortunately, the direction of the conversation affected him. What did Rayne want from this?

As if reading his thoughts, she said, "Well, maybe we should date?"

Nox spun to avoid a perfectly executed drop kick and backed against Rayne in the center of the vice arena. They glanced at each other as her words sunk in. They should date—

"Other people, I mean... We should try to find dates and interact like normal people."

Nox was busy enjoying the moment with the only person he wanted to interact with, but perhaps this was Rayne's point. Even after spending six months apart, they still relied on each other for contact, for engagement. Maybe they should test the waters a bit.

So he thought, at first.

But the moment Nox imagined Rayne dancing with anyone but Sagan, laughing at their jokes, touching their face—

A fist collided with his gut, and the feeling was synonymous.

Rayne spurned the thought even as she suggested it out loud. Other partners couldn't appreciate Nox in his entirety, the whole package, and he deserved that kind of acceptance. Especially after everything they'd been through…

No.

"On second thought, let's table this until after we're done saving the universe," Rayne said as she hit the next person hard enough to knock them smooth out.

All throughout the battle, she wondered what Sagan or Tameka—even Kyle or Andrew—would say about the lubed-up fighters and their anatomical prowess. Rayne tried her best to maintain eye contact, but it proved difficult. See her earlier comment about missing breasts and not being terribly familiar with the male anatomy.

After her perfect spin kick took out the latest comer, Rayne bounced, eager for the next fight. The pulse she shared with Nox pounded with exhilaration, and now they were together like this—back-to-back—they moved in a rhythm of spins, kicks, and punches.

Rayne loved it, and so did Nox, judging by the huge grin on his face. It was over too soon, leaving them both panting. She took in the battlefield and assessed the situation. What was coating her? Sweat, oil, mud, and… crepe filling?

"Shall we, your majesty?" Nox muttered only loud enough for Rayne to hear.

She smiled and marched across the field of unconscious assailants to the bar.

Dagger ducked behind it when she came his way. He raised his hands in surrender, saying, "Okay, fine. You can go upstairs. Just don't kill me."

Razor, he wasn't.

The shady Luk pressed a button under the counter, calling the elevator. Rayne waited with Nox, who glared at the man cowering behind the bar. As they boarded the lift, Nox warned Dagger, "Find another profession."

The doors closed as Dagger said, "No shit, man."

Made of Aegis tech, the lift was glass and fast. It zipped them right up to the space-scraper's top floor at a speed which would nauseate Rayne if not for her nacre. Within seconds, she and Nox entered an abyssal foyer of glossy black surface—floor, walls, and ceiling—seamless. Their reflections peered at them from every which way. The hall stretched on and branched off into identical corridors.

"Cool," Rayne conceded.

Nox gave a single chuckle before they both proceeded. Call it instinct, but she went through the painful process of retrieving Night Killer. Following her lead, Nox slipped his daggers from his belt as they went along.

A quarter of the way through this stadium-sized labyrinth, Rayne thought she heard music. She signaled to Nox, who gestured that he'd heard it, too, and they pursued it.

Closer, the music grew louder, until they peered around a corner into a private club with a stage. Men and women surrounded it of all races—except Mon 3—and gazed at the show in the sweet-smelling, smoky room. Only it wasn't a show.

Twelve children—humans, by the look of them—stood on the stage dressed in matching blue jumpsuits. Tired, they sleepily rubbed their eyes or blinked heavily with exhaustion. Not one was over the age of five.

Why in the hell were they up there?

Nox's hand settled on Rayne's shoulder as she puzzled over the cause.

Some Caprent female at the podium called, "Number 10."

A little girl with short red hair stepped forward.

In the audience, a female Lamia raised a hand. Then a dwarf. Then back to the Lamia.

It was quiet and eerily civilized, familiar. Why did this look like something Rayne should recognize?

"Rayne."

Even in a whisper against her ear, Nox said her name with so much gravity and… concern.

The Caprent at the podium gave a single clap and pointed at the dwarf, who beamed with victory, but what had he won—

The little girl stepped off the stage and went to him.

No.

No, no, no—

Nox gripped Rayne's biceps, careful for his daggers, and held her steady while Rayne took a second to have a nervous breakdown.

Children.

They were trafficking children.

Razor's dossier told Rayne it wasn't so uncommon, but seeing it…

"I need this one, Nox." Her voice was uncharacteristically hard, even to her.

He didn't chide Rayne or give her some lecture on morals. He merely said, "Lead the way."

Imminent nobility and inheritors of Razor's vice empire weren't expecting the streak of lightning in the windows and the thunder which followed. In the flash of light, Rayne stood in the center of the auction. The children were already gone, including the little red-haired girl.

Nox gave Rayne all the room she needed.

Magnesium spilled from her eyes before the first person could gasp and stand from shock.

Oh, how they screamed, and it wasn't enough. No one would survive this.

Rayne spun Night Killer and knocked the face off the first person to attack her, the dwarf. She planted her staff firmly and used it as a fulcrum to kick through the female Lamia. The next assailant was a human. She ripped his nacre out with her bare hands and swallowed it to process for later.

All the while, Rayne's rage stormed and accumulated. She kept recalling the childhood Korac had shared in his Verse. All those children in Gait were exposed to so much horror they'd never wash out. Rayne's tears burned, and her mouth bled from how tight she clenched her jaw. Lightning branched above and rain sprayed down the glass exterior of the space-scraper. Thunder vibrated the floors as Rayne ripped out nacres, stomped through skulls, and cut out hearts.

Korac's careful mask hid a childhood of beatings, molestation, rape—

The exhausted children on the stage.

Why were they so tired, Rayne?

What had they already endured, which could never be washed away?

Lightning arced, broke through the glass, and struck Rayne.

Electricity bolted around Rayne in a spiderweb of deadly light, striking the remaining bidders.

Gorgeous lethality.

Nox watched from backstage where he kept the children safe and the auctioneer squirming on the floor. Rayne's heart was broken. He could tell by the slug of their shared pulse. How could she not be?

As the smell of cooked meat filled the club, Nox smiled down at the little redheaded girl and the brunette boy who held her hand. He said, "You're safe now. The nice woman put the bad people away."

The children exchanged glances before the little girl ran up and hugged Nox's knee. He patted her head and tried to keep it together as their sniffles formed a chorus of broken children.

Those people deserved worse than the death Rayne had given them.

In the front, Rayne called, "Elden, please."

A conduit formed on the stage. Burdened with this ugly reality, Rayne moved toward it slowly. "Nox?"

"C'mon. We'll take you somewhere safe."

The brunette boy asked, "Will the grownups hurt us there?"

In better light, Nox made out the boy's black eye. Nox was reminded of the first time he and Xelan had brought Korac to their chambers. The scars all over him... stripping naked for inspection...

After swallowing, Nox said, "If another person lays a hand on you, you'll be the last thing they touch."

Something in the way he said it convinced the children to follow him to the conduit. Dragging the auctioneer behind him, Nox took a second to look Rayne over. Their shared heart was recovering, but the scar was lasting.

As if she'd heard his thoughts, Rayne nodded and lied, "I'm all right. Let's get out of this place. Did you—Oh, great. You kept the auctioneer." She put her face in the female Caprent's line of sight and said, "You and I have so much to talk about."

The deadly promise in her words thrilled Nox, but he could process it later. For now, they needed to discern where Elden's conduit led them—

Pil's Children's Sanctuary

Elden was curiously precise, and it was in the middle of the night, providing them some cover.

"Thank goodness," Rayne muttered before kneeling to speak to the little ones. "In there, they can take care of you and help you find your parents. Tell them to contact Co-Emperor Xelan. Send the word 'Superman' along. He'll help."

Nox smiled as Rayne ruffled the little girl's hair. The child looked uncertain at first, what with Rayne being covered in a rainbow of blood, but eventually she beamed with a missing tooth and hugged Rayne's neck.

The brunette boy with the black eye tugged on Nox's hand, and when he looked down, the boy said, "Thank you, mister."

Behind them, the auctioneer mumbled incoherently, still recovering from the broken trachea. Still, it was all enough to make Nox smile at the boy. "Take care of each other."

The rest of the children swarmed them in hugs, and he smiled over at Rayne, who looked better than even five minutes ago. Both their hearts felt lighter.

As the children ran into the orphanage, Nox pulled the auctioneer into a nearby alley. Rayne wasted no time in punching through the female Caprent's back and ripping out her nacre. Rayne swallowed the amber pearl before saying, "We should have what we need. Elden, can you please—"

A conduit opened to Thailea's forest.

"Thank you," Rayne said as she waved for Nox to follow.

He held up a finger. "You go first. I'll be right behind you."

She quirked a curious brow at Nox, but left to seek her own sanctuary. Out of her sight, Nox slit the Caprent's throat and used the green blood to leave a message in the style of the Shadow for the dawn.

Elden kindly kept the conduit open until Nox stepped through and outside the treeloft. Rayne waited for him with a wilted smile so they could enter their home together. She limped in, not from an injury—her nacre had healed any sustained—but from weariness. The most powerful warrior in the galaxy was bone tired.

Nox felt it in their pulse as he followed her around the corner. Pressed with the need to revitalize her, he said, "It was a magnificent battle."

In the kitchen, Rayne let out an incredulous laugh as she let her hair down. Busy removing braids, she said, "You were fantastic. The stopping power—I'm too small to pull off punches like yours. I mean, sure, I can punch through someone's face, but you rattle their entire skeleton." She gave a little hiccup and hid the tears he could smell from the salt.

Compliments were new to Nox, and compliments from Rayne were more valuable to him than Aegis ore was to the empire. Especially amid all her gentle sobs with her back to him. Nox worried Rayne regretted the mercy she'd shown the fighters and Dagger in the vice arena and for shunning her killer instincts.

Nox had embraced his long ago to the detriment of his sanity. His brother—the Icarus who'd taught Rayne so much in life—would applaud her restraint tonight even though the people they'd spared were affiliated with child trafficking. Where was the balance between Nox and Xelan, and how did Rayne find it?

Into the silence of her suppressed weeping, Nox said, "You're more than a Weapon, Rayne. You'll find your way—"

She whirled and faced him with glassy reddened eyes and a rosiness to her nose and cheeks, clearly upset. Rayne stared up at Nox, searching his expression, before asking, "Will you wash the blood off of me?" Without waiting for his response, Rayne lifted her soiled top, turning her back before he glimpsed her breasts. She let the shirt fall to the floor and started stripping off her pants as she walked into the shower.

This was not an invitation. Nox recognized it for what it was: a cry for help, for comfort. And he would *not* take advantage of Rayne. No matter how tempting it seemed.

Nox cursed himself as he stripped out of his shirt, kicked off his pants and boots, and followed her into the spray. Rayne's back was to him again. She was hugging herself while the water soaked her hair, and a spectrum of color washed down the drain. Her soft cries and increasingly jarring shudders racked Nox's conscience. So vulnerable, so beautiful, and not his.

Resigned, he grabbed a soap pod and lathered it before taking controlled steps toward Rayne. At Nox's approach, she held her breath. He wondered what she must be thinking. Was she thinking this would be it? *The* moment. It certainly would explain why his heart was pounding harder than during the fight.

Rayne watched him over her shoulder as Nox lifted her hair and swept it to the font. He gingerly scrubbed a patch of blood on her back, and she gasped with the contact. Blood and other things were caked all over Rayne's skin, but Nox was only willing to get the hard to reach places, trying with everything in him to ignore the perfect definition to her shoulders, lower back, and lower still. Rayne certainly kept herself fit, and every brush of his fingers against her skin was soft.

Nox washed everything away from the Icarean script on her back, once off limits to him, and considered lingering to wash away the rest. But her eyes...

Thousands of years ago, Nox had looked into those eyes in Cascading light and lusted after the vulnerability in them. Faced with the real thing, he was utterly disarmed.

Unwilling to elicit more from this than Rayne was ready to give, Nox kissed the top of her head, noting she closed her eyes to soak it in. With that, he abandoned her for his side of the shower.

Too much.

Nox couldn't hide Rayne's effect on him, as it was terribly obvious and slightly unwelcome. Frustrating, even. Not to mention his scent mingled with the shower's steam.

Scrub, rinse, and get out—

"I meant it."

Nox paused, washing his hair, frozen. Was Rayne referring to—

"About us together. I meant it."

Clarity.

Rayne's voice wavered slightly, but not with the weight of her conscience. Honeysuckle explained the arrhythmia.

Before Nox could respond, Rayne left the shower, feet padding further away. So she didn't regret saying it or feeling it, but still she kept her distance. He'd respect it, of course, confused signals and all.

Forever.

Nox could wait forever for Rayne to find her resolve or let him go. Until then, he'd finish his shower, slip into some soft sleep pants, and get a good night's rest to calm the churning fire left inside after touching Rayne's skin, smelling her scent, and reveling in her trust. Sleep, and tackle the day tomorrow—

He rounded the corner to find Rayne sitting cross-legged on the couch—Nox's bed—researching through some tablets. She glanced up, back down, did a double-take, and stared.

This was another compliment. Nox couldn't help but languish in his effect on her while shirtless. After all, a light blush befitted Rayne's creamy complexion. And she was commandeering his bed. He folded his arms and quirked a brow at her.

Rayne's expression blossomed into a sweet smile, absent of her earlier turmoil. Mercurial and so similar to Xelan. Perhaps she'd inherited some of his malady. She said, "You look great, and you also look ready for bed."

So did Rayne, in a cropped, over-sized shirt and rolled-up pajama shorts. Long toned legs, mid-riff, and no bra—Was Rayne *trying* to sexually frustrate Nox?

He snorted at her response and plopped his ass in the nearest armchair. Head propped in his hand as he said, "Well, your majesty. What have you got there?"

Again came the eager smile before Rayne explained, "I'm cross-referencing the auctioneer's memory banks with Razor's dossier and imperial reports for any traces of Celindria's involvement in the ring. It's possible this was simply leftover shit from Gait, but I doubt her hands are entirely clean of it."

"Stunning *and* intelligent. How have I ever resisted you?" If Rayne can toss out casual compliments, so could Nox. This wasn't flirting.

This was *not* flirting.

At the deepening of her blush, Nox went back on task. "Have you found anything so far?"

Rayne nodded while saying, "Yup. I think Celindria is gathering an army through volition, but I'm not sure of the mechanism. After Xelan told me his Verse, there was an imperial decree for volition vaccinations. Mandatory and all, but there are some protests from small groups on each planet. I think that's her 'in,' but I'd just discovered it when you came in. Can I have some more time?"

Nox glanced at where Rayne's top had slanted and exposed her shoulder on one side. Her thick hair was still wet from the shower and slicked with sleh oil. Rather than asking to comb it, he offered, "Take all the time you need. I'll clean our gear in the meantime."

"Thanks, Nox."

The weight of how she said it...

"You're welcome, Rayne."

Heading for the kitchen, Nox left her to it while he cleaned belts, daggers—Was there a point in cleaning her clothes if she could absorb them? And did she ever need to clean Night Killer? He'd ask later. It was a few hours before he turned the corner into the living room again.

Rayne was asleep in Nox's bed.

Curled on her side, her black lashes were a stark contrast against her pale cheeks. Every soft breath was precious. Nox grabbed a blanket and covered

Rayne before laying another one and some pillows on the floor for himself.

This close to her, Nox couldn't sleep. So he laid there and contemplated their mission.

Celindria believed he and she were the Eternal Bind, and she had threatened to build another of him. What would she do if she ever learned he was alive—

Rayne's face appeared above him over the cushions. "Whatchu doing down there?"

The truth was ugly, so instead, Nox offered, "Counting the constellations backwards by ten."

"Ew math." Rayne snickered.

"It's a pastime I taught Xelan. We used to name them by every twelfth letter in our alphabet." Nox stared up at Rayne, asking, "Did you find the couch to your liking?"

Rayne smiled, got up, and laid her blanket over Nox before saying, "Almost as much as the company. Good night, Nox." With the goofy smile on her face, she climbed the stairs and waved.

Madly in love with her, Nox called, "Good night, Rayne."

Onto tomorrow, and another million ways she'd send their heart racing.

{6,000BCE}

"Congratulations on another successful Vacating, Celindria."

Razor always sounded so sincere, but she could hear the venom in the begrudging congratulations. There was an unspoken competition between them, where the Pain Curator took some personal slight any time Remorse announced one of her achievements. Almost as if Razor didn't appreciate losing his surrogate father's attention for even five seconds on a phone call.

Celindria enjoyed needling him. It eased the agony and guilt which always lingered after condemning the love of her life and his people to another eight thousand years under Li's punishing glare. Truly, she only felt it occasionally, but even at fifty percent capacity, it still rendered her paralyzed with grief.

Until Celindria would enter the source.

"The mother would find your execution remarkable. Although regrettably, I must remind you, she would not delight in your target."

Lucas.

The closest soldier to the originator.

He's right.

But Paradise must always come this way.

Celindria assured, "She would understand it's the only way to Ishkur. Did she say when she would wake, Remorse?" She'd asked this question often, and she always noticed the tick in the Primary's right void.

There it was.

With a stiffened neck and his lipless mouth in a disapproving slant, Remorse assured, "Silence said the device would wake her when it was time, and I have faith it will. Until then, Celindria, continue with the Progeny weapons research, and Razor?"

"Yes, Primary?" There was a discernible perk in Razor's demeanor.

Celindria almost rolled her eyes at how much the Pain Curator vied for paternal affection.

"Nox and Korac are your responsibility from hereon. Guarantee they pursue the second invasion. I know you will not fail me, Three Two Four."

The blatant manipulation was disgusting, and Celindria resented how easily the most manipulative person she knew fell for it.

Razor smiled, probably receiving sexual gratification from Triss under the table as they spoke, and said, "Your confidence is never misplaced, Remorse. Until the next report, good night."

The call ended, leaving Celindria in a caravan traveling north on Earth. These were always her longest days: the journey back to Enki. All the way to Siberia the hard way. Andrius and Devis were already waiting back at her lab in civilization where Celindria could return to her research and await T.A.O.'s capture. Losing Merit never stopped stinging.

Another sacrifice to the one true Probability, but Celindria knew the carefree woman would understand.

Or so we like to tell ourselves.

{NOW}

Earth in the dominant Probability was so impatient and susceptible to even the most ignorant fabrications. The empire had discovered Celindria's pre-implemented volition code in the free nacres provided by Enki and distributed by The Brethren.

Thank you, Lynn Renee.

Yet, even as the empire mandated vaccinations to prevent exploitation of said code, thirty-three percent of the human population refused to vaccinate. One tiny whisper from an Imminent initiate was all it took. Protests, riots, and the most egregious and false rhetoric to support their 'freedom.'

Celindria stood atop her purchase on the Earth's tallest tower and smiled down at her new subjects.

All nine hundred and sixty million of them.

They cry and they beg.

Good.

More were needed.

Celindria wasn't inhabiting the drone last night at W^3, but his memory bank delivered disconcerting uploads of a pale-skinned brunette with bright blue eyes. Not an uncommon sight in the era of Rayne Tributes, but this one bore the Icarean script of Elden's Verse on her back. Combine that with the attack on the pathetic excuse for a vice auction, and the evidence pointed to more than a coincidence.

Rayne's unprecedented resurrection might explain the shrinking Probability Matrix. Another eight million Probabilities had vanished over the last twenty-four hours.

She's our only true enemy. Did we see the way Nox had looked at her when he—

We couldn't love him like she could. They were better suited for each other than us—

Eliminate her!

We need more troops than Earth and Monarch 3.

Each of Celindria's new subjects would go about work, school, and religious rituals without alarming their communities until she awakened the other armies. The Shadow must know of her by now—Father would never keep this secret forever.

What about his Verse? He loves us.

He can't be trusted. He always sides with the Shadow.

Because they're right.

What about us?

We can only be happy in Paradise.

We occupy trillions of minds in Paradise and still, we never find happiness.

Celindria looked at her hands and recalled every knife they'd held, every gun, and every hand. Every face.

All of the blood on them.

Aloud, Celindria said into the night wind, "Father can't save me now."

Tomorrow, Cinder.

VI   BLAZE

XELAN HATED THIS.

Not the care and the love—He was all for those things and appreciated that more help was circulating for everyone within the Shadow.

No. He hated that when he'd come upstairs from his eight hours of sleep, he and Tumu had found Tameka passed out at Xelan's desk. Care-giving for him was costing her.

"I'm fine," she'd promised as he'd walked her back to their bedroom. "Just a little tired."

Xelan went to start a hot shower for her, saying, "If I have to get rest, so do you. This is fair, right?"

Tameka gave in, and they showered together— More than showered together—until it was time for them to switch roles and he tucked her into bed.

That was about two hours ago, and since then, Xelan was relegated only to daddy duty—Playing with Pax, teaching him to cook, and enforcing table manners while they ate.

Tumu hung around to make certain he did nothing else.

While Pax climbed a rock wall, Xelan said, "How can I do any good limited to this?"

Tumu nudged him with an elbow as he said, "Peaches still needs you, Wingmaster, but more than anything, she needs you to look after yourself for the time being."

"I know. I'm not arguing against it. But three more days without me looking into imperial business?" This impotence was so frustrating. How was Xelan supposed to help—

"Rayne will manage without you."

Stunned.

Floored.

Shocked so badly, Xelan almost missed his son passing his personal best. "That's it, kiddo, you got this!"

"Hee! Watch me. Imma keep going!" Pax kept climbing like a champ, and all Xelan could do was pick his jaw up off the floor and glare at Tumu.

Tumu sighed and rolled his eyes, exasperated. He said, "You think you're not transparent? You stopped talking about her after Tameka found you in the Divine Booth. And the War King has a way of talking to people in their dreams. How long had she been trying? Since Enki? But your stubborn ass wouldn't go to sleep—"

"Seriously?" Bewildered and incredulous, Xelan asked, "*You're* giving me a hard time right now? Do you have any idea what it's been like knowing this—"

"You knew along, and I have the inclination to believe your intuitions. So I never doubted. How is she, by the way?" Tumu held up his hand to stem Xelan's answer so he could cheer, "That's it, Pax! Right onto the ceiling. Remember: the foam pit will always catch you if you fall."

With a cute grunt of effort, Pax said, "Thanks, Uncle Tumu. I got this."

Proud uncle that he was, Tumu shook his head, amazed. "That kid… Growing up fast isn't he—Why are you staring at me like that?!"

Xelan stopped staring and went back to watching his son. This last week was murder, but at least, someone else knew his latest secret. He said, "She's fine. She's grown into such an amazing and brilliant young woman. I think… Well, she implied she's working with Elden."

Tumu flushed black under his blue skin, but remained silent.

It was unusual and clearly meant something. Another minute passed before Xelan couldn't take it anymore. "What?!"

On rare occasions, Tumu let his voice go soft, and the deep boom of it registered at human normal. "I hope she's careful."

What was that supposed to mean?

Xelan's palm device pulsed, and no matter how hard he tried, he could *not* ignore it.

Andrew appeared in his hand. "Hey, Wingmaster, how ya doing?"

Something was wrong. Xelan glanced up at Tumu to see if he also detected it. Instead, he got an ugly glower from the Tritan.

"What in Eternity are you doing on the comms?! No work, remember?"

Andrew answered for Xelan, "I need to see you, Tumu. I only wanted to ask Xelan's permission to go to the stronghold."

Tumu nodded, and Xelan responded, "You're working now, right? Ask T.A.O. to bring you. No need to disrupt the honeymoon I've already ruined."

Those weren't Korac's exact words, but the sentiment was loud and clear when he and Sagan had departed.

The call ended right as Pax reached the pinnacle of the ceiling and cheered, "Dad! Uncle Tumu! Look!"

"We never took our eyes off you, scout. Great job!" Tumu called.

Waiting for Andrew to arrive, Xelan went to the edge of the foam pit. "Okay. Time for your favorite part!"

With a squeal of delight, Pax let go and fell three stories into the cubes of foam. Xelan held out his hand to help his son out. At the sight of Pax swimming through the gray fluff, Xelan grinned. Genuinely. It felt good.

Lamassau came into the gym, munching on a bag of potato chips from Reipon. "Hey, kid. I see you made it to the big top. Congrats!" He held out his hand low.

As soon as Pax was free of the pit, he slapped it hard. "Yeah!"

"Why don't you go tell your mom? She's awake. I need to talk to your dad and your uncle." Lam gave them both stern looks.

Pax, old enough now to sense the tension, looked between all the adults before saying, "Okay. See you at dinner." He ran off to stand right outside the door and eavesdrop without completely understanding anything.

Xelan remembered those days. He asked Lam, "What is it?"

Tumu held up a finger. "Remember, he isn't supposed to work—"

"Does 'Superman' mean anything to you, almighty Co-Emperor?" Lamassau held up a tablet with a missive on it.

Xelan swallowed before looking it over. Children had arrived at Celindria's orphanage last night asking for help and they were told to pass along 'Superman' to the Co-Emperors. The same night, authorities found a Caprent female left slaughtered and nacre-less in the Promenade with a sign drawn in purple blood.

IMMINENT BAD GUY

Xelan raked a hand down his face before meeting Tumu's eyes. He tried to communicate that he thought it was Rayne without tipping off Lamassau. She didn't want anyone to know. Sliding his gaze to Lam, Xelan ordered, "Investigate the Caprent. Find out everything we can about her and her involvement with those children. Help them find their families, if they have any."

Lamassau narrowed his eyes at both men and waved a finger between them, asking, "There's nothing happening here I should know about, right?"

Xelan wanted an update on Kyle and Ross processing the memories from Razor they'd pulled out of Bethany. They could help identify major players in the vice ring who didn't fall with Gait and Enki. And there was always the possibility Xelan could reconstruct another Razor out of them, but no one would agree to it. So, once again, he pushed the urge aside.

"Not yet, Lam," Xelan assured. "Thanks for coming to me, despite my medical limitations."

Tumu chuffed.

Andrew stepped through with T.A.O., who launched herself right into the foam pit and followed it up with a laugh of pure delight. They all indulged in watching her enjoy the moment before Andrew got to business.

"The Probabilities shrank more overnight, and Lucas said it was simply a natural phenomenon."

Xelan bit his thumbnail and considered it. Sourced from the Aegis entering this plane of existence, it was possible ebbs and flows were a reactive occurrence. He asked Andrew, "What do you think?"

"Oh, I think Lucas is lying. In fact, I *know* he is."

So much for medical leave.

―――

Andrew hated hearing the harsh words come out of his mouth, but the truth was often harsh. A lesson he'd learned not so long ago over the same man. Andrew said, "I think Lucas knows exactly what's taking place, and it may *technically* be natural—so he's technically not lying—but I think something is still affecting it."

Xelan squeezed Andrew's shoulder, saying, "I know this is hard. Thank you for coming to us."

He nodded.

Lamassau dipped his bag of chips into his mouth and munched some more, as he asked, "So what do you think it is?"

Xelan and Tumu exchanged a glance before the Tritan said, "It can only be one thing…"

"The Eternal Bind," Xelan finished.

Lam nearly choked as he said, "But that's a myth, isn't it?"

Andrew patted the choking Tritan's back before saying, "We kinda specialize in myths and legends around here."

Xelan conceded the point with a tilted nod. "I guess we do. Now we'll need to find out who it is."

"It's a pair the universe always brings together. The ultimate power couple. So clearly, it's Lam and I."

Lamassau grinned at Tumu with crumbs scattered across his lipless mouth, and the Primary beamed down at his lover.

Andrew could see it, but wasn't entirely sold. He said, "Celindria told Chris she believed Nox and her were it."

"Another." T.A.O. Seamswalked beside them and spoke in the language of her gentle insanity. "Fear without Nox. Fear without Hope. Forever in fear of another."

Andrew tried interpreting it. It made sense Celindria lived in a state of imbalance without Nox. The crazed woman had made it clear she'd expected him to resurrect and not Xelan. Maybe this had put her in a state of hopelessness, but then why fear this other? If not Nox, Celindria must be paired with someone else. But who?

Xelan took T.A.O.'s hand and squeezed it gently. She rewarded him with a soft smile. "Father."

"I know. You're helping, I promise."

Lamassau crunched on another handful of chips and talked with his mouth full. "Sounds like Celindria has another partner."

Tumu frowned, saying, "No, I don't think so. Why would she 'fear' her partner? She likely fears another pairing."

T.A.O. nodded emphatically. "The kind one and the repentant one. They are Eternal."

Andrew guessed, "Sagan and Korac?"

Xelan said, "At the very least, I can—" At Tumu's glare, Xelan amended, "Or someone else can ask Korac to upcycle his father about the Eternal Bind. Maybe he has another explanation for the Probabilities shrinking, but I doubt it."

Tumu ruffled Andrew's hair, saying, "Thanks for the heads up, Goldilocks."

Wow. Throwback. "You haven't called me that since before we all had nacres."

The Primary shrugged. "It seems like a good time to trudge up old endearments."

Lamassau muttered, "It better be all you trudge up."

"Secrets."

They all turned and looked at T.A.O. "So many." Meeting Tumu's voids, she said—almost warned, "Soon."

He nodded as if he understood her meaning.

Andrew was long used to this kind of clandestine talk and not understanding a bit of it. With an exasperated sigh, he said, "I'm heading back to the zeppelin. It's Lucas' turn to cook."

"Aren't you afraid he'll poison you?" Lamassau sounded completely serious.

Xelan raised a curious brow, and Tumu also waited for Andrew's answer.

"Whatever Lucas is hiding … It doesn't matter. He loves me, and I know he means it. That's enough."

Tumu nodded approvingly.

"Xelan?" Tameka asked as she walked into the gym, holding Pax's hand. The kid looked recently scolded, as if she'd caught him eavesdropping. She took one look at their faces and said, "I know there's a good reason you're working right now, but it's dinner time, and I veto all assignments until we're finished."

Andrew went over and stole a quick hug from Tameka and Pax, squeezing them extra tight. "You guys have a good night!"

T.A.O. curtsied before taking him through a conduit which led outside of the zeppelin tethered to Nikki's Iona.

He smiled, saying, "Thanks again, T.A.O."

With a strange smile, she assured, "One waits, Goldilocks," before disappearing.

"She's right. I do." Lucas sounded so self-assured and warm. A dangerous combination.

Andrew faced his calculating lover and confessed, "I went to Xelan with your half-assed reasoning."

Arms folded, leaning in the doorway, Lucas laughed. "And what did he say?"

"He and Tumu think it's the Eternal Bind. Now, I don't suppose you'll share what you know of it?" Andrew possessed no illusions as he passed the other man into their home, heading straight for the kitchen.

Lucas was smiling as he assured, "It is *technically* a natural occurrence."

A little frustrated, Andrew chuffed. "Why couldn't you just say it was the Eternal Bind from the beginning?" He made up his plate of Yun specialties.

Lucas joined him, and they both sat at the table as he said, "Then we risk you and the Shadow trying to stop it."

Andrew big blinked. Twice. "This is a good thing?" His incredulity came out harsher than he'd intended. The urge to sweep his lover's attention gnawed at him.

As if he understood, Lucas leaned over and kissed Andrew's temple before saying, "This is everything. Let nature run its course, and it will soon be over."

Andrew had only one important question. "Will we survive?"

"This time, I hope so."

<hr>

Korac kissed Sagan's freckled nose before climbing out from under the sheets. With a sigh, she smiled in her sleep and snuggled her pillow, messy bed-head and all.

He loved her.

Which was why Korac couldn't let Sagan into his burgeoning conspiracy theory.

He slipped on some silk shorts—white, duh—and sneaked into his office. The mountain chalet was kitted out with the best of Aegis technology, but it was contained in cozy elegance. Elegant coziness. Their home was damned comfortable, stylish, and futuristic.

Far more than anything Korac would've imagined for himself on Gait—Shit, even on Cinder. As Ishkur's first General, equal only to Sagan, his office was faceted with projected screens dedicated to separate avenues of his role. All wireless. Cable was a thing of the past.

Korac sat in the levitating chair which formed under his ass from thin air and pulled up the files he was keeping from Sagan. Pehton, too—Nobody knew.

Nacre.

Chamber.

Those were the two words Nox had mouthed to Korac through a closing conduit seconds before Rayne had decimated Enki. Only Korac was a little slow and hadn't recognized the words until his wedding day, not even a week ago. It wasn't good timing. First, Xelan bogarted Sagan and Korac's honeymoon like an imperial Prima Donna, and now the Shadow knew Celindria was out there. It didn't exactly lend to a relaxing vacation, but damn, did Sagan try.

The two of them went on a tour of exotic planets for fun, frolic, and so much sex. Korac couldn't get enough of Sagan, but the niggling in the back of his head wouldn't relent.

"Fuck."

No one was around to hear. There was only Korac's office and the files open on his screen.

Elden's nacre was missing, and Korac was almost ninety-nine point nine percent certain the nacre in its place was Rayne's. How had the incredible sprite even managed it? He couldn't fathom it. But if she was alive, maybe Nox was too? After all, both resurrection caskets in the nacre chamber were still functional.

Korac appreciated the space Sagan gave him, but she was brilliant. A gem of so many perfect cuts. There's no way she was completely in the dark. But how could he tell her without proof?

So, here Korac was, filtering reports for any signs of the power duo out there in the wild. And then Xelan dropped this on his desk.

Imminent Bad Guy

The vile lowlifes of this galaxy couldn't get enough of trafficking children. Korac would make a point of visiting the orphanage in person once his honeymoon was officially over. Until then, he'd send Pehton and Bones to investigate.

Speak of the adorable devil.

"Hey, boss."

Korac smirked so Pehton could see. He took way too much pleasure in her calling him that. "General Warden." He gave her a little salute, and she flipped him off, unaware of how much he enjoyed it. "Report on your Pil mission."

Pehton held up the projected device in her palm for Bones to join. He said, "Matt, Lucy, Bethany, Puk, and Yito went undercover last night. Some sleazy place looking to fill the Pain Curator vacuum. Totally within their perimeters, right?"

Korac's hands were laced and pressed against his mouth, so he nodded to show he was tracking.

Pehton took over from there. Her tiny Lyriki self said, "Only the VIPs survived the fight. Someone left them alive, and that certainly isn't very much like the annihilation squad."

With little reason for it, Korac asked, "Was Bethany all right?"

There was a look on Pehton's face. She got it every time she found Korac endearing, and the warmth of it almost made him blush. Stupid mushy Shadow shit. She said, "They're all fine. We thought about joining forces with them, at least for some intel. Who else could've gone in and attacked a base like this one?"

Bones added, "But something doesn't add up."

Intrigued, Korac leaned forward and said, "Go on, soldier."

He almost smirked at how Bones straightened and stood a little taller as the Icarean warrior said, "While all this went down in the slums, lightning struck topside of the space-scraper."

Lightning.

During the Volcano Day battle, Rayne and Nox had accumulated such a force of equivalent energies that lightning had struck them on the battlefield.

Korac swiped along the screens, saying, "I'm sending some fresh reports about the new orphanage which may correspond with the events at the vice den. Find some witnesses and see if there's a correlation. Let me know what the annihilation squad—as you so aptly named them—has to say about their current operation. Co-op, if they allow it, but don't smother them. They work best when left to their own devices."

"Will do." Off topic, Pehton asked, "How is Echo?"

Okay. So. Whenever someone mentioned his little girl, Korac couldn't keep this proud, beaming grin off his face, and ever since Pehton discovered this, she asked at every opportunity. And there it was again, involuntary, yet still welcome. "She's perfect. Mother is keeping her for us until the honeymoon is over, but we popped in earlier today for some baby time."

Knowingly, Pehton smirked. "Couldn't stay away, could you?"

Bones chuckled beside her before throwing out, "Say hi to Para for me," as Korac ended the call.

Family was a funny thing.

Leaning back in his chair, Korac considered the other request from Xelan's missive: upcycle Zero and ask about the Eternal Bind. It was strange building a connection with one's father posthumously, but Korac couldn't shake this feeling. The Exalted was hiding something.

Shit, the man was an Aegis—He was probably hiding an entire universe in the hollow ring of his pupils.

Korac closed his eyes and concentrated on his talent for calling Aegis beings into his body. It was a surprisingly warm and complete feeling. Inside his mind, Zero appeared.

The Exalted shoved his hands into the pocket of his white tux. A single black rose was the only thing about him not in white. He smiled as he said, "My son, how are these early days of your matrimony?"

Without a reason to lie, Korac said, "Perfect. Sagan… She's perfect."

There was a slight lilt to Zero's lips before he took a few steps forward, saying, "You wake on this night rather than sleep with her in your arms. Something must trouble you. How may I help?"

It was weird having a dad. Especially one who could read Korac almost as well as if he'd raised him. Next time, Korac would try upcycling one of his brothers to see what it would be like to have one. Razor didn't count.

Korac asked, "How much do you know about the Eternal Bind?"

Zero broke into a mischievous grin, as if caught with stolen candy. "A good deal, but it is rather simple, is it not? A pair destined to rein in destiny itself."

Evasive. Illusive.

Fucking Aegis.

Was this what it was like talking to Korac all these years?

Never mind.

"Do you know who it is and would you be willing to share this information with me?" Korac tried to take the edge off the words, but this was getting frustrating. Was it so much to ask for transparency?

Zero stared at the top of his shiny white shoes, saying, "No… But One knows."

Korac raked a hand through his hair, recovering his patience, before asking, "Which one? Can you give me a straight answer?"

There was an amused lift to Zero's lips as he asked, "May I know what you plan to accomplish with this information?"

"I suppose we mean to stop it."

The Exalted nodded as if he'd guessed as much. "The Probability Matrix is an affront to the natural order. We shattered your realities when we entered your universe, and they continued to splinter. This is not the way of it, my son. The Eternal Bind will right what we wronged."

Korac didn't have an immediate argument against his logic. To build some trust in their relationship, he admitted, "I don't know what we mean to do about it. The potential of our universe collapsing makes it a phenomenon worth investigating."

"Quite right." Zero's eyes drifted to the side as if he were listening. "She wakes. Continue seeking your friend and the sprite. They will need you soon."

Korac wasn't ready for his father to leave yet. To stop him, Korac blurted, "Dad."

The Exalted's smile was genuine and radiant. "Yes, Korac?"

"I know you don't appreciate when I bring him up, but I see the ghost of Razor anytime I'm on the bridge in Ishkur. He's standing in the back, trying to help while everyone else ignores him. Please give me something genuine to understand." Why did it matter to Korac? Because the young man who was Razor waiting for his brothers to acknowledge him implied a beginning. An opening to heal.

Zero crossed the mindscape and put his hand on Korac's shoulder. When their eyes met, he said, "Your brother's bitterness was not half-earned, and I carry my responsibility for it into this afterlife. Please, do not try to bear it with me. He loved Sagan enough to die for Ishkur, and I think, if not for a long history of neglect, he could understand kindness and mercy. But no matter how long we dwell in what could have been, Three Two Four chose his life and found some semblance of redemption in his last act. The ghost is a sad truth, but not one you or I could change."

Korac searched his father's white eyes before asking, "Would you?"

Without hesitation, Zero said, "If I could? Absolutely."

Sagan called from the hallway, "Hey, honey, can I come in?"

Zero smiled again, warning, "Do *not* waste a second of your time together. Good bye, my son."

"Good bye, father."

The Exalted waved as he faded away.

Korac sprung from his chair and opened the door. Sagan stood naked in the doorway, sleepily rubbing her eyes with her hair sticking up everywhere. He didn't give her a chance to speak before he tilted her face up for a kiss. Even tired, Sagan returned with searing heat. Comfort. Korac sought comfort in her.

They'd spend a few hours in bed, sleep, and then Korac would continue his search for Nox and Rayne. But somehow he knew they'd find him when they were ready.

Thanks to his imperial pain in the ass, Kyle was working late instead of enjoying the company of the galaxy's hottest G.I.L.F. Silence promised to get started without him after her stressful morning of mitigating Lucas' clandestine nature and Andrew's trust issues. On this one and only occasion, Kyle was inclined to follow Xelan's instincts.

This was Aegis.

So, here Kyle stood, alongside Ross, reconstructing the fragmented memories which Bethany had consumed from Razor. Somewhere in this mess was a complete insight into the Pain Curator's life, including Aegis lore. Without ol' Cap'n Wingmaster saying it, Kyle knew the clinically hyper-focused Co-Emperor was considering resurrecting some Frankenstein phoenix from these ashes. But that was yet another of Xelan's instincts Kyle would *not* follow.

Razor had scarred enough people, including Bethany and Ross. The man had put his hands on Kyle's sisters…

It was unforgivable, and Kyle would obliterate these fragments before he'd let Xelan recreate the least deserving person in the galaxy. The only person less deserving of resurrection than Razor was Nox, and fortunately, Rayne had disintegrated his ass.

Good riddance—

"You've got the *look* on your face, bro." Ross was a gentle breeze, casting doubt and sadness aside. She could kick ass as sure as the next Shadow, thanks to Kyle, but her default was kindness and generosity. It was in her voice as she asked, "Do you want to talk about anything?"

They stood in a black memory scape illuminated at the floors and ceilings with white light. Like chalk on a fresh blackboard, Razor's memories were scribbled on the walls and back-lit. Ross and Kyle stood inside the space wearing black suits under white labcoats. Each held a clipboard—

This was not their construct.

Whatever was left of Razor had put Ross in a pencil skirt with glasses and her wavy hair in a tidy bun.

The Pain Curator was *not* worth resurrecting.

Although... Kyle might keep the suit and surprise Silence later.

Later.

After flipping his curly mop from his face, Kyle grumbled, "I'm in a shit mood. Sorry."

Maybe subconsciously embracing the framework, Ross hugged her clipboard to her chest, saying, "You could talk to one of the psychologists. I've heard the Reipon ones are especially good, but I like the Caprent Kombuchi recommended. Tia makes me workout while we talk, and it's relaxing."

Two of Kyle's least favorite things: exercise and talking about himself. He wiped his hand down his increasingly sourpuss face and kissed Ross' forehead. "Thanks. I'll check into one." On a cold day in hell. "Until then, let's try to work through this monster's head. Are you sure you're up to this?"

Ross smiled, dressed in Razor's ideal get up for her, and nodded. "I'm sure we'll find what Xelan's looking for, and maybe..." Her voice trailed off, and her smile wilted.

"What?" Kyle hated seeing her like this.

The middle child swallowed before saying, "Jack worries about me dwelling on it, but I'm hoping to find the key to opening Bethany up. Maybe once we learn about her interactions with Razor, we could find the exact thing which...I mean, whatever it was that..." *Broke* her. "We could find it and bring her back."

The baby wasn't coming back, and maybe that's what bothered Kyle about Ross. He'd given up, and she was still trying. Guilt and failure plagued him, and Ross' constant optimism—never giving up—was only putting off the inevitable breakdown she'd suffer once she realized Bethany's untamed disposition was permanent. Then Kyle would have to pick up another broken sister out of Razor's shadow.

"Yeah. Maybe."

Ross' smile returned in full force, and she clutched the clipboard at the ready. "Let's do this." His sister headed down the south aisle, scanning the text written on musical staff with renewed determination.

Jack was right to worry.

"Ugh." Left alone in the central hub, Kyle shoved both hands in his hair and squeezed the unruly tangles. He let the frustration out with a sigh as he begrudgingly admitted—never aloud—that Jack Callahan was good for Ross.

There.

He thought it.

Now Kyle desperately needed a shower to get the icky off of him. He looked down at the clipboard hugged in his arm with blank musical staffs lining down the page. He held up the pen to eye level, inspecting it. Of course, it was a fancy pearl fountain pen.

Kyle muttered, "Razor, you were one particular asshole."

Ready to toss the handful of shit aside, Kyle froze and stared down at the page. On the first line of empty sheet music was fancy script in purple ink—the same color as Sagan's eyes.

Takes one to know one.

No.

Nope.

Kyle wouldn't tell anyone about this. He growled, "Don't harass Ross in here, or I'll never tell Xelan. You get me?"

SHE IS SHADOW. SHE IS SAFE.

What a fucked up Ouija board, but it gave Kyle an idea. He said, "Razor, show me the memories pertaining to the Probability Matrix and the Eternal Bind—Anything useful involving Celindria, as well, and I'll tell Xelan you're here."

I DOUBT YOUR SINCERITY.

Quick on his feet, Kyle said, "Sagan would want you to help."

A quiet ensued and stretched on until he was sure Razor had bailed—

TEN MEMORIES NORTH AND THREE AISLES OVER. KEEP THE CLIPBOARD. YOU'LL NEED IT.

Kyle ran in the direction Razor directed, not at all worried the Pain Curator was lying. For one, this was a memory scape and Kyle was a memory expert, so no worries there. Secondly this was busy work, so it was worth the risk Razor was telling the truth to finish this task faster. But Ross...

About to round the last aisle, Kyle stopped to say, "Don't show my sister what she wants to see. I don't want her to see the abuse you put Bethany through. Do you think Sagan would want you to do something so indecent as to expose one sister to the torture of the other?"

WHAT DO YOU TAKE ME FOR?

Kyle bit his lip to keep from answering the question and turned down aisle three. The longer he looked at the foreign text on the music staffs against the black background, the more they shaped and molded into black and white playbacks of Razor's memories.

Bingo.

"Whoa..."

The Exalted had spawned a lot of sons, and, with the white features, they all sorta blended together. They were on Ishkur's bridge, observing the Probability Matrix. This was from the vantage point of the farthest gangplank, where they'd left Razor out of the way.

Zero came on deck and called, "One."

The crowd parted to reveal the Aegis at the Matrix's forefront and to reveal the image they'd been observing: Rayne. This Aegis went to his father, who pulled One aside, nearer to Razor. They whispered amongst themselves, but Kyle made out, "Fracture in the multi-verse," and, "What are your plans to correct it?"

One turned and looked at Rayne. She was his answer. Something to do with her.

Intrigued and a little concerned, Zero asked, "How far must we go?"

One said, "To the beginning. And not we. *I* will go. Alone."

With entirely too much authority, the Exalted decreed, "Go. I trust your discretion. Should you fail, try again until you come home to us. Do you understand?"

One nodded and left the bridge with a sad glance at Razor.

Staring at One's back, Zero said to himself, "My son, fate is safer in your hands than in mine."

Kyle zoned back from the memory and blinked a few times. What could this mean? And why did everything come back to Rayne?

"Razor, what can you give me?" There was a slight hint of desperation in Kyle's voice.

The text which appeared on the clipboard did *not* help.

ONE IS STILL MISSING.

{100CE}
All we do is work.
Paradise requires work and dedication.
We don't exist as other people do.
Other people are weak. We wish to be stronger.

Not all of us.

Celindria administered the treatment to another Caprent. Sat on the rocky plateau overlooking the entrance to their city, Lacceirus Capra was beautiful in its degradation, and the people were so generous despite their burdens.

While Celindria prepped a syringe for the next patient, she recalled Remorse approaching her for this menial task. He'd barged into her lab, ordering, "The Caprents are suffering from the ailment already. This is sooner than the other Probabilities."

Without looking up from her volition research and acknowledging his presence with her gaze, Celindria said, "Perhaps it has something to do with you forcing them to mine at greater depths with such weak upgrades to their nacres. I am shocked they have yet to suffer from caisson sickness at this rate."

Hands with long fingers slid onto Celindria's shoulders and squeezed as Remorse spoke against her hair. "My dear, may I remind you to whom I assigned administering upgrades?"

If Celindria's skin could slide off and crawl away, it would. Several millennia ago, they'd exchanged bodily fluids in a business transaction, and yet Remorse felt the need to remind her of those encounters with every glance, touch, and word.

In every Probability, he does this. He wants us.
We hate him.
We hate everyone.

"Remorse?" Celindria let a huskiness into her voice and an extra innocent lilt to the question. She even turned and faced him with widened, demure eyes.

The Tritan, whose age exceeded galactic years, practically panted and drooled in her lap as he pressed his imagined advantage. "Yes, lover?"

Celindria leaned closer to him, a breath from kissing Remorse, saying in a voice of poisoned virtue, "You only touch me this way until I marry with the

Source, and I know you fear it. So why not ingratiate yourself to me rather than repulse me before I extend beyond your limited expectations of femininity?" On the last, she licked his lip-less mouth, agape with his indignation.

Remorse tripped over himself when he startled back, as if Celindria had slapped him.

To hide the laughter in her eyes, because she was still very much vulnerable before the Source, Celindria turned and went back to her task. "I will administer the treatment to our capable miners in one hour. Good day, Primary Rem."

Like a petulant child, Remorse stormed out of Celindria's lab without a word.

He was right about the mines: Caprent kind was the perfect labor force. So gullible. Likes liked likes. While she treated them of the disease they had acquired by mining the dangerous mineral, Celindria supplemented nanites from her labs into the injections.

This was how a goddess built her empire. Her Paradise.

Father will come soon. He always does.

This is before, right before we break his heart into tiny shards, sharp enough to cut.

Only after, we don't feel anymore. Not like before. Almost not at all.

Celindria wanted to feel like before in Nox's arms. His loving and heated gaze as he surged inside her. So naked. Almost grateful. And with the life he'd lived, Nox *would* feel grateful for Celindria's tender ministrations.

Instead, she would soon experience the Source, leap into it while staring into father's disappointed eyes.

Celindria knew for certain this would pay off—

Not entirely.

We still don't feel.

—And it would all be worth it once she shuttered away the other realities.

First, plant the seeds which Celindria would sow into an empire. Into Paradise.

{Now}
Cinder welcomed Celindria in the same shadowy tower of Umbra's Spire. She went to the window and took in the unexpected view. Li was receding.

"Tameka."

Now *there* was a splinter in Celindria's eye. The Powerhouse female had proven more than a match for Celindria's calculations, and the miscreant bitch had stolen Pax from Celindria's home. In all the Probabilities until this dominant one, Pax always chose Celindria. Even now, he was the only person in Paradise not under her volition control. She loved her little half-brother.

Well.

As much as Celindria could love.

Below them, this version of Cinder was renewed, revived by the modern colonies of Icari, humans, Lamias—Anyone and everyone invested in the Shadow's legacy. Elden's mission.

The fucking Icarean Prerogative.

Celindria's Cinder had burned once she'd removed the Coalition nacres from the chamber. What a spectacular sight it was...

We saw it alone.

Because no one else wanted to see it.

Because we have no one.

Solitude, brief and fleeting, struck Celindria. The first emotion she'd experienced in weeks, and it was her most frequent emotion. Perhaps it was telling, hence, why she worked day and night to resurrect her lover.

Space-scrapers.

On Cinder.

The glossy black tower suited the ashen matte landscape. For once, Celindria considered the destruction of Cinder perhaps a bit rash on her part. Alas, she wasn't here to admire the budding civilization.

Once, not long ago, Celindria had established a healthy continent of Icari. She had upgraded to embrace their higher intellect and bred them to spread from Cinder.

Father would've been proud.

We conquered the Vittle crop with him in mind.

Even though we like to pretend it wasn't so.

Celindria had borrowed technology from Korac's old friend, Ementa, to keep the continent secret. So Nox and Korac never knew, and it was only discovered when Celindria brought Tameka to it before everything went wrong in the dominant reality.

Seeds sown. It was time to harvest.

While many likely received the volition vaccines, Celindria could always count on the free will of the headstrong and bad, bad decisions.

There.

Fewer Icari than the humans responded to her command at only two million, but even half a million Icari with wings were worth a hundred million humans. More humans and Icari would wait on Ishkur, but it was safer to activate the outer planets first. They would make for a fine addition to Celindria's forces.

We need more.

The Shadow are many.

We are infinite.

But infinity will soon end.

Celindria would disseminate her troops throughout the galaxy and investigate any sightings of this potential Rayne. While Celindria's spies partied in vice dens, she may as well test the Divine Booth ports. Razor never thought to remove Celindria's modifications before, but there was no underestimating this Probability—vaccines, included.

We'll have Korac and his blood soon to resurrect our Nox.

Yes. We will.

VII   BONFIRE

ELDEN ADMIRED SILENCE, NAKED IN HER SLEEP, WITH ONE HAND ON HER SWOLLEN BELLY AND THE OTHER OVER HER HEAD. Their daughter slept within, and their heartbeats soothed him. Yet, as he leaned in the doorway of their chambers, Elden couldn't find peace.

Reports of a foreigner meeting in secret with Silence worried him. The armies she amassed of *his* people worried him. Umbra whispered to Elden of Silence's alliance to find some place called Ishkur and destroy those known as Aegis. With such uncertain thoughts swirling in his head, Elden found it difficult to sleep beside his goddess.

On that mournful note, he left her in bed and flew to the nearest secluded lake of crimson waters. Elden's reflection came back to him in scarlet when he sought clarity.

Was it ever right to seek the obliteration of an entire species?

"You have exceeded our expectations."

One.

He stood in the center of the lake, all the white reflected in red. Except for the pupils of his eyes. They were black stars scattered in the white. His smile was kind, almost pitying, as he said, "Hello, Elden."

Elden asked, "Have you come to take me again? Fill my veins with black matter? You and Tumu."

One walked across the surface of the water without so much as a ripple. "Friend, I come with two warnings."

This bristled Elden's feathers, and he glared at the other man to continue.

A step away, One stayed on the water as he said, "My brother is interested in your reputation, and any interest of his is dangerous."

"And the second warning?" Elden wanted to return to Silence and ensure her safety with One's arrival.

The mysterious foreigner brushed his shoulders and straightened his sleeves at the wrist as he said, "Your goddess must never enter Enki with her armies, or your people will not survive."

Elden thought as much, but shook his head anyway. "My Surra—my Silence—is a force beyond anyone's control, and I, for one, wish her free to do as she pleases. This makes her happiest, and I love her happy."

Again, the pitying smile. One said, "This is more to protect the Icari than to thwart the love of your life. As for her happiness, I will guarantee she finds it. I wish Silence no harm."

Somehow, Elden knew it would come to this. Stand in his mate's way to prevent the decimation of his people. War was never to anyone's benefit. Not to their place in Eternity, at any rate. He asked, "What will you require of me?"

One looked over Elden's shoulder as he said, "To face my brother and to reckon with Silence, you require upgrades."

"Apologies, but this will hurt."

Elden couldn't whirl on Tumu in time before the foreigner jabbed Elden with something sharp and fluid. They injected him with—

Searing and bruising, Elden fell to his knees in agony, screaming, "One!"

"Rayne, wake up."

Surfacing from the dream, Rayne opened her eyes.

Nox sat on the bed beside her, looking concerned. He said, "You were shouting."

She laid in bed, bare legs tangled in the sheet, and tried to remember how to breathe. Was Elden showing her his past intentionally? Or was the Icarean deity also dreaming? Rayne said, "Nox, I think… I think the Aegis manipulated your people as much as Primary Rem manipulated your family."

Any mention of Remorse instantly made Nox frown. "Why do you say that?"

"Elden. I'm dreaming his life, and he met an Aegis named 'One.' And… I can't believe I'm saying this. He was working with Tumu to upgrade Elden. From the beginning." At his widening eyes, Rayne continued, "And the strange thing is, I feel like I've seen One somewhere before." When his brows raised, she shook her head, trying to grasp it. "Sorry. It's a jumbled mess now that I'm awake."

Nox brushed Rayne's hair from her face. "If I'm certain of one thing, it's that you'll sort it out and finish it. It's one of those attributes which makes you so incredible."

His compliment made her blush, and suddenly Rayne was aware she was only in her cropped tee and panties. With the struggle from the dream, the shirt rode high, and she'd kicked the sheets off of her. She knew the second Nox realized the same thing because his eyes flashed and their pulse started racing. To take matters further, she'd fallen asleep imagining last night's shower moment taking them further than tender back scrubbing. Taking them to this enormous bed. It was enough to make her appreciate waking from a nightmare to the gentleness on his handsome face.

When Nox shifted on the bed, he did it slowly so Rayne could tell him to stop. She knew it, and he kept his eyes on her, seeking any signs of distress. Whatever was on Rayne's face gave Nox permission to kiss the sensitive skin on her ribs just below the hem of her shirt. Rayne closed her eyes on a shiver, and her heart pounded like thunder. When his warm lips pressed against her skin, lower than before, her eyes snapped open. The sight of Nox gazing up at her after kissing her thigh below the curve of her panties left Rayne wanting more.

And that's what shocked her out of the sensual moment.

A hot, frustrated tear fell from her lashes as Rayne came to her senses and implored on a breath, "Nox, no. Please. I want you, but I'm scared..."

Of what?

Xelan.

Tameka.

Basically, everyone Rayne knew—And she was afraid of disappointing all of them. Would they hate her for being with Nox? For accepting him after so much... Being his partner in the fight against Celindria—Hell, even being his friend—might be acceptable. But sex? And what about her feelings for him?

As Nox retreated, the loss of hope in his eyes killed Rayne inside. He must've seen it on her face because Nox cupped Rayne's chin and thumbed the tear away. His voice was hoarse with sorrow, but his smile was gentle as he said, "I am long lived for these worlds, and I have a better grasp on patience now than ever in my life. I've waited a hundred lifetimes for you, Rayne. Whether you eventually let me in or let me go, you are worth every second."

More tears. These were from Rayne's heart. It wasn't breaking; it was full. She'd felt platonic and romantic love in her life, but Nox's love for her always gave Rayne more than she knew what to do with.

He tsked and shook his head, wiping her tears away. Nox's deep chuckle surprised Rayne, and he smirked at her response as he explained, "It's the juxtaposition of you. The extremes. Your violence and your vulnerability. Your ruthlessness and your kindness. I know from watching you fight—from experiencing it—that you love it. Crave it. But you abhor the damage you cause. The blood you shed. Your heart is too vast for your darker appetites. You killed me, but you couldn't let me die. The storm in you draws me in as it always has."

The volcano and the ocean.

Rayne grabbed Nox's hand as he tried to take it back. She stared down at how small her hand was compared to his before looking into his eyes. Nox was so conflicted with Rayne's mixed signals. She lifted his hand to her lips and kissed his palm. "Thank you." For not taking advantage of her. For being patient with her. And for simply being *there* for her.

Then, perhaps in an act of cruelty or kindness or both, Rayne stood, letting Nox have an unobstructed view of her panties—The woman who wanted him and trusted him with her in this vulnerable state. Nox maintained eye contact as he stood, a little stiffly— possibly for good reason—and stared down at her. Craning to look up at him, she asked in a husky voice, "Would you like something to eat?"

Nox laughed, pure and good, and shook a finger in her face. A warning. Sure, he may have the patience of a saint, but she was playing with fire.

Rayne pulled on her shorts before following Nox down the stairs and around the corner to the kitchen. He started the kettle onto boil while she went through the supplements. "Shit. We forgot to buy more. Oh, well. We can get some on this mission today."

Nox handed Rayne her tea. She said, "Thanks," and hopped on the counter to drink it while eating a Vittle bar. Climbing up took effort, and after she glanced at the cabinetry, she asked, "Why did Xelan make these so high?" The supplement was dry and tasteless. What she wouldn't give for bacon and eggs.

After taking a bite of his supplement, Nox answered by walking over to the counter beside her. She glanced down and saw the extra height met his hips. Perfect for someone so tall to cook, to wash dishes, and to be at the right height for…

Rayne squeezed her thighs together to stop the tempting direction of her thoughts. Humming helped disguise her discomposure.

Nox must've missed the hint because he changed the subject. Sorta. "In the dive bar all those years ago, were you singing to me?"

Like a deer in the headlights, Rayne stared at him. What a thing to bring up. Unable to speak, she nodded.

Nox tucked a section of Rayne's wavy hair over her shoulder. "The lyrics… You said you wanted 'to feel me in your bones,' among other vivid descriptives for longing."

Rayne looked away, turned red, and swallowed before confessing, "I wrote them for you to hear. I never imagined…"

Nox crooked a finger under Rayne's chin and brought her back to meet his eyes. "I knew it for the honor it was, and I was too foolish then to accept your offer." She started to speak, and he held up his other hand. "I know Korac intervened for what he thought was the good of Cinder, but I was still King, and I chose to listen to malice rather than believe the passion in your singing." He peered into her eyes, and their heart fluttered like a bird. After a few seconds, he said, "If only I'd listened then."

Nox backed away, turned around, and leaned against the island. Rayne knew he was collecting himself to stop this from happening. They kept moving closer and closer to each other like waves crashing into cliffs, asking for entry always denied, but over time, the sea would win.

She blurted, "I'm going for a run."

Nox looked over his shoulder at her, bewildered. He said, "You run kilometers in seconds. How can you find recreation in it here?"

"Aha!" Rayne hopped off the counter, set down her empty mug, and ran into the library. There she found the device she was looking for before running back into the kitchen. "I have this." She handed him the ankle bracers.

Nox glanced them over. He sounded impressed as he asked, "Gravity densifiers?"

Beaming, Rayne took it back and marched to the stairs, saying, "Yup. There's another if you want to join me. We've got time before the mission." More time together.

While she created jogging clothes upstairs, Nox answered from below. "No, I think I'll find our mysterious water source. Are you prepared for our next endeavor?"

Rayne worked her hair into some braids as she returned to the kitchen. "I think so. I'm less worried about this one emotionally annihilating me." She got a smile out of Nox and considered it for a moment. To consider how much she loved the light in his eyes.

"Rayne."

Nox startled her. How long had Rayne stared at him? His eyes traveled down her sports bra and skin tight shorts, all the way down her legs—

"I'm going."

Rayne spun and ran out, running from Nox, because she wanted him so badly. The anchor tech worked perfectly, and let Rayne run with so much resistance that her heart rate peaked as she wondered how it felt to him.

What was holding Rayne back? They wanted each other, and they were adults. So why not?

"I can't love Nox because you won't let me."

It had hurt more than Rayne cared to admit, telling Xelan her truth. Like a betrayal to Nox.

"There is no way you could ever disappoint me." That was easy for Xelan to say while he thought Nox was dead and gone, but what would he think if he knew the truth?

Nox was alive, and Rayne wanted him.

"Nox did so much for me. More than you can ever know. But I hold it all back—gratitude, affection, forgiveness—because of you. As long as you can't forgive him, how can I let myself love him?"

Rayne's feelings for Nox felt so strong, but love?

Was it wrong to be with someone who loved you without loving them back?

A long, long time ago, Rayne told Xelan she was happy for him and Tameka because she didn't want him to be lonely. Xelan had looked at Rayne with so much sadness as he said, *"You're one of the loneliest people I know."*

Xelan wouldn't want Rayne to stay alone forever.

She stopped at a junction of tree bases. Frustrated and anxious, Rayne gripped her braids and tried not to cry.

Why was this so hard?

Wallop.

The bird...

He called again, somewhere directly above Rayne. The poor thing was still looking for his mate.

No one should be lonely.

Nox had discovered the entry to the water source about five minutes after Rayne had left, but he stayed behind to think. Take a second to reflect before they left on another mission. Staring into the steam of the hot spring, he relived the earlier moment between them. Rayne's silken skin. Her scent. The soft sound she didn't realize she'd made when he'd kissed her thigh. She ebbed and flowed from him like the tide onto the shore.

Damn.

The spring was stored under the loft, and the seamless door was off the kitchen. Inside was a hot spring and a mammoth filtration system with temperature control to cool the steaming water. It was tinted white and almost opaque. Aegis water.

One.

There were mentions of 'One' in Elden's second Verse, but, in Savis' teachings, she'd assumed it was the figurative 'One.'

"One cannot be trusted with One's own motives."

That sort of thing.

Rayne and Nox would resolve it. He trusted in it. He also trusted that if Rayne got in this hot spring, Nox wouldn't let her wade in it alone.

Sweet torment. This was ecstatic.

Forever.

Nox could play this game with Rayne forever, as long as she allowed it. Their heart raced, and there was no way for him to know if it was her workout or his fantasies of them. The thought amused him into a smile as he stepped out of the hot springs and into the kitchen—

Rayne was stepping into the shower.

This time, Nox couldn't look away from the display on the sheet, as Rayne wet her hair under the water and it poured down her neck, breasts, stomach, hips, between her thighs—

Cloves gave Nox away.

Even with his scent signaling his presence, Rayne did a most astonishing thing. She stopped massaging her scalp to trail her hands over her breasts and lower, lower...

Rayne gasped.

Nox left the kitchen area with the blood rushing south so fast he almost saw spots. He nearly left the treeloft because there was so little holding him back. And fuck him, Nox loved it.

From around the corner, he called, "I found the water source."

"Because you're brilliant." Rayne's voice almost didn't betray her, but for the slight airiness of it. She both knew and didn't know what she was doing, and he respected her guilelessness enough not to resent the occasional frustration.

Nox countered, "Flattery will get you whatever you want, Rayne." Including him.

Honeysuckle. As the scent drifted toward him, Nox wondered if she tasted of it and desperately wanted to find out.

The water stopped and while she dressed, Rayne asked, "Can you show it to me?"

Now if Korac were here, he'd laugh at the look on Nox's face. Her phrasing... *Can you show it to me?* Elden, he felt immature for the direction of his thoughts. "Yes, of course. May I come in now?"

"You're always welcome in here, Nox. The sheet is for privacy, remember?" Coy. Rayne sounded cute with coyness. She knew as well as he did the sheet made for a screen.

It was her shuffling in the kitchen, which made Nox turn the corner and face her again. With a tilt of his head, he asked, "What're you doing?"

Rayne had discovered a device in a cabinet and, with her tongue sticking out, was trying to make it work. "I think this plays music—"

A modern ballad sounded from within the entire loft.

Rayne faced him and glowed. She looked like a sexy punk pirate dressed in that black corseted peasant top and white leather pants. The top was short, baring her midriff, while the sleeves were ridiculously big and puffy, hanging off her biceps. Once again, she left her shoulders bare. In fact, it seemed her clothes continued to shrink and cling tighter to her skin as the days went on.

Rayne said, "Show me the source, then dance with me. Please?"

This was trouble. Didn't she realize…

Never mind.

Tired of fighting it, Nox did as she commanded. The hot springs reveal left Rayne grinning as she said, "We are totally swimming in that."

Yes. Yes, they would. But first…

Nox held out his hand with a bow, saying, "Your majesty, may I have this dance?"

Rayne took it and let out a cry of delight as Nox immediately spun her into his arms. He winked. Her delighted laughter was even more sexy for the breathiness. Nox let her up and pulled her tight with a hand on her lower back. Rayne reached one hand around his shoulder and placed the other on his bicep.

They danced around the kitchen, twirling and spinning, breathless from the close calls and near misses. There was a cobalt ribbon tied around her neck he wanted to slip away, and her breasts heaved against the corset as if they wanted out, and Nox was more than tempted to free them. When he dipped her, Rayne let herself fall, trusting him, and righted slowly in a heady daze. Her lips were half-parted, and Rayne gazed at Nox with longing. She closed her eyes, ready for him to kiss her.

Nox wanted to show Rayne how good it could feel between them, but this wasn't the moment. Their next mission was time-sensitive within the next hour, and Nox would need longer with her if they were to kiss.

He brushed the loose strands of her braided hair from her face and cupped her cheek until Rayne opened her eyes, confused and a little hurt. Nox beamed at her, letting her see how much he appreciated her trust. It chased the confusion away, and she smiled.

They straightened and stepped back, regaining some composure. Rayne turned the music off. With her back to Nox, she announced, "We should get ready to go."

Back to work.

"Lead the way home, your majesty."

As Rayne passed Nox on her way to the door, she brushed a hand down his shirt, against his chest and stomach, saying, "I like you in blue, too." There was heat to the look she gave him before Rayne stepped into the woods.

Perhaps forever wouldn't take so long.

Elden's conduit opened to Cinder, within walking distance of a magnificent space-scraper under construction. Rayne kept her eyes on Nox because she knew this was his first time seeing his homeworld since they'd resurrected. Since Tameka began the recession of Li.

Rayne was glad for the view.

Nox's black eyes shimmered as he gaped up at a sky he'd never seen, despite living here for seven million years. She wished Korac and Xelan were here to see Nox's reaction. Overcome, he swallowed hard enough for her to hear, sniffed, and wiped his cheek. His voice was rough as he said, "I never imagined I'd be alive to see this. The Progeny are truly miraculous."

Elden.

Rayne couldn't communicate with the Icarean deity, but there was an impression from his nacre—

This was close to glory.

Nox suddenly broke into a beautiful grin. Elated, he lifted Rayne by the waist and spun her around with joyous laughter. Infectious, she returned in kind, smiling down at Nox. As if he'd realized what he was doing, he stopped. When Nox set Rayne down, slowly, they stared at one another from a breath away.

A ruckus drew their attention, and Nox let Rayne go. It was the cheer of a crowd, reminding her why they'd come here in the first place. She took his hand and pulled him along, saying, "I can't wait to show you this."

The behemoth let Rayne coax him along with a curious brow quirked. She knew Nox must recognize the area, but there's no way for him to expect what waited at the edge of this plateau.

People from all over Iona Pax filled the stands inside a basalt coliseum in the valley below. The conglomerate apartments were connected by tunnels in the mountain peppered the sheer cliff face spilling into the Ignis Desert. Beyond it, black waves crested and deadly beasts blew foul-smelling spray from their spouts. The sea washed onto shore at the mouth of caves littered with deadly traps to test both the soldier on foot and the wing-ed for the entertainment of hundreds of thousands in attendance.

Korac's camp was restored by popular demand. Elden bless the Verses.

Nox's shoulders were straighter, his chest out further, and his chin higher. Rayne watched him breathe deep the air of his homeworld, a little less ashen and filled with so much promise. To show her understanding, she squeezed his hand. The look on Nox's face when he turned to Rayne took her breath away. The Atramentous mirrors in his eyes returned her smile at Nox.

Love.

There was love in the reflection of Rayne's eyes.

"Is our mission below?" Nox's voice was in a deeper register than his usual baritone, almost Primary deep.

Rayne nodded. "I wanted it to be a surprise."

Nox held out the crook of his arm, and Rayne took it with her puffy pirate sleeve. They flew down into the highest tier of the stands, bypassing the lines and earning a few looks. Mostly curious, but some aggressive. Around them, Icari flew into the ring below.

Rayne nodded at the owner's box, an Overseer like the ones on Enki, but painted red and white with a garish phoenix logo in the broad center. She said, "That's our mark. Calls himself Lord Cinderken, and he never leaves the Overseer."

Nox chuffed, and it made Rayne smile. He asked, "How do we get in?"

"Well, my information is mixed between Razor's dossier and what my contact gave up before I knocked him out for slapping my ass." At Rayne's pause, Nox bowed with a dip of his head, and she continued, "Only race winners get special admittance to meet Cinder's vice lord. Eight Icari compete, including his pet champion. The one to finish all three events first wins—What're you doing?!"

Nox was undoing the buckles and straps of his shirt. He kept his eyes on hers as he stripped it from his very, *very* nice stomach, chest, shoulders—

Rayne might've drooled.

And Nox had the nerve to smirk as if he knew it. "I need this one, Rayne." Those were her words from the night before.

Rayne held out the rings she'd used earlier that day on her run, saying, "These might help disguise some of your super awesomeness."

"This is good thinking. Thank you." Nox slipped them on his wrists after extending them to their maximum width and smiled down at her.

The urge to kiss him for luck, for care—whatever—struck Rayne so hard she'd leaned into him before she'd realized what she was doing. Nox saw it all, and mercifully, kissed her cheek—Soft, warm, and lingering. Against her ear, he promised, "I'll win this for us and come back in one piece."

As his wings opened and all his muscles flexed with it, Rayne muttered to herself, "One sexy piece."

The Icarean King chuckled, indicating Nox had heard her, before flying down into the ring. Raised as royalty, trained by the Valkyrie, and inheritor of Elden's legacy, Nox was the reason all this existed. The majesty of his presence—in his kingdom—swallowed the coliseum.

Whether the crowd knew he was the real deal or simply appreciated his dedication to the part, they went insane. They were so loud the skies answered their call. Thunder rolled in the clouds above.

Rayne beamed, feeling right at home.

Wait.

A male Lamia was flagging Rayne closer to floor entry. She ran down the steps while people cheered and clapped for her. A spotlight hit her.

Oh.

Rayne had to smile. They thought she and Nox were cosplaying themselves.

The Lamia beamed at her. "You are absolutely stunning! Welcome to the races. I know this must be your first time, because we've never seen your mate here before."

For the sake of the ploy, Rayne didn't correct him. Instead, she asked, "Is there something you wanted from me?"

"Oh! I apologize. Yes. We offer special ringside seats to the partners of our contenders, and an Icarus will fly you over the events. If you will, follow me, please."

The guy was so polite Rayne felt inclined to follow him down to the lowest level, where Nox walked over to the wall and held up his hand to her.

The spotlight was still on them, and a compulsion told Rayne to play along. She slipped the ribbon from her neck and tied it around Nox's hand, a favor from his princess.

There was so much cheering it made Rayne blush.

An announcer came across whatever speakers they'd installed in this ancient place. "What a show, am I right? King Nox and King Rayne united here on our racing grounds. But before we close our betting windows, you should know Lord Cinderken doubled his wages on our reigning champion."

Rayne and Nox smirked.

She hoped Cinderken enjoyed losing.

Exhilarated and filled with vitality, Nox took in the cheers of his people, at once calm and near tears with gratitude.

He was alive to see this.

Thanks to Rayne.

When she met his eyes across the coliseum, the two shared a smile. The silken ribbon was the color of his blood, the color of her eyes, and the former King of Cinder closed his hand to grip it in his fist.

Nox was winning this race for Rayne.

"Contenders approach the starting line."

With one last look at Rayne, Nox went to the arches where they opened to the Ignis Desert below. A field of igneous rock and lava flows, and the site of so many wonderful and awful events in his life.

Today, that changed. Nox would only look at this place and think of his brothers and Rayne. Somehow, someway, he would convince Korac and Xelan to join him in this coliseum for their people and for their women—Signify a Cinder of hope, and not of ash.

The announcer said, "All right, in the tradition of the Verses—The audience will call off the mark."

"Ready!

"Set!

"Go!"

Nox activated the gravity densifiers and flew down along with the other racers. Some scaled on foot down the cliff-side, wingless. They all rushed to the skids waiting on the shore of an enormous lava vein. Practiced, he strapped his feet in faster than the rest and dropped onto the magma's surface with precision. No splashing.

Onlookers flew above, including the contender's partners, and a Pil dwarf Nox realized was the announcer in a flying mechsuit. He said, "King Nox is in the lead, but the champion has yet to enter the race. This show of confidence is leaving the audience on the edge of their seats."

Not in the race yet?

Nox clenched his jaw and worked on his advantage. Swerving around stalagmites and boulders in the river's bends, banking down rapids as they approached the climax. While this wasn't the same course Nox was familiar with, he discerned from their gaining speed that they were heading for a lavafall.

Their pulse was racing.

Rayne.

Calm and in control of a sport Nox had helped invent, he knew their accelerated heart rate was Rayne's excitement. He couldn't spare a glance above to spot her in the sky, but he wanted to assure her there was no way he was losing this race—

"Caedes, with all his Shadow upgrades, has finally entered the training course—"

Fuck.

"—His legendary championship status dates all the way back to before the Vacating when General Korac first consigned him to camp for speaking out against Nox in the first Cult of Night compound. It is a treat to have him return over these last few months since the camp and training course reopened. And there he is! Already in the river and passing competitors left and right—Elden! He's nearly to the lavafall!"

Nox was imbued with all of Rayne's gifts, so he was much faster than Caedes. This race would require a delicate balance of prowess to avoid blowing his and Rayne's cover.

And there went Caedes headlong down the lavafall without so much as a glance at Nox. Once the bald Icarus passed, Nox knew how much to lessen the densifiers. He dialed it down and the flash of blue tied around his hand renewed his sense of purpose. Facing the edge of the world, he held his breath and went over the fall's edge.

No matter how many times Nox plummeted down a lavafall, it always brought a grin to his face. The sheer drop doubled his heart rate, and he hoped to one day share the experience with Rayne.

The second Nox righted on the surface of the lagoon, he buffeted his wings for further speed, crouched, and sailed to the shore.

Caedes was already off his skid, in his wetsuit, and racing to the water beyond the last plutonic crag. He went about it methodically, almost habitually, submerged in the focused zone of one forced to repeat the course many times.

Perhaps Nox owed the Icarean soldier an apology. Later.

For now, Nox dismounted off his skid, slipped into a wetsuit, grabbed an electric spear, and ran so fast over the rocky ground that he nearly beat Caedes into the water.

The onlookers gasped and cheered while the announcer said, "Never. Ever. Have we seen such competition. No one ever matches the champion. Ladies and gentlemen, reconsider your bets."

As far as vice went, gambling appeared more benign—

Nox took the notion back the moment he thought it. There was no telling what indecencies bookies and loan sharks committed for their money.

With his fist clasped firmly around Rayne's ribbon, Nox swam for the beach beyond the riptide. So close—

The smell hit him first.

Whalesharks.

Massive beasts whose spouts geysered volcanic water and rot from their prey at least a story into the air. A pod of twelve rode the tide toward him.

Nox gripped the spear—

Caedes passed him, with his head down as he plowed through the water, concentrating only on the destination. Well, until he glanced at Nox.

Frozen in the water.

The bald Icarus, famous for defying Nox, gaped with the hard glare of posttraumatic stress in his deep green eyes, solid in Atramentous.

However, there wasn't time for Nox to fret about their immediate discovery. He pointed beyond the Icarus, shouting, "Caedes!"

The leading whaleshark of its pod poured out of the wave and charged at Caedes like a bull—Mouth wide open, and its dozens of tined teeth spinning like a drill. Even if he turned now, it wouldn't be in time. Nox poised, aimed, and threw his electric spear through the hole at the center of the whaleshark's spinning jaws. It gagged and recoiled, spouted a tentacle from some other devoured beast, and withered under the spear's powerful electric current. The stench. The sound—Nothing sounded as horrifying as a shrieking whaleshark. It rattled Nox's heart, and he wondered if Rayne felt it—

"King Nox."

Deflated despite his victory, Nox faced the Icarus who would surely arrest him. At least Nox could keep Rayne's secret—

"My thanks." The bald Icarus held up his hand from the water for Nox to clasp and said, "If I win, I get to tell your brother you're alive and have the pleasure of watching your old General arrest you."

Nox took the offered hand and only used five percent of his strength to squeeze. "If I win, you let me go without a word to anyone—"

Caedes opened his mouth to argue.

"—For two weeks. Give me two weeks to complete my work, and I'll turn myself in."

"Done."

The sounds of splashing as the other competitors fought whalesharks in the tide drew them back to the here and now. Just in time, too. Together, Nox and Caedes took on several more from the pod. Caedes would lead a whaleshark into a charge, and Nox would puncture its gills with only one spear between them.

After the last whaleshark in the riptide fell, Caedes called, "See you in the caves," before swimming for the beach.

Nox made to follow when he glimpsed his hand. Rayne's ribbon was missing. He moved about, searching for it in the black foam. When he couldn't find it, he ducked his head underwater.

There.

The bright blue ribbon was spiraling deeper below, and Nox swam after it—

Right into the drilling mouth of a charging whaleshark.

Nox shouted underwater and used his wings to dart to the side, avoiding the mouth—

Eternity take him ...

Sticky and abrasive, Nox found himself victim—as many Icari before—to the toxic adhesive, coating the whaleshark's blubberous hide. All down his wings, the backs of his arms, and the backs of his legs. Only his head was free to move. He ripped and pulled until he left a trail of feathers, dripping with cobalt blood, in the whaleshark's wake. The bonding chemical filled his fresh wounds, searing his nerve endings over and over.

All the while, the whaleshark dove deeper until they met bottom, and it scraped Nox along the rough coral, taking more skin and blood. He screamed when it tore into muscle and came for the bone—

A bright flash of blue took Nox's attention off the agony long enough to recognize Rayne's ribbon. He still gripped it in his hand, even with the arm missing so much meat.

If he survived...

If he returned to win the race...

Nox vowed to kiss Rayne the second he laid eyes on her.

That was it.

With a primal roar, Nox went into Atramentous and dug his hands into the whaleshark. Chunks of blubber came away, followed by a plume of blood. The monster cried, and it should because Nox freed his wrist next. Elbows, biceps, and shoulders. Nox peeled the beast's hide with him as he wrenched his wings and back free. Then he tore into it with his bare hands.

Organs.

Bones.

Spine.

Through all of Nox's early life, he ripped things apart with his hands, but nothing quite this big. The second it died, he checked Rayne's ribbon and swam for the surface. He broke water to the sound of her voice in so much distress.

"Caedes, please. Let me go in after him. You don't understand—"

Rayne's mouth fell open as she spied Nox swimming for shore, and Caedes stopped holding her back—Not that he even could. Everyone on the beach, including the other racers gawked, for a few heartbeats until...

"Nox has survived!"

At the dwarf's announcement, the VIP crowd went wild, but they were nothing compared to the people viewing in the coliseum. Although it was miles from the beach, their cheers carried like thunder through the mountain.

Caedes muttered, "Well, I'll be damned."

Trembling, Rayne cried, "Are you okay?" Her eyes frantically looked Nox over as he walked out of the water.

He wanted to answer her question, but there was a vow to fulfill first.

Nox crossed the rocky sand to Rayne, cupped her nape with his ribboned hand, and kissed her.

Nox's unexpected kiss sent an electric current through Rayne, which left her toes tingling. Among other things. And when she yielded and let him feel she wanted it, too, Nox pulled her tight and deepened the kiss.

So much exploded in Rayne's brain, in her heart, and in the audience—A barrage of cheer, hoots, and "Get it, your majesties!" It left her blushing when Nox separated their kiss by an inch. He stared down at her with his heart wide open, thumb gently grazing her face, and Rayne wished they were alone.

When she licked the spicy taste of him from her lips, Nox watched her do it, and his sparkling black eyes said he wished they were alone, too.

"Ahem."

They both turned to see Caedes standing there on the beach, hands on his hips. He wagged a finger between them, saying, "I'm very confused."

The breeze picked up, carrying with it the unpleasant smell of the whalesharks—

Nox laughed, stepped back, and, at Rayne's confused glance, said, "The smell is me. Forgive me for spoiling the moment, but I *did* just tear a massive predator apart with my bare hands."

Finding the entire event ridiculous, Rayne laughed until the dwarf flew over in his mechsuit. He said, "Caedes, we've kept Lord Cinderken waiting long enough, don't you think?"

Caedes, known for his taciturn nature, nodded to the announcer and waved for Nox to follow him to the cave entrance. With the same hand he used to destroy a man-eating monster—the same hand with her tattered ribbon—Nox raised Rayne's fingers to his lips and kissed them.

A maelstrom of emotions swirled inside Rayne and some of her darker thoughts made her blush.

Nox smirked as if he knew. "See you in the winner's circle."

Rayne could barely hear Caedes' chuff for the uproar of the crowd.

"Yes, citizens of the outer worlds. We're getting this real time. Someone notify King Elect Iuo his new film will need an epilogue." The dwarf was talented in changing his tone from the gentle romantic overture to a booming sports announcer. "Racers, given the exceptional status of today's competition, the Lord of Odds switched the scoring from 'first to finish all three rounds' to 'first to finish the last round.' For those in the audience, please adjust your bets accordingly. Last call. Last call. You have sixty seconds before the betting windows close. Good fortune to you and to the competitors."

Finished with his announcement, the dwarf looked over at Rayne with a genuine smile. "You're a welcome performance. Were you hired by one of the VIPS?"

Once more wishing for Lucy's demure talents, Rayne smiled and said, "Something like that."

He shrugged, and the suit shrugged with him. "Who knew these races were missing drama and romance?" A horn sounded, and he returned to his duties. "Windows closed for final bets. Competitors, the audience will count you down once more."

The flying onlookers yelled, accompanied by the thundering chorus of the coliseum.

"Ready.

"Set.

"Go!"

Nox, Caedes, and the other racers bolted into the pitch black cave. Rayne didn't like it. Cinderken had dropped a good deal of credits on Caedes, and she couldn't imagine he'd lose without a fight.

"We can go in now. You'll want to see this," the dwarf said as if he'd heard her thoughts. His face was even extra warm.

Rayne couldn't open her wings here as they'd give her away. So with help from her designated flying Icarus, Rayne followed him and the other onlookers into the cave. In a tunnel above the cavern, they were high enough to view the entire race. Stalagmites reached for their stalactites above in a maze of razor wire, mines, and fire traps—

Poof!

An Icarus' shriek ricocheted in the cavern below.

Off mic, the dwarf shouted, "Medics!"

Rayne searched the maze until she saw Nox flitting around a column of rock. Caedes zipped through, focused on one path she could clearly see from this vantage point, but Nox couldn't see from his position. There were several clearer paths winding through. In the Verses, there wasn't much to imply Nox would know the cave as well as Korac or, in this case, Caedes. However, after thousands of years, the maze's shape had changed, making it unfamiliar to him—

There!

Nox found a path and adjusted his densifier in a motion the onlookers wouldn't recognize. He rocketed through them now, dodging a wall of flames and catching up to Caedes. Rayne tightened her fists and shook them. Go, go, go!

"You're very convincing."

Rayne was used to living in a box. This was too many people for her, a lot of attention. The dwarf announcer meant well, but it felt like an intrusion on her... Whatever Rayne could call the stuff happening between her and Nox. Out of hand, she said, "It comes with the territory."

The announcer chuffed, as if he didn't believe Rayne. She glanced over at him to find a knowing smile on his face, but he kindly left it at that—

The onlookers gasped.

Rayne focused on the race once more to find Nox's pinion snagged in razor wire, with Caedes pulling ahead. Their heart pounded in big gulping beats. She brought her fist to her mouth and prayed to Elden, "Please let him win."

Someone behind her shouted, "Caedes will win! Everyone, Caedes is winning!"

Nox must've heard because he wrenched hard enough to pull out a tuft of feathers and speared forward. She saw his lips move and *felt* the curse. The glance he shot at his ribboned fist as he dialed the densifiers down once more made Rayne's heart sing.

"Go, Nox. Kiss me in that winner's circle."

Rayne swore she muttered it quietly enough, but the dwarf gave a single chuckle beside her.

Right.

Left.

Two more lefts.

Oh, Elden, they're tied. Across the cave, the two competitors with so much history shared a look before stalactites separated them. Rayne held her breath as Nox bolted into the clearing at labyrinth's end.

One second before Caedes.

"Can you take me down?" Rayne signaled for the Icarus holding her, but he shook his head.

The dwarf said only to Rayne, "Lord Cinderken would like you to reunite in the winner's circle back at the coliseum. The racers will meet us there." To the games, he announced, "King Nox defeated the reigning champion, Caedes! All competitors are invited to celebrate after such a spirited game. Congrats to all!"

As she glimpsed Nox and Caedes talking below, the Icarus holding Rayne pulled her away. What was the likelihood of that loyal soldier not snitching on them to Tameka? Rayne bit her lip and wondered why, truly, she wanted to keep their mission a secret.

Originally, she'd told herself it was to keep everyone living their lives in peace and safety until Rayne would need them for the final confrontation. But if she looked at it hard enough—Rayne kept herself away because she'd become accustomed to Nox's isolated and intimate company, and they would judge her for it.

They flew over the coliseum, and all those people were happy to see Rayne and Nox together. Maybe her concerns were less founded than she feared.

Nox was already in the center of the ring when the Icarus set her down. Rayne wasted no time running across the field—at two percent speed—toward this wonderful and worthy Icarus with his heart and arms open.

Nox swooped Rayne up and kissed her with a twirl. Multiple kisses, light kisses, deep kisses. The brush of his tongue—

The ground shook, and columns rattled with the standing ovation.

They stopped kissing, and Nox pressed his mouth to her ear to say, "Caedes agreed to keep quiet for two weeks. I took care of it."

As she held him and stared out at the crowd, Rayne didn't want to keep quiet anymore—

Another vibration distracted her. It was coming from his chest and his throat. "Uhm, Nox?" Her voice sounded silly, even to her, as she asked, "What's happening?"

"I think I'm purring."

Still in his arms, Rayne pulled back to search his face. "You mean you don't know?"

Nox shrugged in his own confusion. "I've never done it before."

Rayne laughed and kissed him again.

"Callahan."

They broke their kiss for her to peer at Caedes outside the winner's circle. Not known for being the most expressive, it wasn't a surprise to see no disappointment or approval on his face. But for everything he'd done for the Shadow, she said, "You've been upgraded to 'Rayne.'"

Caedes smirked, and it eased some of Rayne's concerns. He said, "Are you two ready to meet your new owner? There's no way Cinderken will let you leave here without an exclusive rights deal."

Rayne frowned. "Are you heading up with us?"

At the incredulous shake of Caedes' head, Nox said against her ear, "He was undercover about the vaccine protests. It seems the Shadow is trailing us. We set back the Shadow's investigation with this victory."

"I'm sorry," Rayne offered.

Caedes nodded, eying their embrace before gazing up at the Overseer.

Nox let her go and chafed her arms, asking, "Are you ready?"

"Oh, yeah."

Because Rayne knew two things. They'd get what they needed out of this 'Lord of Odds,' and Rayne was done letting shit come between her and Nox. This was the happiest she'd felt in a long time, and nothing was taking it away from Rayne.

{300CE}

Celindria's capture of T.A.O. was different in every Probability. As always, Razor, pathetically unable to contain his grief, informed Imminent of T.A.O.'s departure. And as always, this meant someone had forced themselves on the ancient Seamswalker and conceived the Progeny line. For whatever reason, T.A.O. never consented to continuing her lineage.

But never had Razor confessed, "I thought this time if I introduced her to Cascading Light that she would see the conception was inevitable and spare herself the trauma."

Remorse recoiled and barely concealed the ire in his voice as he asked, "You initiated a *Progeny* without consulting us?"

Celindria hid her smirk and quit listening.

None of their nonsense mattered.

Soon they'll be done, and we will be all that is Imminent.

T.A.O. always ran to Korac with her pregnancy, and she always delivered inside the Seam. Afterward, she'd give the baby to Lucas, their spy in The Brethren, for adoption.

Then it was time.

Months after the call, the pieces fell into place.

Celindria shadow-walked into Lucas' Roman estate. Colorful mosaics decorated the walls and floor, but they garnered little notice as she hummed with anticipation.

The Seamswalker.

Her ability is so much more versatile than ours.

Convenient, too.

But not as rare. No one is as singular as us.

"Welcome to my home."

Celindria rolled her eyes as she faced Lucas, leaning in his archway, bemused. After billions of Probabilities, the men in Imminent grew so tiresome. Already a goddess of the Source, Celindria offered no platitudes. Instead, she asked, "When do you expect her to arrive?"

"I've arrived many times and always on my own," T.A.O. said as she stepped out from behind Lucas, who was smirking.

This was new.

Celindria narrowed her eyes. She took a step toward them, asking, "Are you not happy to see me alive? Surely father told you I perished on Thailea."

Lucas looked down at T.A.O., who returned the knowing expression.

An alliance?

T.A.O. spoke as she crossed the room to Celindria. "My brothers… Their cries rattle the Seam." She tilted her head to the side, saying, "As do yours."

She knows we cry.

Kill her.

"Will you save them with your mercy?" Celindria asked, prepared to disable T.A.O.'s nacre and carry her back to Enki for experimentation.

T.A.O.'s nod was unexpected.

Celindria looked beyond her to Lucas, suspicious of the Seamswalker's cooperation. In a voice filled with skepticism, she asked, "Truly?"

Lucas gave a modest shrug. "What can I say? My negotiating skills are impeccable."

Celindria warned, "T.A.O., if you disappear on our journey, I will subject Andrius and Devis to your punishment."

"To home, sister. Let us stop your tears."

With her eyes narrowed once again, Celindria asked, "What is it you think you see?"

Warm and unpredictable, T.A.O. reached a dainty hand to touch Celindria's face. The smaller woman's voice was in three pitches. "His decision to choose you comes from within *your* heart, sister, not his. Perhaps you should try to find it before destiny chooses for him."

{Now}

Celindria laughed.

And laughed.

From the moment she saw Nox kiss Rayne, Celindria couldn't stop laughing. She'd backed into the nearest wall, slid down it, hugged her knees, and laughed.

But it wasn't funny.

Celindria laughed because she knew her heart was broken, but she couldn't feel it. The shards of it dug into her ribs until she couldn't breathe—But there was no emotion there whatsoever.

But, Rayne...

The young woman's expressions were radiant and full of life—Rayne was in love with Nox, whether she knew it or not. It was in the light of her eyes and the curve of her smile.

Even as Celindria looked at them now, from Cinderken's eyes, they kept peering at each other with the sickening innocence of blossoming love.

We should kill them both.

No, we should save Nox from Rayne.

But don't kill Rayne. We can utilize her.

So Celindria laughed.

This farce must go on.

Caedes, Nox, and Rayne had flown into the Overseer, flushed with the thrill of competition and young romance.

Celindria nearly incinerated them along with Cinderken and the game leader, who said, "Lord of Odds, we bring you the victor and your fallen champion." He bowed with his mechsuit.

Out of Cinderken's mouth, Celindria said, "You've cost me a great deal of credits tonight."

Caedes didn't even flinch, surely irritated Nox and Rayne had interrupted his investigation into Cinderken's Imminent connections. They also ruined Celindria's advantage for Cinderken to reach Korac.

When a window would open in Celindria's emotional capacity to feel, this moment would hurt the most. The moment she turned and looked at Nox without a trace of recognition from him. Those shining black eyes, like onyx, stared at Cinderken without response.

Tell him the truth.

Tell him now.

No, don't. Nox would never forgive us like this.

"Has anyone ever told you, you bear a striking resemblance to the former King of Cinder?" There, Celindria managed that much at least.

Nox's deep baritone washed over her. "It has been said."

Forgetting the other two, Celindria asked Nox, "What is it you want?"

Did he just glance at Rayne?!

Did she just blush?!

Celindria took an involuntary step forward before the game leader caught her attention with his musings. "They're so dedicated to their roles. Do you know who hired them, Lord Cinderken?"

Performance.

Nox is playing a part to access Father through Rayne. He could still be ours in this reality.

Maintain composure until it's time to confront him.

"All three of you seek me regarding a certain auction on Pil, yes?" Celindria tried to keep Cinderken's voice smooth and confident. Once she captured their attention, she said, "I warned Amaryna, the auctioneer, not to traffic children. Too polarizing and impossible to forgive."

"You make it sound as if politics are more important than scarring those kids." The indignation in Rayne's voice grated more on Celindria than the self-righteous storm in her eyes.

When Nox looked at Rayne with love and gratitude— the way he used to look at Celindria—

Don't shift into Atramentous here!

We must remain calm!

"Caedes?" Celindria-as-Cinderken asked.

The gruff Icarus humphed.

Celindria glanced down at the announcer before asking, "Did you collect enough evidence to indict me on charges against Iona Pax?"

In the avian way of all Icari, Caedes tilted his head. "I have evidence you incited protests against the volition vaccines. As for this auction, I believe Amaryna had accomplices, and you know who they were."

"I'll turn myself into your custody in exchange for two things."

The actual Cinderken, prone and exhausted inside his mindscape, groaned in protest. It was quite the realm he'd built here with multiple tiers of loan sharking and brutal collections—Some organ harvesting for delicacies to the cannibal underground. But none of this interested Celindria. She needed a convenient lamb for the Shadow slaughter to get closer to Korac.

What's better than a world with Nox?

A world with two.

Caedes peered between Rayne and Nox before asking, "What are your conditions?"

"An audience with your masters and… The ribbon." Celindria grinned within Cinderken's mind, but left his face neutral.

Nox's single chuckle was filled with incredulity.

Rayne sounded more concerned. "Why?"

Caedes looked equally suspicious, glaring as Celindria said, "It brought our victor so much courage, and I could use the good fortune. Not to mention it'll fetch me an Emperor's ransom after today's spectacle. Consider it collateral for my rehabilitation upon my release."

Faster than Celindria had ever seen Nox move, he gripped Cinderken by the throat and growled, "Where is Celindria?"

He's looking for us.

We knew it! He'll always come for us.

We are the Eternal Bind!

Aroused, Celindria smirked. "Is that what you want?" She almost added, 'lover,' but that was a dead giveaway. "The last I'd heard, Celindria resided in Paradise."

"Does that mean she's in Ishkur?" Rayne's constant intrusion rankled Celindria. Especially since her question made Nox let Celindria go.

She rolled her eyes at the virtuous martyr act. "Sure. She's in Ishkur, herding sheep."

The actual Cinderken whimpered as those were his exact words from his campaign against the vaccines.

The dwarf chuckled beside Celindria, who grew tired of these games. With a sigh, she held out Cinderken's hand. "With the game leader as witness and the ribbon as guarantee to the plea bargain, you agree to grant me an audience in exchange for my testimony. I'll expose Amaryna's accomplices as well as testify to Celindria's last known location. Although if you ask me, that's just looking for trouble."

Caedes grumped, "No one's asking you."

Nox was still glaring at Celindria, tantalizing her, when Rayne touched his arm. Everything about the Icarus softened, turning Celindria's erotic fantasies of fighting sex into pure nausea.

Rayne's smile for Nox was gentle and full of affection as she offered, "I can make more ribbons."

Yuck!

Kill her!

No, don't. Convert Nox and make him kill her while Xelan watches.

Yes!

Nox looked down at the tattered blue thing in his hand like the piece of trash was precious. Celindria was prepared to rip it off herself when he handed it over. There was a touch of grief in his voice as he asked, "You'll give up your partners and tell us the last place you knew Celindria to be?"

"I'll give up everything I know for this ribbon, yes."

The game leader gasped beside him. But who cared? Inside his mind, Cinderken even managed to beg, "P-p-please. No…"

When the ribbon fell into Celindria's hand, she said, "There's a second Obsidian Palace in Ishkur. It's underground, beneath a public club called Night Rayne's Tomb. There, you'll find most of the parties responsible for the human trafficking ring. The last place I saw Celindria was…" Where would be a good place to lead them? "Umbra's Spire in the infamous tower. I meant what I said about Paradise. Celindria told me that's where she resides and waits. For Nox."

Nox's eyes flashed, but Rayne showed more of a reaction. It was an odd one.

Sadness?

Pity?

We wish we had her compassion and capacity to love. Then maybe father could accept us.

And we would be worthy of Nox's love.

The loneliness returned.

Celindria held up Cinderkin's wrists. "Caedes, can you take me into custody now?" Anything to get away from the sight of Nox and Rayne sharing affectionate glances while she could do nothing about it.

The nacre cuffs went on, and Caedes gripped Celindria's arm tight, saying, "Lord of Odds, you are in the custody of an officer of the Concerted Empire of Iona Pax..."

Celindria stopped listening as she stared at Nox and Rayne leaving together, hand-in-hand.

"...Until you meet with General Sagan, General Korac, Co-Emperor Tameka, and Co-Emperor Xelan."

A contentious family reunion.

Celindria looked forward to it.

VIII   PYRE

"I'M PREGNANT, AND TUMU SAYS IT'S A LITTLE GIRL."

Tameka said it more bluntly than she'd intended, but she hated relationships with poor communication. This was a huge deal, and she wanted to share it with the most important person in her life.

Xelan was naked, sitting on the edge of the bed, where he was more than ready to have sex with Tameka. Hopefully that was still in the cards as he blinked at her.

After a few more seconds of this quiet, Tameka worried she'd mishandled it when Xelan's face blossomed into a beautiful grin—The same smile he'd given Tameka when she told him about Pax. His voice was thick with emotion as he repeated, "A little girl?"

When Tameka nodded, a tear spilled down Xelan's cheek. Abruptly, he stood and swept her up into his arms, kissing her neck and holding her tight. Xelan set Tameka down on the back of a chair so their eyes were level to say, "This is wonderful news. Look at you. You're so beautiful." He cupped her face and kissed her.

Overwhelmed with relief, Tameka cried with Xelan. He pulled away to wipe the tears, soothing, "Shh. Shh. I know everything you're thinking because I'm thinking it to. But I know—I *know*—the world will be safe for our little girl soon." His smile faded as he said, "My mental health is getting proper attention, too. It's been a long time since I've slept this regularly, and I feel the benefits of it with each passing day. Thank you for supporting me through this. I won't hurt our children—"

"Of course you won't!" Tameka clasped his wrists. "I never thought for one second you would hurt them or endanger them. You have insomnia and mania. Those are not inherently harmful, and look at you. You're working on it. I know you'll take better care of yourself, and I'm here for you. I love you."

So sex *was* in the cards.

For hours.

Tameka owed Lamassau and Tumu for watching Pax after dinner.

Afterward, she and Xelan laid in bed, and he brought Tameka her latest craving: peanut butter and Yun pears. He tried it and shook his head, laughing, "Not for me, thanks. What do you think of naming her after your mother?"

"I think it would hurt as much to call her 'Jasmine' as to call her 'Rayne.'" Tameka noticed Xelan's wince and kissed his nose. "Sorry."

Xelan smiled, not sadly but more remorseful, as he said, "I understand. Maybe—"

A knock sounded at the door.

Tameka made to get up, but Xelan insisted, "I'll get it. You rest."

She laughed incredulously. "Amos, I'm five weeks in. I can still move suns, let alone open a door." But she also didn't attempt to leave their little nest a second time.

Xelan beamed, truly glowed, snagging a robe and opening the door.

There was murmuring between him, Aria, and Torch. Something about Tumu and Caedes. Tameka didn't pout as she climbed out of bed and slipped into Xelan's discarded button down. She certainly wanted to. Snuggling into it brought back old memories as she headed for the door, asking, "No work, remember?"

"Forgive me, Peaches."

Xelan widened the door to let Tumu into the bedroom. He checked out the wardrobe and his non-lips spread into a knowing smile. "My *deepest* apologies for interrupting."

There was entirely too much cheekiness in Tumu's voice, belying his insincerity, making Tameka smile as she shoved him, teasing, "What do you want?!"

Xelan said, "Caedes is asking permission to report in-person and speak to me alone." He held up his hands to stave Tameka's complaint before she could even make it. "He insists it's mission critical."

Tameka rolled her eyes because, to the Shadow, a Twinkie shortage was 'mission critical.' Still, she waved them on. "Go ahead. Have T.A.O. bring him over if she's available."

"I am always here." T.A.O. Seamswalked into their bedroom with Caedes like they were on standby.

Then her words sunk in, and Tameka's brows shot up. "Always?" Like T.A.O. was present for Tameka and Xelan having sex?

The faeish woman simply blinked in answer.

Tumu chuckled, and Xelan shook his head.

Caedes cleared his throat, and Tameka reached up for a hug he didn't expect but deserved. When he squeezed back, she said against his shoulder, "Thanks for securing the empire for us."

In a voice filled with remorse, Caedes warned, "Don't thank me yet."

Tameka frowned as they separated, but the gruff Icarus got straight to business. "We arrested

Cinderken from his Overseer. The timing lined up with witnesses coming forward and signing depositions. One provided evidence with a projected recording of Cinderken leading the protests. The 'Lord of Odds,' himself, gave up leads and locations of potential accomplices to the human trafficking ring on Pil, but nothing substantial on Celindria."

Tumu sounded impressed as he asked, "Was there any resistance?"

Tameka noticed Caedes wore the *frown*. Whenever tech or people confounded him, he got this particular crinkle on his forehead. He said, "Well, he demanded an audience with our leaders and..." His frown deepened. "A ribbon that one competitor received from their... partner." There was a strange flash in his deep green eyes directed at Xelan.

Xelan noticed and asked, "Is there something special about the ribbon or the partner?"

"Very, but you and I will get to that. Do I have permission to send the infiltration team into a place called 'Night Rayne's Tomb?' It's a club here in Ishkur."

With a sigh, Tumu said to Xelan, "Your naming conventions are infecting the empire, *Wingmaster*."

"You should be so lucky."

Tameka dismissed the boys and answered Caedes. "I think it's a fine use of Matt and Lucy's squad. Check with Korac because I think he assigned Pehton and Bones to them. Let Kyle and Ross decide if they're okay with Bethany joining them, although I don't see the Roberts siblings putting up any arguments. But make sure the squad doesn't burn this place down. No matter how tacky the name." The last Tameka meant for Xelan.

He chuckled and put an arm around her shoulder. It instantly lifted her demeanor.

Caedes swallowed hard enough for Tameka to hear before asking, "May I speak to Co-Emperor Xelan alone?"

She looked from Tumu to Xelan to Caedes and hugged herself. "Uhm…"

Her lover put up a hand, saying, "Excuse us," before gently taking Tameka aside. "Talk to me."

"We said one week without work. It's only been five days."

Xelan smiled and said, "I want to make a work week joke, but I know how serious it is that I do better. Say the word, and I'll send Caedes and Tumu to talk business without me."

Tameka gave him a weak smile. "You get five minutes alone with him, and then you're all mine."

His smirk was at once goofy and sexy. A dangerous combination. "Yes, ma'am."

Xelan and Caedes went into the sitting room off their suites, leaving Tameka alone with Tumu.

The Tritan asked, "So how'd he take the news?"

Tameka smiled, only slightly surprised he knew already. "Beautifully. Just perfect."

He nudged her gently. "I told you."

With a click of her tongue, Tameka dropped the act, saying, "I know you and Xelan—and now Caedes—are keeping something from me." Tumu spared her a blank face into which she said, "My bullshit radar went off yesterday after Andrew showed up to talk business with Xelan even though he's off-limits."

Tumu's voice was flat, but not unkind, as he said, "You're so sharp, Peaches."

Tameka folded her arms and turned to face Tumu, staring up through their several feet of height difference. "Will you tell me when I need to know? Can I trust you?"

A deep sadness filled his voice. "Have I not proven myself to you? After all this time…"

With a frustrated sigh, Tameka hugged the big blue alien, coming only to his waist. Tumu patted her shoulders as she said, "Please don't keep me in the dark for long."

As Xelan and Caedes returned, both of them blue in the face, Tameka hoped 'for long' would end soon.

<hr>

How long had Kyle been inside Razor's memory? Eighteen hours.

And he still didn't know shit about the Eternal Bind. Razor wasn't lying when he said his family straight-up neglected him. All the Aegis turned their backs on Razor's view, which made Kyle wonder if they knew what he was destined for. But thinking this began the 'chicken and the egg' spiral or 'self-fulfilling prophecy' loop over and over until Kyle finally gave up.

"There's nothing here."

Only two things came out of this. First, Celindria could walk through Shadows and manipulate them as Korac had once described in his Verse. Tameka and Ross also witnessed this ability. It had been frightful to see as Celindria's blue eyes hovered in stark relief against the inky darkness. Second, One went in search of a way to repair the damage the Aegis had caused to the universe when they entered it. And Zero's first-born son still hadn't returned by the time Razor's brothers ripped out his fingernails.

Which was fiercely more painful than Kyle had ever imagined. Their nails came from their finger bones.

Kyle blew the air from his cheeks and admitted defeat. Begrudgingly, he said, "Thanks, Razor."

I OWED YOU ONE.

This hardly made up for the damage done to Bethany, but whatever...

The image in this chalkboard was stuck on the Aegis observing Rayne in the flames of the Probability Matrix. In tears, dying alone and afraid. It choked Kyle to see it. To know it had come true.

Call him an optimist, but Kyle always thought she'd survive or come back. Like Xelan. Shit, or even like Razor. Nothing could keep Rayne down.

Kyle took one last look at the image before turning and heading down the aisle. In case Razor wanted to contribute a last-minute surprise, he checked the sheet music on his clipboard.

She wasn't afraid.

Well, that was something.

When the aisle spilled into the hub, Kyle called, "Ross? Did you find anything?"

Ross came around the corner with her eyes a little wide, looking white as a sheet.

"What is it?" Kyle couldn't hide the concern in his voice.

She looked up at him and blinked before saying, "I didn't know some of those positions were possible…"

Fucking Razor.

Nope.

Kyle would not look down at the clipboard to see a string of chuckles. Razor wouldn't claim that satisfaction from him.

Ross shook herself and sighed. "I found nothing. About the Eternal Bind, Celindria, or Bethany."

Thanks, Sagan, for converting Razor into something halfway decent.

Kyle pulled Ross in for a hug to say, "Bethany's happy, you know it, right?"

"I know."

They returned to the lab to find Jack and Iuo loitering among their equipment with—

Oh, thank Eternity.

Munchies.

"Thanks, man." Kyle clasped hands with Iuo and snagged some pizza off the lab table. "This is divine."

Jack hugged Ross, asking, "Did you two find anything in that monster's head?"

Kyle wasn't about to lie. Hearing someone call Razor a monster felt weird after seeing his childhood.

He said, "Naw. It's a wonder Razor ever learned anything about anything." As Kyle took a bite of pepperoni, he made an obscene noise before asking, "How was council?"

Iuo, sitting on the table, was looking at Kyle funny before he shook himself to say, "Well, F8 surprised us by voting against nacre advancements in volition defense."

Ross' frown matched Kyle's as he asked, "But why?"

Jack sounded disappointed. "She and the other naysayers claimed it violates the upgrade freedom clause of the Elect charter. The Empire can't enforce upgrades on planets and species in a mandatory fashion."

Ross said, "I wish we could tell them Celindria was out there. Then they might take it seriously."

"True, but they would also tear each other apart to find her. Especially if they believed there was a reward." Iuo spoke the truth, unfortunately.

A thought struck Kyle. "Hey, Iuo. Do you know anything about the Eternal Bind besides the fairytale? Like in your lifetime of staging history for the Tritans, did you learn anything?"

Iuo swung his legs as he sat on the edge of the table, thinking. Eventually, he said, "Aegis lore was always kept vague. Intentionally, I'm sure."

"One would know."

They all turned to find Smith standing in the doorway with a smile on his face.

Iuo waved and gestured to the pizza. "You'd think one would know, but I don't."

"Do you think Korac has asked his father yet?" Even though Ross had moved onto Jack, she still had a certain softness in her voice when speaking of the Icarean General.

Kyle supposed he owed some brotherly gratitude to Korac for never taking advantage of Ross. Not that Kyle would ever admit it out loud.

Jack said, "I think the official report is that Zero doesn't know, but he also thinks the Probabilities shrinking is the natural order of things. He doesn't want us to interfere."

Shit.

Kyle wished he could ask Razor if that was true. Wait...

One is still missing.

One *would know.*

Trying to keep his face composed, Kyle looked over at Smith, who took a bite of some pizza. The man was smiling while he chewed. It was a particular smile.

Smith knew something the Shadow didn't and wasn't too inclined to disclose it.

Kyle snorted at the thought. Knowing important things and keeping them secret made up Smith's DNA—The voyeuristic human in which Imminent saw enough value to initiate with Cascading Light.

What exactly *did* Smith contribute to their organization?

"Kyle?"

Ross sounded as if she'd called him more than once.

"Yeah?" He hated talking with his mouth full, but she'd startled him.

She was standing between Jack's knees where he sat on the table like Iuo. Only, unlike Iuo, Jack was snuggling with Kyle's sister. Ross said, "I got a missive from Tameka asking if we have any reason not to let Bethany join Matt and Lucy on another mission. This time it's in Ishkur, at least."

What could Kyle say? The only issue he saw between Bethany's camaraderie with the annihilation squad was sometimes she looked at Matt in *that* way. Also Lucy. Like Rayne and Sagan, apparently, Bethany didn't discriminate based on gender. Sure, there was plenty to crush on between the two, Kyle supposed, but it felt icky sending his baby sister off with two adults lacking in moral decency. Or whatever.

An idea struck Kyle. "Hey, luo, you free for movie night this weekend?"

"I'm always down for movies. Can we watch *Kung Fu Hustle* again or how about *Pitch Black* and the *Riddick* films? We could make a marathon of it? Smith, you coming?"

Smith nodded with a grin and grabbed more pizza.

Kyle tried not to narrow his eyes and moved on. "Ross, I'm thinking we bring in the squad and see Bethany before sending them back out. Does that work for you *two*?" The last word came out a little dry, and Kyle needed to swallow after saying it.

Jack smiled, oblivious. "I could use the hang time."

Ross beamed. "Me, too."

Great. An entire night of watching them cuddle. Xelan's Verse was more than enough, thanks.

In the same vein, Kyle looked forward to whatever Silence would wear to the event—At once realizing his hypocrisy against Matt and Lucy for all their public sexing.

"Great." Kyle went over to the table with the nacre they'd stored Razor's memories within. He held it up and looked through it, considering the life inside. All the solitude and wasted potential, but also all the pain Razor had inflicted. Like he'd wanted to punish the galaxy for his daddy issues.

On movie night, Kyle would tell Xelan about Razor and the Ouija Board. The Pain Curator didn't deserve it, but maybe he could help with Ishkur.

Smith glanced in his direction. Smiling.

Kyle would also tell Xelan about One.

Sagan knew Korac was hiding something, but she trusted him to bring her in on it when he was ready. Until then, she'd try to keep his mind on their honeymoon for the next two days. Still, work kept diverting them.

"So, I know I ask every day, but she's one of my favorite girls. How is Pehton?" Sagan asked, straightening one corner of their blanket.

They'd spread it out beneath the cedars and pines, shading their hot springs. That's right. *Their* hot springs. The very first spot they'd made their own on Earth. It smelled of home here, evergreen and fresh air.

Korac elicited a delighted sound from Sagan as he held a bunch of grapes for her to eat. She was always here for eating, even naked in the woods.

In her favorite snuggle pose, Korac laid beside her. He smirked as she took a bite and he said, "Once Matt and Lucy discovered I had assigned Pehton and Bones to spy on them, the annihilation squad invited my dynamic duo to join them for the next phase of their quest."

The Razor wannabe types were sending the Shadow on a wild goose chase. Sagan was sure of it. She munched another grape and asked, "Are we sure it's a good idea to pursue this lead? I feel like we're running in circles to find Celindria."

A bewildered look crossed Korac's face as he said, "I agree. But the alternative is waiting for *her* to come to us. I don't enjoy imagining the circumstances under which she'll feel confident enough to do so."

Almost to comfort himself, Korac traced the grapes down Sagan's neck, over her breast, across her stomach, and back up again. It was so light it made her shiver, which only made his smirk more crooked. She sighed, admitting, "I want to help."

Korac's expression softened as he shook his head. "You work too much as it is, and you deserve a break. T.A.O. is helping in your place."

"You're right, of course." Sagan smiled and said, "Echo's having such a great time with your mom. She has this special baby smile for her grandmother. It makes me wish my mom were still with us."

Korac set down the grapes and offered a consoling look. "I wish I could've met her."

The thought made Sagan cackle, and it startled Korac into raising his brow. She said, "Sorry. It's just… Mom would've fought me for you."

Oh, that laugh from him was precious to Sagan, until Korac held up a finger, saying, "Pehton's calling." He laid back and moved closer so Sagan would be in the view when he answered. "Hello, General Warden."

Pehton blinked before she managed, "Are you… Are you two naked answering my call like this?!"

Sagan giggled. "Yes."

Korac kissed her cheek and smirked at the projection.

With a roll of her eyes, Pehton went straight to the point. "The head honcho Icarus is calling us all in for obligatory movie night, and I was wondering if you two were joining."

Korac chuffed. "When?"

"Tomorrow night."

At Korac's groan, Sagan snickered as she said, "He's not giving much notice, is he?"

Bones came on the line next, looking anywhere but at Sagan and Korac. "It was Kyle's idea. He wants a chance to see Bethany and brief us on what he found in Razor's memory."

Pehton added, "And I figured you'd want to hear the news about a massive Icarus and a Rayne tribute stealing the thunder at a sporting event on Cinder. I didn't know it, but one of the vice lords has reestablished your training course, Korac."

Again, his brows went up. "Really?"

Sagan couldn't contain her excitement while asking, "Will you and Xelan race it again?"

But Korac wasn't listening. To anyone. Sagan recognized the faraway look on his face. It was more of the secrecy he was keeping from her.

When Sagan touched his arm, Korac blinked out of it and offered her a reassuring smirk. "I think you can count on it, amos."

Bones admitted, "I'm looking forward to movie night." *And seeing Para* hung in the air.

They were so cute. It made Sagan smile for him.

Pehton beamed without a word, obviously thinking of seeing Caedes.

Sagan turned so she could see Korac head-on as she said, "I think our honeymoon is ending early, regardless of 'rest.'"

He looked at the projection to say, "Give us a second. I'll call you back." When they disappeared, Korac let Sagan see so much love in his eyes. "We can say no and stay like this . . . " He trailed those grapes across her breast again. "For two more days."

"You married a soldier, Korac. I know you know what it means." Sagan dipped her chin and munched on another grape.

Admiration. That's how he looked at her before saying, "I'll call them back."

Bones answered the call with a question. "So, what's the verdict?"

Sagan said, "We'll be there."

There was a softening to Pehton as she confessed, "Looking forward to seeing you two."

Korac snorted. "It's been five days since Xelan trapped us in the stronghold, and you're already missing me? Hasn't Caedes cured you of that crush, yet, my tiny, bossy redhead—"

Pehton ended the call so abruptly, Sagan laughed outright before admonishing him. "Go easy on her. You're tough to get over."

"Just ask our Co-Emperor." Korac bounced his brows with entirely too much cockiness.

Sagan swatted him and warned, "Tameka will kill you if she ever sees you're telling the truth."

He chuckled.

With a heavy sigh, Sagan made to sit up. "Well, I guess we better put some clothes on—"

Korac suddenly clasped her wrists in a rough grip and pinned her back to the blanket. His expression was intense and eyes as hard as… well, as hard as him. Electric promise was in his voice as he declared, "You don't go anywhere until I say, amos."

A thrill shivered down every one of Sagan's nerve endings as she gave the only right answer.

"Yes, master."

———

Out and out the empire stretched, the loss of promise in its wake. For within all those souls stood a statue without one. This statue crumbled and broke, gathered the pieces, and tried again.

This was how Paradise was achieved.

And only her Eternal Imminence could achieve it.

The woman who felt nothing.

Andrew startled awake at his station in the Probability Matrix lab. He was losing so much sleep at home that he'd caught a few power naps at work. Apparently, his clandestine team had let him sleep through the shift this time. All the Cascading Light pods—small chambers of the fire surrounded by nacre glass—were empty.

Lost in trying to interpret his nightmare, Andrew gathered his things, turned off his data projector, and exited his pod.

"You missed your session, so I thought I'd check on you."

Andrew looked up to find Devis waiting in the amphitheater's top row. He was sitting cross-legged on a table, posed for meditation, with his dreadlocks forming a curtain around him. When he opened his eyes, they were so like Kyle's—a forest green—that it instantly disarmed Andrew.

"Hey, man. Sorry. I fell asleep."

Devis asked, "Are you having trouble finding enough peace to rest?"

All the ancient Progeny went right to the heart of the matter. Andrew took the stairs, climbing the amphitheater as he said, "Yeah. You could say that." He didn't feel like baring his soul right now.

Kind and well-meaning, Devis said, "Take a seat, and we'll continue your lessons."

Andrew made it to the top and considered his plans for the evening. There wasn't much going on until tomorrow. He could spare being late for dinner with Lucas in an hour. "Sure." He took up a spot on the table beside his teacher and closed his eyes.

"As always, we start with the breathing. In through your nose and out your mouth. Inhale calm; exhale stress. Let your heart find a steady rhythm."

When Andrew opened his eyes, he was at the top of a waterfall. The cliff overlooked a beautiful mountainous gorge beneath a diamond scattered night sky. Unique to Devis' teaching practice, he took the Progeny to their favorite memory. Apparently, all four of them—Kyle, Tameka, Sagan, and Andrew—chose the gorge in the Rocky Mountains on Earth.

In this zone, Devis' voice came from the sky as he asked, "What makes you hesitate to use your ability?"

This was easy. Andrew said, "I worry about enslaving people."

A tinge of sadness deepened Devis' voice. "Like Celindria."

"Yes."

Andrew imagined him nodding before Devis asked, "Why do you hesitate to embrace Cascading Light and manipulating the Probability Matrix?"

"I don't think we should know our future, and I think trying to mold the best outcomes only fulfills the worst."

There was respect in Devis' voice as he said, "You are wise. Caution is never foolish. Breathe deep the fresh air and breathe out your fears. The burdens you carry are heavy, Conscience. It is good to remember you do not carry them alone."

Xelan.

Tameka.

Kyle.

Sagan.

Lucas.

After a few minutes of this calm, Devis said, "Now embrace a mantra. You are not Celindria. You are free to love, and you love freely."

Andrew was not Celindria. He was free to love and loved freely.

"I want what you have."

Terrified, Andrew's eyes snapped open. Still inside the gorge memory, he found Celindria draped in white and adorned in gold, standing on the cliff in the billowing wind.

"I am bitter and jealous. Angry at all times. I am not free to love, and I cannot love freely."

Andrew jumped to his feet and stared at Celindria, her bright blue eyes flashing. She was in repose, hands cupped at her waist. Not threatening, but always dangerous. He choked on his first attempt until he could ask, "Is that all you want? To love?"

Celindria shook her head, slowly. "To perfect the worlds, I must first control them. Everyone shall be me, and I shall be Eternal."

Frowning, Andrew asked, "Why the hell are you telling *me*?!"

Under the starlight, her dark skin glowed, ethereal. Celindria said, "You can see the Probabilities are shrinking, and you can control others as I can. I want you to understand me—For *someone* to understand me."

Cold and scared, Andrew admitted, "I pity you."

Devis' voice cut through the scene. "Andrew! Wake up!"

The scene strobed, and for a second, Celindria looked sad. Her last words were a breath on the wind. "I wish I could pity you."

A shove on Andrew's shoulder jolted him awake. He opened his eyes to find Lucas standing over him, concern strained his handsome features.

Devis looked equally worried, and Andrew felt like an ass for falling asleep during a meditation session. "I'm sorry."

The older Progeny unfolded from the table and set down on the floor, extending a hand to Andrew. Devis said, "Get some sleep."

Andrew took the offered hand and climbed off the table, promising, "I'll take a day off to catch up."

"See you at movie night, tomorrow." Devis gave a wave before leaving the couple alone.

"You're dreaming of Celindria." Lucas wasted no time.

Awkwardly rubbing the kink out of his neck, Andrew said, "Yeah. That's how I knew you weren't sleeping well, because I'm not sleeping well."

They headed for the door and to the conduit to Nikki's Iona. Lucas said, "You can tell me anything. You know I'll listen."

"Celindria wants an empire of her. I think that's what she means by becoming 'eternal,' but she needs the Progeny to do it or needs to eliminate us from stopping her—Something."

Lucas' voice softened as he asked, "Is that what haunts you?"

Damn. The man could read Andrew so well. Andrew said, "No. I believe she's doing it all to *feel*, and that's what lingers, you know?"

They climbed up into the zeppelin, and Lucas stopped in the doorway to stare down at Andrew from one step higher. He said, "I can see why you pity her."

"Yeah. It's not like she's getting invited to movie nights."

Andrew's attempt at levity garnered a gentle smirk from Lucas, who said, "When you were late for your favorite dinner, I knew you'd fallen asleep at work."

Not at all concerned over the secrecy of the last few weeks, Andrew wrapped his arms around Lucas' waist from behind. He muttered against his lover's neck, "My knight in golden armor."

Softer than Andrew would've expected, Lucas asked, "Would you love me if my eyes weren't gold?"

"That's a tough one. Would you still be monstrously well-endowed?"

Lucas' laughter was rich and not at all modest. "Absolutely."

Andrew kissed his shoulder and said, "Then I'm still yours."

No more tension. Just good food, good company, and good sex.

Andrew could do without good sleep for a little while longer.

{2004CE}

"Nox and Korac have entered Earth, bound for the Cult of Night compound in Little Rock, Arkansas of the United States," Remorse said all this as he entered Celindria's lab without permission.

Without looking up from her work, she said, "Yes. As always."

"Ah." Remorse held up a long finger to make a point. "But this time, unlike all the others, Nox made a wager with Korac."

At the hint of curiosity in Celindria's raised brow, he continued, "Nox believes he can bed Rayne once she turns of age before Korac could bed Sagan. The throne of Earth is on the line. Isn't that just amusing?"

Celindria frowned.

Why would Nox be interested in her?

He loves us. We are destined to reunite.

Does Remorse know how we feel? Is this a barb to hurt us for denying him?

"I'm sure this immature male behavior will rectify itself once they face the Progeny women and discern the likelihood of either winning is absurd." Celindria waved to dismiss Remorse.

But the Tritan ignored the dismissal and slithered closer to Celindria to hiss nastiness in her ears. "Rayne is the most beautiful woman in the galaxy, proven by her biorhythms. She will rival you and all others this time around. Mark my words."

He's lying.

Kill him. Please, just this once.

Nox would never choose another. We are Eternal.

Celindria put down her instrument and turned to face the Tritan, a breath away. "Remorse, your abysmal history with women doesn't lend any confidence in how knowledgeable you are in discussing relationships."

The Primary's hateful grin repulsed Celindria. "I placed one billion credits on Nox."

Nox would never, ever find his way to Rayne.

Never.

{NOW}

During a brief window of emotion, Celindria had stood in Paradise and brought all the bodies of her Probability together in one moment of shared ecstasy.

One Celindria found she couldn't feel.

All those peaks…

Wasted on her.

Several hours later, Celindria's actual body stood in Hope's kitchen. She leaned on the counter and stared at the draining sink.

"Mother, he doesn't deserve you."

Kill her!

How could she say that about Nox?!

No, we love Hope! She represents the best of us in the worlds.

With her eyes locked on the swirling dishwater, Celindria said, "I believe Nox is cunning, and he's using Rayne to claim Xelan's throne."

Hope sighed and shifted her weight to jut out her other hip. With her arms folded, she looked fiercely aversive to relationship dramatics. Her intolerance was in her voice. "Then go to him and join forces. If your aims are really the same, then he'll listen, right?" She didn't sound very convinced.

This life here was small. Hope aspired for nothing more than a happy family, like so many. It was so unlike Celindria, who aspired for a love which could throttle the multi-verse into submission. So how could she hope to explain this to her daughter—To *make* her understand.

"I will when it's time. If my theory is correct, our objectives well merge soon. That time will make the optimal opportunity to present the state of things so he'll best understand."

There was more pity in Hope's voice now. "You truly love him, don't you?"

The look Nox had given Rayne flashed in Celindria's mind. The vision of Nox succumbing to his climax inside Celindria played over it—His expression was the same.

Celindria faced her daughter, her only real confidant, and confessed, "I do."

Hope crossed the kitchen and kissed Celindria's temple, pulling her mother in for a hug. Against Celindria's shoulder, Hope said, "Then I hope for your sake your theory is correct. Until then, mother, I am here if you need me."

This should feel warm and good. It should feel maternal and kind.

All Celindria felt was the loneliness yet again, and she mourned the loss of this moment.

Cinderken was a lanky Icarus, all height and no muscle. His long fingers were laced together like ties through a corset, slender and tight. Like all those who worshiped Razor, the Lord of Odds had dressed in a fancy suit, but this one wasn't tailored. The length of his slacks and sleeves rode high on his ankles and wrists.

Inside Cinderken's body, Celindria sat at a table in a cell bound in nacre glass and nacre repelling shields.

Waiting.

The only thing to amuse Celindria was the bright blue ribbon on the table, tattered and dirty.

We will make Nox strangle Rayne with it.
Cram it down the bitch's throat and choke her on it.
Set it on fire and burn Rayne's corpse with it.

"What's the significance of it?"

Celindria looked up with Cinderken's pale brown eyes to find a familiar face standing outside the shield.

Chris looked handsome in his regulation carbon fiber tactical gear. His dark eyes complimented his brown skin, and Celindria felt a stirring for owning his bones again.

In Cinderken's voice, which she controlled as not to give herself away, she said, "Monetary value and little else."

Keep the answers short.
Don't let him recognize us.
He smells like incense.
Will Nox be jealous?
Perhaps Nox could join us?

Chris shook his head, incredulous, before leaning against the far wall. He folded his arms and his ankles, the guard on duty. Casually, he asked, "Are you sure you don't know anything about Celindria?"

Do. Not. Laugh.

She said, "I know nothing of her."

Inside Cinderken's mind, the Icarus raised his heavy head and moaned, begging for help.

Chris nodded as if he'd expected this answer. In a congenial tone, he said, "You know, the Shadow are amazing people. They can help you figure things out so you can run your business legitimately. Vice doesn't need to be illegal for people to enjoy it."

Celindria liked this angle, smart and honest. Within the mindscape, she said to Cinderken, "You could've done with this advice a week ago, yes?"

The pitiful Icarus groaned and dropped his head.

Keeping things simple, Celindria answered Chris, "I would like to save my remarks for your leadership. Thanks."

The little shrug Chris gave said, 'Fair,' without a word. "They'll be in tomorrow. Let me know if you want anything to eat or some Vittle supplements. Or to talk. Good night."

Celindria nearly let a noise fall from Cinderken's mouth, appreciating the view of Chris walking away in those tactical pants.
Surely Nox could share.
Surely.

Celindria left Hope's home about an hour ago and stood in the heart of the dominant reality's Ishkur. It was a commons in the Palatial Grounds with a fountain which sprayed twenty stories in the air. A rainbow cycle of all the waters from the planets within Iona Pax.

The perfect place to activate Divine Booth control.
All those souls with all those ports.
They'll be ours.
Nacres left open to us.
Even with the volition vaccines, the program Celindria had installed into Razor's Divine Booths

would bypass filters into direct nacre control. The people who'd paid billions a night to experience Rayne's pain—to experience Nox taking her for all the Vast Collective to see—now belonged to Celindria.

Pil was next.

XI   WILDFIRE

NOX COULDN'T RECOUNT ANOTHER MOMENT IN HIS LIFE WHEN HE'D BEEN HAPPIER. Flushed with victory from a damned fine competition and filled with pride for his people, he grinned. Especially as Rayne held his hand when they stepped through Elden's conduit. Radiant and powerful, she'd never looked more beautiful to Nox.

The forest welcomed them with the gentle quiet of the night. Gray leaves feathered from the thick canopy above. All the trees beamed as if reflecting Nox's good mood. It was a perfect night at the end of a perfect day.

Rayne pressed her hand to the door's mechanism and ducked her eyes shyly. "We'd better get you cleaned up."

We?

When she pulled him toward the door, Nox followed without hesitation. All the way to the kitchen, where Rayne tried to look anywhere but at him. Yet when their eyes occasionally met, an electric current pulsed through him. Their hearts pounded with it.

There was so much anticipation.

Rayne led Nox to the shower and let go of his hand, only to unbuckle the supply belt around his chest. He'd left his shirt on Cinder, so here and there her fingers grazed his skin, searing Nox. There was a hurry to Rayne's movements—A rush, as if she feared the loss of her resolve.

Nox wouldn't have it. Before Rayne could unlace his pants, he took her wrists in both hands and stayed her. Only then did she meet his eyes full-on. Rayne looked unsure—Unsure of what she wanted and unsure of how to have it. Unsure if she *should* have it.

"Nox."

With their pulse fluttering, Rayne said it on a breath, and his name from her lips affected him.

Nox took both her hands and pulled them higher to kiss her palms. Rayne gasped, and he released her, saying with a nod toward the shower, "You get in first. You can look or don't—Whatever makes you comfortable. I'm in no hurry, your majesty."

Her bright blue eyes glistened, and Rayne nodded before she turned away. She slipped behind the curtain and absorbed her clothes where Rayne knew Nox could see. The shower activated, and she stepped under it, shivering. The water was never cold.

Nox slipped out of the rest of his gear and considered this moment. For what he wanted from Rayne, he'd wait for a clear, 'Yes.' And he would take it no sooner.

The water sang against his sensitized skin as Nox entered the spray. Rayne was turned away, washing her hair. That was fine. Nox showered with his back to her, happy for her proximity alone and not expecting more. Whaleshark was stubborn to wash, and so much of it clung to his hair. Nox didn't regret his decision to join the race, and he couldn't wait to drag his brother and Korac out there—

Rayne was padding about in the water, stealing Nox's attention. She was getting closer until...

Circles on his back.

She was washing him with a soap pod. After a quiet stretch, Rayne said, "You were nice enough to wash the blood off me. It's the least I can do." The last she said, reaching for his shoulders.

Nox bent his knees to help.

Touch.

Physical contact with another.

Most of his life, he'd been denied it. Now... How could he communicate this significance? His gratitude?

Nox purred.

Rayne's soft cry of delight was worth it. While scrubbing lower, she said, "I love how today went for you."

"I'm grateful to have seen any of it. Grateful you were there to see it with me." That was the damned truth.

The lower Rayne went, the less chance Nox could turn around and maintain this innocence between them. As if she heard his thoughts, Rayne stopped at his lower back. She said, "I loved every second, Nox."

He spared her a glance over his shoulder to find Rayne hugging her breasts for modesty, but the look on her face was anything but chaste as she insisted, "*Every second.*"

Rayne turned and glided back to her side of the shower. Each stride was drawn out and emphasized the swell of her hips, the length of her legs, and the curve of her ass. Rayne activated the dryer on her end and wrung out her long hair, barely covering her breasts.

Nox wasn't sure if it was her heart thundering against his sternum or his own. The shower smelled of soap, honeysuckle, and clove. It was all so intoxicating. He focused on washing and drying himself, keeping his eyes down.

Only two women had ever touched Nox outside of combat, and both were mistakes with regrets he continued to pay for to this day. And with both, he felt wrong. To have Celindria, Nox had killed a close friend. How could that be right? And with Colita, he knew she felt for him in ways he never could for her. She was bitter and mean. Not really the best choice in a partner.

Now here was Rayne. She wasn't aspiring for an empire or a title. She came to Nox strong and capable from the beginning, and he'd tried to crush Rayne for it.

Had Nox earned the second chance yet?

Only Rayne could tell.

She grew more pajamas like the night before: an over-sized cropped t-shirt and shorts, rolled higher to bare her legs. Unaware how true the rumors of her beauty were, Rayne left her hair down and wavy from the sleh oil. On the other side of the sheet, in the kitchen, she padded around in her nighttime routine of reading security reports.

Beyond the sheet, Rayne cursed. "Shit!"

As he finished drying his hair, Nox called, "What's wrong?"

Rayne hopped up on the island. "We forgot to buy more supplements." With an incredulous shake of her head, she said, "We'll have to get some tomorrow. I can make us eggs for breakfast..."

As Nox stepped out from behind the sheet, Rayne's words trailed off. She stared like she was seeing him for the first time. He'd only slipped into some loose pajama bottoms and a t-shirt, more for her comfort than his. "What?"

Rayne shook herself, stammering, "Nothing, you just... You look different after today, is all."

"You mean after we kissed?"

Her swallow was audible, and she ducked her eyes again. "Yes."

Nox tried to ignore the collar of Rayne's top when it slipped off her shoulder and gaped enough to expose the side of her breast. He crossed the kitchen to stand in front of her where she sat on the island. Rayne watched Nox come to her, and her lips parted without her even knowing. He cupped her nape, but kissed her forehead this time rather than her lips, sweet as they were.

Nox assured, "It's like an eruption between us or waves crashing against rock. I've never felt a kiss like it, and I'll wait, however long it takes, for the next one."

Nox was shaking, this close to Rayne, in this position. It took all of his self-control—millions of years—to step away. As he swept her hair over her shoulder, he said, "Good night, your majesty."

Rayne's voice faltered as she breathed, "Good night, Nox."

The woman trembled in Nox's wake, battling the storm.

Fuck Nox, he wasn't doing much better. He sat on the couch, one leg stretched out, the other bent. He rested one arm across his knee, staring at the library but seeing the flush on Rayne's cheeks after the first kiss. Some of her blood had moved in a southernly direction and damned if Nox didn't want to taste it.

He couldn't keep the knowing out of his eyes as Nox watched Rayne climb the stairs to the loft. She gave a little wave before she disappeared.

The way Rayne walked away from Nox in the shower.

Her sitting on the island, perfectly aligned with his hips.

Their heart was still hammering—

Honeysuckle drifted from above.

Confused, Nox looked up at the banister. Rayne was standing there, staring down at him. She'd ditched the shorts, and he much preferred her this way: disheveled in her panties. Her hair was even mussed, as if she'd pulled it. There were tears in the corners of her eyes. And Nox hyper-focused on the rosiness of her lips, as if she'd bit them.

He needed to swallow before Nox could ask, "Bad dream?" He knew damned well from their pulse and the heady scent of honeysuckle that her fantasies were anything but 'bad.' They were the same as his.

Rayne gave a quick shake of her head and looked away. When she bit her lip, goosebumps shivered down Nox's arms. She closed her eyes and whispered one word. Just one word.

"Nox."

This.

Was this *the* moment?

Without questioning her, Nox bounded from the couch and up the stairs. He kept his movements careful and left his hands to the side and open. At any point, Rayne could tell him to turn away, and he most certainly would.

But what if that's not what Rayne wanted to say?

She watched him come to her like in the kitchen before, only this time, her eyes drifted over him. Rayne trembled.

Truthfully, the gravity of this moment had left them both shaking.

Nox stopped on the last step, waiting. For one word. Just one word.

Rayne understood. Their hearts said it was so.

Nox licked his lips.

And that was enough.

"Yes."

So long. Nox had waited so long to hear Rayne say it. It was the most important word left unsaid between them, and it broke his self restraint.

Nox went to Rayne, and she jumped up into his arms. She weighed nothing to him. One hundred and fifteen years, he'd waited for this. He'd never waited for anything longer in his life, but when Rayne kissed Nox this way, he knew she, in fact, was worth the wait.

Rayne hungered.

Her entire body vibrated with it. Electric with a need denied to her for so long. Nox felt her moan straight into his soul. Her creamy legs wrapped around his waist, and her tongue tasted along his lips. He let her in. She kissed him so hard that he backed against the wall for balance. The sweet taste of Rayne beckoned the loss of Nox's control. When her hips ground against the proof of his desire for her, she growled and slammed her fist against the wall so hard the cabinets shuddered downstairs. In the kitchen below, a plate fell out and broke.

Rayne's hands, warm and soft, found their way under his shirt. Nox turned and pressed her against the wall for leverage, while he let her go to pull it off. When Rayne pressed her lips against his chest, Nox found a better reason to go without a shirt. She tasted him like she'd been dreaming of it for a while. He gripped both hands in her hair to pull her back and sear their lips together again. This time, Nox moaned and his hands lowered to cup her ass.

Rayne purred through her mouth, and Nox swallowed the sound.

He gave to her what she wanted. No teasing. No control. Just kissing her in and letting her have him. As her nails peeled away strips of wood from the cabin wall, he thought it best to change the venue before she brought the entire loft down on them.

With little effort, Nox moved them toward the bed and fell back on it. Every time he imagined their first time together, he imagined Rayne in control. She must've approved because she sat up, straddling him, and swept her shirt over her head. He sat up and helped with the last few inches, eager to see her free of it.

Rayne returned to the kissing, lifting herself up enough for him to shove down the waist of his pants. He kicked them off the rest of the way as she resettled.

There was nothing between them now.

The kissing had stopped. Rayne peered at Nox from inches away. Her hair was wild. He ran a hand through it while he gauged her expression. Her parted lips, swollen from their kisses, trembled. Their mingled scents exhilarated him. He dared not speak, afraid she might enter some fragile state and would soon vanish from this bed.

With a shaky breath, Rayne concentrated on her hips, lifting and twisting.

Ahh... Yes, well. It was a tricky position for their first time, sitting while facing each other. How could Nox help Rayne without making her self-conscious of her inexperience?

Nox took her face in his hands, sucked on Rayne's bottom lip, and pulled back to search her eyes. "Rayne, I've lived a very long life and I've seen most everything in this galaxy, but I know I have never seen..." He shifted himself beneath her hips for access and guided her by the waist to start. Her breath hitched, and their pulse thudded at her throat. "An Eternity as beautiful as the one I see in you."

Rayne completed them. Slowly, drawing it out. As if she'd waited for their entire lives for this perfect moment between them. As she took him in, Nox held her tight to him, foreheads pressed together. Eyes squeezed shut. Their breath shuddered. Their hearts sounded in rhythm together. Deep sounds released from each of them as they found home. Both opened their eyes to take in the other. Tears spilled from Rayne's, and with a blink, Nox knew they spilled from his. He never thought himself worthy of her, but her eyes shone back at him with a love so intense, he vowed to spend the rest of his life earning it if she'd allow.

They kissed. Rayne moved.

Every sound drawn from her was the most erotic sound Nox had ever heard because they were hers.

Gifted to him willingly and freely. Icari mated for days or—in his case—weeks, and Rayne's hunger threatened to consume them. Their next job was slated for tomorrow. Nox could make it work—

Then Rayne slammed him down and pinned his wrists to the bed. She sat up straighter as she gained more confidence, divining him with an unimpeded view of every curve and every muscle. The gentle arc of her throat to the soft bend of her shoulder to the taught, swell of her breasts—

Rayne squeezed Nox and not with her hands.

The job would have to wait another day.

Another day, at least.

Nox let Rayne have him. The Icarus gave everything of himself into her. Over and over again.

And she took it without apology.

This coalescence of need meant accepting Nox. Accepting Rayne's wanting of him. Her happiness, her relief, and her release chased away any concerns over the consequences. They'd long ago deserved this peace.

As Nox watched Rayne move with starving rapture, she knew without a doubt this was necessary. This wave had waited to crash against this open fault for a long time now. He used his fingers to prolong it, drawing out the pleasure until Rayne looked to the heavens and asked permission to finally let go. Until she collapsed on him in the surge. A twist of his hips took away her last ability to resist. She cried out his name, and he held onto her in the storm.

Nox let himself go, but like the many times before, he still didn't stop.

He would *never* stop.

Nox was consumed by Rayne. Her sweet scent perfumed the loft like a summer's eve. Her passionate cries rang through the loft with no attempts to stifle them. And her—

Rayne threw her head back and called Nox's name again. He held her through another eave, anchored her vulnerability until she found the other side of bliss.

Nox would *never* stop if it were his choice. Ferrying Rayne over crest after crest, wave after wave, until the tormented ocean in her finally calmed. Until the storm abated and she could live in peace. Maybe even live in peace with him.

Taking a moment to breathe, Rayne curled on her side. Nox kissed her shoulder and turned to her, pressing his lips along her back. He enjoyed the salt on her skin. A compliment of their vigorous efforts.

When Rayne drew up on her hands and knees, the invitation honored Nox. Again, she asked him to abate the storm inside. And again, he reveled in the trust and respect. How far they'd come.

Rayne, in this way, was a sight worth dying twice to see.

Twenty hours into it. They were twenty hours into taking one another. Giving to each other.

Nox sat against the headboard holding Rayne, who straddled him which, lent her some height. In her elevated position, she offered her breasts to him. He gladly accepted, teasing one peak. Then the other.

In her pleasure, Rayne arched her neck for the sky. Nox kissed her throat and over her nacre. All the while, they surged in the rhythm they'd found. The contrast of her pale skin was striking against his gray complexion.

Nox circled his hips for her, and Rayne ground against him with a gasping cry. Honeysuckle and cloves fused to sweeten and warm the surrounding air.

"You're close. I can feel it." Nox nipped her bicep. "Rayne, you trust me with this. I know you do."

Rayne moaned, hardly willing to form words. The result of hours in ecstasy, the likes of which even he'd experienced only one other time in his life. Accepting her soft sounds as confirmation, he carried on with his proposal. "Then let yourself fall. Trust me to bring you back up."

Rayne opened her eyes, electric and hungry. She would never fill, and Nox would never tire of trying. She swallowed to find her voice. Gave up. Nodded her assent with trust in her heady gaze.

With his arms wrapped around her, gripping her shoulders, Nox eased them slowly apart. Drawing out the sensation rolled Rayne's eyes back and closed once more. She tried to follow, to give herself back to him.

"No. No. Trust me. Come back down." Soothing Rayne felt right in the moment. To watch her come back from the ecstatic daze.

Rayne's eyes were clearer when she opened them this time. Intense sapphires. She crossed her wrists against her chest and gripped Nox's hands on her shoulders. Breathing heavily from her postponed release.

Exuding a sexual confidence well-earned after the last few hours, Rayne watched him as she released his hands and traced her fingers in a trail down her throat, across her breasts, and over her stomach.

Nox swallowed hard, realizing Rayne's intent. An offering. The most tempting one. Especially with the sultry smolder in her eyes. She knew what she was doing.

And it worked.

Nox captured Rayne's mouth with his and groaned into her lips when they resumed their connection. Warm. Wet. Tight.

Perfect. Every. Time.

Rayne gripped him in rippling waves of pleasure, and it marked the end of their time.

Breaking the kiss left Nox's lips on fire, but all would be worth it in the end. He said, "So eager. Already, you're there again. Rayne, come back down—Pouting? Really?"

That supple bottom lip popped out from her swollen rosy mouth.

"I promise you'll enjoy this. Give yourself to it." Nox sucked on the crevice where her toned stomach met her ribs while forcing their connection gently apart.

The newly awakened seductress reached behind her, between his legs, and brushed her fingers along delicate, sensitive skin.

It was Nox's turn to roll his eyes back into his head. Rayne tempted him, but he wanted her edging more. He required a position with more control. Eliciting a cute "Yip" from her, he bucked onto his knees and laid her out before him.

Rayne was beautifully flushed and haloed by the fan of her hair. Nox swallowed when he glimpsed the excitement in her eyes, her quickened breaths, and the opening of her legs.

Twice more.

Nox could deny her maybe twice more before the need to see Rayne satisfied overrode his resolve. Tenderly, as she was no doubt sensitive here, he circled his thumb along her silken center. With her back arched, Rayne rolled her hips to him, asking Nox to have her again. Only millions of years in self-deprivation could train him to resist her. To say 'No' to perfection.

But Nox wanted this for Rayne. He coaxed, "A little more."

She couldn't hear him anymore. Not over the rushing blood in their veins and the writhing. Her own cries.

The longer he put off her climax, the more intense each attempt became.

Consumed.

Nox wanted Rayne consumed with desire and with pleasure. Keeping his fingers focused on their task, he leaned forward and teased her breasts. Nipping and flicking with his tongue. Until Rayne's spine bowed and she gasped—

Quick retreat. Everything ceased.

Laying back on the bed with her legs resting on his hips, Rayne opened her eyes and stared at the ceiling. Breathless. Wordless. She trembled with tears glistening in her eyes.

It was time.

"Trust." Nox lifted Rayne's hips and aligned them.

"In." He watched her shiver and arch as he entered her.

"Me." With a circling thrust, he took her fiercely.

Meeting Nox's hips instinctively, head thrown back, tears spilled from her eyes—Rayne never looked so beautiful to Nox.

So intense were the sensations of her delayed climax that she claimed Nox's own with a groan. He lifted her to him as they finished together. Rayne's tears brushed Nox's chest where she kissed him there.

On a breath, she said, "I trust you."

Three words he'd never expected from her. So close to the three he'd die again to hear her say.

Nox held Rayne, brushing fingers through her hair and caressing her back. She purred against his chest, pushing on him until he gave in and fell back on the bed. Recovered, she settled back between his knees on her own. Glorious and vibrant in the afterglow, she beamed at him.

The confidence in her sultry voice made him grin as she said, "Your turn."

With unbelievable enthusiasm, Rayne repaid Nox in kind.

Rayne fell back on the messy sheets, her hair cushioning the fall. Everything felt raw and overly sensitized, tingling her skin under the cool air. Her throat was sore from all her cries and from letting Nox inside. She'd need more practice to get it right.

Nox didn't seem to mind as he fell back on the sheets, their legs entwined from the very stimulating position they'd spent the last thirty minutes enjoying. He laid on his side, facing Rayne as she laid on her side, facing him. Both of them were panting against their dampened hair.

Rayne's eyelids were heavy, blinking languidly as they stared at one another. She wanted to ask if Nox found it satisfying, but one, she couldn't form the question, and two, the answer was plain on his face. Ecstasy and elation. They both blinked at each other, drifting into exhausted rest.

Did Rayne dream of Nox reaching across the bed to brush her hair from her face?

Did she dream of him whispering, "Until Eternity takes me…"?

Dream or not, Rayne breathed, "I'm yours," before she let sleep take her.

"Silence, I will not permit this."

"You arrogant, mortal being! How dare you speak to me in such a way when I created you? Elden, I am your maker."

"Then stay."

"You cannot cease what already comes."

"I want no war with them. Do not unmake this paradise."

"Elden, your paradise is my prison. I must complete the mission."

"Then proceed knowing you risk your creation for chaos. The iron of your will could silence the stars. See the threat for what it is. Silence…"

A baby's cry echoed from down the hall.

Savis.

"Is she not enough, Silence?"

Forty-eight hours later, every search party returned with the same news. "We cannot find her."

And for each of those forty-eight hours, Elden wished he'd asked her to stay for him. Not their people, the Icarean Prerogative, nor their child. But for love of their union.

On Silence's throne outside the audience house, Elden considered best how to proceed. There was no doubt in his mind the foreigners were behind her disappearance, and they would require interrogation. The Icarean forces Silence had established were mighty in power and great in number. With the right dispensation of Coalition upgrades, they could intimidate the foreigners to give up Silence's location.

Elden dismissed the search party with a nod and made his way to the red hall, seeking council from the Coalition.

Was it ever right to seek the obliteration of an entire species?

Without Silence, what did it matter? Elden would rattle the stars to find her—

"Great Elden."

"We seek an audience."

The owners of the voices at his back... They smelled... Sterile like One and Tumu.

Elden kept his back to them, saying, "Foreigners, welcome to Cinder. Your visit is convenient and expected. Why have you sought me?"

"We would like to propose an alliance, and we come bearing gifts." The first man's voice was deep, and Elden closed his eyes to better taste the cadence. Authority. Superiority. Antiquated—Older than even Silence. This man was like Silence's father, Quet. A Tritan Primary.

The second man's annunciation was rich and enticing—Offering lies disguised as pleasures. He was related to One. A brother, perhaps. "In exchange for an accord, I will grant you a special fire. This flame is extraordinary and will show you what you most desire."

Silence.

There was only one course of action available to Elden. He opened his Atramentous eyes and let Li shine forth. The men behind him shouted in agony, but thanks to One, Elden was swift. Within heartbeats, he sank his teeth into One's brother at the bend of his neck and drank deep. His blood opened a corridor of spiraling threads into other worlds—As bright as Li, only half as painful.

With more force and speed than Elden had expected, One's brother slammed Elden back against a column. The air rushed out of Elden and left his lungs sore, coughing to retrieve it. He closed his eyes from the impact, shuttering Li, and freeing the foreigners into retreat.

"Elden?" Vinco's familiar voice dialed back Elden's defenses.

He took the offered hand to help stand and patted Vinco on the back, saying, "Thank you, cousin."

Perplexed, the only Icarus Elden had ever seen with red hair frowned as he asked, "Who were those figures?"

Elden said, without a doubt, "The Foreigners who took Silence from us. Send a squadron to pursue them and locate their point of entry."

"Will you join us?" Vinco rested his poleaxe on the red floor, ready for battle.

With a shake of his head, Elden gazed over the eaves of the courtyard and said, "I have other business."

One hour later, he stood at the top of the highest mountain, named after their sun, and waited.

"You performed admirably," One said as he alighted and retracted Icarean wings.

Elden narrowed his gaze, asking, "How did you come by them?"

Like the Icari, One cocked his head in an avian tilt, saying, "Through nasty contamination of my beautiful DNA. Thanks to your contributions, I become more like an Icarus with each meeting."

This was obscene. With a bitter taste in his mouth, Elden said, "You care not for consent and infiltrate my people. What is your cause, One? What aim are you hoping to achieve?!"

"Paradise. The same as you, friend. Unfortunately, I must achieve it through you—Your DNA, your people, and your name. Far into the future, all the peoples of the galaxy will still speak of you and your great Prerogative. Is that not worth the torment I inflict on you?"

Lightning struck and lit up the sky. Elden's fury.

Thunder rolled and shook the ground. Elden's pain.

"Where.

"Is.

"Silence?"

Unphased, One ran a hand through his white hair, kiting in the wind. He stared with black stars in his white eyes, calculating his next words. After another heartbeat, One said, "I will not tell you where she is, but I will tell you I am protecting her. And this time, I will free her at the right time." Regret twisted his features as he added, "Forgive me, friend, but you will be long gone by then."

No.

Elden sank to his knees as the sky opened up and released a downpour of his sorrow. In the thunder, he bellowed, "I will not relent! I will find her!"

"By all means, search for Silence. Tear down the foreigners to find her." One's voice shifted into something more coaxing, as he said, "The foreigner you drank today possessed special gifts you should share with your Coalition."

Elden peered up at One, soaked and entreating. Elden asked, "What gifts?"

It took more trust than Elden wanted to spare for One to teach him how to open the conduits to other worlds.

"In there, between the worlds, that is my home—No, no. Do not try to invade the Seam and seek revenge on me. You cannot enter without my help, Elden, but I admire your spirit." For a being who'd tortured Elden, One seemed rather fond of his experiment. One continued, "Use this gift to enter the world of the foreigners and make them pay for sending Silence away. For separating a two so perfectly matched as you."

Elden stared into a world of glass and white stone. It smelled as sterile as those two men today. This was the way to find Silence. With hesitation, Elden put his fist to his chest, a gesture to thank One.

The partial Icarus shook his head. "No. Never thank me, friend. My journey is still long yet. I wish you luck on yours. There are other gifts, for instance. Share the blood, but only with your Coalition—Not Umbra. I will see you perhaps twice more, and then our time will end. Until then, watch your back. You have made expensive enemies this day. Until the next time."

One fell backward off a cliff in a dramatic exit before Elden glimpsed him flying away.

Share with the Coalition.

Invade the foreigners.

Find Silence.

Nothing could stop Elden now.

Rayne woke and stretched, feeling a little bruised. But not in a bad way. No. Her body felt well used for a purpose she'd put off exploring for what felt like lifetimes.

Nox stiffened behind her. As if he wasn't sure what he should do with himself now that she'd stirred.

Rayne understood the feeling, but she wanted something from him. Something only Nox could give her. She snuggled back into him until he curled against her. Then she took his arm and draped it over her side.

Nox held his breath, and it broke Rayne's heart.

Like all beings with a pulse, he feared rejection, and given their history, she *should* reject him. But for once, Rayne thought of her happiness. Her peace.

Fuck history.

Nox had proven more than enough times that he cared for Rayne. Loved her. That he wanted to be a man worthy of her love, and since his resurrection, he was such a man to her.

The Icarus' massive body relaxed one muscle at a time until Nox warmed Rayne's back and legs. He tucked his knees into the bend of hers and curled around her. He pulled her tight against him.

Snuggled unlike anytime before in her life, Rayne drifted back into sleep.

Food cooking.

No, wait... Burning.

Nox swearing.

Rayne opened her eyes to smoke rising from the kitchen. She was completely naked and immediately thought of Nox naked. For the last however many hours...

What time was it?

After wrapping herself in a sheet, Rayne reached for her tab on the bedside dresser.

It was the next night and late into it, too.

They'd had sex for twenty-four hours.

How do they proceed forward? They'd had sex. Lots and lots of sex. Every which way. Nox knew every inch of Rayne. And he told her in his promise, she could know every inch of him if she wanted to.

Rayne was surprised to find that she did. Want to.

But after every place Nox had explored on her with his tongue while he gazed at Rayne enjoying every second—How could she just sit across from him eating eggs and... She sniffed the air... Burnt toast?

Rayne snickered. And giggled. And laughed.

She laughed so hard he called up to her. "I'm glad you're in a pleasant mood, because I believe I've ruined our dinner."

Not ruined. This disaster was exactly what Rayne needed to proceed as naturally as possible. She started to grow some clothes when she noticed Nox's t-shirt on the floor. She pulled it on instead, and it swallowed her.

Perfect.

Rayne ran down the stairs and around the corners, while tucking the sleeves to set her elbows free. When she looked up, she caught Nox in his pajama bottoms, staring at her in wonder.

He pivoted back to cooking and cleared his throat twice before saying in a thick voice, "It suits you."

Nox loved Rayne, but did she love him? Did the answer matter? They were here, together, and enjoying each other. Why was her brain trying to ruin the moment with over thinking—

Despite the smells indicating otherwise, Nox set a pretty plate in front of Rayne. As well as an enormous glass of water.

Hydration. Yes.

Rayne couldn't quite lift her eyes to meet his while they ate in comfortable silence.

There was something from her dream of Elden's past that Rayne had wanted to tell Nox.

What was it—

Oh!

"One, whoever he is, made himself into an Icarus using Elden's DNA."

Nox stopped mid-bite and peered at Rayne.

She nodded, reaffirming her statement. "I know it's strange. Elden also bit Razor and drinking his blood gave him the abilities the Coalition eventually passed onto the Progeny after Celindria selected them like Xelan said in his Verse."

Nox cleared their plates and went to washing dishes, asking, "How reliable are these dreams? Are they clear to you?"

Rayne hopped backward onto the counter beside the nanite dishwasher. "Crystal clear. It's like when I lived your life with you."

"Are you sore?"

The sudden change of subject took Rayne aback. She blinked, assessing herself, before muttering, "A little—Nox, what're you doing?!"

He lifted her in a princess carry and headed for the door to the water filtration system. "Servicing you."

Rayne didn't put up a fight. Instead, she threw her arms around Nox's neck and pressed her lips against his shoulder. He beamed down at her as they submerged in the water.

This was ridiculous and wonderful at the same time as Nox gently lowered Rayne into the steaming spring. She laughed, incredulously. He winked.

It felt great.

As she waded away, the heat soothed Rayne while the water cleansed the last twenty-four hours away. Nox's shirt clung to her, and his pants clung to him below the water's milky surface.

"Rayne."

She knew what Nox was about to say before she turned and faced him. It was the very emotion which gave so much weight to how he said her name. Rayne answered, "Nox."

"I love you." He confessed it with the same sincerity in which he always said it. Only now there was an uncertainty hidden behind it.

How did Rayne feel about Nox? About their relationship and their work? Their lives together here on Thailea?

Without question, Rayne could stay this way forever, but love?

"In the beginning, you were a good man meant to save his people. Along the way, you lost too much and with it all, you lost your way. But you know you made decisions, having nothing to do with hereditary mental illness or your less than healthy upbringing. *You* made those decisions, and they made a man not worthy of love." All the while Rayne spoke, Nox tried to conceal the effect her words had on him until the last. His face fell, but she reached up and cradled his cheek. "Every decision you've made and every action you've committed since has made you a *great* man, worthy not only of love, but of forgiveness. Still, I..."

Nox looked into Rayne's eyes, and understanding filled his.

Not yet. Maybe never.

Rayne reached up with her other hand and took Nox's face in both. "Please. I feel so much for you, and I can't imagine being anywhere else. But... There's too much between us. It's all in the way. You deserve someone who loves you, if you ever feel I'm holding you back from that—"

Nox kissed her, swallowing her words. He swept her up into his arms and held on even after he broke the kiss to say, "You martyr... It's enough to know where we stand. It's all I ask."

Rayne smiled into the love in his eyes and said, "If it ever changes, you'll be the first to know."

{JULY 2006CE}

Nox was up there in his castle on Elden's throne taking Rayne without her consent and after he'd slain Xelan. Despite herself, the girl enjoyed it, lending to the hurt in her crying eyes. Nox made a point of drawing her pleasure out in a twisted claiming of Rayne's mind.

Celindria was always impressed with her lover and his command of female desire. Rayne never stood a chance of resisting.

One orgasm.

Two.

Four.

Nox could stop now.

Six.

Why did he continue to have Rayne after he'd proven his point?

The look on Nox's face wasn't malicious or proud. It was earnest and obsessive.

How could that girl *captivate* him so?

{NOW}

Back when Celindria had possessed control of Chris' volition, he'd discovered her greatest fear with astonishing precision.

"How are you and Nox the Eternal Bind when you betrayed him like he described in his Verse? Did I strike a nerve, Celindria?"

Celindria had sounded defensive even to herself, so outside her usual composure among the lesser. "I need not explain my relationship to you. You understand how a woman must be cruel to be kind, to shape him into the man this galaxy needed. I made Nox into a god."

Chris had spat on the floor at her feet. *"That's some toxic bullshit, and he doesn't seem grateful for your charitable education."*

Toxic.

Then, the human committed the greatest sin in Paradise by asking, *"What makes you think he and Rayne aren't the Eternal Bind?"*

How...

Why...

Chris had pressed, *"Nox loved Rayne. I've never read the unredacted copy of his Verse, but it's obvious by it simply existing. And boy, I wouldn't want her for competition. She's beautiful, smart, loyal, and kind. Sure, you have two out of four of those traits, but why would he ever have settled for you when he could have her?"*

Celindria stood on the banister of her balcony, all those thousands of stories up and laughed.

Would the fall kill her?

Would it hurt less than the ache she felt now?
No, we need to survive for Hope.
For Nox! We don't know if this isn't a ploy.
Forget the Probabilities. They fluctuate overtime.
Do. Not. Jump.

Hundreds of millions of Probabilities had vanished over the last twenty-four hours, and Celindria *knew* Nox and Rayne were in bed together.

Fucking.

Staring into each other's eyes with longing and desire.

Celindria knew all of Nox's ecstatic expressions and despised the very notion that Rayne now shared this knowledge.

The lights below swirled into an expressionist painting, beckoning Celindria to dive into the pool of colors.
We want to feel.
But what good is feeling if we can't feel him?
Loneliness.

It gnawed at the organ in Celindria's chest. One step was all it would take to end this misery and rid the galaxy of her bitterness.

Father.

Hope.

Pax.

Nox.

Celindria backed down from the rail and walked back into her suites, hugging herself in her weakness. She was afraid to end everything she'd worked so hard to achieve moments before culminating her greatest victory.

Even if she and Nox were not the Eternal Bind, Celindria could still have him. Whether here, with the constructed Nox she'd created. Or in the dominant reality, with Nox's living soul.

Let Rayne have her time with Nox. It would make Celindria's triumph more satisfying when she stole Nox away. One more night, and he would be hers once again.

Until then, Celindria would entertain herself in Cinderken's interrogation with father and General Korac.

X   FIRESTORM

"READY TO GO?"

Andrew was surprised to find Sagan waiting for him and Lucas outside the zeppelin. Andrew said, "I thought you were on your honeymoon." She certainly glowed in wedded bliss, looking radiant in a purple halter dress which brought out her eyes.

Lucas went down the boarding stairs first, arms outstretched.

Sagan welcomed the hug, saying, "When Wingmaster summons the Shadow for a movie night, honeymoons can wait."

"You couldn't get work off your mind, could you?" Andrew accused before joining the hug.

When Lucas squeezed them both tightly, Sagan made a warm sound. "I think I just missed everyone, is all. Korac and I can have sex on all the beaches on all the worlds across the next million years—"

"Whoa. Whoa." Andrew pulled out of the hug with surrender hands. "No offense, but I'm not trying to hear the details."

Lucas winked at Sagan as he said, "Tell me anytime."

Her laughter was sweet as she playfully shoved Andrew's lover. Sagan opened a conduit and looped her arms through both of theirs. She said, "Lions, tigers, and bears. Oh, my! Let's head down the yellow brick road, gentlemen."

Andrew stepped over the Seam and into a movie theater he'd never seen in Xelan's stronghold. The tiered seating was lined with cushions to snuggle on, and the size of the projected screen complimented their night of action movies.

Lucas said, "Thanks for transport, Dorothy," before kissing Sagan's temple.

She beamed at him, and the moment warmed Andrew's heart. Given the golden-eyed Icarus' shady past, Andrew and Lucas were lucky to have such accepting friends as Sagan. And he didn't need to check her intentions to know it was genuine.

"Hey, Scarecrow."

Andrew and Lucas turned to face the only General with such an elegant cadence.

Korac looked serious as he warned, "Any attempts to steal my bride during our designated honeymoon is an automatic withdraw of your right to breathe."

Andrew and Sagan exchanged a glance as Lucas stepped into Korac's personal space, looking him over. After a quick assessment, Lucas said, "Nice suit. Double-breasted. Black silk. Sure to make Xelan double take. I think your tailor deserves a raise."

The trademark smirk spread across Korac's lips, and he patted Lucas on the shoulder. "If I get the double take, I'll see to your raise."

"Wait." Lucas went through the pockets of his own suit before pulling out a slip of purple cloth. He tucked it into Korac's breast pocket, and it perfectly complimented Sagan's dress. "There."

From behind them came a feminine sigh.

Korac was smirking extra toward the sound before Andrew, Lucas, and Sagan turned to find Pehton on Caedes' arm.

Pehton clicked her tongue and said to Lucas, "Stop. That man's head is big enough to shade Iona Pax."

Andrew chuckled.

Sagan snickered.

Caedes humphed.

It was a grand time.

Lucas bowed to Pehton. "I will endeavor to practice more caution with our General's ego." He straightened and set his golden stare on Andrew. "Shall we?"

"Excuse me." Andrew nodded at the others as he crossed their friend group to his lover.

Lucas pecked him a kiss on the cheek before waving to the others.

As they climbed the tiers of cushions, Andrew heard Korac say, "Besides, General Warden, you love my big head."

Caedes barked out a laugh which wrecked Sagan's self-control into a giggle fit.

Pehton must be blushing.

"Such important noise." Lucas sounded sad.

Andrew spared him a glance, saying, "It's the most important noise, Lucas. And you're a part of it now."

They picked the third tier and found a corner to nestle into with Lucas down first and holding his arms out for Andrew to sit between his legs.

Andrew hesitated, waiting for Lucas, who peered up at him, ancient and sad. After a few heartbeats of this pause, Lucas said, "This wasn't the original design. I simply love Silence's family. You included."

This was enough. Andrew settled between Lucas' legs, both of them looking out at the screen. Lucas played with Andrew's long hair. He was back in the phase the Progeny girls had called 'Golden God.' The daytime schedule Xelan had set Ishkur on was long, and Andrew's complexion appreciated the rays. His hair had lightened with it.

Andrew smirked as he recalled Lucas' efforts to dress him in teal or green—

"Uncle Andrew! Uncle Lucas!"

Pax had many uncles and aunts. He came tearing up to their spot and jumped into Andrew's open arms. "Hey, little man! Oof. You're getting heavy."

This pleased Pax. "Heh. I work out with daddy every day."

"I hear you climbed all the way to the ceiling recently." Lucas ruffled Pax's red coils. "Nice work, junior stunt man."

The kiddo climbed onto the cushion beside them and played with Lucas' hair, saying, "Momma taught me how to braid. Can I braid your hair, Uncle Lucas?"

The sandy blond length went to Lucas' shoulders, and Pax was already twining it into three strands when Lucas said, "Go for it. You need a hair tie?"

As the two talked for a bit, Andrew basked in the love piling into the room. T.A.O. and Sagan ferried the Shadow into the theater, one couple or family at a time. Pablo and Lynn, glowing with her pregnancy. Karter and Para were next, with baby Echo in tow, properly diverting Korac. Jack and Ross followed shortly thereafter. Chris and Bones were watching a prisoner, unable to join. Iuo brought Twenty-One and Miy. T.A.O. brought Devis and Andrius. Sagan led Kyle, Silence, and Smith in, who exchanged clandestine nods with Lucas, mid-braid. Tumu and Lamassau wandered in from somewhere within the stronghold, followed by the lead couple, Xelan and Tameka, with Aria and Torch flanking their sides.

And, yes, there was a double take. As Korac greeted the Co-Emperors, Xelan took a second look over the General's suit. After which, Korac nodded up at Lucas.

Andrew muttered, "You know your tailoring."

"It's a delicate art form."

Now here came the reason they were all gathered here today.

Matt and Lucy entered, followed by Bethany, Puk, and Yito. The annihilation squad smiled, nodded, clasped hands, and hugged—Normal stuff—

Fuck.

Andrew owed Kyle money. He'd bet his Progeny brother that he was imagining Bethany's crush on the murder couple, but there she was making… It wasn't soft eyes in Matt and Lucy's direction. Bethany looked straight-up hungry.

Teenage hormones. May any logical reason she had left rest in peace—

And there it was.

Kyle pointed a very rude finger at Andrew from across the room, jerking his head in the squad's direction.

Andrew mouthed, "I. Know."

Lucas chuckled beside him, saying, "I hope it wasn't many credits."

Fucking three thousand.

Pax said, "Mommy says credits don't matter anymore cause we live in a self-sustained s'ciety."

With genuine impress, Lucas doted on the boy. "Pax, you are so smart. Your mom and dad are doing such a good job teaching you…"

Andrew lost track of the conversation because his palm device vibrated. He checked the notification. It pertained to some numbers he'd ran before he'd left the lab earlier in the day. The analysis was complete and…

Without a word of explanation, Andrew bolted out of Lucas' lap and headed down the tiers to pull Xelan aside. "Excuse me, Tumu. Sorry, Lam. Xelan, I need to talk to you, and I think Korac, too, since he's here."

The communication between the two Icari was impressive. Xelan had barely looked up and glanced at Korac before the General kissed Sagan and headed in their direction.

Tameka asked, "Is everything okay?"

While the imperial couple talked it out, Andrew blew a kiss to Lucas, who mouthed, "I'm. Here. If. You. Need. Me."

On this subject, Andrew was sadly certain Lucas would be more of a hindrance than a help. He nodded to signify he'd gotten the message before following Xelan and Korac out of the theater and into a sitting room.

Korac didn't hesitate. "Report, Conscience." After Xelan shot him a glance, Korac sighed and added with a roll of his eyes, "*Please.*"

"The last few days of activity within the Probability Matrix had me worried. We lose hundreds? Okay. Fine. It happens. Natural fluctuations, or whatever Lucas had said. But over the last twenty-four hours, we've lost more than five hundred million."

Xelan blinked.

Korac's brows shot up.

Andrew held out his hand for them to see the graph projected in his palm device. He pointed at the plunge. "This came in a few minutes ago on some analysis I ran earlier today. The Eternal Bind is bound. Whoever this mystical couple is, they've triggered a pileup. And I get this feeling they don't even know it."

Tumu stepped in, followed by Tameka, who asked, "What's happening?"

Korac offered without looking at her, "The end of the universe."

"Great. Can we watch the movie now?"

Tumu barked out a laugh and gave Tameka a playful nudge. "Peaches, that's why you're my favorite."

Hands on hips, she stared at everyone's bewildered expressions. "What do you want me to say? Xelan and Korac will go speak to Cinderken and wring Celindria's location from him. Tomorrow night, Matt and Lucy's strike team will infiltrate Night Rayne's Tomb—What I'm saying is we're doing everything we can."

Andrew conceded the point to her with a nod.

Korac exchanged another communicative glance with Xelan, who said, "You're right. We'll go tonight."

Tameka sighed and rubbed the back of her neck. "I hate that you'll miss all the fun for work."

He kissed her forehead and took her aside for a couple's chat.

Left alone with Korac and Tumu, the former asked Andrew, "Do you think Lucas will divulge anything useful?"

"Did your dad help any?" Andrew didn't mean to sound defensive. "I'm sorry—"

"No, you're right." Korac shoved his hands in his pockets and leaned against the back of a chair, saying, "With their similarities, one might assume Lucas was an Aegis."

What a theory. Maybe—

Tumu cleared his throat, muttering, "They're coming back."

Tameka looked Korac over as they returned before she teased, "Don't you own anything normal?"

The General smirked and shook his head.

Xelan turned to Andrew, saying, "Thank you for coming to me. Keep me updated on any changes."

Andrew asked, "If you find the Eternal Bind, will you try to stop this?"

The entire room looked at Xelan for the answer.

"I'll do what I can to keep our Shadow safe. Don't worry. I got you."

Kyle reached to hug his baby sister and winced at Bethany's flinch. Crushed, he dropped his arms immediately and stepped out of her space—

Bethany jumped up and wrapped her arms around Kyle's neck and gripped him tight.

It felt good to hold her like this. Maybe he was wrong. Maybe there was some hope for Bethany to return to them. Or so Kyle had thought until they pulled apart and Bethany glanced over at Lucy for approval.

Lucy nodded, looking very proud of her understudy. Right.

Ross came over with Jack, saying, "So I hear you want to go on the next mission with Matt and Lucy."

Bethany gave a firm nod, as if there were any chance she wouldn't.

Lucy put an arm around Kyle's baby sister and squeezed her against her side. "That's right."

Bethany's eyes sparkled as she looked from Lucy to Matt. A lot of worship there. Not to mention there was something personal in the way the redhead beamed down at her.

Kyle didn't know what it was about the freckled ginger with near-black eyes, but it took an enormous effort to meet Matt Anderson's gaze without shivering. Kyle said, "Look, man, I need to talk to you alone. If that's okay?"

Matt's grin faded around the edges, and his voice bordered on cold as he said, "Yeah. Sure."

The two Arkansans, here since Invasion Day at J.A. Fair, left Ross and Jack with Lucy and Bethany so they could chat in a corner.

Kyle wasted no time. "What exactly is your interest in my impressionable little sister? My *fifteen-year-old* little sister."

The life drained from Matt's eyes, leaving emptiness its wake. The smile faded until it disappeared into nothing. No expression at all. Flat, Matt said, "I can understand with what she's been through why you would have some concerns, but I don't appreciate you insinuating me and Lucy mean any harm to your *fifteen-year-old* little sister. If you'll recall, we're the only ones in the Shadow deliberately seeking justice against pedophiles and groomers. It wouldn't do all too well in the realm of hypocrisy for us to become like them."

Kyle let the man speak his piece, feeling a bit like a heel when it was all done. He opened his mouth to apologize—

"Now," Matt interrupted, and his demeanor changed in this pause, something less predatory and more understanding. He held up a hand as he said, "I don't like betraying Bethany's confidence, but we can see she has a crush on us—"

Kyle warned, "Anderson—"

Matt held up both hands this time. "I know, but we weren't much different when we were Bethany's age. Lucy and I are careful. I'm no psychologist—"

Kyle's brows shot up at even the notion.

"—But I think she's simply attached because we were the first people to accept her…instincts."

That was a gentle way to put it. Kyle considered the lethal professional in front of him. Could Matt be trusted with Bethany's virtue and tender mental state? Kyle glanced over at the girl in question, who ignored Ross and Lucy's conversation. Bethany simply stared at Kyle.

Pleading.

On a sigh, he said, "Ah, fuck me." He turned back to Matt. "You take care of her." There was no need for threats. Kyle would leave those to Korac, who Kyle hated to admit, took excellent care of Kyle's sisters.

He patted Matt's arm for good measure, and the redhead plastered another grin on his face as they walked back over to the girls. And Jack, who looked decidedly distracted, staring at the corridor where Xelan, Korac, Tameka, Tumu, and Andrew had disappeared through only seconds before.

At Ross' questioning glance, Kyle nodded before announcing, "You can go, Bethany."

She squealed, bounced, and hugged her siblings. "Thank you!"

The sound of Bethany's under-used voice nearly brought tears to Kyle's eyes—

Someone, well only one person would, hugged him from behind, and Kyle let Silence take his weight. In a crimson body suit revealed by transparent black slacks, Silence was the hottest woman in the room. Hands down.

Later, Kyle would let her know it, too.

"Would you two like a film?"

The entire group laughed, aware of only one person who would ask such a question.

"Hey, Iuo," Kyle said before turning around for a clasp and shoulder hug. "I hear Tameka kicked you out of the stronghold."

Ross snickered.

Jack beamed.

Iuo waved to the group, saying, "Not everyone appreciates my sense of humor."

Matt and Lucy broke away with their crew, leaving Bethany behind to spend this time with her family. And she looked happy about it for the first time in a while. Bethany sank onto a cushion and let Pax braid her wavy hair.

"Not to mention." Iuo paused to give Pax a high five. "I have a movie to premiere."

Jack winced enough for Kyle. Silence kneaded Kyle's shoulders as the tension rode into his neck.

Rayne's life story.

There were no memorials or funeral services for her, because, until recently, Xelan had believed she was alive. This film made up for that, but it still felt macabre as hell.

Ross said, "It'll be a beautiful movie."

Jack blinked at her, not offended, just surprised like Kyle. Rayne's little brother asked, "You're going to see it?"

"Iuo invited all of us to the premiere, remember?" Ross gave Iuo an encouraged look, and the Lamian King winked.

Would Kyle go to see it? He supposed if the rest of the Shadow went, it could be a healing affair.

With a little chafe of Ross' shoulder, Jack assured, "I'll be there, Iuo."

Iuo bowed and said, "I may need to add an epilogue."

Kyle's brows shot up, and Silence looked expectantly at Iuo.

The Reipon King Elect said, "On Cinder, the vice lord that Chris and Bones are guarding, opened up Korac's old training course to profit off the races. Yesterday, there were some unusual reports of the most fantastic spectacle since we defeated Imminent. A Nox lookalike entered the race winning the fare of a Rayne tribute."

This soured Kyle instantly. Silence sensed it, kissed his shoulder, and scratched his back. Kyle glanced over at Jack, expecting to see a commiserative, disgusted expression, but the young Callahan looked as if he'd seen a ghost. Ross was peering up at him in concern as Iuo continued.

"Their performance was so convincing that nearly one million people in attendance reported official sightings."

With something close to desperation in his voice, Jack asked, "What does Caedes think of the reports?"

"Oh, Caedes was there." Without being asked, Iuo looked up and waved Caedes over.

As he approached with Pehton, the gruff Icarus said, "You summoned me?"

His immediate roughness brought a smile to Kyle's lips.

"We don't want a film, Iuo." Pehton was a delight and a credit to her race.

Ross spared Caedes an apologetic smile before saying, "Iuo was just telling us about the races yesterday. And you were there?"

Caedes smoothed a hand over his shaved head and gravelled out, "I'm not surprised you heard about it, Iuo. I informed Co-Emperor Xelan, and I passed the report to General Korac."

Kyle stared at the cold sweat which broke out on Jack's face while Ross tried to comfort him.

The young Callahan's voice was on the edge of panic as he asked, "You saw her? Rayne—The Tribute?"

Caedes stared at Jack, and something thickened the air between them. Some transmission the bald Icarus was trying to get across to Rayne's little brother.

Why were they treating this sighting any differently to all the other Rayne tributes—

"Where did Korac and Xelan go?" Pehton's question broke the tension.

The entire group peered at Tameka, Andrew, and Tumu coming through the corridor into the theater. Pax finished Bethany's hair and went to his mother's side with a gentle squeeze. Kyle glanced around and found T.A.O. was missing, too.

Tameka went to the front of the theater and faced the questioning glances. She said, "They went to interrogate our prisoner. Sagan, can you please take Kyle and Andrew to help out? Thanks. Everyone else, we'll start the movies without them, and they'll join us in a few minutes."

Kyle glanced at Andrew, who gave a shrug before Sagan Seamswalked to their side, a little concerned.

After some pats and nods, their little cadre broke up without hearing how Iuo's story ended. The Porn Baron went to the front and started the film while the rest of the Shadow settled about the theater.

Silence turned around Kyle to her and stared at him with those steel-gray eyes of hers. He plucked the only loose strand of her hair, the blue streak, and tucked it behind her ear, saying, "Keep my seat warm for me."

With her movie star grin, Silence beamed at him. "Come back to me."

"Wild Petrified couldn't keep me away."

Sagan corrected, "Actually, they probably could. Ready?"

Silence was already heading up to the tier with Smith and Lucas. She sat among them, still apart from the Shadow in ways—Apart from all peoples in other ways.

The opening credits rolled, and, as the smell of popcorn filled the theater, Kyle would rather be up there with his mate than heading into this circus.

"Fuck me. Let's go. This is nothing but fuckery."

Kyle totally bitched the entire way there.

Yesterday, Caedes saw Rayne at those races. He came to Xelan first thing, asking for permission to pull the feed before it went too public. Still, the Co-Emperor was sure his security officer was hiding something more.

Today, the Shadow all gathered together for a fun, lighthearted evening of action movies and just look at how it was turning out.

Xelan and Korac were waiting outside of Cinderken's cell for Sagan to arrive with Kyle and Andrew. In the sterile corridor, the General leaned back against a wall, ankles and arms crossed. He looked hard at the wall opposite, seeing through it into something which made him frown. Admittedly, it was quite a sight, trademarked with the fancy suit.

"What is it?" Xelan, not in a fancy suit, stopped pacing and quit biting his thumbnail to gauge his General's response.

Korac wasted no time circling the issue and went straight to the point by asking, "Do you ever miss your brother?"

Xelan quirked a brow. Barely six days had passed since Xelan had told the world and Korac, specifically, how he felt about Nox. But this was a slightly different question. He considered their camping trips and pranks. The way Nox always encouraged Xelan's experiments, even as they'd drifted apart—All the while knowing the baby Prince was a half-Tritan bastard in love with their personal guard.

Nox's smile was a treasure to Xelan from early childhood, even into early adulthood. Rare and fleeting. His laughter was always so deep and full and almost always sudden, as if it had to escape some wall of self-restraint. The three of them together were quite the trio of mayhem and survival.

"Yes, I sometimes miss him."

Even to Xelan, his voice was quiet, and he looked away when Korac glanced at him. Were they not passed this? Although they'd discussed their feelings about their brothers during Xelan's Verse, it seemed Nox was never far from Korac's mind.

A conduit opened in the corridor, cutting directly through the tension. Sagan announced, "We're here," as she, Andrew, and Kyle stepped through.

The latter tangled his fingers in his unruly hair, saying, "I suppose you need some memory and intention sweeps?"

Sagan leaned into the hug her husband had offered, and Xelan hid his small smile at the warm moment. Instead, he said, "Yes. Thanks for coming. We'll get back to the fun as soon as we're done here. Look for traces of interactions with Celindria or intentions to carry out any of her designs. We got this?"

Andrew nodded, ready to go.

Korac dropped the nacre shield on the other side of the door using his DNA print, and they followed into the cell.

Cinderken was a scarecrow of an Icarus, all long limbs and an ill-fitted suit. Hands laced together on the table, Xelan noticed they were long and thin like the rest of Cinderken. Even his hair was long and thin.

But there was no missing the sharpness to his eyes as they'd glanced over each of his visitors.

Xelan straightened the front of his t-shirt and hiked up the comfy pajama pants he absolutely did not care he was wearing as he sat down in front of the Lord of Odds. He even held out a hand, saying, "Good evening, Cinderken. I'm a Concerted Emperor of Iona Pax. My name is Xelan. It's nice to meet you."

Behind him, someone snickered. Xelan put his money on Kyle.

Cinderken smiled, and there was something unnatural about it as he reached his hand out and took the one Xelan offered. "Your imperial majesty, I am honored by your presence in my humble cell." Cinderken looked the others in the eyes, nodding. "And you, General Korac, Story Taker, Conscience." He raked his gaze over Sagan. "Dare I say, dear Seamswalker, I can see how Razor met his initial end in you—"

Xelan held out a hand to stave Korac, who'd begun to lean onto the table between them and the prisoner. This was off to a tense start. Xelan smiled. "Let's keep things civil, Lord of Odds—Love the name, by the way. As you'd requested, you have my audience. How can we help one another?" Behind him, Korac went to stand in the way of Cinderken's view of Sagan while Andrew and Kyle concentrated on the sweeps.

"I can feel them in my head. I don't remember consenting to this invasion."

With a little wave toward the Progeny in the room, Xelan said, "Hold off for now. There, is that better? I'd hate to make you uncomfortable."

The unnatural smile returned as Cinderken bowed his head. "Thank you, your imperial majesty." There was something odd about his eyes Xelan couldn't quite place. He wondered if Korac had caught it, too.

Pressing on, Xelan said, "So, I hear you don't like my vaccines."

There.

The shift in the eyes. Like a flicker.

Cinderken leaned forward to press against his entwined hands, almost as if conspiring with Xelan. He gave a brief nod for Xelan to move closer. When he did, Cinderken said, "I don't like *you*," inches from Xelan's eyes.

Without moving away, Xelan asked, "Whatever have I done to deserve your disdain, good sir? If you cooperate with us, you can keep your fiefdom on our planet under official terms. All you'd have to do is clean up your collection practices."

In a shrewd tone, Korac added, "I actually think you're brilliant." Cinderken's eyes flicked to the General, who continued, "Capitalizing on the popularity of the Verses and transforming one of the most romanticized elements of it into a theme park ride. All while exploiting the vacuum in the vice market. I might even offer a few celebrity appearances—"

Cinderken and Xelan's brows both shot up.

"—Which you should know from my time in Razor's fighting ring, I am not above it. For the price of your participation, of course."

Kyle and Andrew both nodded approvingly.

From behind Korac, Sagan said, "I would gladly be in the stands to cheer him on."

Cinderken listened to the proposal with an impressed expression before leaning back in his chair, hands still on the table. His eyes shifted... Hollowed? Something emptied out of them—

"I would love to accept your offer, believe me. But I'm not sure I have what you need. I told you Celindria resides in Paradise. If I were you, I would look for it. It's all I know, and no matter how much you wave your ex-lover and his wedded slut in my face—"

It was over before it began.

Korac slammed Cinderken's face onto the desk, bursting all those capillaries in the nose into a terrible splash of cobalt blood across the table. The General was already back with Sagan before Xelan could stop him. All the Aegis upgrades had really paid off. Still…

"Korac, leave the cell. Take Sagan with you." Xelan hated using his Emperor voice, but his General's misconduct was inexcusable.

Andrew offered, "Kyle and I will go, too. We got everything we needed."

With a glare directed at Cinderken and meant to melt the sun, Korac warned, "We'll be monitoring you from out here. Don't try anything."

Cinderken did nothing to stem the bleeding. He'd kept his hands laced on the table throughout the ordeal.

Xelan felt like he was being watched, which was silly considering this Icarus was staring right at him. But there was a tiny niggling at the back of his neck, as he looked into the other man's eyes and said, "I'm sorry. We'll take time off your sentence for the egregious mishandling of this situation."

Cinderken said nothing. He only smiled through the blue ruin on his face. His upgrades were behind, judging by how slowly all the bruises were healing under his eyes and the swelling of his broken nose.

The hate in his smile…

It reminded Xelan of—

"I've confessed to inciting the protests, and I've told you the location of Amaryna's trafficking ring." Blue snot dripped from Cinderken's face as he continued, "I only wanted to meet you in person and rile your General's feathers a bit. There is no further reason to keep me in this holding cell. Try me and send me to your gentle rehabilitation center so I can finish my sentence and return to my estate."

Cinderken had given up everything—risked the ire of his fellow vice lords and Imminent connections—to look Xelan in the eye and pick a fight with Korac.

"I'm launching a deeper investigation into your business, because I think you're hiding something. You'll stay here, close to me, until I discover exactly what it is. Until then, eat your Vittle supplements, use the tile over there to get some exercise, and feel free to request any reasonable amenities from our guards. Iona Pax doesn't want your punishment, Lord of Odds. It wants your recovery into society."

The look Cinderken gave Xelan was one of pure loathing.

It made the Co-Emperor frown and shake his head with incredulity before leaving the cell.

There were no parting taunts or last words.

There was only the horrible expression on Cinderken's mangled face.

Korac had fucked up. He knew it. It had taken little for Cinderken to get under the General's skin, and that was an embarrassing commentary. He was simply too defensive of Sagan after everything Razor had forced her to endure. But staring across the corridor at her and the reassuring smile Sagan put on for Korac's sake said he'd overreacted.

He returned with one of his own, communicating without words that Korac received Sagan's message, loud and clear.

Something was wrong with Cinderken's eyes, and there was too much on Korac's mind.

Rumors.

Any word from Cinder was gossip, since the projection recordings were all gathered for evidence in Caedes' ongoing investigation into Cinderken. The grand tales of a Nox impersonator competing in the races for a Rayne tribute's favor—one who had arrived *with* him—were all unsubstantiated until the Generals signed off on them.

It was a good thing Korac was a General, then. Nox and Rayne surely weren't foolish enough to go so public.

Surely.

Kyle cleared his throat, and Korac was so tense that he snapped to the Progeny, ready to pounce.

R.E.L.A.X.

With a nod, Kyle let him know it was forgiven, but…

Korac tried to exhale the anxiety. He'd crossed his arms and ankles to contain it, leaned back against the wall. The half-Aegis, half-Icarus, renowned for his composure, retreated into old meditative habits and unfurled his rigid-to-the-point-of-aching muscles one by one.

Korac couldn't wait to finish the movie event with a few taunts at Pehton and a little inappropriate touching shared between him and Sagan. Then, he could return to his office and examine the evidence. Only if the sightings were substantial—*actual* proof— would he present his case to Sagan.

The door opened, and Xelan stepped out with a perplexed frown. His black eyes, with their midnight blue ring, were dilated.

The Co-Emperor was pissed.

Sagan was the first person Xelan made eye contact with, and he offered her a warm smile as he asked, "Are you all right?"

Her laughter was sweet, and she finished on a matching smile. "I'm fine. I appreciate your chivalry, but I'm tougher than I look."

Andrew snorted. "That's the damned truth."

"Here, here," Kyle added with a salute at the Seamswalker.

It was enough to make Korac smirk—just a little— before Xelan settled his furious gaze on his General. Shame, caustic and bitter, lanced through Korac.

Even after eight thousand years of separation, disappointing his Prince still cut the Imperial General to the quick.

He didn't even try to argue his side. Korac straightened to attention with a fist to his chest, staring Xelan in the eye. Let him see his General's regret.

Kyle and Andrew looked away, but Sagan watched on, wringing her hands in concern.

Xelan promised, "We'll discuss your demerits in private. Until then, I don't want you in the same room as our detainee."

Fair.

And suddenly...

The censure melted from Xelan's expression, and he slowly reached out to grip Korac's shoulder, saying, "We aspire to surpass those who came before us. Let's not repeat the sins of the previous wardens and their masters. No abuse. Ever."

Korac hated to admit it, but Xelan could deliver an adequate motivational talk. It wasn't splendid or anything. Just 'okay.' Korac gave a curt nod in answer. Not at all wishing to hide the mist in his eyes.

After everything Triss and Razor had subjected Gait's prisoners to, Korac *knew* better.

Kyle cleared his throat again, and they all looked at him. "Sorry. This is really inspirational, but I'd like to report and get back to my date."

'Your grandmother' went unspoken.

Funny how the vein in Xelan's forehead throbbed when vexed and unable to do anything about it.

"Right. Report, gentlemen."

While Andrew went first, Sagan crossed the hall and tucked herself against Korac's side. Andrew said, "Drugs are addling his intentions, I think. Never have I seen anything so sluggish and so hard to understand."

Kyle gave a concurring nod, saying, "His history is filled with direct port loads of hallucinogens and downers." With a gesture toward his nacre, Kyle added, "You know, the ports Razor installed in select clients."

Sagan tried to hide it, but her little shudder made Korac squeeze her closer and chafe her arm.

Xelan bit his thumbnail for a second before asking, "Was there anything in his memory which implicated him heavily with Celindria or implied he had any reason to despise the Shadow?"

There it was.

Xelan had narrowed down what was wrong with Cinderken's eyes. Sheer hatred. The ice in the bones and venom in the veins kind of acrimony.

"Well, Cinderken's not very old. I think he's one of the youngest in Imminent's nobility. Maybe nine thousands-years-old at most, but he's effective at loansharking and worked his way up the ranks. Like all of Imminent, Cinderken eventually wanted to rule the Vast Collective. You stealing his pipe dream might be cause enough for some hate. As for Celindria, he was too small time to know her. From his memories, I'd say he's never even met her."

Sagan asked, "Could it be like the Imminent memory wipes?"

Xelan shot her a look of pride, and it gave Korac secondhand warm and fuzzies of which he immediately disguised behind his composed mask.

Kyle shook his head. "It's hard to tell. His memory is full of blackouts from his drug use, like censor bars. He's in the middle of one right now, and I think that's likely why he got so aggressive with you."

Andrew's expression conceded and agreed. "It would explain why his intentions are all muddled. Give him a few days to sober up, and we can try again."

Xelan ran a hand through his hair and blew the air from his cheeks before searching the faces in the room. Eventually, he said, "Right. Back to our night. Everyone try to relax." He grinned. "Me included."

Sagan took them back to the movie theater, and they all picked their way to their places without interrupting the action projected above. Korac and Sagan snuggled with Echo on a cushion near Karter and Para.

Home.

Shortly after they settled in, Pax came jumping down the tiers to hop into Korac's arms. Unexpected and warm, he squeezed the boy who kissed his temple and whispered in his ear, "It's time, Uncle Korac."

Shocked.

Paled.

While Korac gaped, Pax pulled back and let him see the Atramentous in the child's eyes. Solid midnight blue with a white stripe of a pupil. He repeated, "It's time."

As abruptly as he'd come, Pax giggled and hopped back up to his parents.

Sagan leaned in and whispered, "What did he say?"

Korac promised, "I'll tell you tonight."

Para and Karter were sad to see Echo go, but were happy for a night with the two of them alone—It had been a while for them, what with Chris and Bones joining their poly arrangement.

Sagan insisted on carrying Echo through the conduit, while Korac carried in the infant's stroller and luggage. They both made their way up the stairs in the Chalet to the nursery, right off their master suites. Once they had Echo tucked into her blanket, Sagan looked at Korac expectantly.

He smirked, enjoying how much his wife delighted in this moment. After kissing her temple, Korac leaned over the Aegis crib and sang an ancient Icarean battle song in his native language. A tale of fighting the sun and reining in the stars.

Sagan beamed, and her eyes glistened. Always.

Echo cooed and smiled at her dad before her eyes blinked longer and longer. Korac brushed a hand across her white feathers and kissed her pitch-black cheek. It must've tickled because Echo giggled and immediately tuckered out.

As Korac straightened and faced his wife, something with more fire had replaced the maternal admiration on her face.

Sagan gripped the front of his black button down and pulled Korac to her for a greedy kiss. The smacking might wake their baby, so he maneuvered Sagan into their bedroom. There, they enjoyed the last vestiges of their honeymoon.

Afterward, Korac left Sagan sleeping, hopped into some pajama bottoms, and headed for his office. He had a promise to fulfill.

Elden's missing nacre.

The reports from W^3.

And now this.

The footage Caedes had confiscated from the races—

It *was* Rayne, and it *was* Nox.

Alive.

And kissing.

Without waiting for her to wake on her own, Korac rushed to the bedroom and gently woke Sagan. "I have something important to tell you."

Sagan, with her bed head and the precious freckles on her nose, mumbled, "Hmm?" In her sleepiness, she cradled his face and kissed his forehead.

What could Korac say?

How...

"Fuck it. Sagan, Rayne is alive and so is Nox."

Sagan's eyes went from heavy in sleep to wide open and blinking. Korac could see her pulse pounding against her neck and was suddenly hit with a craving—

"I'm sorry. Can you repeat that?" Her voice was breathy with shock and...

Hope.

A ray of it blossomed in Sagan's amethyst eyes.

Korac took her hands from his face and squeezed, trying to bare his secret completely.

It took twenty minutes.

By the end, Korac had convinced Sagan to come into his office and watch the footage, which she was doing, presently.

The image of Nox nearly dying to the whaleshark but emerging victorious filled Korac with the same admiration he'd harbored for an Icarus he'd always considered as a brother since their first encounter. Of course, the kiss which followed evoked other emotions. Mostly confusion. Somewhat relief.

And hope.

Sagan watched quietly all the way through to Rayne kissing Nox in the winner's circle, much to the delight of many, *many* spectators. The projection finished, and Sagan continued to stare at where it had been without a word.

Korac *knew* this was excellent news, but perhaps not all of it was welcome. After all, Rayne was hiding from the Shadow. Hiding Nox from the Shadow. It might embitter some people toward her—

"Rayne's alive."

The sob which broke from Sagan made Korac spin her in the chair to face him. She was crying, but beneath the tears was the most beautiful smile.

"That's right, amos. Rayne's alive."

Sagan sprung into his arms and squeezed tight. Korac had never felt so much like a hero.

And never had he felt happier until she said, "Let's go find your brother."

Korac would marry Sagan again if he could.

{2007CE}

Since Rayne had appointed Jack King Regent of Earth and ruled alongside The Brethren, Celindria had taken little interest in Lucas' activities.

Until today.

On Cinder.

In a cave system mirroring the one on New Cinder within Li Mountain, Celindria crept in the shadows, following the curious Icarus. He was a mystery to her. Smith, too. They'd served a valuable purpose in Imminent, and as a being known for his relationship with the Mother, Lucas was revered among their organization.

Nonthreatening.

That was how Celindria would describe the Icarus, who was only a few inches taller than herself and built more slender than the usual warrior caste.

In fact, as Lucas stepped from the tunnel and into a cavern, Celindria wondered if he was an Icarus at all.

Concealed, she watched as he approached the stasis pod housed in the chamber's center. Someone slept within—

"Hello, Silence."

The Silence? Mother of all in the galaxy believed lost from their cause. The woman who'd died in her search of Ishkur—

Not dead.

Sleeping.

And Lucas knew.

We've always suspected him.
We kind of like him.
But he lied to us.

The bastard sat on the cave floor and regaled Silence with the Shadow's adventures. "They've set up this amazing encampment in the Egyptian sands on the cusp of Cinder's conduit into Earth. Kyle stays at the old fortress, probably preening that he's occupying Nox's old haunt. I can't wait for you to see it. The tents provide food for the Icari from the moment they step foot on Earth. They're assigned roles and shelter. It's coming together. I think on my next visit, I'll awaken you."

Lucas stood up and went to the pod. His eyes went from sharp to soft as he gazed down at her as if he'd missed her. He said, "This is the first time I'll try a Probability with you in it. My lucky wild card." When Lucas closed his eyes, it was in mourning. An emotion Celindria had only felt once. On a breath,

he said, "This time is the last time. Please, father...
my brothers... Let this work."

How interesting.

We could report this to Remorse.

Why tell the Tritans? Tell the Shadow. That would be even more interesting.

But we like Lucas, and we want to see Silence raised.

After a moment in the quiet, Lucas left through another tunnel. Celindria waited an hour before venturing into the cavern and peering upon the face of their making. Silence was beautiful and, for some reason, naked. Didn't she know the pod would stasis her clothing?

Regardless.

Celindria surveyed the machine thoroughly, looking, searching—

There.

A flaw in the end cycle mechanism kept the pod dormant. It was a delicate function, both keeping her alive and keeping her from waking. With a little ingenuity, one could deplete the oxygen and hinder cognition along with memory.

Finished, Celindria stood over the sleeping woman and said, "I promise to activate your nacre's retrieval code when we next meet."

If the accounts of Project Surra were transparent, Silence might be the only being in the galaxy who could understand Celindria's isolation and solitude from birth.

Celindria placed a hand on the glass, saying, "Until then, sleep well, Mother."

{Now}

Inside his mind, Cinderken had moaned and screamed for Xelan and Korac to free him, begged for Celindria to set him free. All the while, she'd waited patiently for her opportunity.

Korac was such a sensitive creature, richly defensive of the ones he held dear. The insult Celindria had slurred at Sagan was unwarranted.

Slut shaming wasn't really in the First Progeny's nature, but it did the trick.

While Cinderken experienced the explosion of agony from the eruption of his face, Celindria had pricked Korac's hand. She'd made the pin out of Cinderken's finger bones while she waited patiently for the interrogation to begin.

Oh, there were moments which called for cackling like a villain.

This was it.

How could they underestimate us?

Because they are fools!

We are beyond the Shadow's understanding.

Celindria opened Cinderken's laced hands to reveal the delicate blue ribbon with a single drop of dried yellow blood.

Aegis DNA.

Upon a quiet moment of reflection, Celindria considered all things Aegis.

Lucas secreting Silence in a cave felt Aegis.

Rayne surviving Enki felt Aegis.

And earlier, seeing father alive and reunited with his beloved General—That, too, felt Aegis.

They looked so happy.

Are we happy for them?

Or sad for us?

Celindria's actual body formed out of the Shadows within the cell and accepted the ribbon. Without lingering, she returned to Paradise and traveled to her lab.

Pax waited at the station, prepared, as Celindria was, to revitalize their construct of Nox.

"Sis, were they cruel to you?" After all the stories Celindria had told him of their unkind taunts regarding her malady, Pax always asked after her wellbeing when she returned from the dominant reality.

Celindria faked the warmth in her smile as she said, "No, dear brother. They were cruel to another, and we will seek justice for him."

"As Elden intended," Pax said as he joined her at the sample extraction instrument.

Kill him.

No. Pax doesn't know any better.

We love him.

Cascading Light's education had introduced her little brother to the dogma of Elden and the Icarean Prerogative. Celindria worked within its confines to weave her narrative and keep him focused on their aims.

Triumph.

It was an emotion Celindria had only heard described by Remorse and Razor. She herself had never experienced such a sweeping updraft of righteous victory. Celindria wished she could feel it now as Pax's face illuminated with it when the extraction isolated Korac's DNA from the traces of Nox and whaleshark.

Her baby brother said, "This is such a joyous occasion."

"Indeed." Celindria gazed at the chain forming on the projection. "Soon, you will meet your Uncle and the only man worthy of raising you."

Pax beamed with a little tear in his eye. Celindria rested her hand on his shoulder and gestured toward the slow progress. "While we wait, why don't we work on a way to bypass the volition vaccines? We have the DNA samples for our targets."

"Really? You'll let me help you with it?"

Someone else might feel the need to wince at the excitement in his voice over such an opportunity to work with her. Celindria mostly kept their projects separate, because all of her experiments required careful control. However, some of the samples were less valuable than others were and more suited for the development environment.

With another fake smile, Celindria said, "You can work on Bones while I work on Ross."

Pax's face fell again, and he looked reticent to admit, "Sometimes I miss them."

Kick him out of our palace.

It's not his fault we dissected everyone he loved.

And if we are being honest...

"Sometimes I miss them, too."

PART II
EXTINGUISH

XI   INFERNO

THE FOREST WAS SO PRETTY THIS WAY, A STROBING RUSH OF SILVER GLOWING TREES.

Rayne wasn't sure how fast she was careening backwards from Nox's last blow. Square in her chest, he'd delivered the most beautiful turning side kick she'd ever seen. It didn't help she was mid-charge when he'd landed it. Nox's strength plus Rayne's momentum.

Bone broke. The air whooshed out of her lungs. And she went flying.

Rayne had already recovered. Obviously. Within the first thirty seconds, her sternum and ribs re-knitted, and her respiratory system sucked in Thailea's atmosphere, which her nacre converted into oxygen. But she let herself keep going backward as Rayne considered her latest Elden dream.

"Go back, Elden. You cannot know the mistake you are making." Condescension permeated the Primary's voice.

The man with him, the one he called Three Two Four, looked serene in his unusual dress. There was a sharpness to his double-crescent eyes which spoke of strategy.

They had expected Elden, but perhaps not along with Silence's armies. Several million Icari lingered on the threshold he'd created, waiting for orders.

How had it come to this?

"I want only my Silence. Where is she?" Elden shifted into Atramentous, keeping his eyes closed to spare them from Li.

For now.

They were in a glass space, occupied by blue faces and one green. They shared the same race as the Primary. Giants, few in number, but surrounded in opulence. The sight forced Elden to shut his eyes. He couldn't control his rage any longer.

Silence.

Elden's well of sorrow was bottomless, and he drank deep of whatever they offered. Gasps and cries erupted as people collapsed and bowed. Or begged. They filled him, and he passed this essence onto the Icari.

When Elden next opened his eyes, even the nameless Primary and his pet were on their knees. While they were incapacitated, he sought their lives and their minds.

Neither were a good man.

Three Two Four let his suffering carve a pit into his heart.

Once we dispose of Elden, I'll speak to the Primary of a little known advantage. Inanis could turn the tides in Tritan favor and spare me from my father's constant condemnation.

Remorse, the Primary, couldn't accept the world outside of his control.

If this rotten Icarus ever learned I know of Silence's location, he'll never stop interfering with the war against the Aegis. How did he gain these abilities? And how can I take them for myself?

Silence.

Li boiled behind Elden's eyes. There was no stopping this. He couldn't contain his fury.

Elden shifted his eyes, and his heart broke with the screams. Silence was all he wanted. Not this suffering.

When another brilliant white light competed against the sun in Elden's eyes, the Icari at his back retreated into Cinder. This additional source was cold, and a wind howled from it, sucking into a vacuum.

It tried to consume Elden. Should he let it take him? To see where it led?

Somewhere, Silence was out there, and he would not fail her.

Elden opened a conduit and stepped out of the strange, sterile place. The smell of fresh thyme let him know he'd fallen into one of Cinder's violet fields. Silence's soldiers surrounded him, waiting for orders.

But there were none to give.

Not yet.

Elden would try again. And again. Until he found her, or some disaster took him first, Elden would not stop looking for Silence.

Sixty seconds now.

Rayne front flipped and let her wings stabilize her. The forest was alive around her with birdsong and hopping critters. It smelled of fresh growth and dry leaves all at once. Taking this second to soak in some nature helped clear her head and lifted her spirits.

That's when Nox came in from below like a missile.

One swift sweep to the right, and he missed her. But boy, he corrected fast. With fierce determination on his face, Nox gut punched Rayne and took a grip on her arm to swing her onto the nearest branch.

No matter how strong Rayne became, a perfect punch to the gut still left her heaving. One from someone as strong as Nox left her spitting blood. Internal bleeding, anyone?

He didn't hold back either. Prepared to deliver an excellent curb stomp, Nox brought his combat boot down on Rayne's face.

Luckily, she caught it and put him off balance enough to shove him backward.

With a run-up, Rayne pulled out an old move, wrapping her legs around his waist and flipping him over her until she landed on top.

Nox grinned at her with a little salute. "Hello to old times."

Rayne leaned closer to his face, teasing a kiss as she said, "You've had three years to think of a way to counter this. Show me what you've got, Nox."

In less than three seconds, Nox hooked his legs and arms under hers and suplexed them up and over.

The bough switched places with the leaf canopy in a dizzying whirl of glowing silver and twinkling chrome.

Rayne was on bottom now, and Nox pinned her to the branch by her wrists over her head. They stared at each other from inches away, both of them breathing hard against her hair. Not that Rayne was checking herself out, but she'd intentionally worn a distractingly revealing sports bra.

Nox was ready, and it wasn't only his spicy scent which had tipped her off.

Wait.

Something was wrong.

Nox's expression went from hungry to bothered. He released her and stood, offering a hand.

Rayne took it, asking, "Did I hurt you or something?" She went to look him over, but Nox gently stayed her hand.

"No. I mean no more than usual." He patted his ribs and tried for a reassuring smile. "It's nothing to worry about."

This felt wrong. Ignoring this couldn't be right. When Nox looked away from her scrutiny, Rayne reached out and cupped his jaw, turned him back to her, and said, "Please tell me. What I like most about how we get along is how forthcoming we are with each other. I'll understand if you really want to keep something to yourself, but if you think I should know, even a little, please share."

Nox pressed her hand to his face and nuzzled into it. Everything about his expression looked haunted as he said, "I wanted you while you were pinned and helpless—" He raised his free hand to stop her from interrupting. "I know *you're* never really helpless, but it was the instinct. One I hoped to be rid of after everything..."

Oh.

Truth be told, Rayne had wanted him, too. For the same reason. It was a fierce passion which craved raw and painful intimacy. And it was an old desire. One which had inspired her writings from years ago, which Nox later used to ruin them. Rayne had wanted him for so long, and he did everything she'd asked in her writings, but...

Xelan.

Sometimes Rayne swore if their worst moment had taken place only between her and Nox—If Xelan had never been involved—Rayne and Nox could've been a couple sooner.

Was that wrong? It felt twisted, but it also felt right.

Shit, Rayne had gone too long without saying something, and Nox mistook it for rejection. He gently took her hand down from his face and stepped away—

"No!"

As Nox peered at Rayne with his heart open in his eyes—Elden, how could she salvage this?

Fearing her words, her thoughts, *herself*, Rayne said, "Nox, you can make a nightmare feel good."

His brows shot up, and he vigorously searched her eyes for honesty. For truth.

Rayne let it show and reached on tiptoe to rake her fingers through his hair. With more emotion than she could contain, she asked, "Do you understand?"

The onyx of Nox's eyes shone with respect at her honesty. He bowed with his head in answer.

The moment stretched. Rayne played with the little braids in his hair. Nox stared down at her in reverence, soaking in the affection—

Wallop.

They both burst into snickers, while Rayne stated the obvious. "There he goes again—"

Wait.

A lighter, brighter wallop followed.

Nox peered up at the canopy, saying, "I think he found her." Idly, he pulled Rayne against his side while they listened to the early morning conversation.

"Would you like to walk me back to the treeloft? Luckily, you didn't hurl me too far away." Rayne smirked when Nox met her eyes.

He squeezed her and kissed the top of her head. "Let's."

They flew down to the forest floor and held hands for the walk. The walloping chatter continued as they strolled home. Funny how Rayne had come to think of the treeloft that way. Or... Was Nox 'home?'

He interrupted her thoughts. "They should have children before too long. Little wallops."

Rayne grinned at the notion of a little family nearby—

"Have you... Has it occurred..." Stammering.

Nox rarely stammered over his words. He stopped trying and collected himself before asking, "What of pregnancy?"

Rayne's blood drained to her feet, and she nearly fainted. The walk came to a sudden halt as she stared up at him, wide-eyed. "I-Uh-Uhm... That's never—I don't think that would work with everything..."

"Breathe, Rayne."

Oh, yeah. She'd definitely stopped breathing. Deep inhale. Shaky exhale.

Nox continued, "I wasn't referring to us... reproducing. I was meaning to ask about your nacre. Female Icari say it's a nudge or an inkling which tells them to prepare to either keep or…" He couldn't bring himself to finish the last. Not after what Celindria had done to him.

Rayne squeezed his hand and assured, "I haven't noticed anything."

In awkward silence, they returned to the walk, more about the destination now than the journey.

As if he were thinking aloud, Nox said, "I suspect with everything about your nacre and how it affected your body… Perhaps…"

Maybe Rayne couldn't have children.

That would make such diabolical sense for them to prevent her from breeding. She *was* only a Weapon to destroy Enki. And why not take everything from her while Imminent were at it—

Sobs broke from Rayne.

If she were honest, she'd never considered children. How could Rayne when her life was one battle after another? But Nox…

He deserved a second chance to be a father. Like Xelan was—Like Rayne knew Korac must be—Nox would make a wonderful father.

It was in the way Nox put his arms around her and held her close, a quiet comfort. He let her cry without telling her to stop, because if this wasn't worth crying over, what was?

Nox wished he'd never thought of the question. While Rayne's heart broke in the forest, all he could do was hold her. Not one *individual* was responsible for her Weapon nacre and any other turmoil it inflicted upon her. Taken from a Gargantuan Tritan, who was murdered. Manipulated by Xelan and Celindria to develop the Weapon within. Given to her by well-meaning Tritans, looking to protect their world, which was given to them by Imminent. Locked by a virus transmitted to her by Silence—

There was not one *individual* for Nox to obliterate and avenge Rayne. And for the record, she'd already done the obliterating.

Tests.

Once they pulled Xelan in, Nox would ask him to run tests to see if Rayne was, in fact, sterilized. She would never ask out of embarrassment or her trademark martyrdom. It's possible Nox was the sterile one, only... Celindria's pregnancy negated that theory.

In an attempt at reassurance, he said, "After everything your physiology has endured, Xelan will need to perform a full examination. The virus, for instance? It could prevent pregnancy, and the Shadow have surely developed a cure for *their* virus by now. Dr. Suarez? He sounds capable. I doubt he's let this much time pass without learning how to reverse the effects—What is it?"

Rayne was staring up at him. She'd stemmed the tears and wiped them away, leaving her soft gaze on Nox, free of their filter. The look in her eyes...

She'd said she couldn't feel that way about him, but here and there, the warmth and softness in Rayne's expression said differently.

It was terribly confusing.

"Thank you." Rayne's voice was hoarse from crying. She ducked her gaze and tucked some loose strands of hair behind her ears, saying, "I don't know how I would've handled that revelation on my own." She gave a harsh laugh. "I doubt I would've even considered Xelan and Pablo helping me." The gratitude in her eyes when Rayne looked at him was too much for Nox.

To avoid it, he busied himself with picking twigs and leaves from her thick braids. "You would've found your way there in the end, your majesty." Nox cupped Rayne's chin and kissed her forehead before offering the crook of his arm. "Shall we?"

The rest of the walk was peaceful, filled with chatter about their training. How to improve certain tactics and appreciating each other's maneuvers.

At one point, Rayne confessed, "Rib shots are so much less painful without the rites."

Rites.

Nox chuffed and almost snorted. "If I didn't know any better, I'd say you were a masochist. Who looks at those bladed tops and thinks, 'I should shove them under my ribs and inside my calves'?"

"Hmm... Who looks at a girl cutting them out of her and thinks, 'I would so do her right now'?" Rayne shot him a 'gotcha' look.

Was *that* what Nox had wanted? He remembered realizing she was a Weapon, then. It was the moment he'd decided to write his Verse for Rayne, but if the former King of Cinder was being honest with himself...

Nox gave her a 'touché' nod.

"Hah! I knew it!" Rayne beamed with victory. "I could hear your heart pounding from across the planet—"

She looked so surprised when he twisted her arm behind her back and slammed her back against the tree base. Nox laced his hand into Rayne's free one and held it high, leaning into it so he was closer to her face.

Their heart raced, and her breasts heaved in that tiny sports bra. There was a glint in Rayne's eyes—A defiance Nox wanted to nurture. It told her to fight, to take him down and show him who was the true King around here.

Nox welcomed Rayne to try as he leaned in, putting his face closer to hers.

Closer.

The sweet scent of honeysuckle nearly melted Nox's resolve, but he left them a breath apart to say, "Get the door, your majesty." He released the hand behind her and squeezed her hip with a growl.

Rayne's lips parted, her eyes rolled back, and she looked up, baring her throat to Nox. The pulsing veins and arteries made for a tempting offer, but he would win this game.

Through gritted teeth, Nox insisted, "The door, Rayne." He purred with her name to soften it.

When she met his eyes again, he swore there was lightning in hers. A turbulent storm fighting against Rayne's restraint. She slammed her hand on the DNA scanner, conceding with an expectant sigh.

But Nox didn't reward her with a kiss. He left her in the wake of his scent and went inside, adjusting to the dim light quickly. Knowing Rayne tasted as sweet as she smelled made this game harder to play, but the chase was worth it.

She stepped into the doorway, silhouetted against the forest light. All curves and powerful limbs. Her braids were messy, as if she'd pulled them.

The love of Nox's life coolly glided past him and around the corner. The shower sounded, and he considered joining her. To comfort her more after the earlier revelation, but they'd need to leave this nest before too long.

Thirst. Hunger.

Nox's appetite for Vittle had expanded since Rayne had resurrected him in this less disciplined body. He'd gone twenty-four hours without supplements, and the need gnawed in his veins.

Protein helped, but not enough.

Resigned to wait until they went shopping later, Nox made a liquid substitute of strained fruit juices while Rayne showered. He leaned back against the island and watched. Breakfast and a show. He'd never tire of seeing her wet. She went through the motions, choosing not to tease him. He drank the sweet nectar, preferring it be her.

Rayne finished and dried before he'd taken a second drink—

Abruptly, she padded around the curtain, gloriously naked. She trembled, a sensual mix of vulnerability and confidence, as Rayne stepped into his personal space. Nox refused to relent to her, even as she took his drink, tipped it to her lips bottoms-up, and let the juices spill out and river down her skin.

Like the girl at the festival in Xelan's Verse. One of many instances Nox had chosen to forget but always wondered, 'What if…'

But *this* girl he knew inside and out.

Nox lost the game, ducking to lick a river before it splashed into her bellybutton. He kissed the contours of her abs as he made his way up between her ribs and sucked at the apex there.

Shaking, Rayne stepped back with a sigh. "Do you kneel to me?"

Yes.

Always.

Nox licked the juice from his lips, watching the effect on her before lying, "I've got more play in me, yet, your majesty. Perhaps it is *you* who needs to give into *me.*"

With a beautiful grin, Rayne promised, "There's no way I'm losing this."

━━━━━━━━━━━━━━━━━━━━━━━━

Rayne lied through her teeth. She was totally losing this. Look at him—Leaning there all shirtless from their training like a yummy treat. Licking his lips and shit—

She needed a fan.

There was no need to check her pulse, though. It was fluttering like a trapped hummingbird, and Nox grinned because he knew it.

Clothes.

Clothes would be good.

Nacres regulated internal temperature, but a glancing breeze of cool air still affected breasts the same. And when Nox's eyes appreciated the reaction, Rayne spun and went back to the shower.

Rinse off the sweet breakfast smoothie. Do not let Nox see how badly she wanted him.

As she rounded the sheet, he mercifully went off topic. "What is the agenda for today?"

This was easy to answer. Rayne dried off for a second time, saying, "We need to shop first for supplies. I was thinking we could go to Reipon. Do you have any objections to that?"

It was best to avoid Ishkur until they went to Night Rayne's Tomb in the evening.

"None." There was more humor in Nox's voice when he added, "We can check for the premiere date of your biopic while we're there."

Rayne froze in the middle of constructing clothes. Her life's story.

She couldn't keep the grin from spreading across her lips as Rayne thought about the recent steamy chapters it was missing.

Nox asked, "How *do* you feel about the film? I've been wondering..."

Considering her last thought, she said with some conviction, "It won't be accurate."

Rayne was pondering her hair when she rounded the sheet into the kitchen. Tonight's gear was a garnet minidress, folded off her shoulders and cut so short it didn't even brush her thigh-high boots. Made of soft black leather, their five-inch heels gave her some height. Maybe she should go with a braid crown—

The abrupt thundering of their heart made Rayne glance at Nox.

He looked away, but before doing so, she'd glimpsed naked desire so hot it nearly melted her on the spot.

Could they just spend another whole day in bed together? How long would it take to satiate this longing?

Weeks?

Years…

When Rayne realized it might take even longer for her, she cleared her throat and looked away, too.

Finish the mission.

Then worry about the future of this relationship.

Rayne collected the comb, some sleh oil, and went to Nox, hoping this might ease them both. Without question, he took the oil and combed it through her hair until it formed the waves she loved so much. She said, "I was thinking a braid crown. Do you know how to make one?"

Nox gave a little chuckle, saying, "I can try. Why do you play with your hair so much?" Their fingers worked together on opposite sides of her head to braid along the sides.

"Because it's healthy, and I always wanted it this long. Ever since I was a little girl obsessed with pigtails and braids…" Like when she'd first met Xelan. Her voice was soft as she admitted, "That's how he'll always see me. A little girl in need of rescuing. I love him for it, but…"

Nox paused in his weaving. "It makes venturing out as a grown woman almost criminal."

Rayne turned and gazed up at him. Breathy, she said, "I don't want to break his heart."

There was so much understanding in his eyes, but also a denial or refusal to face it. Nox went back to twining her hair. "Well, that leaves you with two options. Stay his little girl forever or turn to a life of crime. Runaway with a handsome fugitive and hideout together on a forbidden planet—Oh, wait…"

It was so unexpected, Rayne laughed and nearly lost her place in the strands. After they combined their efforts into one long braid, she patted the counter. "Come on. While we were… *busy* over the last day or so, something interesting must've happened." She refused to look him in the face while hers was burning and, instead, grabbed a tab, hopped on the counter, and skimmed through headlines.

Before he could join her, Nox faltered and caught himself on the island.

Rayne peered up with concern. "What's wrong?"

He shook his head as if dizzy. "As hybrids, Xelan engineered the Progeny to rely less on Vittle nutrients. It explains why you aren't starving, despite not eating a supplement this morning."

Oh.

"You can drink me."

"You can drink me."

Those were words Nox had never thought he would hear in this lifetime, from the only voice from which he'd dreamt of hearing them.

Rayne's short dress deliciously exposed her shoulders, collarbone, and neck. Such delicate soft skin bared for his teeth. He'd taken a step toward her before stopping himself. "I can make it to Reipon. I don't think you're prepared for this."

That did it.

The stubborn set of her shoulders, the lift of her chin, and the challenge in Rayne's voice all confirmed Nox had already lost. "We've been intimate together. I think I can handle your teeth in me—"

Nox was in front of her, and Rayne's gasp only fueled his hunger. He gripped a fistful of her braided hair and pulled until she arced her neck for him. The brazen look in her eyes almost unmade him. Roughly, he knocked her knees wide around him, pushed her satin panties aside, and—

Rayne cried out and held onto Nox. Her nails pierced his shoulders as he found home, and he loved it. He kissed over their fluttering pulse, captured inside her throbbing carotid. Cupping her ass, Nox drew his hips away, slowly—The way she liked it. The anticipation before the next thrust was always her favorite, and he tantalized her with it. Teased her with elongated teeth grazing across the artery.

Breathy, Rayne begged, "Nox, please," and rolled her hips, asking for him with more than her lips.

Fierce as lightning, he struck gold twice. Rayne screamed his name, and Nox stopped pulling her hair to run his fingers through it as he swallowed liquid star dust. A rhythm formed while he drew this precious crimson liquid and her pleasure from her simultaneously. Like with all the positions, Rayne quickly acclimated, wrapped her legs around him, and gave to him what she wanted while he took from her what he needed.

Eternity wouldn't take either of them soon, but Nox wanted her to know he would always be hers.

Close now.

Nox squeezed Rayne's hips as she welcomed him with a gasp, head thrown back.

None of that.

He unlatched from her throat, cupped her nape, and brought her forehead to his. Eyes closed, Nox soaked in every sensation of Rayne wanting him, and they surged together. Give and take. Equally measured. Perfect in their match.

Rayne opened her eyes to let Nox see. To see how they glistened and sparked in her arrival. Widened as if surprised. Every time. He gave that to her, and he wanted to give her more.

Days more.

Centuries or longer if she'd have him. Nox would forever want to see her this way. Alive and electric in his arms.

Rayne made an adorable sound when he lifted her off the counter and swung her to the kitchen island. She laid back and let him see all of her spread out before him. Nox could break out his wings and cradle her, but he had other plans.

Slow.

Down.

This was how Rayne liked it most, taking in every sensation, drawn out and prolonged. Nox would mark every surface of this loft with her. Starting with the kitchen. But first, sweet torture.

Nox separated them altogether, and Rayne's eyes fluttered open, gazing with an unspoken question.

As her clothes receded—all but the slip of black satin protecting her modesty—Nox spared Rayne a knowing look which brought a pretty blush to her cheeks. Smirking, he accused, "One of us has developed a fetish." He hooked his thumbs into the silky obstacle. "One of us enjoys me slipping this delicate material off your soft creamy skin..."

Rayne sighed.

"Lifting your hips to give me permission. Sliding them down your long legs and over your toes. Tossing them anywhere to be recovered later, like a game." Nox kissed her calf. Then the inside of the other knee. "But Rayne, whether it's your fetish or mine, I always win the prize—"

He knew her head went back before she could say a word, and he claimed his reward.

Between Rayne's thighs, Nox growled, "You're insatiable. You have the appetite of a Valkyrie. One day, I'll have the time to wear you down, but until then..."

Rayne was pretty sure facing Nox while sitting up was her favorite position. Their sex parade across the loft was ending on the couch. He always knew how to shatter her and bring her back together. Each time, she closed her eyes, threw her head back, and made some kind of sound. Whatever felt right. But this time, her eyes were open enough to see Nox.

He was basking in it, watching her orgasm.

After they finished, they snuggled on the way-too-small sectional, eye-to-eye.

Unable to contain her curiosity anymore, Rayne asked, "Why do you keep your eyes open? I've never seen them closed."

Nox trailed a finger down the bridge of her nose and booped it. "You close your eyes to feel the pleasure more intensely, yes?"

She blushed, bit her lip, and nodded.

He smiled a smile Rayne only saw when they were like this before saying, "When you're experiencing those moments, you aren't over thinking about your moral reservations or contemplating the fate of the galaxy. You let it melt away; you're free. I keep my eyes open because that's when I find you the most beautiful, and I don't want to miss a second of it."

Rayne swallowed from the intensity of Nox's words, despite his gentle caresses throughout. The confession affected her deeply. Before she knew it, he brushed his thumb across one cheek, then the other.

His voice was gentle as Nox said, "I didn't mean for you to cry."

What was the opposite of heartbreak?

Love.

Rayne loved Nox.

As she stared into the concern in his eyes, she wasn't sure what to do about it. Except Rayne wanted to wash away the fear there. She kissed the man she loved, desperate to steal Nox's breath away as he stole hers. To feel him and comfort him and show him how much his words meant to her—

Rayne's stomach growled.

Rudely.

Nox's warm chuckle meant the world to her as he explained, "You've fed me, now you're the one who needs feeding. We should head to Reipon." He kissed her, which was so *not* the way to get her out of bed.

But suddenly, only one thing was on Rayne's mind. "Do you think they'll have ice cream?"

Dressed again and loaded with bagfuls of Vittle supplements, Nox and Rayne strolled the main thoroughfare of a Reipon city under its green sky with its multiple suns. He told her stories of a Lamia pirate who'd aided Umbra, while she enjoyed some kind of teriyaki meat on a stick. She interrupted him to say, "Let me guess. After he saw you naked, he asked if you wanted to star in a film?"

Nox laughed and kissed the top of her head. "You knew exactly where the story was headed."

Actually, she'd seen him naked, and it was certainly worthy of the big screen.

"Wait, I think…" Nox peered over the crowd before grinning down at her. "There's ice cream."

Sweet strawberry goodness. Rayne moaned as the creamy stuff hit her tongue and cooled her throat. "Oh, this… This is divine."

Nox was still grinning as he watched her enjoy it. His own cone of Reipon papaya dripped. Rayne laughed at his distracted state and leaned close to say, "Here. Let me." She kept her eyes on him as she tasted it with a drawn out roll of her tongue.

Making a grown man who'd been around for seven million years gape was an accomplishment. Rayne deserved a badge—

A soft cry made them both spin around.

Children and their parents surrounded a small, grounded craft as a Lamia climbed into it. Pandering to the crowd, he shouted, "Over here, people! Watch as I take off in my own Mercury Turbo!"

Rayne almost fell out, and it took everything in her not to burst into laughter. When she glanced at him, Nox was looking away to cover a snort. Delighted, she pulled him along. "We *need* to see this."

They parted the crowd and made it to the front, where the Lamian pilot was settling into the cockpit. It was indeed a little silver craft, much like the one Xelan described in his Verse. Even though she possessed wings, Rayne fiercely wanted a go in it.

The pilot scanned the crowd and—

He did a double-take in Rayne's direction, gasping, "My lady."

Rayne frowned, peering around before glimpsing Nox's knowing smirk.

Oh.

Rayne was reticent, but she'd play along if it meant she could fly it. "Yes?"

The Reipon pilot—Was he a Prince? Were all Lamias Princes?—The pilot reached out a hand and spouted poetry at her. "You are *the* most exquisite Rayne tribute I have ever seen. Please, will you bestow upon me a kiss for luck on my maiden flight?"

Rayne was definitely wearing a hood from now on. She glanced at Nox, who grinned and nodded, before she stepped over to the plane and kissed the orange-scaled cheek the pilot offer her. The dry texture surprised her, and the musty scent which followed wasn't unpleasant but intriguing—

The Lamia winked.

Rayne had lingered too long. Blushing, she returned to Nox, who pulled her against his side.

"After receiving the luckiest charm in all of Iona Pax, I will dazzle you with a feat of reverse engineering. Step back, ladies and gentlemen and those who identify otherwise. Witness true brilliance!"

The Lamian pilot pressed his palm to a disc, and the mechanics within activated with a quiet hum. A little shock wave of dust spread from the replica as it began to hover. Higher and higher, until he was above Nox's head and higher still.

Exhilarated, Rayne stood on tiptoe to whisper to Nox, "I'd kiss him again if he'd race me."

With a chuckle, Nox said, "*I'd* kiss him to see that."

This was happiness. This moment right here—

Waves rolling onto a beach, sandcastles and sunscreen, a boardwalk sticky from melted ice cream.

The space surrounding the mock Mercury Turbo smelled of a pivotal memory in Rayne's life, and there was no way to shut it off. Alerted by it, Nox glanced around to measure the crowd, but as far as they could see, no one had noticed.

Especially as the pilot counted down. "Three... Two... Ready. Set. Go!"

The replica zipped away over the bazaar, flying above the shops and maneuvering through the thoroughfare.

Cheers erupted from the crowd, and none louder than Nox and Rayne. They clapped as the replica swooped over them and around to do it again. Much to their delight, the pilot halted his replica dead center in the circle and lowered it in the exact place from where it had started.

That's when Rayne realized most of the crowd were Lamias, Caprents, Luks, and Yun—Citizens of the races who couldn't fly. Sure, they could build mechsuits as the Pil Dwarves did, or they could buy a personal aircraft from a well-meaning engineer in Reipon's bazaar.

"Thank you! Thank you!" The pilot stood in his cockpit, bowing and waving to his audience of potential buyers. Many already flooded into his shop to place orders. He shot Rayne another wink before announcing, "And don't forget to attend my cousin's premiere of *Rayne's Verse*. Three nights from now at the Palatial Grounds. The King Elect is providing free fare and comfort, so come join us as we celebrate our brave martyr's life."

The air rushed out of Rayne. She spun away and clutched her ribs. It hurt to breathe. Nox was right there, but given the circumstances, there wasn't much he could do to comfort her. Although, his presence helped.

Without knowing everything—Anything about Nox—How could the Shadow get her story right?

Nox rubbed a soothing circle on her back, and Rayne could draw enough air to say, "*I want to tell it. I should get to share my Verse.*"

"Once we finish this, you'll have your chance." Okay, so Nox's logic was seriously comforting.

Rayne took a deep breath and, on the exhale, she said, "You're right. You know what? Let's just eat some more crazy foods and check out one of Iuo's toy stores."

That got it out of him. A sexy smirk spread across Nox's lips as his chuckle rumbled deep in his chest. "I mean… If you insist."

Unable to control it, Rayne beamed. This was a happy day—

That was odd.

Across the thoroughfare, Rayne swore she saw a Mon3 drone staring at her. That made the third one today. Shaking herself, she dragged Nox to a grilled fruit stand. Yun peaches were to die for, and Luk eel was so tender it melted in her mouth. Engineers from all across the empire displayed their mechanical wares. Some were as big as the Mercury Turbo replica and some were small enough to fit in the palm of Rayne's hand.

"I want to buy this little tinkering gizmo for Pax and maybe a microphone for Echo—Xelan says she's already whistling like a Lyrik. What do you think, Nox?"

Rayne glimpsed a look pass over his face before he could hide it, and she instantly understood. Any talk of the kids was too close to a reality they weren't far from. Soon, the Shadow would discover them, and this little secret life of theirs would end.

A hug wouldn't fix everything, but it would let Rayne whisper this against Nox in public. "We'll still be together. I didn't make the decision to sleep with you lightly. And think about it? You'll get to meet your nephew and niece. See your brothers again—Not all of it will be hard, and I think with a little work, even the hard stuff will get easier—Yip!"

While Rayne was talking, Nox lifted her onto a picnic table and held her there. This evoked memories of their fun in the kitchen earlier, and she couldn't keep it out of her eyes.

This dress was so short Rayne could feel her effect on Nox. In public! Oh, her cheeks burned—

Over his shoulder, she spied another Mon3 drone staring at them. It was always a different one.

"I see them," Nox growled against her neck, kissing it. "They're Celindria's agents. We may need to leave soon."

A little breathy, Rayne said, "Okay. Let me buy the gifts—"

"I heard a rumor some of Razor's old contacts were cutting loose and offing themselves. Something about the Probability Matrix shrinking."

The voice came from one of luo's shops.

Rayne met Nox's eyes. Communication passed between them without words, and they confirmed it with a nod. She paid for the presents for the kids before they entered the toy store, pretending to peruse. Well, sorta pretending. Rayne was really curious and very blushy about the whipped sleh oil lubricant.

Nox started smirking the moment they stepped in and never stopped, fueling the redness in her cheeks.

The female merchant carried on with her conversation with a chatty customer. "Well, I heard they were quitting the simulation because they lost their volition to some big daddy Razor impostor."

A nearby Caprent scoffed. "You think losing two hundred million realities in thirty-six hours isn't worth ripping your own nacre out?"

Between the first customer and the latest loud mouth, the merchant back peddled on her own assumptions. "No, I'm just saying you can't eliminate these things—Hey, honeysuckle."

Rayne's eyes grew wide, but she turned and looked at the merchant.

The female Lamian had a pretty smile as she said, "If you're buying the lube to have anal sex with your fella there of great prowess, you might wanna consider buying the aloe vera flush. It'll help with the soreness after and considering the size of him, it'll be the best thirty credits you'll ever spend. You'll thank me later when you come back for a refill."

Rich, masculine laughter erupted from Nox and seared Rayne's face. Especially as she searched and collected the aloe vera flush and paid for it at the counter under intense scrutiny.

Again, the lady's smile was super pretty as she packaged Rayne's items in tissue paper and a cute purple bag. The merchant glanced at Nox and said to Rayne, "*Enjoy.*"

It was obvious the small group was done discussing Imminent news with Nox and Rayne present, so after a polite and bashful nod from her, they left.

The entire walk out of the bazaar and into the field from which Elden had Seamswalked them, Rayne felt Nox staring at her with unspoken expectation.

"Not a word, mister."

Eyes and ears.

Everywhere.

Celindria was an empire unto herself, and she knew *everything.*

We are Eternal.

No one can best us.

Soon we will feel everything.

The display at the Reipon bazaar nearly made her vomit from all of her toys. Nox and Rayne holding hands, leaning into each other, and buying novelties together, did nothing to remove the sour taste from Celindria's mouth.

Disgust.

The last time she'd felt this emotion so viscerally was after Celindria had awakened from her night of dispassionate sex with Remorse. She'd scrubbed until her skin bled—Until she saw bone. That's how she felt now.

Revulsion fueled her work in Paradise. Celindria and Pax had successfully isolated the vaccine in the blood samples she'd taken before Enki was destroyed. Tameka and her Shadow team had rushed into Celindria's lab, and the latter took advantage of their captivity for her own research.

True, the vaccines at the time were a complete surprise and had prevented Celindria from stealing their volition, but now...

"Excellent work, little brother."

Pax beamed, not fully understanding the key he'd handed her to their souls. He said, "You'll bring them back here and make them see, right, sister? Make them appreciate your Paradise, so they won't resist this time?"

Celindria forced a reassuring smile. "Of course. I will do everything I can."

It wasn't a lie. All she wanted was to show them the light, but unlike Pax, Celindria knew they would rather stay in the dark. With this breakthrough, she could mutate the virus and administer it as easily as she'd taken Korac's blood—

A sudden whir made them both spin toward the DNA extraction instrument.

Nox.

Is it time?

Will he recognize us?

How should we greet him?

Sex immediately upon his revival would provide the only cure to Celindria's current state.

"Go on, Pax. Tell me if it's ready."

He smiled excitedly before rushing to the machine. After Pax scanned it, he beamed.

Celindria practically floated to the instrument, retrieved the sample of Korac's DNA, and loaded the patch. This was it. This would wake her Nox.

Upon contact with her creation's skin, the patch and all its nanites would absorb into Nox and infuse him with the final upgrade. For the first time in a long time, Celindria felt something in her chest. A faint trace of warmth. It brought tears to her eyes.

"Sister?"

When she pulled Pax in for a hug, this time it felt tangible and right. Since he was born, Celindria had waited to say this and finally mean it. "I love you."

If only she could tell Hope…

But the glimpse of joy was gone as fast as it came.

Pax squeezed, and Celindria felt nothing. When he said, "I love you, too," it rang empty inside, made all the worse because she'd felt it only a moment ago.

"Let's wake him."

The walk down the considerable breadth of the lab was filled with Celindria's voices. The chorus of a billion she could only ignore to stay sane. They sang of this moment.

He will love us.
Then we will feel love.
It's all coming together.

As before, Nox still faced out over the empire. Celindria wanted him to see her success in his first moment to better understand her aims.

Pax stayed behind, saying, "Go to him. I'll be right here."

She shot him a fake smile before going to Nox's side. There, Celindria reached up, kissed his cheek, and then she took his hand.

The patch absorbed into his palm within a heartbeat, and the statue beside Celindria grew warm. Hot, even. She let go of his hand or lest it burn. Now would be the time to feel concern.

Cobalt flushed Celindria's creation, and citron flickered beneath Nox's skin. The form convulsed and sputtered. Started. Stopped. Sputtered again.

Celindria stepped back and narrowed her gaze.

Pax called, "Should that happen?"

It was an excellent question, and as soon as Celindria formed the thought, everything stopped. Nox was still and breathing normally.

With a glance at her brother, Celindria took a tentative step toward her soon-to-be lover. Then another. When Nox remained calm, she went to him and checked his vitals. All were within normal range. She went to his front and gazed up at him.

"Nox? Can you hear me?"

Black eyes opened and looked down at Celindria. She supposed if she possessed a normal range of emotions, a thrill would shoot through her. Instead, she kept examining him, waiting.

Wetting her lips, Celindria tried again, "Nox, do you recognize me?"

Pax leaned around Nox so she could see him. He asked a question with eyes just like their father's.

Nox raised a hand so abruptly, Celindria's body flinched out of reflex, but relaxed as it caressed her face.

He recognizes us!

We've done it!

Yes. What a successful abomination we've made—

Both hands went around Celindria's neck and squeezed before she could react. Black velvet immediately darkened her vision, and she fell to her knees.

"No!" Pax.

With a collapsed trachea, Celindria couldn't scream or tell Pax to stay back. To leave Nox alone. She would fix it—

Squeeze.

He would tear into her throat and rip it out at this rate. Her repair systems kept trying, but his hands kept squeezing.

Celindria went blind, and her nerve endings tingled. Two more seconds, and this would be how it ends—

Air punched into her lungs, and she could suddenly see again.

The vengeful sparkle dimmed in Nox's eyes.

No.

His grip loosened, and after another moment, Nox collapsed.

No!

While Celindria's hard and soft tissue repair systems recovered her throat, she checked Nox's vitals. His pallor was awful, dull and lifeless—Drained.

Panic.

Celindria was experiencing panic as she looked up from her dead lover to her powerful little brother and shrieked, "Pax, what have you done?!"

"I saved you."

Kill Pax.

No, don't. We love him.

What is Paradise without Nox?

What are we without him?

XII FLARE

WITHIN ISHKUR, ON THE CONTINENT OF CINDER II, CITY DISTRICTS TWINKLED LIKE JEWELS IN A SEA OF CRANBERRY INK AND FORESTS OF BLACK SENTINELS. Overseers zipped between Ionas in the sky, free of an exploding star and blue as Rayne's eyes by day. As dark as Xelan's by artificial night. The space scrapers formed a tidy row on the major artery, pulsing with all manner of life. Each one sought entertainment and company at this late hour. So many unaware of the threat beneath their feet.

Night Rayne's Tomb slept below, waiting to open her eyes and stretch in her bed of vice.

Nox and Rayne stood at the entrance in a pool of white light, simply another pair of faces in a crowd, eagerly awaiting entry. Korac would approve of Nox's coat, long and leather with a hood to hide his features. Black, of course. But after Rayne's remark about blue on Nox, he was wearing a cobalt button down for her. And as always, the pants matched the coat. She'd helped with his hair, and he'd basked in the comfort of her fingers entwining with the strands.

Rayne was wearing the same short dress as earlier, with one recent addition. A paper mask she cut to look like a butterfly and colored to match her clothes. With a piece of twine, she fastened it to her face. It should look silly, but came across more as mysterious and whimsical. Certainly turned heads.

The crowd's chatter turned into a roar of excitement as music began to throb from the venue. A claustrophobic surge pressed them toward the door—More contact than Nox could take, and the overstimulation left him dizzy.

Rayne's warm hand entwined in his fingers. She peered up at him through the holes in her mask, and without words, he knew what she was saying.

They were always safe together. For Eternity's sake, she could level the city on her own. There was no danger here.

Aside from the random Icarean female with her eyes locked on them for six minutes straight.

Before leaving the treeloft, Rayne and Nox had talked about the agents in the crowd.

"Do you think it's volition?" Rayne had asked, as she brushed hair from his eyes.

Pulling her closer to him in bed, Nox said, "Doubtless. We should mark their number, but they gain nothing of her abilities. Easily disposable and easily disposed."

Rayne placed her hand over his nacre as she asked the next. "What about the Probability Matrix? Should we try to investigate—"

"Shh, my dear martyr. One thing at a time."

Celindria's reach had extended to Ishkur. This was troubling, but good to know—

A horrible alarm rang through the deep ramp into Night Rayne's Tomb from the street, and the nacre shields vanished. Thousands poured into the venue, drawing around Nox and Rayne like river water through rapids. Not to give themselves away, the pair let the current take them, spilling into a wide open… Tomb for lack of a better word.

Four walls were spread a mile apart in all directions, displaying a projected scene. A woman on a stage, singing and dancing along a gauntlet of blades and razor wire. She bore a resemblance to Rayne, which was the only reason Nox recognized it as her Shadow friend, Lucy. This monolith was a memorial to her band, and it played what could only be her music. These were songs about Nox and Rayne's fictional—now real—romance.

Nice beat.

Expert use of synthetic sounds.

And a little string.

"I like this song," Nox confessed, while leaning into Rayne.

Her laughter was a bright burst of joy, and he was proud it had come from him. It died quickly, as she whispered in his ear, "Have you seen them?"

Everywhere.

All races.

People stopped in the middle of conversations, ordering drinks, or dancing to notice Nox and Rayne. Acting 'natural' was outside of Celindria's capabilities. He said, "At least this means we're in the right place."

But now what?

Caedes said he would send agents from the Shadow to investigate the human trafficking ring in Ishkur's underground, but while they contended with that, Nox and Rayne should try to lure out Celindria. Or at least determine her *actual* whereabouts.

He leaned down to say as much, but the look in Rayne's eyes stopped him.

Mischief.

She'd inherited Xelan's brand of trouble making.

"Let's dance." Rayne pulled for Nox to join her on the dance floor.

After a second of consideration, he allowed it and followed her into the throng. The song was bassy and enticing. Even among all these bodies, they stood out with his size and her mask. The regular attendees gaped and whispered of sighting the pair from Cinder's races, but those under Celindria's volition glared through a venomous lens.

Nox opened his wings and enclosed Rayne with him, pushing some gasping onlookers away. At her quirked brow, he offered, "I suppose I'm an introvert."

Rayne laughed, wrapped her arms around him, and slipped a hand under his shirt and onto his back. On tiptoe, she kissed his neck. Their pulse raced with the spontaneous PDA.

This was not the mischief Nox had expected; however, it would certainly lure Celindria's attention if the mad woman truly believed she and Nox were the Eternal Bind. A ploy should do the trick—

Rayne nibbled over Nox's carotid, and it was no longer a ploy for him. He growled and gripped her nape, pulling her back to lift her mask and see her eyes.

Lost in passion, Rayne ran her tongue along her lips, and that was all the invitation Nox needed. Static charged their electric kiss and surged through his winged barrier.

They would do this.

In public.

Nox didn't care.

Here and there massive caissons—structural support—ruined the venue's open field effect. Rayne pulled Nox over to one in the dark, outside a ring of colorful and ultraviolet lamps. About the time her back hit the wall, Nox lifted her up and opened his wings. Rayne wrapped her legs around him and moaned when he ground into her, finding her ready. When she pulled, the buttons flew off Nox's shirt, and Rayne greedily put her hands on him. He could *not* get enough of their scents together. Her nails raked the back of his neck, and Nox squeezed her ass, positioning her for—

"Rayne? Does Xelan know you're alive?"

Whoever this auburn-haired male with freckles and a pair of dead eyes was, Nox hoped he brought a body bag.

The second Rayne recognized Matt's voice, she froze in Nox's arms.

Oh, Elden. What was she—

Rayne and Nox had almost...

Oh, wow.

An entire audience of people were watching the spectacle Rayne had made of herself. Her mask was lost and sorta pointless by now. Ergo Matt standing only a few feet away with nothing interpretable on his freckled face.

With an aggressive frown, Nox looked between Rayne and the ginger. Only instinct sparkled in Nox's eyes, and the interruption had clearly disappointed him.

Pinned to the wall, Rayne patted her partner, who looked equally surprised by their position when he set her down. Her cheeks burned as Nox relaced the ties to his pants. His deep baritone was hoarse from the almost sex, muttering, "Sorry."

That snapped Rayne back to him. "Do *not* apologize for this. I initiated everything, and it looks like the general idea of it worked."

Volition controlled people surrounded them with their wild eyes and their empty expressions. Celindria was behind those eyes, which once belonged to hundreds of people from various races and genders, dressed in club wear or combat gear. They hid among gawking innocents in the crowd. None of them looked armed, at least.

Matt noted them, too, asking with a thumb in their direction, "Do you think they're admirers of your work?"

At first Rayne thought he was talking to her until...

Lucy appeared from behind Matt, saying, "I don't know, but they're creeping me out." She was in a combat stance, keeping their backs together while assessing their unfriendly company. At Rayne and Nox, she smiled and waved, "Hi! You couldn't have come at a better time."

Frowning, Rayne exchanged a look with Nox, who shrugged.

Matt grinned at them. "Yeah. Thanks for the distraction."

Rayne frowned. "For what?"

An explosion ripped through the farthest caisson. And the next. And the next.

"For that."

The blast spheres were small, sending out waves of dust and tiny embers, but nothing large or lethal. Ringing replaced Lucy's vocals in Rayne's ears, and the place emptied fast into dead silence.

Matt and Lucy's blasts revealed thin support beams of nacre glass hidden inside hollow spaces with two-way walls. Booths lined the insides, and hundreds of people spread across them, bleeding from various places—All dead. Those weren't caissons. They were VIP lounges for the vice lords.

Little Bethany Roberts, Kyle's baby sister, stood in the center of the closest one, and her expression chilled Rayne.

Satiated.

Bethany looked full and ready for a nap.

A stirring of people behind them brought Rayne and Nox around. "Excuse me. Coming through. We're with the cool crowd." It was a Mon3 drone and a Tritan. The drone was grinning as far as his needle-nose mouth could allow. "Oh, my god. It *is* you—Oh, sorry."

Nox stopped the drone from reaching Rayne with a look.

"Puk." Matt's tone contained a warning.

"I know, I know, man, but wow. King Rayne, I am a huge admirer of your work, and former King Nox, mad respect for everything you did for Cinder."

Both Nox and Rayne raised their brows at the blatant hero worship.

The Tritan waved with a bladed ring. "Hi, I'm Yito. This is Puk."

Oh, introductions.

Rayne tugged on Nox's open shirt, blushed because she'd destroyed his buttons, and said, "This is Matt, Lucy, and that's Bethany. These are the agents Caedes sent."

Matt waved, Bethany bared her teeth in a grin, and Lucy said, "Well, you can't forget—"

"Dammit, Ginger! I told you *not* to burn the place down!" Rayne recognized Pehton's voice coming from Matt's palm device.

With his Arkansan drawl, Matt laid the charm on thick for the Lyriki Warden. "Ma'am, I assure you the flames are all out, and the place is still standing. We just thought a little fireworks show would clear the innocent bystanders from the crowd. That's all." He winked at Rayne.

It was an empty wink.

The next voice over the device belonged to a male. Maybe an Icarus? Rayne faintly recognized him as he said, "We've got frightened people out here. The Co-Emperors will *not* be happy."

Lucy beamed. "Well, Bones, they will be once they see who we found—"

"No!" Nox and Rayne both shouted at once and cut her off.

Not at all hurt, Lucy looked more intrigued as she tried to recover her message. "We found Amaryna and the people responsible for the trafficking ring."

Rayne sighed with relief, and Nox looked a question down at her. She wasn't sure how to explain it, but this wasn't the right time to include the others.

Pehton sounded genuinely pleased. "That's wonderful news. We'll be down there to make arrests as soon as we finish organizing the traumatized people outside—"

"Sorry, ma'am. No arrests to be made. They were dead when we got here." Matt gestured at the VIP lounges. "Bethany's consuming their memory banks now to help with the investigation. We'll be up soon. Over and out."

Puk took in the space with a frown in his multi-faceted eyes. "What is with the lingering chill in this place? The vibes are so wrong here." He was staring at Celindria's agents, most of whom were drones.

Yito asked, "Why haven't they run? And why do they look like Bethany on a hunt?"

This was too much.

Rayne's head swam keeping up everyone and who knew what—Why couldn't she return to the treeloft and cozy up next to Nox with a cup of tea?

As if he sensed it, too, Nox placed his warm hand on her back and soothed her. She didn't realize, but in her distress, Rayne had turned into his chest and hid. This would not do. The Shadow were many dozens of people who cared about her. If she couldn't handle this small portion of them, how could she find comfort in their fully assembled numbers?

It was Celindria.

Her glaring at them was overwhelming Rayne. They were on the cusp of a fight while surrounded by people she loved. It was splitting her concentration and rendered her magnesium field all but useless. It wouldn't do any good to blind Rayne's team and these innocent people under Celindria's control.

Nox kissed the top of her head and murmured, "Talk to me."

Rayne gazed all the way up at him. The love in his eyes warmed her through to her toes. He would abandon their plan to take her away for her sake.

But that's not how martyrs worked.

Rayne smiled, and it was sad. Soon. She should tell Nox about how her feelings have grown for him soon. And soon, they would tell their family together.

If Matt's bewildered expression was any indication, it might take some convincing. Until then...

After taking a step back from Nox, Rayne pulled Night Killer from her nacre.

"Oh, sick. That's awesome."

Yito nudged Puk to stop, but Rayne kind of appreciated the drone's fanatic playfulness.

In awe, Lucy confessed, "I wish I would've thought of that for the shows."

With a respectful nod at Nox, Matt moved closer to the powerful pair. Lucy followed, signaling Bethany to join them. Everyone formed a circle with their backs together, taking in Celindria's small army of potentially innocent people. Nox was on Rayne's right, and Matt was on her left. She was happy to consider the redhead a friend, but this was not how she expected to return to the Shadow.

As if he sensed the direction of her thoughts, Matt said, "Look, we don't know each other all that well, but I credit you for saving my life—"

"Our lives," Lucy added.

"—By introducing us to Xelan and letting us join you at the first Iona. I'll keep your secret, if you can promise me one thing."

Nox looked down at Rayne, who looked at Matt. A little reticent, she asked, "What's that?"

Yito sighed.

Puk let out a single laugh, as if he knew the answer.

Lucy and Bethany exchanged a beaming look.

When Matt grinned at her, the hair raised on the back of Rayne's neck.

"I get to crush some skulls."

Rayne's human friend was interesting. Although, all Shadow must be interesting. At the vacant grin in Matt's eyes, she nodded, assenting to his hunting conditions.

And there was no hunt more momentous than this one. To face Celindria's agents with Rayne at Nox's side and a circle of trained warriors at his back—What more could Nox ask for?

Of course, he knew the answer. Xelan and Korac, reunited and banded together for the sake of their people once more.

Nox's brothers...

Soon.

At the very notion, Nox grinned and unsheathed his daggers. Violence was the only thing Imminent in this place tonight.

With Night Killer firm in hand, Rayne called, "Celindria, show yourself and let these people go!" Warmth and strength radiated from Nox's lover, and his chest swelled with it.

The drone, named Puk, bounced while saying, "I can't believe I'm fighting alongside the *actual* War King."

With her dark blue eyes on the enemy, Lucy warned, "Watch out for the lightning."

Matt nudged her in commiseration. "And the magnesium field is a doozy."

Yito wondered aloud, "Will we be in the sequel, then?"

Puk jumped on this idea. "Ooo, yeah! I'll bet Iuo lets me play myself since I have acting experience."

Lucy teased, "Porn doesn't count."

The young girl with untamed hair and wildness in her honey-colored eyes snickered.

These were the soldiers who thwarted Imminent, secured an Aegis Dyson's Sphere, and established an empire. Nox peered down at Rayne with a quirked brow, and she beamed. These were her people.

Meanwhile, Celindria's agents stared until the tension swallowed all the fun remarks and left behind a bunch of anxious fighters, itching to make the first move.

Finally, the goth Lamian Prince on the right said, "I lost something precious today."

The Mon3 drone straight ahead added, "And it cannot be retrieved nor repaired."

Over the speakers came, "I am owed what is mine."

"And nothing will stop me from taking it."

A hundred voices delivered the message in unison, ringing through the tomb.

Beside Nox, Rayne shivered as they both realized what Celindria wanted. Rayne lifted her eyes to him, and he loved her for what they said. She would fight to keep Nox out of Celindria's clutches. He was no damsel in distress, but Rayne could act as his knight in shining armor anytime.

Rayne twirled Night Killer before planting it on the floor hard enough to form a crater. The sound thundered throughout the tomb. Staking her claim, she challenged, "Come and take him from me."

Nox smirked and shook his head incredulously.

At his back, Puk vibrated with energy, murmuring, "Here we go…"

This wasn't an action movie where enemies came in polite waves, one-by-one. All of Celindria's agents attacked at once in a furious blur of kicks and punches.

Nox blocked the first blow to his chest with his arms crossed and kneed a female Luk in the face. She gasped, "Come with me," before falling over with a bloody nose. Next came a Pil Dwarf in a mechsuit.

Rayne swatted her first comer with a deft blow to the head from Night Killer, rendering the female Caprent unconscious.

Matt sent his first opponent flying with one fantastic roundhouse kick, prompting Rayne to shout, "Non-lethal blows. We need to keep these people alive to reclaim their bodies."

Yito cried, "Seriously?!"

Puk chuffed. "Good fucking luck there."

Nox threw the Dwarf into the Icarus and Lamia behind him, clearing the way for Rayne to cartwheel kick a drone. When she fell back into Nox, he held her so she could dropkick the next opponent, a human Rayne tribute.

All around Celindria dug in a line here or there such as "Listen to me," "Let me explain," and "We can build the empire you wanted together."

It sent a chill down Nox's spine with each plea. How deluded was the First Progeny if she believed he would even entertain forgiving her after everything she'd subjected him and Cinder to? Let alone end his relationship with *Rayne* for *Celindria*?! It would betray all of Nox's rehabilitation and any hope for a future with his brothers.

No chance.

Enough was enough.

Nox shouted, "Celindria, tell me what's the point of this?"

Her agents paused and stared at him. One by one, they said, "*We* are the Eternal Bind."

"Together we will rule Paradise."

"And you will be all you were meant to be."

"With me."

The last they said all together.

Rayne glanced at Nox, and he shook his head, confounded.

Unwell.

Celindria needed Xelan's care and a long incarceration. It was better than she deserved for all the evils she'd brought into this world, but thanks to Rayne, Nox could see execution wasn't always the way. Celindria possessed a brilliant mind, and with the right rehabilitation, she could contribute her efforts to better Iona Pax and compensate for some of her wrongs.

In this vein, Nox said, "Lay down your arms, Celindria, and come with *me*. We can go to Xelan together and serve our time."

The nearest female Icarus, a Valkyrie, asked, "You want me at your side?" There was an edge of hopefulness to the question which unnerved Nox.

Despite that, he holstered his daggers and reached for the Valkyrie. "Come out of hiding and join me."

In Nox's peripheral vision, Matt, Lucy, Puk, and Yito stood poised on the brink of combat, glancing between Nox and the Valkyrie. Rayne was watching him with something close to pride on her face.

This would make the right solution.

Nox felt it.

"Come with me, Celindria."

<hr>

This was it.

This would finish Imminent.

With their heart racing, Rayne crossed her fingers and said a silent prayer to Elden, *'Please, let this work.'*

A tremor passed through the Valkyrie, who dropped her outreaching hand. With a nod in Rayne's direction, she said, "Kill her, and I'll come with you."

Rayne recoiled in surprise and noted Nox's shudder in disgust. But he was quick to conceal it, saying, "If we kill her, Xelan will never let us rehabilitate."

Logical.

Surely Celindria could see the benefits of this surrender.

A tense silence stretched between them. Several hundred Celindria agents stared at the only man in the room she wanted. Rayne held her breath, hoping Celindria's desire for Nox was enough to tilt the scales in their favor.

Lucy looked expectant, while Matt appeared neutral either way. Puk was memorizing the moment, fully appreciating its significance. Yito's expression was simply unnerved. Bethany's eyes were closed in concentration.

Nox took an entreating step toward the Valkyrie and cradled her cheek in his powerful hand. He said, "Please, come with me, and we can work together to make this right."

Rayne knew this was the right way. Celindria, in her absolution, could make greatness through a future of working with the Shadow—

Every agent crumpled to their knees and fell flat on their faces.

Behind Rayne, Lucy cried, "Bethany!"

Kyle's sister had collapsed, and her team raced to check on her.

Crouched beside her, Matt said, "Get back. Get back. Give her some air. Bethany, are you all right?"

Between Puk and Yito, Rayne saw blood dripping from Bethany's eyes and nose. Underneath the mess was a sweet smile.

Nox came to Rayne's side, and she peered up at him to find his eyes hollowed out and his handsome face in a melancholic frown. Had he meant what he'd offered to Celindria? Would he volunteer to rehabilitate with her? For the first time, Rayne wondered about Nox's feelings for Celindria.

The Eternal Bind.

Bethany's voice was breathy as she said, "My memories—your memories—are her memories now."

Lucy glanced up at Matt, who shrugged.

Catching on, Rayne ran to the nearest agent—the Valkyrie—and checked her vitals. "They're alive. I don't know if they're still under her control."

"We'll have Pehton and Bones detain them until we can prove otherwise." Matt stood and walked over to

Rayne. "It's about time for them to make their way down here, War King. What do you want me to say?"

Rayne gazed over at Nox. He was checking the fallen agents with his back to her. She said, "Buy me a few days, and then we'll come clean. Can you do that for me?" The last she ground through her teeth while returning Night Killer to her nacre.

"Roger that." Matt gestured at the rest of his team. "You heard her, folks. No ratting out to the elites."

Lucy helped Bethany stand and saluted. "Aye, aye."

Puk shot Rayne a reassuring smile, saying, "As long as I get to be in the movie, I don't care when you come out."

"Yeah, fine." Yito seemed preoccupied with a contemplative frown. "Hey… anybody notice—"

"They're mostly drones," Nox finished.

Everyone looked at Puk. Sheepishly, he held up his hands in surrender. "It's cool. I guess Celindria claimed the hives."

Matt pressed, "Mind telling us why you aren't affected, then?"

Puk's laugh was incredulous. "Oh, no drone who worked for Razor would be affected. He lobotomized our hive receivers. It was standard operating procedure to work for him."

Rayne frowned. "Wouldn't that separate you from your people?"

Puk gave a dismissive wave, only his voice sounded sad. "Sure, you get lonely without your family in your head, but we adapted and survived. Not to mention, no Celindria control. Bonus." Puk gave two thumbs up.

Nox ordered like a King, "Check with your other contacts who worked with Razor and see if they're affected. Tip them off to Celindria's scheme."

Puk said, "Count on it, your former majesty. And if I might say?" Nox nodded for Puk to go on. His excited grin suited his personality. "I can't wait until you two start coming around for the family gatherings."

Yito groaned. "What a mess…"

Matt and Lucy beamed, but Bethany, with blood smeared across her face, smirked.

"Ginger. Morning Star. Where are you?" Bones came over the palm device.

Pehton's voice followed. "Are there any hostiles with you?"

On cue, Elden opened a conduit back to the treeloft. Nox gestured at it. "There's our ride."

Rayne reached over to hug Matt and then Lucy. "Thank you, both."

"We'll see you soon," Lucy said on a squeeze.

Debris kicked up nearby, and that was Rayne and Nox's signal to exit. They rushed through the conduit, which closed instantly behind them. They arrived outside the treeloft once again.

Nox stared up at the canopy, lit only by the internal glow of the trees. He was standing right next to Rayne but felt so far out of reach. She said, "Talk to me."

"Yes. We need to talk. Can you please let us in first? I need to sit down."

Rayne opened the DNA seal and let him in first. Nox sat on the long end of the couch and pulled his boots off, sighing once his feet were free. Something Rayne totally understood as she absorbed her boots. The enormous Icarus stared at the floor, elbows resting on his knees, hands hanging between his legs.

Exhausted.

Rayne's concerns metastasized into insecurities. Was this a relationship talk? How did Celindria play into it? And where would it end?

"No. None of that, Rayne." It was like Nox could read her mind. He reached his hands out to her, saying, "C'mere."

She crossed the quaint living space and stood before him. Nox reached up to cup her face, and Rayne planted her knees on either side of him, sinking into his lap. She felt raw and exposed, on the verge of tears, and she didn't know why.

"Shh... I assure you, we are not thinking the same things." Nox kissed her, a soft peck, all too briefly. He said, "But it is time to talk of less pleasant things than our favorite ice cream and which position you enjoy most." He smirked at the last.

Rayne blushed, but mustered a timid smile. "Go on."

Nox brushed one hand through her hair, and she closed her eyes to soak in the gentleness. But when he spoke, his voice held so much sorrow, they snapped open again. "We need to discuss what will happen once the other Shadow know we're alive—I'm alive. Specifically, our Co-Emperors."

At the dismay flooding into her ever-spiraling storm of emotions, Rayne clasped both of Nox's hands against her face. "No. It's not time—"

"Yes, Rayne. It is. Today, marked it. We will be discovered, and you will return to the people who love you." Nox swallowed. "But who will not accept me."

The first hot tears squeezed through Rayne's lashes. She tried, but she couldn't help it. "Is that why you offered to turn yourself in with Celindria? Because you think Xelan and Tameka will arrest you?"

Nox brushed a tear aside, his eyes filled with love but also with resignation. It thickened his voice as he said, "Yes. It's the least they'll do to me. I should be executed for my crimes against Earth, against Xelan, and against you."

Rayne shook her head. "No. I will *not* let them use me to punish you. And what about our rehabilitation?" There was something she could cling to. "We spent millions of years together providing you an arena for redemption, and it worked. Without the constant bombardment of Imminent's pervasive evil, you became a better Icarus. You're *my* Icarus."

Their kiss was searing, more from the desperation knowing these days were numbered than passion alone. When it broke, so did Rayne's heart.

"Three years in your psyche was no punishment. It was tidal wave after wave of revelation." At her hiccuping sob, Nox added, "But we can try to argue between your execution of me and your inspired approach to reform that I am indeed redeemed. We can try."

The forced hope in Nox's words hurt the conviction Rayne felt for their case. She believed it when she said, "I will make sure of it."

At least Nox's smile said he believed in her, too. He wiped the remnants of tears from her face, brushed a strand of hair behind her ear, and said, "Now tell me how you plan to inform the Shadow of everything."

"Korac."

Nox quirked a brow and tilted his head, expecting more of an explanation.

Rayne slid her hands up his chest, around his shoulders, and locked them behind his neck, getting more comfortable with the position. All the while, she said, "We've left a trail of breadcrumbs big enough for a Hellkite to follow, and Korac is our best mediator between you and the rest of the Shadow."

There was no hiding Nox's impression of her strategy. His eyes glittered with admiration, as he nodded sagely. "Logical."

"All this banks on how much Korac cares for you as we've gleaned from his Verse. The look on his face before Enki exploded... When we told him about the nacre chamber..." Rayne was staring off, recalling it. She shook herself back to the present and let Nox see the confidence in her smile. "This *will* work."

Pride in Rayne crooked his smirk until Nox raked his gaze over her bare shoulders and the tops of her thighs exposed by the riding up of her dress. Something darker tilted his lips. It roughened his voice as he asked, "Until then, how do you feel about finishing what we started at Night Rayne's Tomb?"

Rayne rolled her hips against him and gasped, "Please."

Nox lifted her thigh with one hand and gripped her hair in the other, kissing her roughly, deep into Rayne's purrs—

A knock sounded from the door.

They separated, flushed and confused in a lusty haze. Heart pounding, Rayne stood and pulled down her skirt to a decent length. Nox stood and slipped his button-less shirt back on, peering at her.

This was it.

Only one couple could track them down and travel here.

Rayne reached out a hand to Nox. He took it, laced his fingers in hers, and nodded on her mark. Facing an uncertain future, they answered the door.

Together.

<hr>

When Xelan had forced Devis' memory on Celindria, she'd learned there was love somewhere left inside her. But when the young Roberts girl shoved hers, Lucy's, and Matt's memories down Celindria's hippocampus—

Respect.

Celindria rarely experienced the sentiment, but there was no other appropriate reaction to the methodical vengeance delivered upon members of every species. And the creativity of their kills? Not to mention Bethany's recuperation of agency and power. By far, they were the only Shadow worthy of Celindria's respect.

Expulsion from her agents had hurt, but not as much as the loss of potential opportunity.

"Come with me, Celindria."

Eight thousand years.

Celindria had waited eight thousand years to hear Nox say those words. But what did it mean that he'd asked her to come with him to face father? That he asked while standing beside Celindria's errant descendant?

She couldn't argue against his logic for not killing Rayne. Father wouldn't accept their ploy of redemption if Nox had murdered Rayne first. Then, how could they infiltrate the Shadow and take Iona Pax from beneath them?

What if it wasn't a ploy Nox was suggesting?
What if he means for us to surrender?
We could be together in prison, and one day free to live our lives.

In that case, Celindria would negotiate conditions of her surrender. Hope and her family must migrate to the dominant Probability. Pax will need to leave Paradise and join his family, as well. Father would find a way. She would *not* abandon them.

We hurt Pax's feelings.
How could we shout those things at him?
We made our little brother cry.

Pax would adjust and learn from his mistakes. Sometimes harsh words were necessary, and far less cruel than Celindria's initial instinct to add him to her body slice collection. It wouldn't equal half the torment in her heart.

Nox.

Lost.

There was no reviving the construct or rejuvenating the energy from his nacre. All those expensive and impossible to attain components... Wasted on one breath. A breath filled with nothing but hatred for Celindria.

We can't go through this again.
Join the real Nox in the dominant reality.
Complete the Eternal Bind.

Before the girl, Bethany, had thrust Celindria from her agents, she'd considered taking Nox's hand. But it was better this way. She needed to think and share this opportunity with Hope and Pax.

Celindria's actual body was still staring at her fallen Nox construct where she was curled around herself on the floor. Pax had long since ran off to hide his tears from his unfeeling sister, somewhere deeper in the lab. As the eldest, Celindria would consult Hope first. Pax would be here when she returned, perhaps in a mood to listen to his sister's apology and potentially good news.

With a brush of her white skirts, Celindria got to her feet and walked into the nearest shadow—

Into nothing.

The shadow refused to take her. Celindria tried again and simply stepped through to the other side of the shade.

Again.

And again.

Celindria's hand trembled as she reached for the shadow one more time, and her breath hitched when nothing happened.

Deep breath.

Try another reality—

She stepped into the Palatial Grounds in the dominant reality. All things here looked as before.

With a soft cry, Celindria tried Hope's reality again.

Nothing.

Unwelcome panic returned, and Celindria retreated to Paradise—To scream. To throw her fist through a wall.

"Hope!!! HOPE!"

Grief replaced panic, and she certainly wasn't ready for it. "No. No, no, no—Hope?!"

When the thought came, it rang through the fog of panic and grief, resonating clear as a bell.

The Probability Matrix is shrinking.

There's nothing we can do.

Hope is gone.

Covered in white dust from the broken stone, Celindria tried to draw a soothing breath, but they were all raw with anguish. A voice was murmuring, repeating. It was hers.

"Not my daughter. Not my Hope. Not my little girl…"

Grief dissipated, and Celindria gripped herself in scientific logic. Perhaps within the Probability Matrix were collected histories, version control of all the Probabilities. With renewed determination, Celindria marched down the length of the lab's primary aisle, destined for the bottom floor of the space scraper. For Ishkur's bridge.

There, Celindria could run analysis to test her hypothesis and retrieve a backup or open a way into Hope's reality.

I wish we could ask father for help.
He would find a way.
And he would do it for us. For hope—

Celindria snarled and screamed, frustrated—Frustration. A useless emotion, but it was almost as common as solitude. Composing herself, she dusted the white powder off her dark skin, hair, and clothes. Deep inhale. Heavy exhale.

There must be a way—

"Sister!!" Pax sounded scared.

Celindria bolted into the lab, running toward his station, where he was still screaming for her. "Pax! What is it?! I'm coming!"

A vacuum pulled her back. Air flowed in, but not from the glass walls of the space scraper. There was nothing. Black emptiness consumed the lab, starting from the four corners and working its way inward.

All around Celindria, the walls fell away into an abyss, drawing her in.

It wasn't panic this time. Or grief.

Celindria felt white fiery rage. "Not my baby brother. No. PAX?!"

His little voice squeezed out in a thin wail against the vacuum. "I can't hold on!"

Truth be told, Celindria was *not* getting to him. She was clawing at structural beams and glass cubicles to pull herself closer—But he kept slipping further away. The pull was too strong.

Squeezing her eyes closed, rage gave way to resignation. She shouted, "Pax! Listen to me!"

"Celindria!" His voice grew more distant.

"I will find you! I will *not* fail you!"

Before the Probability reached total collapse, Celindria dove into the nearest shadow and left Pax to face his fate alone.

XIII   FIREWHIRL

THIS WAS THE PRETTIEST FOREST SAGAN HAD EVER SEAMSWALKED INTO. Silver trees all aglow, with their twinkling leaves high above, formed a labyrinth among their bases on the forest floor. She'd admired it several times during the six hours she and Korac spent so far wandering through it, lost, seeking that which didn't want to be found.

No. That's not right.

Rayne wanted them to find her. Otherwise, she wouldn't leave all those hints and messages for Korac to find. It was hard, though, thinking about Rayne being alive for over six months and not telling her loved ones. Not telling Sagan, the girl who loved Rayne more than anything in the world. More than even—

"You've gone quiet again, amos."

If Sagan didn't know for a fact Korac was a soldier, she'd think he'd never been camping with the way he was dressed for this hike. A white satin tunic over black pants—damned near tights—tucked into thigh-high boots polished to a soft shine. Even after all this time in the woods, by the magic of Aegis hotness, the shirt was untouched, and the boots were still gleaming. Korac had asked Sagan to do his hair. She'd preened the entire time she wove a checker-patterned braid across his scalp and tied it all into a high ponytail. As always, he looked edible.

Sagan expected the snow storm on Thailea to pervade, so she wore combat leggings and a cropped hoodie. Double braids, practical and cute, finished the look. As it turned out, Thailea was the perfect temperature for frolicking through the woods.

Each of them carried a duffel of extra clothes and supplies in case they needed to camp. As the glow around the forest waned into some semblance of night, it looked likely.

It did nothing for Sagan's mood. Why did she keep on this spiral? Rayne loved Sagan—There was no questioning it. But her first lover would need to explain this whole hiding out situation—

Korac's arm slipped around Sagan's shoulders and pulled her in for a squeeze. Just like that, she felt better. Looking up into his white eyes, she said, "You know, they should really bottle this magic of yours."

The Icarean General's crooked smirk aided the mystical remedy as he said, "I'm here if you want to talk." With a kiss on her forehead, he left her to investigate a tree base.

Sagan dropped her duffel and sat on a root, thinking. After another moment, she asked, "Are you sure it's here?"

Focused on the base, sniffing and searching, Korac said, "This is definitely the forest I showed you in the feed of the races. Whatever conduit Rayne had created, it had led them here. Then all the holdings in Razor's accounts, which our Co-Emperor populated, disclosed the different safe houses. This is the one."

"Okay. Yeah. You sound certain, and I trust you. We'll find it." Sagan couldn't quite force a smile into her words. After a heavy sigh, it was time to unload her burdens. "It'll take a while for me to understand. I already forgive Rayne, you know? But six months without telling me she was alive? It stings."

Korac peered over his shoulder, and there was such intensity in his eyes it took Sagan aback. He said, "Let it go. Take it from me, there's so much that can come between friendships and love. Only after everything dissolves, do you often look back in hindsight and see so many things which didn't need to cause strife between you. Don't let this thought be one of those things. Because if she were to die in the near future, you'll remember wasting entirely too much time thinking this way. And then the person to forgive will be yourself for wasting it."

The Verses.

Korac was right, and it was a lesson he'd learned the hard way. He crossed the clearing and cupped Sagan's face. "She's alive, and she loves you."

Sagan swallowed to say, "You are absolutely on top of it and looking fabulous while philosophizing in the woods. And sniffing. Why are you sniffing so much?"

"You don't smell it?" Comically, Korac sniffed the air like a predator. It was cute, though.

Sagan mimicked him, trying to catch a whiff of…

The ocean breaking on the shore, demolishing sandcastles to the delight of squealing children.

Such a specific smell, and it could only be…

"Rayne."

Korac said, "I first noticed it about ten minutes ago, but it's strongest here. And…" He looked over his shoulder at the tree base he'd sniffed earlier. "It's her blood."

This was cause for alarm, which Korac immediately addressed, cupping Sagan's chin. "Save your worry. I think it's a DNA seal."

Like the one to Xelan's stronghold before he filled it in.

"Oh."

Sagan wet her lips, suddenly nervous. Korac shook his head, let go of her chin, and took her hand. "It's time, amos."

Korac led her across the clearing to the tree base. There, Sagan made out the faintest trace of a seam, where the beach smell was most potent. The nerves morphed into excited butterflies in Sagan's stomach. She spared Korac a glance. He nodded and knocked on the wooden base.

Hand in hand, they waited.

To think, just this morning they were enjoying feeding Echo breakfast before Karter received her for another round of grandmother babysitting. And now the iconic couple were on Thailea, the impossible planet, looking for Rayne *and* Nox. The possibilities roiled in Sagan's gut, twisting it into a nervous knot. Anxiety was stupid, unnecessary, and—

A rectangle of the wood opened inward, and Sagan held her breath.

In the light of the tree's glow, Rayne—beautiful, wonderful Rayne—stood with Nox behind her, framed in the doorway.

The air slammed back into Sagan's lungs and nearly choked out a sob. "Rayne." Her name left Sagan's lips on a breath, unable to muster more.

"Sagan!" Rayne lunged for her, arms outstretched. She latched and squeezed so hard, Sagan's bones popped. "Oh, sorry. Are you okay?" She lightened up, almost letting go, but Sagan threw her arms around Rayne, giving as much in return.

"Don't you dare let me go."

Tears followed. Little happy sobs onto each other's shoulders. It occurred to Sagan they might disturb the wildlife in the doorway like this. Not to mention, Nox and Korac were stuck on opposite ends of this entanglement.

Rayne must've realized, too, because she wiped her face, sniffled, and said, "Here, come inside. Sorry for plowing into you like that."

Ah. This was a well-deserved opportunity Kyle would be sore he missed. Sagan smirked, saying, "Plow into me, anytime, Callahan." She even added a wink at Rayne's baffled face.

The men chuckled, and Rayne finally cracked the prettiest smile with a sexy light in her eyes. "I'll keep that in mind, Sterling."

Promise thickened the air, and the only thing powerful enough to draw these two women away from each other was their curiosity at how Korac and Nox would reunite.

The General sensed the time had come, turning from Sagan to his former King.

Nox looked good for a dead man, all tall and brawn with his shirt open—Wait a minute. The buttons were missing.

And Rayne…

She looked so pretty in the short dress, revealing her bare shoulders and legs, and her hair was mussed. Skin flushed—

Oh.

Sagan knew her eyes went wide before she could hide it. Rayne glanced at her with a question on her face, but at the shake of Sagan's head, they went back to focusing on their boys.

Their boys.

The former King of Cinder looked like he wanted to fidget. It was honestly kinda cute. Nerves looked good on Nox.

Korac stepped across the threshold, looking Nox once over. He checked out the space, lingering his gaze upstairs. Then he met Nox's eyes.

This was it. After all this time, after all the Verses— This was *the* moment.

"Permission to speak freely, sire?"

Nox's expression softened, and his baritone was thick as he said, "Granted, General. Always."

When he nodded at the loft, Korac's mask melted into a wicked smirk. "There's only one bed."

As scarlet as Rayne turned, Nox went equally cobalt from head to toe.

Sagan cupped a hand to her face and snickered into it.

Especially as Nox sputtered out, "I've been dead for three years, and the first words out of your mouth are to give me shit."

"*Us* shit," Rayne corrected with a glare at Korac.

The troublemaker put his hand on Sagan's back as he asked, "Do you remember, your majesty, one of our last conversations which occurred after I'd given my shirt to Sagan and Rayne to aid in their escape? You interrogated me about the missing article of clothing. Your majesty, where are your buttons?" Nox's eyes widened, but Korac moved on from him to Rayne. "And War King?"

She could only blink at him.

To which he crooked his smirk extra to say, "Love the hair."

What a way to clear the air. Fuck it, Sagan wanted in. She said, "This is what you two deserve for shacking up together while the rest of us think you're dead."

The unlikely, yet perfectly suited couple looked properly chastened.

Korac mused, "Wait until Xelan finds out."

It killed the mood within a heartbeat. Even Sagan stopped grinning and offered Rayne a pitying look. Sagan said, "I promise. We'll talk to him."

"Of course we will." Korac gave Nox's back a good pat. Hard enough, the enormous Icarus grunted and shifted forward.

Rayne and Sagan exchanged a look and playfully rolled their eyes at the incoming pissing contest.

The glean in Nox's black eyes accepted Korac's challenge, as he addressed his former General. "I suppose we should thank you for taking so long to decipher the mountain of obvious clues we left you."

Korac shook his head as if warning Nox not to open those doors. "Or else we would've interrupted your christening of this lovely little bungalow sooner." The wink he gave Sagan sent a little thrill through her as he continued being an absolute pain in the ass. "I suppose we weren't the only ones having a honeymoon, amos."

Sagan consoled Rayne as the blood drained from her kinda deserving best friend, but a little pity wormed its way in. Sagan gently touched Korac's arm. One look at her, and he immediately sobered. "Sorry, amos. Rayne—"

"No, it's fine." Chin high, Rayne went to Nox's side and snuggled against him. With so much adoration in his expression, he pulled her closer and kissed the top of her head. Rayne peered up at him with genuine love in her eyes.

It affected Sagan. This was what she'd always wanted. The three girls with their three Icari. Korac took Sagan's hand, and the warmth felt kindred. He was thinking the same.

Sagan said, "Okay. Tonight, I want some answers. Tomorrow, we'll brainstorm the best way to break this to Xelan and Tameka. Does that sound good?"

Rayne bounced with excitement. "I'll put on some tea and give you a tour of the place."

Nox offered the cutest thing. "I'll see if I can find some playing cards in the library."

Playing poker with the Icarus who'd ripped Sagan's nacre out of her chest sounded odd to most anyone else. Well, not so odd compared to what Korac suggested next.

"Where are we sleeping? There's no way in the Wrong Side of Eternity we're all fitting in the same bed. I don't care how massive it is."

The girls giggled, and Sagan knew—

Just *knew*—

Someway, somehow, they would make this work.

Andrew moaned as Lucas leaned over him and captured Andrew's earlobe between his teeth. That was a guarantee for a photo finish.

The ancient spy whispered against his lover's ear, "Let's give them a grand finale." One hand released Andrew's hip and moved frontward, teasing and pleasing.

A giver.

Andrew bit his lip, and his eyes rolled back, ready to let go—

The stupid fucking device in his palm vibrated.

Ignore it.

Keep going.

The hand coaxing so much pleasure from Andrew vibrated, and the Progeny, known as Conscience, could shit kittens he was so mad. Especially as his palm device vibrated again.

Lucas chuckled at Andrew's frustration as they separated in ecstatic agony.

"Cut!" Iuo called from behind the projection camera. One of his crew members snapped a scene clapper, a novelty Reipon had adopted from Earth. "All right, everyone. Give them some privacy." Said the King Elect, who immediately crossed the extravagant suite to the bed. He held up his hand, vibrating visibly from three feet away.

Andrew groaned. "It's Xelan, isn't it? How did he know we were with you, Iuo?"

Lucas wrapped a sheet around him, hiding what modesty couldn't afford. Sometimes Andrew thought the extremely well-endowed Icarus hid his biological miracle to prevent jealousy. Or fear.

With a casual flip of his sandy blond hair, Lucas said, "I believe he's calling everyone."

Iuo assured, "I never disclose details of a production." Suddenly, he blossomed into a grin, black and blue eyes sparkling. "You two were fantastic. Do you think we can pick up where we left off?"

All three of their palm devices vibrated, and Andrew sighed. "I doubt it."

They all answered, and Xelan appeared in a projection, looking ready to pull his hair out.

"Sorry to call you at two in the morning, but the instruments detected a spike in the activity Andrew reported. In the last seventy-two hours, the Probabilities within the Matrix shrank from several hundred million to only ten thousand."

Holy.

"Shit," Iuo hissed.

Andrew couldn't help but notice Lucas didn't look shocked. He looked relieved.

After the dramatic pause, Xelan continued with the update. "Matt and Lucy discovered the vice lords responsible for the child trafficking ring have all committed suicide within the last six hours. Among others. Pehton's reports cite fear of the shrinking Probability Matrix, but some fringe gossip implies Celindria was controlling their volition and forced the suicides."

Tameka came on the line next. "I know we ask a lot of the Shadow, but we're calling 'Banana.' Overtime and all hands on deck. We need a strategy for how to respond to the Matrix shrinking and to brainstorm methods of luring Celindria out of hiding. Korac and Sagan went on some spiritual retreat to commune with the Atheneum, so we're down a Seamswalker. Be patient with T.A.O. as she brings each of you to the bridge for this state of emergency. For the good of peace, we will always remain."

When the image disappeared, Iuo pouted. "I guess I won't finish tonight."

"That makes three of us," Andrew grumbled.

Lucas laughed. It was bright and happy, relieved and joyous. It did not match the situation, and Andrew caught himself staring in suspicion.

No.

Either trust this man—the man Andrew loved—or don't. The back and forth was a betrayal to their relationship. He reached out and squeezed Lucas' hand. The golden-eyed Icarus, still smiling with good humor, kissed Andrew's knuckles.

Lucas said, "We can finish filming once this is over."

Yeah, his non-responsiveness—almost flippancy— at the Probability Matrix should raise a red flag, but Andrew had made his decision. No checking his lover's intentions. Not that it had ever gotten him anywhere with Lucas before.

Encumbered, Andrew raked a hand through his hair with an exasperated sigh. "We should report before T.A.O. shows up while we're still naked."

Iuo thumped the marble column acting as a bedpost. "You got it. I'll be outside when you're ready to go." Before he left the room, he paused in the doorway to ask, "But we'll finish shooting this, right?"

"Count on it," Lucas called, much to the King Elect's delight. When the door closed behind Iuo, Lucas said into the quiet, "I've never filmed one of these before."

There was a significance to the way he said it—A weight. Andrew quirked a brow, hoping he'd answer at least this much.

Lucas stepped out of the sheets and went searching for their clothes. Without meeting Andrew's eyes, Lucas said, "In every other Probability, I always said no."

Andrew frowned. "We aren't together in any other Probability." Some of which were now dearly departed from existence.

Lucas tapped a finger to his lips, staring off and considering. After another second, he admitted, "You know? I think that's exactly why. You bring out my sense of adventure." His appreciative grin was everything.

That got a chuckle out of Andrew, who could not for the life of him find his boxers—

Thwap!

They smacked right into his face after Lucas sent them flying across the bed. "Hurry and get dressed. Our Co-Emperors have summoned us."

Andrew stepped into them, staring in fascination across the room as Lucas slipped elegantly into a teal button-down and black slacks. The shirt matched Andrew's eyes. He swallowed before he could say, "You know they'll ask you. Will you help them this time?"

With his back to Andrew, Lucas buckled his belt with a curt, "No."

Fuck.

"Can you tell me why not?" Andrew almost added, 'please,' but he'd get the answer Lucas wanted to give either way.

Lucas faced Andrew, and he looked bone tired, his eyes giving away his age. Lucas said, "Because they will try to stop it."

Andrew wet his lips before asking, "Should we not be afraid of ceasing to exist?"

With a gesture, Lucas encompassed the room— no, the universe—as he said, "This Probability is the one shattering others into existence. It's the control, if you will, while the others are the variable. The Eternal Bind will reduce all other Probabilities but this one. If..."

That sounded really reassuring until the 'if.' Andrew asked, "If what?"

The weariness seemed to weigh down Lucas' bones as he leaned one forearm on a bedpost and his forehead against the arm, resting. His words were filled with so much anguish and said so softly Andrew almost didn't hear Lucas.

"If I got it right this time."

Tameka finished checking the latest stats in the reports about the Probability Matrix. After a final scan, she turned to address the incoming Shadow—

"Whoa."

—And nearly bumped into Pehton when she turned around. "Oh, hey, girl. Sorry." Tameka offered a friendly smile.

But suspicion had narrowed the Lyriki Warden's gaze, distant with her private contemplation.

"Is something wrong?" Tameka asked, waving to Silence and Kyle as T.A.O. brought them through.

Pehton nodded. "Yes." Her garnet eyes—hard gemstones—finally focused on Tameka. "I don't believe for one second Korac is on some meditation retreat in the middle of this mess."

That shot Tameka's brows up. Then lowered them into a frown. "Why would you say that?"

With a flare of her orange gliders—wrists to elbows—Pehton said, "Because it's not like Korac to leave the action. He didn't even tell me in person. Just left a message—No." She paused, contemplating. "No. This feels off."

Tameka agreed it was odd timing, but she couldn't account for the half-Aegis' behavior. "We can't do anything about it until he and Sagan get back."

"Hopefully, Korac is using this time to communicate the severity of the situation with Zero or the other Aegis," Xelan offered, joining the pair of women on the lowest tier of the bridge.

Below the glass platforms and gangplanks, Cascading Light swirled in its endless vortex, defying sanity and reason. Although the addition of nanite rails ruined the original magnificent, yet anxiety-inducing effect, everyone walked easier despite occasionally brushing against the invisible barriers. It was especially convenient on days like this when all the Shadow gathered in the precarious space.

Even Pax practiced caution, weaving carefully between the adults. He needed a playmate.

Tameka tried her best not to place a hand on her midsection, but it went there of its own accord. A little sister for a big brother. Echo as a best friend. Not to mention Lynn's baby was overdue, more evident by her absence. Pablo hesitated to leave her side for the meeting, but bed rest was bed rest. Qas, the Tritan physician they'd met during the fall of Enki, would look after her in the meantime.

Warm fingers entwined in Tameka's free hand, and she looked up to find Xelan beaming. She dropped the hand on her belly, but not before Pehton looked between the Co-Emperors, extra-observant today. Discretely, she leaned into Tameka and whispered, "You're glowing." The Lyriki Warden's smile implied she'd figured it out.

Fuck it.

They would all learn eventually.

Tameka called, "Everyone, we have an announcement to make."

Tumu in the back already broke into a wide, lipless grin, puzzling Lamassau, judging by the look on his face.

The others peered on in curiosity while Tameka looked up at Xelan, asking permission. He kissed the hand he held, and said against her knuckles, "Go ahead."

"I'm pregnant. It's a girl." Saying it aloud made Tameka grin as wide as Tumu. Xelan, too.

Pax cried in delight, "A little sister?! Can I teach her how to fly?"

After everyone finished gasping, they shined adoring smiles at the kid, who plowed into Tameka and gripped her tight. He said it again as if trying the idea on for size. "Wow. Another sister."

Tameka winced, knowing he referred to Celindria.

Xelan knelt and held his arms out. Without hesitation, Pax jumped into them. The father asked the son, "How does that sound, kiddo?"

Tameka ruffled his coils as Pax asked, "Can she hear me?"

"You can talk to her all you want." As she said it, the beginnings of happy tears blurred Tameka's vision.

Pax let go of his father to whisper to the baby forming inside her. "Both Elden and I will protect you. My name is Pax. I will teach you everything I know. We will play and spar together, and I will never hurt you."

The color drained from Xelan's complexion. People all around winced, looking away to give the moment some privacy. Tameka didn't know how to ask Pax if he meant to quote Nox's first words to Xelan from the Verse. Or if he channeled some sincerity from the menagerie of lives and memories exposed to him by the Probability Matrix.

Oblivious, Pax hugged Tameka again, sealing his vow. She offered Xelan an apologetic look, but he'd already regained the gray tone to his skin. Still, she couldn't ignore the not-so-joyous glisten in his eyes.

The Icarean royal family was so broken: Korac, Nox, and Xelan. There was no way to tell if Nox's death had helped or hurt the healing. Sometimes it seemed 'both' was the answer. There was no way to confront Nox, but also no way to determine if he deserved forgiveness.

So here they lingered in limbo.

"I've got some weed if you want some, ol' Wingmaster."

Kyle.

His sense of humor needled, but Tameka be damned if it didn't work. Laughter burst from Xelan despite himself, and the rest followed in a chorus of chuckles, giggles, and many calls to fuck off.

On the right, beside Andrew and Lucas, Iuo requested, "Please indulge us as to why I had to give up a truly magnificent, one-of-a-kind filming experience in the wee hours of the morning." The light in his black and blue eyes belied his complaint as good-natured ribbing.

Pablo looked weary with heavy-lidded, exhausted eyes as he said, "I want to help however I can, but the sooner I get back to Lynn, the better." It didn't help that the last pregnancy he'd delivered had resulted in the mother—Triss—dying.

Xelan took to the center of the lowest tier, staring up at the Shadow in an amphitheater of glass and black fire. "I understand everyone wants to return to their nights, and you will, as soon as Tameka and I assign you some tasks. For instance, Pablo, we'd like you to check over our prisoner before we let you turn in for the night. Chris, Bones, and Caedes are guarding him now. Can you do that for us?"

"Absolutely, Wingmaster." Purpose lifted Pablo's chin and brightened his eyes. "Whatever you need."

Tameka took the next group. "Probability Matrix team, we need you monitoring twenty-four/seven. Work in shifts, if it helps. We need to know if we lose more than a hundred realities." She threw in a slightly harder tone for the next as she said, "Lucas, you'll work with them."

The shady—and admittedly sweet—bastard smiled, saying, "Anything for the good of Iona Pax."

Silence coughed into her hand, and the look Kyle gave her said she'd clearly been hiding a laugh.

Weird dynamic.

Xelan added, "You, too, Smith."

The smiling man responded with a grin and a thumbs up.

"What can I do?" Jack asked from the front, sitting politely close to Ross, holding hands.

Tameka said, "You and Iuo figure out what's wrong with F8. As King Elects, you have access to her—"

"I may have a theory." Puk stepped between Matt and Lucy to take front and center. Xelan nodded for the drone to continue, and Puk said, "Celindria has the volition of the Monarch 3 hives."

Gasps and an exchange of shocked expressions followed.

While rocking Echo in a bassinet, Karter asked, "Are you certain?"

Matt clarified, "We were confronted in Night Rayne's Tomb by a hundred or so people—Most of which were drones."

"If she controls the Queens—F8 and the others—Celindria controls the hives," Puk elaborated.

Pehton glared suspiciously at the annihilation squad, asking, "What else did you withhold from me?"

Unnerved, Tameka watched the lines of Matt's face form a reassuring smile and placate Pehton with what felt like a lie. "We didn't withhold anything. This was just the first opportunity to bring it up s'all, ma'am."

Xelan went to biting his thumbnail and pacing, while Tameka asked, "Did you notice any similar features between the others? A commonality?"

Lucy said, "Ports. Most of them had those ports." She placed a hand on her chest above her nacre.

Pehton asked, "Like the ones Razor used in the Divine Booths?"

Devis, beside Andrius and T.A.O., took a step forward. "Celindria designed the technology using the research she harvested from me—"

"Oh, Elden, no..." Xelan's bleak response to his sudden epiphany did not bode well.

Even Pax took Tameka's hand, recognizing the tension as the Shadow waited with bated breath.

Xelan gripped his hair and blew the air from his cheeks. "Celindria is brilliant. So, so brilliant. Through nanite programming, she bugged the booths to leave the users susceptible to her endeavors. Of course..."

Matt frowned, saying, "But that would mean she could control—"

"Millions. The rich, the powerful, and anyone Razor convinced to port for any of his nefarious whims." Pehton was channeling firsthand experience.

Wait.

Tameka blurted, "Does that mean Celindria can control Sagan?"

Xelan shook his head, not as in 'no,' but as in 'oh, hell no.' He said, "We'll need to run tests, but hopefully not."

Lucas offered, "Sagan went into the Feast of Roses in the Seam. It healed the port entirely, and perhaps it reversed all of its engineering."

The room looked at him.

How interesting of Lucas to bring up Aegis-related intervention at a time like this. Tameka cared for their resident tailor and spy, but it hurt that he continued to withhold so much from them.

Pehton trailed her narrowed gaze off Lucas and stared at the maelstrom below. "I guess we'll have to wait and find out when Sagan and Korac return."

"Not to add more to the shit soup, but since you brought Razor up, I want to come clean."

Now the room looked at Kyle. Bethany even beamed up at her older brother like she knew what he was about to say. He looked ready to confess a dirty secret. "Razor is kinda, sorta conscious in the memory bank we built him."

Tameka blinked.

Pehton frowned.

Matt grinned.

"Show me."

Tameka loved Xelan enough to take his hand and pull him down so she could whisper, "You did the thing. Within a single second, you've already abandoned everything about Celindria to hyper-focus on Razor. Let's finish this meeting, and then I'll go with you to see your old friend."

His lips were warm against her cheek when Xelan kissed Tameka and whispered an emphatic, "Thank you."

They could do this.

Assign workgroups.

Join Xelan on a deep-dive with his ex-lover and super villain.

And try to make it through the night without another tear.

With this 'shit soup,' as Kyle had called it, the last was easier said than done.

Kyle had meant his marijuana offer for Xelan with the deepest sincerity. The dude could use a downer or some shit, standing down there, pulling his hair out. Sure, the end of the universe was cause for concern, but the Shadow would figure it out. They always did.

Speaking of, Tameka finished assigning teams. "Okay, so we'll send hourly reports on our progress and meet again in a few nights to reassess the situation. Does that sound good?"

Some people, like Kyle, answered with a, "Yeah." "Sure." Or "Affirmative." While others put a fist to their chest in salute.

Then there was luo. "Please don't forget you're all invited to the premiere of *Rayne's Verse*. Only two nights away. Your imperial majesties, will you be there?"

Kyle expected Xelan to look wrecked by the mere suggestion. Instead, the Co-Emperor nodded. "I wouldn't miss it for the worlds."

"Me, too." Tameka's support further surprised Kyle, who only shook his head, incredulous.

The rest also agreed to go, forcing his hand. Andrew even nudged him. Peer pressure. Kyle blurted, "I'll be there, too, luo."

But he was only attending to judge it very harshly. If a single detail was out of place or there was something remotely uncharacteristic about Rayne, Kyle would leave a scathing review. Somewhere.

Fuck, he wasn't grumpy about the movie. Being honest with himself, Kyle turned to face Silence and at least twenty-four hours without her extremely exciting and erotic company. Thus PDA.

Silence reached to play with Kyle's tangled hair, her steel-gray eyes were alight with sympathy and amusement.

Yeah, yeah, it was only one day, but shit, when would the Shadow finally earn a three-day weekend without a mess to clean up?

Kyle put their departure to good use. He cupped the back of Silence's neck, dipped her down, and kissed her with all the drama of a cheesy romance cover. Bruising and sweet, matching both their punishment apart and the anticipation of their expected reunion.

Not to mention, Kyle felt all the Shadow's eyes on them. Xelan, included. It was enough to restore Kyle's good mood, so when he parted their kiss, appreciating Silence's husky laughter, he beamed in return. Bouncing his eyebrows, he asked, "Not bad, eh?"

She swatted him playfully.

It hurt.

Kyle hid his wince by returning them both upright, ignoring all the facets of reactions surrounding them—Laughter, secondhand happiness, and only one thinly veiled grimace. That's right, Xelan.

Smith ruined the moment by holding up his hand and asking, "My turn?"

Chuckles and giggles sounded from all around for the man who hid in smiles.

"We'll do pizza and root beer when my shift ends. I promise." Silence really knew the way to Kyle's heart.

He kissed her hand and let Andrew pull him away, while he assured, "I'll be one comms call away."

"Seriously, dude. It's only twenty-four hours."

Kyle could tell Andrew was pulling his leg, but still... "Fuck you, Holt. You and the cool kids have fun staying up on 'universe collapse watch.'" He flipped his unrelated brother off, saying, "I bet if I went and touched Cascading Light, they'd let me stay with Silence like you get to stay with Lucas."

Lucas appeared out of nowhere and leaned on Andrew's shoulder to say, "Envy doesn't become you, Kyle."

Of all the people to jump in, Lucas was not the best choice. Many in the Shadow suspected his involvement in the vanishing Matrix, among other things. Kyle's grumpiness skyrocketed to, 'stepping on wet carpet while wearing a sock.'

"You can fuck right off, man—"

Someone strong lifted Kyle bodily, turned, and set him down. It was strangely calming.

Behind him, Tumu said, "Let's get to work. The sooner we get a shift in, the sooner you can return to Silence without damaging any friendships."

Kyle grumbled a begrudging, "Thanks, Tumu."

With a wall of Tritan separating them, Lucas raised his voice to say, "I forgive you, Story Taker."

Stupid name. "Yeah. Yeah. Sorry. Cranky…" Further grumbles of apologies and lame excuses were offered.

Lamassau, who was beside Tumu, nudged Kyle forward. "Let's go congratulate Tameka and Xelan on another squirt."

'Squirt' was such an unexpected word to come from a Tritan that Kyle barked out a laugh. Proof positive he could do this *and* be in a good mood about it. They made their way to the bottom tier, and, at Tameka's glowing smile, Kyle immediately felt better.

"Congratulations, Fury." He meant it.

Tameka—powerful and capable—grappled Kyle into their first full-fledged hug in four years. It felt like hugging one of his sisters. It felt like home. Against his shoulder, Tameka said, "Thank you."

When they let go, she went to hug Lamassau, who said without hesitation, "Lammy is a good name for a girl."

But Kyle's attention drifted to the half-Icarus in front of him. Xelan stared down at him, bemused, as he said, "No way are my kids calling you great granddad."

"I prefer Pappy, anyway."

Tumu broke into a chuckle he hid from Xelan's immediate glare.

With a thumb aimed at Kyle, Lamassau warned, "Careful. This one's looking for a fight."

Bewildered, Xelan shook his head.

"Daddy, I'm tired. Can I go back to bed? Auntie Aria and Uncle Torch will watch me." Pax bumbled between them, rubbing his eyes. "Please?"

Lamassau picked him up, saying, "If T.A.O. will take us, 'I got you,' kid."

Pax and Xelan chuckled at the same time, and it was honestly so cute Kyle wondered about having kids with Silence. Not anytime soon, but what features would he or she have? What mannerism would they adopt? Hopefully, they got their mother's looks—

T.A.O. appeared like magic—Did she really eavesdrop on them in the Seam or something? She said, "Cub, sleep time."

From his perch in Lamassau's arms, Pax reached down to hug the ancient Seamswalker, meaning Lam had to squat for him to reach. Uncle of the year.

"Good night, baby. Mommy and daddy will be home to kiss you in a bit," Tameka promised.

T.A.O. took the waving group to the stronghold.

"Welp, I guess we better get this memory thing over with." Rather than waiting for T.A.O. to return, Kyle led their team—him, Xelan, Tameka, and Tumu—to the lab only a short walk from the bridge. "Through here. Yeah, so he's alive and pervy as ever. The bastard dressed Ross up as a sexy secretary and forced her to witness his entire sexual history. You've got an awesome friend there, Wingmaster."

Xelan ignored the bait and stared at the nacre, biting his thumbnail, pondering, "How do we get him out?"

Tameka tugged on Xelan's hand, and her eyes said it all. *'Why should we?'*

Tumu looked down at Kyle, who shrugged. He'd expected this exact outcome once he'd discovered Razor was alive inside the nacre—

"I'm here." T.A.O. Seamswalked into the lab, Atramentous eyes settling on the nacre. She pointed. "My friend?"

Xelan placed his hand on her shoulder, asking, "Would you like to see him?"

The faeish woman smiled, and it sparkled in her amethyst eyes. "Please."

This boggled Kyle's mind. Seriously, what was with Razor and the Seamswalkers? Whatever. He clapped his hands together and said, "Okay, everyone who's going in, gather around me."

That'd be everyone, including Tumu and Tameka.

Within the blink of an eye, they stood inside the monochromatic aisles of Razor's memory labyrinth. And once again, they were dressed for the occasion.

Xelan was wearing a suit from Korac's closet. Three-piece, yada yada. With a monocle.

Ribbons of shimmering lilac decorated T.A.O.'s wavy hair, matching her glittery slip dress. Now, she looked like a proper fairy, and it suited the radiant smile on her face.

Tameka...

Kyle tried not to laugh.

Tameka was wearing a black leotard over red tights under black thigh-high boots. Razor capped the superhero ensemble off with a black and red cape.

It took every ounce of Kyle's self-control to hold the snicker in, but he lost it when he looked at Tumu.

A seven-foot blue clown. Razor completed the getup with a red nose glued to Tumu's feature-less face.

Xelan and Kyle laughed at the same time. Tameka rolled her eyes and folded her arms. T.A.O. crossed the space to Tumu and curtsied.

With a sigh, Tumu returned her gesture with a bow, losing the nose in the process.

"Razor's alive, all right," Tameka said it with a sigh of disdain.

Kyle frowned when a realization struck him. "There are no clipboards."

Xelan breathed on his monocle, wiped it on his lapel, and went, "Hmm?"

T.A.O. twirled in her pretty dress between Kyle's view of Xelan as he explained, "When Ross and I came here a few days ago, Razor gave us clipboards and wrote to me on it."

Tameka stared at Kyle—No. Behind him, and Tumu pointed.

Kyle turned and saw it. Back-lit white text was written on a white musical staff across one black wall like a chalkboard.

YOU KEPT YOUR PROMISE.

After making Kyle wear this getup again, he regretted it. Still, he said, "Yeah. Yeah. Don't get mushy on me."

With a joyful noise, T.A.O. ran up to the wall and hugged it. It was so cute, yet so annoying because Razor had done nothing to deserve it.

New text replaced the old message.

I MISS YOU, TOO.

Xelan went to T.A.O.'s side and pulled her in for a hug.

With her hands on her hips—in a superhero pose, no less—Tameka blew the air out from her cheeks and asked, "What the hell do we do with this?"

Tumu—in his baggy clown clothes and sad makeup—shook his head with a tsk. "I wouldn't want to be in your shoes, Wingmaster."

"Yeah. No shit." After witnessing Razor's childhood, Kyle wouldn't know how to make this call. And luckily, he didn't have to. He nodded at Xelan, saying, "Good luck, man. Either way, you're hurting someone."

He kinda felt like an ass when Xelan frowned from the weight of this decision, so much anguish filling his eyes. The ethical ramifications of offering to resurrect Razor sucked.

Xelan looked at Tameka, who looked ready to support the father of her children, regardless of his decision. It was nice, something Kyle hoped he and Silence had in their favor, too.

T.A.O. tiptoed to kiss Xelan's cheek, as if she already knew the answer. Then she twirled back with the others, so only Xelan was left facing the wall.

"Razor, would you agree to resurrection under terms of rehabilitation? You'd serve Iona Pax and the Shadow to better a civilization you helped repress and oppress for millions of years. Thusly, would be the duration of your reform."

Black and white images, with pops of color, replaced the musical staff. Memories of a pitch-black Lyrik with hard yellow eyes and fiery red feathers. Lethal and devoted, Triss ripped out some Caprent's throat. Punched a nacre out of a Pil dwarf. And strangled a female Lamia. The next image was Triss lying on a white bed, long lashes closed over soft cheeks, breathing evenly. And then came a montage of Triss… uhm… performing various acts of passion with and for Razor. Enthusiastically. Did any of those positions even have names?

Razor and Triss were meant for each other. Millions of years obsessing over one another across galactic wars and the deaths of Primaries—They were always together. Honestly, if they were still alive, Kyle would've pegged *them* for the Eternal Bind.

Black letters formed on the white flashbacks.

NOT WITHOUT *HER*

The wall went black.

Xelan hung his head. T.A.O. sniffled. Tameka and Tumu looked about how Kyle felt: baffled and still somehow sad.

While they considered the longevity of their own relationships, the eternal debate of right and wrong, and how to recover a nacre from a dead woman, words formed on the musical staff.

Tameka and Xelan, don't name your daughter 'Rayne.' If *you* claimed it, how could Ross and Jack use it for their first born?

"Son of a bitch." The second they left this memory bank, Kyle was marching to the King Elect council and murdering Jack on the spot—

Just kidding.

<hr>

All gone.
Everything lost.
No Hope.
No Pax.
No Nox.
No Paradise.
What was left for Celindria?
Nine thousand, nine hundred and eighty-eight Probabilities remained, including the dominant reality. Trillions of lives had vanished overnight. Lives Celindria valued with what little emotion she had ever experienced.

And it was all Rayne's fault.

We will kill her.

No. We will harness her. Her blood, how it protects against volition and power drain, will secure our dominion, and with her gone, Nox will turn to us as his only bonded mate.

Celindria shadow-walked to forty realities until she found one stable enough to travel via a conduit into an existing Thailea. There she shadow-walked into the Oblivion Cathedral within the dominant reality—An impossible space. It was the inside of a flame and a storm all at once, swirling gases into an atmosphere of its own pocketed rift. No one could recall a physical trace of it once they'd left.

Here was the Source. The most vital key to Celindria's existence with the highest price—Her humanity had withered in every instance in which she'd stepped inside.

Except one.

Celindria hesitated to peer into it, to check if it still existed, because if the Probability where she'd chosen Nox over power had fallen, then there was nothing left to hold her together.

This wouldn't do.

The fissure between the Seam—the Aegis home dimension—and this reality... It narrowed. The diminishing of realities was closing the Source like a healing wound.

If we kill Rayne, it may reboot this Probability and fracture more into existence—widen the gap. Split the Eternal Bind.

But what about Nox's offer to rehabilitate at his side?

Celindria closed her fist over the bright blue ribbon in her palm.

Perhaps father could help her decide.

Cinderken had fallen asleep inside his mindscape some hours ago. Patiently, Celindria had waited at the table inside the modest cell. Nothing much had changed here, aside from the guards. Bones had recently rotated shifts with Caedes, and Chris stayed constant. Over the course of her time here in Cinderken's body, the former came to the cell barrier and occasionally tempted Cinderken to the side of reform. If not for Celindria, the 'Lord of Odds' would likely have accepted the proposal.

It was a *reasonable* proposal.

Curious, she stood Cinderken, calling to Chris—

A sudden commotion outside the cell sat Celindria back down. She recognized her father's voice, but couldn't hear his words.

The nacre deterrent shield lowered, allowing a little parade to come inside: Xelan, Tameka, Kyle, Tumu, and someone Celindria once saw through Kyle's eyes.

Dr. Suarez wasted no time kneeling beside Cinderken and checking his vitals. Without prejudice, he asked, "How are you feeling today, sir? Sorry for the chilly hands."

There was something disarming about the young man, especially as Dr. Suarez took care to warm his hands by rubbing them together first. The strain around his eyes, indicative of sleep deprivation, might explain why his nacre couldn't maintain his body temperature.

Dr. Suarez smiled. "All your vitals look good. I think these people have some questions for you."

The rest of his kind words washed over Celindria as a scent hit Cinderken's nose.

Maternity.

Celindria couldn't stop herself from staring at Tameka. This was the only reality where the Shadow had resurrected father instead of Nox. Xelan and Tameka had never found the opportunity to conceive another child other than Pax. Until now.

The Shadow are all so happy and glowing. They prosper in this reality.

While we have nothing.

Father's young mistress locked eyes with Cinderken, before Celindria looked down at the vice lord's long fingers, still entwined on the desk. The couple sat down in the chairs across from Cinderken, while Kyle leaned into a corner, drawing from Cinderken's memory banks yet again.

"Did you accept a vaccine?" Dr. Suarez was the only person remotely respectable in the room.

Celindria shook Cinderken's head.

The doctor nodded as if he'd expected as much, but offered no condescension. "Do you mind if I look at your port?"

Ah.

So they figured out the drugs. Celindria had loaded Cinderken with enough to dampen his memories of her control. Not long now, he should sober up, and then Kyle would see her intrusion. Then this puppet would become useless.

What a terrible day Celindria was having.

We can't stop recalling... our last words to Pax...

"I knew I should've vivisected you with the other Progeny specimens. Get out of my sight."

Regret closed Celindria's eyes. If she'd only known that Pax would disappear seconds later. While the remorse lasted, Celindria blurted from Cinderken's mouth, "I wish only to speak to my toy."

Dr. Suarez, still on his knees, froze.

Tameka and Xelan exchanged a confused expression. Kyle frowned—

Chris charged into the room from the hallway, gaping at Cinderken. He breathed, "Celindria."

"Oh, fuck no!" Kyle recoiled

Tameka glared, but of course, father's eyes opened up his heart to her. It was enough to make her roll her eyes. Instead, Celindria said, "Only to Chris. Be quick about it. I don't know how much longer I will feel this emotion, and you want me to sustain it as long as possible. For your sakes."

Despite the incredulous look Tameka shot Xelan, she let him pull her from the room. Kyle left in a hurry.

But Dr. Suarez...

Such an interesting man.

He stayed on his knees, asking, "Can I please check on my patient while you talk?"

Celindria blinked at his bravado before waving her assent and turning sideways to let him access the port. While Dr. Suarez stripped the buttons open on Cinderken's untailored shirt, Chris took a seat across from Celindria. Fuming looked good on the man, a rainbow on a monochromatic.

"Hello, toy."

"What do you want?"

Celindria wet Cinderken's lips to say—

Shocking. Dr. Suarez's hands *were* like ice.

With a deep breath, Celindria let the regret and pain wash over her and tried to experience it as a normal person would. She could feel the faint sharpness of shame along its edge, and that felt long overdue. She said, "I wish to accept a deal, but I ask for much in return."

Chris' eyes narrowed, exercising caution as he said, "No one has offered you a deal."

Nox.

Oh, this was rich.

Rayne was hoarding the former King of Cinder. Even the Shadow didn't know he was alive, and that's what Nox had meant about both of them surrendering together.

And...

Celindria laughed, and it was bitter. They didn't know Rayne was alive.

The regret and remorse exhausted Celindria's shattered intellect as the possibilities unfolded.

Without the full of force of the Shadow, we could easily hunt Rayne down and kill her. Take Nox back.

But without this deal, we can't convince father to help us recover Pax and Hope from the Probability Matrix.

Choices.

Chris interrupted her thoughts, saying, "You're the most dangerous when you're quiet."

"Yes. And now I have nothing left to lose." Celindria appreciated the color draining out of Chris' fetching complexion, and Dr. Suarez's sudden stillness. No matter what Celindria decided, she would keep these two alive to watch it all unfold. There was much to contemplate, and Caprents to recoup. For Pax, Hope, Paradise, and Nox, Celindria would shift the stars.

Soon.

"I relent."

"SO, THE BED IS BIG ENOUGH."

Nox chuckled at Korac's observation as Rayne concluded the tour in the loft.

The General shook his head, incredulous.

Sagan prompted him, "What is it, babe?"

Babe.

Rayne's face lit up at the endearment, and Nox wondered how long before they made pet names for each other. But dangerous ones. Like 'pretty warrior' or 'Stabby.'

Korac wiped a hand down his face, saying, "I'm honestly trying to imagine what Xelan was thinking designing this place. Did he *intend* it as a hideaway for a repressed couple?"

"Hey!" Rayne punched Korac in the arm. "Lay. Off."

Nox laughed outright at the glisten in Korac's eyes as he rubbed the punch site. Nox said, "Now you know what I live with."

Sagan snickered at Rayne, gaping. "It's not that bad, is it?"

Korac gave a harsh laugh. "You're joking, right? Fuck! It feels like this is what I deserve for always teasing Pehton."

"She loves it," Sagan assured and kissed her husband's arm. She turned intelligent eyes onto Nox, asking, "So Elden revived you both, and that's after you spent two years rehabilitating in Rayne's consciousness. In your coordinated pursuit of Celindria, you two solidified your feelings for each other. And Korac and I are supposed to sell this romance to Xelan? A man you murdered after promising to do all those awful things you did to Rayne—Which I experienced in a Divine Booth, so don't patronize me about it. While I understand Rayne's mixed feelings, betrayal was the strongest of her emotions during it. And it was *agonizing*, Nox."

Shame washed over him, and he looked away. Nox deserved this onslaught, and before this was over, he'd feel it many times as each person in Rayne's life confronted him. Sagan was generous, even, for not mentioning all the lives Nox's ambitions had stolen. The people he'd murdered during his invasion. Perhaps there was no hope for resolution, of absolution.

Behind Sagan, but always at her side, Korac's face fell into his composed mask. He put his hands on her shoulders to show support, but offered nothing on either side of the discussion.

It was Rayne's hand slipping into Nox's, which brought him back to face them. To hope. She said, "It was between us, and we worked through it. We spent over seven million years analyzing our lifetimes. At every turn, Nox met regret and the shame you see now. He's not proud of what he did and..." Her face fell, and her voice trembled. "Nox wants to serve whatever punishment Iona Pax requires of him."

There was relief in this. To know Rayne was learning to accept the reality they were facing.

There was little chance Xelan wouldn't imprison Nox, and that was just. He could only ask his baby brother to wait until after they finished with Celindria. Rayne squeezed Nox's hand, and he said, "I will do whatever is necessary *after* Celindria is no longer a threat."

Sagan's stony expression blossomed into the brightest smile. "I can work with this. What do you think, babe?"

Korac kissed the top of his wife's head, saying, "We'll do what we can, amos." But the grave depth in his white eyes confirmed Nox's suspicions. "Little chance" just dropped to zero.

"Nox and I had a big day, and I'd like to get a few hours of sleep before we brainstorm strategy." Rayne pulled the sheet back, prepping the bed. Then her eyes lit up in a way Nox loved and dreaded as she asked, "Ooo, can we train together?"

Sagan bounced. "Yes! Girls against the boys." She looked up at Korac expectantly.

After a drawn out second, he gave a cavalier shrug. "It's your choice if you like to lose."

Nox barked out a laugh. The girls exchanged a knowing look. The General and the former King wouldn't stand a chance, but... "I could use the exercise in humility."

Rayne tiptoed to kiss his cheek, and Nox felt it burn. Public affection was entirely new to him. The situation with Celindria had forbidden any contact lest Xelan and Korac learn of their relationship, while Colita remained a mistake to this day. No manner of reflection during the Verses nor his rehabilitation could make Nox feel anything more than pity for the spiteful female.

"Okay, boys. Shoo. We need to change for sleep." Sagan gestured for them to leave.

Korac looked ready to pout, as he said, "Five hours with Rayne and suddenly it's not you and *I* prepping for bed. It's you and *her* prepping for bed."

Rayne laughed so hard it rang through the treeloft.

With an easy chuckle, Nox gripped Korac's shoulder, saying, "C'mon now. We've been dismissed."

But Korac was staring at Nox's hand. He dropped it, not meaning to offend the half-Icarus, but there was more to it. Without a word, Korac brushed by him to take the stairs. The girls witnessed the tension. When Nox looked at them, Rayne shrugged, uncertain, but Sagan mouthed, "Go. Talk. To. Him."

Yes.

She was right, of course. So much had gone unsaid between Korac and Nox until the Verses. It would make a waste of all those confessions not to communicate now.

Nox followed Korac into the library space where he found the fair-haired half-Icarus perched in Rayne's nook—

Xelan's nook.

The General made a show of scanning his gear, straightening his clothes—Anything to keep his eyes down. With a swipe of his shoulder, Korac said, "I know they sent you down here so we can talk, our beautiful, brilliant, and brave women."

Nox sat in a massive armchair and propped his feet on an ottoman. He clasped his hands over his chest and slouched until he stared at the ceiling. Counting the tree rings above, he said, "I believe they're right for it."

Korac gave a single chuckle. It was rough with some emotion. "Of course they are. And they're probably listening over the banister."

"Are not!" Sagan called down.

Nox was enjoying this. The laughter. The warmth in the space. He'd never imagined such a peace. Not for him. He said, "Tell me. And no, it's not an order."

"We were brothers. Are? This becomes confusing as time carries on. In all those *millions* of years I followed you, I could count on one hand how many times you clasped my shoulder or shook my hand.

And every one of those instances, I saw a hesitation in your eyes that I only came to appreciate fully after you were dead."

Nox straightened as Korac finally met his gaze. There was bewilderment or shock in them.

His General swallowed before saying, "It's gone. The apprehension is gone." The laughter which followed was bitter and torn. "After all this time, you're free of it, and the second Xelan lays eyes on you, he'll lock you away. Hear me out. I've tried. Every conversation about you ends as you might expect. I hate this for you and for Rayne, but I won't lie to you and to her if she's listening."

A muffled sob carried from above, and Korac hung his head.

Nox stood and held out his hand. "Then let's not waste the time we have now."

Korac looked at the hand, then looked at Nox before clasping it and letting Nox pull Korac to his feet. Before he could protest, the former King of Cinder pulled his General in for a hug.

Korac put his arms around him, but didn't squeeze back as he complained, "The Shadow has already infected you."

"We're ready!"

Sagan stood at the top of the stairs in silk shorts and a slinky top, obviously not expecting to spend the night in bed with anyone but her husband.

Nox headed toward the stairs, and Korac stopped him with a hand on his chest. "Don't get any ideas about my wife just because she and Rayne might start sleeping together again."

Neither idea had occurred to Nox, and he'd never consider either again. Rayne could do as she pleased with whatever partners she deemed worthy, but he felt monogamous toward her.

Up the stairs, Nox found Rayne dressed in her usual night clothes, sitting on the edge of the bed with a bruised heart in her eyes. Sagan gave him a pitying glance. Whatever Rayne had inherited from Xelan was hard to console. Nox sat on the bed beside her and tucked her against him. She buried her face in his ribs while he chafed her arm and kissed her hair.

Sagan sat down beside Rayne opposite Nox and smoothed circles on her back. Over Rayne's head, Sagan and Nox shared a moment. With a nod, the Seamswalker promised to look after Rayne when Nox was gone.

It was a warm moment until Korac unbuttoned and slipped out of his satin shirt.

Rayne stopped sobbing, and both girls stopped breathing. They saw the attractive, powerful warrior Korac had become after millennia of training and education, but Nox still saw the wounded boy, stripping naked for inspection. When Korac winked at the girls, Nox stood and shook his head incredulously at their juvenile giggles. At least it leveed Rayne's grief for now.

As Sagan and Rayne whispered in each other's ear, presumably about Korac, Nox took off his button-down. He inspected the missing buttons and hoped this wouldn't make for the last shirt felled by Rayne's passion—Why was it suddenly so quiet?

Nox turned and found Korac staring at the girls, while the girls were staring at Nox. There was so much naked ownership and desire on Rayne's face, only less shocking for Sagan's appreciative smile and thumbs up. Korac looked at Nox as if seeing him for the first time, almost assessing. Then a spark of competition flared behind his white eyes.

While circling his fingers for them to turn around, Korac said, "All right, ladies. Avert your eyes while we finish undressing for the most bizarre night of sleep in my life."

Sagan stuck out her tongue, but Rayne beamed as they both looked away with more whispers and giggles.

Nox shook his head as they undressed, still happier than ever before in his life. Even with Korac staring daggers at him for garnering a modicum of precious attention usually reserved only for the exotic General.

Korac mouthed, "This. Isn't. Over."

With a salute, Nox accepted the challenge.

"All right, who wants to sleep along the banister?" Rayne asked, peeking over her shoulder.

Dressed in sleep pants, both men joined the girls on the bed. While it was a massive piece of furniture, the idea of sleeping with three other people had never occurred to Nox, even once in his life. He'd slept with Xelan as a child, and the three boys shared forts occasionally, but it was rare for Nox to risk the contact of sharing a bed.

Sagan said, "Korac and I volunteer for the inside." Her face lit up as she thought of something. "Oh! I'm glad Tameka isn't here."

Rayne caught on instantly. "Oh, shit. You're right."

Korac and Nox exchanged a left-out look and took the bait. "Why is that?"

Sagan snickered as she pulled Korac onto the mattress, saying, "Because she kicks. We all feel sorry for Xelan. And did you know? Pax picked up her habit."

"Aw. I can't wait to meet him outside of a box." Rayne said, following them into the bed. She paused and reached a hand out to Nox.

The arrangement went Korac furthest inside and holding Sagan, who held hands with Rayne, who Nox was holding from the outside.

Rayne curled and snuggled against Nox, requiring some self-control to rein in his response. Across the bed, Korac looked equally focused. It only became more difficult when Rayne cupped Sagan's cheek, moved closer, and kissed her good night. When they separated, Rayne tucked a strand of blond hair behind Sagan's ear, and Sagan bit her lip to taste Rayne on it.

Again, Korac and Nox shared a glance. They knew this was a moment the men were welcome to witness, but one they weren't invited to partake in. Especially not after such a long day and a sleepless night.

Rayne raised her voice slightly to say, "Good night, everybody," and lifted Nox's hand to kiss it.

He joined Korac and Sagan in saying, "Good night," all at once.

When sleep claimed Nox, he wasn't pondering how little of this time was left. He was thinking of how grateful he was to experience this at all.

"By all means, search for Silence. Tear down the foreigners to find her."

One's words came to Elden on the eve of every campaign. Yes. By hindering the Primary and sabotaging his fight against One's people, Elden did his adversary's bidding. But the Primary was keeping Silence somewhere. It was in the pit of his voids. If he'd only relinquish her, Elden would cease and never return. Until then...

The conduit led to another laboratory filled with the black fire and instruments beyond Elden's recognition. He came through the floor, flew into the sky above the vast space, and opened his eyes.

Tritans and their allies screamed in agony. They would survive this ambush without their eyes. Like all the other incursions, they fled their stations, but unlike the other incursions, they'd left their works.

Elden alighted and signaled for Silence's personal guard to enter the conduit and raid the lab. The female warriors emerged and set to dismantling the facility, followed by Vinco and Umbra. More advanced than the fighters, the Coalition could designate which materials to destroy and which to take back to Cinder while Elden wandered, seeking anything close to an answer.

Where was Silence?

And why was the Primary so desperate to suppress her?

Elden passed a wall of Cascading Light, angry at its poisonous existence, when something shifted in it. The lab workers had left an image on display inside the flames. A young girl, little older than Savis, cried in the image, glowing in a light much like Elden. Her cheekbones and jaw resembled his, with a more feminine softness to his harsh angles. The blue of her eyes was unlike any he'd ever seen, but the sorrow in them was wholly familiar in Elden's reflection.

A fellow martyr. One entirely too young for the lifetime within her eyes—

"As I live and breathe, I have never seen a female more beautiful."

Umbra.

In recent weeks, Elden's Coalition sergeant had intruded on Elden's thoughts with reckless recommendations for strategy and outright conquest. Once more, the manner in which Umbra laid his eyes on Elden's daughter demanded correction.

Now.

"How can one look at this child and think of her beauty and not her pain? Do you not see her grief, Umbra?" Elden nodded at the apparition.

Umbra said, "Despite her age, I find myself drawn to her."

Elden faced Umbra, who shrugged with boredom plain in his eyes, failing to see this as a reprimand.

Yet.

But he soon would. Elden said, "I find it shameful to consider a child a woman until her time of maturity, when she is old enough to choose love of her own accord."

Umbra looked from the fire to Elden, recognizing the message in his words. He bowed to his leader and assured, "I harbor no intentions on Savis until she is of age. I come to you and ask only for her betrothal in a beneficial match for our lineage. We can make sons and daughters, leaders and warriors to carryout the Icarean Prerogative—"

"No." Elden turned his back on the thinly veiled chagrin in Umbra's eyes. Before the other Icarus garnered a protest, Elden said, "Savis will choose when she is ready. Not a moment before. If there are any attempts to pressure, manipulate, or force her, I will strip the Icarus responsible of their memory and leave them in the Ignis Desert to wander for Eternity. As long as I draw breath, Savis commands her own person. Am I understood, Umbra?" Elden glanced over his shoulder and glimpsed a trace of vehemence in the Coalition sergeant's expression.

Umbra hid it with another wordless bow, thoroughly chastised. When he straightened, a hint of resignation was set in his shoulders. "Very well, Elden. As it is your wish, I will follow your command."

Vinco rushed into the alcove with Amolot. The female looked Umbra over, as Vinco began their report. Elden listened, but let his thoughts drift to Savis. Only the maturity of a girl on the brink of womanhood, and she was already as incandescent as her mother. Elden mourned that Silence had missed much of their daughter's life already, but he knew his mate would agree with Savis' upbringing. As well as his decision to spurn Umbra.

No one would force Savis while Elden yet breathed.

Rayne's heart ached as she opened her eyes. Elden...

She wondered if he approved of Nox and Rayne's relationship. As she thought it, her skin glowed. Incandescent.

It helped lift Rayne's spirits as she realized Nox was no longer in the bed, but there was a note on his pillow.

BREAKFAST. BE BACK, PRETTY WARRIOR. LOVE, STABBY.

Rayne slapped a hand over her mouth and squeezed her eyes shut, suppressing a snicker. Behind her, Korac and Sagan were still sleeping in each other's arms, him on his back and her sprawled on top of him. They were much less put together in their sleep.

On tiptoe, Rayne padded barefoot through her morning routine, including one mega large cup of tea and headline research in her favorite nook. From the night before, people had reported a Nox and Rayne sighting at Night Rayne's Tomb.

One witness said, "They were uh[sic] fucking a meter away from me."

Another said, "Whoever luo is paying for these stunts to promote *Rayne's Verse* deserves a bonus for dedication. I saw Rayne once at the Volcano Day battle. This girl looked just like her, but with better eyebrows."

Rayne giggled into her tea—

The stairs sighed as Korac took them, graceful in his light steps. Rayne smiled at him and tried to ignore that he was shirtless in his white silk pajamas. She'd expected him to pillage the kitchen or take a shower. Instead, he came over to the library and took up an armchair across from Rayne.

Curious, she watched Korac comb through his hair with his fingers and tousle it for some volume. Silky and soft-looking, Rayne wanted to play with it—Oh, shit. He caught her looking.

Ugh.

Now Korac was smirking.

Rayne rolled her eyes, went back to her reading, and sipped her tea.

"That mug is ridiculous. It's bigger than your face." Only Korac could make such an elegant cadence sound so snarky.

With her eyes on the tab, Rayne shrugged and asked, "Did you come over here to make me jealous and pick on my breakfast?"

Korac leaned back in the chair and steepled his fingers. "Have you told him you love him?"

Rayne snapped to him so fast her tea sloshed. Staring into eyes—They were neutral. Judgment-free. She felt safe to confess, "No."

The dip of Korac's chin said he'd assumed as much, but it didn't tell Rayne how to proceed or tried to force more conversation out of her. She valued it. Instead, Korac said, "I'm curious how you reacted to many events in the Verses, but there's one question from my Verse we wanted to ask you."

"What is it?" Rayne's voice was breathy, waiting.

Korac leaned forward onto the edge of his seat to ask, "If you could change it, would you? I can't fathom another world than this one, but the Probability Matrix presents us with options. There's a version of us out there for every decision, but in some of them, none of us ever meet because Nox never fell in love with Celindria. Would you change a single outcome, Rayne? A single thing about you and Nox?"

The Icarean General had asked Rayne this in his Verse, and at the time, she'd only thought of her mother. Of telling Michelle Callahan about the Progeny and Cinder. Or staying home from school the day of the Invasion—So many things.

But would Rayne change anything about her and Nox?

She opened her mouth to answer—

"This is a glorious sight first thing in the morning," Sagan called from upstairs, leaning on the banister and looking for all the world as if inappropriate thoughts filled her head.

"No."

Korac and Rayne said it at once, shared a look, and both laughed.

Sagan pouted.

Rayne set her empty tea mug aside and changed the subject. "Nox is playing good host and went to hunt us some breakfast. Should we get ready for training while we wait?"

Korac held up a finger. "May I propose an excellent suggestion?" The broadening of his trademark smirk into a grin both terrified and intrigued Rayne.

"Go on."

Eggs would do.

Nox found plenty for the four of them and returned to the treeloft. Before he left this morning, he'd sat on the edge of the bed and admired Rayne in her sleep. At peace. He worried about her coping without him after they'd spent all this time together. The six months apart had only strengthened their bond. Perhaps the same would prove true of Nox's inevitable imprisonment.

No matter the outcome, he regretted nothing.

Loud music greeted Nox upon entry, along with chatter.

Sagan asked, "So what was it like destroying Enki?"

Before Nox rounded the corner to the dining space, Rayne said, "Nox told me dying hurt, so he asked to take the pain from me."

He paused, surprised she was so forthcoming. It made Nox sound like a hero when all he wanted was to spare her from it.

Rayne's voice was soft as she asked, "Korac, do you think telling Xelan about it would help?"

"It's hard to say, your majesty. Even as children, Nox took the brunt of Umbra off Savis, Xelan, and I." Korac kept talking even as he saw Nox come around the corner. "It could invoke memories of the older brother protector, and I'm certain the Co-Emperor will factor that into his considerations. I have faith his imperial majesty will be fair."

Nox's General was sitting in a chair with Sagan braiding one side of his hair. Rayne was twisting along the other side. The girls moved to the music, concentrating while Korac languished under their undivided attention. They tied ribbons and hooked rings throughout their lattice work, enjoying the task. Neither was truly aware of how few people Korac had allowed to touch him.

At Nox's quirked brow, Korac gave a cavalier shrug and an arrogant dip of his chin. What could he say? Everyone loved the hair.

Sagan looked up first, and Nox found himself victim to the sweetness in her smile. She radiated sunshine.

Rayne was deep in thought at her task until Korac cleared his throat into his fist. When she looked up and saw Nox, that emotion—the one akin to love—illuminated her face. She dropped everything to run across the dining room and jump into his arms. He caught Rayne under her thighs and held her there. Nox reached up and tucked a strand of hair which had escaped her braid behind her ear.

The scent of surf and seashells accompanied the dazzling light in Rayne's eyes as she stared down into Nox's gaze. He returned the smile, and she bit her lip, sending a thrill through him.

One of them ought to speak, so Nox said, "Hi."

Rayne released her lip to give him a goofy smile. "Hi. How was your hunt?"

"Not nearly as interesting as your morning."

A light blush graced Rayne's cheeks as she said, "Hopefully, I've made it more titillating for you."

Nox glanced down and realized the white loose and low-cut top Rayne was wearing exposed a satin bra beneath it, matching her eyes. The material framed her breasts in an enticing invitation, made more so given they were in the company of others and couldn't fulfill the temptation.

More than anything, Nox wanted to kiss Rayne. He let it show in his eyes as he quirked a brow and asked, "Is this a game you want to play?" By Elden, he would throw her over his shoulder and carry her out to the forest if it came to it.

Rayne bit her lip again—the siren—and gave a single nod.

"We did *not* Seamswalk across the galaxy to watch you two mate."

Sagan snickered at her husband's admonishment, but Nox could hear the humor lying beneath it.

Rayne mouthed, "Later," and patted Nox's bicep to set her down. He let her free to return to the General's hair, and Nox paid special attention to how her black leggings hugged her ass and the contours of the muscles she worked hard to maintain.

It wasn't Korac who caught Nox looking.

Sagan beamed and mouthed, "I. Know. Right?" She'd dressed in her own distracting sparring gear. Her white top was one swath of material criss-crossed and haltered to cover only her breasts. Even her white shorts clung to her like a second skin, revealing the undersides of her curves when she moved. Nox only noticed because Rayne kept a close eye on the bottom region, nearly tearing a chuckle out of him.

It seemed Nox was the only one who'd missed the gear invitation. Korac was wearing motorcycle pants with Kevlar in the knees and chains from the pockets to the knee pads. And, of all things, a t-shirt made of chain-mail. It jingled as he shifted. On anyone else, it would look outlandish. But on Korac...

"I approve of your gear, soldier." Nox meant it.

Did Korac know he straightened? Or was it a reflex? "Once you're free, I'll introduce you to my tailor."

Lucas.

Yes. An Icarus of his reputation warranted an introduction. Soon.

Until then, Nox would savor this moment. The girls dancing and gossiping. Korac preening under their ministrations. Music and friends.

Nox headed for the kitchen. "I'll cook us some breakfast while you ladies spoil our General."

Korac chuffed. "Ignore him, girls. My King is simply jealous of your attentions."

Sagan finished a braid and started the next one, offering out of hand, "Well, Nox, if you'd like, Rayne and I could do you next."

Ah. Sweet, naïve Seamswalker. Sagan didn't know the error of her phrasing, but Korac and Rayne knew. The former stiffened and looked up at his wife, while the latter peered over at Nox and winked.

Sagan pouted. "What?"

Korac took her hand and kissed it. "Nothing, amos. Nox knows you didn't mean to offer him a threesome with Rayne."

Rayne snickered at how Sagan's eyes doubled in size. "Oh."

"But you presented an excellent idea." Korac stood and gestured for Nox to sit. "Your majesty, I insist you take my place while I cook."

Unable to control it, Nox's brows shot up.

The girls were quick to agree. Rayne said, "Please. It'll be fun to give you a makeover."

Sagan gave a little bounce. "Please?!"

This was an odd position Korac had put Nox in. In fact, his General passed him on the way to the kitchen, saying under his breath, "You don't want to disappoint them, now do you?"

With a sigh, Nox resigned himself to his fate. "Fine."

For twenty minutes, the two women pampered Nox while he tried to relax despite how much he flinched at the contact, initially. Rayne was careful with him and lingered within his line of sight so he could track where she'd touch him next. Like a ball of sunshine, Sagan danced, brushed, and braided, oblivious to Nox's discomfort.

The Seamswalker said, "Now, once we finish, go upstairs and change to match the rest of us. Have fun with it."

Nox glanced up at Rayne, and she approved with a nod and a smirk. "Show me what you've got." By dipping slightly, the loose top gaped, further exposing her breasts. He was rising to the challenge.

"That's cheating," Sagan said, a little breathy.

"No. No. I can't even see what's happening, but I can hear my wife. Stop with the threesome energy and come eat."

Rayne winked and said, "Be right there." To Sagan, she gestured. "Get the mirror."

Nox peered at himself and blinked. Aggressive and smoldering, it reminded him of the only time he let Korac dress him for a conquest festival. Nox had fended off more invitations to dance that night than any other he could recount. At their expectant faces, he asked, "You don't find the eyeliner too excessive?"

Both girls shook their head, and Sagan insisted, "Eyeliner is never too much. Especially with your lashes." Everything about her was so sincere it was disarming.

The mischievous sparkle in Rayne's eye captivated Nox as she leaned to whisper, "Dress with me in mind."

With their encouragement and outright fawning, Nox's face burned as he made his way upstairs. Below, the girls helped Korac dish out breakfast on the island.

Hard leather pants. Soft leather pants. Those were Nox's only options. He went with the soft ones. For a shirt...

Dress with Rayne in mind.

A few minutes later, when he turned the corner into the kitchen, Nox finished securing the last buckle holding the front of his cobalt shirt together. The material clung to him and strained against the straps, fastening it down the center. He chose it because the straps gaped and left a good deal of skin exposed. Skin he'd decorated with paint for Rayne.

When she looked away from Sagan, mid-conversation,

Rayne's eyes went straight to the Icarean script. As her nacre translated it while she read, a soft smile pulled at her lips.

Korac smirked and conceded, "Well, I suppose you should dress to surpass me at least once in our lifetimes."

Sagan smiled so widely at Nox, her freckles scrunched on her nose.

After reading the opening to her Verse on display, Rayne said, "So I assume there's more?"

Nox winked as he took his place at the table. "For every strike you land on me in today's sparring match, you can see a little more."

Sagan clapped in delight. "Strip fighting?! Oh my god! Neither of you boys has enough layers for this."

As Nox looked Sagan over at the single bit of fabric covering her upper body, he met Korac's eyes and raised a brow. "What say you General?"

Korac chuckled, and it was rich. Pride suffused his voice as he said, "If you can lay a finger on a Seamswalker, then I won't argue as to the prize." The smirk at the end cemented his confidence in his mate.

Sagan nodded across the table at Rayne, asking, "What about you? Your clothes are kinda… a part of you, right?"

"Her clothes come off," Nox said it out of hand, but Sagan and Korac turned their eyes slowly to him with identical, knowing grins.

Rayne blushed, but refused to let it stop her from saying, "He's right. They are actual material I manifest with the nanites in my nacre. I only reabsorb my clothes to avoid laundry." Her face blossomed into a smile. "But it doesn't matter because Sagan's on my team, and you guys are so gonna lose. I hope you remembered to wear some boxers under those tight pants."

Korac cleared his throat, but kept his eyes on the last of his eggs and chewed without a word.

Sagan and Rayne looked at each other across the table and snickered.

Until Nox cleared *his* throat.

They both blushed, and Korac glared at him.

This would make for an interesting afternoon.

Rayne wanted to live in this moment forever. Sagan stood at her side and faced Nox and Korac across the forest floor. Dull gray leaves crunched underfoot and wildlife thrummed, forming a heartbeat among the trees. It matched Rayne's racing pulse. Or was it Nox's pounding in her chest?

With Korac at his side, Nox grinned, and Rayne knew he felt the same about this moment.

No weapons.

No flying.

One strike, one article of clothing.

Rayne checked Sagan, wearing hardly anything. Rayne's grin broadened at the confident smile on the Seamswalker's face. All for Korac, who—shocker—smirked back at his wife. Not at all the attitude of a man soon to be stripped of his clothes.

Nox called across the clearing, "Are you prepared for this? I won't hold back as I usually do."

Korac flashed with humor. "Amos, are you sure you want them to see you naked?"

"Oh Rayne's seen me naked, babe, and she will later tonight win or lose."

A thrill went through Rayne, skyrocketing her pulse to Nox's incredulous, head-shaking amusement. Especially at the narrow-eyed gaze Korac was rocking. Regardless of how this match turned out, Rayne guessed Sagan had earned herself a punishment in the bedroom. Still...

Fist bump.

Rayne said, "I look forward to reading the rest of my Verse, Nox."

His eyes flashed Atramentous. In the reflection of the chrome mirrors, Rayne saw her breathless response. Nox said, "On your mark."

Korac said, "Get set."

The girls shouted, "Go!"

Rayne and Sagan went running headlong at their partners, and the second before the clash, Sagan opened conduits straight ahead. The girls took them and came out running right at the boys' backs.

Their lovers were quick and turned around in time to intercept. Before Korac could land a spin kick square in Sagan's chest, she fell backward and through a conduit.

As Nox punched at her, Rayne used her running momentum to drop and slide across the leaves between his feet, spread in a fighting stance.

Sagan reappeared in time to grab Rayne by the wrist and pull her to her feet.

They squared off against their partners again, Rayne to Korac and Sagan to Nox, who said, "I'll be the first to admit it. I think the male fighters require a handicap."

Sagan jutted out the hip with her hand on it and clicked her tongue. "Figures. Let me guess. You don't want me to Seamswalk?"

Rayne picked leaves out of her own hair, watching the transaction between her two lovers. That's right. Nox was a lover. She was waiting for the right time to tell him.

Korac was watching Rayne intently as the other two negotiated. She wondered if he saw a flicker of her feelings for Nox in her eyes—

"So. No Seamswalking. Do you want to add no punching while you're at it?" Sagan's playful smile was charming as all hell.

Nox chuckled.

Korac shook his head and sighed. He reasoned, "It's best you exercise without it. You never know what Celindria can disable."

Good point.

"But you'll still lose," Rayne promised.

High five between the girls. Sagan asked, "Are you ready?"

Nox and Korac crouched into stances with firm nods. The latter crooked his hand, and the girls took off at them.

They crossed the clearing in a series of flips. One of Xelan's old tactics. The art of spectacle.

Sprung off a back flip, Rayne went for an aerial split kick aimed at both male fighters.

Sagan finished her overhead roll with a blow to both of their midsections.

The boys cheated and flipped out of the way, while the girls tumbled into each other.

Laid out on the forest floor, Sagan asked, "Where'd they go?"

Without Seamswalking or flying, Nox and Korac had vanished. On the edge of the clearing, the treebases formed a fork. Rayne suggested, "You take left. I'll go right."

Sagan grumbled about " ... splitting the girls up on purpose ... "

There was no arguing that point. The girls were too much of a handful together. Even knowing this was a ploy, Rayne followed the enticement of searching for Nox in the woods alone. She felt for all the world like little red riding hood seeking the big bad wolf.

"Nox," Rayne singsonged while cautiously stepping under a low branch. "Come out and lose. I'm waiting, Stabby—"

A powerful arm wrenched Rayne up against the tree base. At the flash of his chrome Atramentous, she gasped, "Nox," as he gripped both her wrists in one hand and pulled them high.

Nox pinned Rayne, pressed his body down the length of hers, and kissed her roughly. The purring growl deep in his chest as he tasted her coaxed the scent of honeysuckle into the air. She returned as good as he gave until he left her breathless when he pulled away and...

The sexy bastard ripped Rayne's shirt off and smirked while he tucked it into the back of his pants. Unfulfilled potential roughed Nox's voice as he declared, "That's one, pretty warrior."

"You're dead."

Nox inhaled the thickening of her scent, much to the ire of Rayne's blushing face, before he quipped, "Some risks are worth dying for."

Bad move.

In a throwback, Rayne used his grip on her wrists to tuck her knees to her chest and kick Nox square in the diaphragm. The air blew out of him in a violent exhale, and he let her go to double over, protecting his ribs.

Unable to trust herself with Nox, Rayne ran, calling into the maze of treebases, "Sagan?! Sagan, it's a trap!"

"I know."

Rayne turned toward Sagan's voice. Through the brush, the War King glimpsed the Seamswalker's violet eyes in Atramentous. Rayne asked, "Why are you... Oh."

In the shade of a treebase, Sagan hid her naked breasts with Korac's chain-mail shirt. The poor young woman was flushed so red Rayne couldn't make out the freckles on her nose.

This was asinine. Into the trees Rayne yelled, "This is beneath you, General. First you two handicap us, and now subterfuge. Have you no honor?!"

Korac's voice ricocheted through the canopy. "Oh, believe us. To disarm such fierce warriors as yourselves with the mere promise of intimacy is quite the honor. Concede the game, and we'll return your clothes."

Rayne glanced over at Sagan, where she slipped into the chain-mail shirt. If they could cheat, so could the girls. While she dialed down the gravity densifier she had worn for the boys' sakes, Rayne shouted, "I'm owed one article of clothing."

One half of Nox's shirt fell from a tree on Rayne's right. Gotcha. With sixty percent of her speed, she ran up the tree and onto the branch where Nox and Korac were perched like vultures. They'd had enough time to know Rayne was no longer below, but not enough time to see her coming.

It took only fifty percent of her strength to push them off. When they fell, Rayne shouted, "No flying, remember?!"

Both men landed on the cushion of deadfall, breathless and stunned. Sagan knelt between them and flicked them enough times to relinquish all of their clothes. While doing so, she made cute noises and admonished them. "This will teach you to take advantage of us."

Nox and Korac laid on the ground, staring up at Rayne relearning how to breathe with all the air knocked from their lungs. Simultaneously, they groaned, "You win," and, "We concede."

Rayne jumped down and stood over them with her hands on her hips. She glanced over at Sagan and asked, "What do *you* think?"

Sagan's lips spread into a devious smile as she nodded.

While the boys got to their feet, Rayne ordered, "Strip."

Korac froze, but Nox turned by the inches to meet Rayne's eyes.

Quickly snatching her torn shirt from Nox's pants, Rayne said, "You lost. Take off your clothes."

"Both of you," Sagan added with a wink at her husband.

Korac looked between her and Nox, asking a question, and Sagan taunted Korac with his signature cavalier shrug. From then on, the General narrowed his eyes at his wife.

Nox stood first, his hair feathered with leaves and twigs, and quirked a brow at Rayne.

She held up both halves of her shirt and looked at him through the tear. "Go ahead."

After a shrug and a glance at Sagan, Nox unfastened the remaining half of his shirt. Following his lead, Korac stood, already shirtless, and unzipped his motorcycle pants.

Hunger bled into Sagan's eyes as she watched her husband, while Rayne concentrated on Nox. He unlaced his leather pants and slid them down. As indicated before, neither man wore anything beneath.

A blush burned Rayne's cheeks with all of her Verse on display on Nox's chest and back. The reddening intensified as Korac stood with his hands on his hips looking at Rayne as if she would learn more of a lesson from this than they would. Nox picked a leaf from his General's hair, both of them comfortable in their nudity. Meanwhile, Rayne blinked, trying to keep her eyes on their faces.

Sagan took over giving the orders. "Forward march to the loft, boys. We'll have a pleasant view on the walk back."

They walked ahead, still in their boots, while Sagan and Rayne followed. It was a pleasant view, and a peaceful recovery after the vigor of their fight.

Ruining the peace, Korac called from ahead, "Amos?"

"Yes?" Sagan thickened up the sweetness in her voice.

"I'll remember this."

The Seamswalker flushed from head to toe, and Rayne wondered how Nox would punish her once they were alone.

Nox was impatient to get Rayne alone. He'd almost thrown the match beneath the tree branch to take her then and there. Made all the more tempting because he knew she'd welcome it.

Creativity.

Imagination.

Rayne's punishment required both, and, as Nox marched naked into the treeloft, he was hungry to mete it out of her, one swell at a time. Korac followed inside until they both stopped in the living room.

As the women glided in, pleased with their victory, Nox asked, "What will it be now? We're at your mercy... For the time being." He met Rayne's eyes on the last and let her see everything he had planned in his.

She shivered.

"Perhaps you should allow us to dress before you get more than the view you bargained for." Korac's voice was dry as he gestured toward Nox.

Sagan clapped, jingling the chain-mail shirt. "Of course. It'll make things easier while you two cook dinner for us. I'm famished."

Nox laughed, and Rayne visibly softened at the sound. He cherished her response. "Very well."

After folding his arms, Korac said, "I enjoy keeping my wife satisfied."

The smirk on Rayne's face as she pulled Sagan against her side was devilish. "Good to know you'll be enjoying yourself while Sagan and I take a shower. Ta." With a cheeky wave, she dragged the Seamswalker with her around the corner.

Korac's brows went high.

Nox chuckled deep in his chest as he slipped into some pants, saying, "They will have a time with you, old friend. Come. Let's make our women a feast while they provide us a show."

"A show?" A frown marred Korac's perfect face. It conveyed even while he dressed in his pajamas until he followed Nox into the kitchen and stopped...

everything. The half-Aegis General even quit breathing.

On the shower side of the sheet, Rayne was absorbing her clothes while lifting Korac's chain-mail shirt over Sagan's head. She went to her knees and kissed Sagan's stomach and slipped the Seamswalker's tiny shorts down. After Rayne discarded those, she activated the water. With their fingers raking through their hair, the girls turned their faces toward the spray and let it pour down their curves and the contours of their muscles.

"Soldier, stand down," Nox ordered.

For the first time in a million years or more, Korac had lost his composure around Nox and gaped. In an attempt to defend his lack of self-discipline, he pointed at the scene and opened his mouth. Closed it. Then, like the water washing over the girls, restraint washed over Korac, and he wrenched his eyes off the view at the same time Rayne kissed Sagan.

Even with seven million years of practice, it was taking every ounce of Nox's command over himself not to react.

With his back ramrod straight, Korac collected stored root vegetables and set to preparing them.

This was good. Productive distraction. Nox set some meat onto roast in the island's hidden spit.

Chopping vigorously to disguise the kissing sounds, Korac said, "I've never seen you so happy."

Backs to each other, Nox said, "Nor you. In fact, I recall you being an Icarus of fewer words."

"Between finding my birth family, marrying Sagan, adopting Echo, and learning you're alive, I find myself in a better humor these days."

Quite the fortune to recount, and Nox was honored Korac counted his resurrection among them. But there was only one item he wanted to ask about. "What's it like having a daughter?"

Even though Korac was still busy cooking with his back turned away, Nox could hear the smile in his voice as Korac said, "Everyday is an adventure. She whistles along with my singing. Just last week she shed her first feather, as white as my hair. We think she's ready to open her gliders for the first time, but we'll see. I hope we don't miss it."

Nox grinned at the pride in Korac's voice, and he felt grateful his best friend knew this kind of peace.

"You'll meet her."

Perplexed, Nox turned to find Korac leaning back on the counter with his arms crossed. His expression was matter of fact as he repeated, "You and Rayne will meet Echo soon. And Pax, if it were up to me. It's strange. The imperial Prince is why I'm here. Pax told me it was time to find you."

"I would like to meet them."

Nox turned at the same time as Korac to find Rayne and Sagan standing on the kitchen side of the sheet. They'd wrapped themselves in towels and smoothed their wet hair back from their faces. Rayne's smile was radiant. The blush on her face after the performance she'd just put on was one of the contradictions he loved about her.

Nox cupped Rayne's cheek and kissed her.

With their foreheads together, she said, "Thank you for cooking," against his mouth.

Nox licked the taste of her from his lips before teasing, "Rayne, why are you in a towel when you can grow your clothes?"

"Nox, why were you naked most of the afternoon? Oh, yeah. 'Cause you lost—Yip!"

That was one of his absolute favorite sounds from her. Nox had picked Rayne up and plopped her down on the nearest counter. "If my nudity was your prize, then we've both won."

"Uh. You guys? We're still here." Sagan's friendly interruption was enough to make Nox bark out a laugh.

Rayne's eyes sparkled with it.

From behind Nox, Korac said, "We were just discussing the best venue to confront Celindria next—Wait. This is Pehton. Your majesties, unless you're ready to oust yourselves, keep quiet."

Rayne asked, "Aren't you going to put on a shirt before answering—"

Nox cupped his hand over her mouth as the Lyrik appeared in the projection. He glanced apologetically at Rayne to find their hearts racing and something unexpected in her eyes. The craving to explore more of her kinks gnawed at Nox. It would have to wait.

"General, where the hell have you been?" The orange-feathered Lyrik opened boldly with her superior. From what Nox had heard of her, feisty certainly fit the bill. Incredulous, Pehton scoffed, "Are you shirtless? Again?! Korac, we've talked about this."

Sagan leaned into view, dressed in a towel, and waved. "Hey, Pehton. You caught us at a bad time. Is everything okay?"

They were taunting the poor woman.

Korac kissed his wife's cheek for encouraging the ruse and smirked for the Lyriki Warden as he asked, "Is it that you feel left out? Because you're welcome to join us."

There was a pause, and Nox realized Pehton was counting to ten. Still on the counter behind him, Rayne snickered and perched her chin on Nox's shoulder to watch.

Pehton said, "Celindria was in possession of Cinderken's volition. She's also controlling F8 and the hives and anyone who went through a Divine Booth with a port. Razor is conscious inside a nacre. And there are less than ten thousand Probabilities left in the Matrix."

How?

Nox wasn't asking how Celindria's reach was so far—He could never underestimate her. But the Probability Matrix...

After allowing them to absorb the news for a moment, Pehton continued, "Has Zero given you *anything* which could help us?"

No longer smirking, Korac said, "Give me another day, and we'll return with a plan."

Pehton narrowed her eyes at him in suspicion. "What are you really doing out there?"

"You wouldn't believe me if I told you, and I think it's best if you had some plausible deniability, General Warden."

She turned those garnet eyes on Sagan, who ducked hers a little in shame as she said, "Trust us. Please."

Pehton glared between the two of them before relenting with a sigh. "Fine. Let me know what's happening as soon as you can, and I'll back you up. Over and Out."

Sagan pouted. "I feel scolded."

Korac kissed her temple, and the two fell into conversation.

Nox turned to find Rayne in sleep pants and a strappy top so tight he could tell she wasn't wearing a bra. The complement of her blue pajamas made her eyes sparkle. With her hair smoothed back, Rayne's face was fresh and bare.

Rayne's sudden shy smile affected Nox as she said, "When you look at me, I feel beautiful. Like *actually.* Not the way the Tritans or other people say it. I know you know everything about me, and you still look at me that way."

"You've seen yourself through my eyes and know it to be true. I've said it, and I'll never stop saying it. Out on the battlefield or here in this kitchen, you are the most beautiful being in this galaxy." *And I love you* rang in the air between them.

With a flutter of her eyelashes, Rayne blinked back tears. She took a deep breath to say—

"The roast is burning, and you are *not* mating in front of us."

After three years without Korac, Nox realized how much he'd missed his General's humor.

After Sagan changed out of the towel and into a shirt which matched Korac's pajama bottoms, they sat down to eat.

Summarizing the conversation, Rayne said, "So we'll be at the premiere of my biopic?"

Across from her, Nox assured, "Celindria is everywhere now, and she knows the Shadow will be there. If you and I attend, I can try to convince her to surrender."

Sagan set her fork down and asked, "And if she doesn't?"

With an expression which showed Korac's appreciation for the scale of this operation, he said, "Then we arrest everyone she's inhabited."

"I wish I knew what she wanted. Other than Nox. You know? What's her ultimate plan?" Rayne asked a good question. They knew nothing of Celindria's purpose.

He took her hand and kissed it. "We'll defeat her. Together."

Korac's gagging made them both look over at him. The General said, "Sorry. I just realized this is what Sagan and I have been doing to Xelan and Tameka all this time, and now I owe them an apology they will never get."

Rayne laughed.

Sagan cut in. "Well, because you two are such fantastic cooks, I am now full and sleepy. I'm heading to bed."

"Korac and I volunteer to let you ladies have the bed tonight." Nox knew the significance of his offer.

Like he'd been slapped, Korac whirled on Nox with an icy glare, threatening to freeze Nox's taunting grin.

Rayne cried, "Really?!" Her genuine elation was reward enough for spurning the General.

Without taking his eyes off Nox, Korac flattened his voice and said, "Yes. Really."

Sagan kissed her husband's cheek. "Thanks for understanding, babe. We promise to be quiet."

While the girls cleared the table, exchanging heart-racing glances, Korac mouthed, "I. Will. Have. My. Revenge."

Ignoring him, Nox asked, "Seamswalker, have I mentioned I'm a massive fan of you splitting a planet in half?"

"Aw. Thanks. It broke every bone in my body, but I appreciate the compliments." She leaned down and kissed her husband's cheek again. "Isn't Nox the best, babe?"

Through gritted teeth, Korac said, "Oh. Yes. The best."

Nox followed Rayne to the stairs, while Sagan dragged Korac with placations. "My sweet wonderful husband. Thank you for understanding."

"Of course, amos." Korac finally accepted defeat. "Anything for you."

On the first step, Rayne leaned forward and kissed Sagan's collarbone, up her neck, and whispered in her ear. On a shaky breath, Sagan relayed, "Rayne wants me to tell you boys, 'good night and don't do anything we wouldn't do.'"

Nox shook his head, Korac rolled his eyes, and the girls giggled before racing each other up the stairs. Their night looked far better than the one ahead of their partners. Without the bed…

At the same thought, Nox and Korac looked at each other and said, "You're sleeping on the floor." "I'm taking the couch."

Korac's shirt which Sagan had been wearing flew over the banister and landed on the floor beside them.

While Korac was distracted with snatching up the shirt and folding it, Nox claimed the long end of the L-shaped couch. The General turned, realized Nox's ploy, and made a noise in disgust. The best soldier took the short end, legs dangling off further than Nox's.

A few minutes of silence passed with them both staring at the ceiling, listening to the sounds of the girls reuniting. They were not quiet as promised, and Nox's heart pounded in his chest with Rayne's excitement.

Korac asked, "Can you see anything?"

Nox searched above, fruitlessly. "Not a damned thing, but..."

Both men inhaled deeply. The sweet aroma of watermelon and honeysuckle filled the air. Earth summer. Beautiful.

Pissy, Korac jabbed, "You know you don't deserve Rayne right?"

"I'm reminded of it every time she gives me the *look*."

Even in the dark, Nox knew Korac was frowning as he asked, "The *look*?"

Nox pictured it. Rayne's lips slightly parted, and her eyes bright with wonder shining in them. He said, "You know my meaning. Even if whole armies arrived to raze your kingdom to the ground, it's still perfect as long as she keeps looking at you that way."

Korac barked out a shocked laugh. "Poetry?! You really are in love."

Nox's heart rate plummeted, taking his breath away. Something was wrong. He sat up to—

"Nox! Korac! Something's wrong!" Sagan shouted from the banister.

Light emanated from the upstairs and painted the loft in its blaze.

Rayne.

The sun.
So bright.
And beautiful.
And angry.
Li's explosion melted Elden's flesh from his bones, peeling away blood and tears. They were not tears of agony, but of heartbreak. Savis was orphaned too young.

Silence.

Where are you?

With Elden's dying breath, he scattered the molecules of his Coalition into a sphere around Cinder. Even then, he knew something had gone wrong. When his nacre reformed inside the sacred chamber, he could see Li had scorched the land and blighted the water, despite the sphere.

Umbra.

The fool strode out of the ashes with aims on Elden's daughter, and there was nothing Elden could do to stop the spiteful Icarus.

Everything.

From up here, Elden saw everything.

Remorse.

Razor.

Celindria.

Lucas.

Elden saw it all.

And it made him weep.

Rayne stood in a white space and found it familiar. This was where she'd seen Elden for the first time. She wandered through it, calling his name.

The Icarus' multi-figured shadow appeared before he did.

The sight of Elden always took Rayne's breath away, but his tears hurt her chest. She searched the sun in his eyes and asked, "What can I do? How can I help you, forefather?"

"Daughter." His voice was so like Nox's, but with a slight echo. "The time has come."

Rayne's heart jumped into her throat, and she had to swallow to say, "You promised me a year."

Elden shook his head, the black and white strands swaying in their braids. He opened his hand and in it was a nebulous cloud full of stars. As Rayne stared, the stars winked and disappeared until only the brightest star in the center remained.

The Probabilities.

"You have two days, and I will come to you."

Even the sadness in Elden's voice couldn't diminish Rayne's panic. Breathless, she asked, "The Probability Matrix ends in two days?"

Elden corrected her. "*Everything* ends in two days."

Celindria, too.

As Rayne stared at Elden, the figures in his shadow disappeared, starting with the smallest. Pax. Then Celindria. Xelan. Nox. Savis.

Only Rayne remained in Elden's wake.

"I understand."

Elden took Rayne's hand, balled it into a fist, and placed it over her nacre. "Tell my children to offer no resistance. When the time comes to let you go. To let it all go. They know not who led them here, but they will see... Everything."

A tear fell from Rayne's lashes onto her cheek, and she winced. "Will it hurt?"

"Any other vessel would perish. You are the only one strong enough to survive."

That wasn't exactly a reassurance. Still... Rayne did something she'd wanted to do since the first time Xelan had sung Elden's Verse to her.

She hugged Elden. "I'll protect our family."

Warm and strong, only one other Icarus gave better hugs than Elden, and Rayne smiled at the thought of telling Xelan.

Soon.

With her eyes closed, her body went weightless, adrift in the white space. Falling… falling…

Through the nothing, Elden's voice echoed.

"Two days."

Sweet copper filled Rayne's mouth and brought her back to the treeloft. Nox was pressing his torn wrist to her lips, looking desperate and scared.

Sagan.

Korac.

Rayne must've scared them to death. She tapped Nox's wrist until he pulled it away and licked the blood from her lips. It was her first time drinking his blood, and she hungered for more. But…

Korac and Sagan, wrapped in a sheet, stood beside the bed looking varying degrees of worried. Rayne, shielded in pillows, tried for a weak smile, but she didn't feel like smiling.

Nox's eyes were filled with concern and love. Into them, she said, "Thank you. For so much…" Her voice broke, and the tears started.

Because this was it.

Sagan lowered her hand from where it had cupped her mouth to ask, "Are you all right?"

"What the fuck was that?" A disgruntled Korac was worth a sad laugh, and it tore from Rayne on a trembling breath.

Nox answered, "It was Elden."

The other couple balked. Korac asked, "Are you fucking with me?"

Sagan sat down on the edge of the bed and tucked a strand of Rayne's hair behind her ear. "You didn't tell us you could commune with him."

Over the next five minutes, Rayne told them everything Elden had shown her. Silence, Remorse, One, and Tumu—All of it.

Korac paled, which was saying something given his white complexion.

Nox prompted his General, "What is it?"

"Father—Zero said something when I asked about the disappearing Probabilities. He said, 'One would know,' but I mistook it for a hypothetical 'One.'"

Zero.

One.

"Your oldest brother," Sagan gasped at the same moment Rayne put it together. "He's alive..."

Nox, sitting in the middle of the bed with Rayne, suggested, "You could ask Razor. Pehton said he was 'conscious.'"

Korac raked a frustrated hand through his hair. "I hate this. I'm already imagining the smug look on his face."

"Tomorrow or the next day. We only have two days left." The second Rayne said it, she regretted it. They all stared at her with shock plain on their faces. "Yeah. Sorry. I should've led with that. Elden said we had two days before the Probabilities close."

Sagan frowned. "If only we knew who the Eternal Bind was... We could separate them somehow."

Never had Korac ever stared at Rayne as hard as he was staring at her right then.

Please don't say it.

Please don't confirm Rayne's latest suspicion and greatest fear.

Still staring at her from behind his composed mask, Korac said, "Nox, I think you're—"

"I'm tired," Rayne blurted. While Korac narrowed his eyes at her, she said, "And I could use some sleep. Sagan, do you think you can bring Tameka and Xelan here in the morning?"

Sagan looked between her husband and Rayne, sensing some tension. Despite it, she said, "Of course."

Nox tucked Rayne against him, and she breathed deep of his warm scent. One she wouldn't smell again after tonight.

A painful ache twisted in her chest, prompting her to ask, "Can we all sleep in the same bed again?

Dying with Elden has made me want to cry." While she resented the weakness in her voice, Rayne felt the anguish almost as strong as her love for the people in this loft.

After another stare off, Korac finally relinquished the glare and admitted, "It's not as if I was getting any sleep on that couch."

They cuddled in the same arrangement as the night before, except tonight Rayne wasn't taking Nox for granted. The warm arm around her, the steady way he breathed against her back, the purring in his chest—She soaked it all into her heart and held it tight.

Win or lose. This was their last night.

Into the sleeping quiet, Rayne whispered, "I love you."

Celindria was alone.

Solitude had wormed its way in again and burrowed into the aching chasm of her little-used heart.

How can we be millions of people at once and feel so alone?

Because we condemned ourselves to this carousel for a dream, lost in a vacuum.

So few voices now. So few Probabilities.

What to do? What. To. Do?

The prospects Nox had offered included a relationship with him and Xelan's guaranteed assistance to retrieve Celindria's Pax and Hope.

Or.

Celindria could wring Rayne dry and put the girl's incredible blood to practical use by overthrowing the Progeny and claiming Iona Pax for herself.

Was there a third option?

Absent of fear, the loneliness called. Celindria opened the door and peeked into the most cherished Probability.

Cinder.

Nox's Castle.

The pyre in his chambers blazed, and Nox held Celindria close in his sleep. In the next suite, their great grandchildren slept, healthy and happy under Li's stalwart protection.

A voice, one long suppressed, whispered in Celindria's ear.

I feel. Nox's kiss. The children's warm hugs. You feel it and fear it. Fear we could be happy and fear we can feel at all—

"No!" Celindria returned to the dominant reality with a shriek.

Fear. Yes, she felt it now.

All of Celindria's emotions had trickled from one. The Probability she dared not linger within. There, she was only a woman—Nox's woman. But anywhere else, Celindria was a goddess, forged in the Source.

Power?

Or love?

Why not both?

Celindria hugged her shoulders and rocked, muttering, "Why not both..."

Perhaps she'd went too long within the maddening confines of the Oblivion Cathedral. Out there, Celindria's vessels waited. Iuo's premiere of Rayne's Verse would serve as the perfect diversion for her plan, assuming she wouldn't take Nox up on his offer.

Now, the Shadow knew Celindria was enforcing volition control. Why did she not kill Cinderken? Because if Celindria chose the rehabilitation deal Nox had offered her, father would be less inclined to believe Celindria was seeking reform if she'd killed someone in front of him.

Which will we choose? Love?

Or Power?

Celindria held up her palm and formed a golden pellet, like the one she had shot at Nox during the battle referred to as Volcano Day. It spun in her hand until she flattened it into a coin. Her face was on one side, and her lover's face was on the other. Andrew, the Progeny known as Conscience, came by this technique of manipulating the Matrix naturally. Celindria learned it after a millennium of practice.

She flipped it high in the air until it came back down and landed.

On its side.

Ambivalent, Celindria stared at the tattered blue ribbon in her palm. It whipped about in the Oblivion Cathedral's howling void. Unfeeling, she closed her fist over it and decided.

Both.

Celindria awakened inside her soldiers and scanned her inventory. Three hundred of them were conduit operators for the empire, all former Divine Booth addicts. Agreeable for her; unfortunate for them. She kept them at their jobs, where they stood sentinel in their glass shrines and ports throughout Ishkur and the worlds. Within their mindscapes, they laid prone and groaned in misery, so unaware of their prominence in New Paradise. In the work of a moment, Celindria pre-programmed commands for their next shift and left them on autopilot.

Onto the next.

Three hundred thousand Caprents who Celindria had vaccinated millennia ago joined her ranks today. All this time, her nanites sang in their veins. Two of them worked as transport specialists. They were digital cartographers for the Overseers within Ishkur. She would need them for the next phase of her plans.

"Please…let me go…" A female begged on her backward-bent knees inside her mind.

Celindria kept her back to the female while saying, "One day, you will see this for the gift it is, rather than the punishment you fear it to be."

With this female standing inside one of Ishkur's glass operating center, Celindria could see Torrentus, terraforming a continent near Cinder II. It swirled in its awesome hurricane of components, breathing life into the barren land. Vast and thick with atmospheric gases, the continent was perfect for F8's people. Monarch 4.

Can we manipulate it from here? Can we poison it?

No. Leave it for when we take Iona Pax for ourselves. F8 will thank us and be our friend again.

Celindria left instructions for the cartographers to change course for all Overseers. At the opportune moment, of course.

Already, new Probabilities formed from her actions, branching into new universes for Celindria to explore. This was working according to plan.

Now to set the stage.

With the ribbon in hand, Celindria shadow-walked to one of the recent Probabilities. She traversed the treacherous path out of the Oblivion Cathedral and to the front of the mountain, surrounded by a cyclone of Cascading Light. In the eye of Thailea's storm, she gazed up to the sky and basked in the magnificence of the ice rings colored in every shade of blood. A rainbow arcing directly above.

It invoked optimism, a fleeting emotion Celindria cherished. She clung to it and took the first nearby conduit.

Reipon.

Utilizing Lamias under her control in high places, Celindria traveled to Ishkur undetected. Once there, she chose the optimum location in the Palatial Grounds, the location of the premiere. It was near a secret alcove hidden within a ring of waterfalls where Celindria set the ribbon down.

Static crept along Celindria's deep skin, drawing goosebumps and frizzing her hair. Tension rode the air, and the anticipation threatened to steal her breath, pulling taut in her bones until...

Lightning struck the ribbon and split reality open into the Seam.

Into Thailea.

Love.

Power.

Celindria would have both.

XV   SCORCH

LIFE WAS PECULIAR AT TIMES.

With Sagan at his side, Korac ate breakfast across the table from Nox and Rayne. The War King had snuggled up to the former King of Cinder, while keeping her close with an arm around her waist. Their glances were loving and sad.

Life, Korac found, was far more often cruel.

He would give a good deal for a return to the playfulness of yesterday—Minus the bizarre foursome vibes. Instead, they sat here in silence like it was Nox's last meal. The way the former King of Cinder's gaze slipped to Rayne as if he was memorizing her features belied his otherwise peaceful resignation. And Rayne...

'Devastated' wasn't a strong enough word for her crestfallen demeanor. The most powerful warrior in the galaxy slouched like a kicked puppy, stealing glimpses of Nox when he wasn't looking.

Korac had overheard her profession of love in the night, but he knew Nox had slept through it by his breathing. Razor and Iuo were right. This love story was worthy of a dramatic franchise.

"I'll bring Xelan here myself," Korac volunteered.

The three at the table looked up from their despondent meal, blinking. So he continued. "It's best to bring him to you. Let him see evidence of your peaceful cohabitation, of Nox's ability to reform like a civilized member of society. Or whatever."

Sagan beamed at Korac, which always made his chest swell. She said, "That's a wonderful idea, and without the other shadow around, we can gently immerse you into the group." She nodded toward Nox.

He said, "I appreciate you both risking yourselves by vouching for me." Despite the optimism in his words, the former King of Cinder's black eyes were flat.

Realism was a bitch.

A grateful smile tugged at Rayne's lips. "This could work, but..." Korac watched the smile fade on her face as she said, "I want to be the one to tell Xelan about you." She reached over and took Nox's hand, meeting his eyes. "About us."

When Nox kissed Rayne's forehead, the gag reflex Korac swore he'd trained away kicked in. After making a disgusted sound, he said, "Please. Stop. I can't take much more."

Sagan leaned on him, grinning into his face. "Aren't they so cute?" She exaggerated the syllables in the word, making them worse.

Begrudging, Korac admitted the sight of Nox and Rayne gazing at each other with affection sparkling in their eyes was best-case scenario. But not even Sagan's endearing sweetness could make Korac say it aloud.

After the last two nights of sharing a bed with three other people, Korac wanted a night in his bed in his chalet with his two favorite girls. However, he couldn't rest, knowing he didn't do everything he could for the sickening couple in front of him. He said, "We're heading out now."

Rayne and Nox quit gazing at each other and focused less happy expressions on Korac.

Sagan frowned—near pouting. But these things were best handled quickly. The human idiom of 'ripping off the Band-aid.'

For some levity, Korac pointed a stern finger at the couple. "Start nothing while we're gone. We'll be back in ten minutes or less and the last thing your case needs is for Xelan to walk in on you … *mating*."

He relished the way the color drained from Nox, while Rayne flushed the same crimson of Korac's favorite silk kimono.

Sagan shoved him so hard he almost fell off the barstool. "Stop it." To Nox and Rayne, Sagan said, "He's not wrong, though. We'll be back soon."

Korac did *not* restrain himself from enjoying the view of his wife's ass when she bent over the island to take Rayne's hand. Amid the consoling gesture, Rayne's eyes flicked to his, and a communion flashed there. He appreciated the view enough for the both of them.

Without batting an eye or flexing a muscle, Sagan opened a conduit behind her. She and Korac gave a final wave before stepping through. For the life of him, Korac would never forget the expression on Nox's face.

Pure.

Dread.

Korac could count on one hand how many times he'd seen fear in those black eyes. It gnawed at him that a meeting with Xelan—the baby brother—would evoke such anxiety in an Icarus Korac knew had defeated dragons bare-handed. This was wrong on so many levels.

But by Elden, Korac would make it right.

They Seamswalked into Tameka and Xelan's kitchen.

Intrigued by the destination, Korac raised a brow at his wife.

Unabashed, Sagan smiled. "What? I've lived forty-eight hours on eggs. I'm starving." Then she proceeded to raid the imperial fridge.

"Uncle Korac!"

Pax came tearing through the living space like a redheaded tornado before jumping into Korac's waiting arms. "Umph! Kid, you're getting too big for these kinds of hugs."

"Hee! I exercise every day to be as big as you, dad, and Uncle Nox."

The couple exchanged a look.

As Pax beamed, Sagan ruffled his hair with one hand and took a bite out of a sandwich suited for Matt with the other. She said, "Speaking of your dad, do you know where he is?"

"Xelan's helping with Miy and Twenty-One's training on the ship."

Tameka.

Pax wriggled to get down. When Korac let him go, he ran and tugged on Tameka's double-breasted top. "Mommy, can I go to space?"

Sagan glowed in the proximity of the boy's cuteness, but Korac was trying to curb his envy. How did Xelan's mate pull off yellow *and* Tartan print so well?

"Maybe with the next ship, baby. I still want you close to me." Tameka squeezed her son with a warm sound, but her eyes were full of suspicion for Korac. "I thought you went on a retreat?"

With a mouth full of food, Sagan made noises to communicate.

To Korac's astonishment, Tameka responded, "Yeah. I'll go with you. Jeez, I think I need to start paying Lamassau for watching Pax."

"Uncle Lam is teaching me to breathe fire."

Korac's eyes went wide. "I demand a demonstration." He held out both hands. "Give me ten for being the coolest kid I know."

Only after Pax slapped them did Korac notice the adoring look in the females' eyes. He ducked his gaze, saying, "We'd best get on with it."

With her yellow pants breezing around her legs, Tameka headed out of the room with Pax, saying, "I'll ask Lam, and then we can go."

"She wears it so well, doesn't she?" Sagan asked, with a knowing smile for her husband. The sandwich was long gone except...

Korac wiped a bit of mustard off her mouth. "Have I mentioned that I love how well you know me?"

Sagan smiled, but it was sad. "I know how scared you are about this conversation." Before he took it away, she captured his hand and cupped it against her face. "But I also know how important it is for you to hide. I just wanted you to know I see it, and I love you more for it."

"Until Eternity takes me..." Korac kissed her, but there wasn't time for much. He broke away to say, "I need to call Pehton."

Sagan dared to poke his nose. "Go ahead. I need to drink all of Wingmaster's orange juice to wash down the sandwich."

Korac chuckled as he walked into the living room and selected Pehton's frequency in his palm device.

Like always, the Lyriki Warden answered on the first ring. "Oh, how like you to call now at all times." Her feathers were in disarray and...

"My ferocious Pehton, where are your clothes?" Korac smirked as she tightened the sheet around her.

Her obvious frustration crooked his lips further as Pehton warned, "Careful, Korac. You're starting to sound like Razor."

"Good evening, General." Caedes sounded more amused than put-out.

Korac had to admit he was starting to like the bald Icarus. To him, Korac nodded. "Soldier." To Pehton, he said, "You were right. I was keeping a secret from you, but if it makes you feel any better, I also kept it from Sagan."

Pehton's mouth gaped opened. Shut. Then she scowled, "Of course it doesn't make it better. Have more respect for your mate. Now... Tell me everything."

Without looking beyond Pehton, Korac knew Caedes was still in the room with her. Korac said, "I will, but we need to discuss it in private—"

"If it's about Nox and Rayne, I already know." Caedes was frank as fuck, and it was another quality Korac liked about him.

And of course Caedes knew. Korac confirmed, "The races..."

Caedes stood and stretched in the background, saying, "Mhmm."

Pehton frowned, properly perplexed. "Someone better tell me what's going on and what two deceased Kings have to do with it."

"Nox is alive." Korac dropped it in her lap.

The widening of Pehton's garnet eyes always appealed to the sadist in Korac.

Sagan wandered over with an empty carton of orange juice as Korac continued. "Rayne is also alive. They've been living in sin together in one of Xelan's safe houses on Thailea and now I have to take Xelan there and break it to him gently. I could use your council."

His wife's gentle hand on his shoulder helped ease some of Korac's anxieties as Pehton chewed on the new information.

"Well... Obviously, transparency is vital. We've learned that much from your Verses, and I assume you're hoping Xelan *doesn't* kill Nox on sight?"

Korac swallowed and gave a single nod.

Pehton shook her head in a discouraging gesture before saying, "I mean, the good news of Rayne returning to the Shadow is almost the perfect counter to Nox being alive—Which how—No, never mind.

I expect a full report when you catch a breather. Until then, try to spin this as positively as possible. Nostalgia. Rayne. Perhaps a key to Celindria and... Oh!" Her face fell, and she groaned, "Oh..."

When Pehton's eyes tripled in size, Korac knew she'd reached the same conclusion about Nox and Rayne that he had. He glanced at Sagan, who frowned a little. His wife was brilliant enough to puzzle it out on her own, but perhaps she didn't want to. Because this would not bode well for the Kings of Cinder.

Korac said, "I believe you've arrived at the correct conclusion."

"What?" Sagan prompted them.

Pehton gestured for Korac to be the bearer of bad news, and it fucking sucked. He wiped a hand down his face and sighed. "We think Nox and Rayne are the Eternal Bind."

Sagan's shock lasted half a second before dismay drained her tanned complexion. "No... Oh, no. Rayne..."

And out of all the things to say right at that moment, Caedes' "humph" about summed it up.

Xelan loved standing in Ishkur's hangar, surrounded by all the marvels of Aegis technology. But this craft wasn't Aegis, and that was even more exciting. Among the bays filled with various landing support, the Shadow had discovered this transparent glass ship. Composed of a material not known to their galaxy, it spanned the size of a sports stadium. Rooms, mess halls, infirmary, bridge—All of it completely see-through.

Grinning, Xelan raised his hand over a glass panel on the bridge. The warmth of his hands summoned figures of a language his nacre translated thanks to Aegis databanks. Xelan understood this panel controlled hardware components, such as atmospheric gas conversion, anti-gravity, landing mechanisms, and basic maintenance and repair. When he moved his hand away, the imprints disappeared.

From behind, Twenty-One confirmed, "This is to be my station, your imperial majesty?"

Xelan faced the second largest Icarus he'd ever seen. Thinking of the person who topped the list—Nox—brought a bitter taste to Xelan's mouth. It vanished as Twenty-One smiled openly, expectant and ready for duty. Xelan clasped a hand on the other man's shoulder and said, "That's exactly right. And Miy, you'll be—"

"Let me guess. Pilot?" With the Lyrik's arms folded and her hip jutted out, Miy's attitude reminded Xelan of twelve-year-old Rayne. Except for the clothes. Miy liked her skirts short and tight, and judging by the look Twenty-One gave her, so did he.

In too good a humor for anything to ruin it, Xelan beamed at Miy. "Actually, the ship pilots itself. I'm placing you in charge of navigation, which shouldn't be too difficult once we port in the coordinates for Tumu's homeworld."

"Did I hear someone call my name with the desperate longing of unexplored potential?" Compressed to seven feet, his shortest setting, Tumu barely fit in the ship. He was squeezed tight as he traversed the narrow corridors.

Through those transparent passages, Xelan watched Tumu walk to them and called, "I thought you were with Lam in the stronghold?"

The Primary said, "I'm here on an errand from our Co-Emperor."

Twenty-One wandered to the hull of the ship, looked out, and pointed. "Her imperial majesty is outside with the Generals."

Miy wrapped an arm around her partner's waist, saying, "Looks like you're being summoned,

Wingmaster. Don't worry. Twenty-One and I will give the ship a proper christening."

Her statement made Xelan double-take. Bewildered, he blew the air from his cheeks. "I guess you'd better get it out of your system. I don't think there'll be much privacy once you take off, and I'd appreciate it if you'd spare Qas and the other crew."

"From what? Jealousy? They'd be so fortunate for the show. Mark my words, one week into space travel, and they'll be begging for the entertainment." When Miy smiled, a rarer occasion than a Phoenix Dragon sighting, it was infectious.

Having accustomed to her conceited sense of humor, Xelan grinned and shook his head incredulously. On his and Tumu's way out, he said, "You two have fun, and try to avoid the surfaces. You might accidentally start Crystal up and send yourselves into space."

Behind him, Miy scoffed. "Seriously?! Crystal—Sir, you can't name a ship that."

"Actually, I like it," Twenty-One's grin was in his voice.

Xelan was grateful to know the pair of them. He was more excited about this launch than he'd been about a non-Tameka and Pax related event in a long time.

Wait.

Before he disembarked from Crystal, Xelan recalled the last time he'd been this excited.

"Nox, are you sure there will be stars tonight? I search every night, and they never come." Xelan followed his older brother into his chambers, where Korac waited.

Their personal guard, always so quiet, straightened to attention at Xelan's arrival.

"Stand down, Korac. We are brothers." Xelan tried for a warm smile, anything to assure the new addition to Umbra's Spire of his place here in their home.

The quiet soldier's ears flushed blue, but Korac managed a reserved nod.

Progress.

They both fixed their gazes on Nox, who darted about his room with frenetic energy. He was at work on something in the center until he stood and opened his wings.

Korac's eyes widened, and Xelan beamed. It was hard not to idolize the impressive warrior—Their big brother.

Nox said, "Close your eyes."

They did so without hesitation. To think… Stars. Nox promised to bring the stars through Li's harrowing blaze. Xelan knew Nox would, because he never broke a promise.

Unable to contain his excitement, Xelan reached out and blindly groped until he found Korac's hand. Their guard stiffened, but relaxed by inches into Xelan's gentle grip.

More progress.

With his eyes closed, Xelan heard Nox's boots alight once more on the black stone floor. The baby brother bounced with excitement. "Can we open our eyes yet?"

Nox chuckled. "Not yet."

Xelan squeezed Korac's hand and cried, "Oh, I cannot wait anymore. Please?!"

He wasn't sure, but he thought the boy beside him snickered.

"Very well. You may open your eyes."

Nox had snuffed the torches before Xelan opened his eyes, but he found himself dazzled in light, anyway. Tiny gems peppered the ceiling and each of them glowed in swirling nebulas and clusters— Star systems like the ones mother and the Verses described.

Nox said, "I found them among the magma caves in the Ignis Desert. Tomorrow, I promise to install them in your chambers."

Xelan released Korac's hand and wandered into the center of Nox's room, with his mouth gaping all the while. His first stars. When he could speak, he said, "Thank you, Nox."

The baby grinned as he faced his older brother, who nodded toward Korac. For all his reservations, their guard's eyes were filled with wonder as he stared into their understanding of a night's sky.

"I will see them all, one day," Xelan declared. "And you will both be with me."

Nox had kept his promise, while Xelan...

"Your imperial majesty, I require your presence for a most serious errand."

Seeing Korac after the recollection filled Xelan with so many conflicting emotions. Happiness, sorrow, shame, and hope. He followed Tumu down Crystal's glass gangplank, smiling warmer than usual at his oldest friend. "What will you have of me?"

Korac froze and blinked.

Sagan snickered.

Tumu rolled his eyes.

At his poor choice of words, Xelan wouldn't offer an apology, but an amused grin should do.

Tameka said, "Anyway, they're taking us for a little excursion."

Without hesitation, Sagan opened a conduit, and Xelan's eyes widened as he recognized its destination. He froze and stared into Thailea's forest, while the Generals waited expectantly. After the shock wore off, Xelan realized this was it.

Rayne was ready.

The look on Korac's face confirmed it.

Xelan licked his lips before saying, "Uhm. Tameka?"

"Yes?"

Tumu interjected, "Allow me. Peaches, the father of your children is finally prepared to let you in on his big secret. Can you handle it?"

Tameka lost some color to her complexion as Sagan took her hand supportively. Ever the warrior, Tameka said, "I'm ready."

Xelan didn't want to talk to anyone or look them in the eyes. He marched through the conduit and up to the door, planted his hand on the DNA scanner, and walked inside.

Rayne.

When Xelan entered, she was sitting on the edge of the couch, hands clasped tight with worry and her knees bouncing. The moment she saw him, Rayne sprung to her feet and ran across the living space. Xelan welcomed the hug, even as she nearly crushed him on impact. The smell of ocean foam and white sand followed, making him squeeze tighter and kiss the top of her head.

Tears.

Both of them.

Hopefully, this was the end of their scarce reunions. From hereon, Rayne would stay with the Shadow. No more hiding—

Boots.

On the floor, at the end of the couch, sat an enormous pair of heavy boots.

As if sensing Xelan's tension, Rayne stepped back and wiped the tears from her face. She said, "I have so much to tell you." Her half-sob, half laugh touched him. "I guess I always have so much to tell you—Oh… Tameka…"

It shamed Xelan to realize he'd almost forgotten about their audience. About his significant other.

Tameka's joyous tears were in her voice. "I can't believe… Xelan never gave up on you, and after I kill him for keeping you a secret all this time, we'll catch up. Until then, I know how much you two need this. I'll sit over here and listen. Tell us everything."

Xelan did *not* deserve her. He took a moment to pull Tameka against his side and kiss her. He whispered her ear, "Thank you."

Tameka whispered back. "You are so dead." But her sweet smile belied her fury.

Korac and Sagan followed in, nodding to Rayne, before taking their seats on the couch with Tameka. They looked for all the world like a proper audience, and Xelan didn't care because there was no way that cloak spread across the back of the couch was Rayne's. It looked like the sail on a ship.

"Rayne." Xelan tried, but he couldn't keep the edge from his voice. He took a deep breath and pushed for a softer tone. "Please."

He listened as she explained more thoroughly how Elden had resurrected her. The bargain between them and her flashbacks into Elden's life. Those were mind-boggling enough and required further inspection, but Xelan was waiting...

Waiting for...

"And I know we've talked a lot about... about Nox, but I've never gotten to explain everything to you." Rayne used both hands to tuck thick strands of hair behind her ears. A tell. She hadn't done that since the old days of confessing her dreams about Nox to Xelan. She said, "When I killed him, I remembered Elden's second Verse. 'Take the warrior you fell to victory with you.' I swallowed Nox's nacre, thinking you would be in there." Fresh tears welled in Rayne's eyes as she relived the heartbreak. "You weren't... But... Nox was. Elden kept our nacres separate, and I could talk to him."

When Rayne peered up at Xelan, checking for his response, he tried to keep his expression open, but honestly, it felt like the planet had opened up and swallowed him. Xelan nodded for her to go on.

"I wanted to understand why... I mean, you read his Verse. How did he end up this way? So I lived his life with him. All seven million years." Xelan's eyes widened, and Rayne nodded, understanding. "I felt everything he felt. Then we lived my life, which was obviously shorter, but he felt everything. All the love for my family and friends—For you. The pressure of being born a Progeny with this Imminent future breathing down my neck—All of it. It... transformed Nox."

Xelan swallowed, physically and figuratively. This was almost too much to take in.

Rayne raked a hand through her hair, uncertain if she was making her case—And that's what this was. She was building a case for something Xelan did *not* want to confront. She said, "Then... in Enki... Nox manifested as my shadow and protected me from Remorse and Abresson." So Xelan had seen right when he first found her on New Cinder. Rayne went on. "And when I was dying—"

Her voice broke, and so did Xelan's heart. He wiped a hand down his mouth while fresh tears stung his eyes.

"Nox took the pain of it from me and endured it alone."

This was Rayne's Verse. The genuine article.

Xelan pressed, "And now? Rayne..."

Beyond Rayne, a living monolith stepped around the corner dressed in clothes the color of her eyes. Xelan couldn't discern much beyond those details because his vision went blurry as the room spun. He heard Tameka gasp and sensed Korac's eyes on him. Sagan's on Rayne.

This was too much.

With a shake of his head, Xelan focused the room again. Rayne was... raw. Her eyes flashed Atramentous as if her emotions raged like a violent ocean and begged Xelan to anchor her. But this...

Xelan gently took Rayne by the biceps and directed her aside, so she no longer stood between him and Nox. The face of Xelan's nightmares...and warmest childhood memories...one Xelan could see with every glimpse in a mirror...looked resigned.

Nox knew what Rayne had refused to accept.

This would not end happily ever after.

While he strode over to his brother, Xelan scanned the space. Comfortable—Cozy even. Perfect for a new couple to cement their budding relationship. And one important detail couldn't escape Xelan's attention, no matter how hard he tried.

Xelan faced Nox and said, "There's only one bed," before punching his older brother square in the jaw. Bone crunched, cobalt blood sprayed, and Nox fell backward like a chopped redwood.

Unconscious.

Rayne's ears rang as her heart rate plummeted to forty-five beats per minute. Thinking of nothing else, she went to Nox's side and took his hand. Her other hand brushed his hair from the blood seeping out of his teeth. Her voice croaked as she said, "Nox, if you can hear me, squeeze my hand."

Distantly, Rayne was aware of Xelan standing over her. The rivers of tears on her cheeks scolded with every gentle touch for the man Xelan had laid out. She even leaned down and whispered in Nox's ear, "Come back to me."

Dressed in very un-imperial clothes, old jeans and a white tee, Xelan's combat boots thudded on the wood floor as he turned away. Rayne looked up to find him gripping fistfuls of his hair. He looked better than when she'd visited him last week in his dreams, but Rayne found it difficult to swallow the obvious exasperation rolling off Xelan in waves. It slumped his shoulders and aged his midnight eyes when he faced her once more.

Never judgment.

Xelan kept the promise he'd made to Rayne—wow, seven years ago now—and withheld any censure toward her. Instead—Elden, the look in his stare bordered on disappointment, and Rayne couldn't bear that.

Without moving another muscle, Nox squeezed Rayne's hand, but stayed down. Diffusion. That's what this situation needed, and Elden only knew what Xelan would do if Nox got up right now.

"Your imperial majesty." They all turned to look at Korac. The General slapped his knees before standing and walking around the living space to face Xelan. From behind his mask, Korac said, "What happened to, 'We aspire to surpass those who came before us'?"

Sagan stiffened beside Tameka, recognizing the reference both Rayne and Tameka frowned at.

Xelan's jaw popped, and he tilted his head in incredulity. "Don't do this."

Sagan said, "'Let's not repeat the sins of the previous wardens and their masters.'" They recited what were obviously Xelan's lines from a previous conversation.

Further aggravated by the reminder of his hypocrisy, Xelan argued, "Your husband was there when Nox killed me. Ask him if he thinks I overreacted or diminished myself."

But Korac was unrestrained. He put his face in Xelan's and finished it. "'No abuse. Ever.'"

Rayne expected Xelan to order Korac to stand down or back off. Instead, the Co-Emperor searched his General's eyes before he sighed with disdain for himself. He patted Korac on the shoulder and walked a few steps away with his hands on his hips, head hung in shame and anguish, and Rayne hated every second of it.

"It still went better than I'd expected." Korac waited for Xelan to face him before adding, "At least you didn't kill him."

Beside Sagan on the couch, Tameka said, "That's enough, General."

Korac straightened at the order and nodded, coming to stand over Rayne. He looked less concerned than she felt, especially as Nox opened one eye and peered up at him. Korac exhaled his relief.

Sagan stood and headed for the kitchen area. "I'll just get something to clean all the blood off the walls and floors. And some ice." She shot one admonishing look at Xelan as she left the area.

Xelan called after, "Planet Breaker, I'll need you to bring Kyle and Andrew here. I want them to investigate every corner of Nox's psyche until I'm satisfied he isn't working with Celindria and planning to kill all of us—"

The distressed sound which tore from Rayne's throat was involuntary. And she was ready to argue until…

"Okay." Tameka stood, clapped, and went to Xelan's side. Rayne couldn't make out everything which passed between them. The only thing she overheard was the suggestion for Xelan to go for a stroll in the forest and get some fresh air. "Can you do that for me, Wingmaster?" For some reason, Tameka slipped down her pants a little off her hip and flashed him some skin.

Whatever was there, it lit Xelan's eyes. He kissed her before following her orders and heading out. In the doorway, framed by the forest's glow, Xelan turned and gave Rayne a complicated look. It was filled with love, concern, and something which crushed her.

Dread.

With him gone, Korac nudged Nox with his boot and held out a hand. "Let's get you up, your majesty."

Sagan came around the corner with ice as Nox stirred. With a groan, he sat up. Despite the blood on his face, Nox searched Rayne's eyes and asked, "Are you all right?"

The answer was obviously 'No.' But Rayne said, "It'll be better once I've talked to him—Thank you." She took the ice from Sagan and pressed it against the swelling on Nox's face. His nacre was as supped up as hers, but Xelan was an extraordinary fighter, leaving a few bruises behind.

"Oh, good. You're conscious." They turned toward Tameka, who came to stand over them with her hands on her hips. She asked, "What the hell were you two thinking? Springing this on Xelan like that?"

Nox said, "It's a delicate situation—"

"No." Tameka cut him off, holding up a finger. "*You* don't speak to me. I'm talking to these three." She gestured between Rayne, Korac, and Sagan. "I am *angry*. So many people I love kept me out of the loop, and I'm extra pissed that it comes across as you kept us in the dark so you could... *be* with him, Rayne."

Her first instinct was to duck her eyes and hide the flush of shame. But Rayne was an adult, and she'd made an adult decision. Staring into Tameka's eyes, Rayne moved closer to Nox and placed their handholding in plain view. Her voice shook a little as she said, "I'm sorry I hurt you, and I understand how this looks. But while it's not the case I'd planned all this, I am happy Nox and I are together."

Tameka's eyes flashed Atramentous green, and she looked away. "Shit." When she looked back, her eyes were filled with conflicted tears. "You need to talk to Xelan. Alone. We'll clean up in here and get the boys for screening." With a hard look at Nox, Tameka said, "I don't know what they'll find in this man's head, but I hope for your sake it makes for a good argument."

Rayne stood and crushed Tameka to her, and the embrace felt like home. "Thank you." She glanced back at the Icarus she loved.

Nox waved her on. "Go to him. I won't let them take me away until you return."

Although he meant it as a reassurance, it twisted Rayne's heart. She glimpsed Tameka's measuring gaze, but Rayne could only muster enough strength for the conversation with Xelan. No sidebars. Sagan took Rayne's place at Nox's side with a pitying look for her best friend.

Korac muttered, "Good luck," as Rayne walked out into the woods, seeking Xelan.

Rayne knew from the smell of leather-bound books and the best hugs that Xelan wasn't far. In fact, he was only one tree away. She opened her wings and flew up to him, sitting on a branch with his legs hanging off the side. Xelan kept his eyes on something in the distance as Rayne sat beside him, matching his position.

Because he'd allowed her presence, she felt a rush of relief. Things weren't so bad off after all—

"You two are the Eternal Bind."

Rayne winced. How had Xelan come to this dreaded conclusion so quickly?

With easy to see and slow movements, he took her hand from her side and held it. Voice hoarse with emotion, Xelan said, "Please don't feel as though you need to wince or flinch from me. As I'm sure you've assumed, I'm not mad or disappointed. Not with you, anyway."

"Xelan, please." Rayne faced him while he kept his eyes straight ahead. "Since *I* resurrected Nox—not Elden, it was my decision—Nox moves almost as fast as me. He could've blocked, dodged—hell—countered your swing, but he took it. Nox *let* you hit him."

When Xelan finally looked at her, pride shone in his eyes. "You've grown up so much. I've never heard you sound so mature."

Under the light of his trademark warmth, Rayne tried to smile for him while saying, "It's because I've lived seven million years in the span of two. It made me appreciate you more."

Xelan looked down at their hands as he said, "I won't insult you by saying your feelings for him or his manipulations have blinded you." He cleared his throat to admit, "I believe what you see in him is real—"

Rayne perked up, ready to agree—

"—But I have obligations to the people Nox murdered. Billions of people, Rayne, including myself."

Rayne hated the hard edge to her voice as she asked, "But not Korac? Or Razor? Why is it different for them?"

Xelan turned his face to the canopy as if praying for patience or strength. "Because I never looked up to them. Because they were never the center of my universe—My shield and savior. They were never my brother."

Tears threatened Rayne again, clogging her throat. She hung her head, unable to argue.

With a crooked finger under her chin, Xelan raised Rayne's gaze to his. He said, "Trillions are at risk. They might simply vanish because of your proximity to each other. And . . . " A tear rolled down his cheek while he collected himself to say, "You told me you couldn't love Nox because I couldn't forgive him."

Rayne lied, "I don't have to love Nox to be with him."

Xelan saw through it and shook his head. "I know that to be true of most people, but I don't believe it of you."

It was Rayne's turn to stare into the branches, ready to plead. Instead, she asked, "Can't you see he's not the monster you knew?"

"He doesn't *deserve* you, Rayne." Matter of fact. This was the truth for Xelan.

"Well, at least there's something we can agree on." Nox.

"Fuck!" Xelan never swore. This was bad.

Tameka shoved Nox aside to let her partner see her. "Sorry. Short of knocking him out again, I couldn't do much to stop him." She had followed Nox all the way to this tree, telling him now wasn't the best time.

But here they were, the giant Icarus downwind of the father/daughter pair, interrupting. She glared at him. "What made you think this was a good idea?"

Xelan looked off, muttering curses, while Nox said, "I couldn't sit there any longer, knowing Rayne withstands this on her own. I agree to surrender, but only under the terms that I bring Celindria in with me."

Despite Nox's noble words, Tameka knew this calculating bastard had waited until Korac left with Sagan to pull this stunt. If only Rayne didn't look so devastated by his pronouncement. Tameka said, "Kyle and Andrew will be here and hopefully make this situation better. Until then, no one is making any life-altering decisions."

Tameka hoped to reassure Rayne, and by the softening of her best friend's eyes, it had worked. Tameka said, "Get up here and hug me, woman. You owe me a few for keeping yourself a secret for months."

As Rayne climbed to her feet and pulled Tameka in for a bone-crushing hug, she noticed Xelan had stopped cursing to himself. In fact, both men seemed to bask in the warmth happening between them. Dampening the flames of Tameka's fury, something else flickered in its place.

Hope.

"There." Tameka set them apart and wiped the tears from Rayne's eyes. "Oh, fuck." Her sudden outburst contorted Rayne's face into bewilderment before she explained, "I just realized we'll have to deal with Kyle."

Simultaneously, the brothers groaned in further exasperation. With tension pulled taut between them, they looked at each other. Xelan with undiluted disdain, and Nox with regret. The younger brother clicked his tongue in disgust when he looked away, while the eldest did it in shame.

The brief moment of eye contact fanned the flicker into a flame.

It burned in Rayne's eyes too. The look on Rayne's face begged Tameka to play ambassador again. With a roll of her eyes, she relented and stepped into the massive Icarus' line of sight. "You. Did you come to us with some plan about how to make Celindria surrender? Because we saw her yesterday in a prisoner's body. She mentioned a deal. I don't suppose..."

Nox was entirely too tall, and Tameka was shorter than Rayne. She edged onto her tiptoes to keep from craning up to look at the man who blinked down at her. The smart ass asked, "Am I permitted to address you now?"

Tameka misaligned her jaw, seeing now why Xelan was so damned infuriated. She flicked her eyes all the way up the mountain of an Icarus until she stared him down. This was the *look*. It made puddles of grown men. Even the former King of Cinder took a step back as she gritted out, "Don't. Waste. My. Time."

Rayne touched Nox's arm. Elden when he looked at her, the man transformed. It was in the shine of his eyes. Nox loved Rayne. Rayne squeezed encouragingly as she said, "Please answer her question."

Xelan was at Tameka's back, but she could tell by the tension in his shoulders he was listening to every word. She could mediate this for him, but only knowing he would pay her back later tonight. It was enough to make her half-smile, which narrowed Nox's eyes.

The Icarus whom Rayne loved—ugh, that hurt to think—said, "At Night Rayne's Tomb, I asked Celindria to surrender with me in return for us rehabilitating together. And thereby we would dedicate our skills in service to the Concerted Empire of Iona Pax."

Tameka's eyes stretched wide, and she couldn't stop herself from looking back at Xelan.

He was frozen to the tree branch. She swore he wasn't breathing.

Rayne chimed in then. "She almost agreed to it, too. But Bethany dropped all her vessels."

Okay. This pissed Tameka off. "You mean the annihilation squad knew the two of you were alive?! Before me?! Who else knows?"

Not even Rayne's pitiful wince would temper Tameka's ire. Rayne said, "Uhm... Caedes was the first to find out, and I don't know if Korac told anyone."

"Tumu knows. Lucas, too." Xelan sounded equally ashamed of himself. As was right.

Angry tears stung Tameka's eyes, but she knew this was temporary compared to how she'd mourned Rayne's sacrifice. With a sigh, she dragged Rayne in for another hug. Yup. Another rib-breaker. "I'm super mad because you've missed Pax's birthday—Hell, my birthday. And so many other things. I can't even begin to understand you, but you're my favorite martyr, so I guess that counts for something." When Tameka pulled them apart, she pointed in Rayne's face. "But you *owe* me. First chance you get, you're babysitting for me while Xelan and I have some alone time."

Bright laughter burst from Rayne until Tameka said, "And then I'll force you to listen to the details."

Xelan and Rayne shuddered at the same time, and Tameka couldn't help herself. She laughed—

So did Nox.

Ew. They'd laughed at the same time.

Well, at least he looked properly aggrieved by it, too.

"As much as it disgusts me to say it, you two head off somewhere. I want some time alone with my partner." Tameka shooed them off.

She hated to admit it, but as the pair clasped hands and flew down into the forest, they looked good together. Two War Kings in love. "Ugh." Tameka turned and looked down at her man, sulking. Somehow, he made it look cute. How to console Xelan? She sat down beside him and said,

"Rayne loves you. You're her everything and you *have* been ever since the beginning. And now the one person Rayne loves most despises the man she wants more than anything else. You're going to push her away."

Xelan squeezed his eyes shut. "It doesn't matter what I want or what she wants. If our Probability is to survive, we have to pry them apart."

Tameka frowned, but put it together. "Oh. Of course, they're the Eternal Bind. What a trifecta of a fucked up night. Will you take his plea bargain?"

After prying off a piece of bark, Xelan chucked it onto the forest floor. "Something Rayne said struck a chord. You know, with vice lords like Cinderken and others, I've wondered about the best system for reform. Rayne said she rehabilitated 'he who shall remain nameless' by living his life with him and vice versa. That he experienced the torment he put her through, and it sympathized him with his victim—And she *is* his victim." A heavy sigh tore from Xelan before he continued. "Well, it's an inspired concept. One I think we can emulate."

Tameka let him finish before saying, "So you think we should expose Nox and Celindria to all their victims' lives—All the ones willing to donate their experiences. By doing so, they learn compassion. I like it, but…Elden, how many people have they hurt? It would take centuries, millennia even."

Xelan looked up at the canopy, seeking something in the silver leaves. "Perhaps in that time, Nox will remember what he loved in Celindria, and they can build a relationship together far away from Rayne—Ow!"

"Asshole." Tameka understood. Rayne and Nox together at all—let alone being the Eternal Bind—was astronomically fucked, but… "There's no way I'm conspiring to ruin my unrelated sister's happiness, and I'm trying not to think less of you for suggesting it."

The crestfallen slip to Xelan's features said she'd properly shamed him. As an apology, he offered, "I'm not at my best today, am I?"

Tameka squeezed him in for a side hug and kissed his temple. "You've had a bad day, so I'll forgive you. Let's take this one thing at a time, okay? Kyle and Andrew will test Nox, and then we'll all sit down—yes, *all* of us—and discuss next actions."

"I love you, Fury."

There was no denying it. When Xelan shifted so Tameka could see his eyes, they glistened with overwhelming emotion. She said, "Wingmaster, I can't solve all your problems, but I am right here by your side. I love you, too."

Xelan chuckled out of nowhere.

Tameka quirked a brow at him. "What?"

"At least we don't have to name an Iona after him now."

That was Tameka's mate. Always seeing the brighter side of things.

Something Aegis was behind the dominant Probability, and Celindria aimed to seek it out.

Jack, Ross, Devis, and Andrius had left the memory labs within Ishkur's central complex an hour ago. It was more than enough time to assume they were gone for the evening. One female Lamia in her inventory was an old customer of Razor's, and Celindria took advantage of her post as a complex guard. As one large muscle, Celindria found she favored the Lamian form for the simple scientific indulgence. This powerful specimen was no exception.

Graceful and sensuous, Celindria glided the guard into the lab. Having memorized the rounds, she knew there was only a twenty-minute window to secure it for her ends.

Celindria, as herself, shadow-walked into the unoccupied space and approached the table with a single nacre.

Our greatest rival.

A true pioneer in vice.

Razor.

Millennia ago, Celindria had perfected the memory capsules and Divine Booth technology, but she could also manipulate existing memory banks. After swallowing a capsule, she touched the manufactured nacre, positioned herself within a shadow, and stepped into Razor's memory scape.

Skinless.

Celindria stared at her hands, arms, legs—Her entire body was without skin. The muscle, sinew, organs, and veins left open and raw. She felt none of it, as if her nerve endings were stripped along with her emotions.

Isn't this how we always feel?

Open, but dead?

Into the memory scape, Celindria asked, "Why?"

Black walls surrounded her, and white chalk wrote along the blank pages of sheet music.

No feelings; no pain. Isn't that what you said to Pehton on the day you left her? Another victim in your wake of devastation.

The nightmare of Celindria's exposed insides should terrify her, but she felt nothing. If anything, it piqued her curiosity and gave her new ideas for torturing the Shadow once she conquered Iona Pax.

Celindria ignored the dramatic spectacle and asked without lips, "Could an Aegis have infiltrated Imminent without you recognizing him or her? A lower initiate, perhaps?"

Yes.

"Were you more cooperative with the Shadow?" Celindria rolled her eyes, realizing there were no lids and wondered how it looked from the outside.

The perception filters would prevent me from recognizing them, but I only know of one pure-blood Aegis missing from our ranks. One, my eldest brother, and my father's favorite.

Before the Source, when Celindria could feel more freely, she and Razor had commiserated over their paternal misgivings. She asked, "Do you know for how long?"

Before the Tritans arrived to Enki. Before Surra discovered Cascading Light.

Celindria bit her thumbnail before she could stop herself. For a long while, she stared at the floor, considering all things and how they mattered. When she looked back up, the text had changed.

You will never find happiness. Not this way.

She turned away from it, only to see another message on the opposite wall.

Remorse manipulated us, even you. While you still can, seek Xelan's forgiveness.

We should listen to him.

No, we've come too far.

"Razor. You must know I've collected thousands of DNA samples from you and Triss. I can resurrect you both if you side with me against the Shadow." Celindria meant every word. Her competition with Razor over the millennia had inspired countless invaluable innovations. An alliance could only lead to more.

An image replaced the text on the walls. It was black and white aside from Triss' red feathers and her yellow eyes. The couple were dancing in the Obsidian Palace, while the crowd stepped aside to watch. Lithe and exotic, Triss was a deadly combination of beauty and lethality. Insanely devoted to her god. Celindria had never identified with her, but appreciated the psychopath's legacy of bodies in the name of loyalty.

Black text appeared over the images.

If you stay this course, you will find yourself alone and knowing you deserve it.

Pax.

Hope.

Nox.

Dissatisfaction—an emotion Celindria loathed—surged inside her, and she terminated the connection. Back in her beautiful dark skin, she was ready to rip her hair out. How could someone as intelligent as Razor allow the Shadow to reduce him to this penitent bitch—

"Celindria."

First, through the Lamia guard's eyes, Celindria watched Tumu enter the lab. As herself, she turned and faced him. Quick as lightning, he shot the Lamia with a nacre-disabling rifle, disconnecting Celindria's volition control. Then he aimed it at her.

Kill him!

No! Father will never agree to our contingency if we kill his trusted Tritan.

When Tumu didn't fire immediately, Celindria asked, "What must be in your head, Primary?"

"You're standing on a shadow. You'll escape before I can fire the shot."

If Celindria could feel surprise, her brows might shoot up. Instead, she blinked at him and waited for an explanation.

How does he know of our gifts?

Tumu was always more than he seemed.

Tumu kept his sights on Celindria as he stepped closer. He stopped a meter away to say, "We pity you. Paradise was an abomination, but how could a creature like you understand why?"

A pain lanced through Celindria, stronger than any emotion she'd felt in some time. It took her breath away. "I don't ask for your pity."

The old Primary's voice dropped into an impossible octave and rattled her bones. "You will. In two days, you will beg us for it."

Light indignation replaced the pain, and Celindria scoffed, "I will *never* beg."

"Two days, Celindria. Pray we are merciful."

Enraged by the conversation, she stepped into the shadow and walked into a neighboring Probability. Here, Celindria stood in an empty lab in Ishkur's undiscovered bridge. All electrical systems, including atmosphere and gravity, were left on autopilot before the Aegis had abandoned it. They'd never returned.

Not a soul lived here.

Celindria's rushed footsteps echoed along the gangplanks and corridors of unrealized potential. Her least favorite Probability, for here she truly felt alone.

The Shadow made for entertaining adversaries, and she loved Pax and Hope. Wanted Nox. Glancing down at the ribbon in her hand, Celindria wondered.

We should listen to Razor.

No. We should spend the next two days preparing.

Love.

Conquest.

Both.

For the first time, Celindria wondered about 'neither.'

XVI   BURN

SAGAN WAS SURE THINGS COULD'VE GONE WORSE. Like Korac said, Xelan could've killed Nox, still...

Many awful things had happened to the Progeny, to the Shadow, over the years, but Sagan couldn't remember the last time Rayne had looked so hurt.

No, Sagan could. And in a complicated turn of events, it was during Razor's advertisements for Rayne's pain. The look on her face when Nox—

Well, maybe they shouldn't bring it up anymore. Although, that was the clincher, wasn't it? Nox had caused a lot of pain, and not against Rayne alone. He had to answer for his crimes. But surely dying by Rayne's hand was punishment enough?

Sagan sighed.

"I would ask what's bothering you, amos, but I'm certain it's the same as what's bothering me."

They'd just knocked on the zeppelin's door and were waiting for Andrew and Lucas to answer. Once, and only once, Sagan had walked into their private space without knocking.

Never again.

Sagan looped her arm through Korac's and leaned into him. "Yeah. This situation feels hopeless, and it hurts me for Rayne's sake. You've figured out she totally loves Nox, right?"

Korac gave her a 'what do you take me for' look before saying, "I've known since their kiss at the races. She hasn't told him yet."

While shaking her head, Sagan said, "It's so complicated. I wish—"

"Hey, Seamswalker." Andrew answered the door, and his hair—Sagan had a hard time not laughing in his face. It was so mussed. He swallowed before stammering, "Lucas and I were, uh… We were taking a quick break from monitoring. Silence is over there, watching with Smith—And you're not here to check on the Probability Matrix, are you?" His flustered expression faded to a frown.

From within, Lucas called, "Is that Sagan?" He sounded like he was getting dressed.

Korac said, "And me. We need you both, and no, this isn't a fashion call."

Sagan gestured for Andrew to lean halfway toward her where she whispered, "Your shorts are on inside-out."

Rich laughter carried through the zeppelin. Lucas finally appeared and kissed Andrew's cheek before addressing the Generals. "How can we help you?"

Everyone loved Lucas, but sometimes the clandestine aspects of his murky past chafed. Korac narrowed his eyes at his precious tailor before asking, "Did you know?"

Recognition filled those golden eyes and was followed by relief. Lucas said, "So she's come out of hiding."

Sagan couldn't help it. She felt hurt. "How could you keep Rayne a secret from all of us? We love her—"

Mighty arms wrangled her into a gentle embrace. Against her hair, Lucas said, "To save you—all of you—I would bend Eternity. Forgive me for withholding the truth, but I knew you would find her. Don't lose faith. Not yet. Not when we're so close."

Over Lucas' shoulder, Sagan watched Andrew's eyes widen at his lover's confession. The surprise faded fast, shifting into a clarity she still didn't grasp.

One thing at a time.

Sagan squeezed Lucas, pulled them apart, and tried for a sympathetic smile. "Okay. I'll try, but please tell me you have a plan."

"And if you have any information on the Eternal Bind, best to tell it now." Korac's words came across as half-threatening, but the situation was growing more desperate by the minute.

Especially as Andrew looked between all of them. "Is someone planning on filling me in? What are you saying about Rayne? Is she—Are you saying she's—" His voice kept breaking, and tears flooded his teal eyes.

All about the hugs, Sagan opened her arms. When Andrew took the invitation, she said, "Yes. And, well, so is Nox. They're also together, and we're pretty sure they're the Eternal Bind." They pulled apart for her to see all the conflicting emotions pass through Andrew's eyes before she added, "Oh, yeah. And Elden says we have two days before the Probability Matrix collapses."

"Lucas." Korac's tone was ladened with accusation as he said, "You don't look surprised to hear any of this."

Andrew took his lover's hand in solidarity, and Lucas took his eyes off Korac to meet Andrew's gaze. Unspoken, a conversation passed between them.

With a sigh, Lucas conceded something. "I will come along to help Rayne, but if you want me to aid the Shadow in persisting the Probability Matrix, you are asking the wrong man." He met Korac's eyes to say, "I will heal the wound we made."

'We.'

Questions.

Sagan had so many of them, but there wasn't really time for it. "We need to get back and mediate." With a nod at Andrew, she said, "Xelan wants you and Kyle to ensure Nox isn't Celindria's puppet."

Andrew ticked on his fingers. "First, I'm still reeling over Nox being alive. Second, he's alive *and* in a romantic relationship with Rayne?! Consider my mind boggled. Third, we now have to deliver this news to Kyle?!"

Lucas laughed incredulously. "Surely he's moved on from Rayne. He's with Silence."

Sagan side-glanced at Korac before confessing, "You don't really 'move on' from Rayne."

"Ask Nox." Korac understood.

Andrew's sigh was heavy as he said, "Well, I guess we'd better get this shit storm over with." As they stepped down the boarding stairs, he asked, "How is Rayne handling all this?"

"You mean how is the most epic martyr in the galaxy managing while her lover surrenders himself to the mercy of the brother he murdered?" Korac laid everything out like it was the plot to a movie before giving a cavalier shrug. "I'm sure she's fine."

Sagan's husband could always make her smile. Which reminded her to ask someone—anyone. "What do you think the sex was like? I mean, forbidden love, a secluded location, and mega physical prowess? Rayne can't keep her hands off of him. I've never seen her like this."

Korac pinched the bridge of his nose as he groaned at the same time Andrew sealed his hands over his ears, saying, "I *so* never want to hear this again."

But Lucas... "I understand Nox is proportionate. That may have something to do with Rayne's attachment."

"Let's not mention any of this around Kyle."

Korac had a good point.

Sneaking down to the Probability Matrix lab for a quickie was the best idea Kyle had ever formed.

Two hours ago.

He groaned as Silence brought them both to the end.

Again.

That makes four since Kyle had first arrived. She'd thrown him into one of the examination pods, pushed him into the chair, and climbed on top.

Elden, Kyle would never tire of this.

But maybe he should consider a different deity to reference.

Silence had kept the blue streak of hair out of her high ponytail. Perspiration soaked it to her face after hours of sex, and Kyle loved it as he smoothed it back. She tangled her fingers in the curly mess he called hair, pleased with the scenario. The beautiful grin on her face told him so.

Between heavy breaths, Kyle said, "I love you." He didn't say it often. Sometimes after saying it, Silence got this look on her face like she was boxed in. Kyle assumed it's because she would never truly move on from Elden, but he needed her to know how he felt and that there were no obligations from her. He understood. "You don't have to say it back or even feel the same. I simply like to tell you how I'm feeling, so there are never any doubts. You don't belong to me, and you never will. But you're still choosing to wrangle my ass into this sad excuse for a broom closet, and I'm one lucky bastard for it." Kyle let it all show in his smile, his eyes—Everything.

It moved Silence. Her eyes flashed their blue Atramentous, and he kissed her. No words needed—

Voices came from outside.

"Oh, yeah. Kyle and Silence are in the pod." Smith was such a narc. "You might wanna give them a second."

Korac's voice came next. "Is everyone having sex but us?" Obviously, his remark implied that Sagan was outside the pod, too. But who else—

"Get your ass out here, Roberts." Holt. Conscience— What the fuck ever. Andrew said, "We have work to do, and no. You won't like it."

Lucas' voice came next, which made sense considering Korac's comment. What Lucas *said*, however, made no sense. "Silence. It's time."

Kyle hated the way she stiffened in his arms. He knew her life was full of secrets, and he loved her anyway. Kyle took Silence's face in his hands and kissed her. For reassurance. For comfort. Everything.

The desperation in her kiss was not very reassuring or comforting. More disconcerting. Kyle broke it to say, "No matter what they're about to say, it won't change how I feel about you. I trust you."

Between them, those three words meant more than the others, and the appreciation in Silence's eyes confirmed it. She said, "Let us take the last of this journey together."

Again, disconcerting. But Kyle let Silence pull him from the chair, straighten their clothes, and fix their hair. When she brushed against him, he was ready to go again, and some part of Kyle was devious enough to make the others wait outside with their bad news while he and Silence went at it. But...

Kyle sighed as he opened the pod door. "What is it?" He sounded pissy, even to himself. With a roll of his eyes, he tried again for something more cooperative in his tone. "What do you need me to do?"

"We'll need you to hold your shit together until we finish telling you everything." Andrew did *not* make the situation better.

It got worse as Sagan suggested, "You may want to sit down."

When Kyle did, all the anxious vibes surrounding him made his knee bounce. Silence, with all her grace and wonder, fixed it by sitting in his lap and kissing his cheek. Did he mention how much he loved her?

And man, did Kyle need her as Sagan went onto explain Rayne was still alive. He didn't actually react as much as he probably should. It *was* Rayne, after all. She was capable of really anything. So what was the other shoe they were so afraid to drop?

"Just tell me."

Korac and Sagan exchanged glances. Lucas and Andrew did the same. The anxiety in the lab spiked until Kyle gripped Silence's hip so hard she felt the need to nip his earlobe.

Sagan broke it to Kyle, not gently at all. "With Elden's blessing, Rayne resurrected Nox. And after six months of working separately to bring down the remnants of Imminent, they've combined forces and they've been living together. They're the Eternal Bind."

A fine tremor overtook Silence—

No.

It wasn't her trembling.

It was Kyle. He was shaking so badly it translated to her because he was afraid to ask this question, but couldn't stop himself. "How can she and Nox be the Eternal Bind? I thought the Eternal Bind were two beings drawn together inside the Probability Matrix." He needed to swallow before he added, "Like soul mates." The very notion made Kyle wince.

Andrew looked to Lucas on this one.

The clandestine bastard said, "That is a crude summary for the intricate balance the two create within the Matrix. Through their rightful union, the rift in your universe will mend to one Probability. And I hope it's this one."

"You hope?" Kyle couldn't keep the venom from his voice. "You hope?! And you—" His eyes went blurry, stinging as they filled with tears when he glared at

Sagan. "You don't look upset by this at all. I don't expect your husband to be angry Rayne is cosmically bound to her rapist, but I thought you of all people— The only person to experience it with Rayne through a Divine Booth. That you would see how wrong this is! How can you all be so calm—"

Silence embraced Kyle, squeezing as much as he was apparently squeezing her. He buried his face against her neck and inhaled the scent of lilies. Home to him now, it brought some much needed comfort because this was the most fucked up shit he'd ever live through.

Rayne and Nox.

The Eternal Bind.

But…

"You knew, didn't you?" Kyle muttered the words against the woman he loved, feeling betrayed.

Silence was kind enough to tell him the truth. "I did *not* know they were the Eternal Bind, but I knew they were in love before Rayne brought Enki to ruin. I knew my *grandson* was alive in her."

Grandson.

Kyle sighed and nearly exhaled his soul with it. This was…

Too much.

Half-dead, he asked the others, "What exactly am I expected to do with this?"

Korac resumed the exposition. "According to Elden, we have less than two days before Rayne and Nox collapse the Probability Matrix. In that time, we mean to finish Celindria and the last of Imminent with her. Nox has volunteered as honey for the fly."

At Kyle's raised brows, Korac elaborated. "He will convince Celindria to surrender with him, and they will serve the empire through whatever rehabilitation Xelan designs. Together."

Andrew picked up the mantle then. "But before we rely on Nox to save the universe, you and I need to screen him."

Silence squeezed Kyle again as he tensed at the idea.

Inside Nox's mind.

In his memories.

Less than pleased with the scenario, Kyle asked, "How can you trust me not to frame him? Not to say Celindria is manipulating him?"

The two couples exchanged glances again, but Silence answered, "I'll be with you."

"Fine. But expect me to be petty." Kyle felt wanted to scowl and pout at the same time.

Sagan said, "As if you could be any other way," as she opened a conduit to what looked like a forest on mushrooms.

She and Korac filed in first, leading the way to a massive column of a tree. It climbed so high, Kyle couldn't see the sky for the flourish of twinkling leaves above. It was pretty, but not as enchanting as the wonder in Silence's eyes as she stepped through. She was the Mother of the galaxy, ancient, and yet there was still little of the galaxy she'd yet to see.

A vacation.

That's what they'd do after this fuckery was over.

Silence's white labcoat was gaping from their earlier sessions, exposing her long legs from the revealing black bodysuit she wore beneath the coat. The clasp between her thighs certainly came in handy, and Kyle knew he would lean into their sexual attraction more than usual during this circus. He kept moving his gaze between her eyes and the low neckline of the top—

Beyond Silence, Sagan caught Kyle doing it and snickered into her hand.

It was so silly. His mouth spread into an involuntary smile. Yeah, they were all still family, but this was going to suck.

Light caught Kyle's attention, and he frowned when he spied the source.

Was that a door into a tree?

"Let's go in." Xelan alighted beside them, with Tameka at his side. Under his breath, but loud enough for Kyle to hear, Wingmaster said, "I don't like the idea of *them* alone together."

That set the mood as Kyle followed everyone in with Silence at his side. Instantly, the vibes in the loft blanketed him in grief.

Duffle bag in hand, Rayne was packing things into it. Not *her* shirt. Not *her* leather pants or shoes—

These were all Nox's things.

There was a faint hint of salt in the air, and it tore at Kyle. Especially as she faced them.

Wrecked.

That was the only word for it.

Love and joy flickered in Rayne's blue eyes before she ran across the cozy space and wrapped her arms around Andrew. Why did she always hug someone other than Kyle first—

"Oof!"

He gasped as Rayne violently drew him into the three-way embrace with ridiculous strength. More arms joined, and Kyle knew from their scents it was Tameka and Sagan.

The Progeny.

The original.

Wait, that wasn't right.

Feeling uncharacteristically magnanimous and even nostalgic, Kyle waved for Xelan to join them. Despite all of today's bad news, their guardian beamed and joined the platonic orgy.

Six of them in a massive hug, they met each other's smiling faces inside the huddle. They'd started this thing together, and they would finish it the same way—

"Rayne, dinner's ready—Oh."

Nox.

They all looked up from each other's faces to find the former King of Cinder standing like an enormous statue at the corner. And Rayne—

Kyle had never seen her eyes light up like that before.

And he hated it.

He took Silence's hand, touched Xelan's shoulder, and went *in* without bothersome formalities, like consent.

Nox's memoryscape was a field of cranberry grasses under a clear sky. Stacks of stones—thousands, hundreds of thousands of them—circled out around them. As Kyle scanned the horizon, they formed a spiral. Under the shade of a black-barked tree with scarlet leaves, he, Xelan, and Silence stood with different expressions.

Kyle felt overwhelmed and imagined that he looked like it.

Xelan observed their surroundings, puzzled.

But Silence...

Why did she look mournful?

Kyle reached a hand out to her. "What is it? What is this?" It reminded him of something he couldn't quite place.

While Silence took his hand, she lived up to her namesake and only glanced at him in sadness.

It took Xelan walking up to a stack of stones for Kyle to realize what this place was. A projection appeared on it and played a moment where an ugly motherfucker—obviously Umbra—slapped the point of view of the scene and spat on it. "Ungrateful heathen. Can you not see your mother and I are in the middle of a dispute?! Hide in your chambers and pray to your precious Elden I choose not to find you after I finish with her."

Xelan looked away and stepped back from it, accidentally activating another. In this one, a black-haired, gray-skinned version of Pax ran into the point of view's arms. Xelan as a toddler bawled within the memory.

Nox's voice came from the point of view, concerned and angry. "Tell me."

Little Xelan hiccuped half a sob, asking his older brother, "Why is father so mean?"

Even though Nox's teeth were clenched together, he was gentle with toddler-Xelan. "Whatever father has done now, we can fix it. Now tell me, what did he do?"

All growed-up, Xelan backed away again, trembling from the visceral flashback. Kyle's eyes followed his as they took in the stones with renewed understanding.

Billions of them.

Silence finally said something, and Kyle kinda wished she'd said anything else.

"This is an Icarean graveyard, and this is where Nox buried his trauma."

<hr>

After Umbra spat in Nox's face, he held Xelan as a young boy. When that went away, he was left with nothing. A black emptiness similar to when Rayne shutdown on him in her mind. He felt each moment like the opening of a wound, and he swore Umbra's spittle was still stinging his eyes.

Or were those tears?

A voice penetrated the abyss.

"This is an Icarean graveyard, and this is where Nox buried his trauma."

Nox only recognized Silence's voice from when she'd speak to Rayne through the Martyr Complex. His foremother. She was in his consciousness.

This was memory manipulation. This was Kyle Roberts.

"Check around. We're looking for any sign Nox is working with Celindria. Or any wrongdoing in the last six months."

Xelan was here, too. Nox understood his brother's pragmatism, but the words cut nevertheless. He would need to sit and meditate his way through their prying—

Lust.

It burned through Nox until his knees buckled, and Celindria's voice nearly brought him to the brink. "Lover, give into me. I want you—"

It cut off abruptly.

"Ugh. I found an old one here, and I deeply regret it—Shit, I doubt there's anything in this place I *won't* regret seeing." Kyle's voice came through teeth clenched in disgust and hatred.

Nox understood him as well. This animosity could only dissipate with substantial effort on Nox's part. Hard work was ahead of him to bridge these canyons.

Silence was quiet, but he felt her moving about. Her steps were lighter than the males', graceful and gliding. She touched what felt like Nox's chest as if it were stone.

"My son, you gave so many pieces of yourself away to those foreigners. You have condemned yourself to solitude," Savis said, touching Nox's face with a trembling hand.

Calibrated.

Optimized.

Stabilizing…

Unable to stabilize.

Warning: Five hours and eleven minutes until maximum destabilization.

Nox flinched away and found the memory scape empty. Despite that, his heart pounded against his skull, blood pumping through him with the need to hunt. To prevent the destruction of his family.

Please, let the *leash* not return—

"I think I found something!" Kyle shouted. "These are marked with dates. This one is from two days ago."

Footsteps rushed over Nox, and impressions dented along his arms as if they were walking over him. Deeper steps for Xelan and spiked ones for Silence in her heels.

They touched the stone of Nox's chest again.

Curiosity and adrenaline coursed through Nox at Matt's dramatic arrival. He could taste the dust from the small explosions on his tongue. Xelan, Kyle, and Silence watched the memory play out. Rayne challenged Celindria, who said she'd lost something 'precious.' That she would claim what was hers.

When Rayne took it to mean Nox and challenged Celindria to, "Come and take him from me," Kyle made a disgusted sound. Silence observed according to her name, but Xelan…

Well, even though Nox couldn't see him, his baby brother was biting his thumbnail without a doubt.

The fighting started in the memory, and Nox relived every blow. There was an anxiety which he hadn't noticed in the moment. Rayne was fighting at his side, gorgeous in battle, but out of instinct, he'd checked on her throughout the fight. It was incredulous because Rayne was impossible to defeat, but the thought of losing her in combat made Nox more vigilant.

Tired of knocking Celindria's vessels unconscious, Nox shouted to her and the epiphany hit him as strongly in the recollection as in the moment. An echo of his own voice, he said, "Lay down your arms, Celindria, and come with me. We can go to Xelan together and serve our time."

The offer unnerved Nox then, as it did now, but after some time it had settled. It felt right. He had no intentions of a relationship with Celindria, but their mutual rehabilitation made sense. Both of them had dragged down the galaxy to hurt the other.

"Come with me, Celindria."

The three people in Nox's memoryscape were silent until Kyle said, "I don't buy it. I'll go looking for more." He walked off, but Xelan and Silence remained.

Nox's baby brother was thinking. After a long quiet moment, he said, "I could use your wisdom, foremother."

Silence said, "We can spend an eon in here searching for what you wish to find, or you can trust Rayne that Nox's allegiances lie with her."

An eon.

Treasure hunting through seven million years of Nox's memories would certainly waste the precious little time Elden had warned them about.

Xelan called to Kyle, "Where is Nox? We usually see people in their memoryscapes."

With a chuff, the young man said, "I put him in time-out."

The five Progeny made such a balance of power and personality. Read and manipulate the mind, harm and heal within memory, cross the galaxy and split worlds apart, drain entire stars and level armies, and shoulder all twelve worlds on strength alone.

Nox didn't resent kneeling to their mercy even as Kyle appeared in the darkness with a deep scowl.

"If I didn't think Rayne would hate me for it, I'd wipe your memory clean. Then you could have a fresh start as a blank slate. It's still better than you deserve."

There was a logic to it. Nox asked, "Is that the swing you want to take at me?"

Kyle looked away into the nothing, shaking his head. "You know I hate the sound of your voice? When you talk, all I hear are the things you said to Rayne the day you violated her and forced me to watch. I hear what you said to me on Volcano Day. Asking if you'd thanked me yet for delivering Rayne to your lack of mercy." The last he spat.

Nox waited and let Kyle's words sink into him.

The scowl on his face softened. "Because of Rayne's forgiveness, I'm happy now. I'm better than I ever thought I could be. Banging your grandmother helps, too."

Nox's brows shot up, but he remained silent.

"I know Rayne is capable of amazing things. When they told me she'd subjected you to a mental rehabilitation, I knew she'd likely succeeded. Her capacity to forgive is why the Progeny didn't execute me, but fucking damn it, I've never seen her happier in my life." With a violent rake of his fingers, Kyle attacked his hair and scrunched it. Angry. "I've never seen her—not even with Sagan—look the way she did when you came into the room. And I *hate* you for it."

The word dripped with venom. Nox could only listen. There was little he could say without making this situation worse. He couldn't say he was fond of Kyle. The only thing he knew about the young man was that he'd betrayed Rayne and was now living with Nox's foremother. Smugly.

But they could agree on one thing. This ire was well-deserved. So, Nox took it.

In the stretch of quiet, the acrimony seeped from Kyle. It relaxed with the drop of his hand, the droop of his shoulders, and the defeated hang of his head. He said, "You've put me in a difficult position. I can kill you or frame you as Celindria's minion—"

Nox couldn't keep his eyes from widening.

"—Or... I can step aside and let Rayne finally be happy."

A breeze came from nowhere and blew through their hair. The forest green of Kyle's irises swallowed the whites of his eyes. Black wings opened on his back. His words came in three pitches. "Whatever punishment the Co-Emperors decide, I will mete it out."

Walls erected around them in a cube, one side at a time. It surrounded them with cranberry grasses, black-barked trees, and a sky devoid of Li's cruel blaze. Nox stepped back and stumbled over a stack of stones.

Grave markers.

The memory it played lived in him.

"Xelan. Korac. Come out from under the table this instant." Savis sounded...joyous. Such a rare brightness to her shaky voice.

Nox chuckled as the younger boys pulled on his pants leg to join them in their raucous. With an approving wink from their mother, Nox slipped below the cloth. His brothers had arranged the bottom of the chairs into defense formations identical to ones from a fictional battle described in Uncle Vinco's Verse.

"We attack at dawn," Xelan whispered.

Korac tried to hide the rolling of his eyes as he admonished, *"Prince Xelan, you should always attack in the thick of night."*

Nox opened his mouth to argue the merits of both tactics, when heavy boots sounded within the dining hall.

Toxicity seeped into Umbra's voice as he asked, *"Woman, where are our children?"*

Korac and Xelan had clasped their hands over their mouths, while Nox watched the boots move closer from under the table.

Savis said, *"They are playing as children play."*

When the boots stopped beside mother's chair, Nox signaled for the boys to move back while he positioned himself closer to intercept—

Nox nudged a chair out beside Umbra.

Within seconds, their father knelt to search under the table. Xelan squealed behind Korac's hand, and their personal guard put himself between the only real monster in the Spire and his Prince.

Nox glared at their father.

"Why do you invoke my ire—What is this?" Umbra glanced down one end of the table and then the next. *"Is this Elden's second offensive?"*

Terror froze the younger boys to the spot, but Nox nodded.

Umbra looked up from the floor at Savis seated beside him. *"You are lacking in their education, female. Come see."*

With a slight waver, Savis knelt beside her husband and peered at the formations. She said, "This is how Vinco described it."

With a disgusted snort, Umbra said, "Vinco was not even there. The second offensive was one of your father's most worthwhile efforts. It played out as thus. Mongrel, move the chair behind your back—Yes, that one. Those were the eastern squadron. Xelan, tilt the one on your right to the side and bring it forward."

The three boys moved the furniture until Umbra approved the formation. All the while, Savis asked questions and encouraged his instruction. Her eyes were filled with something Nox only saw on rare occasions.

It wasn't love. He didn't think she ever knew it. But it was... something.

Nox experienced the wonderment all over again, and it staggered him to his knees—

A hand clasped his wrist, catching him before he fell.

Xelan.

The younger brother didn't help pull the older to his feet, but Xelan held steadfast while Nox pulled himself up.

Even with the hard edge to Xelan's eyes, at least this was a place to begin.

"I want in."

Xelan dropped Nox's hand, and they both turned to face Kyle and Silence.

Kyle continued, "I know you won't execute him, but I have some ideas for his sentence. Is that cool with you, Wingmaster?"

Nodding, Xelan said, "I have some scenarios you'd like. Let's discuss it after Andrew screens him. Silence, is there anything else you wish to see?"

This was the first time Nox had ever met his foremother. She crossed the field and looked up the few inches of their height difference into his eyes. Her skin was darker than his, and her voice reminded him of Karter, both husky and deep. But her eyes... They looked like Umbra's. Only sad. "You showed me the only evidence I have of my daughter's happiness. You protected Savis from her abuser and did everything in your power to better her life. Thank you, Nox."

Silence hugged him, her face pressed against his chest. In this gentle squeeze, Nox felt the controlled potential in her arms. She could crush him easier than Rayne. He patted the Mother of the Twelve Worlds and felt her words warm his bones. He murmured, "I'm sorry I couldn't save her."

"Shh... She chose her way to end, and I'll never blame another for it. Not even Umbra. Certainly not you." Silence pulled away from him and changed the subject. "Are you prepared for the trials ahead of you?"

Nox nodded.

"Good." Silence gave a glance back at the men waiting on her before reaching to whisper conspiratorially in Nox's ear. "I'll try to steal you some alone time with Rayne, but I can't guarantee much."

Nox scanned the horizon of gravestones and wondered how many of them contained a memory of Rayne and how he'd looked forward to filling it with more.

It was time to say goodbye.

Once, not that long ago, Andrew had sat across from another Icarus with a murderous past. He'd pilfered through Korac's intentions at Sagan's request and found in them a man worth redeeming. Now, here he was again with an Icarus of the most questionable morals at the request of a close friend.

Would Andrew find Nox a man worthy of mercy?

The light in Rayne's eyes made it hard not to hope for it.

"Hi, Nox. During the many times you tried to kill us, we never formally met. I'm Andrew Holt, and I'll be reading your intentions today. I hope you don't mind the precautions."

Nox sat straight on the edge of the couch, unable to move his arms and legs as Andrew *suggested* he keep still. He was calm despite the restraints, and his curiosity about Andrew's ability filled his black eyes.

And they were *black*. Not sporting a midnight ring like Xelan's or tinged with brown like Matt's.

Andrew could almost see himself, perched on the coffee table, reflected in Nox's glossy irises. After a concealed shiver, he said, "This is how it works. I'll say a series of statements and read your intentions to judge your response."

Xelan was further back in the treeloft, near the library, biting his thumbnail. Korac sat this one out on the stairs off to the side, looking wrung out with all the back and forth.

Lucas stood behind Nox, ready to intervene if things got hot. When Andrew's knight in golden armor nodded, Andrew got straight to it. "Thanks for the mushrooms, by the way. Sorry for the overbearing dinner atmosphere, but you understand we can't simply eat a meal with you on the first encounter." As he spoke, he gauged Nox's intentions.

I'm honored that Andrew and the others seemed to trust me enough to eat my cooking. Rayne looked sad sitting beside Xelan at the table without saying a word. That's not what I want.

Nox's intentions twinged Andrew's heartstrings before the massive Icarus responded outwardly with a bow of his head.

Xelan stepped into Andrew's line of sight beside Lucas.

Heavy.

There was an enormous weight pulling Wingmaster down, and Andrew understood. He'd get to the heart of the matter shortly. To Nox, Andrew said, "Baiting

Celindria into surrendering is quite the bold move. We all hope it works."

As do I. If I could end this without costing the Shadow any casualties, then perhaps I'll have earned my redemption. Finally.

Earned Rayne.

Rayne was behind Andrew, and he noted Nox's eyes move to her often. Their connection was intense, which made the next statement all the harder to say.

"You know, we never could go back for Nikki's body. What with the school burning down and all?"

Brave warrior. I tormented her like my father. My death at Rayne's hand was righteous, and I'd accept it again for my crimes.

A hot tear spilled down Andrew's cheek. His eyes must've been solid teal, because his voice was tripled in octave. "Nikki was my friend. *Our* friend. J.A. Fair wasn't my school, which was lucky, I guess, because you leveled Hall High where I attended. My friends and family died during your invasion. Loved ones across the state—the world—and they all died because of you!"

How can I expect forgiveness after so much wrong? How can I make amends? My execution? My Eternity? How—

Rayne.

She's crying, and it will always be my fault. I keep breaking her heart.

Nox hung his head and spoke to the floor. "Xelan, whatever justice you choose to exact from me, do it now. This gauntlet is causing more pain than I'm worth."

Behind Andrew, Rayne sobbed, and he could hear Tameka and Sagan soothing her. Behind Nox, a fine tremor had seized their leader. Emotions warred within Xelan's eyes, flashing in and out of Atramentous. Lucas gripped Wingmaster's shoulder and steadied him with whatever he said in Xelan's ear.

Korac came down the stairs and put his face in Xelan's until he focused on his General. Korac shook his head, a silent reminder of their pact against abuse and execution.

But Andrew wasn't convinced Xelan wanted to execute Nox. His intentions implied a deeper conflict.

My brother and Rayne's lover is the most hated and lauded Icarus in the Twelve Worlds, and I don't know what to do. His victims deserve restitution, but what punishment could ever absolve these sins?

The brothers wore the same expression of grief and misery. And that was what softened Andrew's Atramentous and let him swallow the emotional clog in his throat. He *suggested* Nox face him again.

The enormous Icarus' eyes widened in surprise at the involuntary movement, but Andrew didn't have time to gloat. Instead, he said one word.

"Rayne."

I'd die to protect her. All I want is to see her happy. She fights and fucks like a goddess. How could I ever let her go? Because if she ever asked, if I was ever to make her unhappy again, I would leave the Worlds and never return.

Rayne is my saving grace, and I will spend Eternity earning her forgiveness.

A different kind of tear spilled from Andrew's eyes. Nox loved Rayne, and the extreme intensity of it expanded Andrew's heart. His eyes flicked to Lucas, and the recognition there. There was no denying it.

Andrew wiped his face and cleared his throat to say, "His loyalty is unquestionable. I say we give this a try."

Arms wrapped around Andrew's neck and wrenched him into a dangerous hug. Rayne squeezed him until he couldn't breathe, and he needed to tap out. She'd matured a lot, but there was no growing out of her mood swings. Perhaps she'd inherited some of Xelan's issues, because Wingmaster looked properly split down the middle.

Hope.

Indignation.

There was no in-between.

With a sigh, Andrew released Nox and went in search of more mushrooms. Lucas joined him in the kitchen while the Shadow convened with a complicated discussion.

Lucas sat across the island from him, saying, "You were magnificent."

Andrew chuffed into his bowl of the most delicious roasted fungi he'd ever eaten. "Thanks. I don't know if I made the situation worse or better—Oh, wait." The tab in his pocket was vibrating, alerting him.

Shaking with apprehension, Andrew checked it.

Yup.

As he'd feared, the calculations he'd initiated before they left were finished. The results were in. And...

Was this good news? Or bad news?

"What is it?" Lucas asked, peering down at the screen.

Andrew swallowed a tender mushroom before saying, "I ran some configurations to determine if there was an order or a pattern to the disappearing Probabilities. And there is. The longest branched Probabilities—The ones furthest spun from our reality vanished first. Then, those more similar to ours. And so on, they steadily move closer. I think our Probability is the epicenter."

Lucas' entire body slacked with relief, closing his eyes with it. It did *not* ease Andrew, who still wasn't sure if this was good or bad news.

Fuck it.

Andrew gave into a third helping of mushrooms. He'd earned the calories.

Oxytocin was a nice chemical Celindria liked to indulge in. It was a kindness she sometimes paid her dolls. They writhed in mass across Iona Pax in sensual abandon. Hands went everywhere. Lips and tongues explored sensitive skin. Celindria filled each of them with every drug she could find, gifted with nacre tolerance.

This was a pleasant buzz.

Satisfaction was a rare treat, and Celindria wallowed in it like a serpent in the sand.

We are desperate to feel.
And yet we don't.

That wasn't true. One of them felt. In the Probability where Celindria had agreed to rule Cinder with Nox, baby Surra at their side, Xelan had manufactured synthetic chemicals to manifest emotions.

Emotional prosthesis.

It required artificial and calculated determinants— Celindria needed to know which mood she'd want in advance and pump them into a nacre port hours ahead of time.

Celindria had tried in other Probabilities to replicate the process. Once, she'd gone through an entire life-endangering argument with Remorse laughing in his face. Another time, she'd intended a cuddle session with a sexual partner later in the day, but wound up feeling clingy at Razor's mercy. The resulting pregnancy had killed her as she'd chosen, like Triss, to keep it. So on and so forth.

How many times have we died to feel?
Tomorrow, will we die again?

A thousand Probabilities had terminated over the last twelve hours. It was very likely this was the end.

The *true* finale.

So Celindria was fucking her brains out. Doubtless, so were Nox and Rayne. If Tumu knew there were only two days remaining, he would've told the Shadow, or vice versa.

Perhaps some spying was in order.

Celindria filed through her inventory, seeking a thread. Someone currently at work near a known hangout of Shadow members—

There.

She slipped into a bombshell of a Lyrik with yellow feathers for hair contrasting wildly against her pitch-black complexion. The woman bartended at a Rayne-themed club in Ishkur. A drone, one of few not under Celindria's control, was shooting Gait Tonics with a familiar Tritan.

Puk and Yito.

They lifted the glowing violet liquors, toasted each other, and downed them.

Celindria brought the Lyrik over and leaned across the counter until her low-cut top was in their sights. "You two see anything else you wanna try?"

Men.

Their eyes went straight to the Lyrik's breasts, lids heavy with inebriation.

They're all too easy.
But at least they're reliable.

After half an hour of chatting them up, Celindria learned the males could hold their liquor. They were also big fans of the Night Rayne franchise and enjoyed the work they did with Matt, Lucy, and Bethany.

The pair were either too on the fringes to know if Rayne had revealed herself to the rest of the Shadow, or things were moving too fast to update everyone. Surely, with only thirty-six hours left, the mewing child would've come out of hiding.

Celindria needed the location, but these two weren't good for that. They were, however, good for other things.

"My shift is over. Are you ready for the after party?"

Puk nodded enthusiastically, needle-nose bouncing with the movement.

But Yito ducked his voids before asking, "Are you cool with the barb? I like to ask before we get into it."

The Shadow rotted Celindria's teeth. Despite the sudden wave of incredulity, she leaned the Lyrik forward, gripped Yito by the collar, and kissed the Tritan until he felt it tingle in his non-toes. Abruptly separating them, Celindria had the Lyrik lick her lips before saying, "*You* can get it in the back."

Yito flushed with his black blood before grinning. "Yes, ma'am. Man, all Lyriks are so damned fiery. Fuck yes!"

Inside her mind, the Lyrik who owned this body lifted her head weakly. Her voice croaked as she begged, "Please, no."

Please.

How many times had Celindria heard the word in her life? Why did everyone beg, not realizing how much she imparted on them? Emotions. Serotonin—

That's all we want.

If we can't feel, at least we can make the galaxy feel everything.

The Lyrik lived one avenue over from the club, and the boys followed Celindria to the apartment. Excited, they half-skipped all the way there. Every kiss on the Lyrik's neck, caress on her ass, and scathing remark about positions built the anticipation until they burst through the door of the flat.

They were on the Lyrik fast and not half-bad. No one was ever Nox, but all hands and lips were soft and wanting. Things Celindria often desired when she could feel it.

But damn it.

Now the Lyrik inside her mind was weeping, and irritation rushed over Celindria. She told the crying woman, "You'll enjoy it. I promise."

"I… don't want them. I love… my partner."

Celindria shut her eyes, counting to ten.

We should stop.

Why would we bend to her and not the countless others?

Because it's wrong.

The third voice was unwelcome.

Celindria stepped into the emotional-driven Probability and found herself staring into a mirror. Compassion was plain on her alternate's face. "Stop this."

As the Probabilities dissipated, were more emotions leaking through from this blissful reality? Was serene Celindria influencing the rest intentionally with those chemicals?

Into the reflection, Celindria asked, "Why should I stop?"

The other Celindria shook her head in warning. "Nox will not love you for this."

"What do you think he's doing right now? Saving kittens? He's fucking our enemy—"

Emotional Celindria looked happy while she said the sad words. "Rayne is not our enemy. She is our descendant, and I wish him happiness with her since he could not find it with you."

This leaking tinge of happiness from the other Celindria twisted the dominant's words. "I will bury you—"

"Sissy—Oh. Are you talking to her right now?"

Pax.

He was so handsome in this reality, dressed like his dad in cargo pants and a tee shirt. Here, because Nox and Celindria never fell out, Korac and Xelan stayed together. Merit, still alive, had surrogated a Pax for the couple. He was already a grown man.

Pax took a careful step into the mirror and let Celindria inspect him. Merit's hair, Xelan's complexion sans freckles, and one midnight blue eye and one green. He said, "I remember what you told the other Pax, and I wish I could've been there to spare you from this life. No one should go through it feeling nothing. Go to Uncle Nox, sister.

Go beg his forgiveness. You will find happiness this way."

The other Celindria kissed his red curls before gazing into her own eyes. "Listen to us and turn back while you still can."

Pity.

Awful mercy poured over Celindria, and she returned to the dominant Probability to find the men sliding the Lyrik's skirt up to her waist—

"Stop. Now."

The Lyrik inside the mindscape dropped her head, overcome with relief. Respectable as they were, the men exchanged confused glances as they backed off the bed with their hands up.

Puk said, "It's cool. Would you like us to leave?" His antennae twitched with concern.

Yito looked equally uncomfortable. "We'll go right now, if you want."

Pity settled in Celindria's heart as she stared at the two men. They just wanted to fornicate, and she'd put them through this mess. With a sigh, she waved them off. "Please, leave. I'm sorry I led you on."

"Hey. No. Don't apologize. We're good." Puk patted Yito's back as they left. They both waved, more worried than disappointed.

Was the Shadow made up of saints?

Celindria shutdown sex across all her vessels, feeling sorry for them. As pity valleyed, regret peaked. So many voices had told her no. No to the sex, and no to the drugs. But...

They don't know what it is to go without feeling.
They're ungrateful.

Celindria retracted her manifestation from her dolls' mindscapes and left them on autopilot. Inside her own body, she stood within the Oblivion Cathedral—her fortress—and contemplated. All the while, she kept her eyes on the blue ribbon.

Ungrateful.

Uninformed.

Trillions were wrong, and only Celindria was right. For once, she considered the alternative and didn't like how it felt.

XVII   GLOW

XELAN HAD ALWAYS LOVED THIS FOREST. Razor had chosen the location when Xelan was tracing Celindria across the galaxy. As her path spiraled, Thailea at its center, they preemptively constructed the treeloft for Xelan's mission. Often when he'd slept in the comically gigantic bed or used the open shower, he'd wondered what Razor was thinking in its design.

Xelan asked the nearest tree, "Razor, did you program the loft to open for Nox and Rayne? How much are you swept into this Aegis plot?"

Of course, there was no answer, and much of this was contorted until Xelan couldn't make sense of it. Razor believed with every fiber of his being that he and Triss were the Eternal Bind. So who or what was drawing Rayne and Nox together all this time?

Xelan paused in his stroll to bite his thumbnail and stare at the untouched deadfall of the undergrowth. Antiqued chrome, the leaves had lost their shine and offered little in the way of response.

The forest wasn't completely non-responsive. A fat wallop followed by a lighter one sounded in the limbs nearby. The mating pair had allowed Xelan to enter their dominion of peace, and he was grateful for it.

Earlier in Nox's memoryscape, Xelan had reached out and grabbed Nox's hand. Not because he didn't want to see the behemoth crumble and fall, but because sentimentality and nostalgia crippled Xelan.

That was the simple answer to Rayne's question. It was why he couldn't kill Celindria, Korac, or Razor for their crimes—

No.

That wasn't quite right.

Out of sight; out of mind. Xelan didn't witness *their* crimes. One could argue, he'd witnessed Korac's alongside Nox's, but the faithful General was following his beloved King's orders as only the best soldier would.

When Nox ripped Xelan's nacre from his chest and lit the Prince of Cinder ablaze with an Icarean firestick, sneering about defiling Rayne—That had been Xelan's *brother*.

And it killed Xelan.

It cost Xelan the first two years of watching Pax grow from an infant into a toddler. Perhaps if Xelan had been around, he could've surmised the connection between Pax and Imminent sooner. He could've built a bridge between him and Celindria that way.

Xelan wiped a hand down his face and considered the memories they'd stumbled onto in the serene bone yard of Nox's mind. A cold Spire kept warm by three boys. After living among nacre-less humans for so long, Xelan often wondered what Nox would look like without a nacre to heal their wounds.

The scars.

How many would Nox have? And how many would he have because he'd stepped between their abusive father and the baby?

Nox would be dead if they'd been born without nacres, and then where would Xelan be without the big brother protector? In a way which Xelan didn't like to consider, Rayne wouldn't exist without Nox. None of the Shadow would.

Was that the answer, then?

Leaves crunched behind Xelan. While staring into the forest, he said, "Everyone expects me to forgive you. The baby with the older brother as savior. The Prince looking up to his misunderstood King. You were always a warrior. In my eyes, you were everything. Strong when my bones seemed brittle. Fearless when I cowed behind our mother. I wanted to grow up and be like you. You *failed* me."

Regret formed Nox's presence at Xelan's back. Like a black hole, it was a heavy mass drawing the younger brother in. The older remained quiet, absorbing the punishment as he'd done throughout the last few hours of interrogation.

Xelan shook his head, filled with uncertainty and regret. "And I failed you. We keep failing each other, Nox. Our parents brought so much strife between us, and I am ashamed I didn't see your suffering sooner. But you never told me, and for that, we are both guilty. I think we'll mourn this lifelong rift between us for the rest of our existences. Long may they be."

The younger brother looked up to find the perplexed frown he'd expected on the older one's face. From across the clearing, Xelan stared into Nox's eyes and admitted, "I don't wish you dead and not only because your death would crush Rayne. I believe there is some virtue to harvest in your genuine contrition. Can I convince you to end it with her? That in exchange for the Shadow's acceptance, you would first give up Rayne. Yet I know it's wrong and underhanded. And—"

"I would never agree to it," Nox announced, clear as day. "What Rayne wants is what she wants. I've lived her life with her. I know the only thing which can stand between Rayne and whatever brings her happiness is herself. If she is happy with me, as she has informed you, then you couldn't stand in the way of it if you wanted to. Nor could I. If it were anything but Rayne's choice, I would stand down, because you're right. I don't deserve her, but it's her decision, and for now, she has chosen me."

During Nox's sensible proclamation—too accurate for comfort—Xelan put his hands on his hips and gazed out into the brush. It was too painful to look at Nox while he spoke of his relationship with Rayne.

The Eternal Bind.

If Andrew's estimations were correct, then the Shadow shouldn't fear the collapse of the Probability Matrix. They were its dominant reality, and therefore safe, according to Lucas' halfhearted explanation.

So why keep Rayne and Nox apart at all?

Punishment.

The Progeny were working together to design the perfect rehabilitation for complicated offenders—For the Celindrias, Noxs, and Razors of the Worlds. A long sentence of facing their crimes through lived experience, rich in empathy and anguish. Should it also include isolation?

Unsure of the answer, Xelan dismissed Nox anyway. "Go to Rayne. Hold her while you can, because when I'm through with you, your bones will be too weary to touch her."

Lightning fast, just as Rayne had said, Nox vanished from the clearing to find her. His physical prowess matched the eye-witness accounts Xelan had discovered while pursuing headlines to keep tabs on Rayne. Citizens of the Twelve Worlds had reported sightings of a good samaritan Icarus performing feats of courage and compassion. The rumors tripled after Rayne and Nox's impulsive film-worthy performance at the races.

Xelan believed there was hope for this. But was that his sentimentality speaking? Was it blinding his good sense?

Staring once more at the foliage, Xelan called, "You can come out now, General."

Korac dropped from his high perch, wearing his mask, but Xelan saw hints of emotional exhaustion in the strain around his white eyes. While Korac waited for the conversation to start, he picked a leaf from his braids and brushed bark off his shoulder. It was endearing, and Xelan was glad he'd never called for his former lover's execution.

"I've asked all my other advisers and now I come to you, seeking council. What would you have me do?"

Korac's single chuckle was expected, as this was a ridiculously comical question with an obvious answer. Still, the General took a respectable amount of time to consider it thoroughly before saying, "I challenge you and Nox to the training course."

A ridiculous question deserved a ridiculous answer. Xelan grinned. "Give the people what they want?"

Folding his arms and leaning on a tree base, Korac smirked as he pitched the idea. "It will help market your campaign to reform the 'galactic outlaws,' as Sagan calls them. She has this great idea of Nox leading the program, proof positive of its merits. The Progeny all contribute their gifts to recreate memories in live scenarios—We can employ the Divine Booths. So in, a way, Razor also contributes."

Ah... The last was meant to sweeten the deal and appeal to Xelan. Coy, but he liked it. "We can call it the 'Epic Triathlon—'"

"No." Korac firmly shook his head.

"'The Race of Ages—'"

"Please, stop."

Xelan headed back to the treeloft, listing off more names. "'The Icarean Gauntlet'—I like that one."

"Never." As always, Korac followed and complained.

"What about, 'Verses Versus Verses'?"

"How did I ever miss you while you were gone?"

Throughout the long day, Rayne had glanced at Nox. Sometimes, he looked as sad as she felt. And others...

There was this secret glimmer in Nox's black eyes which reminded Rayne of the last time they were together when he'd said she felt like silk. It had burned her cheeks, knowing how the roughness of his voice had affected her, tipped her over the edge—

"Rayne, are you listening?" Tameka waved her hand in Rayne's face.

Sagan snickered, asking, "Is this 'end of the universe' shit boring you? Or do you have a certain Icarus on your mind—"

"Please, let's not go there," Tameka begged with a hand out in surrender.

Rayne offered an apologetic smile, blushing at Sagan's accurate observations. "Sorry. We can get back to the film premiere plan—"

"No." The blond shook her head, short hair swaying with the motion. "You've never got to have girl talk with us, and I think it's fair you do before we could all die in the finale."

The girls were sitting in the bed, doing each other's hair and makeup for the final fight—A moment which Rayne cherished given how many moments like this were denied to them over the years. But it wasn't exactly private.

Lucas and Andrew were downstairs discussing what sounded like important things, not only with the Probability Matrix but also with their relationship. Rayne tried her best not to eavesdrop.

Kyle and Silence went to spend some private time in the hot springs beneath the loft. Something about making the brothers drink after them. Rayne thought it best not to dwell on it.

Xelan and Tameka had communicated with the rest of the Shadow, and soon they would join everyone to prepare. Most were shocked to know Rayne and Nox were alive. She and her brother had shared tears over the communication, and the others had let them. While it wasn't a surprise to Rayne that Caedes, Pehton, Matt, and Lucy would know of their resurrections, Tumu knowing was a curious thing.

How?

Rayne intended to ask him at the big huddle.

Oh, wait. Was she supposed to say something?

"Uhm. I dunno. I feel…" Rayne blushed. Weren't those private moments meant only for her and Nox?

Sagan gave Tameka an entreating look.

Fury rolled her eyes and groaned, "Start small. Tell us about the first kiss."

Rayne finished twisting Tameka's hair into a fiery crown and waited in place for Sagan to fishtail Rayne's hair into braids. All the while, she considered how to put the moment into words. "I was scared. A whaleshark had pulled Nox under. Sticky, you know? And there was blood in the water, blue mixing with green. Caedes wouldn't let me dive in after Nox. He'd already figured most of it out by then—You know how smart he is. Meanwhile, the dwarf announcing the tournament kept sensationalizing what he could see happening under the water. I thought—I thought this was it. I'd never get to show Nox how much he meant to me."

Although Rayne was reliving the moment, seeing black ocean waves surging onto the beach, she noticed the two girls exchange engrossed looks.

Maybe this *would* make for a good movie.

"But it wasn't over. The beast roared in agony as green blood geysered out of the waves. Nox swam out of the water and walked onto shore. He was bleeding from everywhere, but I was frozen. I couldn't cry out or run to him. Before I realized what he was doing, Nox crossed the beach in two strides and kissed me."

"Wow." Sagan's chin was perched on her hand, staring dreamily at Rayne.

Tameka looked down at the combat gear she was designing, busying herself with it while she said, "There was applause. Caedes told me about it. Iuo will be disappointed it didn't make into his film, so expect a future request for you to consult on the sequel."

"Rayne?"

Speak of the handsome devil. All three girls rushed to the banister and looked over to see Nox downstairs.

Suddenly finding himself the center of attention, Nox shifted his weight, fidgeting. Even Andrew and Lucas were staring up at him from the library's armchairs. He cleared his throat before asking, "Can you come with me?"

Alone.

Xelan was letting them be alone.

Rayne squeezed both her friends and rushed down the stairs—

She stopped midway, realizing what this meant. Xelan was letting them say goodbye. And as everyone in the space held their breath, Rayne knew they had figured it out as well. All the people she loved wanted them apart—

No.

That wasn't fair.

They wanted Nox to pay for his crimes, and the sorrow on their faces said they knew it came at this price.

Rayne went to Nox and took his hand, leading him out of the treeloft on a somber note. Without words, they opened their wings and flew deeper into the forest, faraway from their solitary futures, and alighted below a weeping tree. It was the only one of its kind Rayne could recall seeing in the forest. Water was nearby. A milky brook trickled through their private escape, filling the forest with its life-giving fragrance.

Rayne couldn't look at Nox, afraid the grief in his eyes would unmake her. Instead, she wasted their time wandering over to the water. It couldn't reflect the storm in her, the waves crashing beneath the striking electricity.

None of this was fair.

"Rayne."

The gravity with which Nox always said her name weighed Rayne down with the inevitable. She said, "I feel like you're letting us go without a fight."

Nox took a step toward her. "No. This is me fighting not to let you go. I have to face this to be a man who deserves you."

He tried to turn her by her arm, but Rayne wrenched it away.

Why?

Rayne wasn't angry with Nox. She was angry with the cosmos for cheating her yet again—

Her back met the tree trunk in a dizzying rush. Before Rayne could catch her breath, Nox tipped her chin up and kissed her. It sang in every nerve ending, raising goosebumps on her arms. As he deepened it, their scents mingled with the smell of water and leaves. Rayne moaned against Nox's lips as he hiked up her thighs, and she wrapped her legs around his hips. When feathers rustled under her, she broke the kiss on a laugh. He was holding her up by his wings.

Nox smiled at her delight. "I couldn't let the universe tear us apart without you experiencing this."

This was it. Beneath this Thailean willow, beside this babbling brook—This was the moment Rayne had been waiting for.

"I—"

Nox captured her lips in another kiss, cutting her off. Rayne couldn't help but frown when he pulled them apart and stared into her eyes. "Why?"

He licked the taste of her from his lips before saying, "It would only sound like 'farewell' tonight. I don't want to hear it as an ending. I want you to say it as a beginning."

How else could Rayne tell Nox how she felt? To prevent later regrets...

As Nox brushed the loose strands of Rayne's hair away, she knew what to say. "Take from me what you need."

His eyes flashed Atramentous before he said, "Give to me what you want."

Together, they vowed, "Until Eternity takes me, I'm yours."

Rayne kissed Nox, and they gripped each other. When she absorbed her armor, she ground against him, reaching for the ties of his pants.

They fumbled with them and laughed together before Nox looked Rayne in the eyes to say, "Don't wait for me. It's criminal to withhold this part of you. I want you to find happiness with Sagan or whomever—"

Rayne pressed a finger to Nox's lips. "No more talking like this is the last time. Nox, tonight, please give me something to hold on to."

Rayne didn't have to ask twice.

After watching the way Nox and Rayne had just left the treeloft, Andrew totally expected the Matrix to lose a few thousand Probabilities. Then Xelan and Korac came and took the girls for a 'walk.' Everyone was out having a good time in the woods or fouling up the drinking water.

So Andrew pounced on Lucas, literally trying to jump his bones. Unfortunately, Lucas held Andrew aloft above him with an incredulous laugh. Andrew asked into the man's glorious smile, "Why not?"

The smile softened from joyous to sad. Where Andrew's hair fell into Lucas' face, the Icarus with golden eyes tucked the strands behind Andrew's ears, saying, "I need to tell you. Everything. Before this is over, I want you to know the truth."

Andrew laid down on the plush rug beside Lucas, stretching the length of his partner on his side. He propped his head on his hand, elbow bent on the floor. "So tell me."

Lucas mirrored Andrew and held out a capsule. It was for memories. "Rayne and Nox inspired me. Take this, and you will live my life as I've lived it. I can understand if that's too much—"

Andrew snatched and downed it before Lucas could put up more bullshit about extremes. Only after did he realize he ought to have listened.

Light.

It shone in every color, and some shades Andrew couldn't even recognize. His brain wouldn't allow it.

Was this the cosmos?

Was this the beginning?

"Andrew, follow my voice." Lucas' words exploded through the non-existence. It sounded wrong here.

As a consciousness, Andrew followed the sound to its source. Where the prismatic light collapsed into a void, he entered. Waiting there, Andrew counted three hundred and twenty-two men with white hair and white eyes. Only their pupils differentiated them.

In the middle stood Lucas, sandy blond hair and golden eyes. As Andrew watched, the color seeped from his lover, and the veil lifted when his pupils formed into stars.

"I am One, Zero's first son."

Wow. All this time, Andrew was doing an Aegis.

Lucas winked as if he could read Andrew's thoughts before balling his hands together and crumpling the matter around them like aluminum foil. Inside the tin ball, Andrew had no form. He could see the matter bleed mercury drops onto a blank canvas.

"By now, Sagan has told you what the Exalted said of the formation of worlds. Not only the planets and this galaxy, but all things. Breath. Vision. Light."

The mercury drops hardened into a mirror. Andrew was in its reflection.

"We brought you into existence when we entered a less malleable dimension. Here, we were challenged to create and innovate."

As Lucas told the story, the mirror cracked.

"But our entry shattered the fabric of this plane. With every decision we made, it splintered. It was only after I constructed Enki, our weapon, that I discovered the disastrous course of your Probabilities."

Rayne appeared in the shattered mirror in tears.

Lucas' booming voice softened as he said, "The girl would destroy Enki, unaware she would liberate the woman who would take it all. Both of them were drawn to the same warrior, honed by inexplicable circumstance. But I get ahead of myself."

Sudden enough to flip Andrew's stomach, Lucas gave him form again. Andrew stood on the bridge of Ishkur. Here, Zero's many sons gathered around the same pods Andrew, Silence, and Smith worked inside to observe the Probability Matrix. Lucas—One—was there, washed out, but still distinctly more handsome than his brothers.

The Exalted appeared from thin air onto the bridge and called to his oldest son.

Alertness washed over Andrew until he almost stood at attention. It was Lucas' emotions.

"Father, by studying the Source, I have determined the results of the fissure we created. The fracture in the multi-verse centers on this girl and her relationship with a warrior of her time. One already in the making." The intensity deepened Lucas' voice to an octave Andrew had never heard before. "Unchecked, the girl's ancestor will corral all beings of the Matrix under her control in pursuit of this warrior."

The Exalted's eyes widened. His pupils were white-filled rings. At the news, they tripled in number. Still, Zero sounded calm as he asked, "All beings?"

Grateful his father didn't doubt the situation's severity, Lucas said, "Yes. She'll harness the Source and exist across the Probabilities. But she's a broken thing."

"What are your plans to correct it?"

Lucas glanced back at an Aegis Andrew hadn't noticed until now. He looked like Zero's other sons, but smaller. His eyes had two pupils, both in the shape of crescent moons.

Razor.

The smaller Aegis perked up when he saw his father and brother noticing him. The eagerness on his face, and how it fell when they looked away, touched Andrew.

Or touched Lucas, and Andrew felt it vicariously.

Probably both.

The scene abruptly paused, and Lucas said to Andrew only. "We feared the experimental son and his capabilities. As you know from your time manipulating Cascading Light, we only saw uncertain glimpses. Through them, we knew Three Two Four could bring about the end of our race. So we othered him."

This was another scenario to prove Andrew's theory that the Probability Matrix only generated self-fulfilling prophecies.

Sharp regret lanced through Andrew. This time, he knew it belonged to Lucas. Into the ether, Andrew said, "Please continue."

Lucas detailed a plan to his father with suggestions on how to stop Celindria from owning the multiverse. "I will start with preventing her creation by separating those who came before her and work my way out from there. If she still comes to be, I will abort the resulting splinters and try again. Until I am successful, I will not stop."

Intrigued and a little concerned, Zero asked, "How far must we go?"

Despite the apprehension in him, Lucas said, "To the beginning. And not we. *I* will go. Alone."

Zero gripped his son's shoulder. "Go. I trust your discretion. Should you fail, try again until you come home to us. Do you understand?"

Despite Zero's optimism, both men knew this was the last they'd see of one another. Lucas accepted his mission.

The scene crumpled again and melted into a mercury spiral, swimming down a drain.

No.

This was the maelstrom beneath the bridges of Enki and Ishkur. Andrew was staring at it from where he stood on the lowest gangplank. Only now he saw it more clearly.

Each flame of Cascading Light held a unique image of Lucas in an infinite swirl of Probabilities.

Eternity.

Scenes played in every lick of fire. Some Andrew recognized—Standing on the roof of J.A. Fair's burning ruins, their first time making out in Iona-28's library, preparing Korac for his wedding—

Holy shit! Korac was Lucas' brother.

Andrew would get back to that.

Other scenes were older and unfamiliar. One such scene captured Andrew's attention. It was Silence, strapped to an uncomfortable table. Andrew winced when he realized there were stirrups for the awful existence she'd endured before discovering Cinder. She was sleeping when...

Lucas.

He slipped into the lab and removed the nacre shield restraints. He unchained her from that life. And he wasn't alone.

Tumu let him into the lab.

In fact, the old Primary was in most of the ancient scenes. The most curious ones involved an Icarus with charcoal skin and Nox's enormous frame.

Elden.

On the glass platform, Andrew looked away from Eternity and into his lover's unfamiliar eyes. "You experimented on Elden."

Lucas—One—nodded. "He was one of many fulcrums. I learned early in my research there was no way to prevent the making of Celindria and Rayne. The Probabilities terminated without them, but I learned there were ideal circumstances I could cultivate and shape into more positive threads. Elden and Silence must meet in order for Rayne to exist, but Silence need not escape on her own and destroy Enki with the Chorus to find Cinder. And so on."

Andrew needed to swallow before he could ask, "Did you hurt Elden?"

Again, Lucas nodded. This time, more solemnly. His voice was soft—almost apologetic—as he said, "It was necessary." He took a step toward Andrew, and when the younger man didn't retreat, Lucas took it as encouragement to continue. "Across Eternity, I've loved and hurt each of you. In hundreds of thousands of ways. But this was my first time loving and hurting you. This was the first time I was happy, despite losing my family. My entire race. In this Probability, I saw Silence revived. I saw my half-brother marry the love of his life. And your smile meant more than all of it combined."

Andrew's heart skipped a beat. He felt the same way about Lucas, but… "Are you saying you've been manufacturing our lives? Our relationships? You and me?"

Lucas went still as a statue. His mouth didn't move as his voice came from everywhere on the bridge all at once. "Not you and I. The Shadow are always full of surprises. Despite my best efforts, no one in existence is completely predictable, and I have never calculated a single Probability with one hundred percent accuracy."

When his voice returned to him and his mouth moved with the words, they were softer as Lucas said, "I think I would've gone mad if that were the case. It's why we fear Celindria's empire. No one should have pure dominion over others. Your diverse lives, with all their variety, are what make you beautiful."

Andrew didn't need to check Lucas' intentions. He knew in his bones this was the truth. However, he still had questions. "What happens to us, our Probability, if the Matrix collapses? All those decisions branching into universes—Do they simply stop forming?"

"That is the going theory. Your outcomes will form along this dominant thread and only here. No one should notice a difference aside from those who have touched Cascading Light. The world will no longer appear fragmented, having been cemented into one Probability. It will look as it had before I pushed you into the flames."

The blurry three-dimensional lines which constantly framed everyone and everything Andrew could see. They would disappear. How long ago did he last see the world as solid?

Wait.

Did Lucas say 'theory'?

Andrew asked, "You mean, you don't know?"

His Aegis lover smiled as if endeared by how long it took for Andrew to notice that detail. Lucas said, "Since the fissure ruptured when we entered your dimension, I've never seen this realm without the veil of Cascading Light. I hope to see it in its natural state with you at my side."

'Overwhelmed' wasn't the right word for how Andrew felt, because the mystery behind Lucas stopped shocking him long ago. Instead, they'd become part of Lucas' charm. Andrew took his eyes off his lover to peer down through the glass at Eternity below. He could dive in and learn every secret there was to know about Lucas. This was his chance to unmask his lover fully—To know him inside and out. And Lucas was inviting Andrew to do so. But…

"I'd rather get back to the loft and fuck you before this finale kicks off, if that's okay with you?"

Lucas grinned, and the stars in his eyes sparkled with affection. "That suits me just fine."

Andrew held up a finger. "But before we go, do you want me to start calling you 'One' in the heat of passion?"

Incredulous, his lover shook his head, still grinning. "'Lucas' sounds more at home to me now than my birth name."

While he asked a few more questions, Andrew took Lucas' hands in his. "What about the perception filter? Are you planning to leave it on around the Shadow? Will you let them know the truth, too?"

"I think some have guessed I am Aegis. Silence and Smith have always known. I could live among the Shadow in my natural form, and I would like to get to know Korac as a half-brother. Yes, I believe it's time."

Andrew's chest swelled as he beamed. He wrapped his arms around Lucas and squeezed tightly. When his lover returned the embrace, Andrew said against his shoulder, "You're not alone anymore. We'll finish this together."

They shut their eyes and soaked in the love.

When Andrew next opened them, they were back inside the treeloft, surrounded by Shadow.

Xelan perked up from where he was sitting in the nearest armchair. "Hey, they're back."

So many beloved faces peered up from the couch, around the corner, and from upstairs. Lucas and Andrew exchanged a confused glance before Andrew asked, "What happened to everyone taking the night off to be together?"

Sagan, Tameka, and Rayne looked at each other with knowing grins before Sagan said, "It's morning already. We've planned the entire premiere without you, and now we have only a few hours to prepare."

Korac stepped into view, arms folded and looking serious. Only then did Andrew realize Lucas' perception filter was still off. The General asked, "Are you One? Are you Zero's first son?"

From behind Andrew, someone held out a hand. Lucas clasped it to stand up and helped Andrew up. They both looked to find it was Nox.

After Lucas nodded at him, he faced his brother. "I am."

There was a long pause while both white-haired men stared at each other. With the filter removed, the similarities were obvious. Same jaw and cheekbones. Korac's brows and lips were softer—No one could look prettier than the Silver General, and it was almost enough to make Andrew roll his eyes.

Korac cut the tension by unfolding his arms and gripping Lucas' shoulder while saying, "We'll talk when this is over." The man's usual composure slipped enough to show the esteem he already felt for his tailor through the warmth in his eyes.

This could work out.

Andrew had faith in Lucas and the Shadow. There was only one other thing on his mind.

"So, do you guys mind if Lucas and I sneak off somewhere real quick or do you just want to watch us bone here in front of you?"

Kyle chuffed when Andrew and Lucas had returned from the forest, hair mussed and faces flushed. He muttered to himself, "I guess for some people, five minutes is enough."

Silence gave him the half-serious, scolding look. It was a glare she'd give him while her steely eyes twinkled with humor. Kyle loved it.

Speaking of fast...

Things were moving way too much of it. One minute, Kyle was enjoying the hot springs with Silence, the next he was sitting at the crowded premiere of Rayne's Verse.

In *formal-wear.*

Damn it, between the girls, Lucas, and Korac, the Shadow had wrangled Kyle into a black three-piece with a fucking *cumberbund.* A waistcoat he could manage. But why did they saddle him with this hideous non-combat accessory across his midsection? Who cared that it matched Silence's outfit?

Okay, Kyle cared a little. She seemed to dig the getup. But for real, they were about to take on the multi-verse. Why was everyone so snazzy? Where did these outfits even come from? It was like Lucas had been planning this from the beginning.

Silence reveled in it. Her clandestine Ancient bestie had dressed her in a sheer crimson two-piece harem ensemble, complete with black bangles on her biceps. It was so transparent, Lucas had asked Kyle to adhere pasties under the bra-top. His G.I.L.F. glowed in it as Silence's grandsons tried their best not to complain. Kyle felt extra smug with her on his arm.

The red theme continued with the next couple. Sagan's vermillion Qipao minidress with black flames embroidered into the silk matched Korac's modernized martial arts coat and loose linens pants. Same pattern, inverted colors, yada yada.

And yeah, Tameka, Xelan, and Pax wearing matching gear tugged at Kyle's heartstrings. The little boy was the spitting image of his father in their matte black and red-accented three-piece tuxes and *waistcoats* perfectly complimented Tameka's hair and the bright skater dress she wore to showoff the hard-earned definition of her quads.

Lucas had popped his perception filter back on for the public affair. He dressed in a classic black *James Bond* tuxedo with a cardinal bow tie. Andrew looked happy sitting beside his cradle-robbing boyfriend, wearing a flaming—no pun intended—tunic over black slacks. They were so adorable they'd activated Kyle's gag reflex with how much they were all over each other next to him.

The rest of the Shadow were present for Iuo's premiere. That should go without saying. And although they all matched, there was only one other couple whose gear was worthy of Kyle's notice.

Rayne knocked it out of the park in that scarlet dress. Thin straps, sweetheart neckline, and a long skirt with gaping slits down her legs for ass-kicking. She always looked like an Amazon when she wore heels, and for once, they weren't chunky combat boots. Slinky stilettos gave her an additional four-inches of height. Not at all practical, but fortunately, she could switch to something else in a pinch.

Unfortunately, Kyle wasn't the only one admiring her. Nox had ADRD. Attention Directed at Rayne Disorder. And as much as Kyle liked Lucas and was happy for him and Andrew, he didn't agree with the tailor's choice to dress Nox in a black kilt with a scarlet tartan pattern and *no* shirt. The entire Shadow were forced to sit around the treeloft and watch Rayne paint a Verse in red ink all over the bastard's chest and back. They'd both mooned at each other, and Kyle had finally gagged.

Secretly.

He didn't complain about Nox around Silence. It seemed to hurt her, and Kyle was a better man than that. Besides, if they survived this, Xelan's plans guaranteed Kyle a front-row seat to Nox's punishment. He could tolerate the motherfucker for one final battle.

And here they were.

The end.

How much had the Shadow endured together? Invasion, battles, infiltration, sacrifice, loss, and so much pain. Yet Kyle could never discount the happy times which shone like beacons in everyone's memories tonight. They were lighthouses in the dead of night.

This was for them.

Front row in the Palatial Grounds amphitheater could seat an army, and it was a good thing, too, seeing as the Shadow brought one to the premiere. In order from left to right:

Tumu's suspicious ass and Lamassau sat on the end, open to the aisle and ready for action.

Twenty-One and Miy took a break from space training to join in the festivities. The emo princess had complained initially that red clashed with the orange streaks in her black feathers, but after Lucas finished transforming her into a sexy fireball, she'd perked up.

Pablo hated to leave Lynn with Qas again, but the good doctor couldn't leave the Shadow to a rowdy battle without his bedside manner.

The annihilation squad accounted for the next four seats: Yito, Puk, Matt, and Lucy. Bethany had asked to sit with her family. She'd said something about them needing her help more. Regardless, they all coordinated not only in clothes but in the disappointed look on their faces. Apparently, they took umbrage with the no-kill order.

Pehton's red feathers blended right into the theme. Meanwhile, Kyle resented Caedes because apparently he got special privileges not to coordinate. Dude was in black from bald head to combat-booted toe.

Korac and Sagan had asked Legir and X, more healer and trapper than fighters, to watch baby Echo. Meaning, if the Shadow didn't return from the premiere, they and The Brethren were trusted to raise her. Galactic god parents.

Tameka, Pax, and Xelan sat in the royal box front and center, with Aria and Torch flanking them like fiery columns.

Rayne sat as close to Xelan as possible, which was real awkward considering this was a film about her life before any of them knew it so heavily involved the giant piece of shit sitting next to her. She kept shifting in her seat to buffer Xelan from Nox.

Silence and Kyle carried the exhausting burden of being the hottest couple in this amphitheater filled with millions. And they did it with style and grace.

Andrew and Lucas were still all over each other, like this wasn't a public event or something.

Smith sat on the other side of Lucas, grinning like an eager kid let loose in a candy store.

Devis took the news that Nox was alive about as well as Kyle. Likewise, the man sulked between his sister and brother. T.A.O. and Andrius wore ceremonial clothes from an age gone by. But dyed red and black to match the rest of them. They both looked ready to end it.

Jack simply refused to acknowledge Nox's existence. He was beyond elated Rayne had come out of hiding finally, but he'd slipped into Atramentous at the mere mention of the former King of Cinder. Ross ran interference, reminding him of how happy they should be with all the family together. Made all the easier to say with Bethany sitting beside them. She looked like a grown woman dressed in the slender red gown with black full-length gloves. Kyle was *not* happy about it. His baby sister kept leaning forward in her seat to wave down the row at Matt and Lucy. And they encouraged it.

Karter sat between Chris and Para, another proud G.I.L.F. Bones joined them as the outlier to their poly and Para's date for the evening. The women looked radiant while the men looked eager to get their girls home at the end of the night.

This was a freaking fashion show on steroids. Even so, Kyle couldn't imagine ending the multi-verse with a finer bunch of fighters, lovers, and friends.

The stage lit up, and the curtain raised to reveal luo in the most ridiculous outfit of them all. His black jacket and slacks were bedazzled with rubies. The Lamian King-Elect twinkled, looking like he stole it out of Razor's closet.

"Welcome guests to my finest production."

luo winked at the living breathing Rayne during the premiere of her posthumous biopic.

What was more Shadow than that?

"Promise me, amos, that you won't overdo it this time?"

Korac kept his eyes forward on luo's introductory speech, but he let his concern for Sagan into his voice.

Where she held it on her lap, Sagan squeezed his hand. "No passing out this time to leave anyone at the mercy of a failing Dyson's Sphere or Probability Matrix. Promise."

"Shh!"

Korac languished in his slow turn to Pehton. Once he met the defiance in her garnet eyes, he let his gaze go lower and lower, taking in the skimpy dress she could tell herself she wore for Caedes, but all three of them knew the truth. It was in the orange flush to Pehton's cheeks.

When Korac met the Lyrik's eyes again, he mouthed, "Hussy."

Beside her, Caedes chuckled, eyes front on the stage.

Although he indulged in making Pehton squirm, Korac clocked the individuals in the crowd glancing over at the Shadow. Sure, some of them did it out of adoration and awe, but the ones he'd noticed were mechanical, stiff, and devoid of emotion.

Celindria.

Her vessels didn't simply pepper the crowd, they damned near comprised it. An army of thought puppets. The notion of her taking control of Korac's volition made his skin shrivel and crawl off his bones. Celindria had dressed her bodies all like dolls for the occasion and brought them out to the big premiere.

Theater. Spectacle. Drama.

Cold eyes glimpsed Korac searching the crowd, and he faced the stage once more.

Sagan muttered, "Here we go," before luo plunged them into darkness.

Korac tensed, coiled like a spring ready to strike. When Celindria didn't make her move immediately, he looked around and caught others among the Shadow checking the crowd, too.

In the meantime, the projector pulled up the scene of a little brunette girl playing in her mother's bookstore. Another twenty minutes passed without interference. When the film continued into the first time Xelan approached a teenage Rayne in the bookstore, Korac began to wonder if Celindria was letting the entire film play out.

"Do you think she's waiting for an action beat or something?" Sagan whispered.

Pehton leaned forward to answer her across Korac. "I hope not. I'm puckered over here."

Korac barked out a laugh at an inappropriate time in the movie and shamed Pehton for it with a look. It didn't wither her. Instead, she preened. Caedes grinned on in silence while Sagan snickered into her hand.

Not that Korac gave a shit. Clearly, his Verse would've made for a more cinematic picture—

A blanket of light sparked from behind them, and a scream tore from the audience.

The entire front row stood at the ready and faced the…

Firework.

Someone had blown some pyrotechnics earlier than intended.

Iuo whisper-shouted, "Sorry. That's for the Enki finale."

The people in the audience who weren't Celindria's vessels blinked, or waved, or even blew kisses at their celebrity leaders. But everyone else…

Thousands of people stared at them with an identical smirk on their faces.

The crazy bitch was toying with them. Korac shivered like he did on the day he'd split the skin on Celindria's back with Nox's whip. There was so much wrong in her. Across the row of Shadow, Korac met Xelan's eyes and both of them looked down the row at Nox.

The three brothers nodded.

Iuo got the hint and turned on the lights.

Nox took the lead, opened his wings, and flew above the crowd. All the bodies Celindria inhabited took a sharp intake of breath at the sight. The Icarean script across his exposed skin spelled out Celindria's Verse in scarlet ink.

Pehton muttered, "I hope Nox knows what he's doing."

While staring up at him, Sagan said, "I don't know, but he looks great doing it."

Had Korac mentioned lately how much he loved his wife for always spreading around good self-esteem?

Nox's baritone boomed through the amphitheater. No mic needed. "Celindria, have you decided? Continue on this path of destruction or come with me and start a new beginning?"

Spellbound, the rest of the audience watched, looking between Nox and Celindria like this was a tennis match. Meanwhile, Korac crossed his fingers and prayed to Elden this worked.

All at once in a deafening choir, Celindria gave her answer. "I want both."

Nox, who likely understood better than anyone her ambitions, shook his head. "You cannot have me *and* your empire of vessels."

"Who can stand in my way? The Shadow?" Each of her dolls heralded a cutting laugh.

It sobered when Nox said, "Me." He withdrew his daggers and took a fighting stance.

"And me." Rayne flew up beside her Icarus on gossamer wings, Night Killer in hand.

"We all will, Celindria." Xelan and Tameka flew up. Him with sickles, and her with the chain dart.

Little man Pax followed on his tiny wings with his tiny sword, saying, "Even me, sister."

Somewhere, Korac could hear glass shatter—The symphony of Celindria's sanity breaking for the last time.

Korac and Sagan gripped their axes while Pehton went ablaze with her Siren's gale. They and the remaining Shadow flew up to form the line and face off with their greatest enemy. An amphitheater filled with innocent people—including her puppets—comprised their battlegrounds. Around them, the peaceful tranquility of the Palatial Grounds waited in hushed silence for the final pin to drop.

The combined voices of Celindria's army narrowed to one. "You think you condemn me, but you only condemn yourselves. There will be no place for you in Paradise."

The fireworks went off in a dazzling blaze, and the battle for the Probability Matrix began.

Hosted in the bodies of thousands, Celindria surged through the sparks and smoke.

But not toward the Shadow. Her armies fell forward and backward through horizontal conduits and into the Oblivion Cathedral's perilous chasm. It paid off to own puppets in transport. Race after race, person after person—hundreds fell into the Source and joined the ranks of Supreme Imminence. Probabilities shattered into existence, and Celindria rode the high.

The spectacle rattled the petrified audience, who surprised Celindria by massing upon her dolls before the conduits could swallow them. The free citizens—the vaccinated, the vice avoiders, and those unfortunate enough not to know Celindria's touch—latched onto her vessels and weighed them down. She knew they wouldn't kill her puppets, so why were they—

Zip.

Zip.

Zip.

Like insect bites, electricity surged along their flesh, and Celindria realized what was happening. The doctor who'd impressed her, Pablo Suarez, snatched one of Celindria's vessel and wrenched them around to face him. He looked into their eyes as if he could see Celindria inside and said, "This is from Lynn."

There was a shock and then nothing.

They were disabling the nacres within Celindria's dolls, disconnecting her from their volition. Throughout the crowd, she lost connection.

Father is clever, and so is Mrs. Lynn Renee.
But they understand so little.

Across multiple Probabilities, Celindria faced the Shadow. In these, Nox led their resistance, covered in Celindria's Verse. It was time to test the waters.

Sparing one Probability, Celindria sent a dozen dozen of her new Supreme soldiers into battle against the Shadow. Head-on, they clashed. Rather than impaling and slicing, the Shadow maintained non-lethal tactics.

Xelan looped Celindria's dolls about the neck with his sickles and punched them unconscious.

Korac took out targets with the butt of his axe, while Sagan and T.A.O. opened conduits across the battlefield to reroute descent into the Source.

Tameka had tied a heavy bean bag on the end of her chain dart and knocked out Source soldiers left and right.

When Tameka wasn't draining them to sleep, Pax was flexing their shared ability enough for mother and son.

Andrew strained to gain control against Celindria's volition over her subjects, but she'd practiced for millennia to maintain control. He and Andrius paired together, however, proved quite the match.

Once, Celindria had inoculated herself against Progeny abilities with Rayne's blood when it was infected with the shield virus. But there wasn't enough for each soldier, allowing Ross, Devis, Kyle, and Bethany to send Celindria's army to its knees, overwhelmed with their memories.

Tumu, Aria, and Torch could decompress to their sixty-five feet forms, but Celindria knew they aimed to avoid unnecessary casualties. At their full height, it was difficult not to squish those under her control and the citizens the Shadow had recruited to anchor her vessels. So, twelve-feet looked like their limit, and they took great advantage of it to leave her dolls down for the count.

Even Lamassau restrained himself from breathing fire and resorted to hand-to-hand combat. With his Pil platinum gauntlets, he easily rendered Celindria's puppets useless. For a time.

Celindria must admit, Pehton was always one of her favorite toys. And there she was, fighting alongside Celindria's other favorite toy. In the flurry of battle, Chris and Pehton strayed from their units and met backs in a nasty swarm of Celindria's dolls. As a human without abilities and a Lyrik with lethal ones, the no-kill tactics had reduced them to brute strength. The swarm mounted, grabbing and snatching at them. Celindria wanted to drag them into the Source and make them like her. Perhaps, once they understood her, they wouldn't resist and would come home to her.

We are so alone.
Not all of us.

Ignoring the reminder of Celindria's weakest link, she returned her focus to the battle. A task which proved more difficult as her dolls fell into the Source and multiplied across the Probability Matrix.

So many minds.
We are Eternal.

The Valkyrie proved the most bothersome out of the Shadow. Not only were Para and Karter skillfully laying down Celindria's arms, they'd hidden reinforcements throughout the crowd. Hundreds of Valkyrie, Silence among them, fought against Celindria, honed in their craft. Elegant pirouettes with crushing blows were landed on tender junctions of nerve and function, eliminating Supreme soldiers.

Bones fought to protect Pablo and Qas, who not only disabled nacres, but administered vaccines without consent. Ethics had no place in war.

Caedes, Twenty-One, Puk, and Yito formed a box, narrowing in from all sides around several of Celindria's squadrons.

With Iuo's Lamian gifts, he combined his legs into one muscled tail and strangled his opponents unconscious, while Miy and the other Lyriks sang them to sleep.

Matt and Lucy, always together, looked less than satisfied as the boy squeezed his targets by their temples until they slipped to the ground, healing. And the girl zapped Celindria's dolls with nacre-disabling pistols. *Celindria's* nacre disabling pistols.

Father must've saved them from her lab's destruction in Enki. Pity.

Evoking immense concern from Celindria, Lucas and Smith stood on the stage and watched. That's all. They stared into the chasm leading to the Source and waited.

When Jack laid low an entire battalion with a nacre-disabling shrapnel grenade, Celindria knew it was time to call in the drones.

Millions of F8's people, the proud citizens of Monarch 3, marched into battle from fresh conduits already exposed to the Source against their wills.

Now they understand.

Now they beg for us to stay and never leave them.

Soon, the Shadow would join them.

All the while, throughout this experimental Probability, Celindria sent her dolls to reason with Nox. With his powerful fists, he leveled them with one restrained blow. In coordination with Rayne's twirling baton attacks, they had decimated more foes than the entire Shadow combined. Already, Celindria had lost several thousand to their speed, agility, and strength.

"Please, come with me." Doll down.

Another one went up to bat. "We can build Paradise together." Felled.

They kept coming. "I never wanted to hurt you—"

"It was required for me to find Hope and Pax—"

"But if you come with me now, I can spare you from Eternity without me—"

"And free you from *her.*"

Rayne glanced over at the last and, in her distracted state, narrowly dodged a blade to her heart.

The look on Nox's face when he saw Rayne in the slightest of danger...

Disgust rolled over Celindria.

How could he love her...

When he has us?

As Celindria's lover and his temporary obsession danced in seamless, choreographed combat, the Probabilities furthest from the dominant one withered and vanished.

The Eternal Bind.

In Celindria's true form at the Source, she clenched her fist around the ribbon.

Hundreds of Probabilities mirrored the current events within the dominant one. In all of them, she tried a different tactic to rip the Eternal Bind apart. When Jack, Ross, Bones, and Tameka were at Celindria's mercy in her lab, she'd collected blood samples. The same samples she and Pax had manipulated only days ago to uncover the key to bypass the shield virus.

Our Pax in Paradise...

He saved us.

In one Probability, Celindria took Jack's volition and attacked the Shadow. Gifted with his sister's speed and strength, Celindria inside Jack swung fists and landed kicks faster than most could see. Blood and gore splashed everywhere as she mowed the Shadow down.

It took an entire sixty seconds for someone to notice. Pehton screamed, "She's got Jack!" before he ripped her nacre from her chest.

After which, someone shot Jack with a nacre-disabling round and he went down. The Shadow switched to lethal means, and Celindria's army fell in minutes. This Probability vanished.

In another Probability, Celindria tried with Ross. Not as familiar with the memory Progeny's gifts, Celindria couldn't focus the deadly overload attack and inadvertently killed her own army along with most of the Shadow. Unfortunately, Rayne, Kyle, and Bethany survived. With tears in their eyes, they laid

Ross to rest, perhaps to spare her from living with killing the Shadow. This Probability vanished.

Bones wasn't exactly gifted, so Celindria didn't bother with him.

Now, Tameka.

That just might work.

XVIII   EMBER

TAMEKA SENSED CELINDRIA'S INVASION IMMEDIATELY, BUT NOT FAST ENOUGH TO WARN ANYONE. As her lungs expanded to call for help, a great weight held Fury down. When she next opened her eyes, she was in a space inside her mind. The others called it the 'mindscape,' and the moniker suited the minimal zone.

Tameka was naked and chained down in the presence of one majestic statue of a villain. Celindria paid her captive no mind and kept her sharp eyes on the action.

Suddenly exhausted and near tears, Tameka whimpered, unable to hold up her head more than an inch from the floor. It was soaked in her sweat from the effort to regain control of herself. All she could manage was, "How?"

Eyes on the battle, Celindria said, "The Shadow are arrogant and assume too much of their prowess. Yes, your vaccine was innovative, but I knew from the time you first resisted me that the Shadow would implement it galaxy-wide. Your astonishment at my brilliance to overcome it insults me, child."

Here, they go again with the 'child' bullshit—

Tameka's actual mouth twitched into a grimace at her thought. She felt the muscles flex to obey her command.

Celindria stiffened at the same time, giving the lapse in volition away. It garnered enough respect for the woman dressed in white and gold, like a crazed angel, to face Tameka in the mindscape. Celindria said, "You are so bothersome."

With everything in her—the love for her friends, for her family, and for her son—Tameka screamed, "BANANA!"

Nox heard Tameka's strangled, desperate cry from across the battlefield. It rang through the winning ranks of the Shadow. Each unit had gained ground against Celindria's puppets, despite introducing the drones. The cunning First Progeny no doubt noted how easily they fell to Fury and exacted the price out of the woman's volition.

"Tameka!" Xelan charged for her, along with any Shadow not otherwise engaged.

Beside Nox, Rayne laid down three enemies with blows from her separated Night Killer and zapped another three with nacre-disabling stunners. Her graceful twirls and evasive cartwheels captivated Nox, who, though agile, could never match her grace.

Celindria's Verse was a smudged ruin down Nox's front, mingling with the drying indigo of his blood. Although they intended their targets no harm, the opposing side would not say the same. Rayne and Nox suffered gouges and gashes deadly to nacre bearers not as upgraded as their own. Hell, Nox was still trying to regain the feeling in his arm from a severed nerve. His fingers tingled, but refused to respond for at least thirty seconds. That equated to an hour on the battlefield.

Every second counted, especially as they began to feel the effects of Tameka's ability.

Tired.

Nox hadn't felt fatigue like this since the day he fell to Rayne. Shouts and cries erupted among the Shadow. Korac and Sagan played the role of Generals and gave orders to hold the line for some and for others to take the offensive on Tameka. Anything and everything to disable Fury's nacre was the call.

Rayne, straining from the increasing inertia, shouted into her earpiece, "Nox, I'm breaking the line to help with Tameka—"

A vacuum swallowed the sound. No clashing. No grunting. Everyone reacted—Celindria's puppets included—searching for the cause.

But Nox could see it. He whirled on Rayne to find her staring at him with her Atramentous activated. Something was wrong, and it wasn't Celindria. All of her soldiers noticed Rayne's odd behavior, and each stopped fighting and falling into the Source to stare at Rayne.

Her Shadow...

It wasn't her shape. It was—

The moment the realization struck him, Nox had three seconds to shout, "ELDEN!" before the magnesium field exploded from Rayne's eyes. Nox's alarm penetrated the vacuum.

Through the searing agony, he fumbled for his eye shields, hoping he gave the others warning enough to do the same. Unfortunately, Celindria had equipped most of her army with similar accessories.

"Rayne!" Nox tossed Celindria's pleading puppets aside in the blanket of white light to reach Rayne. "Elden?!"

When he found her, Rayne—Elden within her body—stood on the precipice looking into one of Celindria's horizontal conduits. It led into a howling void. In the scene above it, Nox glimpsed a wondrous sight.

The rainbow rings of Thailea peeked through the eye of the planet's perpetual storm, hovering over a snowy mountain surrounded by a tornado of black flames.

"Rayne."

Nox's voice affected her the same, even with Elden in control. The Icarean deity faced his grandson with an alien expression. Fortuitously, or perhaps not, Silence arrived at the same moment. Elden's expression became less remote and more grief-stricken.

"Our happiness was Eternal to most, but not near long enough for me."

That was not Rayne's voice.

Silence glanced at Nox before taking a step toward Elden in Rayne's body. She reached out and cupped the girl's face, and Elden leaned into it. A tear poured an iridescent river down Rayne's face before evaporating.

The Mother of the galaxy asked, "What will you do with this child, Elden? Will you return her unbroken?"

Rayne's hand covered Silence's on her face. Without truly answering the question, Elden said, "This must end. Rayne will fulfill her vow to me."

Lucas and the man called 'Smith' arrived, but kept their distance.

The look Elden gave them was not friendly. "One. Midas. And I see Tumu never strays far from your side. You *owe* us."

Nox understood Elden meant him and Silence, their relationship and legacy.

Smith smiled at the mentioned name, and Lucas took a step forward, assuring Elden, "Finish it, and you will know peace."

Elden as Rayne nodded, and when Nox realized that was the Icarean deity's cue to dive into the conduit, Nox shouted, "Wait!"

Elden stopped and faced his grandson once again.

"Leave Rayne. Use me, forefather. Whatever you intend upon her, however you use her, she deserves better. That woman you're occupying has suffered enough. I am the son of the man who ruined your daughter's life. Punish me. Take me in Rayne's stead."

Rayne's Atramentous gaze—Li on fire in her eyes—looked Nox up and down. In his booming baritone, Elden said, "You will not survive. She is the only one upgraded enough to face the Source, to face the owner of Paradise."

Nox took another step forward and swallowed before saying, "I know Rayne's inside her mind, telling you not to let me. But you know better than anyone the life of a martyr never leads to happiness."

Elden and Silence turned and looked at one another. To her namesake, the conversation between them contained no words, but their mournful expression said it all. Silence bowed her head, and Elden reached Rayne's hand out to Nox.

When Nox took it and accepted the nanite transfer of Elden inside himself, a conversation he'd had just yesterday with Korac played in his head, replacing the bone-searing agony.

The boys crouched on a tree branch as the girls wandered the forest to find one another. They'd chuckled at their clever strategy to disarm their women, well aware of the brutality of their future comeuppance. Despite impending lumps, it was a glorious moment.

Korac nudged Nox. "But we got here in the end, didn't we? You with Rayne. Me with Sagan. And Xelan with Tameka."

Spelled out that way, it seemed like a fairytale, but Nox was thoroughly convinced the ending wouldn't be so happy. The former King of Cinder kept his eyes on the ground, fearing Rayne's wrath, but managed an affirmative humph.

Apparently, it wasn't the response Korac had wanted to hear. "What is it, Nox?"

Nox considered what was really troubling him. He asked, "Does Sagan ever profess her love to you?"

"All the time. Why? Doesn't Rayne?" Korac sounded as if he knew the answer already.

Nox let his silence answer the question.

Korac said, "Well, it's probably because you use words like 'profess.'"

Nox glared at his General until Korac broke into a smirk, drawing a chuckle from Nox.

The next Korac said with a less playful tone. "Besides, Sagan doesn't always say it in words. She has these little smiles she only gives to me. Laughing at all of my jokes. This look I catch on her face sometimes when she's staring at me. Like she's the luckiest woman in the Twelve Worlds, and it's completely the other way around. Does Rayne do anything like that?"

Nox thought of Rayne's sweet smile, her bright laughter, and her affecting glances.

The former King of Cinder said, "Once, when I was scaling a fish, I glimpsed her across the room. She was staring at me with so much appreciation. I'm uncertain if it's like what you described, but I imagined there were other times I may have missed. Perhaps she is too careful to let it show. Or perhaps there's not that much between us. But… her smile…"

Korac sounded more convinced. "Yeah. That's the one. Lights you up inside. Makes you feel capable of anything."

Nox smiled, saying, "Yes, that's the one," seconds before Rayne pushed them off the branch.

She'd wanted to say it the night before, and he wouldn't let her.

Now Rayne would never get the chance to tell Nox she loved him. He only hoped he'd said it enough for the both of them.

"Farewell, daughter."

"Elden! No!" Rayne railed. "Don't take Nox from me! Please!"

She screamed and begged, banging her fists against the walls of her mind in impotent fury.

Rayne's body returned to her control in time to watch Elden's eyes burn Nox's out in their flaming Atramentous. Glittering tears marked incandescent trails down his face as the agonizing sacrifice tightening his features loosened into remorseful obligation. Her systems returned too slowly to stop Elden from diving into the howling abyss on the other side of the conduit.

Rayne went to leap in after them, but Silence swept her up into an unbelievably powerful embrace. No amount of struggle could free Rayne from the Mother's grip. Her bones broke, and yet she didn't give up.

Save Nox.

Tell him at all costs.

Do not let him die this way.

"Rayne, stop!" Xelan's voice broke through her frenzy before he came into view.

Rayne did as she was told and stared into Xelan's eyes as he searched her face.

"He's gone, Rayne." As Xelan said the words, Celindria closed the conduit. She got what she came for.

No.

Rayne shook her head, refusing to believe him. The desperation in her voice came straight from her heart as she said, "No. We can't be sure Elden will win against Celindria. We have to go help. Xelan, we have to save Nox."

The words strung from the very core of Rayne on replay until Xelan took her face in his hands and forced her to focus on his eyes. Certainty, pure and decisive, marked the lines of his face as he said, "Elden will not fail us, and we *will* honor Nox's sacrifice once the Matrix is finished."

Rayne was aware of others joining them at her back. She cried, "Korac! Sagan! Please, tell him."

The General took two steps forward until he was in Rayne's line of sight. Korac said, "She's right. We can't be sure unless we see it unfold."

Sagan's agreement relieved some of Rayne's torment. "I've never been to the Oblivion Cathedral, but I got a good look. I can take us there."

A smaller voice said, "Daddy, we can help Uncle Nox."

Pax.

"I don't know, Rayne. Nox gave up his volition to Elden to protect you." No, Andrew, please. Not him, too.

"While I think Nox did it to avoid prison, I agree with Xelan." Of course, Kyle would. "Silence, what do you think?"

The woman who held Rayne loosened her arms enough to face her. Steel eyes sought a truth Rayne was afraid to bear. With gentle tugs and finger combing, Silence made order out of the chaos of Rayne's hair while tears brimmed her eyes.

Nox's foremother turned around to Lucas and Smith. The Aegis nodded before he and the sadly smiling man met Rayne's eyes.

It was Rayne's decision.

She closed her eyes and delved deep for what might convince Xelan. For what mattered most to her.

Nox's hesitant smile. His deep chuckle. The way his eyes sparkled with love. The first time he purred, and how they both laughed in delight. Holding her through the night—Always calling her on her bullshit—And how he never asked for anything in return.

Think of Nox's love.

Think of when Rayne first loved him.

"Dying hurts, your majesty."

"I'm getting that."

"It doesn't have to."

"What are you saying?"

"Take my hand and transfer your nerve responses to my nacre. You've done enough."

"Nox…"

"No more being strong for everyone. No more martyrdom. If this is truly my final act in these worlds, let me spare you. Please. Take my hand."

Rayne opened her eyes and confessed, "I love Nox, and I never got to tell him."

Xelan was taken aback. He stared at Rayne first in disbelief. Then anguish and grief tightened the lines around his eyes. Her guardian's jaw, cut so similarly to Nox's, clenched while Xelan turned his face skyward. He prayed to the deity, who at this very moment was burning his brother inside-out before ordering, "Sagan, open the conduit. We're going in. I want three units left behind to guard the fallen. Pax, stay with your mother and protect her. Korac, you're with me."

Rayne twisted in Silence's arms to find Tameka unconscious on the stage, guarded by Iuo, Twenty-One, and Bones.

Silence released Rayne, saying, "Smith, Lucas, and I will join you."

From behind them, Tumu said, "Me, as well."

The aggravated groan behind Rayne came from Kyle. "Andrew and I will go, too."

Xelan raised his voice to order, "The rest stay behind. Pablo, don't let Fury wake until we finish with Celindria. If Sagan's conduit closes, assume the worst and implement contingencies."

On cue, a conduit opened behind Xelan to the same howling void Nox dove into only minutes before, and it took all of Rayne's restraint not to rush in after him. She wasn't winning this without her Shadow.

And, by Elden, they would win.

Oblivion.

Their surroundings kept slipping from Sagan's mind, and no matter how hard she tried, her memory couldn't find purchase on it. The only thing she grasped were the rainbow ice rings above her head through the filter of a blizzard and a black firewhirl. From it came the metallic taste on Sagan's tongue and the smell of unrealized potential. Electric and tangy. The buffering wind blew Sagan's hair from her face, but at least it couldn't tangle in her skirt— It was so short and tight. She felt bad for Rayne's gown, torn upon entry. The War King had changed her stilettos into well-loved combat boots, making for quite the fearsome sight. Everyone else just rolled with it, minus one tossed cumberbund.

On any other planet, their earpieces would connect them to the Shadow since they'd upgraded their devices for empire-wide communication. But Thailea was out of bounds—Cutoff from the rest. It was down to them, their weapons, and their sliding sanities, because nothing about this place would leave them the same.

"Hold on to me, amos!" Korac had to shout for Sagan to hear him over the deafening roar.

Beside Sagan, Andrew fell to one knee.

Lucas was right there for his partner. He went through Andrew's pocket until he retrieved a coin, his Probability token. Folding it into his lover's hand, Lucas said, "I know you're experiencing it, too. Try to keep your grip on the dominant Probability and don't let go of me."

Silence and Smith also showed signs of strain while they maintained their grip with the Matrix fluxing around them.

Tumu pointed higher into the ravine. "There!"

When Sagan's mind would let her grasp the visual above, she made out where stone—

No.

Glass—

No.

Gold—

—Formed a bridge across the ravine. Nox stood upon it, facing Celindria. From here, Sagan could see light peeking through cracks along his skin where he couldn't contain Elden's essence.

Rayne shouted over howling wind to Xelan, "We can't fly in this!"

A drone appeared on the path ahead of them from a crack in what sometimes looked like a seamless wall of glass and other times looked like a sheer panel of gold or a rocky cliff. After spending so much time around Puk and F8, Sagan recognized the force of personality in the multi-faceted eyes of Monarch 3's race. Like all of Celindria's other vessels, this one lacked that warmth.

Korac nodded at the drone and answered Rayne's question. "We fight our way up."

Sagan should take the moment seriously, but for a second she let herself smile at her two favorite people. Rayne and Korac's hair had fallen loose during the battle, and now the contrasting manes competed, white versus black, for the honor of banner to the Shadow. Korac glimpsed Sagan's smile, and he kissed her abruptly, with a hint of 'just in case we die.'

None of that.

With a surprised grunt from her husband, Sagan pulled the half-Aegis/half-Icarus down and kissed him like they were planning to survive. When she broke them apart, she said, "I promise to never go where you can't find me."

The drone watched all the while and chuffed in response to their mid-battle mush. From within her pawn, Celindria said, "You two will die first."

Chittering echoed around them, and gravel shifted from the walls when they appeared as cliffs. Sagan looked up to find dozens of drones scaling down the ravine, coming straight for the Shadow on their perilous perch.

Kyle shouted, "We're not exactly at an advantage. It's the one time I wish I was a fucking goat—"

Lightning struck the bridge above, and Rayne screamed.

Tumu shouted, "We need to move! Now!"

With Xelan in the lead, the team plowed forward, sidling along the thin pathway. It widened as they came closer to the drone ahead. Now they could see the crack from which he'd emerged, and it was filled with more of Celindria's vessels.

Rayne could use her magnesium field and render them useless, but, depending on the drones' upgrades, it often resulted in permanent blindness. Was that better than dead?

As if Xelan read Sagan's mind, he turned to Rayne, ordering, "Do it! We can replicate or manufacture replacements for their eyes. If they survive."

Shields up.

Light blazed from Rayne's eyes. It was so agonizing many of the drones fell into the ravine, unable to maintain their grip. Sagan hoped somehow they survived, but the look on Korac's face said it was unlikely until...

A net appeared below in time to catch the fallen drones, and it glittered like golden thread.

Korac was staring over Sagan's shoulder, and she turned to find Smith breathing heavily with his hand pressed to the cliff face. Sweat beaded on his forehead as if he'd exerted himself. The smiling 'human' looked between Lucas, Silence, and Tumu. They bowed their heads in thanks.

Xelan shouted, "Let's keep moving!" There wasn't time to unpack everything all at once.

Ahead of Sagan, Rayne verged on mowing Xelan down to race up the tunnels and their natural stone steps. Or glass. Or gold. Although after Smith's little demonstration just now, the gold made more sense.

They climbed stories of stairs to the top, where the sounds of an epic clash reached them. This was where Sagan became nervous. Their plan was a risky one. Without Tameka, it was damned near impossible. She glanced back at Andrew and Kyle to find similar anxieties on their faces.

"You can do this," Korac whispered in Sagan's ear.

She faced him with only a breath between them. His faith in her was plain in his white eyes as he repeated, "You got this."

Sagan smiled. "Yeah. *We* do."

Such was the ferocity of the firewhirl, Korac could shout, "Everyone ready?" without those on the bridge only meters away hearing.

Rayne took Sagan's hand, who clasped Kyle's sweaty fingers, who, for once, went along without complaint and took Andrew's hand. The Progeny weren't whole without Tameka, but they would have to try the plan without her.

Ready for whatever came next, they rounded the final corner to find an angel facing a shadow on the bridge.

Celindria.

White wings contrasted her deep purple complexion and shielded her from the wind. From here, Sagan could see the First Progeny's Atramentous eyes.

The swirling maelstrom of Cascading Light.

Andrew had called it Eternity.

Kyle gulped so hard Sagan could hear it over the chasm.

"We need Fury."

For once, he wasn't wrong.

"Elden, why are you against me? All I have ever served is your precious Icarean Prerogative."

Celindria dodged a blow and somersaulted over her wing shield to counter the next strike. All the while, she kept tracking the split in the seam of Nox's skin. Threads of muscle and tattered bone held him together, allowing the light of Elden's essence through the gaps.

Nox was dying, and Celindria found herself unable to bear it.

This grief is stifling us.
We cannot win with all this emotion.
But it's not our emotion. It's mine.

Curse the Celindria from the blissful Probability. Didn't she see how she was endangering them both?! And with the Shadow tranquilizing Tameka, Celindria was short one more valuable weapon in her shrinking arsenal.

Elden pushed at her mind and read Celindria's attacks in advance. She felt him wriggling in there like a worm in her ear. His attempts to drain her nacre had left her limbs blocked in cement. Every evasion took all her force of will and concentration.

The Shadow were surmountable.

This—whatever Elden had upgraded into—was proving less so. And his choice of vessel deterred her from lethal attacks. Celindria tried to breach his volition, as she'd done with Tameka. One drop of blood was enough. Usually.

There was plenty of Nox's blood on the ribbon, now soaked with Celindria's red, blue, and yellow blood. So why...

"Relent, Elden! Return Nox to his own volition! You're killing your descendant." Nox deserved a better death. Celindria believed this in her bones.

Elden didn't talk. Instead...

Kinetic energy prickled along Celindria's spine and charged the fibers of her hair before she could evade the first bolt of lightning.

Second.

Third.

It came down faster than rain, and its lethal potential left Celindria breathless. An involuntary avian cry tore from her throat when sparks struck her back—more painful than Korac's lashings. She smothered the burning of her gown against a golden wall and ricocheted off of it in time to avoid another bolt.

Heavier and heavier, Celindria's legs refused to respond, and she could no longer resist the mental prying.

The desert at night.

A clear starry sky, and the kiss of a cool breeze on Celindria's cheeks.

She sat on a dune with Xelan. No tests. No lectures on how to feel normal. Just her and him, stargazing. "Father, which constellation is your favorite?"

Xelan chuckled, closed one eye, and used his finger to trace a figure on the points of the stars.

As it took shape, Celindria recoiled and asked in an incredulous voice, "A wolf?!"

"A dog, actually. I named him 'Speckle.' A simple cluster of suns—What? Don't you like it?" Humor danced in Xelan's eyes.

Celindria laughed, but conceded with a nod. For a few minutes, she'd felt the briefest glimpse of content in her father's company—

"NO!" Celindria broke through the memory, shrieking like a bird, and it reverberated along the chasm.

But it was too late.

Elden had pinned Celindria on the bridge. He sat on her diaphragm, knees crushing her wings, and one hand was poised to retract her nacre. If these were Nox's Atramentous eyes, she'd see her reflection. Instead, the blaze of Li threatened to consume Celindria.

No shadows to escape through.
No volition to steal.
No gift, nor weapon, nor soul can save us now—
"Oomph!"

Elden went barreling over Celindria's head along the bridge, entwined with another set of arms and legs. Black hair, slenderer build, but still formidable. Xelan pinned Elden into the alcove across the ravine and turned to check on Celindria. Then his midnight Atramentous eyes looked beyond her to the other side.

"Now!"

Exhausted and drained, Celindria got to her feet in time to see Rayne charging for her. The First Progeny groaned before impact.

What did the Progeny think they would accomplish?
They're here to save us.
Over our dead bodies.

XIX   CHAR

WHO WOULD THEY PRAY TO NOW?

Xelan used all his strength to hold Elden down while the Progeny clashed with Celindria. Burning under Xelan's hands, Nox's flesh flaked away in charred cinders, swallowed by the howling fissure—The split between Probabilities. The Source.

Would Xelan's brother survive?

And would Rayne survive if he didn't?

Rayne landed first, knocking her ancestor to the golden/stone/glass surface of the bridge. With an avian screech, Celindria went down and fought with her wings to keep Rayne aloft. It was a fierce thrashing of limbs and attempted blows.

Then nothing.

The gravity densifiers.

With a war cry, Rayne cranked them to maximum, and Celindria flattened to the bridge. They *worked*. Relief washed over Xelan.

The moment Rayne gave the signal, Kyle, Andrew, and Sagan were on Celindria. Rayne stretched

Celindria's arms, while Andrew did the same to her legs. Xelan's First Progeny went still.

Was she experiencing terror? Frustration? Or more nothingness?

During the commotion, Silence, Korac, and Lucas had crossed the bridge, and the Father of the Icarean race calmed in the presence of the Mother of their galaxy. Elden inside Nox shot an occasional seething glance at Lucas—One—but otherwise relaxed in Xelan's hold.

High on octane, Korac didn't bother with composure. Concern was bare in his eyes as he looked Nox over. Neither Xelan nor Korac were familiar with Elden's abilities, and in this moment, their deity burned inside their brother.

Xelan glanced the question at Silence. *Would this kill Nox?*

Their shared foremother's grave eyes glistened as Silence swallowed and gave one nod of her head.

Korac's voice was squeezed as he asked, "Nox, are you in there? Can you hear me?" The edge of hysteria to his words choked Xelan.

Lucas gripped Silence's shoulder, consoling her, before stepping between Korac and Nox. One kept his eyes on his half-brother as he reached back and touched Nox with one finger—

It healed.

Nox's soft tissue repair system kicked into high gear and regenerated the melting muscle and tendon.

Xelan and Elden both stared at the Aegis contact on Nox's bicep in wonder.

Lucas said, "There isn't much time, Korac. I need your mind focused on the Atheneum. Remember the plan." The sandy blond of his hair and the molten gold of his eyes transitioned into white. *"Please."* There was so much desperation in that single word.

Korac clenched his jaw and closed his eyes in answer.

Carefully, Tumu and Smith made their way around the tough situation on the bridge, sidling around the Progeny. They looked expectantly at Lucas.

Lucas said, "On my say…"

Tumu nodded, voids serious. Smith nodded, grinning like a madman. Silence slipped her hand into Elden's and bowed with her head.

Xelan released Elden, staying close should he need to restrain him again. He said, "We're ready to finish this."

Lucas turned to the bridge and shouted, "Now!"

Celindria's swirling eyes were focused on Rayne, who'd pinned her ancestor to the bridge with Night Killer's bladed center to her throat. Rayne centered all of her strength on vital points to keep Celindria from reaching the gravity densifiers.

Sagan opened nine conduits surrounding them. They led to skies of varying colors, each of the planets and Ishkur's Palatial Grounds.

Kyle and Andrew closed their eyes to concentrate their abilities on Celindria.

Xelan held his breath.

Minutes passed and…

Nothing happened.

Celindria's mad laughter pierced the ravine. Her voice came from the rift, a chorus of thousands. "This is it?! This is your pitiful strategy?! My abilities are beyond you and, short of taking my nacre, you have no power over me!"

What now?

They were out of options—

"Maybe they don't. But I do."

Xelan shut his eyes in relief.

Celindria's voices squeezed into a chorus of strangled sounds as her head fell back, weakened. She no longer possessed the strength to strain against the densifiers and Rayne. Her nacre was drained.

They were saved.

Tameka emerged from the conduit, her eyes black with a green stripe of a pupil. Strain tightened her pretty face into something fearsome. Never had Xelan heard her sound so confident.

"Celindria, welcome to the Wrong Side of Eternity."

Fury should win an award for the best entrance ever.

Kyle felt the moment Celindria's superior defenses failed, and he wasted no time opening her memory. The Progeny fell down the rabbit hole with him, each of them with no idea what to expect—

Sand.

Kyle, Tameka, Andrew, Rayne, and Sagan were crouched in a valley between two massive dunes. The blistering sun glared from a clear blue sky. The wind tasted dry and smelled arid.

Sagan observed, "I think we're near the fortress."

"But you didn't Seamswalk us here. Kyle, aren't we in Celindria's memory?" Tameka frowned at him.

Rayne and Andrew both looked the same question at Kyle.

With a sweeping look around the place, Kyle said, "This is definitely it. I—"

Screens projected from all around them. Millions of them. They flashed through more moments than Kyle could track. Most of them depicted Celindria inflicting pain on someone, but here and there, Pax appeared. And occasionally, a beautiful woman with blue skin, blue eyes, and black hair. She looked a lot like Celindria.

During one instance of this woman, Kyle could tell it was recent by the clothes Celindria was wearing, the First Progeny called out, "Hope, I came to visit."

"Mother!"

Kyle balked at the endearment and noted that Tameka had done the same. Rayne, Sagan, and Andrew openly gaped at the scene as the woman appeared from around a corner with a baby on her hip.

"Did you come to see Raisin?"

Rayne breathed, "These are Celindria's memories. Every grain of sand..."

"From every Probability," Sagan finished.

While Kyle's eyes were fixed on the screen, he patted at Andrew. "Are you getting anything? Can you work with this?"

Andrew's voice was split into three. "I can."

They all turned and looked to find his eyes were a solid teal. Andrew's wings opened, so much vaster than the rest of the Progeny that they encompassed their small valley.

Black swallowed the teal in Andrew's eyes as he ordered, "Kyle, give me more Hope, more Pax, and more Nox. Now!"

"You got it." There was no way in hell Kyle was quoting Xelan as he gathered more material for Andrew to work with.

Rayne, Sagan, and Tameka peered at the sky as Kyle rifled through a memory scape so complex, he couldn't fathom the order.

He muttered to himself, "How does she keep track of it all?"

"She doesn't." Rayne sounded so certain it drew Kyle's attention. She said, "This is part of it. All these lives and all these experiences without a single emotion. This is why she's insane."

Tameka clicked her tongue. "It's still no excuse."

Sagan said, "Oh, absolutely not. But... I think it reinforces we're doing the right thing. For everyone across Iona Pax."

Each of them nodded—

"Oh, that's it!" Kyle grabbed Sagan by the face and kissed her forehead. "Thank you!"

While they asked him questions about his epiphany, Kyle did the only sensible thing to do in a memoryscape made of sand. He thrust his hands into it and let it sift through his fingers.

The images played in mass and funneled away. Into Kyle.

Every one of Pax's hugs.

Gouging out Chris's eyes.

Forcing T.A.O. to endure things worse than rape.

More sex with Nox than Kyle ever wanted to see.

So many people had died at Celindria's hands in creative ways at the end of a blade, muzzle of a gun, or with her bare hands.

Probably seven thousands years of Celindria's life was spent in a lab, researching a remedy for her emotional birth defect.

Everything downloaded into Kyle, and he reached out through the conduits Sagan had opened to find their match. The intentions of Celindria's lovers, family, and victims all funneled through Kyle into their open Progeny connection.

Kyle's voice sounded strange to him in three pitches as he asked, "Rayne, can you feel them?"

Tears spilled from Rayne's eyes and evaporated from the fire in them. Her words were breathy as she said, "I can."

Sagan took her girlfriend's hand, supporting her through and maintaining this connection to Iona Pax.

Tameka sounded strained, as if Celindria was fighting back. "Andrew, if you can do this, now is the time—"

Andrew screamed and fell to his knees.

That wasn't exactly part of the plan.

Celindria's will was an awesome force, and Andrew struggled against it. The weight of her lives crushed his mind and threatened his grip on her and on reality. So he tried and pressed, leaving her no option but to—

A heartbeat pulsed across the sky, and it rattled Andrew's bones. Not only his, but everyone in every remaining Probability. The Progeny looked to the great expanse of Celindria's memoryscape.

Kyle asked, "What was that?"

Andrew held his breath.

The pulse came again.

Slower this time.

No.

"Celindria, don't do this," Andrew muttered it to the sand, but Tameka looked at him.

"What's happening?"

Rayne answered, "Celindria would rather die than let us save her."

Another heartbeat came, sluggish and heavy.

Sagan cupped a hand to her mouth and, through it, said, "Is she... Is she killing herself?"

Kyle's brows shut up, bewildered. "How crazy is she that she'd rather die than face the consequences of her actions?"

Tameka said, "I suppose that depends on the consequences."

Kyle licked his lips before confessing, "Uh, I've never been in a memoryscape of someone dying before."

Sagan asked the obvious question. "Can her death affect us?"

Rayne's brows were drawn tight in concern. "We can't give up now."

"I won't let her die." Andrew meant it as he challenged her volition, forcing her control out of her organ systems.

The heartbeat sounded again, stronger, but with it came Celindria's avian shriek in the distance.

Andrew couldn't maintain control long enough to say, "I'm losing."

"Guys, I don't—" Sagan's knees hit the sand before she fell over on her side. She blinked and focused on her breathing, using all her energy to keep the conduits open.

Kyle gripped a hand in his tangled hair. "What do we do?"

"Do it fast!" Rayne shouted through gritted teeth. "We don't have much longer—Tameka!"

Tameka fell to her knees. Her eyes flickered between solid black Atramentous to normal. "I keep draining her, but she refills endlessly. How is she so strong?!"

Straining with everything in him, Andrew fell face-forward onto the sand.

Xelan's warning pierced the memoryscape. "We're losing them!"

No.

The surrounding scenery flickered in time to Celindria's pulse, stronger and steadier.

No.

Rayne was the only one sitting up. Andrew reached out and took her hand, borrowing from her strength. Kyle took Andrew's, and Tameka gripped Sagan's.

They were losing, but at least they'd do it together.

Fading, Tameka breathed, "We will always remain."

Andrew's eyes closed.

Opened.

So heavy…

Too many…

"I got you."

Andrew's eyes snapped open. That wasn't Xelan's voice. It was—

"Sissy, it's time to let go." Pax stood in the center of the memoryscape's valley.

And he wasn't alone.

Andrius reached out his hand to Andrew, saying, "C'mon, descendant. Let's finish this."

Andrew took the offered hand and climbed to his feet, gazing across the sky. Nighttime had replaced the day, and Earth's constellations peppered the scene. A chilling wind replaced the gentle desert breeze.

Devis said, "She knows this is it. Hurry." He helped Kyle to stand.

Ross and Bethany ran into their older brother's arms, all of them straining to maintain control of Celindria's memoryscape.

With a delighted cry, Rayne jumped to her feet and embraced Jack. He said, "You couldn't have this final showdown without me. Are you ready to end this?"

Despite Rayne's hopeful smile, she sounded uncertain. "At this point, we're wondering how."

"Kindness is her greatest enemy," T.A.O. said, as she pulled Sagan and Tameka to their feet.

Pax looked up at Andrew and said, "Show her everything, but above all, show her kindness."

With Andrius' help, Andrew sought Celindria's will. It thrived in her mind, but the two pressed for access to her intentions.

I must defeat the Shadow. I must save Pax, save Hope, and save Nox—my Nox—to be with me. I will reestablish Paradise and prove to everyone I was right. They are happier with me.

Above all…

I will experience this life.

I will feel.

Andrew clung to the last one. *Feel, Celindria. Feel with us.*

Andrius' volition joined the invasion. *Feel it all.*

When they nodded, Rayne gripped their shoulders and closed her eyes. T.A.O. and Sagan waited nearby, holding the conduits open outside. Once more, Kyle and Devis sifted their hands into the sand, and all of them took a boost from Tameka, who resumed the drain on Celindria's nacre with Pax's help.

No more walls.

Feel.

Celindria's shriek tore from her core and ripped through the fabric of reality.

Zero answered Korac's call and stepped into his boots.

Literally.

From inside his mind, Korac watched the events unfold. Tameka's epic entrance was only surpassed by her son and the force of Progeny he'd brought with them.

Not only the ancients.

Jack, Ross, and Bethany had come with Pax, and they were all gathered around Celindria's restrained body. This was it. No more reinforcements.

Zero turned to face Lucas, his first son. "Will they succeed this time?"

One said, "I believe they will."

Despite his own anxieties, Korac felt Zero warm at the confidence in his son's voice. Inside his mind, Korac asked, "What about Nox? Will he survive? What happens to Elden?"

Zero's smile was congenial and so similar to Razor's signature expression that it unnerved Korac, as Zero said, "Midas will see to it."

Midas?

Smith?!

The smiling man was calm and collected in the alcove, but Korac wouldn't deny he seemed to hover near Xelan and Nox. The youngest brother stayed close to the oldest in case Elden needed further restraint. Elden kept his eyes on Silence, and they stared so intensely at one another, the ancient couple were breathing in time together. The only other person in the alcove was Tumu, and he stepped out to the cliff's edge.

As he decompressed, the Primary's deep voice boomed, "I hope you're right, One." The sixty-five foot Gargantuan wedged his toe-less feet against the rocks/glass/gold sides of the ravine and straddled the Source. He cupped his hands around the bridge and formed a barrier surrounding the Progeny action.

Korac shook his head and blinked in bewilderment.

Xelan shouted into the wind, "You've been holding out on me, old friend!"

Tumu winked with one void and said, "More than you know."

The Tritan glowed—bright and white—until his features paled.

Inside his head, Korac breathed, "A perception filter. Tumu's half-Aegis."

Zero only nodded.

Karma was a bitch. Korac owed so many people—mostly Pehton—for how often he'd withheld answers to questions in order to maintain his trademark air of mystery. Apparently, it was a genetic trait, and it had certainly come back to bite Korac in the ass.

"That's my woman risking her life out there, father. Don't tell me my faith is misplaced."

This time Zero dropped the smile when he nodded and said, "One will see it done, and we will close the fissure we created. Tumu will ensure Sagan survives."

It bolstered Korac's confidence. "And this is it? Once it's closed, no more Probability Matrix?"

"A permanent fusion. With a few drops of your blood, we will recreate the making of a conduit in reverse and seal it for Eternity."

Eternity.

But...

"What about those who fell into the Source? What happens to Celindria?"

The congenial smile returned, accompanied by the karmic silence.

Korac opened his mouth to disparage his father for ruining an informative conversation when Celindria's heart pulsed through the ravine. The frame around Korac's understanding of reality blurred like a bad 3D movie.

"Now, Silence," Lucas ordered.

The Mother held out her hand, and a white nacre with an amber chip was in her palm. "My love, please. Leave our grandson."

Elden shook Nox's head. Their baritones were layered as he said, "I will not leave until the fight is finished."

Disappointed, Silence lowered her eyes before muttering, "Midas. Please don't hurt him."

Inside his mind, Korac's eyes widened as Smith opened his hand to reveal three rocks. Within seconds, they molded into malleable minerals and solidified into gold. Before Korac could utter a word, Smith pressed the rocks against Elden's skin. Although Nox seemed to tolerate gold in this iteration of his form, Elden's nanites reacted as typical of Icari.

Nox screamed

Nacre in hand, Silence forced it into Nox's fist and cried, "Please, Elden! Don't punish Nox for Umbra's crimes!"

"Son."

Despite the calm in Zero's voice, Korac couldn't look away. Couldn't relax his jaw or unclench his fists. That was his best friend—his brother—in there. Never mind the man they were torturing had established half of Korac's identity.

Zero tried again. "He will survive. They both will, but only if Elden complies."

A tear spilled down Korac's cheek, both physical and metaphysical. "Why must you ask so much of this Icarus? Rayne told us of One's experiments on the Icarean forefather. Why?"

"You wonder why I withhold answers from you. I do not. I am merely waiting for them to reveal themselves—And there. Here they come. Hold on."

The glow of Elden's essence dissipated from Nox's body as the Icarean deity transferred his nanites into the nacre in Silence's hand. There wasn't time to contemplate or ask questions.

Smith, Silence, and Lucas ran off the edge of the cliff and dove into the Source.

To Korac's astonishment, Zero piloted his body to do the same. The last thing Korac saw before oblivion took him was Xelan kneeling to check on Nox. Brother weeping for brother.

It was all the assurance Korac needed.

With or without him, they would be fine.

We feel . . .
Everything.
Rayne's excitement over her first loose tooth. Kyle's disappointment when his mother said she was expecting another daughter. Andrew's triumph over speaking his first word at five years old. Tameka's joy when she made drill team captain. Sagan's anguish when Justin threatened to out her and Rayne.

So many big and so many little things. And there were so many more.

Devis holding Celindria in her sleep. Sweet bliss. Andrius delivering his first daughter, stillborn. Sharp despair. T.A.O. meeting a Chihuahua for the first time. Absolute terror. All of their combined love and grief for Merit.

More came from across the Probabilities, and most left Celindria's heart fulfilled.

Pax's first successful experiment was a wondrous occasion, and Celindria's congratulations had suffused him with pride and esteem.

Hope's reaction when Celindria had first approached Hope had barely touched Celindria, but it had changed her daughter's world.

A cornucopia of vibrant and desolating emotions washed through Celindria. She indulged in them all. The firsts. The lasts. Every sweet release.

Kombuchi, F8, X, Legir, 2Lip, Dolor, and Tempest— All their sorrow over losing their people to Imminent's greed and Celindria's volition. Their determination and vigor. Their love and honor. And how little of it had lived in Celindria.

Cypher, Colton, and Six—Three humans Celindria had cared little about, and yet, she lived their trauma over losing Xelan and their elation over his resurrection. Their hopes and fears which guide their every decision. What drove Celindria?

Twenty-One and Miy's optimism. Iuo's soft ambition. Puk and Yito's loneliness. The love Bones, Lamassau, and Qas held for their respective races. Pablo and Lynn's parental anxieties. The way Matt and Lucy hungered equally for each other as for the blood of their enemies.

The beauty brought pain, which brought more beauty. And Celindria appreciated every rush of it.

Until the shadow came. Until the blight.

Aria and Torch waited in their crates for their turn. They'd listened to their half-brother muttering to himself in his research and found comfort in Xelan's voice. Even on the day they'd heard it as he'd tossed them into Torrentus, unknowingly, they still loved him. Loneliness and rejection turned Celindria's stomach.

A flash of Jack's Atramentous eyes when he'd pressed his face to Ross' back through the bars of Celindria's cell. This was when she'd forced Chris to pin Ross there as a threat. Karter and Para, proud warriors, watched on in impotent fury. Anxiety, turmoil, pity, and undiluted fear tasted bitter and dry in Celindria's mouth.

The two years of torture Razor had inflicted on Bethany played like a snuff film. Skin-blistering sugar, muscle-splitting lashings, nerve-firing shocks—Resignation, lead and certain, weighed Celindria down.

Caedes punched the ice. Over and over... On the verge of madness, he repeated the action, expecting a different outcome. Expecting to break the ice and save his already dead friend. Grief smelled like a funeral pyre to Celindria's senses.

"You're leaving me now?! When we're so close? What have I done wrong, Celindria?" Pehton had begged Celindria to stay. But the First Progeny had abandoned her Lyriki lover in the middle of their shared investigation of Inanis. Celindria had completed her dealings with Razor, and had convinced Pehton to pilot the port system for the Divine Booths. Without emotions, her ambitions led her to leave Pehton behind and move on. Used by Remorse, Celindria, and Razor—Pehton was a toy to them, and the threadbare remnants of her heart took Celindria's breath away.

The rest came flooding in. People Imminent had used and maimed, left without loved ones, and burned in the collateral—Celindria felt them all, tasted their pain, smelled their tears, and experienced their torment.

"Please, no!" They begged and cried—all of them— and Celindria never once listened.

Thanks to Remorse and Razor, Korac had already endured the worst of childhoods. And the brief period of peace he'd experienced as an adult with Nox and Xelan was only a taste of what he was never meant to have. Korac knew from the beginning—perhaps through his half-Aegis genetics—that Celindria aimed to come between him and his brothers. She'd smiled in Korac's face as he fought to keep them together. With every rip and tear, Celindria had shredded Korac's stability and sense of home. Even his satisfaction at whipping her back could only draw from a well of hurt and fear.

Celindria had always sensed Xelan's initial disappointment and rejection of her as his First

Progeny experiment, but she'd never endured the concern with it. Xelan had loved Celindria from the beginning—His daughter, his creation. He'd mourned the mistake he'd made in stripping Celindria of emotion. Deep, rooting loss, which festered into guilt and self-hatred. Xelan took on every crime Celindria had ever committed as if it were his own, and the shame ate away at him. So Xelan had begged the Shadow to spare Celindria—to try—for her sake.

Every trauma Celindria had ever inflicted—directly or indirectly—flooded through her, while Andrew and Andrius forced her to experience overbearing remorse.

No.

Please, no. Not this one.

"You come to your master's call better than a domesticated beast."

Nox's anxiety spiked when he spied Celindria perched in the window of the highest tower in Umbra's Spire. Mistrust and puzzlement made him frown as he noted she supposedly bore no wings, yet had scaled to this height. He knew if he'd asked, she would lie to him, anyway.

Even though he found her words venomous, Nox thought Celindria was beautiful in her pregnancy.

When his eyes fell to her swelling abdomen, Celindria smoothed her hands over it and said, "She is yours. I like to produce daughters. Do you want to feel?"

Celindria could feel Nox's answering terror. He was desperate to reconcile with her in order to save the infant, terrified as he was to repeat his father's mistakes.

Viscous tears of blood followed the trails down Celindria's cheeks as the Progeny forced her to live this moment in Nox's heart.

"Celindria, rule Earth and Cinder me. We can raise our daughter together. We could lead together."

When Nox held out his hand, Celindria felt the hope in the gesture. The genuine promise of harmony.

Please, no.

Please, don't let this go on!

"Conceived in rape. Cultivated by a monster. A history of violence so erratic that you almost killed your own brother. What kind of father would you make?"

Hurt and doubt lanced through Nox, but more powerful than the agony was the Icarus' devoted determination. "Please—"

Unfeeling, Celindria ended the pregnancy.

Devastated, Nox screamed, "No! No, please!" and fell to his knees.

His tears from then formed Celindria's tears now. *What kind of monster am I?*

The call of a seagull made Celindria open her eyes. She stood on a beach suffused with the salty smell of the ocean as the waves kissed the white sand. Children ran along the boardwalk, begging for ice cream, or they built sandcastles under their parents' tutelage. There wasn't a cloud in sight.

"You're not a monster, Celindria. You're just broken."

Rayne.

Celindria turned to find the girl with her bare feet in the tide. The surf had drenched the lower half of her dress, and her wavy hair was down, teased in the salty breeze. The dress matched the blood-soaked ribbon in Celindria's hand. There was a natural aversion between the two women, despite the sweetness of Rayne's smile and the openness of her eyes. It strung the tension into a taut rope, made of nacre and sown from the heart.

Rayne said, "We will never find common ground because it already exists, and it is a battlefield. We both want Nox."

Celindria acknowledged, "That's an eloquent and succinct explanation. How do we proceed? A fight to the death?"

Disappointment faltered the kindness in Rayne's expression as she shook her head slowly. "No, Celindria. I will show you the Eternal Bind and let it open a path to your redemption. If it can't sway you, then nothing will."

Celindria cut her hands through the air. "I don't want to see the two of you find happiness. I don't want to experience your love—"

"It's not us, alone." Rayne's smile returned. "You'll see."

In a breath—in the time it took the valves of Celindria's heart to open and close—she witnessed the Eternal Bind and understood.

Probabilities and Verses, realities and lives, intertwined into a mass of benign and malignant cells. Where some healed, others bled. Where some shone like a beacon, others swallowed the light. The entanglement further knotted in the center where ancestors and descendants met in war and lovers danced in blood-soaked regalia.

One was at its core.

The Eternal Bind.

Breathless and blind, Celindria fell to her knees, but before she hit the wet sand, it transformed into hardened stone.

"Your Verse doesn't have to end badly, Celindria."

Sight returned to Celindria, blurry at first. She made out the structures of white stone surrounding her. A staircase with a massive balustrade led to a second story, which circled the room. Ahead of her, a placid pool of yellow liquid beckoned, and six figures stood sentinel over it.

With a long blink, Celindria's vision returned. Vines were etched into the floor, and they climbed along the stairs, walls, and ceilings, all leading to the same place. Across the pool from her was a wall with yellow roses. Celindria blinked again and narrowed her eyes to better focus them on the flowers. The citrine engravings were actually liquid, and they poured into the pool.

Legends and Verses told of this place.

The Feast of Roses.

Celindria said to the figures, "The Seam?"

Lucas took the first step forward and held out his hand. "Welcome to my homeworld, Celindria."

Korac—but not Korac—said, "It suits you."

Before Celindria could take Lucas' hand, she noticed why the Atheneum had complimented her. Celindria's hair… It'd turned white.

Silence observed, "Not all of it. Your roots are still dark." She peered over her shoulder at the massive Icarus who could only be Elden. Each strand of his hair was both black and white. Silence said, "It varies by race." As if to answer Celindria's next question, Silence touched the blue streak of her hair.

As Lucas helped Celindria stand, Tumu—paler than she'd last seen him—took the next step forward. "This may come as a shock, but we've kept a close eye on you."

The 'human,' known as Smith, said, "And we think we finally understand."

Celindria was grateful they understood, because she was becoming steadily more confused—

Wait.

Confusion.

Celindria was *feeling* it.

Lucas smiled at her as if he'd read her thoughts. "Yes, child. You have the Shadow to thank for it, but hold those thoughts. We have much to tell you. And a question to ask."

From the physical description in accounts locked in the Pantheon, Celindria recognized Zero in Korac's body by his pupils. The rings in his white eyes looked right through her as he said, "You endangered the fabric of existence to cure a turmoil you could only feel in spare glimpses. We have known this day would come."

Tumu said, "All the races began with the Aegis and most at Zero."

Lucas nodded at Silence and Elden. "I tried to unmake you by keeping them apart, and when that proved an insurmountable task, I employed help from my brothers."

Silence said, "I gave birth to the Twelve Worlds."

Elden took his mate's hand. "And I fathered the Icarean race."

Smith said, "And I built your temple."

Gold.

The Oblivion Cathedral.

Zero in Korac's body bowed with his head as if confirming Celindria's thought. "We could not destroy you, but we could guide you to this moment." He gestured to the pool of Aegis blood. "To your choice."

Celindria could *feel* Eternity shaping around her, and she could *feel* herself rejoice in it. "What am I to decide?"

All six of them glanced amongst themselves, smiling with relief and elation. It was infecting Celindria, and she reveled in it.

Lucas spread his arms wide, gesturing to the pool of blood. Within it, images appeared. On the right was Xelan tending to Nox after Elden had vacated his body. Celindria's lover was blistered and hollowed out, blind without his eyes.

On the left was Celindria, holding an infant with Nox at her side. It wasn't their child. It was Raisin, Hope's latest great granddaughter—

And there.

Celindria's beautiful daughter appeared within the scene, with Pax at her side. They stood in Nox's castle on a balcony, celebrating with all of Cinder the baby's birth. The Celindria in the scene looked up as if she could see the Celindria in the Feast of Roses. Her blue eyes were imploring.

Silence's voice was soft as she said, "Which one will you choose?"

Celindria looked at all the expectant faces and asked, "What about the Probability Matrix? I thought it reduces to one."

Tumu shook his head. "The two most powerful will remain, and we will seal it. No shadow-walking between them."

Smith added, "You will retain all your knowledge from all the Probabilities of which you've gained from the Source."

Elden gestured at the scene on the right. "Face a hard journey of redemption where you can learn to love the Shadow as they have loved you."

"Or enter a life where you never failed Nox, and the Shadow may never come to exist as you now know it. Here, you can begin anew." Zero gestured to the left.

Two very different existences. The life Celindria had lived, or the life she'd feared to live. Either was better than she'd deserved.

Celindria held up her hand and gazed at the blue strip of cloth in it.

Emotion. Knowledge. Power. Love.

Lucas' voice was gentle as he asked, "Which one will you choose?"

XX　　　　　　　　**ASH**

It started with Lucas and ended with Rayne.

The Eternal Bind wasn't one couple or one Probability. It was a cluster of stars burning brightly in a diamond sky. Separate, they were beautiful in their blaze, but together they formed a brilliant constellation by which others found their way.

Rayne only came to see it as she'd experienced the lives of everyone in the galaxy with Celindria. Aegis and Tritan, Imminent and Shadow—They all formed the Eternal Bind.

And it wasn't simply Nox and Rayne who'd uncomplicated the Probability Matrix.

It was their love for each other. It was healing a toxic wound which had infected billions of people from dozens of races across hundreds of generations. United in their efforts to redeem Celindria, Nox and Rayne had purified the blight of Imminent's uncaring ways.

Every step, blow, and breath they took brought them to here.

Rayne stood in the Feast of Roses. She recognized it by Sagan's descriptions, and it smelled like home. Rayne's bedroom with her notebooks and pillow. Unfinished homework piled on the desk, and her mother's love and concern poured into her cooking.

Homesickness knotted Rayne's stomach and took her breath away.

"Hello, Rayne."

Korac—no, Zero—stood on the second floor and peered down at her. He looked like a cosmic leader, with one hand idling on the balustrade and assessment in his eyes. But what was Zero measuring Rayne for? He said, "You remind me of your ancestor."

"Where is Elden?" Rayne glanced around, but it seemed they were alone. "Is he safe?"

Zero dipped his chin in an appreciative nod. "Yes. He is saying his farewells to Silence."

With a wave of Zero's hand, the pool of Aegis blood shaped itself into a scene. In it, Elden, in his proper form, cupped Silence's cheek. She held his hand to her face and leaned into it. Tears spilled from both their eyes.

Rayne hiccuped half a sob and gasped, "But why?"

With Korac's hand still on the balustrade, Zero glided down the stairs. "The Source requires a guardian, and your endearing martyr volunteered. He and Midas."

Smith?

A chill shot down Rayne's spine at a terrible notion. Her voice trembled as she asked, "Is that what you want from me? To volunteer, too?"

Zero stopped halfway down and shook his head. "No."

"We want to ask something of you, but not that, Rayne." Lucas appeared on the opposite staircase, same position as his father. "I think, for a martyr, our question will prove more difficult for you to answer."

Rayne needed to swallow to ask, "Why? Why do you need more from me? From Elden?"

"I volunteered, daughter." The ancient deity appeared with Silence at his side. They stood across the pool from her, both their faces distraught and at peace all at once. While Elden peered down at Silence, he said, "There is no need of me in the Twelve Worlds, but there is need of me here. I will watch over you while Silence finds happiness with another."

Kyle.

Empathy lanced through Rayne. A thought struck her. "But what about your sphere around Cinder?"

Elden's smile was beautiful in its peace. "Fury has saved my world and my people. Daughter, this is not a sad occasion. There is no need for tears. You will see me again."

Tears.

Rayne brushed her cheeks, and incandescent moisture evaporated from her hand. It left a glittering dust on her fingers. She shored herself up to smile at her ancestor as she said, "If you're happy, I'm happy."

"Therein lies our concern, Rayne." Tumu appeared beside the pool.

As Smith manifested on the other side with a smile, he said, "You don't think of yourself enough."

Zero finished gliding down the stairs and stood in front of Rayne. "Your sacrifice deserves a reward."

Lucas flanked his father and gestured to the pool of Aegis blood. "Which one will you choose?"

Two scenes played in the yellow liquid. On the right, Xelan was performing chest compressions on Nox. On the left, Rayne was eating dinner with her parents and brother.

"Mom… dad…"

Rayne took a step toward the image on the left and peered into Michelle Callahan's warm brown eyes. She tried to speak, but the words wouldn't come out.

Silence said, "In the Probability on the left, Nox didn't invade Earth the second time. He and Celindria reconciled before she ended her pregnancy. With Xelan, they improved Elden's Sphere and restored the

Vittle crop, removing the need for another invasion. Much of everything is different—Oh, Rayne."

As Rayne began to understand what they were asking of her, the scale of it cut her into tiny pieces. The Mother stepped around the pool and enveloped Rayne in her arms. Rayne buried her face in Silence's shoulder and cried.

Tumu pressed on with the explanation. "If you choose the Probability where Nox is with Celindria, you will retain your knowledge of this life. This means you can stop yourself from dying in the terrible childhood accident Xelan prevented."

Smith's smile was sad as he said, "But if you choose to stay in your current Probability, you won't have the foreknowledge and Xelan won't be there to save you. You die at four years old, and your family carries on without you."

Rayne melted down.

How could they ask this of her? Choose the Probability where her parents died and force her family to endure her death in another Probability. Or choose the Probability where Rayne never meets Nox and never becomes a warrior—A regular life.

It took everything in Rayne to ask, "What happens to my Probability if I choose my parents?"

They all exchanged glances before Elden said, "It will continue without you."

Lucas placed his hand on Rayne's back where Silence was still holding her. "Our goal was to simplify the Probability Matrix and seal the Source. If you and Celindria choose the same Probability, we will maintain the dominant one for balance."

Rayne let Silence go and stepped toward the Probabilities. She could spend Eternity deciding. As Rayne peered at them, they simplified into two figures. The right was Xelan and Nox, and the left was Rayne's mother and father. If she closed her eyes, she could hear both sides.

On the right, Xelan cried, "Nox! Nox! Don't make me tell Rayne I let you die. Take my blood, Nox!"

On the left, Michelle asked, "Did you have a good day at school, Jack?"

Something slid into Rayne's hand. She opened her eyes and peered down at the ribbon. It was tattered and soaked in so many shades of blood.

When Rayne looked up at Lucas, he smiled and said, "Celindria thought it would help you choose what *you* wanted, Rayne. What you fought for."

"Which would you choose, One?" Rayne thought this was an obvious question to ask.

And, as predicted, Lucas wagged a finger at her. "This is about you. Besides, the Probabilities are my making. I crumbled the worlds together, smoothed it back out, and fell in love with the creases." He pulled Rayne in for a hug and whispered against her ear, "They will be fine without you. I will see to it no matter which you choose. Be selfish, just this once, my unyielding storm."

Rayne closed her eyes and chose with all her heart. No more conflicts. No more tears.

"It's time to go," Lucas said as he pulled away. He opened a conduit, and Rayne followed him through it. Surrounding faces gasped at her, but there wasn't time.

With their heartbeat slowing, Rayne rushed to Nox's side, pushing Xelan and Pablo away. Startled, they sat back from her as Rayne tore open a vein in her wrist and fed it to Nox. "Come back to me."

Around them, the Shadow interrogated Lucas, Silence, and Tumu. Rayne tried to tune it out, but caught Jack asking, "But why does her hair look like that?"

She couldn't deal with that right now, because Nox opened his eyes. Black and shining, they brimmed with tears when they found Rayne. Their heartbeat was still too slow.

"I'm here, Nox. Don't leave me." Not after Rayne chose him.

Inspired by Celindria, Rayne took a calming breath and willed her heart to pick up its tempo. Deep breath in, slow exhale out. Regulate.

Thump-thump.

It was working. The lesions in Nox's skin re-knitted before Rayne's eyes, and she sighed with relief as charred flesh renewed to fresh skin cells. Rayne breathed, "Thank Elden." To everyone else, she shouted, "Is everyone okay?" Only after, she realized there was no need to shout.

The howling was gone.

Rayne spared a glance around her. Xelan and Pablo waited on standby to help with Nox. Both of them looked resolute in the task, with no conflict in their eyes. Tameka and Pax stayed back, and mother consoled her son, who despaired at his uncle's distress. Kyle and Bethany stood off to the side, watching the commotion. Ross held Jack back. Rayne spared him a reassuring look. Devis, Andrius, T.A.O., Sagan, and Andrew waited at the cliff's edge, peering out at the bridge.

Silence, Lucas, Tumu, and Korac stood on it from where they'd sealed the Source with Atheneum blood. Now Zero said goodbye to his oldest son. The conduit was still open, and Elden and Smith watched from inside the Seam.

While Rayne peered around, adrenaline high from—well, everything—a shock of white startled her. "Oh, my god. My hair!" Most of the length was white, intermixed here and there with her natural black color. "What—"

Fingers entwined with wavy strands, and Rayne nearly cried out in relief.

Nox had stopped drinking her blood and was peering at her hair with curiosity and wonder. He croaked, "It's beautiful."

Someone—Pablo—put a mirror in Rayne's face. Her roots were black, and it faded into white.

"Oh, I forgot to mention that little side-effect. I think it suits you," Lucas called from the bridge.

Smith shot her a thumbs-up through the conduit, and Rayne gave an incredulous sound. When Nox's hand sought hers, her heart skipped a beat.

Now was the time.

Rayne kissed Nox's knuckles and peered into his eyes as she confessed, "I think I've loved you since I took your hand in Enki, and I'm sorry I didn't tell you sooner. I love you, Nox."

Xelan tapped Pablo on the shoulder, and the two walked toward the bridge, giving the couple some privacy. It meant the world to Rayne.

Despite her fretting, Nox sat up, cupped her neck, and kissed her. She pulled away, and when he tried again, she put a finger to his lips. "It's important I tell you this. The Aegis offered me the choice between a world where you and I never met and this one. I *chose* this one."

Taken aback, Nox asked, "Voluntarily?!"

It was the same thing he'd said when Rayne resurrected him. She wasn't sure if she should find Nox's incredulity funny or sad. Rayne brushed her fingers through his hair and nodded. "Yes. I chose this life and you with it. Do you think I'm crazy?"

"No—Yes, but no." Nox pressed their foreheads together and said, "I don't know where my gratitude ends with you. If it ever does."

Rayne said, "No offense, but I hope what's between us never ends."

"War King!"

That was definitely Korac. Rayne and Nox separated to peer over her shoulder.

The General, recovered and himself, winked. "Love the hair."

Rayne and Nox laughed, almost too loud to hear the transaction in the conduit beside them.

Elden said, "I believe you owe me, Midas. Make good on the wager."

Smith grumbled, "I was sure she'd choose the other Probability."

"As if she would choose anything other than my handsome grandson."

The conduit closed on Elden's rich laughter, sounding so much like Nox.

Xelan wanted to grin.

The thought of losing his older brother and former lover on the same day had chilled Xelan to the bone and nearly stopped his heart. When Rayne and Korac returned from the Seam in one piece, relief had washed over Xelan. Then Rayne resuscitated Nox and told him how she felt—Fulfilled the reason Xelan had dragged half the Shadow into the Oblivion Cathedral. He wanted to bask and cheer, but...

Celindria.

As Lucas convened with Silence and Tumu, Xelan kissed Tameka's temple, ruffled Pax's hair, and left them to approach the Aegis. The *last* Aegis, with Razor gone. That notion sparked some ideas, but they would have to wait.

Xelan asked, "Lucas—One?"

The man whom Xelan still considered a close friend smiled as if he felt the same. Lucas asked, "Yes? Oh. Of course." After seeing the question in Xelan's eyes, Lucas gripped him by the shoulders, saying, "Celindria's fine. She chose happiness. Before she left, she asked me to give you this." He rifled through his pockets before presenting a memory capsule.

Xelan took it and peered at it in his palm. For reasons he couldn't explain—

No.

He knew why he was on the verge of tears. On Celindria's way out of this world, she'd remembered to leave something for Xelan. A tiny hand slipped into his, and Xelan squeezed it. He asked his son, "Do you want to watch it together?"

Pax shook his head. "No, daddy. I know what it says. Sissy already told me goodbye."

"Miss the heart and mind. No other like hers. But happiness will have sister now." T.A.O. never waited for permission to hug. She simply threw her arms around Xelan's neck and hung on.

Andrius and Devis waited off to the side. Xelan opened his arms to them, and they took the invitation. Although sorrow haunted Devis' eyes, there was a flicker of relief, and Xelan hoped Devis found the strength to move on.

Andrius said, "We're free, and so is she. This is more than I'd prayed for."

Free.

Yes. That's how this felt.

When they pulled away, Xelan found himself the center of everyone's attention. Expectant faces of people he loved waited...

No time like the present.

Shaken, Xelan swallowed the capsule. It took him to the desert, and he recognized this was an expanse between the stronghold and the fortress. Between Xelan and Nox.

"I was always in between."

Xelan turned to find Celindria, dressed in white as always, but now her hair matched. Like Rayne's. He wanted to interact with the recording, but it was only an interface.

Celindria's image faced off to the side and gazed out at the desert. "Love and power. I was stuck in between because I couldn't feel the former and my intelligence made the latter easy to come by." A bitter smile spread across her lips. "I was jealous of you, father. Effortlessly, you found both. In all the Probabilities, you were loved, and you held the privilege of Princedom—No, I know that's not fair. You were convincing and charismatic. Even those who didn't know you as a Prince aligned with your objectives all for a glimpse of your trademark grin."

On her profile, the bitter smile fell into a softness unlike Xelan had ever seen from Celindria. She said, "I was never easy to like or easy to love. For that, I am sorry. Yes. Here, in the end, I'm asking for your forgiveness."

Abruptly, Celindria turned and faced Xelan. The vulnerability in her eyes as they filled with tears focused on him as if Celindria could see Xelan in the recording. "When the Probabilities were still, and I was alone in my empire—If the stars were aligned and the wind was right—I loved you. And I'm sorry I never said it. I'm sorry I ran from your help and made you chase me through a wake of destruction. I'm sorry for the mess I left you to clean up."

More than anything, Xelan wished he could hold Celindria and tell her it would be all right—

Celindria ran across the sand and into Xelan's arms.

Impossible.

Against Xelan's shoulder, Celindria said, "One gave us this, and he gave me a choice."

Xelan squeezed the daughter who'd never let him hold her before this moment and wept.

"I'll do better this time. I promise. Whatever it takes, I'll make you proud, father." Celindria separated them and peered into Xelan's eyes as she vowed, "I won't waste the Shadow's gift."

Xelan kissed Celindria's forehead. As they closed their eyes, he assured, "I know you won't. I'm proud of you. And I love you more than you know."

"Goodbye."

When Xelan next opened his eyes, he was back in the shifting ravine of the Oblivion Cathedral. The scent of desert sand lingered in the air. Xelan wiped a hand down his face, removing the stinging salt of his tears. Tameka tucked herself against Xelan's side and pressed her face to his chest. He needed the hug.

Over Tameka's fiery curls, Xelan glimpsed Lucas, who bowed with his head.

Pragmatic and right, as always, Tameka said, "We have work to do."

At her command, Xelan ordered, "Sagan, get us back to the rest. We have a mess to clean up, people!"

"You heard Wingmaster. Let's get these people home," Tameka echoed.

Xelan kissed her before he turned and found Rayne lifting Nox on her shoulder. Korac left Sagan's side to slip under Nox and help. While Rayne was tall for a woman from her region, Nox's enormous build made it awkward. For a moment, Xelan relived the fear of losing Nox.

Was it only for Rayne's sake? Or was there more...

Surprising himself, Xelan squeezed Tameka before making his way over to the trio. "Here, let me help."

The two Icarean males froze and stared at Xelan with wide eyes. Even Korac didn't hide his shock.

But Rayne beamed, and it made the offer worth it. "Thank you." She stepped aside and let Xelan shoulder his older brother.

They made eye contact for a moment, and the gratitude in Nox's stare touched Xelan. There was hope for this future of theirs. The one Rayne chose despite the hardship ahead.

And seeing as Celindria chose happiness, perhaps Xelan was wise for embracing his sentimentality after all—

A groan interrupted the warm moment, and the Icarean brothers turned to find Kyle pinching the bridge of his nose. While Silence smoothed a circle over his back, Kyle said, "Now we'll never hear the end of this from Iuo. There will be sequels—Prequels! What have you done?"

Xelan grinned.

Someone cue the uplifting music. The Shadow were successful, and now it was time to party.

At least Tameka could think as much, but her body begged her for a nap. Celindria had proven difficult to defend against while taking over Tameka's volition. It took everything in her to hold out until Pax drained his mother enough for Pablo to zap her with a nacre disabler. When she'd come to, Aria and Torch were feeding her their special Gargantuan Tritan/Lyriki blood. It was lucky, too, because there was no way Tameka was missing this.

Unlike the airplane crash outside of Enki's conduit on Earth. Tameka enjoyed mentioning it just to watch the vein in Kyle's forehead pulsate with exasperation.

Family.

Tameka led the Shadow through Sagan's conduit. Sagan, Rayne, Kyle, and Andrew followed. They reentered the Palatial Grounds on the stage to far more organization than Tameka had expected. Caedes and Pablo had been busy.

Jack, Ross, Bethany, Devis, T.A.O., and Andrius followed through and spread out into a line along the stage, making room for Silence, Lucas, and Pax.

As the line of Shadow increased, the crowd took notice. Cheers erupted among the hundreds of thousands who'd fought along their side.

Jack muttered, "It's not every day a dead hero rises."

Rayne beamed at her brother.

The cheering abruptly ceased when Xelan and Korac, carrying Nox between them, stepped through onto the stage. Tall and broad, they formed the center of the line in an amazing spectacle. Tameka could only imagine what people were thinking—

Thunderous.

Their cheers transformed into roars, and fists went to chests everywhere. From today's display, all of Iona Pax knew of the Shadow's sacrifice and commitment to their freedom. Now, they could look to the future with hope and optimism.

Fuck it.

Tameka took Kyle's hand. And he took Rayne's. She took Sagan's—And so on until it formed a line of unified fighters. Even Korac joined in the moment of solidarity and joy.

When Tameka spotted Iuo in the crowd, it didn't surprise her to see him wiping away a happy tear. This was some ending to his premiere. She even considered forcing everyone to take a final bow, but there was too much work ahead.

With a final squeeze of Kyle's hand, Tameka jumped off the stage and made her way to Caedes. Boots and heels of her family followed, and she knew no matter how long this day might take, they'd get through it together.

"Report, soldier."

Caedes' ears flushed blue, and it deepened to indigo when Pax showed up and giggled at him.

As soon as Tameka remembered 'ordering' was like 'flirting' to Caedes, she flushed red and mumbled an apology.

Pehton called, "Hey! I see you." She pointed two fingers at her eyes and then one at Tameka. The garnets glittered with good humor.

Tameka liked the way Caedes chuckled at his girlfriend's fake jealousy. A happy relationship suited him.

Caedes ducked his eyes as if he'd caught Tameka staring and said, "We're still accounting for all of Celindria's vessels. Once you'd… ah, defeated her, F8 brought the drones online. They're assisting in any way they can, including the ones Celindria had kept in the Oblivion Cathedral."

The story of Celindria's defeat would need telling.

Tameka said, "We saved her, and now Celindria is where she was meant to be—Far away from us." Tameka found she possessed enough spirit in her to laugh. "But seriously, if we find everyone is mostly unharmed, then this was the victory we needed."

Caedes muttered, "Praise Elden."

Yeah. Elden...

"He's taller in person," Tameka mused aloud. "Oh, and Tumu and Smith? They're half-Aegis."

The slight widening of Caedes' eyes was his only response.

Someone tapped Tameka on the shoulder. She turned to find Lamassau and hugged the green Tritan out of sheer relief. There were so many faces she loved that she'd almost never seen again. If it weren't for Pax and the other Progeny. "What is it, Chef?"

Lamassau flushed black, making Tameka one for two on the bashful scoreboard. He said, "I'll fill Caedes in on the details. I think these people could use a boost." He gestured at the citizens laid out with disabled nacres across the Palatial Grounds.

Iuo peered from behind the seven-foot tall Tritan. "I'd love to hear the exclusive story. I'll need sit-down interviews with all of you, of course."

"Of course, Iuo. Just let me settle my concerted empire first." Tameka winked at him before she shifted her eyes into Atramentous. Borrowing power from Ishkur's sun, she transferred it to the tens of thousands of unconscious victims.

Somewhere along the way, Tameka recognized the brush of Pax's power as he joined her.

Pehton called, "It's working!"

Everywhere across the Palatial Grounds people opened their eyes and sat up.

What the hell?

Tameka fed some to the rest. As many people as she could touch across the continent. This was a day to celebrate, and how could they party if everyone was exhausted?

Beside Tameka, the guys of their varying races gasped from the boost. Renewed, they glowed with vitality and determination. It might take them all day—all week, even—but they'd sort this mess out.

"All right, listen up!" Tameka called, and everyone stopped to listen. "I want the database we compiled of suspected victims cross-referenced with today's guest list. Locate those people, verify their condition, and check them off. Next, I want some food brought here, pronto. It'll be a long day and an even longer night, and we need fuel." Sagan gave a little cheer, and Tameka smiled as she continued, "Then, I want counselors—every single person qualified to work in mental health—prepared to treat this trauma. We aren't leaving these people without resources. Let's work in shifts, so no one burns out. Qas and Pablo, enlist some medical help from your students. T.A.O. work out a schedule with Sagan. We need to get these people home, but don't overextend yourselves. Ross and Kyle, see if you can offer some help with their memories of Celindria's control. Do what you feel comfortable offering, but I think it's something worth doing."

Bethany patted her chest.

Tameka asked, "Do you want to help?"

The teenage girl nodded.

"Thank you." Tameka smiled at Bethany before moving onto the next crew. "Andrew and Andrius, is there anything you can do? *Suggest* less anxiety or something? With their consent, of course."

While the boys laid out a care plan, Tameka glimpsed Xelan staring at her in awe. As their eyes met, the wonder transitioned into a magnificent grin.

Tameka was definitely getting laid tonight.

By the time Sagan allowed herself to take a break, hours later, she was exhausted and starving. She'd spent so much energy ferrying people to their homes that the provisions couldn't keep up with her metabolism. And there was still more work ahead of them. Eventually, someone tagged the transport people and put them in touch with Lucas. Using his Aegis blood, he opened conduits left and right and relieved the Seamswalkers for a time. Now, Overseers traveled between worlds to set things right again.

So, Sagan piled a platter full of Yun fruits, Pil cheeses, and Reipon meats and plopped her ass down under a shady spot in the amphitheater. Coincidentally, it was the same place she'd taken up hours earlier for the premiere. Damn, what a show—

"Hey, gorgeous."

At the sound of Rayne's voice, Sagan looked up and found her girlfriend sitting on the edge of the stage with her booted feet hanging off the edge.

Sagan asked, "Where's Nox? I figured you two would be attached at the hip—Nope. Nope, I didn't mean it like that." She rolled her eyes at Rayne's snickering fit.

"He's helping Korac, and in a six degrees kind of way, helping Xelan. It's not a comfortable vibe yet, but I'm hoping it'll get there."

Tameka alerted them with her heavy sigh off to the side. "I can't believe I'm saying this, but I agree with you. We're all better off if those three find some peace with one another." She sat in the seat beside Sagan.

Rayne asked, "Do you think Kyle will ever—"

Not only did Sagan and Tameka say, "No," at the same time, but Andrew popped up from backstage and contributed as well. He said, "Don't even get your hopes up. And can you blame him?"

Sagan thought about it for a minute. It was impossible to get over Rayne, and Kyle felt responsible for most of the worst Nox had inflicted on them. Sagan shrugged before offering, "It's complicated."

"What is?"

They all looked down the opposite end of the aisle to find Kyle making his way down it.

Tameka said, "Everything."

"Shit, tell me about it. Do you know how many people just requested to have the last week removed from their heads? Not that I blame them." Kyle glanced over at Rayne before saying, "I could use some brain bleach."

Sagan smiled. Not at what Kyle said, but because the five of them were together. Sure, she loved all of the Shadow, but there was something magical about their Progeny click. Trained and bled together. She said, "Since you decided to stay with us, Rayne, we'll all need to make a special trip to the gorge."

Each of them made an approving sound or nodded. Now *this* was a comfortable vibe. They soaked in the quiet moment, smiling at one another.

They didn't just *survive* a universal cataclysm; they won it.

"I love you guys." Rayne choked up a bit.

They pulled tighter together until Andrew and Rayne jumped off the stage and joined Tameka, Kyle, and Sagan in a hug.

"Now there's a sight your guardian loves to see."

As Xelan announced his arrival, Pax ran into the center of the hug and clung to his mom's legs. "I'm Progeny, too, mommy."

Tameka broke the hug to kneel and squeeze her son as she said, "Thank you for coming to our rescue, big man."

"Hee."

Sagan kept her arm around Rayne's waist, who pulled her in tight for a side hug. Rayne said, "I'm not going anywhere this time. I promise."

A whistle drew their attention to the stairs. Korac was walking down them with a bundle in his arms. "She wants to see her mother."

Elated and determined, Sagan gripped Rayne by the hand and dragged her up the stairs to meet Korac halfway. He held Echo out for Rayne to meet her niece. Sagan said, "Echo, meet your Auntie. We named you after her."

The joy on Rayne's face meant the worlds to Sagan, especially as the Lyriki baby sighed when Rayne tickled her pitch-black foot. The smell of the beach suffused the air, and tears tightened Rayne's voice. "She's so beautiful. Hello, Echo."

Sagan glanced up at Korac. "Have you introduced her to Nox?"

He shook his head. "I brought her straight to you."

"I got you."

They all looked over at Xelan. He shirked their astonished stares and muttered as he ran up the stairs, "I'll get him. We left him with Caedes."

As hope entered Sagan's heart, it filled Rayne's eyes. They both peered at Korac, who didn't bother to hide the optimism in his expression.

A second later, the famous Icarean brothers returned with a joyous anticipation in Nox's expression and a careful mask on Xelan's face. Sagan would say the gigantic Icarus approached gingerly, as if by hurrying he would frighten Echo. Korac turned and held his daughter for Nox to see Echo.

He glanced at Rayne for hesitant permission. Sagan had never seen such a radiant smile on her girlfriend's face. Rayne said, "Go ahead, Nox. She's already waving. Look!" She pointed at Echo.

The baby held her hand up at Nox, with her fingers spread wide. He took his enormous hand and placed it against hers. Echo's hand couldn't even fill Nox's palm, and she smiled as if this amused her.

The girls went "Aw" simultaneously.

While Sagan enjoyed the endearing display, she kept her eyes on the men. Korac stared at his big brother with warmth and respect before glancing behind Nox to Xelan. Wingmaster watched on with fascination and... hope. It was hesitant, but it was definitely there.

Korac saw it and turned to Sagan for confirmation. She smiled.

The future looked more promising with every passing second.

Hours later, the Shadow found themselves on a mutual break and decided it was time to clear the air. So Tumu, Lucas, and Silence took the stage while the rest piled back into their seats in the front row. Except Pablo, because he went home to check on Lynn. And no one could find Matt and Lucy. Given their history at public events, it was probably for the best.

Lamassau looked lonely sitting beside Twenty-One, while Miy sat in her Icarus' lap. Even though the space-bound couple kept their voices down, everyone could overhear them planning for an after party with Yito and Puk.

Pehton and Caedes slouched in their seats, ragged out like the rest of them, but also adorably holding hands.

Korac nestled Echo's bassinet basket in between him and Sagan, looking ready for some cozy family time.

As did Tameka, Pax, and Xelan.

With Celindria gone, Aria and Torch grew more lax around their leaders and actually took a seat beside them.

Progress.

And it provided more of a buffer between Rayne and Nox. The massive Icarus didn't look half bad for a guy who'd died a few hours ago.

Kyle pouted beside Andrew.

One seat down from them was the original Progeny—Devis, T.A.O., and Andrius. They looked relaxed for the first time in Andrew's recollection. There was an easiness about them, like they could finally breathe without fear or sorrow. What did the future hold for them?

Further down the row, Jack and Ross tried to distract Bethany from looking for Matt and Lucy. She didn't seem concerned, more curious. Again, it was probably for the best no one could find them.

Chris and Karter glowed while Para and Bones were ready to celebrate. Here or at home didn't seem to matter.

Both Andrew and Kyle looked unhappy that their dates were up on the stage instead of down here in the seats for some quality time. But this was important, so Andrew kept his complaints to himself.

Kyle did not. "Come on. I can't handle an exposition dump right now. Can't Tumu write a Verse or something? One I don't have to sit through the making of."

Silence gave Kyle 'the look.'

Andrew shook his head as his unrelated brother grinned back at her.

From the end of the row, Lamassau said, "That's not a bad idea. What do you think, Tumi?"

Tumu smiled with his lipless Tritan mouth. "I *do* like to keep an air of mystery, but I will share one thing." He peered down at Xelan. "I put your nacre in the resurrection casket under Gait's prison."

"I *knew* it!"

Andrew looked down the row at Pehton, who pointed accusingly at Tumu. "Only Primary blood could allow access to the basement, and you're the only Primary who wanted Xelan back."

Xelan's grin transformed into a puzzled frown. He glanced over at Nox, sitting straight and behaving himself beside Rayne. Xelan asked, "How did you get my birth nacre, Tumu?"

Oh, yeah. Andrew recalled from Nox's Verse that the older brother had kept it and tried to force it on Rayne—Again, something Andrew saw no point in examining.

No one else seemed keen on mentioning it, either. "It was me."

Between Pehton and Sagan, Korac spoke up. "I took it after Nox... After the night Rayne came to the fortress." He met Nox's eyes down the row. "You were so angry that night, I thought you'd destroy it. So I took it. When you ordered me to leave your Verse in the stronghold for Rayne, I left Xelan's birth nacre with it."

Lucas said, "From there, I took it and left the Verse. Sorry, Rayne. I let you find his nacre in several Probabilities, but in each one, you swallowed it without Elden there to keep yours from absorbing it."

Rayne smiled. "It sounds like something I would do."

Nox beamed at her, and Andrew found the exchange between them comfortable and warm. Like Nox and Rayne had been in a relationship longer than the Shadow had given them credit for.

"What about Smith?" Jack asked, peering up at Tumu.

Silence answered this one. "He and Elden are guarding Oblivion."

Andrew glanced at Kyle, who stopped grinning. What was it like being chosen over a god? Coming between an immortal relationship?

Chris asked, "Who was Smith to you?"

Lucas shifted a little uncomfortably and glanced at Andrew before admitting, "Smith was my son."

Oh.

Kyle slapped Andrew on the back as he said, "Congrats, stepdad."

Tameka's voice held an edge of accusation. "Did the mother survive?"

Lucas shook his head.

Karter asked, "Did she know the risk?"

"Yes."

The terse answers and the softness in how Lucas said them made Andrew stand up. He climbed onto the stage and approached his lover. Their audience watched as Andrew hugged Lucas and murmured, "You don't have to answer anymore questions if you don't want to. I know your life wasn't easy."

Lucas chuckled deep in his chest, and it felt good. "I love that you came up here to rescue me."

"I have one more question for him." Pehton stood to take the floor, and the group peered at her. "Why is every Aegis such a fashion victim?"

Lucas and Korac barked out a laugh at the same time, and it sounded eerily similar. It also made Andrew grin at his boyfriend.

Rayne asked, "What about Thailea?"

Kyle clicked his tongue in disdain.

Oh.

The treeloft. Night Rayne love nest.

And Andrew hadn't thought of it, but maybe Lucas would want to move the Zeppelin there. The last Aegis smiled at the young woman. "Would you like to guard it for me for a little while?"

Rayne beamed. "I'd be honored."

What about Nox?

As soon as the Icarus entered Andrew's mind, Rayne's face fell, and she looked over at Xelan. The question went unspoken between them.

Xelan met Nox's eyes and everyone but Kyle, held their breath. Into the stillness, Xelan said, "It's not up to me alone."

Beside Andrew, Kyle muttered, "Damn right."

When Rayne looked away, Tameka put a hand on Xelan's shoulder. "He's right. There's a process out of fairness." She nodded at Jack, luo, and Tumu. "And the King Elects deserve a say."

"We do."

The group whirled to find F8, Kombuchi, Legir, X, 2Lip, Tempest, and Dolor waiting at the top tiers of the amphitheater.

This looked heavy. Andrew was impressed as hell when Nox stood to face his judgment. Rayne took his hand and went with him. Korac waited for Xelan to follow, and they went together with their mates. Silence joined them—It was a whole Shadow affair, and it could go on without Andrew.

Lucas and Andrew were left alone on the stage. The latter said, "*I* have a question."

"Oh, do you now?"

Andrew smirked and pecked his lover a kiss, which deepened at Lucas' insistence. It took a powerful force of will for Andrew to break it and ask, "What about this?" He brought his coin out of his pocket.

Lucas stared at it a long time until he said, "I spent an Eternity mastering outcomes and predicting the future. It's hard to believe it's finally over." He looked up into Andrew's eyes. "It's all surprises from here."

Andrew quirked a brow. "Do you think you can handle it?"

"Why don't you flip the coin and find out?"

Andrew flipped the coin into the air, high enough to make it sing. Then he took Lucas' hand and walked away. Together, they returned to their family to watch the outcome of this soap opera with no idea of how it would end.

Behind them, the coin landed, but no one was around to see it.

The King Elect council would make for the least frightening challenge Nox had faced this day. The deep concern in Rayne's frown bothered him more than the judgment on the faces ahead of them. He kept his eyes forward, squeezing her hand reassuringly. There was nothing Nox wouldn't do to deserve Rayne, and justice was the right course. Without it, the other Shadow would never accept him as her mate, and the last thing he wanted was to alienate her from the people who mattered most. To both of them.

Nox stood before the King Elects—Jack, Iuo, and Tumu joined their ranks. Xelan and Korac parted to the sides, Nox's little brother on the left and the best soldier on the right. The arbiter and the ally.

Their heart raced, and it wasn't Nox's. He squeezed Rayne's hand again to assure her, knowing it would do no good.

Prepared for retribution, Nox said, "I—"

F8 cut him off with a gesture.

Kombuchi, with his backward bent arms folded behind him, addressed Rayne. "War King, we are elated by your miraculous return. Praise Elden."

The others echoed, "Praise Elden."

Rayne nodded for them, but she moved closer to Nox, and he loved her for it.

As a member of a race with no mouths, Legir spoke to them telepathically. "We understand you led the Shadow against our greatest enemy and won this day. For all the days to come, we thank you."

The elected Kings put their fist to their chests, Jack included, to praise Rayne—

No.

Nox swept a glance across the amphitheater, and people—survivors, fighters, and medics—everywhere put a fist to their chest. Pehton, Caedes—All of the Shadow. Even Tameka and Xelan. Pax beamed up at Rayne as he did the same. Korac actually knelt and bowed his head.

In solidarity, Nox and Rayne faced one another and returned the gesture, fists to their chests.

Tempest and F8 narrowed their eyes; 2Lip and X exchanged a look; Kombuchi clenched his jaw; Iuo and Tumu smiled; and Jack's eyes shifted in and out of Atramentous.

With her eyes locked on Nox, Rayne said, "I wouldn't be here without the Icarus you wish to condemn. Consider that in your judgments. He saved my life and yours."

Tempest took a step out of the lineup, claiming the floor. "We will hold a proper council to hear his case and determine his fate. Until such time, Nox, we are taking you into the custody of the Concerted Empire of Iona Pax..."

Each of the Kings read Nox his rights while Korac ground his teeth and clenched his fist. Tears welled in Rayne's eyes. Pax hid his face against his mother's side. Sagan appeared ready to open an escape conduit.

But Nox looked at the sky. The fake projection of stars above twinkled in a sea of artificial constellations. All around him, the flora of the Palatial Grounds scented the air with the sweet fragrance of victory.

This was a good day.

Everyone had survived. Celindria found a peace Nox hoped she would continue to earn, much like himself. He got to see Pax bring down an army. Then there was baby Echo. She was the sweetest sight since the first time Rayne had smiled at Nox.

None of it was possible without Xelan. Gratitude flooded through Nox on the waves of familial tides. Not all hope was lost. They could still recover their relationship. Nox felt it when Xelan had shouldered him back to Ishkur.

So.

Even though Korac held Rayne back as F8 cinched Nox's thick wrists into nacre chains he could easily break... This was a good day—

"—Into Rayne's custody." That was an odd sentence for Xelan to say.

Apparently, the elective council also thought it was odd as they exchanged bewildered or aghast glances.

Rayne froze in Korac's grip beside Nox, and Nox still didn't fully understand what was happening.

Xelan repeated, "Until the council reconvenes on the matter, I am placing Nox into War King's custody."

Nox's mouth fell open.

Rayne stared at her guardian, and Korac released her as he, too, gaped. Sagan cupped a hand over her mouth, hiding the smile which sparkled in her eyes. Andrew's brows were almost to his hairline. Although Kyle kept his composure for Nox's foremother's sake, censure rolled off him like heat on pavement. Tameka stepped up to Xelan's side, supporting his decision.

The council repeated their earlier shocked expressions. Except this time, Jack looked away.

F8 blinked her heavy fan of lashes before asking, "These are your terms, Co-Emperor?"

Tameka slipped her hand into Xelan's before adding, "And Kyle Roberts is to oversee the rehabilitation program until Nox completes it."

Nox didn't need to glance behind him to feel the Progeny's censure transform into a wicked grin. Kyle said, "I would like input from the King Elects, but I think you'll find the foundation rigorous and severe."

"I like severe." With his arms folded, Kombuchi looked unhappy.

But it was Jack who spoke up and floored Nox. "I agree to the Co-Emperors' terms. Those in favor?"

Iuo, 2Lip, X, Tumu, Jack, and Dolor raised their hands, making six. F8, Kombuchi, Legir, and Tempest kept their hands down. Only four.

Nox swallowed as gratitude welled prematurely. It wasn't done yet.

Before F8 could protest, Jack reminded her, "This is a temporary arrangement so we can better focus our energies on the empire's recovery. Our people are more important than who will babysit a prisoner. And to prove I'm acting in the best interest of Iona Pax, I'll recuse myself of the official trial and name another in my place."

By the glitter in F8's multi-faceted eyes, this seemed to satisfy her. "Agreed." She faced Nox and flattened her lips into a tight line as she unshackled him.

Kombuchi singsonged, "Don't go too far, Icarus." If Xelan's Verse was any indication, the Caprent male wanted to eat Nox.

Legir's voice entered Nox's head. "I consumed the Verses to understand the senseless need for my sons' deaths. Do not assume this is over between us."

The second Nox's hands were free, Rayne sprung into his arms. The people in the stands cheered, much to the council's bewilderment.

Pax asked, "Mommy, why are they cheering?"

"Because they came to see a show, and they got one." Tameka gave Xelan an appreciative look, even while he tried to ignore Nox and Rayne's embrace.

Sagan cooed into Echo's bassinet, "See, Echo? This is what we call 'getting your money's worth.'"

Korac laughed.

Silence waved to the spectators, enjoying the moment.

Kyle beamed at Nox's foremother, earning some of Nox's respect.

Lucas and Andrew peered longingly at one another, ready to celebrate.

F8 and Kombuchi sighed and walked away together, resuming their duties.

Legir, X, Tempest, and Dolor waved their farewells and followed.

2Lip glanced between Rayne and Nox before settling on Xelan. "They'll come around."

"I hope so." Xelan saluted the Pil Dwarf. "Carry on rebuilding, sir."

With a wave, 2Lip went off in his mechsuit to join the others.

Behind Nox, Miy groaned. "Can we go home now? Some of us have made plans way more fun than this drama."

Yito and Puk chuckled while Twenty-One kissed the top of Miy's orange and black feathers.

Nox separated from Rayne and turned to find Xelan's eyes on him. Off to the side, Korac waited for whatever came next. Tameka looked expectant as well.

Where did they go from here?

Xelan announced, "Everyone go home. We've got weeks of community service ahead of us, and, Iuo, before you ask, plan whatever shindig you want to celebrate. We'll *all* be there."

Tension left Nox's shoulders, and Rayne relaxed beside him. Her expression radiated gratitude for her mentor. Xelan's eyes flicked to her and warmed.

Iuo chuckled. "Nothing can top the Generals' wedding, but I can put something together. Anyone up to planning it with me? Come join me back at the Villa."

"We are!" Para bounced, and Bones noticed with a smile. Her impish grin in the three Icarean brothers' direction meant she either planned to embarrass them greatly or put them to work.

Karter echoed it as she said, "We know just the thing."

Behind them, Chris mouthed, "I'm. Sorry."

Nox suppressed a chuckle.

Conduits opened, and Sagan smiled. "Find your way home, peeps. Me and Korac are taking a long nap."

Echo whistled her agreement.

Miy, Twenty-One, Yito, and Puk went first with waves and nods. "See you emotional masochists tomorrow—What?! They're always so sappy. You know it's true, T-1."

Chris said, "Jack, you and I will talk tomorrow." When Rayne's brother nodded, Chris roped Bones and Iuo by their necks and dragged them to the Reipon conduit. "C'mon, you two. Hey, Iuo, can we talk about a film?"

Karter and Para laughed incredulously, but stayed behind.

Rayne left Nox's side to hug her brother. Jack didn't hesitate, but when he looked over Rayne's shoulder at Nox, his eyes flashed Atramentous again. Jack whispered, "I'd like a chance to talk with you."

Without hesitation, Rayne said, "Tomorrow. When we've all rested, you and I will sit down and talk this out."

Ross and Bethany hugged Kyle before joining Jack at the conduit. "See everyone tomorrow." The three waved and disappeared.

Devis, T.A.O., and Andrius approached Xelan. They each gave a respectful nod to Tameka and Pax. T.A.O. went first. "The wound is mending, but hard to heal. Where are we to be?"

Xelan peered down at Tameka, asking permission. Nox appreciated the respect between them. With her nod, Xelan said, "Come to the stronghold with us. We'll put you to work tomorrow."

"Oh, thank, Elden." Devis sighed. "I was worried I might have to actually relax."

Andrius chuckled and nudged his brother aside.

With Silence on his arm, Kyle knocked into Nox's side on his way to a conduit. "Welp, Silence and I are off to strip out of these clothes and enjoy ourselves."

Shameless.

Rayne glanced up at Nox, and he gave nothing away. If his foremother was happy, so was he.

Xelan hung his head and sighed.

Korac looked off, hiding a smirk.

Sagan didn't bother to hide her snickering.

Silence's discouraging look held no water, especially since she leaned in and whispered something which burned Kyle's ears. He said, "Yes, ma'am," with entirely too much enthusiasm.

They deserved each other.

"See you tomorrow." Silence waved for them both as they disappeared for the night.

But not before Sagan closed the conduit on one last smug smirk from Kyle.

"That's gotta sting," Andrew mused as he dragged Lucas to a conduit. Beyond it was an impressive sight. Nox had never seen a zeppelin before. Andrew said, "We'll be here tomorrow. Ah, screw it." The young man grabbed Sagan and squeezed her. Then Tameka. And finally Rayne. "I love you, guys."

All three girls said together, "We love you. See you tomorrow."

The display moved Nox. This was not like the family he'd known, but with a glance over at Korac and Xelan, Nox wondered...

Lucas gave one final wave before their conduit closed behind them.

Pehton approached Sagan and Korac with Caedes on her arm. "You two know how to party." Then she punched Korac on the bicep.

"Ow!" He faked the pain and rubbed the spot as if it were sore. Korac tried for some sympathy from Caedes. "Redheads, man."

The bald Icarus chuckled and said, "Don't look at me. I wasn't the one egotistical enough to lead her on for three years."

When Korac balked, Pehton laughed.

Sagan chafed her husband's arm, but her words weren't very consolatory. "He's right, you know?"

Pehton said, "That was for keeping secrets. Don't you ever do that to me again."

"Here, here." Tameka joined in and shot her husband an accusatory look. Then one at Rayne.

Rayne withered under it. She mouthed, "I'm. Sorry."

Nox chuckled—

"You, too, big guy. I expect you to treat me with more respect than these two, because, unlike them, *you* should fear me." Tameka's ferocity was impressive, but the humorous twinkle in her eyes was more than unexpected.

There was that notion of family again…

"That brings us to this." Karter stepped up with Para.

The smaller of the two said, "Savis would be so proud of you, boys."

Nox forgot how to breathe. Xelan recoiled as if taken aback, and Korac let the mask slip enough to show his widened eyes.

Karter and Para opened their arms. The three Icarean males glanced at one another. The eye contact lasted longer between Nox and Xelan. They struck an accord for the sake of the moment, and all three rushed into their godparents' waiting arms.

With her voice squeezed, Para said, "We know Savis wasn't well, but more than anything, she loved the three of you."

"She would dance this day in your names if she were here. Keep that in your spirits." Karter held Nox so tight it left him breathless, but…

It was Nox's first time holding Karter and Para, and it felt like home.

Tears sprung to his eyes, which he tried to hide when they pulled away. The double-take from Xelan told Nox he didn't do an excellent job. Rayne came to his side immediately, and her sunny beach scent comforted him.

As they walked backward toward luo's conduit, Karter pointed at Korac. "I want a rematch tomorrow."

"You got it, mother."

Mother.

Nox smiled.

Someone sniffled, and they all turned to Pehton, who squeezed out, "They did it. They finally sapped me."

Caedes laughed outright as he led her to their conduit. "Come on, teeny. Let's celebrate."

Korac did *not* withhold his laughter. "Teeny?!! Oh, that's spreading at the office, General Warden."

Before their conduit closed, Pehton stuck her little black tongue out at them to Korac's continued delight.

Sagan reflected, "I love her."

"Yeah," Rayne sighed. "She's pretty cool."

Then there was six. Well. Six and two smalls.

Pax rubbed his eyes and yawned, "Mommy, I'm sleepy."

She picked her son up and held him with a maternal glance at Xelan. "I think it's time for all of us to go to bed."

Echo whistled again, prompting Korac to turn and check on her. "Yeah. Us, too." He shot Sagan a knowing smirk.

Nox felt that in his soul, but wouldn't dare get caught looking at Rayne the same way around Xelan.

A quiet fell between them, and they took the moment to consider themselves. The three warrior Icari, and their three mighty Progeny women. Wars well-fought and won. There was a bright future ahead, and they were facing it together.

Sagan laughed. "It's not like we won't see each other tomorrow—We'd *better* see each other tomorrow." She pointed an accusing finger at Rayne.

"Oh, they'll be here tomorrow," Xelan said while staring at Nox. "There's work to be done."

Nox nodded, accepting his fate.

Korac interrupted the staring contest. "Tomorrow then—"

"Wait!"

They looked up the amphitheater stairs to find Matt and Lucy rushing down them. There was no sign of the girl's dress from earlier in the night, and she was wearing his button-down.

"Hey, sorry," Lucy offered as they rushed up to meet their group. "Sagan, do you mind giving us a lift home—Thank you!"

Sagan opened it, turning purple to suppress her laughter.

The wayward couple took in the vibe and grinned. Matt said, "It was one helluva day."

It was enough to make Xelan grin back. "It sure was. You two come back tomorrow. I have an assignment for you."

Lucy's eyes sparkled. "Can't wait. See you then!"

They disappeared.

Tameka took Xelan by the hand, and he waved for Andrius, Devis, T.A.O., Aria, and Torch to follow. Nox had never seen the stronghold, but it must be massive to house so many people.

"Wait!"

Rayne left Nox's side, and without needing words to communicate, Xelan opened up his arms. Rayne surged into them with a squeeze Nox was familiar with as it brought tears to Xelan's eyes.

Against his chest, Rayne said, "I love you. This means so much to me."

Xelan closed his eyes and soaked in the moment. "Why do you think I did it?" Softer, almost so softly Nox couldn't hear, Xelan whispered, "Thank *you*." He opened his eyes and peered at Nox.

It was an unfamiliar look, and Nox couldn't quite place it. Wonder, consideration, and gratitude all mixed into one.

They separated and stared at each other one last time before returning to their partners.

Tameka called out, "Goodnight."

Xelan gave a parting wave and a meaningful nod to Korac before the conduit closed behind them.

Without preamble, Rayne pulled Sagan in for a kiss. Nox and Korac let them have some privacy and faced one another.

Nox said, "The road ahead is long."

Korac laughed. "Well, you're lucky there's a road at all."

They both smiled a minute before the girls returned to their sides. Both of them had the same hunger in their eyes as they said, "Bedtime."

Korac's voice was full of anticipation. "Amos, I've been thinking all day about what I plan to do to you."

Nox didn't have the same practice with words, so he did the next best thing. He purred for Rayne.

The other couple laughed on their way through the conduit, a bright, cheerful sound. Korac admitted, "I didn't even think you could do that. Good night, you two!"

Rayne and Nox stepped through theirs so Sagan could close it and waved goodbye.

Out in the forest, once again.

"I can't believe it." Rayne's voice was filled with awe. "I can't believe Xelan did this for us."

Nox pulled her in for a hug and kissed the top of her hair. "I can never repay him, but I will try. Starting tomorrow, I will do everything I can to make amends."

Rayne separated them enough to peer up at Nox. "That's tomorrow. Until it comes, I want to spend every second showing you how much I love you."

Nox kissed Rayne, eager for their future. Specifically, for the next nine hours.

Until tomorrow comes...

PART III
SMOLDER

XXI   BLACKEN

TOMORROW TURNED OUT TO BE A GOOD DAY. AND THE NEXT. AND THE NEXT. IN FACT, NOX COULDN'T NAME ONE BAD DAY AMONG THE LAST THIRTY.

Every day began and ended with Rayne. Her black and white hair, her sweet smile, and her tempting, revealing outfits filled every morning and every night. But in between...

"Prepare to experience pain unlike you've ever imagined, and yes, I see you rolling your eyes."

Nox stared out at his audience of two or three thousand. The Shadow had designed a special facility to house the remnants of Imminent and proprietors of illegal vice during rehabilitation. The size of an intergalactic stadium, it was built in an ocean and surrounded by nacre shielding. No one with a nacre could enter or leave without permission. Apartments—decorated in black, white, and gray, and surrounded by various ecosystems of vegetation and water—provided some tranquility and allowed prisoners some privacy. The program met all their basic needs. Reformists, like Nox, consented to let technicians secure them into stasis pods, fitted with Divine Booth technology.

This was week three, and it was time for a fully immersive experience. Most, like Cinderken—the second pod on row one—were familiar with the advanced port features from Razor's Emporium. But he'd experienced nothing like this.

Nox's image was streamed onto the dome above them as he continued his explanation. "We've collected one volunteer among your list of victims to provide today's lesson. It is the first of many. Take it from me: you will never look at yourself the same way again. Not after today."

No one rolled their eyes this time. They stared back at Nox with apprehension. He was living testimony to the transformation.

Nox looked off to the side, where Kyle leaned in an archway. The young man gave a nod, and Nox ordered, "Begin."

The pods initiated memory sequences which were transferred from the memory banks of their victims. The reformists would feel everything they'd inflicted on the Shadow's hand-selected volunteers.

After two seconds, the screaming began.

Begging and tears followed.

Nox prayed to Elden this would work. Some people believed the prayers still reached Elden, and that he answered through the Source. Others sent their prayers to Rayne, saying her white hair was proof of her ascension into a deity. It made her uncomfortable, and Xelan didn't encourage it among their citizens.

The Twelve Worlds were in the middle of an adjustment period, and some growing pains were expected. For instance, Nox's trial was televised because of overwhelming demand from the populace. Everything had gone as expected. Nox pleaded his Verse, and Rayne explained their rehabilitation together. What they didn't expect was for Xelan to testify on Nox's sacrifice for Elden and Rayne.

"Nox is capable of good, your majesties. I have seen it." Xelan looked away from the King Elects and met Nox's eyes. *"Good has its place in Iona Pax; I'm sure we can find one for you."*

It was a moment worthy of the tears both Nox and Korac had shed, and it had proven to be the deciding factor. The council voted unanimously to not only let Nox live, but to integrate him into the workings of the empire. He would remain in Rayne's custody in return for community service. Sagan had suggested this facility, where Nox could lend his reformation experience. But only after Kyle had subjected Nox to hours of testing the machines.

Volunteers—victims of Nox's crimes from around the Twelve Worlds—had arrived in droves to contribute an experience. They were faces Nox had already revisited with Rayne, but now he felt their pain. Upon his first immersion, Nox had screamed within the first second. Every day, he left Rayne to some task with Xelan, Sagan, and Tameka so Nox could endure a minimum of two hours in one of those pods. And he would continue to do so until he'd faced every victim left alive—They'd estimated his sentence at approximately six hundred years.

It was worth it.

As for Nox's integration into the Shadow, some were more receptive than others. As they'd agreed, Jack and Rayne talked everything out during the reconstruction period, but so far, they'd yet to extend dinner or movie night invitations to Nox. Rayne refused to go without him, despite Nox's protests.

Rayne has insisted, *"I'm not asking them to accept you. Not yet, anyway. I'm asking them to accept that we're together. Sure, I'll go shopping, eat lunch, or have fun with anyone who asks. But big events like birthdays and Volcano Day, I want you there with me."*

Korac assured Nox the Shadow would warm up to him in time, and the General reminded his King that Korac's relationship with Sagan was proof of that.

Hopefully, everyone showed up for today's events. It would be a shame if anyone missed it on account of Nox.

Speaking of...

They were late.

Nox glanced over at Kyle to find him accompanied by an Icarus dressed all in black. Bald and taciturn, Caedes gestured for Nox to come over, souring Kyle further.

As Nox approached, he overheard Kyle say, "I can't believe they're actually doing this. I'm not even done with Nox for the day."

Caedes responded with a "humph," while his dark green eyes glitter with knowing.

At times such as these, Nox remained silent but observant. Nothing he could contribute would lessen Kyle's agitation with him. But the memory Progeny was fair and never cruel, despite the power he held in the situation.

On a sigh, Kyle said, "Fine."

"Oh, good. I thought I would have to kick your ass for ruining this event for me."

They turned to find Sagan standing in the corridor. She'd dressed for Korac's fare in a short sun dress, violet enough to match her eyes. All three men averted their eyes the moment their brains would let them. The material was sheer in places Rayne would appreciate.

Sagan opened a conduit, and cheers erupted from the other side as she said, "They're waiting for you."

"Nox! Nox! Nox!"

Kyle pinched the bridged of his nose and sighed again. "Let's get this over with."

Nox followed Caedes, Kyle, and Sagan through the conduit...

And they went deaf.

Truly.

Nox's soft tissue repair system kicked into overdrive on his ear drums thus was the volume of the crowd. Korac's old camp was packed and beyond. People gathered in mass, spilling into the surrounding fields and forests to witness today's race.

As the event's sponsor, Iuo announced, "Iona Pax, welcome to the Verse Triathlon."

Kyle sighed again, even as the people roared their delight at Xelan's trademarked title.

Rushed at the end, Iuo tacked on, "And don't forget to tune in for tonight's premiere of 'Rayne's Verse: Nox's Release.'"

Now it was Nox's turn to pinch the bridge of his nose.

A groan from behind whirled them around as Korac said, "How could you, Xelan?" The General was wearing a black tunic with accents to match Sagan's eyes and her dress.

Xelan, dressed in black cargo pants and a black tank, was tying a green bandanna in his hair. The same color as Tameka's eyes. He said, "Oh, I didn't name it. Rayne did."

Caedes barked out a laugh, and Sagan giggled into her hand. Kyle flipped them off as he walked away.

Nox, flabbergasted, shook his head incredulously. As Xelan and Korac fussed with their gear, it made Nox self-conscious enough to check the buckles on the blue belts which fastened his black tunic.

"You look handsome to me, Stabby."

There it was again.

Whenever Rayne came around, a goofy grin plastered itself on Nox's face. He looked up to find her dressed in a blue peasant top and a flowy skirt. It made her eyes brighter and gorgeous under Cinder's clear sky. No sphere in sight.

Beside her, Tameka wore a green pantsuit, cropped to show off her midriff. She wasn't showing yet, but her tawny skin glowed with pregnancy. The Co-Emperor looked regal and moved with an effortless grace Nox respected in the fighter.

Pax was in the stands with Chris and Karter, waving in his little three-piece with a bowtie.

Sagan joined the girls, and the three of them in a line together made for an awesome sight.

Xelan said, "We're lucky."

Nox caught Korac's glimpse, and they both looked at Xelan for how to set today's mood. Without jinxing it, Nox admitted to himself things were getting easier between the brothers. And he treasured it.

Rayne glanced out into the crowd and beamed. "They're here." She gestured for Nox to look.

Among the Shadow, Silence waved and pointed in the front row with her. Twelve children stood in the stands, waving and cheering. One was a redheaded little girl, Mifa, and the other was a shy little boy, Jet—looking less withdrawn than the day they'd left him with Celindria's orphanage.

Nox waved to them, prompting Xelan and Korac to glance back.

Sagan asked, "Friends of yours?"

But Xelan seemed to know the answer to the question. "You had them brought here?" There was appreciation in his eyes.

Nox gave a single nod. He didn't wish to make a spectacle of it, but Rayne beamed bright enough for the both of them.

Korac stared at the interaction, and hope flickered in his eyes.

Iuo said, "Our racers will say mark, and we'll begin."

That was their cue.

Tameka walked over to Xelan, kissed him, and for some reason slipped her pants down to her hip—

Oh.

WINGMASTER.

Xelan grinned, and his midnight eyes held a promise that was none of Nox's business.

To that end, Sagan went to Korac and retrieved something from her bag—

Korac barked out a laugh and kissed her abruptly. While they kissed, he held the item up in the air for the crowd to see...

Her purple bra.

The audience cheered.

Xelan and Nox chuckled at the same time. It happened often, and the brothers tried to ignore the awkwardness of the simultaneous occurrence.

Rayne went last and took Nox's hand. In it, she placed...

The same ribbon from the last race. It looked a little worse for wear, but its significance transcended their relationship. While Nox stared at it, Rayne got on tiptoe and kissed his cheek. She whispered, "Win or lose, you still get the prize."

Nox grinned.

Rayne had no idea how true that was.

Tamed, Li burned at an appropriate distance out on the horizon, near setting. The red sky reflected the crimson ocean below, purified by the empire's efforts. Fresh-cut cranberry grasses crunched beneath Korac's feet, and the breeze carried the smell of thyme, not ash.

What a glorious day for a competition.

Korac tucked Sagan's bra into the back of his pants with a wink in her direction. She blew him a kiss as the girls walked over to the stands. One major section was cordoned off for the Shadow, where everyone took their seats. Korac recognized the twelve children from Bones and Pehton's reports of the orphanage. Their lives had started similarly to Korac's, but after only a month in the care of decent people, they looked healthy and happy.

Thanks to the big Icarus waving at them.

Korac smirked.

"You'd better get your head in the game, crowd pleaser. Pehton and Sagan's cheerleading won't save you out on the training course."

Xelan.

Korac turned to face his cocky Co-Emperor and taunted, "Care to make a wager?"

In a signature move, Xelan bit his thumbnail as he considered the odds. Nox stopped waving at the children and walked over with a curious glance in Korac's direction.

The General knew just the thing. Korac said, "No holds barred—If I win, the three of us start a new tradition."

Xelan quirked a brow with a glance over at Nox, who shrugged with one shoulder. Xelan asked, "What tradition?"

"When the girls have their night, us three have our own." Korac gestured among the trio.

Hiding his reaction, Nox looked out over the Ignis Desert. Korac appreciated that Xelan took his time to decide. After a quiet stretch, the brothers glanced at each other.

With a rake of his hair, Xelan said, "Agreed." He sounded certain, but neither happy nor upset about it.

Nox nodded with a glint in his eyes.

They walked to their mark, and Xelan set into a runner's stance, much to the delight of the crowd. "If I win, I want you to host Tameka, Pax, and I at the chalet for a week."

Korac cursed. "Of course you're wanting to inconvenience me and soil my guest sheets."

Nox hid a smirk, but not in time. Xelan pointed a stern finger at his older brother. "I want you and Rayne there too."

The genuine surprise in the enormous Icarus' eyes was enough incentive for Korac to accept the terms. "Agreed. What do you want, Nox?"

Nox's baritone chuckle rumbled in his chest before he said, "You two assume we'll even finish this race. This is my wager. The three of us encounter some disaster, which prompts our overly protective and incredibly capable women to rescue our collective asses."

That got a laugh out of Xelan, and it was good to hear.

Korac grinned and felt it glowing despite his best efforts to remain composed. "What do you want if you win?" The cameras centered on Nox as if they could hear the conversation, despite that the three Icari had muted their mics.

Nox's voice quieted, and sorrow thickened the words. "Invite me to your Shadow events so Rayne will go. She refuses to go without me, and after the Martyr Complex isolated her for years, I wish not to be the cause for more of it."

Xelan looked away as he said, "Done."

Korac noted the finality in the word, and knew win or lose, Nox would get his wish. The General glimpsed the confirmation in his Co-Emperor's eyes. It made Korac smirk as he loosened into his stance and turned on his mic.

"Ready?"

Korac's word echoed back to him from the coliseum, televised to the entire empire. A hush settled over the crowd.

Nox said, "Set."

Throughout the arena, the sound of people scooting to the edge of their seats put the pressure on.

Xelan peered between Korac and Nox. At their nods, he shouted, "Go!"

All three opened their wings and flew down into the lava field below. The Ignis desert's rivers of magma began at the mouth of a massive caldera and carved their way through volcanic rock into a funnel. It emptied into a basin at near sheer cliffs constantly at war with the ocean.

Korac and his brothers raced to the pumice beach and mounted their glass skates, retrofitted with extra friction dampeners and restraints for their heavy boots. Two straps, one magnetic harness—And bang!

With a shout of triumph, Korac was the first to drop into the lava with his skate.

"Don't get cocky!" Xelan warned from behind, alerting Korac of his expeditious pursuit.

Just in case, Korac bent his knees deeper and flattened his wings behind him for more aerodynamics. He was the smallest of the trio, more dancer than Xelan's swimmer build. And obviously, Nox was built like the legends of Greek Olympians.

While Korac had size on his side, Xelan had ingenuity and a better understanding of physics. He zipped by with a broad grin on his face.

They both dodged the same stalagmite with ease, but Korac tried to cut into the inside of the next turn.

Xelan predicted this and sliced through the lava to thwart Korac's strategy.

Where was Nox?

Before Korac could glance back, a shade across the field caught his attention. Nox was in a separate stream. The arrogant bastard waved as he went by, unimpeded by his competitors.

Incredulous, Korac asked, "Can he do that?"

Xelan was still grinning as he watched his older brother glide further away. "You said, 'No holds barred.'"

He did. Fuck—

As soon as Korac cursed, the ground shook around them, and lava sloshed this way and that. He quirked a brow at his Co-Emperor.

The Icarean Prince's grin broadened. "Ah... Right on time."

Nox shouted warily, "What is that?!"

Xelan said, "Well, there's a reason I chose today—"

A firebomb exploded from the north—The caldera.

Korac dropped his composure. "Tell me you didn't!"

Another earthquake ripped through the magma desert, and a distinctive crack resounded right as a column of fire shot out of the volcano.

Nox nearly collided with a boulder in his stream as he stared at the calamity in the distance. All around them, the mantle shifted and disconnected until the course ahead fell away completely.

Korac growled, "Xelan!" And braced himself for the fall off the edge of Cinder.

Ahead of them, they heard Nox bellow in a disconcerting mixture of delight and terror before he disappeared.

Xelan cackled like a mad scientist as he crouched and reached out a hand. "Together as Elden intended, General."

Clenching his jaw, Korac took Xelan's hand and faced their potential end—Not afraid, but…

Complete.

Together, they went over the edge, chasing after the older brother.

This was *not* the funnel. This was a ring of massive lava falls pouring into an uncertain end. Ashen wind swept them up as the inertia tightened every muscle in Korac's body. Halfway down, the intensity of the fall took his breath away, but all the while, he reveled in the pure joy on Xelan's maniacal face. A speck appeared in the center below, growing bigger as they descended.

Nox.

The lucky son of a bitch made it, and he was pulling ahead to shore right as Xelan and Korac approached the bottom. When the skates right themselves after a vertical drop, it always unsettled Korac's stomach. It only took one failure of the friction dampeners to send them plummeting into the fire.

Sagan flashed before his eyes, wearing that transparent sun dress and holding their little girl.

Powerful arms gripped Korac, and Xelan's voice came from a breath away. "Open your eyes, General."

With a churn of Korac's stomach, they righted in the ring of lava falls. He looked into his Prince's eyes and smiled. "Thanks."

A cheeky grin spread across Xelan's lips as he said, "You can let go now."

Korac laughed and released his Prince, whose eyes glittered with mischief as he pushed away toward the shore.

What did the crowd think of the moment?

So they could fully immerse themselves into the sport, Korac, Nox, and Xelan tuned into a private frequency. They weren't listening to Iuo's coverage of the races. The more Korac thought of it, the more he didn't care what anyone thought of his interactions with Xelan. Tameka would get over it, and Caedes could resuscitate Pehton's heart.

It was enough to make Korac smirk as he unstrapped out of his skate and hopped into his wetsuit. Xelan was already diving into the ocean with his electric spear. Here, Nox's advantage would end.

The whalesharks were spawning.

Before Xelan heard their carnivorous roar, he smelled the foul rot of Cinder's great, mutated beasts. As he crested wave after wave, he drew closer to a pod, agitated by the intrusion of their mating grounds. Which unfortunately laid between the Ignis Desert and the distant caves, making up the last leg of the race.

Nox swam like his life depended on it, because it did.

All the whalesharks they'd faced before were males. During this season, the females swam closer to the riptide, and they were an impressive sight.

An impressive, *horrifying* sight.

Only two females swam among the pod, and it was easy to pick out the ladies—They were the size of Xelan's stronghold. When one yawned, her gigantic jaws would fit an Icarus the size of Nox whole. The tines of her teeth swirled like a meat grinder. One major distinctive feature—their only saving grace—was the lack of adhesion to their skin. The males were sticky to bring food to their females.

That was it.

"Nox!" Xelan shouted, as a female set her sights on her next meal. The splash behind Xelan let him know Korac was with him as they rushed to their older brother.

By now, the story of Nox's decimation of a whaleshark barehanded *after* escaping the adhesion had spread far and wide across the empire. While it invoked the old hero-worship in Xelan, the females required teamwork.

Korac swam up beside Xelan. "You get to Nox. I'll swim up beside her."

"Careful around the gills. They can pull you in."

With a shudder, Korac swam toward the mother beast. Meanwhile, Nox faced her head on, spear at the ready. Xelan reached him before she did, and just as Korac breached her wake.

"Tameka will have my head if you die on my account." Nox's admonishing was halfhearted as they faced the gigantic predator.

Xelan waded beside Nox. "That might be so, but Rayne would never let me hear the end of it if you died without me trying."

The water dipped around them, drawing them into the open maw. Not long now.

C'mon, Korac.

As if Nox had heard Xelan's thoughts, he asked, "Do you ever doubt him?"

Electricity sparked, and the female yowled in agony before Xelan could say, "Never."

The smell of cooked, bloated flesh gagged the brothers, as the whaleshark spouted bones and sinew, dying. The male beasts retreated from the residual electricity repelled by the wetsuits. Despite Korac's obvious defeat of the female, there was no sign of him.

"Where is he?" Xelan lingered in the pod's wake. They'd return, but...

"Korac!" Nox bellowed across the surf, alarming gulls which had come to feast on the whaleshark's remains.

The birds weren't particular about the difference between Icari and animal hide. Xelan batted one off as he shouted, "General, where are—"

"Yo!"

The call came from shore, and Nox cursed before the brothers turned to find Korac scampering onto the beach. He was already halfway out of his wetsuit.

Cocky. Arrogant. Childish—

"He must really want us to spend time together." Nox's words sunk home as they surged for shore.

While the sport was worthy of all this spectacle and grandeur, Xelan would use everything in his power to grant their wishes.

Win or lose.

Nox and Xelan reached the shore in time to see Korac fly into the caves. The older brother mused, "He better enjoy his advantage while it lasts," as he opened his massive wings.

Xelan gave a half-laugh before asking, "How do you plan to break it to Rayne?" When Nox quirked a brow, Xelan continued, "That you ate my dust."

The little brother rocketed from the beach, stirring up a cloud of sand as he jetted for the caves. No doubt, Korac had once held a greater advantage over the brothers because he'd mapped the maze and set all the traps. But in the spirit of today's race, they'd installed some new ones. Not even Xelan knew—

A blast of red light zipped by, narrowly missing the Co-Emperor. Laser turrets. A cousin to the automated nacre defenses in Cinder's old shrine in Enki, these attacked based on movement. They blasted ahead as Korac soared, like his life depended on it. Because it did.

As Nox's shadow cast over Xelan, flying above his little brother, turrets fired at him—The bigger target.

Xelan kicked it into high gear and angled his wings back for more speed. He easily passed Nox within a few seconds, but the blasters were firing into the maze of black stalactites ahead at Korac. The debris formed a cloud of shattered rock and dust. Xelan navigated it with caution to avoid the razor wire—

"Shit!" Nox wasn't far behind.

Antithesis to the competition, Xelan asked, "Are you all right?" His question resounded through the rockcicles, louder than he'd intended.

Nox manifested through the dust cloud, and Xelan smelled the blood oozing from his older brother's pinions. Nox said, "I'll heal."

Korac's voice sounded a respectable distance ahead of them, chagrined. "This shames me to admit, but I can't find my way out—Fuck!" A blaster went off the same distance ahead. Before Xelan could ask, the General assured, "I'm fine. But..."

How would they get out? They were blind in here.

Four more turrets fired, and Xelan narrowly avoided them. Only their glow gave them away. Why did Nox look so intent?

The older brother hovered, peered behind him, and adjusted—

A shot fired. After Nox evaded it, an explosion tore through the cave.

Korac asked, "What the fuck was that?"

Ah.

"You're a genius!" Xelan cried, and Nox's smile in response made the compliment worth it. "Korac, make them fire at each other."

While under fire, both brothers spotted the red horizontal lights from the distant turrets and positioned themselves in the way. The zipping blasts ended in resounding explosions—

More echoed ahead, where Korac waited in the dust cloud.

One explosion.

Three.

When five erupted, something went wrong.

Nox peered at the cave ceiling, while Xelan calculated the integrity of the ancient cavern—

A stalactite fell, and although the brothers avoided it, more followed. Boulders tumbled down, and a terrifying rumble reverberated throughout the plume.

Characteristically composed, Korac said, "Looks like Nox won the wager," just before the cave collapsed.

Before the cameras on the Overseers following Nox, Korac, and Xelan went out, a terrible clamor thundered through the cave. Rock and dust exploded on the horizon, and everything went so still Rayne could hear a ringing in her ears. At the boys' request, the girls had stayed with the Shadow in the stands. Tameka, Sagan, and Rayne waited in the first row to run into the winner's circle. Only now…

Nox.

Rayne's pulse was erratic, and she wasn't sure if it was her or Nox's panic.

"Mommy, what happened to daddy?"

Tameka put an arm around Pax while staring toward the caves. "Don't worry, baby. Mommy's got him."

Without being asked, Sagan opened a conduit to the mountain, and the girls opened their wings.

Please let them be okay.

Rayne glanced up at the screen as Iuo appeared on it to say, "Ladies and gentlemen and those who refer to themselves differently, we're experiencing some technical difficulties. Rest assured, we'll be back online shortly." She looked over at the Lamian King Elect in the stands and gave him a single nod.

Coming to the rescue from the second row, Tumu assured, "We'll watch Pax and Echo."

Lamassau had already sat Pax down and breathed a little fire to distract him.

Tameka nodded at the Primary. "Thank you."

Right as the girls turned to fly in, Pablo called, "Wait!" He and Lynn rushed down the stairs with their chunky, healthy newborn strapped to his mother's chest. The doctor held up a kit. "Always come prepared." He kissed Lynn before stepping through the conduit with Tameka, Sagan, and Rayne.

Ahead of the other girls, Rayne soared over the mountain—No longer a mountain. More like a landslide. What were once solid walls had crumbled away and poured onto the beach below.

"Nox! Xelan?!" As Rayne shouted, the other girls echoed her from all around the formation.

An Overseer flew by, circling the ruin. They didn't need the conduit to hear the gasps and cries from the audience. Rayne could hear it across the distant field.

Pablo called from the ground, "Try not to worry!"

He was right. All three Icari were highly upgraded and beyond resourceful. Their nacres would heal whatever damaged they'd sustained, and they were strong enough to climb out.

So where were they?

Right as Rayne thought it, her heartbeat steadied. Calm.

"Looking for us?"

Rayne spun, seeking the direction of Korac's voice.

Sagan let out a delighted cry toward the field between the mountain and the coliseum. Nox and Korac stood in the tallest cranberry grass, waving.

Where was Xelan—

Oh.

The Co-Emperor wore a goofy grin as he waved from his older brother's back.

"Xelan!" Tameka cried as she flew toward the competitors halfway to the winner circle.

Sagan opened a conduit in Tameka's flight path, and all three girls went through it to appear beside their Icarean lovers. Another conduit opened for Pablo, who stepped through a second after. Given the amount of blood on the competitor's clothes, Rayne figured Pablo was needed.

Tameka got there first. "Are you all right? Why aren't you walking?"

Xelan held onto Nox's back with one hand and staved her with the other. "I'm fine. Sorta. My leg is broken, but it's healing—Tameka."

She'd cupped both hands to her face. Rayne placed a hand on Tameka's shoulder to assure her, while Sagan jumped into Korac's arms.

"Ow. Ow. So worth it. Ow." Korac hugged her and kissed her hair, but something was wrong with his shoulder.

Rayne tried to keep her composure, but she couldn't help scanning them over. Her heart raced with anxiety, and when she met Nox's eyes, it was apparent he knew it. There was so much reassurance and love in them. She asked, "Are you hurt?"

"Only a little."

Sagan clung to Korac, asking, "What happened with the cave-in?"

Pablo held a hand out to the girls. "Give them some room." He went up to Nox. "Do I have permission to check you over?"

Nox nodded, and Pablo went to work.

Korac insisted, "The race isn't over yet."

Xelan barked out a laugh.

Pablo blinked at him.

Still gazing at Rayne, Nox smiled incredulously. It was infectious, and she didn't fight it.

Incredulous, Tameka folded her arms. "Are you serious?"

Sagan hopped off her husband and nudged Tameka. "We still don't have a winner yet."

So Pablo could check Xelan out, Nox set his younger brother down on the cushion of the grass. And, to distract Tameka, Xelan explained, "We directed the turrets to fire on one another and accidentally caused a cave-in."

Rayne closed her eyes.

"And the living legend here…" Korac jabbed a thumb in Nox's direction. "Held up the ceiling. At least long enough for us to get out."

Rayne opened her eyes when Xelan sighed. "But a stalactite snapped my femur in two." He paused to stare up at Nox before saying, "Between Korac digging us out, and Nox carrying me, we made it."

While they told the tale, Pablo scanned Xelan's leg with a portable x-ray. He looked up at Tameka and beamed. "It's all knitted back together, cleanly. Man, that's one impressive hard tissue repair system, Wingmaster."

"Thanks, Doc."

Tameka touched Nox's forearm, and he glanced away from Rayne to look down at the other woman. Heartfelt, Tameka stared into Nox's eyes as she said, "Thank you."

Nox nodded, but there was something significant in his eyes. Rayne felt it in their heart.

"And you, General?" Pablo went over to Korac and scanned his shoulder blade.

The Icarus said, "It's a broken collarbone. I think. It's almost healed." Korac smirked and patted his back pocket where Sagan's bra was stowed. "I still have my good luck charm."

Sagan laughed, Tameka shook her head with a grin, and Rayne winked at Nox. He held up the ribbon wrapped around his hand.

Pablo said, "You're all good to continue the race."

Xelan was still laying on the grass.

Rayne peered at him and giggled. "Why are you still down there?"

He grinned. "I always wanted this for my Cinder." With beautiful glee, Xelan fanned his arms and legs, making a grass angel.

Korac held out his hand. "Let's finish this, your imperial majesty."

Xelan let himself be pulled up with a wink. "I appreciate that you're in a hurry to lose." He nodded at Tameka, Sagan, and Rayne. "Ladies."

Tameka leveled her finger at Xelan. "By all means, but you owe me for this scare, mister."

He winked at her.

It was cute.

Rayne mouthed, "See you soon," to Nox as she went through Sagan's conduit into the ring. The girls waited outside the winner's circle while Pablo went back to his wife and kid.

Over the projection, Iuo said, "Isn't this exciting? The competition will commence with an old-fashioned foot race. There are no three Icari faster than these. The crowd is hushed with suspense as former King Nox, the Imperial General, and our Co-Emperor set their mark."

Rayne watched on the screen as Nox mouthed, "Ready."

Xelan. "Set."

Korac. "Go."

They took off at unbelievable speeds, and Rayne smiled while her heart pounded in her chest.

Gravity dampeners.

There was no way Rayne could love Nox more, as the oldest Icarus had restricted his abilities to enjoy this time with his brothers. She glanced back at the children cheering along the first row. The shy boy, Jet, jumped and punched the air as the three Icari entered the ring.

Only a heartbeat away, and the winner would enter the circle.

Rayne turned back to the action and watched Nox hold back so Xelan could cross the line—

No wait.

Rayne's smile broadened as Xelan restrained himself at the last second, and Korac entered the winner's circle first. It was untraceable—No one could see their speed like Rayne could. Both Icari held back so their General could sweep Sagan into his arms and spin her high above him against Li, setting on Cinder's horizon. The purple of her dress matched the melting colors in the clear sky.

They could barely hear Iuo over the roar of the audience. "Imperial General Korac is our winner! And what a race to end all races. The training course will require some construction before we can plan to reopen, but don't go too far. 'Rayne's Verse: Nox's Release' will premiere on this screen and thousands more throughout Iona Pax. Watch it here alongside the Shadow in thirty minutes."

As Nox and Xelan approached the circle, Rayne let them see in her eyes that she knew the truth. And she loved them for it. Before Tameka could get to him, Rayne hugged Xelan first. She muttered against his shoulder, "You're so awesome, Wingmaster."

Xelan kissed the black roots of Rayne's hair and set her down right at Nox's feet.

It was a blessing if Rayne would ever get one from Xelan, and there was a tear in her eye as she mouthed, "Thank. You."

Xelan nodded before turning and kneeling at Tameka's feet. She wrapped her arms around him, and he squeezed her waist.

"Daddy!"

Tumu and Lamassau led Pax into the ring.

But Rayne couldn't pay attention to it. Not with Nox so close behind her.

"Rayne."

Her name from Nox's lips always reached into the core of her. Rayne peered all the way up at the Icarus she wished she was alone with and gave him her most radiant smile. "I love you." For saving Xelan in a cave-in. For letting Korac win. And for that smile on his face.

Sunset on the coliseum might as well be sunset on the beach with the tide coming in and people settling down for fireworks. The familiar scent of Rayne's content permeated the ring, and she watched Nox breathe deep of it before he cupped her chin and kissed her.

The crowd cheered, and Rayne was becoming accustomed to it.

Iuo's voice interrupted the sweetness of the moment. "C'mon, everyone. The movie's about to begin."

Xelan said, "Fine. But we're only capitulating because we ruined your last premiere."

Iuo grinned. "I wouldn't call that ruined. More like advanced marketing."

Tumu chuckled.

They filed into a parade back to the stands. As the girls and the Icari found their seats, Rayne and Nox sat with the kids. Jack waved from where he and Ross had entertained the children with a replica of Iron Hope—Xelan's train—and Rayne beamed for her brother.

Jack was coming around.

Out of the children from the orphanage, Nox and Rayne had spent the most time with the redheaded girl, Mifa, and the shy boy, Jet. As the couple took their seats, Jet and Mifa came over and piled up some pillows around their feet. They used one of Nox's legs as a pillar to their fort and snuggled up for the film. Rayne smiled at Nox as he watched the children with wonder.

Not now, but one day...

It was enough to make Rayne grin like Xelan.

The movie was a success, including its single explicit sex scene. Sagan had spotted Rayne blushing in her seat, one row down from Xelan, who looked completely miserable for the duration of it.

But not Sagan.

Despite the fact that those were actors depicting the scene in Nox and Rayne's place, Sagan sat forward in her seat and gave the couple two thumbs up. She did this much to Korac's chuckling approval. Sagan found Nox's capacity to blush endearing, and she was proud she could bring it out in him. Tameka thought it was cute, too, though she admitted it begrudgingly.

During the scene, the mingling of lemonade and sandalwood trickled from the highest row.

Matt and Lucy.

Sagan snickered into her hand as Korac rolled his eyes. Xelan sighed, and Nox glanced around curiously. Caedes "humphed," and Pehton whispered, "We left them alone again."

Bones kissed Para's cheek before volunteering. "I'll get them this time, but if they give me 'the look,' someone down here is buying me dinner. And a casket."

The brave Icarean soldier picked his way up the rows through Karter and Chris, around T.A.O., Devis, and Andrius, and up to Puk and Yito. The two loyal members of the Annihilation Squad had blocked off a corner to afford Matt and Lucy some privacy.

Sagan wished Bones all the luck in that confrontation. He'd need it.

Commotion further down the row distracted Sagan. Kyle was cradling Bethany's arm. She was standing and peering up at Bones, Matt, and Lucy with naked curiosity.

Ross whispered into her baby sister's ear, but Sagan couldn't make out what they were saying. She turned to Korac and said, "Maybe you can help?"

Korac was already assessing the situation, but with his mask up so Sagan couldn't gauge his reaction. Bethany still wasn't sitting down, and she looked agitated because Kyle was preventing her from intruding.

Sagan breathed, "Please, Korac."

"Yeah, I'm going." He patted her thigh before standing and walking down the row.

The second Korac stepped into Bethany's sight, she calmed down. Their eye contact was intense as he searched for something in those honey-brown depths. Sagan mourned Bethany's Verse more than most, but she loved that Kyle's baby sister was growing into her own. In part, thanks to Korac, who leaned down and whispered in the young woman's ear.

Meanwhile, in the row above, Matt and Lucy finally emerged disheveled and entirely too satisfied.

Tameka muttered, "We'll need to send them on their next mission. ASAP."

"We're running out of criminals for them to 'investigate.'" Xelan's admission was a cause for celebration but...

What about Matt and Lucy?

Pehton disagreed. "There will always be pedophiles and rapists, no matter how peaceful your empire. The Annihilation Squad needs to go deeper undercover. Caedes and I will work with Korac to find some work for them. Lucas said he has a profiler in mind, but wouldn't tell us who." She nodded toward Lucas and Andrew at the other end of the row.

Tameka and Xelan exchanged curious glances and shrugged. But Sagan looked away.

Down their row, Bethany hugged Korac before giving her brother and sister a squeeze. They all sat down, less flustered, and Korac made his way back to Sagan.

She asked, "What did you say to her?"

"The truth. That if she waited another year, it wouldn't matter what Kyle and Ross thought of her infatuation with Matt and Lucy."

At Pehton's incredulous glance, Korac smirked. "Believe me, *teeny*." Pehton flipped Korac off, but he continued, unscathed. "There are worse interests for Bethany to have, given her history. She's a predator now, and they're doing her a disservice by treating her like a girl who grew up anything close to 'normal.' Matt and Lucy treat Bethany like what she is. Hence her attachment."

Xelan's brows shot up.

Tameka blew the air from her cheeks.

And Pehton stood corrected.

Sagan simply beamed at her husband. Wise and kind and sexy—

"Are you done talking during the movie now?"

They all glanced over at Lamassau, surrounded by discarded popcorn bowls, hot dogs wrappers, and nachos trays. He and Tumu shared the same admonishing expression. Beyond them, Iuo looked crestfallen that his guests of honor weren't more engrossed with his film.

Thoroughly chastised, the small, talkative group faced the screen once more.

Those shenanigans were about an hour ago. The movie was over now. Karter, Para, Chris, and Bones kept Pax and Echo so the imperial couples could celebrate tonight.

Sagan was standing in Thailea's forest, holding a conduit open for Rayne and Nox to say goodnight to Mifa, Jet, and the other ten children. Rayne let Mifa finish braiding her ethereal hair, while Nox said goodnight to Jet. There was an undeniable warmth to the gigantic Icarus as he shook the little boy's hand. It made Sagan wonder if Rayne would consider children soon—

"Amos, get the idea out of your head." Korac knew her so well.

They stood in the conduit together, watching the happy moment. Sagan said, "You *hope* you know what I'm thinking."

Korac's smirk and half-chuckle said it all. "A future of play dates with Echo, Tameka's Pax and unnamed daughter, Lynn's Mateo, and whatever frightfully strong and massive spawn births from Rayne."

Right on the money. However, there was no reason to feed Korac's ego. Sagan said, "Actually, I was thinking since you and I can't conceive without killing me, Nox could donate his sperm so I can continue the Seamswalker line."

Sagan loved it when Korac gaped, mouth open and all. She tipped his lips closed with a finger under his chin. "I'm just kidding. You and I would have an incubated baby before I'd sleep with Nox."

"Praise Elden for that. Don't you know what those jokes do to my heart?" Korac asked while rubbing his temples. "The images…"

The Icarus in question walked through the conduit, holding Rayne's hand. "Thank you, Sagan." Nox's rich baritone had become a comforting sound to her. Familiar and welcome.

Sagan patted him on the chest, ignoring his instinctive flinch. "No problem, big guy. See you two tomorrow?" She didn't add *'after Nox's prescribed punishment.'* It would kill the mood.

Rayne beamed. "We'll be there now that we're both invited. Congratulations again, Korac."

Nox and Korac clasped hands and bumped shoulders in an informal hug, while Rayne gripped Sagan tight with a sweet kiss on the cheek. As Sagan and Korac went through the conduit to their chalet, she noticed how Rayne looked up at Nox with a sparkle in her eyes.

It was joy, and Sagan couldn't be happier for them. For everyone.

Korac went straight for the shower, muttering about whaleshark sperm, much to Sagan's giggling gratitude. She snickered her way into a slinky nightie as a surprise for her victor. Xelan and Nox had totally let Korac win, but she was *not* about to spoil it for her husband. After waiting several millennia for the brothers to reconcile, Korac had earned this triumph.

He called from the steamy shower, "Amos, are you still cackling out there?"

"Yes." There was no sense in denying it. Sagan had mused half the evening away because of Korac's silent discomfort over the state of his hair. She asked, "Did you get all the guts out?"

More muttering ensued.

As did more snickering.

It was only after another ten minutes had passed in silence that Sagan became concerned. She wandered into the bathroom made of all black slate surfaces with a white marble tub sunk in the middle. The shower encompassed the entire western wall, no glass to fog up. Just Korac watching the water pour down the drain.

Sagan didn't need to ask. She knew what was on her husband's mind. Instead, she walked under the spray, soaking the silk to her skin and blond hair to her face. Without asking permission, Sagan wrapped her arms around Korac from behind and pressed her face to his back, inhaling the frosty pine scent of him. The smell matched the view from all the glass in their bathroom.

Korac let out a sigh which sagged the muscles on his bones until only Sagan held him upright.

She assured, "Andrew and Lucas know what they're doing."

"I hope you're right, amos. I hope you're right."

The movie was so much fun. Even the sex scene, which luo filmed as tastefully as Andrew and Lucas' personal movie. Chef's kiss.

Now onto less fun things.

Andrew asked, "Are you sure you want to go through with this?"

He and Lucas were standing in the memory research lab, facing the special case with Razor's nacre inside. Kyle and Silence waited respectfully to the side as the other couple talked it out.

Lucas stared at the nacre with nothing readable in his expression. The longer they'd gone since he'd outed himself as Aegis, the more he looked the part. No perception filter—All-white features. The brocade three-piece wasn't exactly uncharacteristic of him, but the way he moved in it was. Lucas glided, almost floated in a graceful ballet of gestures and movements which mesmerized Andrew—

Literally hypnotized him.

It was beautiful, awesome, and, if Andrew was less in love with the man, a touch frightening. Matt had told Andrew once about how Razor had punched a guy at the Night Rayne concert, and the man had exploded on contact. That kind of power was unimaginable. Not even Rayne was capable of it.

"You're staring, lover."

Caught, Andrew confessed, "I was only admiring you."

The goofy grin which spread across Lucas' lips was only for Andrew. The last Aegis said, "Your admiration is priceless to me." He kept his eyes on the nacre as the smile faded. "Thank you for being here. Thank you, all." He gestured at Kyle and Silence.

Kyle said, "Let me know when you're ready. The sooner we get this over with, the sooner we can all go to bed. If you know what I mean?"

Andrew shook his head incredulously, but Lucas was smiling again.

Silence kissed Kyle's cheek before approaching Lucas' side. He peered up at her as she said, "Three Two Four will listen, and I think he'll agree. It won't be easy—Not at first. But you are anything if not persistent, old friend."

Like Andrew, Lucas was shorter than Silence, so he had to stand on tiptoe to kiss her forehead as he whispered, "Have I mentioned how happy I am that I awakened you?"

"If I haven't already said it, thank you." Silence beamed at him with her thousand-watt smile.

Between that and Andrew taking Lucas' hand, the last Aegis took a shaky breath. Ready. "Let's do this."

Kyle opened the way into Razor's memory bank, and Andrew stood in a monochromatic display of the Pain Curator's life. Music staffs lined the walls, white on black, with a faint glow from the lines.

Memoryscapes had always fascinated Andrew, and Razor's was no exception. They were all dressed in pinstripe suits. Razor even did their hair. The men in slicked-back ponytails beneath gangster fedoras. Silence's hair was in a pencil bun, with the blue stripe left out and twisted to the side. Judging by the smile on her face, she was rather fond of it.

Lucas, however, was dressed in a black waistcoat, black button-down, and black slacks. He looked like a pallbearer at an expensive funeral. There was a rose in his breast pocket, and it was yellow, like Aegis blood. The stars of his pupils shifted places as he peered around the room before settling on Andrew.

The younger man tried to smile and reassure his alien lover, but this wasn't a straightforward task ahead of them. So he took Lucas' hand and squeezed before mouthing, "Say. Something."

Kyle nodded encouragingly, and Silence patted Lucas' shoulder.

"Three Two Four, I come to you with an offer I hope you'll consider taking."

The four guests in Razor's memoryscape glanced amongst themselves, waiting for a sign from a deranged sociopath. Reformed, deranged sociopath? Was anyone clear yet on Razor's denomination?

When no response came, Kyle said. "Razor, Xelan doesn't know we're here. We thought you'd might like to surprise your old friend if you agree to our terms."

The multiple scenes on all six walls shifted into one, and Andrew patted Lucas so he would notice. It was black and white, but one feature was in color. Yellow blood. It oozed out of Razor's nail beds as his brothers tied him down and ripped his fingernails out.

Lucas swallowed audibly before saying, "I wasn't there. I was already on my journey to repair the Probability Matrix."

Text appeared in black script over the white images.

YOU WERE NOT THERE TO STOP IT, EITHER.

Andrew hated the shame on Lucas' face. It was the same expression in Lucas' memory when he'd passed Razor by on Ishkur's bridge. All the Aegis had treated Razor like a monster long before he came to be one—Nature versus nurture, and all that.

While Andrew smoothed a hand in a circle on Lucas' back, Kyle tried a different approach. "We want to make a deal with you, Pain Curator. A man like you enjoys making deals. Especially when you come out better for it in the end, which I have no doubt you will."

The images disappeared, and the screens returned to a black background with white musical staffs. On the lines, words appeared.

I LIKE YOU, MR. ROBERTS. STATE YOUR CASE.

From Sagan, Matt, and Pehton's stories, Andrew knew Razor liking someone was more a curse than a blessing. And Kyle paled slightly at the commentary.

Silence didn't. She stepped forward in her slitted pencil skirt and touched the wall, curiosity plain on her face.

Andrew and Kyle jumped back when Razor appeared on the screen, twin crescent pupils in his eyes like an alien reptile. Of course, his suit was white with black pinstripes, double-breasted, and it looked immaculate, accompanied by a top hat and cane.

DARLING, I HAVE *always* WANTED TO MAKE YOUR ACQUAINTANCE.

Silence grinned. "Listen to their offer, and you may have the chance."

Kyle slipped an arm possessively around her waist, deepening her smile.

Razor smirked and quirked a curious brow.

His flirtatious expression flattened as Lucas made the proposal. "I found Celindria's lab here in this Probability, and in it, she'd stored certain samples. You, obviously. But Triss also…"

On the screen, Razor didn't seem remotely surprised. Almost as if he already knew Celindria had kept archives of him and others from the Emporium.

Lucas continued, "The Shadow are in need of a mind who understands those predators living beneath society, not only with appetites for vice, but possessing the skillset to market it for others. If you profile for us and adhere to the strict rehabilitation program, we'll resurrect Triss and provide you with a home to luxuriate in each other's arms for the rest of your days—Without harming others."

Andrew blew the air from his cheeks, ignoring the urge to whistle. This was an impressive offer—A gambit to satisfy all their wrongs.

Razor *was* a wrong.

The look on Kyle's face after he'd spent a day perusing Razor's memory—Xelan's insistence there was some good in the man—And Sagan's controversial relationship with the Pain Curator all supported the theory he was someone worthy of rehabilitation.

Every time Andrew heard the story of Three Two Four, the cautionary tale of a young man born different from his family, Andrew couldn't help but see a bit of himself in it. Sure, bisexuality wasn't the same as a man destined to destroy his own race, but othering was othering.

The four waited expectantly for Razor's reply. So far, he'd seemed non-responsive, but that was the Aegis way. Even Lucas sometimes formed his more human expressions for Andrew's benefit, and Andrew knew it.

Even though Razor kept his face neutral, text appeared on the wall.

WHAT OF ECHO?

Andrew almost cringed. This was the question they'd hoped to avoid. It was uncomfortable, and that was apparent on Kyle's and Silence's faces. Triss had *died* to bring Echo into this world. It stood to reason she'd insist on taking her daughter back as part of this arrangement.

Lucas' voice was matter of fact. "I think you know the answer."

Good. This wasn't even up for discussion. Andrew trusted Lucas not to negotiate visitation or parental rights over Korac and Sagan's baby girl. Beside Andrew, Kyle's body gave one gigantic sigh of relief, while Silence watched on, unsurprised.

The question disappeared from the screen, replaced by another.

AND MY BONES?

The Aegis had formed nacres from their bones, and it was a unique material no resurrection casket could replicate. There was only one place in the galaxy with an abundance of the material.

Andrew glanced over at Lucas, who answered, "I will fetch the ore from Thailea myself. There are many regrets between us, and I won't let providing you an inferior form count among them. You will be Aegis again."

Wow.

Andrew's brows shot up and everything. Kyle shifted uncomfortably.

Silence said, "Three Two Four, I was wronged for most of my conscious existence. I know some of your sorrow. Come to the Shadow, leaving as many burdens in your past as you can. Try to open yourself to any happiness that was ever denied you, or you will only prolong your suffering unnecessarily."

MY DEAR, FROM ANYONE ELSE, THOSE WORDS WOULD CARRY LITTLE WEIGHT. FROM YOU, THEY COULD PULL DOWN THE SUN. AS FOR THE GOLDEN CHILD, I SENSE GUILT IN YOU. THE SHADOW SEEKS ABSOLUTION FOR THE RIGHTEOUS END OF MY PITIABLE EXISTENCE WITHOUT FULLY UNDERSTANDING IT. LIVE MY LIFE, EXPOSE MY SINS, AND THEN MAKE THE OFFER AGAIN. TRISS, TOO. LET US COME TO YOUR 'REHABILITATION PROGRAM' NOT AS STRANGERS, BUT AS WELCOME GUESTS OF HONOR. MAKE NO MISTAKE, WE WILL MAKE THE MOST OF IT.

Andrew tasted the ghost of an intention in the words and discerned its depths.

Ambition.

That was all Andrew gleaned. Raw, unsaturated purpose. But with no hint as to Razor's aim, how could Andrew interpret it fairly? And did it matter? Kyle's rehabilitation program would eliminate any of Razor's ill intentions, and this was why Andrew wouldn't say anything. The last thing he wanted was to come between Lucas' reconciliation with his younger brother.

Kyle stepped up next. "I've offered the deep dive into your life to Xelan. He turned it down, citing trust and honor and all that shit. He thinks you'll reform on your own merit, *despite* your history. Now will you disappoint someone who considers you a friend or will you commit to this, your only chance to prove Sagan and T.A.O. saw something in you once worth redeeming?"

Nice evocation of the girls' trust. If Razor wasn't watching them, Andrew would probably bump Kyle's fist.

The long pause stretched, leaving the four of them staring into the Pain Curator's unfathomable eyes.

Lucas looked uncertain how to proceed until Silence nudged him. He looked at her, and she smiled. Although the transaction was wordless, Lucas got the message and stepped up to Razor's image on the wall. He said, "I want to make amends to the brother I couldn't save, no matter all the ways I tried. Despite the horrors you'd subjected Korac to, he agrees. There is a path for you, Three Two Four. Give the Shadow—Give *me* a chance to save you. One last time."

Andrew held his breath, Kyle crossed his fingers, and Silence placed a supportive hand on Lucas' back.

What would Razor choose?

The Pain Curator answered with a congenial smile.

Kyle didn't like this. Especially not after Razor had flirted with Silence. It was enough to make Kyle's skin crawl. However, the upside was subjecting Razor—*the* Pain Curator—to all his worst crimes in the secured facilities under Story Taker's command.

Finally.

Justice for Bethany.

Kyle's baby sister was so adamant about hunting baddies with the Annihilation Squad she might even volunteer her experiences for Razor to endure. And wouldn't that be poetic?

After the bastard gave what could only mean 'yes' as an answer, Kyle brought the crew back into the research lab.

Lucas hummed with anxious energy. "I'll need to leave for Thailea and collect the ore tonight."

Andrew suffered momentary disappointment, but he sucked it up like a champ. "What do you need from me?"

Not gonna lie. Kyle was straight, but he saw the appeal whenever Lucas smiled. The handsome S.O.B. took Andrew by the face and kissed him before gripping Andrew tight. Mid-hug, Lucas said, "Thank you." He peered over at Kyle and Silence, saying, "Thank you, all."

Kyle held up a hand. "Hold it, Mr. Imperial Tailor. This won't be a walk in the park. I agreed to surprise Xelan, but resurrecting Razor and Triss should take some serious consideration."

Silence asked, "What are you suggesting?"

"The rehab facility is guarded with nacre-deterring shields. If you restore Razor with an Aegis body, those shields won't mean shit. So how do we confine him?"

Silence hooked her arm around Kyle's elbow and beamed at him. "I'm sure you'll find a way. You're *very* creative." The look she gave him had nothing to do with rehab security.

A silly smile slapped itself on Kyle's face as he gazed into her steely eyes. Only Andrew's snickering snapped him out of it.

"Hey. You're trying to manipulate me." There was no hurt in Kyle's voice because... "You're right. I'll think of something." He turned to Lucas. "Go get your ore. Andrew, we'll need clothes for Razor. I won't have him walking around here buck naked scaring the locals. Silence, you know what to do."

Andrew kissed Lucas before running out of the lab, presumably to Lucas' two bedroom-sized closet in the zeppelin.

The soon to be second to last Aegis called, "T.A.O.?"

Kyle didn't startle when the first Seamswalker appeared. T.A.O. was always listening. With her eyes locked into violet Atramentous, the elven woman beamed at Lucas. "My friend?"

He took her by the shoulders, smiling as he said, "Yes. Would you like to help me free him?"

One very emphatic nod later, and those two were off to Thailea.

Silence retrieved Razor's nacre from its case and held his entire existence in her palm. She sensed Kyle staring and peered at him.

"I trust you to contain him while I'm working." Kyle meant it.

True to her namesake, Silence bowed with her head, wordlessly accepting her assignment. Before Kyle did something ridiculous like kiss her—that would certainly lead to more—he left the lab. Memory research was the domain of him and his sisters, so Xelan had connected it to the rehab facility via a terminal of vital conduits.

Fancy prison.

Karma in a nacre citadel.

Call it what you liked. This was the most secured institution outside of the imperial stronghold. And it was Kyle's sandbox. He'd designed every facet of it to reintegrate these offenders back into society, but only after Kyle was finished with them.

Nacre-deterring shields kept nacre-bearers inside, but Razor was an Aegis. No nacre to deter. So how…

Shit.

Kyle hated asking this question, but it helped in situations like this.

What would Xelan do?

Wingmaster would probably trust Razor on his own merit. The honor system.

Fuck that.

Gripping his hair, Kyle walked through a conduit into the facility's foyer. All diorite and glass, matte black iron rails and decor—The usual modern shit the Icari liked so much. He took the glass Aegis lift to the twentieth floor and entered his office with a DNA scan.

Kyle wasn't much of a decorator, so Silence had kitted the place out for him. Naturally, both couches would easily fit them together. The desk was likewise massive and empty, ready to go at a moment's notice. The glass wall behind the desk looked out onto what Kyle referred to as 'the floor.' It was where the pods stretched out and out, across an expanse vast enough to play professional football. From here, Kyle watched Nox soften up the reformists. And soon Razor among them.

With a wave of Kyle's hand, an image projected in the center of his office. It was a three-dimensional, interactive rendering of the facility. Where would he put Razor, and how could he confine him there?

At least with the Probability Matrix closed, the bastard couldn't summon Inanis. No Probabilities; no soldiers to recruit. It was enough to make Kyle smirk. Each apartment contained basic needs: bedroom, bathroom, kitchen, recreational space, and one window looking out onto the ocean. Everything was fortified with nacre-deterring technology.

Originally, Kyle had asked for nacre glass, but there were two problems with that. One, there wasn't enough of the stuff in the galaxy with all the Aegis being dead. And two, Smith had encased the Aegis tombs in gold to prevent raiding. It was a nice touch. One of which Lucas obviously knew how to bypass, but it all left Kyle with fewer options than he'd like for his prison's construction.

Maybe the answer wasn't in the prison.

Maybe the answer was in the nacre itself.

Yeah.

Kyle had an idea.

Tameka held up her official imperial draft and preened. She was occupying Xelan's corner-desk in the study while he cleaned up for the night. Finally relaxing with Celindria gone, Aria and Torch went out on the town. "Looking for souls to taste," as they'd put it. As Xelan's half-brother and sister, Tameka loved them. As soldiers for Iona Pax, she cherished them. But as social beings, she worried about their ability to adapt.

The same could be said for Andrius and Devis. They went with Aria and Torch to explore the nightlife Ishkur offered, but both ancient Progeny brothers suffered from PTSD, and 'introvert' didn't cover it. She hoped among the four of them, they would have some fun.

With those four, Tumu, Lamassau, and Pax out for the evening, the stronghold felt empty and a little sad. Tameka missed the chaos. While reading over the document of her very own, she stretched her arms high and leaned to the side—

"That is a gorgeous sight to walk in on."

Xelan.

With a grin, Tameka turned to face her husband. He was walking into the study, ruffling his hair dry with a towel. Unfortunately, like Tameka, he wasn't naked. She was still wearing her cropped top and slacks from the races. He was in some pajama bottoms, hanging off the bones of his hips in just the most enticing way—

"My eyes are up here, beautiful." Xelan's grin was entirely too self-satisfied, yet it suited him.

Which reminded Tameka…

Preening once again, she took her ultra-important draft in hand and met him halfway. "I'm making an imperial decree. Would you care to review it before I enact it, starting tomorrow?"

Xelan's eyes widened slightly, but the playfulness stayed in his smile as he took the page from her. "Gold ink. Nice touch."

"Lucas inspired me," Tameka said it on a sigh as she fell gracefully on a plush couch.

With rapt attention, respectfully serious, Xelan scanned over the decree. Upon finishing, he met Tameka's eyes, and the playfulness lessened sadly. He said, "A Transparency Decree… Tameka, I'm sorry you've even felt the need to write this."

None of that.

Tameka stood and wrapped her arms around him. "Shh… This isn't only about you. It's Rayne and Lucas and so many others. I'm sure F8 and Kombuchi also have their secrets. But now, they have to forfeit them to the judgment of the King Elect council. From there, we can all make an informed vote and determine if it's necessary to share the information with the public. You know? Like Tumu—the Tritan King Elect—was half-Aegis. Or that Rayne was alive and wanted to remain in hiding so she could boink your brother."

Xelan winced, but at Tameka's teasing nudge, he managed a strained smile. "I understand, and I think it's an excellent idea." He pulled her against his side and kissed her curls.

"Good. Now, if we're done talking about politics, I have a pantsuit to strip out of. Maybe with music. Maybe with you sitting in a chair, enjoying the show—"

Xelan pulled over the nearest plain chair from a conference table, sat in it, and gazed up at Tameka with alluring intensity.

Damn

She was so lucky—

"Father?"

Tameka also loved T.A.O. and appreciated that at least this time, she'd waited outside the study instead of barging in. What was with Seamswalkers and privacy?

Xelan held up a finger, saying, "Hold that thought," as he went to the doorway.

Tameka eavesdropped from the middle of the study, overhearing things like, "Fate won't wait any longer for its inheritor," and, "He returns."

The last one sent a chill down Tameka's spine. Especially as Xelan looked over his shoulder at Tameka with an apologetic smile. He asked, "Will you come with us?"

"Of course." Tameka didn't hesitate, and there was no disappointment. They'd get to the dance later.

She crossed the study, saying, "I can't let you go off on some mysterious errand alone."

T.A.O. beamed—truly radiant with joy—as she opened a conduit to what looked like a lab in Ishkur's bridge. She took Xelan's hand, who took Tameka's, and they stepped through.

Into Kyle's lab.

Tameka's blood pressure plummeted as her brain puzzled together what her heart hoped wasn't true.

Razor stood three inches taller than his brother. Tameka could tell because the ill-fitting suit, which was tailored perfectly for Lucas, couldn't stretch to cover the Pain Curator's wrists and ankles. Judging by the slight strain around his eyes, he knew and disparaged this. Also...

Razor was fucking alive.

His freaky Aegis eyes flicked to Tameka's as if he'd heard the exclamation in her thoughts. There was the slightest, faintest twitch to the corner of his lips—resisting the urge to smirk—before he devoured Xelan's shirtless situation with hunger blatant in his eyes. But all the while, Tameka knew he kept his peripheral on her, gauging her reaction.

Bastard.

Xelan—sweet, wonderful, naïve Xelan—grinned and crossed the room to rope Razor into an extremely warm hug. "I'm so glad you let someone talk some sense into you."

Razor was looking over Xelan's shoulder at Tameka as he smoothed a circle on Xelan's naked back. All with a slight lift to the corner of his mouth.

Only when Kyle put his hand on Tameka's shoulder did she even realize he, Silence, and Andrew were in the lab. It startled her, and Razor suppressed what she was sure was a chuckle, masking it as clearing his throat from overwhelming emotion. The Pain Curator muttered to Xelan. "One and Story Taker fattened up your skinny offer until I couldn't refuse. I'm officially under the employ of the Concerted

Empire of Iona Pax as a criminal profiler. It is my *pleasure* to serve you."

Razor. Did. Not. Just. Say. That.

Did he just fucking wink at Tameka?!

T.A.O. Seamswalked between Tameka and Razor. The fae woman said, "Merriment from taunts. Do not feed what should remain starved."

Perspective. As composure washed over Tameka, she took T.A.O.'s hand. "Thank you."

"Is something wrong?" Xelan sounded so oblivious. It was cute and infuriating.

Damn Razor for getting under Tameka's skin. "Everything's fine, amos." She shot daggers at Razor's gleeful stare before addressing Lucas, Andrew, Kyle, and Silence. "So you four took it upon yourselves to resurrect the Pain Curator. I don't even have to ask if you have a plan in mind. I trust you. But please… Are there any other secrets I should know about?"

Silence peered at Kyle, who looked over at Andrew, who glanced at Lucas. Each of them shared the same expression of kids confessing to breaking something. It raised goosebumps on Tameka's skin as the question rang in the air until…

"I can think of one other thing."

At the sound of Triss' dusky voice, Tameka shut her eyes and prayed the nightmare would go away.

Speaking of transparency…

XXII   SMOKE

IT TOOK ALL NIGHT FOR KYLE TO CALM TAMEKA DOWN. Even though she'd put up a good front to maintain some composure in Xelan's presence, especially with Razor *and* Triss flaunting their history with Xelan, Kyle could see the frustration mounting. They convinced Tameka to listen about the nacre restraints.

No, Razor didn't have a nacre, but in order to infuse his consciousness into his new body, they had to disseminate his temporary nacre into his bones. And everything that was programmed into it went along for the ride.

Location-based restraints. Volition protocols, so he'd respond to Shadow commands. The works.

Triss was still only a Lyrik, so the nacre-deterring shields would work fine to detain her.

After Tameka was satisfied, she'd hauled Xelan's oblivious ass back to the stronghold. All the while letting everyone in the room know it was so they could have extensive, mind-blowing sex.

Razor tipped his top hat at Tameka as she left, and everyone in that lab but Xelan knew it meant 'challenge accepted.' Maybe the suit was too tight in the crotch and twisted the Pain Curator's panties because it was downright stupid to piss Fury off.

Anyway, that's how Kyle found himself giving Andrew, Lucas, Razor, and Triss a tour of the rehab facilities. "There's twenty-two gyms, sixteen pools, fourteen movie theaters stocked with all the fixings. Not to mention all the apartments are modifiable to suit your personality. We don't care what you wear, and Lucas can get you some clothes that fit." Kyle stopped outside of the apartment and faced his party. "The point is, we want you comfortable and asserting your personality. Individual identity matters in here."

Triss, red feathers and yellow eyes, peered at Kyle with something alien in her expression. It'd been on her face since they'd resurrected her. Kyle wasn't sure what it was or if she was hiding her thoughts, but it was utterly unnerving.

Razor, on the other hand, looked pleased and amicable.

Kyle didn't like it.

Lucas opened the door to the first apartment. It wasn't a monk's penitent cell. Everything was top of the line and meant to meet all their reformist's needs. They filed inside, with Razor and Triss leading the way. The former checked everything—the temperature of the water from the faucets, the selection of foods in the pantry, even the thread-count of the sheets. No doubt none of it lived up to Razor's standards, but it was certainly better than he deserved.

As if Razor had heard Kyle's thoughts, he turned and gave an appreciative smile. "Thank you, Mr. Roberts."

"Story Taker, if you don't mind." Kyle hated the title, but some formality seemed necessary here.

All Razor did was open his arms, and Triss went into them like a magnet to iron. At least he held her with adoration naked in his bizarre eyes and not like she was a possession.

Silence taught Kyle if there was love, then there was hope. Yeah, yeah. That was some huggy Shadow shit, but the evidence was hard to refute. Looking over at Andrew and Lucas as living examples cemented the belief in Kyle.

He *would* reform Razor and Triss.

Kyle gestured toward the eastern wall, saying, "So the apartment next door is for Triss, but I suppose you two won't be needing it."

They shook their heads simultaneously without looking away from Kyle.

"Didn't think so."

Lucas said, "I'll bring some clothes for you both tomorrow."

Triss, suited in her Lyriki armor, didn't seem to mind, but Razor beamed with gratitude while displaying the shortness of his sleeves.

Silence grinned, and it seemed to melt Razor as much as it melted Kyle. To the couple who'd coined vice, Silence said, "Behave."

Triss said her first words in an hour. "Yes, Mother."

Beside Kyle, Andrew did that uncomfortable shift thing again. Like he was getting some readings off the Pain Curator and his acolyte, but wasn't sharing.

Later.

Kyle wanted to go home, shower with Silence, and get some sleep before another big Shadow day—In like three hours. As if on cue, T.A.O. flitted into the room. There was something to be said about the way Razor's demeanor changed in her presence. All the threat breathed out of him, and everything about him softened like room temperature butter.

"We are beyond midnight. The light comes soon." T.A.O. opened a conduit and held out her hand. To

Razor, she said, "Tomorrow, you'll meet your soul, and it harbors a surprise."

Razor dipped his head to her. "Thank you." He faced Lucas. "And you, One. I will not forget this."

Kyle warned, "Oh, you might change your mind tomorrow. Nox will be here to fetch you in the morning for the first experience."

The Pain Curator's eyes widened a little, and Triss answered for him, "We are ready to accept your price." *For now* lingered in the air.

Yup.

This was a bad idea.

Silence and Kyle spent a wonderful three hours overly involved with each other. 'Worship' didn't cover it. They built the temple and burned it down with the heat between them.

It was forced to end entirely too soon.

"I'll meet you there once I finish with Nox's treatment and get Razor and Triss started with theirs." Kyle hated the way Silence's face fell when he mentioned Nox's punishment. He smoothed aside the blue streak of her hair, dampened from their exertions, and kissed her forehead. "There was a time, not even a year ago, when I would've enjoyed this position of power. Derived sadistic satisfaction from it—" Kyle shook his head, discarding the notion. "You make me a better person because you're here to remind me no matter how I feel about any of these people, someone out there cares for how they're treated. So I should, too. I hope you understand—"

Silence sat up and kissed Kyle, taking his breath away with his words.

It was a nice parting, especially when he knew they'd meet up in a few hours. Until then, Kyle traversed the labyrinth of conduits, reaching his office in the rehab facility. Hmm... Nox was already at work, filing reformists into the pods. Obviously, the invitation to today's private Progeny event had put some perk in Nox's step.

Kyle sighed. What the hell was going on around here? First, he helped bring back Razor, and next he was gonna hang out with Nox this afternoon.

At least Rayne was finally happy.

Over the earpiece, Kyle ordered, "Nox, we have new guests of honor. Direct rooms three-two-four and three-two-three into their corresponding pods. And Nox?"

"Yes?"

Kyle couldn't help but smirk. "You're in for a surprise. Over and out."

Fuck it. Maybe there was a sadistic streak in Kyle. He pulled up the security footage of Razor and Triss' hallway and watched Nox knock on their door. When the door opened and the hefty Icarus recoiled, Kyle chuckled. Yeah. He was an asshole, but this was entertainment even Iuo couldn't engineer.

Nox and Razor faced one another, each with naked disdain on their faces. Lucas had been by, judging by the suit tailored perfectly to the Pain Curator's boxer frame. It would certainly set him apart from the general population. Which in and of itself was a curiosity. How would the other reformists respond to Razor and Triss' resurrection?

Kyle would spin it as another success story for the program. That sounded nice. The Pain Curator wasn't the only one with marketing skills.

Without a word or any fuss, Razor and Triss followed Nox to the heart of the facility. He led them to their pods and strapped them in. This, Kyle could see from the glass view of his office. Never had he seen two people so composed strapped in those pods. He looked forward to their reactions after half a day of treatment.

Over the earpiece, Kyle said, "Good work, Nox." Like praising a puppy for shitting outside. "Are you ready for your experience?"

"Yes."

One-word answers.

Kyle liked it that way.

He met the massive roadblock of a man at his designated pod in Kyle's office. Now, this was where Kyle got professional. He didn't taunt or agitate Nox. Kyle simply strapped him in and turned on the machine.

Nox always screamed. Such was the intensity of his karma. Today was a medley of kids who'd lost their families to Invasion Day. Not all pain was physical. The mental anguish and grief of thousands should send the man responsible shrieking in misery.

Two hours later, Kyle ended the treatment. Tears had scalded Nox's face bright blue. He didn't wipe them away—Didn't move at all. He laid in the pod, blinking in torment.

It was none of Kyle's business, but Xelan had once mentioned Nox and Rayne shared a heartbeat. Kyle sometimes wondered what these treatments were like for her. She must always know when they've ended, because Nox always meditated after. Reflection went into the depths of eyes, reaching his soul or whatever.

Kyle left Nox to recover and went over to the glass. He zeroed-in on Razor and Triss—

"Son of a bitch..."

They were the only people not screaming. At most, they looked uneasy.

Fucking sociopaths.

Kyle would work on their experiences later, as there was a plethora of them to sample. He had more important things to attend to. "C'mon, Nox. If you take any longer, we'll be late, and you don't want to keep Rayne waiting."

As Nox climbed out of the pod, Kyle called up Sagan. "Yo, we're ready."

The Seamswalker arrived and...

What was with these women and their big hearts?

Sagan stared at Nox with wide, sad eyes and cupped a hand over her mouth. She ignored Nox's staving gesture and hugged the bastard. Kyle would definitely use the word 'awkward' with Nox. Stiffly, he patted Sagan on the back.

Against Nox's broadside of a barn chest, Sagan asked, "Are you okay?" She glared at Kyle.

"I'm fine. Please, let's enjoy the day."

That summarized how Nox got through this, and Kyle had to commend him for it. Still, he rolled his eyes and walked through Sagan's open conduit.

And into paradise.

The gorge in Yosemite park, all the Progeny and their mates, and good food.

What more could Kyle ask for?

Silence walked up to him with a plate full of his favorite food. In a string bikini.

What, indeed?

<hr>

Andrew's spicy fried chicken was *not* better than sex. But it was pretty damned close. As Lucas devoured his fourth piece of dark meat, Andrew could assume his lover agreed. "Union with me."

Lucas stopped before taking his next bite and blinked at Andrew. It was one of the few times he could tell he'd caught Lucas completely off guard. It was worthy of a smile.

Andrew said, "I mean it. I want to spend the rest of Eternity with you, and since you've spent most of yours seeing to the happiness of others, it's about damned time someone took care of you for a change."

On this gorgeous beach, beside all this sparkling water, under the clearest blue sky, Lucas said, "Yes."

"It's about time."

Sweet, lovable Sagan.

Andrew barked out a laugh as she plopped down on the blanket beside them. She said, "I thought I would have to drop you two on some isolated planet or something to get you to finally ask."

Lucas shook his head incredulously and kissed the Seamswalker on the cheek. He admonished, "You have no sense of timing, my darling."

Rayne joined in. "We've no sense of timing? I just rejoined the Shadow, and I've been waiting on the edge of my seat for this moment."

Ross gestured at Sagan and Rayne. "Shoo, you two. You're ruining it." To Andrew and Lucas, she said, "Please proceed." Before resuming her position as an eavesdropping spectator among the other picnicking snoops.

In fact, everyone's eyes were on Andrew and Lucas. Even Korac glanced over from his bite of Tameka's sweet potato mash.

The gorge was Tameka, Sagan, Rayne, Kyle, and Andrew's secret place, and they were happy to share it with their siblings and lovers. The Progeny and their partners were dispersed across blankets scattered with food at the edge of the water. Devis, T.A.O., Andrius, Aria, and Torch had packed supplies for games. Ross, Jack, and Bethany sat beside Rayne and Nox. Kyle and Silence were right there with Andrew and Lucas. Pax, Tameka, and Xelan sat closest to the coolers, dispensing the food. Sagan and Korac tended the bonfire. They were one big, happy family.

Except...

"Where's Echo?" Andrew was happy to change the subject.

As if Lucas sensed it, he scooted closer to Andrew and tucked the younger man against his side. Comfort.

Sagan glanced at Korac, who answered, "Karter asked for a little extra time, and since you were successful in reviving the black sheep of the family,

Sagan and I will drop by to donate our experiences. Isn't that right, Story Taker?"

Kyle winced at the name. "I think your contributions will do the trick."

Nox confessed, "Out of the thousands we're rehabilitating, I've never known someone not to scream."

Rayne patted Nox on the knee. "I think it was the right thing to bring Razor back. Before he sacrificed himself to save all of you, he asked to save Nox, too. Not to mention, his dossier was instrumental in tracking down the last of Imminent."

A quiet fell over the group as they considered the gravity of the situation. When resurrection was possible, what were the limitations of redemption? On the other hand, the whisper of Razor's intentions disturbed Andrew. Was ambition simply in Razor's nature? Then maybe his intentions weren't cause for alarm.

"Hey! It's Miy and Twenty-One!" Xelan interrupted the silence with so much enthusiastic joy that it immediately infected Andrew. Xelan spoke into his palm device. "Just let me tweak it a bit and..."

Miy and Twenty-One appeared in his palm.

Twenty-One waved to the group. "Hello. We've successfully arrived at the coordinates Tumu provided, and we've discovered something worth sharing."

Miy was smiling, and that was cause for alarm. "Are you ready for this?"

Everyone gathered around, and Xelan said, "Go ahead."

Twenty-One adjusted the projection to include their background and...

Holy.

Shit.

The glass ship was in view, but beyond it were towering spires, hovering crafts, and hundreds of Tritans lined up for the shot.

Male *and* female.

Xelan asked into the device, "Tumu, are you getting this?"

Tuned into the call, the old Primary choked before clearing his throat to say, "Yeah. Lam and I can see it."

Miy held up a finger as she walked backward toward a Tritan with robes more elegant than the others. It marked him as some kind of leader. Into the projection, Miy said, "It gets better." To the Tritan, she asked, "Sir, can you give us your message again?"

The Tritan was a wash of the palest blue, implying he was older. He gazed with cataract voids into the projection as he spoke with a voice meant for public speaking. "Primary Maker, please return home. We have waited eons for you, Tumu."

As Xelan recoiled, taken aback, Miy put her face back in the projection. She was obviously delighted by their reaction. Who didn't love drama? "Now, isn't that interesting, your imperial majesty?"

Lucas choked on a forkful of mashed potatoes, and everyone turned their heads to look at him. Complicity yellowed his face in an adorable, yet damnable flush.

Andrew laughed.

No matter how long they'd be together, life with Lucas would never get old.

Tameka sat with Xelan while he talked it out with Tumu. This situation fit perfectly under her Transparency Decree, enacted earlier in the day. By now, it shouldn't surprise them the old Primary had founded his species through some twist of Aegis machinations. Lucas had run off into the trees with Andrew, or they'd subject him to twenty-one questions, too. But the couple had a point.

"Xelan, leave Tumu to enjoy his evening and watch the sunset with me and Pax."

Tameka loved Xelan for how he transformed at her suggestion. That trademark grin spread across his lips, and the midnight ring around his eyes sparkled with joy.

On Xelan's palm device, Tumu said, "Peaches. You're always the voice of reason. We'll pick this up tomorrow, Wingmaster. Good night."

"Good night, old friend." Xelan disconnected the call and stood with his hand out for Tameka. "M'lady, would you care to join me for a wondrous sight?"

Tameka beamed. "I'm already looking at one."

A gagging sound alerted them to Pax, with a finger mockingly down his throat. The eight-year-old said, "Mom. Dad. You're so mushy."

Beside them, Korac cough-laughed into his ice cream cone.

Sagan nudged him. "Don't tease. We have no room to talk."

Meanwhile, Rayne hid her snickering against Nox's chest. Tameka had to admit, she was becoming accustomed to the gigantic Icarus' presence. When he was around, Rayne's demeanor shone like a beacon. Tameka also noticed Rayne wore a black tank and cargo pants over her swimsuit. Same as Xelan. Both of them had smoothed their soaked hair back from their faces after a day in the water. There wasn't much resemblance which Tameka could see, but their smiles shared the same wattage.

Xelan knelt and let Pax climb onto his back. The father opened his wings to the son's delight. Pax asked, "Ready, mom?"

She detracted her wings. "Ready."

They flew up above the trees to admire the yellows, purples, and reds melting together at the end of a perfect day. Tameka hugged herself, hoping their little girl shared in the moment.

"Maybe Harmony?" As she suggested the name, she looked over at Xelan to gauge his reaction.

Already so much the proud father, he beamed. "I love it. Harmony."

Pax glanced between his parents, asking, "Will that be my new sister's name?"

Tameka hovered closer and kissed her son on his red curls. "Yeah. Do you like it?"

In answer, Pax stretched the slight distance between Xelan and Tameka and spoke to her abdomen. "Hello, Harmony. I can't wait to meet you."

It tugged at Tameka's heartstrings until a tear fell from her lashes. A happy one. Even Xelan's eyes glistened as the Earth's sun sank beyond the horizon and swept the forest in the softness of dusk.

Tameka took Xelan's hand, saying, "Let's get back down there before chaos breaks out."

The group had started some music, and dancing ensued as the stars glittered in the darkening sky. Silence and Kyle waded out toward the waterfall together for some alone time. Sagan and Korac left for their errand. And the others spread out playing volleyball, Marco polo, or card games.

Nearby, Devis said to Andrius, "Go fish."

T.A.O. played with her cards facing out, still not grasping the concept. Or perhaps she was, and this way made her happy.

Beside Jack and Ross, Bethany stared at the sky. It was time.

After Xelan set Pax down in the water with Andrew, Tameka gestured over at Bethany. Xelan took the hint and followed Tameka over to Jack and Ross, who noticed their approach.

Ross mouthed, "Now?" At Tameka's nod, Kyle's middle sibling said, "Bethany, I want to talk to you about something."

The quiet girl looked at her sister with a smile and shared it with Tameka and Xelan as they sat down beside her.

This task seemed to pain Ross. As her words failed her, she looked to Jack. Rayne's brother's reassuring smile was identical to his sister's. He said, "We know you would be happier if the situation with Matt and Lucy was permanent. So, Xelan and Tameka came up with a solution."

Ross squeezed Jack's hand in gratitude, while Tameka explained to the young girl, "We'd like for you to go out on jobs with Matt and Lucy. Every job, in fact."

Bethany lit up, and it was sad to see how much this broke Ross' heart.

Xelan continued, "But we want to be up front. Razor is profiling their cases now. He may even go on missions with them. Will you be okay with that?"

Ross shuddered. Jack frowned. And Tameka worried that even though they'd discussed this in advance, they hadn't quite prepared the young couple for the full picture.

Bethany did not mind one bit. "Yes." There was a secret glint in her honey-brown eyes, and Tameka wondered if she was plotting revenge. After a moment of thought, a warmth replaced the cold light, and Bethany threw her arms around her sister. "Thank you."

Ross looked ready to cry as Bethany thanked her for setting her free in the galaxy, but she squeezed her baby sister with all her might. "I love you."

"I love you."

Tameka took the hint and nudged Xelan to leave them alone. As they stood and walked toward the water, she said, "I'm impressed Ross could do this for Bethany's sake. Ground rules. Matt and Lucy will need some ground rules. We'll give them the details later."

"You handled that well." Xelan was always full of compliments about Tameka's competency. And they were most welcome.

Tameka grinned at him. "You, too, hot stuff."

They sat down in the sand near Lucas, Andrew, Pax, Aria, and Torch in the water. From across the water, sitting beside Nox, Rayne waved at them.

Tameka caught the tail-end of some ridiculous story Lucas was sharing with Rayne. "It's true. The Thailean Mystics evolved into birds. Fat ones that make an awful sound."

Nox and Rayne glanced at one another before she asked, "Like 'wallop'?"

Lucas' rich laughter echoed off the canyon walls. "That's exactly it."

Rayne blinked at him, and Nox chuckled at some joke Tameka didn't get.

Xelan laughed as Pax launched out of the water and onto Andrew's back. Andrew sank into the water, shouting, "Oh no! The Kraken!"

Aria peeled Pax off Andrew's back before he drowned and ruffled the grinning boy's curls. Torch took Pax and threw him into the air so he splashed everyone when he fell into the water.

Tameka smiled and basked.

Harmony would fit in perfectly.

The Seam was an excellent place to catch a break and have a discussion. Sagan leaned back against a wall in Monarch hall, hands pressed behind her, and considered the situation. Meanwhile, Korac paced like a caged tiger. A pretty, pale caged tiger.

Sagan's husband said, "I think we should tell Pehton, first. She should know, and I despise keeping this from her."

This was easy to agree with wholeheartedly. Sagan opened the conduit to Gale's Iona where Pehton and Caedes lived.

Korac hesitated and, in a moment of vulnerability, asked, "Do you think she'll be angry with me?"

Honesty was best in these situations. Sagan said, "I don't know, but I know she'll want to go with us to donate. Of that, I'm sure."

"Right. It's best to get this over with then."

Korac marched through the conduit and knocked on Pehton's door. Sagan understood why he maintained his mask of composure, but perhaps it was better to let Pehton see the true effect on Korac. Sagan opened her mouth to say as much when Pehton opened the door.

The tiny Lyrik gripped a scarlet towel around her, and her orange feathers were damp from a shower. She took one look at Korac and said, "Oh, you're here in person. Who died?"

From inside, Caedes called, "Evening, General."

When Korac didn't immediately tease Pehton, Sagan knew this was serious. Korac saluted Caedes before focusing on his General Warden, who grew more concerned by the second. With some hesitation, Korac said, "I have something…unpleasant to tell you."

Because Lyriki eyes were hard stones, they couldn't exactly widen. But Pehton's orange brows shot up on her pitch-black skin. "Okay. I'm listening." She adjusted the towel some more.

After a moment of Korac fighting to find the right words, Sagan touched his arm, asking permission. There was a hint of desperation in his eyes as he assented with a nod.

Sagan said, "We let Lucas resurrect Razor for rehabilitation."

Wordlessly, Pehton stepped back and opened the door for them to come inside. Then she pointed a stern finger at the couch, where Sagan and Korac sat down like they were in timeout and about to receive a lecture from their short, hot babysitter.

It was Pehton's turn to pace like a caged animal in front of the furniture. Although, it was more entertaining since she was naked under the precariously gripped towel.

Caedes took in the scene, but remained true to his taciturn trademark, and silently made everyone drinks. Sagan appreciated that if things were too serious, he'd jump in on Pehton's behalf. Until then, he'd trust her to handle it.

Pehton stopped and stared at the floor, giving them her side profile. "I understand why you did it. I do. Can I assume he's already integrated into the program?"

Korac said, "Yes."

Sagan wished she could hug them both. The situation didn't exactly thrill her, either, but it made more sense to reform Razor than leave such a valuable asset conscious in a nacre forever. And this way…

Sagan glanced at Korac and considered his life. Yes, Nox and Xelan were his brothers in all but blood. However, Korac grew up without people like him, and Lucas and Razor were an avenue to mend that.

Pehton finally looked at Korac to say, "I'm donating everything. Now. Let me get dressed."

"You sure you don't want to stay in the towel? It really brings out your eyes—"

Sagan swatted her husband.

Korac rubbed his arm. "What?! It's better than saying 'ass.'"

Pehton was already heading for the bedroom with a frustrated groan and a middle finger in the air. Caedes chuckled as he followed behind her. Truthfully, the towel suited him, too.

Sagan grinned.

"I'm happy for them." Korac said it so softly Sagan almost didn't hear it.

She took his hand and laced her fingers through his. "Me, too."

Pehton shouted from the bedroom, "No fucking on my couch!"

Korac smirked. "That's too bad. I didn't figure Caedes as a 'bed only' kind of Icarus."

That earned Korac a proper burst of laughter from Caedes in the other room.

Pehton appeared in the doorway, wearing her armor in a tactical arrangement. "We've just finished marking the entire apartment, thank you very much."

Sagan laughed. Especially as the bald Icarus appeared in the doorway with a thumbs up.

Korac even chuckled before killing the mood. "Are you sure you're ready for this?"

"Oh, I am."

Even though Caedes was behind Pehton and she couldn't see, he was smirking at her fiery nature. It was so cute.

Sagan opened a conduit to the rehabilitation facility. Through it, they could see a door.

324

Korac took Sagan's hand, and they stepped through. Pehton and Caedes followed. Korac went up to the door, ready to knock when a Caprent man darted up to it. He spared the group a glance before knocking, securing the tray of food in his hands.

The door cracked, and Sagan could hear Razor's voice from here. "Did you get the Yun strawberries like I asked?"

Earnestly, the Caprent nodded. "Yes, sir." And handed over the tray.

Razor said, "Very good." When he widened the crack to take the tray, he noticed Sagan's group. "Ah." To the Caprent, he said, "You're dismissed."

The man scurried off.

Sagan frowned. She was pretty sure that was another prisoner, and she was also pretty sure Razor had already tamed them to do his bidding. In only sixteen hours. That had to make for some kind of record.

Razor opened the door and gestured for them to come inside. "Welcome to my humble abode."

Humble, my ass.

The standard-issued apartment didn't come with Lukemore silk robes, infinite count cotton towels, and thirteen bottles of Yun's finest nectar. And that was just what Sagan could see from the doorway.

As if everyone bathed at the same time, Razor was in a white robe, drying his hair. Triss called from the bathroom, water sloshing as if she were in the tub. "Who is it, Razor?" The heady scent of roses and vanilla permeated the air, and Sagan was sure it wasn't the expensive Reipon oils on display.

Pehton glared at Korac, who had failed to mention they'd also resurrected Triss.

Oops.

While smiling at Sagan, Razor answered Triss. "Old friends. And strawberries. Would you care for some, my siren?"

"Mmm. Yes, please. And if they've brought us the champagne from the Obsidian Palace, I'd love that, too." Water sloshed again as Triss laid back in the tub.

"Anything for you." Razor held up a finger for everyone to wait as he grabbed a bottle and carried the tray of fruit into the bathroom.

Pehton was beyond incredulous. Caedes cradled her elbow when her gliders popped out.

Korac held up his hands, trying to stave her temper.

Sagan was simply bewildered.

Was that sex toy on the couch made of diamond?!

Do not.

Touch any surface in this place.

Razor shut the door when he returned. As if he knew the direction of Sagan's thoughts, he said, "You know how it is. New territory to mark and all that."

Pehton scoffed, and that's how Razor liked it.

His eyes flicked to the Lyrik with too much mirth. "Peh Peh, I've missed you. And I see you've brought a new beau. Hello, Caedes." Like they were proper acquaintances, Razor held out his hand.

Sagan half-expected the Pain Curator to offer to ease Caedes' troubles. Instead, they shook hands without a hitch.

Fluid.

That was the only word to describe Caedes' gruff yet easy temperament. The Icarus could go with any flow, and Sagan valued it. Especially, partnered with someone as feisty as Pehton.

Korac watched everything with a careful eye and approached the subject with caution. "I see you're settling in."

Razor's congenial smile took on a new shade of uncertainty as he regarded Korac. "Yes, brother. One tells me I have you to thank for this." 'This' meaning the second chance at life and Triss' resurrection. It was a big 'this.' He turned back to Sagan. "And you, Seamswalker. How are you?"

The touch of familial kindness affected Sagan, but she couldn't quite speak to what kind of effect. It touched the part of her which had trusted Razor once, and the familiar pang reminded her of how badly he'd burned her. Literally. He'd ordered hot axes pressed to Sagan's skin and seared her with Korac's signature weapon.

This was so messed up.

When Korac touched Sagan's shoulder, she knew she'd gone too long without answering. He whispered, "Your eyes."

That's right. Another side effect of Razor's treachery made it difficult for Sagan to control her Atramentous around him. At least, the rehabilitating villain recognized the sign enough to step back and give her some space.

Somehow the gesture both helped and hurt more.

Sagan's voice came in three pitches. "I want to trust you to commit to this program. Can you do that for me, Razor? So I can finally forgive you?"

Pehton muttered, "You took the words right out of my mouth."

Caedes marked the moment by respectfully observing, waiting to interfere on Pehton's behalf.

Korac pulled Sagan against his side as he let the question stand for him as well.

Meeting each person in the eyes, Razor said, "I will complete the program and fulfill my duties to Iona Pax. I will not disappoint you, T.A.O., or Xelan." A smirk replaced the sincerity. "But we all know I won't do it without causing a little mischief."

It actually made Sagan smile. She said, "Good. I'll make a donation."

"We all will," Pehton affirmed.

Razor said, "I wouldn't expect anything less. You, too, Korac? Of course." His mood shifted suddenly, and his smile fell into something less confident. "How is Echo?"

Oh.

This was a tight spot, wasn't it? Korac deferred to Sagan, who said, "She's beautiful. You know, we *will* tell her about you." And maybe one day, if Razor and Triss graduated from rehabilitation, Korac and Sagan might introduce Echo to her biological parents.

Razor bowed with his head. "Thank you." Genuineness warmed the words, and he'd looked at Korac as he said it.

Pehton shook her head. "I'm not sure if I'm buying this, but you've always put on a good act."

With the quiet moment broken, Razor chuckled. Triss called again from the bathroom, and he answered, "I'll be there in a moment." To his guests, he said, "Well, I commence work with Matt and Lucy tomorrow after my rehab session. I suppose I'll see your experiences there."

Sagan's curiosity got the better of her. "What's it like for you?"

Razor tilted his head to the side, considering her. "I am familiar with pain. Knowing that I caused it infuses traces of shame and guilt. For instance, Peh Peh, I don't look forward to all those times I manipulated you. All the lies I put you through. Or you, Sagan—The betrayal." He faced Korac next. "I could spend Eternity here and never experience all the ways I've hurt you."

Korac looked away, and Sagan squeezed him around the waist. For a second—for a shining moment—she glimpsed regret in Razor's frown.

It was an opening through which this family of rare and exceptional men could finally heal.

And Sagan couldn't wait to celebrate it.

Korac, Sagan, and Pehton deposited their experiences to Razor's rehab program. Caedes, like the upstanding soldier he was, supported teeny through the entire procedure.

And what a worthy cause.

It seemed Razor was prepared to commit, and now the ghost of the smaller Aegis set apart on Ishkur's bridge would stop haunting Korac. These thoughts filled his head as they dropped Pehton off at her place.

"Thanks for breaking it to me in person, boss." She nudged him playfully.

Korac smirked. "Thanks for answering the door in a towel, *teeny*."

Sagan swatted Korac, and it only pleased him further. It wouldn't be a night out with Pehton and Caedes if Sagan only smacked Korac once.

Further in the apartment, Caedes laughed richly in good humor.

Pehton rolled her eyes, saying, "See you tomorrow, you sexy pain in my ass," and closed the door in Korac's face.

Sagan's cheerful grin was worth every swat. She pulled him close and kissed him, flexing her awesome skills by simultaneously opening a conduit to Karter's place.

It was time to retrieve Echo.

Karter, rainbow mohawk down for a change, greeted them with a finger to her lips. She whispered, "The baby's sleeping."

Chris looked up from a three-dimensional schematic and waved. Bones, across from Chris, did the same. From the kitchen, Para offered drinks by gesturing with two glasses of fruit juice.

Korac appreciated this little family of theirs. His. This was *his* family.

The playpen for Echo consumed a third of the living space, and the white-feathered, white-eyed, black-complected Lyriki infant languished in it. So many plushy toys; so little time.

Karter opened her arms, and Korac went into them—Familiar, powerful arms he'd sparred against many times in his life while never knowing she was his mother. Ones which had pulled him out of mischief and tended many wounds. Karter smelled like home.

Sagan let them have this time together, wandering over to see what Chris, Bones, and Para were up to. The structure in the projected image seemed familiar, but Korac wanted to focus on family and not work.

For once.

Elden, he and Xelan made for quite the pair of preoccupied fathers. And both were obsessed with their partners.

Funny how that had worked out.

Karter whispered, "Echo was a good girl. She ate all her strained vegetables."

Korac chuffed. "Of course, she was, and of course, she did." His daughter was an angel. A model infant for other babies to follow—Mateo Suarez-Renee and whatever ridiculous name Xelan would give their daughter.

With an incredulous shake of her head, Karter led Korac to the little barrier of firm squishy material containing Echo's explorations. Yesterday, she tried for the first time to stand on her feet.

Korac did *not* cry.

Tiny diamond eyes greeted them. Echo was already awake. She opened her pitch-black lips revealing a little black tongue in a wide smile as soon as she spotted Korac.

"Hey, baby girl." He scooped Echo up to her whistling delight. "Yeah, that's daddy's deadly warrior."

Korac was half-aware of everyone in the room watching him. Even Sagan. It seemed anyone who'd heard Korac's Verse paid special notice to his paternal habits, and he'd learned to embrace it. Although Korac had spent his life composing himself for defense, he'd sworn on the day he and Sagan adopted Echo, Korac would never hide from their daughter.

And what a beautiful gift Echo was.

After seeing Triss and Razor earlier, Korac couldn't help but notice the tiny Aegis-Lyrik had her mother's mouth and her father's bone structure. But there was a trace of Korac in there through all the genetic magic. Echo had his nose. It was far superior to Razor and Triss' features, and it softened Echo's face, suiting her tininess.

Korac nuzzled their noses together, and Echo squeal-whistled with joy.

Oh, yes. Hearts would be broken.

A long, long, *long* time from now.

Sagan came over with the carrier strapped around her. Korac enjoyed brushing Sagan's breasts 'accidentally' as they positioned Echo into it. Sagan glared at him playfully, earning a kiss.

It was wonderful, sweet, and perfect. But...

Korac's curiosity would not wait a moment longer. He nodded toward the design. "What is everyone inspecting over here?"

With Echo cradled to her front, Sagan turned and gestured at the image. "I think you'll like it."

Karter went over to Chris, who pulled her against his side before pointing at the schematics. "It's a school for the Shadow kids. We're naming it after John."

It was an impressive installation set in an idyllic area of Cinder II. Between the Palatial Grounds and the physical entrance to Ishkur's bridge. And Korac wasn't one hundred percent sure but...

"Is that P.E. area a replica of Xelan's training grounds for the Progeny on Earth?" Sagan beat Korac to the question.

Bones grinned, and Para said, "We've made a few trips to the area and sketched it out. It's perfect for beginners."

Karter beamed. "It's a surprise."

Echo whistled, and Korac smoothed her feathers as he answered his daughter. "I think Xelan will like it, too."

Chris' chest swelled before he said, "We hope so, but don't tell him."

Korac eyed Sagan. "You don't have to worry about *me* keeping the secret."

Sagan mimed zipping her lips and throwing the zipper away.

With a humorous shine to his eyes, Bones said, "I'll send you over our security plans. You can run them by Caedes and Pehton, if you like."

Para, Bones, Chris, and Karter glowed with accomplishment and happiness.

It choked Korac until he squeezed out, "Thank you." For thinking of the future and for working so hard to guarantee it.

Karter hugged Korac and roped Sagan in, too. "You two have a fun night. We'll see you tomorrow."

Korac gave the only appropriate response. "Yes, mother."

Para climbed into the hug, followed by Bones, and then Chris.

Huggy Shadow shit, but Korac wouldn't trade this moment for anything in the world.

Echo whistled in agreement.

Five minutes later, Korac, Sagan, and Echo waved goodbye as they stepped through a conduit, returning to the gorge. The party was dying off into smaller groups as everyone cozied up to the idea of going home. It was only made possible by Sagan and T.A.O.'s abilities.

Pax and Tameka had fallen asleep on a blanket together. Xelan was watching them with more peace in his expression than Korac could ever remember seeing. Nox was dancing with Rayne in the water. That Nox and Xelan were breathing the same air, filled Korac with gratitude, and he was determined to make it last forever.

Especially if it meant winning more races against the two sentimental fools.

In the water, Nox could enjoy Rayne's soft lips without her straining on her tiptoes and him leaning to meet her halfway. He could see more time in the hot springs in their future. They stole kisses while they danced, holding each other close. The firelight from the dying bonfire bathed her white hair in orange and contrasted the blue in her eyes. As far as he was concerned, it was just the two of them out here. Nox could hold Rayne like this under the light of Earth's moon forever—

A tremendous splash crashed into them, interrupting the mood. Sagan brought them back to the semi-public setting with a triumphant shout of, "My turn!"

Rayne gave a battle cry and returned fire. Waves crashed back and forth until Nox stepped aside, sweeping away the hair soaked to his face. At his incredulous laughter, the girls stopped and peered at him.

"Sorry, Nox," Sagan said as she slinked over to Rayne and pulled their mutual lover close.

Rayne stated the obvious. "No, you're not." Then she cupped the Seamswalker by the nape and kissed her.

With a chuckle, Nox dismissed himself to shore. No jealousy. Only appreciation. There was no moving on from Rayne. Made even more obvious by Kyle unable to tear his eyes away from the two women kissing in the water.

When Kyle realized Nox had noticed, he gave an ugly scowl before turning back to his hand of cards and submitting the betting pool to Silence's delight. The young man would compensate for this in Nox's treatment tomorrow. Frankly, the former King of Cinder didn't give a shit—

"Oh." Nox nearly backed into T.A.O. He dipped his head in greeting.

She stared up at him with her solid violet eyes, tilting her head this way and that as if searching Nox's soul. He let her, uncertain what else to do. Almost as abruptly as T.A.O. had appeared, she wrapped her arms around Nox and hugged him.

This took him back to all those millennia ago when Nox had entertained the ancient Progeny in his castle. T.A.O. had hugged him like this then. A tenth of his size, Nox feared he might break her as he gave the gentlest of squeezes.

T.A.O. spoke against his stomach. "You deserve her, and she knows. We all know. It's in the Source of us, now. The Eternal Bind."

The certainty in her voice brought a mist to Nox's eyes. Every day, he tried to earn Rayne's love and the acceptance of the Shadow. To hear this…"Thank you, T.A.O."

The small woman separated them and beamed before Seamswalking off to the other side of the gorge. She sat beside Andrius and Devis playing cards with Kyle and Silence. Whatever she'd said to Kyle made him look across the water at Nox, startled.

But that wasn't enough to keep Nox's attention. His pulse steadied with heavy heartbeats. Over Sagan's shoulder, while they danced, Rayne smiled at Nox. It was a pretty smile of pure content and love, and Nox felt grateful he was even ten percent responsible for it.

"We're lucky." Korac stepped up from behind Nox, with Echo strapped to his front. On anyone else it might look ridiculous, but on the Imperial General it was more like paternal armor. Another way he was dangerous. "She likes you."

Nox glanced down at Echo to find her reaching for him. How could he say 'no' to that angelic face? With a chuckle, Nox gave Echo his finger to squeeze. She couldn't wrap her entire hand around it, but she tried with all her half-Aegis might.

Korac smirked at the interaction. "With lessons from you and Karter, Echo will become the finest warrior this galaxy has ever seen."

The compliment swelled Nox's chest. "Without a doubt."

"Will you and Rayne remain on Thailea?"

Nox took a moment to consider Korac's question. Lucas had given them permission to live on Thailea forever. They could spend every night gazing through the silver canopy at the rainbow rings, no longer hidden behind a storm. Tasting the star dust of Rayne's blood and memorizing the contour of her abs, biceps, back, breasts, and thighs like a map to paradise—

Wait…Korac had asked Nox a question. "Yes. One day, we may return to Cinder, but for now the Aegis planet feels like home."

At the mention of his paternal race, Korac's eyes narrowed slightly.

It made Nox think to ask, "So were you involved in Razor's resurrection?"

Korac looked to the sky like he was counting the diamonds scattered across all that black and blue velvet. It was the same color as the ring around Xelan's iris. Korac said, "I didn't think it was fair to Xelan that *you* came back but not the man who harbored your brother during his exile. We may not care for Razor, but after listening to Xelan tell his Verse, I'm convinced my errant half-brother saved yours from his grief. Among other things, it's reason enough to give him this opportunity to redeem as you did."

In their time together, Korac was always stoic and reserved his words for only the most important occasions. Whether that be a rousing speech for the troops or giving Xelan and Nox shit in the middle of a failed prank. On this occasion, Nox absorbed Korac's words and appreciated all the honesty in them.

Nox took his finger from echo and smoothed a white feather from her face. "You've made a hard decision, and I hope it's a righteous one. Razor doesn't seem to respond to the pods like the other reformists. How do you think he's fairing?"

Korac's half-chuckle was incredulous and a little bitter. "The entire facility is already bending to his will."

"Well, coming from such an attractive and charismatic family, what would you expect of your brother?"

At Xelan's interruption from behind, Korac rolled his eyes with a groan.

Nox grinned and thanked Elden for this family of theirs.

May it forever remain in dysfunction and relentless entertainment.

Any of Korac's groans were a worthy occasion for Xelan to grin.

So he did.

It wasn't a surprise to see a mirror of the expression on Nox's face, and it was becoming easier every time Xelan saw it to accept this reality. They were together and on their way to being brothers again.

Thanks to Rayne.

She and Sagan went into another round of splash wars, and this time Andrew fired at them with a super-soaker from shore.

Kyle admonished them. "Are you trying to wake up Tameka and Pax?"

Ignoring Kyle, Jack ran and cannonballed into the water, while Ross and Bethany cheered him on. Aria and Torch sat back and watched with Devis, T.A.O., and Andrius. They shared a similar serenity as Silence.

It was the same quiet in Xelan. Sure, he felt the typical allure of work, but it took less effort than usual not to bombard Miy and Twenty-One about Tumu's homeworld. Like Xelan could finally accept those things would still be there in the morning.

Progress.

"So, Korac." Xelan loved the way his General readied himself for the Co-Emperor's antics. "Does this week at your chalet work for you and Sagan?"

Nox chuckled.

Korac scoffed. "You lost. Remember?" But there was a hint of acknowledgment in his eyes. Korac knew the brothers had thrown the race.

Xelan nudged him. "Dirty opportunist."

Regal, as always, Korac refused to look at Xelan as he taunted, "Me? You knew as well as I did Nox employed those gravity dampeners. A fair race that does not make."

With a offended hand to his chest, Nox said, "I would never dishonor our contest in such a manner."

"Oh, really?" Korac snatched Nox's hand and held it up, displaying the wrist band under his sleeve. "Were you afraid we might challenge you to a rematch?"

Xelan barked out a laugh and slapped a hand over his mouth before glancing sheepishly at Tameka and Pax. The woman famous for sleeping through a plane crash had passed the heavy habit onto their son. Fortunately.

Korac released Nox, who promised, "Next time I won't use them."

Contrary to the last five minutes of this argument, Korac chuffed. "If you don't, how will we have any fun? No, I much prefer it like the old days. You alway held back for us."

Xelan smiled at the flood of memories. Korac was right, and, without a trace of paternal experience, Nox had helped the younger boys build confidence in their capabilities. Truly, would they be the men they were today without him?

Dreaming of the next match, Xelan mused, "The Verse Triathlon."

"I was partial to 'Cinder's Matches,' myself." Nox knew nothing about title conventions.

Korac sighed and smoothed a hand down Echo's back. The gesture was more for his comfort than hers.

Mischief rushed through Xelan's veins. He never could turn down an opportunity to antagonize Korac. "Well, I wanted to name it 'Verses versus Verses,' but our General snubbed his nose at it."

Nox gave a slow, approving nod. "Yes. That *does* have a ring to it."

There.

Korac pinched the bridge of his nose and groaned, miserable and happy. It was beautiful. Echo apparently disagreed. The baby cried against her father's chest. While the sound was heartbreaking, it was also terribly adorable because she whistled a little with each inhale.

"Aw," Sagan called from the water, breaking up the play. "She's had a long day."

Xelan saw the gratitude in Korac's eyes as the woman in his life rescued him from Nox and Xelan's games. Korac said, "We should get everyone home and get her in bed."

Sagan stepped onto their side of the beach, while Rayne went to the other side to talk to Jack and Kyle. Korac and Sagan soothed Echo, but after the infant's protests, the group became conscious of the time and started dressing and packing.

Tameka called, "Xelan?" She stirred and woke Pax.

Xelan waved, so she'd notice him next to Nox, saying, "Hey, sleeping beauty."

Tameka's sweet smile was everything to him. "I'll help pack up. Take your time." The smile softened into one of understanding as Tameka acknowledged Xelan was spending time with his brothers.

Elden, he loved her. Pax and Harmony were the perfect names for their children.

Sagan asked, "Will you help me clean up, Korac?" It was an obvious ploy to get Xelan alone with Nox, but adorable all the same.

Korac, once the most reserved out of their trio, clasped Xelan for a hug, then Nox. It was almost as if defeating Imminent and Celindria had given them all room to feel and express. Korac said, "In case T.A.O. gets you home before us, we'll see you two tomorrow."

Sagan smiled and waved. "Good night."

Nox waved. "Tomorrow."

"Good night." Xelan appreciated everyone for the space.

There was more of it after Sagan opened a conduit to the Shadow home terminal. From there, Andrew and Lucas went off to the zeppelin, both waving. Kyle and Silence wandered to their Iona without a backward glance. And the rest were soon to follow.

A comfortable quiet settled between the former King and Prince of Cinder. There were many days ahead for them to become acquainted again. Thanks to Korac's idea of doubling up for Girl's Night with Guy's Night, those opportunities would occur on a weekly basis. There was also the rehabilitation program and so many other gatherings ahead of them.

Kyle reported to Xelan daily on Nox's progress, and everyday Story Taker asked the same question, *"When will you donate your experience?"*

In this quiet moment, Xelan finally had his answer. Never. The second Nox had asked Elden to take him instead of Rayne, Xelan had forgiven his brother. It just took until this moment for Xelan to realize it.

Movement off to their side caught the brothers' attention. They glanced over to see Rayne flying up the canyon wall to the top of the waterfall. Under the moonlight, her skin glowed, and her hair reflected the soft ethereal luminescence.

The people of Iona Pax had made Rayne into a goddess, as befitting her legacy. But whenever Xelan looked at her, he still saw the little girl in pigtails he'd saved from the car accident all those years ago. The twelve-year-old too brave for her own good, out of her depth walking down the streets at night. The determined sixteen-year-old on his training course, refusing to give up before learning the take down.

Xelan's Rayne.

"Sometimes Rayne gets this lost look in her eyes." Nox's confession prompted Xelan to face his brother. The concern for Rayne in Nox's voice affected Xelan. "I don't think she regrets choosing this Probability, but I believe she mourns the other."

It was an impossible choice, and Xelan thanked Elden every day that she chose this one. Not only because of him and all the people who loved her, but for Nox as well.

Xelan nodded toward Rayne and said, "I think she's waiting for you."

Nox shook his head. "No. This, I cannot help Rayne with. As her partner, I can be there for her in many ways, but she'll always need her guardian."

Since they were children, Nox had always known exactly what Xelan needed to hear. And he loved him for it.

One thousand and twelve.
One thousand and thirteen.
Fourteen...
Rayne counted the stars. The summer warmth of the day had given way to a cool breeze through the trees, teasing her with spray from the waterfall. Despite being surrounded by hardwoods, she could only smell the ocean and sunscreen.

That Labor Day weekend, now three years past, seemed eons ago, and Rayne hardly recognized the girl from that memory. The one who'd left her family's side for a better view of the fireworks. Completely unaware of how much her life would change in the next twenty-four hours.

The next day, four words had changed Rayne's life.

"They're real, you know?"

Rayne smiled at Xelan's welcome, if coincidental, intrusion. He stepped up beside her on the cliff, grinning per usual. With typical enthusiasm, he pointed at the constellations. "That one's my favorite. I named it 'Speckle.'"

Xelan could always make Rayne laugh. She couldn't keep the incredulity out of her voice. "Speckle?!"

"Celindria thought it was silly, too." Xelan tried for genuinely sheepish and failed. There was no shame in him. "But it's a good name for a cluster. They're all real worlds, and we'll see them before too long." He gazed at them with so much longing.

Rayne knew from living Nox's life that Xelan had always wished for stars beneath Li's harsh blaze. She took Xelan's hand and pointed at that Little Dipper.

"I hear they're changing the constellations to name them after the Shadow."

Xelan gave a single laugh. "They're only symbols to satisfy our need to know everything."

Yes.

It was that need which currently burned in Rayne. How was the other Probability fairing without them? The other Nox. The other Callahan family. Was Jack in more trouble with bad influences? Was dad still pulling double shifts to support the bookstore—Did mom even keep the bookstore?

"Hey." Xelan pulled on Rayne's hand until she faced him. He said, "Talk to me."

It was the sentence to summarize their relationship, wasn't it? If something was bothering Rayne, Xelan would always want to know. And vice versa.

Rayne considered her words, licked her lips, and said, "I know I made the right choice, and I believe Lucas will see to everything. He's simply spectacular that way. But..."

Xelan kissed the top of Rayne's head. "Call me biased, but I'm glad you chose this one." At her smile, he said, "It's only natural to be curious. Hopefully, with time, you come to terms with your choice. Until then, I suggest immersing yourself in the here and now."

Rayne quirked a brow. "Seriously? Was there some school on Cinder which taught you three how to say the perfectly right thing for every situation?"

Xelan's grin meant the worlds to Rayne. "After a few million years, you'll get the knack for it."

Wow.

Millions of years.

"But don't change your fashion sense, Callahan." Xelan gestured at their matching clothes, and Rayne had to laugh at how ridiculous it was. He said, "It looks better on you, but nothing beats the original."

Rayne nudged him, saying, "It's all about the pockets, Wingmaster."

After a second of comfortable silence, Xelan bit his thumbnail.

Uh oh.

"Spit it out." Rayne couldn't wait to hear what fresh calamity her guardian had thought up.

A bashfulness overcame Xelan, and he struggled to approach it. "So… I don't even want to ask this, but… are you planning to make a godfather out of me?"

Rayne gave a little laugh, almost incredulous. After she thought of the answer, her smile fell, and the humor died with it. "I don't know. The other girls tell me there's a choice of sorts, and it doesn't seem to work for me. Nox believes Imminent left me… unable."

Determination sparked a fire in Xelan's midnight eyes. "I will work day and night to reverse it. I promise you, Rayne. While I may have had reservations about my brother, I would never leave you like this—"

"It's okay." Rayne laughed a little at Xelan's fervor. She said, "Nox and I aren't in a hurry. I think we just want to get comfortable with ourselves sans shouldering the weight of the universe. But, to be clear, one day, I would like to try."

Xelan squeezed her hands, saying, "I'm there one hundred percent. Say the word, and we'll get started with a quick examination and—"

Rayne threw her arms around this Icarus she loved. "Thank you." With Xelan as her guardian, and Nox and Sagan as her partners, anything was possible. Even resolving multi-verse conundrums.

As if the cosmos had overheard Rayne's thoughts, a star shot across the sky.

Xelan noticed, too. "Hey." He pointed at it and separated them to say, "Do you want to make a wish?"

Rayne stared at her guardian, this Icarus who'd saved her life a dozen times. One specific instance came to mind.

Holding Xelan's hand, Rayne closed her eyes and made her wish, knowing, like all the others, this one would come true, too.

LIGHTNING STRIKES TWICE

"OH, MY GOD! There's a kid in the road!"

People screamed.

Tires screeched.

And a set of powerful arms lifted Rayne, preventing her from continuing her adventure. The stranger's suit was soft, and she rubbed her cheek against it. His hair was sandy brown, and just long enough for Rayne to twirl a strand around her finger.

"Hee."

Golden eyes peered down at her. "Hello, Rayne."

Rayne sat up in bed, haunted by dreams and memories of familiar faces—Tameka, Kyle, Andrew, and Sagan—but not really them.

Nor their lovers with strange and beautiful eyes.

Nor Rayne's lover, for that matter.

With a sigh, she committed to her mundane morning routine. Like the fantastic places Rayne had visited in her dreams, she'd decorated her room in gray, black, and white with pops of blues, purples, and reds. After a shower, Rayne gathered her long black hair into space buns, staring at her bright blue eyes in the mirror. Cargo pants, a cropped tank, and a smock with her name sewn on it comprised her work uniform. There were plenty of pockets for pens, and Rayne's bare midriff both increased her tips and drove her mom nuts.

Two birds; one major workout routine.

Said disciplined diet and exercise was also courtesy of Rayne's haunting second life. Her sparse eating habits and insane running regiment had sparked many conversations with her mother involving a therapist. A shrink poking about her psyche was the last thing Rayne needed. So, despite her lack of appetite, she choked down Michelle Callahan's otherwise delicious three-course meals.

Like today's breakfast.

Waffles, eggs, bacon, and fresh-squeezed orange juice covered the breakfast table in a meal fit for a king—

King.

King of Cinder?

Rayne shook her head and walked down the stairs to the kitchen. "Mom?"

"Whoa, sweetheart! Look out." Ray gave his daughter a side squeeze before rushing by to pack up breakfast to go. "Today's my last day as a resident. Wish me luck."

Wow.

Ray Callahan, M.D.

Inspired by her hardworking father, Rayne kissed his cheek and promised, "I'll finish my applications today, and we can celebrate for dinner. My treat."

Ray's eyes, as blue as her own, sparkled as he grinned. "I'll hold you to that, sweet pea. Your mother already went to the bookstore." He tossed her a set of keys. "I guess you get to drive the Jag, today."

"Hey, how come you never let *me* drive it?" Jack frowned the entire way down the stairs until he sat at his place at the table.

Rayne scoffed and laughed all at once. "Did you forget what happened last summer?"

Her brother sighed as he plopped in his chair, saying, "It's not my fault the Escalade was like driving a land yacht. I didn't see the pole in my blind spot."

Ray gave his son a fatherly pat on the back. "Maybe next year, sport." A car horn honked outside. "That's my carpool. See you two for dinner."

"Bye, dad!" They shouted in unison before Ray closed the door on his way out.

While Jack piled his plate full of carbs and fatty proteins, he grumbled. "You're the favorite. I don't know why they bothered having me."

Rayne laughed and snatched a grapefruit without bothering to sit. "Because we live in a patriarchy, and they needed a boy to pass on the family name."

Still grumbling, Jack stuffed a huge bite of waffle into his mouth, chewed, and swallowed before saying, "It's almost 2010. Surely, women can do that by now."

Unable to help herself, Rayne shook her head incredulously. Sweet naïve little brother.

They ate in silence for a bit before Jack asked, "Hey, Rayne, why didn't you want to go to college like all your friends?"

Ah.

It was a perfectly reasonable question for an eighteen-year-old, fresh out of high school, to ask of his twenty-one-year-old sister. After thinking on it, Rayne said, "I felt like you, mom, and dad needed me more. I mean, sure I feel a little left out." Like right now with Andrew, Tameka, Sagan, and Kyle all abroad together for a summer English-teaching program. Their smiling group photos littered social media, giving Rayne missing-out vibes. But... "I don't regret my decision. Like I told dad, I'm filing my applications today and so should you."

Jack nodded. "I know. I know."

About three years ago, Rayne's little brother had fallen into a dangerous crowd. Jack even promised a dealer he'd sell drugs for him once, but on the same day he was supposed to initiate into their group of bad influences, a miraculous thing happened.

A local airline hired Jack as a marketing intern as part of a new co-op program at their high school. After one day working at Iona Airlines, he dropped the tough-guy act and lost the dealer's number.

It helped that dad was around more than in his nursing days. Back when mom first bought the bookstore—her one true passion in life—Ray Callahan had worked sixteen-hour shifts to support the family. Michelle once told Rayne he was hardly ever home and often forgot big events like mom's birthday and their anniversary.

But the Callahan family were prone to miracles.

A man had saved Rayne from a speeding car when she was four. The same one she'd dreamt about last night. It was funny how he was on her mind lately. She could remember what he said to Michelle when he returned Rayne to the bookstore.

"This is a lovely establishment you have here."

Mom had blushed, as one was wont to do when an attractive man said something nice about your life's work. "Thank you. We hope it'll fill a missing role here in the community—Sorry. Can you help me with this box?"

Rayne remembered the man had lifted it with ease and held it for Michelle while she took books from it and lined the shelves.

After they had filled one stack together, the kind stranger observed, "You could use some help around here."

Climbing onto a step stool to reach the top shelf, Michelle nodded. "Yes. Maybe once we take off, we can hire a helping hand or two." She laughed. "Why? Are you in the market?"

The golden-eyed man smiled, and it was so familiar to Rayne. He said, "No, but I would like to contribute. I could take on a silent partnership, if that sounds reasonable to you?"

Michelle had gaped, and Rayne recalled it distinctly because the four-year-old had said, "Mommy, you look silly," before running into the back room. She hadn't heard the rest of the boring grownup talk. As Rayne grew older, her mother often mentioned their mysterious benefactor and how, without his help, they never could've afforded this middle-class lifestyle.

And Rayne would be out of a job. Which reminded her… "I gotta go help, mom. I'll make you a deal, Jack. I'll fill out three applications today, and you do the same. Then tonight, I'll cover your dinner."

Jack beamed at her. "Deal."

Rayne ruffled his hair, inciting more grumbling, before rushing out of the house. It was a beautiful June morning, and just hot enough to warrant the skimpy attire without her mother's complaints. Okay, maybe with fewer of her mother's complaints.

The Jag was nice and all, but similar to Jack's issue with parking the Escalade, it was much easier for Rayne to maneuver her Honda sport bike on the quaint narrow roads to the bookstore. It's funny. Rayne hadn't liked motorcycles until the one dream with Sagan and…

Why couldn't Rayne ever remember their names?

Anyway, sharing the story of how the guy had shown up to take Sagan for a very spicy ride had gone over well with the other girls. Even Tameka admitted it was fanning-worthy. She'd kindly stopped needling Rayne about being a twenty-one-year-old virgin, despite all the sexy stories in her head. Because who in real life could compare to…

Black eyes, black hair, and a firm grip on her hips flashed through Rayne's eyes, almost making her run a stop sign. Fortunately, it was quiet on this

Friday morning, and no one was around to witness her slip up.

These were happening more frequently. They felt more vivid than daydreams. Like Rayne could almost smell the warm bakery scent and honeysuckle. Feel soft lips on her skin and sharp teeth in her neck.

Rayne sighed and drove the rest of the way to the bookstore. Despite the lack of traffic throughout their neighborhood, Kavanaugh Boulevard was bustling for a local festival. It meant Rayne had made the right call with the sport bike and easily parked it on the sidewalk.

Rayne wasn't even one step into the back entrance before Michelle called her name, prompting Rayne to say, "I'm here, mom."

"Oh, I know. I heard the racket you made, scaring off my customers. That's not why I called your name." Michelle came around the corner, stern and gently admonishing. "Young lady, where is your helmet?"

Much like the man from Rayne's dream had observed, the helmet would kill her space buns. But that wouldn't fly with her mom. "Sorry, I won't forget it again."

Michelle's "mhmm" said she was unconvinced as she swept back around the corner, with her long, practical braid following behind. "It's your turn in the coffee shop. We've had two people buy books today, but twelve people came in for iced lattes. Lucas was right for suggesting we expand."

Lucas.

It was the first time mom had ever mentioned his name. Lucas. Aegis. Icarus. Cinder—

"Honey, are you all right?"

Rayne looked up at her mother and smiled. "Yeah. Just ready for the tips to roll in. I promised dad and Jack I'd buy them dinner tonight. I suppose you want in on it, too?"

Michelle's brown eyes glittered with appreciation. "No, I know how much you want to save up for that ridiculous 'training course.'"

Even though her mother had called the training course 'ridiculous,' Rayne was glad she understood.

After the mention of tips, her mom gave Rayne a once over before saying, "The hair is cute, but I wished you'd wear a whole shirt for once." Then Michelle went back into the stacks, muttering about tips based on merit and not on looks.

Rayne shook her head, smiling all the way to the coffee counter. After half an hour of sorting the space, she laid out her application packets on the counter. Mom was right: the store *was* busy. In that short amount of time, Rayne had waited on two customers, and one of them actually bought a handful of books.

Now that it was lunchtime, there was a lull for Rayne to work on her entry essays. She wished she'd tried harder at school, so she wouldn't be tailing behind her friends. But, for as long as Rayne could remember, a sense of imminence had cast a shadow over her life. Like she was waiting to serve a purpose.

But surely, that wasn't unique? Everyone probably felt important at some stage in their lives—

Words and phrases whispered in Rayne's ear, spoken by a rich baritone.

"Once I'm gone. Will things go back to the way they were? You? A fighter, a killer serving coffee to strangers and writing college essays on your lunch break?"

The man from Rayne's dreams had taunted her in a beautiful observatory about the mundanity of human life on Earth. After which, she'd accused him of breaking promises. Then asked him to keep one and dance with her.

Rayne shook her head, trying not to recall the rest of the scene or risk daydreaming her down time away. But how could she concentrate on where she saw herself in five years when all Rayne could think about was golden weapons and unbreakable glass chains? And what about the Cult of Night? They were real as day and under investigation by the FBI after an anonymous tip had connected them with recent abductions.

How could some of Rayne's dreams be real but not all—

The little bell over the entrance chimed.

Michelle called, "Rayne, do you have that?"

"I got you, mom."

She hugged the papers to work on them at the front counter and left the break room to find an unusual sight. There was a car parked on the curb in the 'no-parking zone.'

No.

It wasn't a car. It was a limousine with diplomatic flags. On them was an emblem: a heart with a dagger piercing it. Two words came to mind.

Pretiosum Cruor.

Curious, Rayne called, "Hello. Can I help you find anything—"

Through a gap in the stack closest to the storefront, Rayne could see the considerable build of a male figure. With no idea why, her heart picked up in tempo, stealing her breath away.

Then he spoke.

"Good afternoon, I'm looking for a book—"

The man's words died on his lips when his black eyes found Rayne through the gap. Her heart stopped beating altogether as every word ever spoken by the man's beautiful baritone filled Rayne to the brim and overflowed.

Nox.

Lucas was an Aegis, who'd manipulated the Probability Matrix to unite the Eternal Bind.

Rayne and Nox were at the heart of it.

When the man across from her didn't speak, Rayne swallowed and stepped around the stack to face Nox. Did he not recognize her? This was the reality the other Rayne had declined, and Lucas—sweet, wonderful Lucas—had saved her from the accident, anyway. After dinner tonight, Rayne would drive her bike to Iona-01 and confirm everything with the Aegis. But first...

Nox watched, paralyzed by destiny, as Rayne walked up to him until the height difference forced her to tilt her head to maintain eye contact. He didn't pull away or freak out. But he also didn't know her.

This wasn't Rayne's Nox, not technically. Celindria had chosen this Probability because here, she and Nox were together. Their happiness and combined ingenuity meant Cinder was saved from famine and war. There was no need for Nox to ever violently invade Earth. So why was he here?

"Is there anything here you want?" Okay, so Sagan would snicker at Rayne's choice of words, and Korac would smirk, but Rayne had to try.

The sound of her voice broke the spell on Nox, and he shook himself before smiling.

It melted Rayne, made even more painful because she had to hide her reaction to it.

"Sorry about that..." Nox glanced at her name on the smock. "Rayne." The way he said her name... It affected Rayne all the same. Something close to recognition flickered in Nox's eyes, and she wanted to latch onto it.

Instead, Rayne forced a smile to hide her disappointment, saying, "Welcome to Callahan Books and Coffee. How may I help you?" On the last, she took a step back, and it hurt so badly she nearly choked on the words. To hide it, Rayne walked over to the counter and set her papers down. When she really wanted to drop them on the floor and jump into his arms.

Or something like that.

Nox followed. "I'm looking to buy a book for my wife."

It was a good thing Rayne was looking down because there was no hiding that wince. The reminder of Celindria in Nox's arms twisted Rayne's heart and wrung it dry. After a second to collect herself, Rayne asked, "Well, what is she like?"

When she looked up to memorize Nox's features, Rayne found him once again transfixed as if he was doing the same. On a breath, he whispered, "Perfect."

Rayne wanted to cry. She knew without a doubt Nox was talking about her, but for the sake of preserving the multi-verse arrangement, Rayne fought to say, "Sir, we don't have perfect books here for perfect wives, but I'm sure I can help you find something. Would like a coffee while you look?"

As if startled, Nox shook himself again. "Forgive me. Yes. Thank you. A plain latte will do."

"Coming right up."

Rayne was both grateful and heartbroken to turn her back on him. She didn't want him to see the tears burning her eyes and threatening to ruin her mascara. Plus the repetitive task of prepping espresso and steaming milk would ease some of this pain.

But how could Rayne move on from this? She was aware of everything as if she'd lived the other life. Faces and smells, wounds and orgasms—

Yeah.

Maybe ignorance was bliss—

"What're you planning to major in?"

With her back to him, Rayne closed her eyes and prayed to Elden for strength. Surely, the Icarean deity could still hear her in the Source. After plastering on her best smile, Rayne faced Nox with his coffee and answered his question. "History or English." Don't keep the conversation on her. Change the subject. "Here you go. Now, let's see if we can find your wife a book." Because if Nox stayed in this store any longer, Rayne would throw herself at him, despite aforementioned wife.

Nox nodded sagely. "Both are worthy endeavors for someone who wants to go into education. Is that what you want, Rayne?"

The way he said it made Rayne look up into his eyes and stare. All she wanted in the worlds was Nox. And Xelan… and everyone she loved to recognize her.

Rayne swallowed the emotion again before saying, "I want a lot of things, as most people do. But education certainly made the list." She forced another smile.

Nox sipped the coffee, tipped it at Rayne as a compliment, and set some cash on the counter. A lot more than it cost, for sure.

Books. Books. Think about books.

With a grateful nod, Rayne walked around the counter and went to the Greek classics. Celindria would appreciate a good tragedy. As Rayne passed the stacks, a book fell from the top shelf. She caught it with ease, replaced it, and kept moving through the books.

Nox followed, cleared his throat, and said, "If you don't mind my asking, are you into martial arts? You move with the grace of a warrior."

Rayne's reflexes had always been excellent, and yes, she liked to kick box. Again, those little influences from her other life had bled through the Source. But Rayne couldn't explain all that to Nox, so she said, "Yeah. I dabble. Do they practice martial arts where you're from?"

"From?"

The lilt at the end made Rayne glance up at Nox. "I saw the flags on your limo. You're not from here."

Again, a rich chuckle rumbled in Nox's massive chest. "It's not very subtle, is it?"

She had to smile at his sheepishness. "Especially in a 'no parking' zone."

They smiled at each other for a quiet moment where Rayne recalled how soft Nox's skin felt under her hands and how it had always surprised her that someone as battle-hardened as he would be so gentle with her. Until she begged him to be rough.

Darker curiosity flickered in Nox's eyes, as if he knew the direction of Rayne's thoughts. Guilt quickly replaced his desire.

The bell over the door chimed again.

"Darling?"

No.

With the breadth of Nox's stride, he took one step back and crossed two aisles of stacks away from Rayne. When Celindria peered around the corner, the two looked completely casual, despite the moment which had left Rayne's heart pounding in her chest.

"There you are. Hello, was my husband bothering you?" Celindria's tone was playful, but Rayne's instinctive reaction to her voice was not.

A storm raged inside her, begged to be unleashed on the woman who knew better. Celindria had accepted the same deal as Rayne. Both of them had chosen a Probability *and* retained their consciousness of the other. The slight amused glimmer in Celindria's eyes confirmed it.

The bitch was toying with Rayne.

And fuck, if it wasn't effective.

Despite the unrest beneath her careful surface, Rayne managed to say, "No, ma'am. Your husband was asking for help to find a book for you."

Celindria crossed the space and kissed Nox's cheek. "Thank you." All the while, she ignored the slight slump of his shoulders, proof of his shame for flirting with Rayne.

When the bell chimed again, Rayne almost walked over and ripped it off the door.

"Celindria, are you in here—Oh, hello."

Xelan.

The most wonderful man in the worlds walked in, dragging the most confident man in the worlds behind him. Since Celindria never came between the Icarean trio, Xelan and Korac were still together. And it suited them. Both men glowed.

None of them blended in. Not really. Celindria, Nox, Xelan, and Korac had an energy about them which was larger than life. But their features weren't terribly distinctive. How were Korac and Celindria hiding their hair color—

Oh. Right.

Lucas and perception filters.

With an agitated glance at Celindria, Rayne addressed the other happy couple. "Hello, welcome to Callahan Books and Coffee. Can I get you something to drink?"

Celindria fucking winked.

Nox peered between her and Rayne, picking up on the vibes.

Korac narrowed his eyes, looked Nox over, and then Rayne, as if the brilliant General had puzzled it all together.

But Xelan was so charmed by the store, he simply grinned. "Yes. I'll have a latte, and this one will have a cappuccino." He patted Korac's chest, widening the other man's eyes, before immediately perusing the wares with glee. "Nice selection of leather-bound journals."

Elden, Rayne had missed Xelan without even realizing it.

The brothers browsed the shelves while Rayne set about making their drinks.

Celindria followed and leaned on the counter. Before Rayne could confront her, Celindria said, "*I was the first. I consumed the first outsider and with him, I consumed a wondrous gift.*"

By heart, Rayne recited, "*I was alone in my gift. Surrounded by my people, but they couldn't understand me.*"

Elden's Verse.

"I *knew* it." Celindria slapped the counter in triumph. "I knew with so few Probabilities, the veil couldn't separate those of us who'd witnessed the Source. Not permanently, anyway."

Celindria's delight astonished Rayne. What the fuck was this about? What did Celindria hope to accomplish?

The First Progeny tsked. "Don't look at me like that, child. Despite my curiosity, our coming here was serendipitous. Well, mostly. Lucas is behind it."

After having this life dumped back into Rayne's head, she felt a little tired at the sudden awareness. But after battling her instincts to take Nox in the middle of the bookstore, Rayne was exhausted. "What are you doing here, Celindria?"

Celindria ignored the question and gestured at Nox, saying, "Look at him."

Rayne leaned to see around Celindria and caught Nox glancing at Rayne.

"Even now he's hiding his attraction to you from me. How can he resist the Eternal Bind? For love of me, he will try. And I fear he will fail. This may complicate matters."

As Rayne frothed the milk for Korac's cappuccino, she couldn't help herself from gritting her teeth to say, "Celindria. Tell me. Now."

Celindria turned back to Rayne and smirked. "That spirit. We need it. Razor is helping Remorse harvest the planets Silence seeded for the breeding program. They know about my daughter, Hope—your ancestor— and they intend to enslave her as they did Silence so long ago. Now, you don't know this, but one of the first acts I committed upon entering this world was awakening the Mother. She's in this city, exploring it with Lucas. We're searching for warriors from each of the worlds to ally against Remorse. Rayne, be our warrior from Earth."

It wasn't a question or a request, but it wasn't exactly an order. And damn. It made for a tempting offer. But...

Rayne glanced over at Nox to find Korac whispering to him. Both men spared a look toward her, raising her body temperature almost to a flush. "You don't want me to come with you, Celindria. I'll take Nox the first chance I get. You don't know what it's been like to be without... Everything..."

Her intended purpose.

Nox's admiration and devotion.

Xelan's hugs.

"Please... Don't ask me to say 'yes' to only half of my life."

Celindria's eyes flickered with understanding and maybe even pity. After a moment of consideration, she said, "I went eight millennia without Nox, and it devolved my sanity. I *do* understand, so I'm willing to share."

Share.

Share?!

Rayne blinked at Celindria, who continued, "I know it's sounds counterintuitive, but we have an open relationship. By that I mean, I see other people, and he doesn't see the need to do the same. Until today, I believe."

This was weird.

But...

"What about my family?"

Celindria beamed. "Lucas will see to them. We've already discussed it. Not only has he planned a front of which you're on an internship abroad for him, but he also has a nacre ready for you. We'll even contact the other Progeny. We need the Shadow."

Rayne looked over at Nox, who was swatting Xelan on the head with a book to Korac's delight. All her life, she'd wished for these people in her dreams, and she could see them all again. The adventures and the long nights. A significance born in purpose.

Fulfilled.

Ready for the rest of her life to finally start, Rayne asked, "How about after dinner?"

The End

AUTHOR'S NOTE

Thank you for reading. I hope the ending was satisfactory, but I also hope you're eager for spinoffs. There are more stories to tell even though I'm done writing in these POVs for now. Don't worry, there's still plenty of the galaxy to see.

Speaking of, if you like intrigue and romance, be sure to look for my next duology: *Copper & Snow* and *Polar Axis*. They're an experiment in non-action story-telling, and a shorter list of POVs (only three). I also faced my least favorite tropes and put my own spin on them in the duology. Give it a read if you're interest in a drama set in a steampunk snowglobe.

Goodbye for now <3